HARD-BOILED

AN ANTHOLOGY OF AMERICAN CRIME STORIES

HARD-BOILED

AN ANTHOLOGY OF AMERICAN CRIME STORIES

Edited by

Bill Pronzini and Jack Adrian

Oxford   New York

OXFORD UNIVERSITY PRESS

1995

Oxford University Press

Oxford   New York
Athens   Auckland   Bangkok   Bombay
Calcutta   Cape Town   Dar es Salaam   Delhi
Florence   Hong Kong   Istanbul   Karachi
Kuala Lumpur   Madras   Madrid   Melbourne
Mexico City   Nairobi   Paris   Singapore
Taipei   Tokyo   Toronto

and associated companies in
Berlin   Ibadan

Copyright © 1995 by Bill Pronzini and Jack Adrian

Published by Oxford University Press, Inc.,
200 Madison Avenue, New York, New York 10016

Oxford is a registered trademark of Oxford University Press

Library of Congress Cataloging-in-Publication Data
Hard-boiled : an anthology of American crime stories /
edited by Bill Pronzini & Jack Adrian.
p.   cm.
ISBN: 0-19-508499-3
1. Detective and mystery stories, American.   2. Crime—United
States—Fiction.   I. Pronzini, Bill.   II. Adrian, Jack.
PS648.D4H375   1995
813'.087208—dc20   94-43055

Since this page cannot legibly accommodate the acknowledgments,
pages 527–530 constitute an extension of the copyright page.

1 3 5 7 9 8 6 4 2

Printed in the United States of America
on acid-free paper

ACKNOWLEDGMENTS

All these individuals have, in one way or another, to a greater or a lesser extent, aided in the putting together of this volume. To them all, the editors extend heartfelt thanks: Bob Adey, Connie Aitcheson, Mike Ashley, the staff of the Bodleian Library in Oxford, England (in particular, Richard Bell, Head of Reader Services, and his deputy Alison Northover, Christine Mason, Jackie Dean, Rosemary McCarthy, and John Slatter of the Nuneham Courtney out-station), John Clute, Richard Coombs, Alastair Durie, Liza Ewell of Oxford University Press, Ed Gorman, Douglas Green, Martin H. Greenberg, E. R. Hagemann (who probably knows more about *Black Mask*, its contributors, and the hard-boiled movement in general than any other critic), Stephen Leadbeatter, Marcia Muller, Kim Newman, William F. Nolan, David Pringle, Roger Robinson, the late and much lamented Robert Sampson, Andy Sawyer, John F. Suter, Peter Tyas, and Gene Zombolas.

During the course of preparing this volume, Jack Adrian suffered a near-fatal heart attack, which added more than somewhat to the project's timeline. He would like to acknowledge a debt of unusual gratitude to Oxford University Press's Linda Morse and Liza Ewell for their lasting enthusiasm and enormous patience during trying times.

CONTENTS

HARD-BOILED

AN ANTHOLOGY OF AMERICAN CRIME STORIES

INTRODUCTION

The only significant fiction in America is popular fiction. . . It is from Chandler and Hammett and Hemingway that the best modern fiction derives.

KENNETH REXROTH

How does one define hard-boiled crime fiction?

Not easily. The very label "hard-boiled" makes it difficult, if not impossible, to come up with a precise and concise formulation. The term has been used and misused by readers, writers, and critics so often that, as with most literary labels, it has become virtually meaningless.

A more worthwhile approach is to list some of the elements contained in commendable crime stories of this type. These elements are not the only ones, to be sure; but for us they are the most vital. The more of them that an author incorporates into a particular work, the greater the work's merit.

The hard-boiled crime story deals with disorder, disaffection, and dissatisfaction. Throughout the genre's seventy-year history, this has remained a constant and central tenet. The typical hard-boiled character (if not the typical hard-boiled writer) has a jaundiced view of government, power, and the law. He (or, sometimes, she) is often a loner, a social misfit. If he is on the side of the angels, he is likely to be a cynical idealist: he believes that society is corrupt, but he also believes in justice and will make it his business to do whatever is necessary to see that justice is done. If he walks the other side of the mean streets, he walks them at night; he is likely a predator, and as morally bankrupt as any human being can be. In the noir world, extremes are the norm; clashes between good and evil are never petty, and good does not always triumph, nor is justice always done.

A hard-boiled story must emphasize character and the problems inherent in human behavior. Character conflict is essential; the crime or threat of crime with which the story is concerned is of secondary importance.

It must be reflective of the times in which it was written, providing an accurate, honest, and realistic depiction of its locale (whether urban, suburban, or rural) and of the individuals who inhabit that locale. Even more important, it must offer some insight into the social, political, and/or moral climate of its era. It must, as critic David Madden has written, "reflect [its] world in a way that is at once an objective description and an implicit judgment of it." Entertainment alone is not a sufficient raison d'être.

Even though it involves some type of violent crime, a hard-boiled crime story must not use unmotivated violence or violence for the sake of sensationalism. The mere threat of brute force is often sufficient.

It must have, in Benjamin Appel's phrase, "living people talking a living language," however harsh, cruel, or obscene these people and that language may be.

It should generate, as much as possible, what Raymond Chandler called "a smell of fear."

The presence of these various elements was one of three criteria we used in selecting stories for *Hard-Boiled: An Anthology of American Crime Stories*. The second criterion was a given story's familiarity and accessibility to today's readers. Many hard-boiled tales have been anthologized in recent years; some, such as Chandler's "Red Wind," have been overanthologized. Wherever possible, therefore, we chose stories that either have never before appeared in an anthology or at least have not been reprinted too recently. In a few instances, where the work of such icons as Chandler, Dashiell Hammett, and Ross Macdonald is limited in quantity, and either still in print or at any rate easily obtainable in other sources, we chose representative stories that, in our opinion, have had the least amount of exposure.

The third criterion was the authors themselves. While we considered it necessary—indeed, crucial—to include a wide range of the form's major practitioners, at the same time we grew aware, as we researched various magazine and book sources, of how much excellent neglected fiction they contain by writers not known to us (such as William Cole and James Hannah). As a result, in preparing the final table of contents, we decided that although preference should be given to those individuals whose body of work has defined, shaped, and influenced American hard-boiled crime writing over the past seven decades, it was imperative to include stories by lesser-known authors.

We run the risk—as all anthologists do—of excluding favorite stories or favorite authors. Our choices will certainly not please all readers; we would be amazed if they did. Nevertheless, it should be pointed out that some writers were omitted because of space limitations, while other notables in the hard-boiled tradition were left out simply because they produced no short pieces worthy of the distinction, or they wrote short stories that in our estimation do not have the quality of their longer works.

Although the hard-boiled story as we know it today was born in the 1920s, hard-boiled writing did not spring fully fledged from that antisocial maelstrom of the years between the two world wars. It was a mélange of different styles and different genres, and its heroic figures can be traced back a hundred years earlier, to both the myth and the reality of the western frontier. The history of the United States abounds with larger-than-life loners whose accomplishments, whose very survival, depended on an uncompromising toughness and a willingness to enter into struggles against seemingly insurmountable odds: Daniel Boone, Kit Carson, Davy Crockett, Jim Bridger, Mike Fink, Jim Bowie. Such rugged individualists inspired the creation of mythical heroes—Paul Bunyan, for instance—and of fictional men of action. Both James Fenimore Cooper's Natty Bumppo and Herman Melville's Captain Ahab are hunters driven by forces outside themselves, and in that sense are perfect paradigms of the modern private eye. Even Mark Twain's Huck Finn, and certainly Jack London's Wolf Larsen, have elements of the hard-boiled knight in their makeup.

Similarly, American history is filled with scoundrels and outlaws; persons motivated by greed, lust, and power; persons who hold human values and human life in little regard: William Bonney, John Wesley Hardin, Belle Starr, Herman W. Mudgett, and all the little-known and long-forgotten grifters, gamblers, confidence swindlers, whores, thieves, and paid assassins who inhabited the towns and cities, followed the railroads westward, and flocked to the gold-mining camps. These figures likewise inspired nineteenth- and early-twentieth-century authors, among them Mark Twain, Bret Harte, Frank R. Stockton, Upton Sinclair, and O. Henry. They, too, are the antecedents of the individuals who live in the pages of the modern noir story.

Literary writers were not the only ones energized by both heroic and villainous men and women and their deeds. Writers of popular fiction were equally motivated, in particular during the last four decades of the nineteenth century, when the "dime novel" pioneered by New Yorker

Erastus Beadle revolutionized mass-market publishing. The first of Beadle's slender, cheaply printed story booklets appeared in June 1860. Compulsory education in most states had created a growing number of readers, many of whom were more interested in escapist entertainment than in literary fiction and could not afford the 25 cents for which paper-covered novels were then sold. Beadle's Dime Novel Library was an instant success and spawned scores of competitively priced series from other publishers.

Early dime novels were melodramatic tales with historical, sea, and frontier settings; but in the 1870s, stories of street life in New York City and Philadelphia came into vogue, and soon afterward, into this milieu, the mass-audience detective story was born. "Old Sleuth, the Detective" appeared in *Fireside Companion* in June 1872 and was soon followed by dozens of other investigators of every conceivable occupation and based in every major city from Boston to San Francisco. Not all were men, either; successful series featured such women sleuths as Round Kate and the Western Lady Detective.

By today's standards, the dime-novel detective story was pallid juvenile fare. There was little character development; for the most part, the protagonists were ciphers, with neither moral code nor personality. The streets and alleys they prowled were those of hack writers' imaginations. Even the most popular and best-known of the dime-novel manhunters, Nick Carter (whose twenty-year career began in 1886 in *New York Weekly*), offered little in the way of realism, humanity, or social conscience. These characters were detectives in name only, in only the barest sense progenitors of the tough-guy hero of the twentieth century. Yet it was their devotion to justice and their feats of derring-do that paved the way for their hard-boiled offspring. Cheap-fiction publishers of the early twentieth century would not have been so quick to promote the crime story if it had not been for the enormous followings built up by the dime-novel sleuths.

Another development in the birth of the noir crime story, this one of major proportions, also began in the nineteenth century. Frank A. Munsey, a tightfisted magazine publisher of adventure stories for young adults, decided in 1895 to revamp one of his publications, *Argosy*, in two distinct ways: first, by turning it into an all-fiction magazine aimed at adult readers; and second, by printing the new *Argosy* on rough wood-pulp paper, which was much less expensive than the smooth paper stock that was standard for periodicals of the time. The conversion to wood pulp allowed Munsey to print and circulate a greater number of copies of *Argosy* and his other magazines. The move was rewarded by a substantial increase in sales. By the turn of the century, *Argosy*'s circulation topped 80,000 copies a month, and by 1910 it had soared to 250,000 copies.

Munsey's rivals—chiefly, Street & Smith, which had supplanted Erastus Beadle and his partner, Robert Adams, as the predominant supplier of dime novels—soon brought out seven- by ten-inch pulp-paper magazines of their own. Many more so-called pulps were introduced during the 1910s: at first mostly general fiction publications, and then an increasing number specializing in categories such as Western stories and, beginning in 1915, detective stories. The first detective pulp was in fact a conversion of Street & Smith's thriller, *Nick Carter*, which in its new incarnation featured the adventures of other sleuths in addition to Nick Carter. With the exception of love-story magazines, the pulps were aimed primarily at a male readership; for this reason, especially from the 1920s onward, they were given vividly colored enameled covers whose artwork usually depicted scenes of high melodrama. Mass-market readers overwhelmingly preferred this new form of cheap fiction; dime novels and their cousins, flimsy story-paper weeklies, were virtually extinct by the end of the 1920s.

In 1920, another important development occurred, ironically enough as the long-range result of a decision by a pair of literary entrepreneurs, H. L. Mencken and George Jean Nathan, who would later sneer openly at hard-boiled fiction. Mencken and Nathan were co-owners of the *Smart Set*, a glossy "magazine of cleverness" that was in constant financial trouble. They sought to subsidize it by publishing a pulp monthly that they called *The Black Mask*—"a lousy magazine, all detective stories, [that has] burdened Nathan and me with disagreeable work," as Mencken complained in a letter. Under their brief auspices, *Black Mask* was largely stocked with mannered, drawing-room-type mystery stories. It attracted women readers as well as men (one of its early enthusiasts was reputedly Woodrow Wilson), and its sales were substantial enough to allow Mencken and Nathan to sell it after six months for $12,500, a tidy profit on an initial investment of $500. The new owners, Pro-Distributors Corporation, appointed George W. Sutton and then P. C. Cody as editors. Cody, in particular, transformed the magazine into one that featured crime stories in American settings (along with adventure and Western stories). *Black Mask*'s "new look" attracted two young writers whose work would have a strong impact on the hard-boiled form, one briefly and the other lastingly.

"Three Gun Terry," a tough-minded story by Carroll John Daly, was printed in the May 15, 1923, issue. Just two weeks later, Daly's byline topped the first fully realized private-eye tale, "Knights of the Open Palm," an anti–Ku Klux Klan diatribe that starred a violent, poorly educated, somewhat sadistic loner named Race Williams. Readers embraced Williams with such fervor that Daly was encouraged to bring him back fifty-two times over the next dozen years. In a 1930 readers' poll, Daly was judged *Black Mask*'s favorite writer.

Despite his popularity, Daly was a crude and badly flawed writer. He was cursed with a tin ear where speech patterns of the day were concerned and possessed no talent at all for characterization. His action sequences (on which all his tales relied heavily) were invariably implausible, his plotting was weak and obvious, all his characters seem hewn from the same block of wood, and the East Coast environs in which Race Williams operated were no more authentically portrayed than were those in the dime-novel detective stories.

A far more literate and polished writer, whose detective was modeled on a real-life Pinkerton agent and whose stories were set in a sharply and believably drawn northern California milieu, was Dashiell Hammett. His first Continental Op story, "Arson Plus," was published in the October 1, 1923, issue under the pen name Peter Collinson, four months after Race Williams's debut. It was Hammett's third appearance in *Black Mask*, the previous two having also carried the Collinson byline. His second Op novelette, "Crooked Souls," published two weeks after "Arson Plus," was Hammett's first appearance in the magazine under his own name. Altogether, the Op was featured in two dozen *Black Mask* stories, plus the serialized versions of *The Dain Curse* and *Red Harvest*, from 1923 to 1929. *The Maltese Falcon*, Hammett's hugely influential novel, in which San Francisco private eye Sam Spade pursues the fabulous jewel-encrusted black bird, "the stuff that dreams are made of," was also serialized in *Black Mask* before its publication in book form in 1930.

Hammett's position as patriarch of the hard-boiled crime story owes as much to the efforts of Joseph T. "Cap" Shaw, who took over the editorship of *Black Mask* in 1926, as to his own considerable talent. Shaw, a retired army captain and friend of new publisher Ray Holland, was unfamiliar with the magazine; in fact, he had never read any pulp magazine prior to assuming his editorial duties. He did not care for what he found in previous issues: he felt that the contents lacked direction. The one *Black Mask* writer whose work he did like was Hammett, and it was Hammett he chose as the model for what he thought the magazine should be—one devoted to a new type and new style of detective writing.

The subject matter with which Hammett dealt and on which Shaw would focus *Black Mask* was not the bloodless crimes of Victorian-era mysteries or the hack-generated imaginary felonies of the dime novels; it was genuine sin and vice, of the sort their readers saw all around them and read about in their daily newspapers. The 1920s were a lawless decade, for this was the era of the Volstead Act, the Eighteenth Amendment to the Constitution, which expressly forbade the brewing and distilling of all intoxicating alcohol. Prohibition, however lofty the motives and intentions behind it, was a staggering legislative and human blunder whose ramifications are still being felt three-quarters of a century later. The illicit manufacture of and trafficking in liquor was a winked-at commonplace, and illegality became an accepted norm. This nationwide amorality—crime almost as a way of life—allowed the underworld to organize and grow strong enough for its corruption to reach into the highest levels of government and society. Feud as they might, kill one another as they did, Alphonse Capone and his gangster cohorts flourished in a climate of violence, brutality, and unconstrained social and commercial vice. It was inevitable that the hard-boiled-fiction movement, given the leadership of individuals such as Hammett and Shaw, would also grow and flourish against this background of disorder and disaffection.

Shaw would later define the *Black Mask* prose style as "hard, brittle . . . a full employment of the function of dialogue, and authenticity in characterization and action." A fast tempo and "economy of expression" were two other ingredients. (Neither Hammett nor Shaw invented the style, of course. Its emphasis on dialogue, its use of vernacular, and its basic colloquial rhythm were offshoots of the styles employed by Sherwood Anderson and Ring Lardner and polished and simplified by Ernest Hemingway. What Hammett brought to it was "romantic realism," in Ellery Queen's phrase: he placed his stories against a stark background; peopled them with men and women who seemed truly to sweat, bleed, and ache; and made the pursuit of justice a noble as well as a necessary goal.)

Over Shaw's ten-year editorial reign, he developed a nucleus of writers who adhered to—and in some cases refined—what would come to be known as the *Black Mask* school: Raymond Chandler, Frederick Nebel, Raoul Whitfield, Paul Cain (George Sims), Horace McCoy, Dwight V. Babcock, George Harmon Coxe, Norbert Davis. These writers created heroes who were worthy of Cooper's Bumppo and Melville's Ahab—true rugged individualists who believed that murder will out, who were determined to see law and order prevail no matter what the cost. Chandler's Carmady, an early version of Philip Marlowe, was one such creation. Others were Nebel's police captain MacBride and Kennedy of the *Free Press*; Coxe's crime photographer, Flashgun Casey; and Whitfield's private detective, Ben Jardinn.

It should not be thought, however, that Hammett and his followers wrote for any high-minded or didactic purpose, or to any grand design. Although there was in their work the dominant element of "taking murder out of the library and putting it back on the streets where it belonged," in Chandler's celebrated phrase, these writers were essentially storytellers, aiming their wares at a large and sympathetic but by no means uncritical audience. It was incumbent on them to produce stories that gripped, entertained, surprised; otherwise, the stories would not be bought and published. Thus even though the writers were working with realistic material and in a fresh idiom, to some extent they still relied on past detective-story traditions, motivations, and (often enough) clichés.

The best of the craftsmen under Shaw's tutelage were so adept at their lessons that they soon graduated to other, higher-paying media: glossy-paper magazines, novels, radio scripts, Hollywood screenplays. Some of their creations also went on to success outside the pages of *Black Mask*. Ben Jardinn was featured in one of the better early Hollywood private-eye novels, Raoul Whitfield's *Death in a Bowl* (1931). Flashgun Casey enjoyed a wide following in a series of novels by George Harmon Coxe, as well as in his own radio show, *Casey, Crime Photographer*, in the 1940s. Curiously enough, the toughest of all the hard-boiled characters to come out of *Black Mask*, Paul Cain's Gerry Kells, was neither a hero nor a detective; Kells, in fact, was in many ways the first true antihero in noir fiction—a murderous, amoral gambler and racketeer whose base of operations was the Los Angeles underworld. Five interconnected stories featuring Kells were joined in the 1933 novel *Fast One*, a rock-hard tale that is arguably the harshest and most relentless of all the hard-boiled crime novels.

With Shaw at the helm, *Black Mask*'s circulation increased dramatically at the end of his first year and peaked in 1930 at 103,000 copies a month. Predictably, its early success brought on imitators, including Fiction House's short-lived *Black Aces* and Popular Publications' long-lived *Dime Detective*. By the mid-1930s, however, Shaw had lost or was about to lose most of his major writers—Hammett, Nebel, Whitfield, Coxe, McCoy—to the more lucrative and challenging media; only Chandler remained. Circulation had fallen off, and financial cutbacks were imminent. One cutback was to be in Shaw's salary; he objected vehemently, and in the fall of 1936 he was relieved of his editorial duties. (In sympathy, Chandler quit *Black Mask* as well. His last few pulp crime stories appeared in *Dime Detective* and in Street & Smith's *Detective Story*.)

Despite the efforts of new editor Fanny Ellsworth, sales of *Black Mask* continued to decline, and in 1940 the magazine was sold to Popular Publications. It ended its life rather ignominiously in 1951, as a second-string title in Popular's chain of detective pulps, behind *Dime Detective*, *Detective Tales*, and *New Detective*. But the *Black Mask* school remained the hard-boiled standard for all pulp crime fiction during the last twenty years of the pulp-magazine era, and for much of the hard-boiled fiction—short stories and novels alike—that has been published since.

The tough crime story was not limited to publication in pulp magazines or the tough crime novel to publication within the mystery and detective genre, once the Roaring Twenties gave way to the Depression thirties. Grinding poverty, unemployment, homelessness, bank and small-business failures in alarming numbers, ongoing police and political corruption and rampant gangsterism, violent clashes between union organizers and management scabs in both industry and agriculture—these were the social ills of the Great Depression. Combined with a vast westward migration from the Midwest and the Dust Bowl of Oklahoma and Arkansas to California's "promised land," these real-life trends gave rise to a different type of hard-boiled fiction that was more solidly rooted in the literary mainstream. Some of the period's angriest and most savagely realistic short stories were published in such "quality" magazines as *American Mercury*, *Story*, *Esquire*, *Harper's*, and *Liberty*. Many mainstream novels of the 1930s had grim themes, in particular those that championed the cause of the proletariat; many dealt wholly or in part with violent crime, often in a bitterly existential fashion. A few, although treated less than respectfully by critics of the time, have endured and achieved the status of classics: James M. Cain's *The Postman Always*

Rings Twice (1934), Benjamin Appel's *Brain Guy* (1934), Horace McCoy's *They Shoot Horses, Don't They?* (1935), Edward Anderson's *Thieves Like Us* (1937), Richard Hallas's *You Play the Black and the Red Comes Up* (1938), and James Ross's *They Don't Dance Much* (1940).

With a few exceptions, the 1940s were a static decade for the hard-boiled crime story. Good work appeared in genre and other magazines, but most of it was formulaic and none of it broke any new ground. A number of talented writers made their debuts in the crime pulps, among them John D. MacDonald, Day Keene, and David Goodis; their primary contributions would come later, however, in the novel form. Easily the grittiest of the decade's novels was Jonathan Latimer's *Solomon's Vineyard* (1941), a work so tough-minded and sexually explicit that no American publisher would take a chance on it in its original form; it was first published in England (where its dust-jacket blurb trumpeted: "It's got everything but an abortion and a tornado," neglecting to mention that one of the things it does have is necrophilia). Its first publication in the United States was not until nine years later, in a heavily expurgated paperback edition retitled *The Fifth Grave*. The original text did not see print in the United States until 1982, and then only in a limited edition of 326 copies from a small press.

A scattering of very good private-eye novels—and one seminal private-eye novel—were published in the 1940s. The very good ones include Norbert Davis's fast and funny *Mouse in the Mountain* and *Sally's in the Alley*, both published in 1943 and both featuring Doan and his Great Dane, Carstairs; Leigh Brackett's Chandleresque *No Good from a Corpse* (1944); the first three Paul Pine adventures by John Evans (Howard Browne), *Halo in Blood* (1946), *Halo for Satan* (1948), and *Halo in Brass* (1949); the first of Wade Miller's Max Thursday novels, *Guilty Bystander* (1947); and the first Lew Archer investigation by Ross Macdonald (Kenneth Millar), *The Moving Target* (1949).

The decade's most influential hard-boiled detective novel is Mickey Spillane's Mike Hammer debut, *I, the Jury*. When this book was published in 1947, it had an immediate and profound impact on noir fiction. Action, sex, and vigilante justice were nothing new to the private-eye tale: Carroll John Daly (an admitted influence on Spillane's work) had introduced this provocative mix more than twenty years earlier in his Race Williams melodramas, and other writers, including Hammett and Chandler, had utilized it with varying degrees of emphasis and success. But no one presented sex, violence, and the personal vendetta in such a heady stew as Spillane in *I, the Jury*: savagely, implacably, and with the most cold-blooded (or hot-blooded, depending on one's perspective) dénouement in the history of the genre—an ending guaranteed, as more than one critic has pointed out, to enrage any feminist.

I, the Jury, and such subsequent Mike Hammer novels as *My Gun Is Quick* (1950), *Vengeance Is Mine* (1950), and *Kiss Me Deadly* (1952), sold millions of copies and opened up the hard-boiled market to hundreds of mimics in the 1950s and 1960s. Spillane's work, far more than that of any other writer, dictated which sort of crime fiction was to be published as paperback originals over the next twenty years. And his influence on hard-boiled mysteries as a whole, whether one likes the idea or not (many readers and critics find the Mike Hammer stories repellent), cannot be ignored or underestimated.

Fawcett Gold Medal was the first of the softcover publishers to specialize in original, male-oriented category fiction. When the first Gold Medal novels appeared in late 1949, editors Richard Carroll and Bill Lengel had already assembled (and would continue to assemble) a stable of some of the best popular writers of the period by paying royalty advances on the number of copies printed, rather than on the number of copies sold; thus writers received handsome initial payments, up to four times as much as hardcover publishers were paying. Into the Gold Medal camp came such established names as W. R. Burnett, Cornell Woolrich, Sax Rohmer, and Wade Miller; such first-rank pulp writers as John D. MacDonald, Bruno Fischer, Day Keene, David Goodis, and Harry Whittington; and such talented newcomers as Charles Williams, Stephen Marlowe, and Gil Brewer.

What the Fawcett brain trust and the Fawcett writers succeeded in doing was adapting the tried-and-true pulp formula of the 1930s and 1940s to postwar American society, with all its changes in lifestyle and morality and its newfound sophistication. (This, too, was what Spillane had done and would continue to do in his Mike Hammer novels.) Instead of a bulky magazine full of short stories, Fawcett published brand-new, easy-to-read novels in a convenient pocket-size format. Instead of gaudy, pulp-style cover art, Fawcett utilized the "peekaboo sex" approach to catching the reader's eye: women depicted as either being nude (as seen from the side or rear) or showing a great deal of cleavage or leg or both, in a variety of provocative poses. Instead of printing hundreds of thousands of copies of a small number of titles, Fawcett printed hundreds of thousands of copies of many titles in order to reach every possible outlet and buyer. As a result, many Gold Medal novels, particularly in the early 1950s, sold more than a million copies each.

Fawcett and the best of its competitors—Avon, Dell, Popular Library, Lion—may have been selling pulp fiction, but it was an upscale variety. The novels they brought out were short (generally about 50,000 words), fast-paced, and action-oriented. They were well written, well plotted, peopled by sharply delineated and believable characters, spiced with sex, often imbued with psychological insight, and set in vividly drawn, often exotic locales. The best of these paperback originals were in fact the apotheosis of pulp fiction—rough-hewn, minor works of art, perfectly suited to and representative of their era. Notable individual titles include Jim Thompson's harrowing excursion into the mind of a serial murderer, *The Killer Inside Me* (1952); John D. MacDonald's *The Damned* (1952); David Goodis's *Street of the Lost* (1952); Gil Brewer's *A Killer Is Loose* (1954); Harry Whittington's *Brute in Brass* (1956); and Jack Dillon's Hemingway pastiche, *A Great Day for Dying* (1968). A number of long-running noir series were also launched and developed as paperback originals during the 1950s and 1960s; among these were the Eighty-seventh Precinct novels by Ed McBain (Evan Hunter), begun with *Cop Hater* (1956); Chester Himes's Harlem police procedurals, featuring Coffin Ed Johnson and Grave Digger Jones and begun with *For the Love of Immabelle* (1957); and the antihero Parker created by Richard Stark (Donald Westlake) and begun with *The Hunter* (1962).

While the bulk of the softcover originals published in the 1950s and 1960s were concerned with violent crime of an interpersonal nature, a percentage of them—and a larger percentage of hardcover novels and short stories—embraced larger themes: Senator Joseph McCarthy's anti-Communist witch hunt, widespread fear of nuclear annihilation, rampant urban juvenile delinquency, drug addiction, and the threat of organized crime (the hearings held by Senator Estes Kefauver's Special Committee to Investigate Organized Crime in Interstate Commerce, which were nationally broadcast on radio and television in 1950 and 1951, opened the American people's eyes not only to the threat but also to the underworld's deep and longstanding ties to local political officials). In response, heroic struggles against the Red Menace were the stuff of such novels as Mickey Spillane's *One Lonely Night* (1951); grim accounts of juvenile gangs filled Hal Ellson's *Tomboy* (1950), Benjamin Appel's *Life and Death of a Tough Guy* (1955), and Harlan Ellison's *Rumble* (1958); drug addiction was examined in Ellson's *The Golden Spike* (1952) and

Alexander Trocchi's *Cain's Book* (1960); the effects of organized crime were chronicled in Louis Malley's *Horns for the Devil* (1951), Harry Grey's *The Hoods* (1952), and Appel's *The Raw Edge* (1958). Many hard-boiled novels—and such documentary-style films as *The Captive City* (1951) and *Big Jim McLain* (1952)—treated their subject matter in highly sensationalized and inflammatory fashion, in keeping with the some-what frenzied atmosphere of the period. The same was even more true of the hard-boiled short story.

In the same way that pulp magazines had brought about the decline and fall of dime novels, paperback originals and the new medium of television sounded a death knell for the pulps. All major pulp titles were extinct by 1954. The new domain of the hard-boiled short story, in the late 1950s and throughout the 1960s, was the digest-size detective mag-azine. *Ellery Queen's Mystery Magazine* (*EQMM*) had been well estab-lished since 1941, but only occasionally did its editor-in-chief, Frederic Dannay, include a genuinely gritty tale; Dannay was not a proponent of the form (except for Hammett's work, which he admired extravagantly). The time was ripe for a new outlet devoted solely to the form, and in 1953 one came along: *Manhunt*, a showcase for tough, downbeat, violent stories of "the seamier side" of contemporary life. *Manhunt*'s premier issue, dated January 1953, featured the first installment of a new serial by Mickey Spillane, "Everybody's Watching Me," plus short fiction by such established names as William Irish (Cornell Woolrich) and Kenneth Millar (Ross Macdonald) and such future stars as Evan Hunter. Sales far exceeded the expectations of its publisher, Michael St. John, and its ed-itor, John McCloud—nearly 500,000 copies of that first issue—and in-stantly established *Manhunt* as the new standard bearer.

So successful was the magazine in the early to mid-1950s that St. John and McCloud were able to elicit hard-edged original stories from Erle Stanley Gardner, Rex Stout, Fredric Brown, and other respected mystery writers, as well as from a surprising array of literary figures: James M. Cain, Nelson Algren, Erskine Caldwell, James T. Farrell, Charles Jackson, and Ira Levin. A plethora of *Manhunt* clones with tough, staccato titles that almost verged on self-parody soon crowded the newsstands: *Ac-cused, Hunted, Pursuit, Guilty, Trapped, Two-Fisted, Sure-Fire, Justice, Suspect*, and four from Manhunt's own publishing company: *Verdict, Menace, Murder!*, and *Mantrap*. Few of these lasted more than a handful of issues. A small number survived the decade (mainly those, such as *Guilty* and *Trapped*, that specialized in brutal stories about juvenile delinquents), but even that group had all but disappeared by the end of 1962.

Manhunt reigned for a scant few years; by 1959, its quality and its circulation had fallen off radically, as a result of editorial and financial mishandling, apathy, and changing reader tastes. The last important author and story to appear in its pages was Raymond Chandler's Philip Marlowe tale "Wrong Pigeon" in the February 1960 issue; the story had been unpublished in the United States, although it had appeared in England as "The Pencil." Few writers of note contributed material to *Manhunt* from 1960 onward. It lingered until 1967, most of the time as a bimonthly under different ownership. When it finally died it was a ghost of its former self, publishing reprints from its heyday and generally poor original stories by unknowns.

Mike Shayne Mystery Magazine (*MSMM*) and *Alfred Hitchcock's Mystery Magazine* (*AHMM*), both founded in 1956 and both moderately successful as purveyors of genre crime stories, were the main inheritors of the post-1960 hard-boiled short story. Neither specialized in the form, however, though the preponderance of selections in most issues of *MSMM* could be termed hard-boiled. Now and then, a new periodical devoted to noir fiction would appear—notably, *Ed McBain's Mystery Book* in 1960 and *Mystery Monthly* in 1975—but these had short runs.

The last issue of *MSMM* was published in 1985. Since then, the hard-boiled short has had no regular forum. One quarterly magazine, *Hardboiled*, is currently in existence, but it is semiprofessionally produced and has a limited circulation. *EQMM* and *AHMM*, the last of the mystery digests, publish hard-boiled stories now and then, as do such magazines as *Playboy*. Theme anthologies of original stories have provided another inconsistent market. Among anthologies of this type are four published under the auspices of the Private Eye Writers of America: *The Eyes Have It* (1984), *Mean Streets* (1986), *An Eye for Justice* (1988), and *Justice for Hire* (1990).

It is in the novel form that the hard-boiled story has had the most growth over the past quarter-century, in large part as a response to the Pandora's box of disorders afflicting modern society: the insidious and epidemic presence of drugs and drug trafficking, random violence, AIDS, homelessness, the abortion issue, child abuse, spousal abuse, and rape. Until the constraints placed on writers by society's moral guardians began to relax in the early 1970s, such issues had to be treated either in oblique, often superficial fashion or not at all. Today's writers of hard-boiled fiction have far more latitude than their predecessors did to examine their subject matter honestly and incisively, as frankly and at whatever depth they deem necessary. Their work not only is more searching and therefore more powerful than that of their predecessors, but is erasing the line of demarcation between genre crime fiction and literature. In effect, the hard-boiled crime story has grown into adulthood, and in the process has attained some of the wisdom and insight of adulthood. To say that it is capable of attaining a great deal more is to bestow on it both high praise and the challenge of responsibility.

In the 1970s and early 1980s, several notable detective characters entered the field, among them Lawrence Block's alcoholic former New York cop Matt Scudder, in *Sins of the Fathers* (1976); James Crumley's Shugrue, in *The Last Good Kiss* (1978); Jonathan Valin's Cincinnati private eye Harry Stoner, in *The Lime Pit* (1980); and Loren D. Estleman's Detroit-based Amos Walker, in *Motor City Blue* (1980). The emergence over the past fifteen years of the female private eye (and such offshoots as realistically portrayed women cops, probation officers, and lawyers) has broadened the hard-boiled form's scope and horizon; with relatively few exceptions, it had been a male-dominated subgenre, in terms of both its writers and its readers. The best and most popular of these tough new women sleuths are Marcia Muller's Sharon McCone, who made her debut in *Edwin of the Iron Shoes* (1977) as the first fully realized female private eye created by a woman; Sue Grafton's Kinsey Milhone, who first appeared in *A Is for Alibi* (1981); and Sara Paretsky's V. I. Warshawski, whose initial investigation was *Indemnity Only* (1982).

Most significant among recent nonseries noir novels are those that address major social issues. Jonathan Kellerman and Andrew Vachss have each written harsh condemnations of child abuse, in such novels as *When the Bough Breaks* (1985) and *Hard Candy* (1989), respectively. In *Bitter Medicine* (1987), Sara Paretsky pulls no punches in addressing women's health issues. *The Silence of the Lambs*, Thomas Harris's 1988 bestseller, unrelentingly probes the psychology of the serial killer. The mounting controversy surrounding illegal immigration is the subject of Marcia Muller's *Wolf in the Shadows* (1993). Sexual harassment is the central theme of Linda Grant's *A Woman's Place* (1994), and sexual exploitation of women through pornography is the topic explored by Lia Matera in *Face Value* (1994).

This introduction would not be complete without a brief mention of film noir. Film has proved fertile ground for the hard-boiled movement from the 1930s to the present day. During the 1940s and 1950s, directors seized on the grim and at times unremittingly bleak visions of Cornell Woolrich, James M. Cain, and David Goodis, among others, and transformed them into minor masterpieces of moody, shadow-filled filmmaking. There are dozens of film noir classics; a few of the outstanding examples based on hard-boiled fiction include Jacques Tourneur's *The Leopard Man* (1943), taken from Woolrich's *Black Alibi*; Edward Dmytryk's *Murder My Sweet* (1944), adapted from Raymond Chandler's *Farewell, My Lovely*; Delmer Daves's *Dark Passage* (1947), whose source was a book of the same title by David Goodis; Fritz Lang's *The Big Heat* (1953), based on a William P. McGivern novel of that name; and Stanley Kubrick's *The Killing* (1956), adapted from Lionel White's *Clean Break*.

Over the past decade and a half, both directors and writers in the United States have become increasingly aware of the hard-boiled genre, reinterpreting old noir favorites such as James M. Cain's *The Postman Always Rings Twice* (first filmed in 1946 and remade in 1981 from a taut David Mamet script); updating novels by hard-boiled writers of the 1950s into dazzling screenplays, as Donald Westlake did with Jim Thompson's *The Grifters* (published in 1963, filmed in 1990); or creating entirely new works so immoderately vicious that they exceed by a considerable degree the old conventions of cinema noir. The current high priest of designer violence is director and writer Quentin Tarantino, who plunders the plots of old films and 1940s pulp fiction and reshapes them into a purely 1990s product that resonates with aberrant and often stomach-churning brutality. The idea behind the work of auteurs such as Tarantino is that cinematic violence is both fun and cathartic, a concept that has a certain validity. In the process, however, characters lose their humanity and become mere symbols, and as Dashiell Hammett once implied in a letter to Cap Shaw, it is difficult to relate to a symbol no matter how cleverly or wittily the symbol behaves.

A final word about the stories we have selected for inclusion.

The reader will note that we have taken several from the 1930s and several from the 1950s, while other decades are more sparsely represented. The imbalance is deliberate. The 1930s were the single most important decade in the form's development, thanks to Hammett, Chandler, Shaw, and numerous others. The 1950s was its renaissance decade, the first in which mystery-genre specialists were able to shed some of the restrictions of style and content created by hard-boiled crime writing's pulp origins and stretch its limits in inventive new ways. In terms of volume, more first-rate works were published during that ten-year span than during any other.

The 1990s may prove to be the form's third most important decade. Certainly the novels and stories that have been published thus far foreshadow another renaissance period in which contemporary authors will expand its boundaries even further. It may well be that editors of future anthologies of hard-boiled stories will want to give much greater emphasis than we have to this final decade before the millennium. If so, then its promise will have been fulfilled.

DASHIELL HAMMETT
(1894–1961)

As Raymond Chandler states in his essay "The Simple Art of Murder," Samuel Dashiell Hammett "wrote at first (and almost to the end) for people with a sharp, aggressive attitude to life. They were not afraid of the seamy side of things; they lived there. Violence did not dismay them; it was right down their street."

To put it another way, Hammett was the trailblazer, the founding father of the hard-boiled form. Every other writer of hard-boiled fiction, past and present, including those who have made major refinements or opened important new veins, is a prospector mining the goldfields that he established.

There are those who would argue that Sam Spade, hero of the single most influential private-eye novel, The Maltese Falcon (1930), is Hammett's greatest character, while others opt for the mildly inebriate husband-and-wife team, Nick and Nora Charles, of The Thin Man (1934). But most aficionados—the editors of this volume included among them—accord that distinction to the Continental Op. Fat, fortyish, and the Continental Detective Agency's toughest and shrewdest investigator, the nameless Op was based on James Wright, assistant superintendent of the Pinkerton Detective Agency in Baltimore, for whom Hammett worked during his fourteen-year stint (1908–1922) with the agency. The Op's methods, if not his cases, are based on real private-investigative procedures of the period. For these reasons, the Op stories are more starkly realistic than any of Hammett's other fiction.

The first Op story, "Arson Plus," appeared in the October 1, 1923, issue of Black Mask under the pseudonym Peter Collinson. Two dozen Op stories followed over the next eight years; the series ended with "Death and Company" in the November 1930 issue. Four of the stories constituted The Dain Curse, though they were published separately rather than as a conventional serial, and another four separate stories made up Red Harvest. Both novels were published in book form in 1929. The remaining Op yarns were reprinted by Ellery Queen in a series of digest-size paperbacks in the late 1940s and early 1950s, and several were later collected in The Big Knockover (1966) and The Continental Op (1974), the only two volumes of Hammett's stories to be authorized by his close friend and literary executor, Lillian Hellman.

"The Scorched Face" was first published in the May 1925 issue of Black Mask. (Curiously, in a blurb for the story, editor Philip C. Cody referred to the Op as "the Continental Sleuth.") This is arguably one of the three or four best Op tales, for not only does it have, in the words of Ellery Queen, "savagery, style, sophistication, sleuthing, and sex," but it offers three additional S's: a sharp surprise stinger in its final sentence.

B. P.

1 9 2 5

THE SCORCHED FACE

"We expected them home yesterday," Alfred Banbrock ended his story. "When they had not come by this morning, my wife telephoned Mrs. Walden. Mrs. Walden said they had not been down there—had not been expected, in fact."

"On the face of it, then," I suggested, "it seems that your daughters went away of their own accord, and are staying away on their own accord?"

Banbrock nodded gravely. Tired muscles sagged in his fleshy face.

"It would seem so," he agreed. "That is why I came to your agency for help instead of going to the police."

"Have they ever disappeared before?"

"No. If you read the papers and magazines, you've no doubt seen hints that the younger generation is given to irregularity. My daughters came and went pretty much as they pleased. But, though I can't say I ever knew what they were up to, we always knew where they were in a general way."

"Can you think of any reason for their going away like this?"

· He shook his weary head.

"Any recent quarrels?" I probed.

"N—" He changed it to: "Yes—although I didn't attach any importance to it, and wouldn't have recalled it if you hadn't jogged my memory. It was Thursday evening—the evening before they went away."

"And it was about—?"

"Money, of course. We never disagreed over anything else. I gave

21

each of my daughters an adequate allowance—perhaps a very liberal one. Nor did I keep them strictly within it. There were few months in which they didn't exceed it. Thursday evening they asked for an amount of money even more than usual in excess of what two girls should need. I wouldn't give it to them, though I finally did give them a somewhat smaller amount. We didn't exactly quarrel—not in the strict sense of the word—but there was a certain lack of friendliness between us."

"And it was after this disagreement that they said they were going down to Mrs. Walden's, in Monterey, for the weekend?"

"Possibly. I'm not sure of that point. I don't think I heard of it until the next morning, but they may have told my wife before that."

"And you know of no other possible reason for their running away?"

"None. I can't think that our dispute over money—by no means an unusual one—had anything to do with it."

"What does their mother think?"

"Their mother is dead," Banbrock corrected me. "My wife is their stepmother. She is only two years older than Myra, my older daughter. She is as much at sea as I."

"Did your daughters and their stepmother get along all right together?"

"Yes! Yes! Excellently! If there was a division in the family, I usually found them standing together against me."

"Your daughters left Friday afternoon?"

"At noon, or a few minutes after. They were going to drive down."

"The car, of course, is still missing?"

"Naturally."

"What was it?"

"A Locomobile, with a special cabriolet body. Black."

"You can give me the license and engine numbers?"

"I think so."

He turned in his chair to the big roll-top desk that hid a quarter of one office wall, fumbled with papers in a compartment, and read the numbers over his shoulder to me. I put them on the back of an envelope.

"I'm going to have this car put on the police department list of stolen machines," I told him. "It can be done without mentioning your daughters. The police bulletin might find the car for us. That would help us find your daughters."

"Very well," he agreed, "if it can be done without disagreeable publicity. As I told you at first, I don't want any more advertising than is absolutely necessary—unless it becomes likely that harm has come to the girls."

I nodded understanding, and got up.

"I want to go out and talk to your wife," I said. "Is she home now?"

"Yes, I think so. I'll phone her and tell her you are coming."

In a big limestone fortress on top of a hill in Sea Cliff, looking down on ocean and bay, I had my talk with Mrs. Banbrock. She was a tall dark girl of not more than twenty-two years, inclined to plumpness.

She couldn't tell me anything her husband hadn't at least mentioned, but she could give me finer details.

I got descriptions of the two girls:

Myra—20 years old; 5 feet 8 inches; 150 pounds; athletic; brisk, almost masculine manner and carriage; bobbed brown hair; brown eyes; medium complexion; square face, with large chin and short nose; scar over left ear, concealed by hair; fond of horses and all outdoor sports. When she left the house she wore a blue and green wool dress, small blue hat, short black seal coat, and black slippers.

Ruth—18 years; 5 feet 4 inches; 105 pounds; brown eyes; brown bobbed hair; medium complexion; small oval face; quiet, timid, inclined to lean on her more forceful sister. When last seen she had worn a tobacco-brown coat trimmed with brown fur over a gray silk dress, and a wide brown hat.

I got two photographs of each girl, and an additional snapshot of Myra standing in front of the cabriolet. I got a list of the things they had taken with them—such things as would naturally be taken on a weekend visit. What I valued most of what I got was a list of their friends, relatives, and other acquaintances, so far as Mrs. Banbrock knew them.

"Did they mention Mrs. Walden's invitation before their quarrel with Mr. Banbrock?" I asked, when I had my lists stowed away.

"I don't think so," Mrs. Banbrock said thoughtfully. "I didn't connect the two things at all. They didn't really quarrel with their father, you know. It wasn't harsh enough to be called a quarrel."

"Did you see them when they left?"

"Assuredly! They left about half-past twelve Friday afternoon. They kissed me as usual when they went, and there was certainly nothing in their manner to suggest anything out of the ordinary."

"You've no idea at all where they might have gone?"

"None."

"Can't even make a guess?"

"I can't. Among the names and addresses I have given you are some of friends and relatives of the girls in other cities. They may have gone to one of those. Do you think we should—?"

"I'll take care of that," I promised. "Could you pick out one or two of them as the most likely places for the girls to have gone?"

She wouldn't try it. "No," she said positively, "I could not."

From this interview I went back to the Agency, and put the Agency machinery in motion: arranging to have operatives from some of the Continental's other branches call on the out-of-town names on my list, having the missing Locomobile put on the police department list, turning one photograph of each girl over to the photographer to be copied.

That done, I set out to talk to the persons on the list Mrs. Banbrock had given me. My first call was on a Constance Delee, in an apartment building on Post Street. I saw a maid. The maid said Miss Delee was out of town. She wouldn't tell me where her mistress was, or when she would be back.

From there I went up on Van Ness Avenue and found a Wayne Ferris in an automobile salesroom: a sleek-haired young man whose very nice manners and clothes completely hid anything else—brains for instance—he might have had. He was very willing to help me, and he knew nothing. It took him a long time to tell me so. A nice boy.

Another blank: "Mrs. Scott is in Honolulu."

In a real estate office on Montgomery Street I found my next one—another sleek, stylish, smooth-haired young man with nice manners and nice clothes. His name was Raymond Elwood. I would have thought him a no more distant relative of Ferris than cousin if I hadn't known that the world—especially the dancing, teaing world—was full of their sort. I learned nothing from him.

Then I drew some more blanks: "Out of town," "Shopping," "I don't know where you can find him."

I found one more of the Banbrock girls' friends before I called it a day. Her name was Mrs. Stewart Correll. She lived in Presidio Terrace, not far from the Banbrocks. She was a small woman, or girl, of about Mrs. Banbrock's age. A little fluffy blonde person with wide eyes of that particular blue which always looks honest and candid no matter what is going on behind it.

"I haven't seen either Ruth or Myra for two weeks or more," she said in answer to my question.

"At that time—the last time you saw them—did either say anything about going away?"

"No."

Her eyes were wide and frank. A little muscle twitched in her upper lip.

"And you've no idea where they might have gone?"

"No."

Her fingers were rolling her lace handkerchief into a little ball.

"Have you heard from them since you last saw them?"

"No."

She moistened her mouth before she said it.

"Will you give me the names and addresses of all the people you know who were also known by the Banbrock girls?"

"Why—? Is there—?"

"There's a chance that some of them may have seen them more recently than you," I explained. "Or may even have seen them since Friday."

Without enthusiasm, she gave me a dozen names. All were already on my list. Twice she hesitated as if about to speak a name she did not want to speak. Her eyes stayed on mine, wide and honest. Her fingers, no longer balling the handkerchief, picked at the cloth of her skirt.

I didn't pretend to believe her. But my feet weren't solidly enough on the ground for me to put her on the grill. I gave her a promise before I left, one that she could get a threat out of if she liked.

"Thanks, very much," I said. "I know it's hard to remember things exactly. If I run across anything that will help your memory, I'll be back to let you know about it."

"Wha—? Yes, do!" she said.

Walking away from the house, I turned my head to look back just before I passed out of sight. A curtain swung into place at a second-floor window. The street lights weren't bright enough for me to be sure the curtain had swung in front of a blonde head.

My watch told me it was nine-thirty: too late to line up any more of the girls' friends. I went home, wrote my report for the day, and turned in, thinking more about Mrs. Correll than about the girls.

She seemed worth an investigation.

Some telegraphic reports were in when I got to the office the next morning. None was of any value. Investigation of the names and addresses in other cities had revealed nothing. An investigation in Monterey had established reasonably—which is about as well as anything is ever established in the detecting business—that the girls had not been there recently, that the Locomobile had not been there.

The early editions of the afternoon papers were on the street when I went out to get some breakfast before taking up the grind where I had dropped it the previous night.

I bought a paper to prop behind my grapefruit.

It spoiled my breakfast for me:

BANKER'S WIFE SUICIDE

Mrs. Stewart Correll, wife of the vice-president of the Golden Gate Trust Company, was found dead early this morning by her maid in her bedroom, in her home in Presidio Terrace. A bottle believed to have contained poison was on the floor beside the bed.

The dead woman's husband could give no reason for his wife's suicide. He said she had not seemed depressed or . . .

At the Correll residence I had to do a lot of talking before I could get to Correll. He was a tall, slim man of less than thirty-five, with a sallow, nervous face and blue eyes that fidgeted.

"I'm sorry to disturb you at a time like this," I apologized when I had finally insisted my way into his presence. "I won't take up more of your time than necessary. I am an operative of the Continental Detective Agency. I have been trying to find Ruth and Myra Banbrock, who disappeared several days ago. You know them, I think."

"Yes," he said without interest. "I know them."

"You knew they had disappeared?"

"No." His eyes switched from a chair to a rug. "Why should I?"

"Have you seen either of them recently?" I asked, ignoring his question.

"Last week—Wednesday, I think. They were just leaving—standing at the door talking to my wife—when I came home from the bank."

"Didn't your wife say anything to you about their vanishing?"

"No. Really, I can't tell you anything about the Misses Banbrock. If you'll excuse me—"

"Just a moment longer," I said. "I wouldn't have bothered you if it hadn't been necessary. I was here last night to question Mrs. Correll. She seemed nervous. My impression was that some of her answers to my questions were—uh—evasive. I want—"

He was up out of his chair. His face was red in front of mine.

"You!" he cried. "I can thank you for—"

"Now, Mr. Correll," I tried to quiet him, "there's no use—"

But he had himself all worked up.

"You drove my wife to her death," he accused me. "You killed her with your damned prying—with your bulldozing threats. With your—"

That was silly. I felt sorry for this young man whose wife had killed herself. Apart from that, I had work to do. I tightened the screws.

"We won't argue, Correll," I told him. "The point is that I came here to see if your wife could tell me anything about the Banbrocks. She told me less than the truth. Later, she committed suicide. I want to know why. Come through for me, and I'll do what I can to keep the papers and the public from linking her death with the girls' disappearance."

"Linking her death with their disappearance?" he exclaimed. "That's absurd!"

"Maybe—but the connection is there!" I hammered away at him. I felt sorry for him, but I had work to do. "It's there. If you'll give it to me, maybe it won't have to be advertised. I'm going to get it, though. You give it to me—or I'll go after it out in the open."

For a moment I thought he was going to take a poke at me. I wouldn't have blamed him. His body stiffened—then sagged, and he dropped back into his chair. His eyes fidgeted away from mine. "There's nothing I can tell," he mumbled. "When her maid went to her room to call her this morning, she was dead. There was no message, no reason, nothing."

"Did you see her last night?"

"No. I was not home for dinner. I came in late and went straight to my own room, not wanting to disturb her. I hadn't seen her since I left the house that morning."

"Did she seem disturbed or worried then?"

"No."

"Why do you think she did it?"

"My God, man, I don't know! I've thought and thought, but I don't know!"

"Health?"

"She seemed well. She was never ill, never complained."

"Any recent quarrels?"

"We never quarreled—never in the year and a half we have been married!"

"Financial trouble?"

He shook his head without speaking or looking up from the floor.

"Any other worry?"

He shook his head again.

"Did the maid notice anything peculiar in her behavior last night?"

"Nothing."

"Have you looked through her things—for papers, letters?"

"Yes—and found nothing." He raised his head to look at me. "The only thing"—he spoke very slowly—"there was a little pile of ashes in the grate in her room, as if she had burned papers, or letters."

Correll held nothing more for me—nothing I could get out of him, anyway.

The girl at the front gate in Alfred Banbrock's Shoreman's Building suite told me he was *in conference*. I sent my name in. He came out of conference to take me into his private office. His tired face was full of questions.

I didn't keep him waiting for the answers. He was a grown man. I didn't edge around the bad news.

"Things have taken a bad break," I said as soon as we were locked in together. "I think we'll have to go to the police and newspapers for help. A Mrs. Correll, a friend of your daughters, lied to me when I questioned her yesterday. Last night she committed suicide."

"Irma Correll? Suicide?"

"You knew her?"

"Yes! Intimately! She is—that is, she was a close friend of my wife and daughters. She killed herself?"

"Yes. Poison. Last night. Where does she fit in with your daughters' disappearance?"

"Where?" he repeated. "I don't know. Must she fit in?"

"I think she must. She told me she hadn't seen your daughters for a couple of weeks. Her husband told me just now that they were talking to her when he came home from the bank last Wednesday afternoon. She seemed nervous when I questioned her. She killed herself shortly afterward. There's hardly a doubt that she fits in somewhere."

"And that means—?"

"That means," I finished for him, "that your daughters may be perfectly safe, but that we can't afford to gamble on that possibility."

"You think harm has come to them?"

"I don't think anything," I evaded, "except that with a death tied up closely with their going, we can't afford to play around."

Banbrock got his attorney on the phone—a pink-faced, white-haired old boy named Norwall, who had the reputation of knowing more about corporations than all the Morgans, but who hadn't the least idea as to what police procedure was all about—and told him to meet us at the Hall of Justice.

We spent an hour and a half there, getting the police turned loose on the affair, and giving the newspapers what we wanted them to have. That was plenty of dope on the girls, plenty of photographs and so forth, but nothing about the connection between them and Mrs. Correll. Of course we let the police in on that angle.

After Banbrock and his attorney had gone away together, I went back to the detectives' assembly room to chew over the job with Pat Reddy, the police sleuth assigned to it.

Pat was the youngest member of the detective bureau—a big blond Irishman who went in for the spectacular in his lazy way.

A couple of years ago he was a new copper, pounding his feet in harness on a hillside beat. One night he tagged an automobile that was parked in front of a fireplug. The owner came out just then and gave him an argument. She was Althea Wallach, only and spoiled daughter of the owner of the Wallach Coffee Company—a slim, reckless youngster with hot eyes. She must have told Pat plenty. He took her over to the station and dumped her in a cell.

Old Wallach, so the story goes, showed up the next morning with a full head of steam and half the lawyers in San Francisco. But Pat made his charge stick, and the girl was fined. Old Wallach did everything but take a punch at Pat in the corridor afterward. Pat grinned his sleepy grin at the coffee importer, and drawled, "You better lay off me—or I'll stop drinking your coffee."

That crack got into most of the newspapers in the country, and even into a Broadway show.

But Pat didn't stop with the snappy comeback. Three days later he and Althea Wallach went over to Alameda and got themselves married. I was in on that part. I happened to be on the ferry they took, and they dragged me along to see the deed done.

Old Wallach immediately disowned his daughter, but that didn't seem to worry anybody else. Pat went on pounding his beat, but, now that he was conspicuous, it wasn't long before his qualities were noticed. He was boosted into the detective bureau.

Old Wallach relented before he died, and left Althea his millions.

Pat took the afternoon off to go to the funeral, and went back to work that night, catching a wagonload of gunmen. He kept on working. I don't know what his wife did with her money, but Pat didn't even improve the quality of his cigars—though he should have. He lived now in the Wallach mansion, true enough, and now and then on rainy mornings he would be driven down to the Hall in a Hispano-Suiza brougham; but there was no difference in him beyond that.

That was the big blond Irishman who sat across a desk from me in the assembly room and fumigated me with something shaped like a cigar.

He took the cigar-like thing out of his mouth presently, and spoke through the fumes. "This Correll woman you think's tied up with the Banbrocks—she was stuck-up a couple of months back and nicked for eight hundred dollars. Know that?"

I hadn't known it. "Lose anything besides cash?" I asked.

"No."

"You believe it?"

He grinned. "That's the point," he said. "We didn't catch the bird who did it. With women who lose things that way—especially money—it's always a question whether it's a hold-up or a hold-out."

He teased some more poison-gas out of the cigar-thing, and added, "The hold-up might have been on the level, though. What are you figuring on doing now?"

"Let's go up to the Agency and see if anything new has turned up. Then I'd like to talk to Mrs. Banbrock again. Maybe she can tell us something about the Correll woman."

At the office I found that reports had come in on the rest of the out-of-town names and addresses. Apparently none of these people knew anything about the girls' whereabouts. Reddy and I went on up to Sea Cliff to the Banbrock home.

Banbrock had telephoned the news of Mrs. Correll's death to his wife, and she had read the papers. She told us she could think of no reason for the suicide. She could imagine no possible connection between the suicide and her stepdaughters' vanishing.

"Mrs. Correll seemed as nearly contented and happy as usual the last time I saw her, two or three weeks ago," Mrs. Banbrock said. "Of course she was by nature inclined to be dissatisfied with things, but not to the extent of doing a thing like this."

"Do you know of any trouble between her and her husband?"

"No. So far as I know, they were happy, though—"

She broke off. Hesitancy, embarrassment showed in her dark eyes.

"Though?" I repeated.

"If I don't tell you now, you'll think I am hiding something," she said, flushing, and laughing a little laugh that held more nervousness than amusement. "It hasn't any bearing, but I was always just a little jealous of Irma. She and my husband were—well, everyone thought they would marry. That was a little before he and I married. I never let it show, and I dare say it was a foolish idea, but I always had a suspicion that Irma married Stewart more in pique than for any other reason, and that she was still fond of Alfred—Mr. Banbrock."

"Was there anything definite to make you think that?"

"No, nothing—really! I never thoroughly believed it. It was just a sort of vague feeling. Cattiness, no doubt, more than anything else."

It was getting along toward evening when Pat and I left the Banbrock house. Before we knocked off for the day, I called up the Old Man—the Continental's San Francisco branch manager, and therefore my boss—and asked him to sic an operative on Irma Correll's past.

I took a look at the morning papers—thanks to their custom of appearing almost as soon as the sun is out of sight—before I went to bed. They had given our job a good spread. All the facts except those having to do with the Correll angle were there, plus photographs, and the usual assortment of guesses and similar garbage.

The following morning I went after the friends of the missing girls to whom I had not yet talked. I found some of them and got nothing of value from them. Late in the morning I telephoned the office to see if anything new had turned up. It had.

"We've just had a call from the sheriff's office at Martinez," the Old Man told me. "An Italian grapegrower near Knob Valley picked up a charred photograph a couple of days ago, and recognized it as Ruth Banbrock when he saw her picture in this morning's paper. Will you get up there? A deputy sheriff and the Italian are waiting for you in the Knob Valley marshal's office."

"I'm on my way," I said.

At the ferry building I used the four minutes before my boat left trying to get Pat Reddy on the phone, with no success.

Knob Valley is a town of less than a thousand people, a dreary, dirty town in Contra Costa County. A San Francisco–Sacramento local set me down there while the afternoon was still young.

I knew the marshal slightly—Tom Orth. I found two men in the office with him. Orth introduced us. Abner Paget, a gawky man of forty-something, with a slack chin, scrawny face, and pale intelligent eyes, was the deputy sheriff. Gio Cereghino, the Italian grape-grower, was a small, nut-brown man with strong yellow teeth that showed in an everlasting smile under his black mustache, and soft brown eyes.

Paget showed me the photograph. A scorched piece of paper the size of a half-dollar, apparently all that had not been burned of the original picture. It was Ruth Banbrock's face. There was little room for doubting that. She had a peculiarly excited—almost drunken—look, and her eyes were larger than in the other pictures of her I had seen. But it was her face.

"He says he found it day 'fore yesterday," Paget explained dryly, nodding at the Italian. "The wind blew it against his foot when he was walkin' up a piece of road near his place. He picked it up an' stuck it in his pocket, he says, for no special reason, I guess." He paused to regard the Italian meditatively. The Italian nodded his head in vigorous affirmation.

"Anyways," the deputy sheriff went on, "he was in town this mornin', an' seen the pictures in the papers from Frisco. So he come in here an' told Tom about it. Tom an' me decided the best thing was to phone your agency—since the papers said you was workin' on it."

I looked at the Italian. Paget, reading my mind, explained, "Cereghino lives over in the hills. Got a grape ranch there. Been around here five or six years, an' ain't killed nobody that I know of."

"Remember the place where you found the picture?" I asked the Italian.

His grin broadened under his mustache, and his head went up and down. "For sure, I remember that place."

"Let's go there," I suggested to Paget.

"Right. Comin' along, Tom?"

The marshal said he couldn't. He had something to do in town. Cereghino, Paget and I went out and got into a dusty Ford that the deputy sheriff drove.

We rode for nearly an hour, along a county road that bent up the slope of Mount Diablo. After a while, at a word from the Italian, we left the county road for a dustier and ruttier one. A mile of this one.

"This place," Cereghino said.

Paget stopped the Ford. We got out in a clearing. The trees and bushes that had crowded the road retreated here for twenty feet or so on either side, leaving a little dusty circle in the woods.

"About this place," the Italian was saying. "I think by this stump. But between that bend ahead and that one behind, I know for sure."

Paget was a countryman. I am not. I waited for him to move.

He looked around the clearing, slowly, standing still between the Italian and me. His pale eyes lighted presently. He went around the Ford to the far side of the clearing. Cereghino and I followed.

Near the fringe of brush at the edge of the clearing, the scrawny deputy stopped to grunt at the ground. The wheel-marks of an automobile were there. A car had turned around here.

Paget went on into the woods. The Italian kept close to his heels. I brought up the rear. Paget was following some sort of track. I couldn't see it, either because he and the Italian blotted it out ahead of me, or because I'm a shine Indian. We went back quite a way.

Paget stopped. The Italian stopped.

Paget said, "Uh-huh," as if he had found an expected thing.

The Italian said something with the name of God in it. I trampled a bush, coming beside them to see what they saw. I saw it.

At the base of a tree, on her side, her knees drawn up close to her body, a girl was dead. She wasn't nice to see. Birds had been at her.

A tobacco-brown coat was half on, half off her shoulders. I knew she was Ruth Banbrock before I turned her over to look at the side of her face the ground had saved from the birds.

Cereghino stood watching me while I examined the girl. His face was mournful in a calm way. The deputy sheriff paid little attention to the body. He was off in the brush, moving around, looking at the ground. He came back as I finished my examination.

"Shot," I told him, "once in the right temple. Before that, I think, there was a fight. There are marks on the arm that was under her body. There's nothing on her—no jewelry, money—nothing."

"That goes," Paget said. "Two women got out of the car back in the clearin', an' came here. Could've been three women—if the others carried this one. Can't make out how many went back. One of 'em was larger than this one. There was a scuffle here. Find the gun?"

"No," I said.

"Neither did I. It went away in the car, then. There's what's left of a fire over there." He ducked his head to the left. "Paper an' rags burnt. Not enough left to do us any good. I reckon the photo Cereghino found blew away from the fire. Late Friday, I'd put it, or maybe Saturday mornin' . . . No nearer than that."

I took the deputy sheriff's word for it. He seemed to know his stuff.

"Come here. I'll show you somethin'," he said, and led me over to a little black pile of ashes.

He hadn't anything to show me. He wanted to talk to me away from the Italian's ears.

"I think the Italian's all right," he said, "but I reckon I'd best hold him a while to make sure. This is some way from his place, an' he stuttered a little bit too much tellin' me how he happened to be passin' here. Course, that don't mean nothin' much. All these Italians peddle *vino,* an' I guess that's what brought him out this way. I'll hold him a day or two, anyways."

"Good," I agreed. "This is your country, and you know the people. Can you visit around and see what you can pick up? Whether anybody saw anything? Saw a Locomobile cabriolet? Or anything else? You can get more than I could."

"I'll do that," he promised.

"All right. Then I'll go back to San Francisco now. I suppose you'll want to camp here with the body?"

"Yeah. You drive the Ford back to Knob Valley, an' tell Tom what's what. He'll come or send out. I'll keep the Italian here with me."

Waiting for the next west-bound train out of Knob Valley, I got the office on the telephone. The Old Man was out. I told my story to one of the office men and asked him to get the news to the Old Man as soon as he could.

Everybody was in the office when I got back to San Francisco. Alfred Banbrock, his face a pink-gray that was deader than solid gray could have been. His pink and white old lawyer. Pat Reddy, sprawled on his spine with his feet on another chair. The Old Man, with his gentle eyes behind gold spectacles and his mild smile, hiding the fact that fifty years of sleuthing had left him without any feelings at all on any subject.

Nobody said anything when I came in. I said my say as briefly as possible.

"Then the other woman—the woman who killed Ruth was—?"

Banbrock didn't finish his question. Nobody answered it.

"We don't know what happened," I said after a while. "Your daughter and someone we don't know may have gone there. Your daughter may have been dead before she was taken there. She may have—"

34

"But Myra!" Banbrock was pulling at his collar with a finger inside. "Where is Myra?"

I couldn't answer that, nor could any of the others.

"You are going up to Knob Valley now?" I asked him.

"Yes, at once. You will come with me?"

I wasn't sorry I could not. "No. There are things to be done here. I'll give you a note to the marshal. I want you to look carefully at the piece of your daughter's photograph the Italian found—to see if you remember it."

Banbrock and the lawyer left.

Reddy lit one of his awful cigars.

"We found the car," the Old Man said.

"Where was it?"

"In Sacramento. It was left in a garage there either late Friday night or early Saturday. Foley has gone up to investigate it. And Reddy has uncovered a new angle."

Pat nodded through his smoke.

"A hockshop dealer came in this morning," Pat said, "and told us that Myra Banbrock and another girl came to his joint last week and hocked a lot of stuff. They gave him phoney names, but he swears one of them was Myra. He recognized her picture as soon as he saw it in the paper. Her companion wasn't Ruth. It was a little blonde."

"Mrs. Correll?"

"Uh-huh. The shark can't swear to that, but I think that's the answer. Some of the jewelry was Myra's, some Ruth's, and some we don't know. I mean we can't prove it belonged to Mrs. Correll—though we will."

"When did all this happen?"

"They soaked the stuff Monday before they went away."

"Have you seen Correll?"

"Uh-huh. I did a lot of talking to him, but the answers weren't worth much. He says he don't know whether any of her jewelry is gone or not, and doesn't care. It was hers, he says, and she could do anything she wanted with it. He was kind of disagreeable. I got along a little better with one of the maids. She says some of Mrs. Correll's pretties disappeared last week. Mrs. Correll said she had lent them to a friend. I'm going to show the stuff the hockshop has to the maid tomorrow to see if she can identify it. She didn't know anything else—except that Mrs. Correll was out of the picture for a while on Friday—the day the Banbrock girls went away."

"What do you mean, out of the picture?" I asked.

"She went out late in the morning and didn't show up until some-where around three the next morning. She and Correll had a row over it, but she wouldn't tell him where she had been."

I liked that. It could mean something.

"And," Pat went on, "Correll has just remembered that his wife had an uncle who went crazy in Pittsburgh in 1902, and that she had a morbid fear of going crazy herself, and that she had often said she would kill herself if she thought she was going crazy. Wasn't it nice of him to re-member those things at last? To account for her death?"

"It was," I agreed, "but it doesn't get us anywhere. It doesn't even prove that he knows anything. Now my guess is—"

"To hell with your guess," Pat said, getting up and pushing his hat in place. "Your guesses all sound like a lot of static to me. I'm going home, eat my dinner, read my Bible, and go to bed."

I suppose he did. Anyway, he left us.

We all might as well have spent the next three days in bed for all the profit that came out of our running around. No place we visited, nobody we questioned, added to our knowledge. We were in a blind alley.

We learned that the Locomobile was left in Sacramento by Myra Banbrock, and not by anyone else, but we didn't learn where she went afterward. We learned that some of the jewelry in the pawnshop was Mrs. Correll's. The Locomobile was brought back from Sacramento. Mrs. Correll was buried. Ruth Banbrock was buried. The newspapers found other mysteries. Reddy and I dug and dug, and all we brought up was dirt.

The following Monday brought me close to the end of my rope. There seemed nothing more to do but sit back and hope that the circulars with which we had plastered North America would bring results. Reddy had already been called off and put to running out fresher trails. I hung on because Banbrock wanted me to keep at it so long as there was the shadow of anything to keep at. But by Monday I had worked myself out.

Before going to Banbrock's office to tell him I was licked, I dropped in at the Hall of Justice to hold a wake over the job with Pat Reddy. He was crouched over his desk, writing a report on some other job.

"Hello!" he greeted me, pushing his report away and smearing it with ashes from his cigar. "How go the Banbrock doings?"

"They don't," I admitted. "It doesn't seem possible, with the stack-up what it is, that we should have come to a dead stop! It's there for us, if we can find it. The need of money before both the Banbrock and the Correll calamities, Mrs. Correll's suicide after I had questioned her about the girls, her burning things before she died and the burning of things immediately before or after Ruth Banbrock's death."

"Maybe the trouble is," Pat suggested, "that you're not such a good sleuth."

"Maybe."

We smoked in silence for a minute or two after that insult.

"You understand," Pat said presently, "there doesn't have to be any connection between the Banbrock death and disappearance and the Correll death."

"Maybe not. But there has to be a connection between the Banbrock death and the Banbrock disappearance. There was a connection—in a pawnshop—between the Banbrock and Correll actions before these things. If there is that connection, then—" I broke off, all full of ideas.

"What's the matter?" Pat asked. "Swallow your gum?"

"Listen!" I let myself get almost enthusiastic. "We've got what happened to three women hooked up together. If we could tie up some more in the same string—I want the names and addresses of all the women and girls in San Francisco who have committed suicide, been murdered, or have disappeared within the past year."

"You think this is a wholesale deal?"

"I think the more we can tie up together, the more lines we'll have to run out. And they can't all lead nowhere. Let's get our list, Pat!"

We spent all the afternoon and most of the night getting it. Its size would have embarrassed the Chamber of Commerce. It looked like a hunk of the telephone book. Things happened in a city in a year. The section devoted to strayed wives and daughters was the largest; suicides next; and even the smallest division—murders—wasn't any too short.

We could check off most of the names against what the police department had already learned of them and their motives, weeding out those positively accounted for in a manner nowise connected with our present interest. The remainder we split into two classes; those of unlikely connection, and those of more possible connection. Even then, the second list was longer than I had expected, or hoped.

There were six suicides in it, three murders, and twenty-one disappearances.

Reddy had other work to do. I put the list in my pocket and went calling.

For four days I ground at the list. I hunted, found, questioned, and investigated friends and relatives of the women and girls on my list. My questions all hit in the same direction. Had she been acquainted with Myra Banbrock? Ruth? Mrs. Correll? Had she been in need of money before her death or disappearance? Had she destroyed anything before her death or disappearance? Had she known any of the other women on my list?

Three times I drew yesses.

Sylvia Varney, a girl of twenty, who had killed herself on November 5th, had drawn six hundred dollars from the bank the week before her death. No one in her family could say what she had done with the money. A friend of Sylvia Varney's—Ada Youngman, a married woman of twenty-five or -six—had disappeared on December 2nd, and was still gone. The Varney girl had been at Mrs. Youngman's home an hour before she—the Varney girl—killed herself.

Mrs. Dorothy Sawdon, a young widow, had shot herself on the night of January 13th. No trace was found of either the money her husband had left her or the funds of a club whose treasurer she was. A bulky letter her maid remembered having given her that afternoon was never found.

These three women's connection with the Banbrock-Correll affair was sketchy enough. None of them had done anything that isn't done by nine out of ten women who kill themselves or run away. But the troubles of all three had come to a head within the past few months—and all three were women of about the same financial and social position as Mrs. Correll and the Banbrocks.

Finishing my list with no fresh leads, I came back to these three.

I had the names and addresses of sixty-two friends of the Banbrock girls. I set about getting the same sort of catalogue on the three women I was trying to bring into the game. I didn't have to do all the digging myself. Fortunately, there were two or three operatives in the office with nothing else to do just then.

We got something.

Mrs. Sawdon had known Raymond Elwood. Sylvia Varney had known Raymond Elwood. There was nothing to show Mrs. Youngman had known him, but it was likely she had. She and the Varney girl had been thick.

I had already interviewed this Raymond Elwood in connection with the Banbrock girls, but had paid no especial attention to him. I had considered him just one of the sleek-headed, high-polished young men of whom there were quite a few listed.

I went back at him, all interest now. The results were promising.

He had, as I have said, a real estate office on Montgomery Street. We were unable to find a single client he had ever served, or any signs of one's existence. He had an apartment out in the Sunset District, where he lived alone. His local record seemed to go back no farther than ten months, though we couldn't find its definite starting point. Apparently he had no relatives in San Francisco. He belonged to a couple of fashionable clubs. He was vaguely supposed to be "well connected in the East." He spent money.

I couldn't shadow Elwood, having too recently interviewed him. Dick Foley did. Elwood was seldom in his office during the first three days Dick tailed him. He was seldom in the financial district. He visited his clubs, he danced and teaed and so forth, and each of those three days he visited a house on Telegraph Hill.

The first afternoon Dick had him, Elwood went to the Telegraph Hill house with a tall fair girl from Burlingame. The second day—in the evening—with a plump young woman who came out of a house out on Broadway. The third evening with a very young girl who seemed to live in the same building as he.

Usually Elwood and his companion spent from three to four hours in the house on Telegraph Hill. Other people—all apparently well-to-do—went in and out of the house while it was under Dick's eye.

I climbed Telegraph Hill to give the house the up-and-down. It was a large house—a big frame house painted egg-yellow. It hung dizzily on a shoulder of the hill, a shoulder that was sharp where rock had been quarried away. The house seemed about to go skiing down on the roofs far below.

It had no immediate neighbors. The approach was screened by bushes and trees.

I gave that section of the hill a good strong play, calling at all the houses within shooting distance of the yellow one. Nobody knew anything about it, or about its occupants. The folks on the Hill aren't a curious lot—perhaps because most of them have something to hide on their own account.

My climbing uphill and downhill got me nothing until I succeeded in learning who owned the yellow house. The owner was an estate whose affairs were in the hands of the West Coast Trust Company.

I took my investigations to the trust company, with some satisfaction. The house had been leased eight months ago by Raymond Elwood, acting for a client named T. F. Maxwell.

We couldn't find Maxwell. We couldn't find anybody who knew Maxwell. We couldn't find any evidence that Maxwell was anything but a name.

One of the operatives went up to the yellow house on the hill, and rang the bell for half an hour with no result. We didn't try that again, not wanting to stir things up at this stage.

I made another trip up the hill, house-hunting. I couldn't find a place as near the yellow house as I would have liked, but I succeeded in renting a three-room flat from which the approach to it could be watched.

Dick and I camped in the flat—with Pat Reddy, when he wasn't off on other duties—and watched machines turn into the screened path that led to the egg-tinted house. Afternoon and night there were machines. Most of them carried women. We saw no one we could place as a resident of the house. Elwood came daily, once alone, the other time with women whose faces we couldn't see from our window.

We shadowed some of the visitors away. They were without exception reasonably well off financially, and some were socially prominent. We didn't go up against any of them with talk. Even a carefully planned pretext is as likely as not to tip your mitt when you're up against a blind game.

Three days of this—and our break came.

It was early evening, just dark. Pat Reddy had phoned that he had been up on a job for two days and a night, and was going to sleep the clock around. Dick and I were sitting at the window of our flat, watching automobiles turn toward the yellow house, writing down their license numbers as they passed through the blue-white patch of light an arc-lamp put in the road just beyond our window.

A woman came climbing the hill, afoot. She was a tall woman, strongly built. A dark veil not thick enough to advertise the fact that she wore it to hide her features, nevertheless did hide them. Her way was up the hill, past our flat, on the other side of the roadway.

A night wind from the Pacific was creaking a grocer's sign down below, swaying the arc-light above. The wind caught the woman as she passed out of our building's sheltered area. Coat and skirts tangled. She put her back to the wind, a hand to her hat. Her veil whipped out straight from her face.

Her face was a face from a photograph—Myra Banbrock's face.

Dick made her with me. "Our baby!" he cried, bouncing to his feet.

"Wait," I said. "She's going into the joint on the edge of the hill. Let her go. We'll go after her when she's inside. That's our excuse for frisking the joint."

I went into the next room, where our telephone was, and called Pat Reddy's number.

"She didn't go in," Dick called from the window. "She went past the path."

"After her!" I ordered. "There's no sense to that! What's the matter with her?" I felt sort of indignant about it. "She's got to go in! Tail her. I'll find you after I get Pat."

Dick went.

Pat's wife answered the telephone. I told her who I was.

"Will you shake Pat out of the covers and send him up here? He knows where I am. Tell him I want him in a hurry."

"I will," she promised. "I'll have him there in ten minutes—wherever it is."

Outdoors, I went up the road, hunting for Dick and Myra Banbrock. Neither was in sight. Passing the bushes that masked the yellow house, I went on, circling down a stony path to the left. No sign of either.

I turned back in time to see Dick going into our flat. I followed.

"She's in," he said when I joined him. "She went up the road, cut across through some bushes, came back to the edge of the cliff, and slid feet-first through a cellar window."

That was nice. The crazier the people you are sleuthing act, as a rule, the nearer you are to an ending of your troubles.

Reddy arrived within a minute or two of the time his wife had promised. He came in buttoning his clothes.

"What the hell did you tell Althea?" he growled at me. "She gave me an overcoat to put over my pajamas, dumped the rest of my clothes in the car, and I had to get in them on the way over."

"I'll cry with you after a while," I dismissed his troubles. "Myra Banbrock just went into the joint through a cellar window. Elwood has been there an hour. Let's knock it off."

Pat is deliberate.

"We ought to have papers, even at that," he stalled.

"Sure," I agreed, "but you can get them fixed up afterward. That's what you're here for. Contra Costa County wants her—maybe to try her for murder. That's all the excuse we need to get into the joint. We go there for her. If we happen to run into anything else—well and good."

Pat finished buttoning his vest.

"Oh, all right!" he said sourly. "Have it your way. But if you get me smashed for searching a house without authority, you'll have to give me a job with your law-breaking agency."

"I will." I turned to Foley. "You'll have to stay outside, Dick. Keep your eye on the getaway. Don't bother anybody else, but if the Banbrock girl gets out, stay behind her."

"I expected it," Dick howled. "Any time there's any fun I can count on being stuck off somewhere on a street corner!"

Pat Reddy and I went straight up the bush-hidden path to the yellow house's front door, and rang the bell.

A big black man in a red fez, red silk jacket over red-striped silk shirt, red zouave pants and red slippers, opened the door. He filled the opening, framed in the black of the hall behind him.

"Is Mr. Maxwell home?" I asked.

The black man shook his head and said words in a language I don't know.

"Mr. Elwood, then?"

Another shaking of the head. More strange language.

"Let's see whoever is home then," I insisted.

Out of the jumble of words that meant nothing to me, I picked three in garbled English, which I thought were "master," "not," and "home."

The door began to close. I put a foot against it.

Pat flashed his buzzer.

Though the black man had poor English, he had knowledge of police badges.

One of his feet stamped on the floor behind him. A gong boomed deafeningly in the rear of the house.

The black man bent his weight to the door.

My weight on the foot that blocked the door, I leaned sidewise, swaying to the Negro.

Slamming from the hip, I put my fist in the middle of him.

Reddy hit the door and we went into the hall.

"'Fore God, Fat Shorty," the black man gasped in good Virginian, "you done hurt me!"

Reddy and I went by him, down the hall whose bounds were lost in darkness.

The bottom of a flight of steps stopped my feet.

A gun went off upstairs. It seemed to point at us. We didn't get the bullets.

A babble of voices—women screaming, men shouting—came and went upstairs; came and went as if a door was being opened and shut.

"Up, my boy!" Reddy yelped in my ear.

We went up the stairs. We didn't find the man who had shot at us.

At the head of the stairs, a door was locked. Reddy's bulk forced it.

We came into a bluish light. A large room, all purple and gold. Confusion of overturned furniture and rumpled rugs. A gray slipper lay near a far door. A green silk gown was in the center of the floor. No person was there.

I raced Pat to the curtained door beyond the slipper. The door was not locked. Reddy yanked it wide.

A room with three girls and a man crouching in a corner, fear in their faces. Neither of them was Myra Banbrock, or Raymond Elwood, or anyone we knew.

Our glances went away from them after the first quick look.

The open door across the room grabbed our attention.

The door gave to a small room.

The room was chaos.

A small room, packed and tangled with bodies. Live bodies, seething, writhing. The room was a funnel into which men and women had been poured. They boiled noisily toward the one small window that was the funnel's outlet. Men and women, youths and girls, screaming, struggling, squirming, fighting. Some had no clothes.

"We'll get through and block the window!" Pat yelled in my ear.

"Like hell—" I began, but he was gone ahead into the confusion.

I went after him.

I didn't mean to block the window. I meant to save Pat from his foolishness. No five men could have fought through that boiling turmoil of maniacs. No ten men could have turned them from the window.

Pat—big as he is—was down when I got to him. A half-dressed girl—a child—was driving at his face with sharp high-heels. Hands, feet, were tearing him apart.

I cleared him with a play of gun-barrel on chins and wrists—dragged him back.

"Myra's not there!" I yelled into his ear as I helped him up. "Elwood's not there!"

I wasn't sure, but I hadn't seen them, and I doubted that they would be in this mess. These savages, boiling again to the window, with no attention for us, whoever they were, weren't insiders. They were the mob, and the principals shouldn't be among them.

"We'll try the other rooms," I yelled again. "We don't want these."

Pat rubbed the back of his hand across his torn face and laughed.

"It's a cinch I don't want 'em any more," he said.

We went back to the head of the stairs the way we had come. We saw no one. The man and girls who had been in the next room were gone.

At the head of the stairs we paused. There was no noise behind us except the now fainter babble of the lunatics fighting for their exit.

A door shut sharply downstairs.

A body came out of nowhere, hit my back, flattened me to the landing.

The feel of silk was on my cheek. A brawny hand was fumbling at my throat.

I bent my wrist until my gun, upside down, lay against my cheek. Praying for my ear, I squeezed.

My cheek took fire. My head was a roaring thing, about to burst.

The silk slid away.

Pat hauled me upright.

We started down the stairs.

Swish!

A thing came past my face, stirring my bared hair.

A thousand pieces of glass, china, plaster, exploded upward at my feet.

I tilted head and gun together.

A Negro's red-silk arms were still spread over the balustrade above.

I sent him two bullets. Pat sent him two.

The Negro teetered over the rail.

He came down on us, arms outflung—a deadman's swan-dive.

We scurried down the stairs from under him.

He shook the house when he landed, but we weren't watching him then.

The smooth sleek head of Raymond Elwood took our attention.

In the light from above, it showed for a furtive split second around the newel-post at the foot of the stairs. Showed and vanished.

Pat Reddy, closer to the rail than I, went over it in a one-hand vault down into the blackness below.

I made the foot of the stairs in two jumps, jerked myself around with a hand on the newel, and plunged into the suddenly noisy dark of the hall.

A wall I couldn't see hit me. Caroming off the opposite wall, I spun into a room whose curtained grayness was the light of day after the hall.

Pat Reddy stood with one hand on a chair-back, holding his belly with the other. His face was mouse-colored under its blood. His eyes were glass agonies. He had the look of a man who had been kicked.

The grin he tried failed. He nodded toward the rear of the house. I went back.

In a little passageway I found Raymond Elwood.

He was sobbing and pulling frantically at a locked door. His face was the hard white of utter terror.

I measured the distance between us.

He turned as I jumped.

I put everything I had in the downswing of my gun-barrel—

A ton of meat and bone crashed into my back.

I went over against the wall, breathless, giddy, sick.

Red-silk arms that ended in brown hands locked around me.

I wondered if there was a whole regiment of these gaudy Negroes— or if I was colliding with the same one over and over.

This one didn't let me do much thinking.

He was big. He was strong. He didn't mean any good.

My gun-arm was flat at my side, straight down. I tried a shot at one of the Negro's feet. Missed. Tried again. He moved his feet. I wriggled around, half facing him.

Elwood piled on my other side.

The Negro bent me backward, folding my spine on itself like an accordion.

I fought to hold my knees stiff. Too much weight was hanging on me. My knees sagged. My body curved back.

Pat Reddy, swaying in the doorway, shone over the Negro's shoulder like the Angel Gabriel.

Gray pain was in Pat's face, but his eyes were clear. His right hand held a gun. His left was getting a blackjack out of his hip pocket.

He swung the sap down on the Negro's shaven skull.

The black man wheeled away from me, shaking his head.

Pat hit him once more before the Negro closed with him—hit him full in the face, but couldn't beat him off.

45

Twisting my freed gun hand up, I drilled Elwood neatly through the chest, and let him slide down me to the floor.

The Negro had Pat against the wall, bothering him a lot. His broad red back was a target.

But I had used five of the six bullets in my gun. I had more in my pocket, but reloading takes time.

I stepped out of Elwood's feeble hands, and went to work with the flat of my gun on the Negro. There was a roll of fat where his skull and neck fit together. The third time I hit it, he flopped, taking Pat with him.

I rolled him off. The blond police detective—not very blond now—got up.

At the other end of the passageway an open door showed an empty kitchen.

Pat and I went to the door that Elwood had been playing with. It was a solid piece of carpentering, and neatly fastened.

Yoking ourselves together, we began to beat the door with our combined three hundred and seventy or eighty pounds.

It shook, but held. We hit again. Wood we couldn't see tore.

Again.

The door popped away from us. We went through—down a flight of steps—rolling, snowballing down—until a cement floor stopped us.

Pat came back to life first.

"You're a hell of an acrobat," he said. "Get off my neck!"

I stood up. He stood up. We seemed to be dividing the evening between falling on the floor and getting up from the floor.

A light switch was at my shoulder. I turned it on.

If I looked anything like Pat, we were a fine pair of nightmares. He was all raw meat and dirt, with not enough clothes left to hide much of either.

I didn't like his looks, so I looked around the basement in which we stood. To the rear was a furnace, coalbins and a woodpile. To the front was a hallway and rooms, after the manner of the upstairs.

The first door we tried was locked, but not strongly. We smashed through it into a photographer's dark-room.

The second door was unlocked, and put us in a chemical laboratory; retorts, tubes, burners and a small still. There was a little round iron stove in the middle of the room. No one was there.

We went out into the hallway and to the third door, not so cheerfully.

This cellar looked like a bloomer. We were wasting time here, when we should have stayed upstairs. I tried the door.

It was firm beyond trembling.

We smacked it with our weight, together, experimentally. It didn't shake.

"Wait."

Pat went to the woodpile in the rear and came back with an axe.

He swung the axe against the door, flaking out a hunk of wood. Silvery points of light sparkled in the hole. The other side of the door was an iron or steel plate.

Pat put the axe down and leaned on the helve.

"You write the next prescription," he said.

I didn't have anything to suggest, except, "I'll camp here. You beat it upstairs, and see if any of your coppers have shown up. This is a God-forsaken hole, but somebody may have sent in an alarm. See if you can find another way into this room—a window, maybe—or manpower enough to get us in through this door."

Pat turned toward the steps.

A sound stopped him—the clicking of bolts on the other side of the iron-lined door.

A jump put Pat on one side of the frame. A step put me on the other.

Slowly the door moved in. Too slowly.

I kicked it open.

Pat and I went into the room on top of my kick.

His shoulder hit the woman. I managed to catch her before she fell.

Pat took her gun. I steadied her back on her feet.

Her face was a pale blank square.

She was Myra Banbrock, but she had none of the masculinity that had been in her photographs and description.

Steadying her with one arm—which also served to block her arms—I looked around the room.

A small cube of a room whose walls were brown-painted metal. On the floor lay a queer little dead man.

A little man in tight-fitting black velvet and silk. Black velvet blouse and breeches, black silk stockings and skull cap, black patent leather pumps. His face was small and old and bony, but smooth as stone, without line or wrinkle.

A hole was in his blouse, where it fit high under his chin. The hole bled very slowly. The floor around him showed it had been bleeding faster a little while ago.

Beyond him, a safe was open. Papers were on the floor in front of it, as if the safe had been tilted to spill them out.

The girl moved against my arm.

"You killed him?" I asked.

"Yes," too faint to have been heard a yard away.

"Why?"

She shook her short brown hair out of her eyes with a tired jerk of her head.

"Does it make any difference?" she asked. "I did kill him."

"It might make a difference," I told her, taking my arm away, and going over to shut the door. People talk more freely in a room with a closed door. "I happen to be in your father's employ. Mr. Reddy is a police detective. Of course, neither of us can smash any laws, but if you'll tell us what's what, maybe we can help you."

"My father's employ?" she questioned.

"Yes. When you and your sister disappeared, he engaged me to find you. We found your sister, and—"

Life came into her face and eyes and voice.

"I didn't kill Ruth!" she cried. "The papers lied! I didn't kill her! I didn't know she had the revolver. I didn't know it! We were going away to hide from—from everything. We stopped in the woods to burn the—those things. That's the first time I knew she had the revolver. We had talked about suicide at first, but I had persuaded her—thought I had persuaded her—not to. I tried to take the revolver away from her, but I couldn't. She shot herself while I was trying to get it away. I tried to stop her. I didn't kill her!"

This was getting somewhere.

"And then?" I encouraged her.

"And then I went to Sacramento and left the car there, and came back to San Francisco. Ruth told me she had written Raymond Elwood a letter. She told me that before I persuaded her not to kill herself—the first time. I tried to get the letter from Raymond. She had written him she was going to kill herself. I tried to get the letter, but Raymond said he had given it to Hador.

"So I came here this evening to get it. I had just found it when there was a lot of noise upstairs. Then Hador came in and found me. He bolted the door. And—and I shot him with the revolver that was in the safe. I—

I shot him when he turned around, before he could say anything. It had to be that way, or I couldn't."

"You mean you shot him without being threatened or attacked by him?" Pat asked.

"Yes. I was afraid of him, afraid to let him speak. I hated him! I couldn't help it. It had to be that way. If he had talked I couldn't have shot him. He—he wouldn't have let me!"

"Who was this Hador?" I asked.

She looked away from Pat and me, at the walls, at the ceiling, at the queer little dead man on the floor.

"He was a—" She cleared her throat, and started again, staring down at her feet. "Raymond Elwood brought us here the first time. We thought it was funny. But Hador was a devil. He told you things and you believed them. You couldn't help it. He told you *everything* and you believed it. Perhaps we were drugged. There was always a warm bluish wine. It must have been drugged. We couldn't have done those things if it hadn't. Nobody would— He called himself a priest—a priest of Alzoa. He taught a freeing of the spirit from the flesh by—"

Her voice broke huskily. She shuddered.

"It was horrible!" she went on presently in the silence Pat and I had left for her. "But you believed him. That is the whole thing. You can't understand it unless you understand that. The things he taught could not be so. But he said they were, and you *believed* they were. Or maybe—I don't know—maybe you pretended you believed them, because you were crazy and drugs were in your blood. We came back again and again, for weeks, months, before the disgust that had to come drove us away.

"We stopped coming, Ruth and I—and Irma. And then we found out what he was. He demanded money, more money than we had been paying while we believed—or pretended belief—in his cult. We couldn't give him the money he demanded. I told him we wouldn't. He sent us photographs—of us—taken during the—the times here. They were—*pictures—you—couldn't—explain*. And they were true! We knew them true! What could we do? He said he would send copies to our father, every friend, everyone we knew—unless we paid.

"What could we do—except pay? We got the money somehow. We gave him money—more—more—more. And then we had no more— could get no more. We didn't know what to do! There was nothing to do, except—Ruth and Irma wanted to kill themselves. I thought of that, too. But I persuaded Ruth not to. I said we'd go away. I'd take her away—keep her safe. And then—then—this!"

She stopped talking, went on staring at her feet.

I looked again at the little dead man on the floor, weird in his black cap and clothes. No more blood came from his throat.

It wasn't hard to put the pieces together. This dead Hador, self-ordained priest of something or other, staging orgies under the alias of religious ceremonies. Elwood, his confederate, bringing women of family and wealth to him. A room lighted for photography, with a concealed camera. Contributions from his converts so long as they were faithful to the cult. Blackmail—with the help of the photographs—afterward.

I looked from Hador to Pat Reddy. He was scowling at the dead man. No sound came from outside the room.

"You have the letter your sister wrote Elwood?" I asked the girl.

Her hand flashed to her bosom, and crinkled paper there.

"Yes."

"It says plainly she meant to kill herself?"

"Yes."

"That ought to square her with Contra Costa County," I said to Pat.

He nodded his battered head.

"It ought to," he agreed. "It's not likely that they could prove murder on her even without that letter. With it, they'll not take her into court. That's a safe bet. Another is that she won't have any trouble over this shooting. She'll come out of court free, and thanked in the bargain."

Myra Banbrock flinched away from Pat as if he had hit her in the face.

I was her father's hired man just now. I saw her side of the affair.

I lit a cigarette and studied what I could see of Pat's face through blood and grime. Pat is a right guy.

"Listen, Pat," I wheedled him, though with a voice that was as if I were not trying to wheedle him at all. "Miss Banbrock can go into court and come out free and thanked, as you say. But to do it, she's got to use everything she knows. She's got to have all the evidence there is. She's got to use all those photographs Hador took—or all we can find of them.

"Some of those pictures have sent women to suicide, Pat—at least two that we know. If Miss Banbrock goes into court, we've got to make the photographs of God knows how many other women public property. We've got to advertise things that will put Miss Banbrock—and you can't say how many other women and girls—in a position that at least two women have killed themselves to escape."

Pat scowled at me and rubbed his dirty chin with a dirtier thumb.

I took a deep breath and made my play. "Pat, you and I came here to question Raymond Elwood, having traced him here. Maybe we suspected him of being tied up with the mob that knocked over the St. Louis bank last month. Maybe we suspected him of handling the stuff that was taken from the mail cars in that stick-up near Denver week before last. Anyway, we were after him, knowing that he had a lot of money that came from nowhere, and a real estate office that did no real estate business.

"We came here to question him in connection with one of these jobs I've mentioned. We were jumped by a couple of the Negroes upstairs when they found we were sleuths. The rest of it grew out of that. This religious cult business was just something we ran into, and didn't interest us especially. So far as we knew, all these folks jumped us just through friendship for the man we were trying to question. Hador was one of them, and, tussling with you, you shot him with his own gun, which, of course, is the one Miss Banbrock found in the safe."

Reddy didn't seem to like my suggestion at all. The eyes with which he regarded me were decidedly sour.

"You're goofy," he accused me. "What'll that get anybody? That won't keep Miss Banbrock out of it. She's here, isn't she, and the rest of it will come out like thread off a spool."

"But Miss Banbrock *wasn't* here," I explained. "Maybe the upstairs is full of coppers by now. Maybe not. Anyway, you're going to take Miss Banbrock out of here and turn her over to Dick Foley, who will take her home. She's got nothing to do with this party. Tomorrow she, and her father's lawyer, and I, will all go up to Martinez and make a deal with the prosecuting attorney of Contra Costa County. We'll show him how Ruth killed herself. If somebody happens to connect the Elwood who I hope is dead upstairs with the Elwood who knew the girls and Mrs. Correll, what of it? If we keep out of court—as we'll do by convincing the Contra Costra people they can't possibly convict her of her sister's murder—we'll keep out of the newspapers—and out of trouble."

Pat hung fire, thumb still to chin.

"Remember," I urged him, "it's not only Miss Banbrock we're doing this for. It's a couple of dead ones, and a flock of live ones, who certainly got mixed up with Hador of their own accords, but who don't stop being human beings on that account."

Pat shook his head stubbornly.

"I'm sorry," I told the girl with faked hopelessness. "I've done all I can, but it's a lot to ask of Reddy. I don't know that I blame him for being afraid to take a chance on—"

Pat is Irish. "Don't be so damned quick to fly off," he snapped at me, cutting short my hypocrisy. "But why do I have to be the one that shot this Hador? Why not you?"

I had him!

"Because," I explained, "you're a bull and I'm not. There'll be less chance of a slip-up if he was shot by a bona fide, star-wearing, flat-footed officer of the peace. I killed most of those birds upstairs. You ought to do something to show you were here."

That was only part of the truth. My idea was that if Pat took the credit, he couldn't very well ease himself out afterward, no matter what happened. Pat's a right guy, and I'd trust him anywhere—but you can trust a man just as easily if you have him sewed up.

Pat grumbled and shook his head, but, "I'm ruining myself, I don't doubt," he growled, "but I'll do it, this once."

"Attaboy!" I went over to pick up the girl's hat from the corner in which it lay. "I'll wait here until you come back from turning her over to Dick." I gave the girl her hat and orders together. "You go to your home with the man Reddy turns you over to. Stay there until I come, which will be as soon as I can make it. Don't tell anybody anything, except that I told you to keep quiet. That includes your father. Tell him I told you not to tell him even where you saw me. Got it?"

"Yes, and I—"

Gratitude is nice to think about afterward, but it takes time when there's work to be done.

"Get going, Pat!"

They went.

As soon as I was alone with the dead man I stepped over him and knelt in front of the safe, pushing letters and papers away, hunting for photographs. None was in sight. One compartment of the safe was locked.

I frisked the corpse. No key. The locked compartment wasn't very strong, but neither am I the best safe-burglar in the West. It took me a while to get into it.

What I wanted was there. A thick sheaf of negatives. A stack of prints—half a hundred of them.

I started to run through them, hunting for the Banbrock girls' pictures.

I wanted to have them pocketed before Pat came back. I didn't know how much farther he would let me go.

Luck was against me—and the time I had wasted getting into the compartment. He was back before I had got past the sixth print in the stack. Those six had been—pretty bad.

"Well, that's done," Pat growled at me as he came into the room. "Dick's got her. Elwood is dead, and so is the only one of the Negroes I saw upstairs. Everybody else seems to have beat it. No bulls have shown—so I put in a call for a wagonful."

I stood up, holding the sheaf of negatives in one hand, the prints in the other.

"What's all that?" he asked.

I went after him again. "Photographs. You've just done me a big favor, Pat, and I'm not hoggish enough to ask another. But I'm going to put something in front of you, Pat. I'll give you the lay, and you can name it.

"These"—I waved the pictures at him—"are Hador's meal-tickets—the photos he was either collecting on or planning to collect on. They're photographs of people, Pat, mostly women and girls, and some of them are pretty rotten.

"If tomorrow's papers say that a flock of photos were found in this house after the fireworks, there's going to be a fat suicide-list in the next day's papers, and a fatter list of disappearances. If the papers say nothing about the photos, the lists may be a little smaller, but not much. Some of the people whose pictures are here know they are here. They will expect the police to come hunting for them. We know this much about the photographs—two women have killed themselves to get away from them. This is an armful of stuff that can dynamite a lot of people, Pat, and a lot of families—no matter which of those two ways the papers read.

"But, suppose, Pat, the papers say that just before you shot Hador he succeeded in burning a lot of pictures and papers, burning them beyond recognition. Isn't it likely, then, that there won't be any suicides? That some of the disappearances of recent months may clear themselves up? There she is, Pat—you name it."

Looking back, it seems to me I had come a lot nearer being eloquent than ever before in my life.

But Pat didn't applaud. He cursed me. He cursed me thoroughly, bitterly, and with an amount of feeling that told me I had won another point in my little game. He called me more things than I ever listened to before from a man who was built of meat and bone, and who therefore could be smacked.

When he was through, we carried the papers and photographs and a small book of addresses we found in the safe into the next room, and fed them to the little round iron stove there. The last of them was ash before we heard the police overhead.

"That's absolutely all!" Pat declared when we got up from our work. "Don't ever ask me to do anything else for you if you live to be a thousand."

"That's absolutely all," I echoed.

I like Pat. He is a right guy. The sixth photograph in the stack had been of his wife—the coffee importer's reckless, hot-eyed daughter.

W. R. BURNETT
(1899–1982)

It has been written that if W[illiam] R[iley] Burnett's major novels are judged solely for their influence, he was one of the most important writers of his time. His first novel, Little Caesar (1929), about the rise and fall of Rico Cesare Bandello of Chicago's Little Italy, was the prototypical gangster saga. It inspired numerous other writers and Hollywood filmmakers, created a new subgenre, and helped make film legends of James Cagney, Edward G. Robinson, and Humphrey Bogart. Public Enemy (1931), They Live by Night (1948), White Heat (1949), The Godfather (1972)—all are direct descendants of Little Caesar, as is Burnett's 1941 classic, High Sierra, which added poignant elements of humanity and high tragedy to the gangster story. Similarly, The Asphalt Jungle (1949) and its 1950 film version also established a subgenre, that of the "big caper novel," which flourished in the 1950s and 1960s and which still has its proponents and practitioners.

Burnett's novels may fall short of art when judged solely on their literary merits. But as critic George Grella says of Burnett and his work: "He may be the single most successful writer on the notion of the criminal as the emblem of an era. He provides some of the most dynamic and apposite metaphors for the life of America in the twentieth century."

All the first-rank novels by Burnett were written before 1950. In addition to those cited above, others of note include Dark Hazard (1933), Nobody Lives Forever (1943), and two historicals: Saint Johnson (1930), the first substantive novel about Wyatt Earp and the gunfight at the O.K. Corral, and The Dark Command (1938). Such post-1950 novels as Vanity Row (1952), Round the Clock at Volari's (1961), and Good-bye Chicago (1981), his last published fiction, are competent but undistinguished. Between 1931 and 1963, Burnett wrote numerous screenplays not only for A films such as High Sierra (1941), with John Huston, and This Gun for Hire (1941), with Albert Maltz, but also for lesser, B movies.

Burnett's output of short stories was small, and all but one were penned early in his career. "Round Trip," which was first published in Harper's in 1929, the same year Little Caesar appeared, is likewise a gangster story. Just as the novel does, this quiet little tale of Chicago *enforcer George Barber (born Giovanni Pasquale Barbieri) and his eventful Toledo vacation tells it like it was in the days of Al Capone, Frank Nitti, and Rico Cesare Bandello.*

B. P.

1929

ROUND TRIP

It was about ten o'clock when the lookout let George in. The big play was usually between twelve and three, and now there were only a few people in the place. In one corner of the main room four men were playing bridge, and one of the center wheels was running.

"Hello, Mr. Barber," the lookout said. "Little early tonight, ain't you?"

"Yeah," said George. "Boss in?"

"Yeah," said the lookout, "and he wants to see you. He was grinning all over his face. But he didn't say nothing to me."

"Somebody kicked in," said George.

"Yeah," said the lookout, "that's about it."

Levin, one of the croupiers, came over to George.

"Mr. Barber," he said, "The Spade just left. He and the Old Man had a session."

George grinned and struck at one of his spats with his cane.

"The Spade was in, was he? Well, no wonder the Old Man was in a good humor."

"How do you do it, Mr. Barber?" asked the croupier.

"Yeah, we been wondering," put in the lookout.

"Well," said George, "I just talk nice to 'em and they get ashamed of themselves and pay up."

The croupier and the lookout laughed.

"Well," said the croupier, "it's a gift, that's all."

Somebody knocked at the entrance door, and the lookout went to see who it was. The croupier grinned at George and walked back to his chair. George knocked at Weinberg's door, then pushed it open. As soon as he saw George, Weinberg began to grin and nod his head.

"The Spade was in," he said.

George sat down and lighted a cigar.

"Yeah, so I hear."

"He settled the whole business, George," said Weinberg. "You could've knocked my eyes off with a ball bat."

"Well," said George, "I thought maybe he'd be in."

"Did, eh? Listen, George, how did you ever pry The Spade loose from three grand?"

"It's a business secret," said George and laughed.

Weinberg sat tapping his desk with a pencil and staring at George. He never could dope him out. Pretty soon he said:

"George, better watch The Spade. He's gonna try to make it tough for you."

"He'll try."

"I told him he could play his I.O.U.'s again, but he said he'd never come in this place as long as you was around. So I told him goodbye."

"Well," said George, "he can play some then, because I'm leaving you."

Weinberg just sat there tapping with his pencil.

"I'm fed up," said George. "I'm going to take me a vacation. I'm sick of Chi. Same old dumps, same old mob."

"How long you figure to be away?" asked Weinberg.

"About a month. I'm going over east. I got some friends in Toledo."

"Well," said Weinberg, "you'll have a job when you get back."

He got up, opened a little safe in the wall behind him, and took out a big, unsealed envelope.

"Here's a present for you, George," he said. "I'm giving you a cut on The Spade's money besides your regular divvy. I know a right guy when I see one."

"O.K.," said George, putting the envelope in his pocket without looking at it.

"Matter of fact," said Weinberg, "I never expected to see no more of The Spade's money. He ain't paying nobody. He's blacklisted."

George sat puffing at his cigar. Weinberg poured out a couple of drinks from the decanter on his desk. They drank.

"Don't get sore now," said Weinberg, "when I ask you this question, but listen, George, you ain't going to Toledo to hide out, are you?"

George got red in the face.

"Say . . ." he said, and started to to rise.

"All right! All right!" said Weinberg hurriedly, "I didn't think so, George, I didn't think so. I just wondered."

"Tell you what I'll do," said George; "get your hat and I'll take you down to The Spade's restaurant for some lunch."

Weinberg laughed but he didn't feel like laughing.

"Never mind, George," he said. "I just wondered."

"All right," said George. "But any time you get an idea in your head I'm afraid of a guy like The Spade, get it right out again, because you're all wrong."

"Sure," said Weinberg.

After another drink they shook hands, and George went out into the main room. There was another table of bridge going now, and a faro game had opened up.

The lookout opened the door for George.

"I won't be seeing you for a while," said George.

"That so?" said the lookout. "Well, watch your step wherever you're going."

George got into Toledo late at night. He felt tired and bored, and he didn't feel any better when the taxi-driver, who had taken him from the depot to the hotel, presented his bill.

"Brother," said George, "you don't need no gun."

"What's that!" exclaimed the taxi-driver, scowling.

"You heard me," said George. "You don't need no gun."

"Well," said the taxi-driver, "that's our regular rate, Mister. Maybe you better take a street car."

Then he climbed into his cab and drove off. George stood there staring at the cab till it turned a corner.

"Damn' hick!" he said. "Talking to me like that!"

The doorman took his bags.

"You sure got some smart boys in this town," said George.

The doorman merely put his head on one side and grinned.

There were three men ahead of George at the desk, and he had to wait. The clerk ignored him.

"Say," said George, finally, "give me one of them cards. I can be filling it out."

The clerk stared at him and then handed him a card. George screwed up his mouth and wrote very carefully:

Mr. Geo. P. Barber,
Chicago, Ill.

The clerk glanced at the card and said:

"You'll have to give us an address, Mr. Barber, please."

"Allard Hotel," said George. "Listen, I'm tired, and I can't be standing around in this lobby all night."

"Yes, sir," said the clerk. "About how long will you be here?"

"I don't know," said George. "It all depends."

As soon as George was settled in his room he unpacked his bag and undressed slowly. He still felt tired and bored.

"Some town," he said. "Why, the way them birds act you'd think this *was* a town."

He turned out the lights, lighted a cigarette, and sat down at a window in his pajamas. It was about twelve o'clock and the streets were nearly empty.

"Good Lord," he said; "why, in Chi it's busier than this five miles north."

He flung the cigarette out the window and climbed into bed. He lay thinking about The Spade and Weinberg. Finally he fell asleep.

He woke early the next morning, which was unusual for him, and discovered that he had a headache and a sore throat.

"Hell!" he said.

He pulled on his clothes hurriedly and went across the street to a little Italian restaurant with a green façade and an aquarium in the window. The place was empty. He sat down at a table in the front and stared out into the street. A waiter came over and handed him a menu. The waiter was tall and stooped, with a dark, sad face. He studied George for a moment, then addressed him in Italian. George turned and stared at the waiter. He did not like to be reminded that he had been born Giovanni Pasquale Barbieri.

"Talk American! Talk American!" he said.

"Yes, sir," said the waiter. "You a stranger here?"

"Yeah," said George.

"I seen you come out of the hotel, so I thought you was."

"Yeah," said George, with a certain amount of pride, "I'm from Chicago."

"Me, too," said the waiter. "My brother's got a plumbing shop on Grand Avenue."

"Yeah?" said George. "Well, I live 4000 numbers north on Sheridan."

"That so? Pretty swell out there, ain't it?"

"Not bad," said George. "Say, what do you do around here for excitement?"

The waiter smiled sadly and shrugged.

"That's what I thought," said George.

"If I ever get me some money I'm going back to Chicago," said the waiter.

George ate his breakfast hurriedly and gave the waiter a big tip. The waiter smiled sadly.

"Thank you. We don't get no tips around here like that."

"Small town, small money," said George.

The waiter helped him on with his overcoat, then George returned to the hotel. He didn't know what to do with himself, so he went to bed. When he woke up his headache was worse and he could hardly swallow.

"By God, if I ain't got me a nice cold," he said.

He dressed in his best blue-serge suit and took a taxi down to Chiggi's. Chiggi was in the beer racket and was making good. He had a new place now with mirrors all around the wall and white tablecloths. The bouncer took him back to Chiggi's office. Chiggi got up and shook hands.

"Hello, George," he said. "How's tricks?"

"I ain't starving."

"In bad over in Chi?"

"Me? I should say not."

Chiggi just grinned and said nothing.

"Listen," said George, "does a guy have to be in bad to leave Chi?"

"Well," said Chiggi, "the only guys I ever knew that left were in bad."

"Here's one that ain't."

"That's your story, anyway," said Chiggi, grinning.

The bouncer came and called Chiggi, and George put his feet up on Chiggi's desk and sat looking at the wall. From time to time he felt his throat. Once or twice he sneezed.

"It's a damn' good thing I didn't come over on a sleeper; I'd've had pneumonia," he thought.

Chiggi came back and they organized a poker game. George played listlessly and dropped two hundred dollars. Then he went out into the dance hall, got himself a girl, and danced a couple of times. The music wasn't bad, the floor was good, and the girl was a cute kid and willing, but George wasn't having a good time.

"Say," he thought, "what the devil's wrong with me?"

About two o'clock he left Chiggi's, got a taxi, and went back to the hotel. It was raining. He sat hunched in one corner of the taxi with his coat collar turned up.

He went to bed as soon as he could get his clothes off, but he didn't sleep well and kept tossing around.

At eleven o'clock the next morning he came down into the lobby. He went over to the mail clerk to ask if he had any mail; not that he was expecting any, but just to give the impression that he was the kind of man that got mail, important mail. The girl handed him a sealed envelope with his name on it. Surprised, he tore it open and read:

> . . . as your stay is marked on our cards as indefinite, and as you are not listed among our reservations, we must ask that your room be vacated by six tonight. There are several conventions in town this week and it is absolutely necessary that we take care of our reservations. . . .
>
> W. W. Hurlburt, Asst. Mgr.

"Well, tie that!" said George.

The girl at the mail desk stared at him.

"Say, sister," he said, "where's the assistant manager's office?"

She pointed. He went over and knocked at the door, and then went in. A big, bald-headed man looked up.

"Well?"

"Listen," said George, "are you the assistant manager?"

"I am," said the big man.

George tossed him the letter.

"Sorry," said the big man, "but what can we do, Mr. Barber?"

"I'll tell you what you can do," said George; "you can tear that letter up and forget about it."

"Sorry."

"You think I'm going to leave, I suppose?"

"Well," said the big man, "I guess you'll have to."

"Oh, that's it," said George, smiling. "Well, try to put me out."

The big man stared at him.

"Yeah," said George; "try to put me out. I'd like to see somebody come up and put me out. I'll learn them something."

"Well, Mr. Barber," said the big man, "as a matter of fact, it is a little unusual for us to do anything like this. That is, it's not customary. But we were instructed to do so. That's all I can tell you."

George stared at him for a moment.

"You mean the bulls?"

"Sorry," said the big man. "That's all I can tell you."

George laughed.

"Well," he said, "I'm staying, so don't try to rent that room."

He went out, banging the door, ate his dinner at the Italian restaurant across the street, talked with the waiter for a quarter of an hour and gave him another big tip; then he took a taxi out to Chiggi's. But Chiggi had been called to Detroit on business. George had a couple of cocktails and sat talking with Curly, the bouncer, about Chicago Red, who had once been Chiggi's partner, and Rico, the gang leader, who had been killed by the police in the alley back of Chiggi's old place. At four o'clock George got a taxi and went back to the hotel. All the way to the hotel he sat trying to figure out why he had come to Toledo. This was sure a hell of a vacation!

The key clerk gave him his key without a word, and George smiled.

"Bluffed 'em out," he said.

But when he opened his door he saw a man sitting by the window reading a magazine. His hand went involuntarily toward his armpit. The man stood up; he was big and had a tough, Irish face.

"My name's Geygan," said the man, turning back his coat. "I want to see you a minute. Your name's Barber, ain't it?"

"Yeah," said George. "What's the song, flatfoot?"

Geygan stared at him.

"You talking to me, kid?"

"There ain't nobody else in the room that I see," said George.

"Smart boy," said Geygan. "Come over till I fan you."

"You'll fan nobody," said George. "What's the game?"

Geygan came over to George, whirled him around, and patted his pockets; then he lifted George's arms and felt his ribs; then he slapped his trouser legs. George was stupefied.

Geygan laughed.

"I thought you Chicago birds packed rods," he said.

"What would I do with a rod in this tank town!" said George.

"All right," said Geygan. "Now listen careful to what I say. Tonight you leave town. Get that? You birds can't light here. That's all. We've had some of you birds over here and we don't like you, see? Beat it and no questions asked. You stick around here and we'll put you away."

George grinned.

"Putting it on big, hunh?"

"Yeah. You better not be in the city limits at twelve tonight or . . ."

"Listen," said George, interrupting, "you hick bulls can't bluff me that easy. Just try and do something, that's all. Just try and do something. You ain't got a thing on me."

"All right," said Geygan.

Geygan went out. George took off his overcoat and sat down in the chair by the window.

"Can you beat that!" he thought. "It's a damn' good thing I got my rods in the trunk. Why, that mug actually fanned me. Yeah. Say, what kind of a town is this, anyway? No wonder Chicago Red hit for home!"

He got up and unlocked his trunk. There was a false bottom in it where he kept his guns and his liquor. That was safe. Well, they didn't have a thing on him. Let them try and put him out. All the same, he began to feel uneasy. But, hell, he couldn't let these small-town cops scare him.

He was taking off his shoes when somebody knocked at the door.

"I wonder what the game is," he thought.

Then he went over and opened the door. Geygan and two other plain-clothesmen stepped in.

"There he is, chief. You talk to him. He won't listen to me."

"Say," said the chief, a big gray-haired man, "they tell me you've decided to prolong your visit."

"Yeah," said George, "indefinitely."

"Well," said the chief, "if you want to stay here, why, I guess we can accommodate you. Fan him, Buck."

"Say," said George, "I been fanned so much I got callouses."

"That's too bad," said the chief. "Go ahead, Buck."

Buck whirled George around and gave him the same kind of search Geygan had given him, with this difference: he found a gun in his hip pocket, a small nickel-plated .32. George stared at the gun and began to sweat.

"Geygan," said the chief, "you didn't do a very good job."

"I guess not," said Geygan.

"You never found that cap pistol on me," said George, staring hard at Buck.

"Will you listen to that, Buck!" said the chief. "He thinks you're a magician."

"Why, you planted that gun on me," said George. "That's a hell of a way to do."

"Well," said the chief, "when your case comes up, you can tell it all to the judge."

"My case!" cried George.

"Why, sure," said the chief. "We send 'em up for carrying rods here."

George stood looking at the floor. By God, they had him. Wasn't that a break. Well, it was up to Chiggi now.

"Listen," said the chief, "we ain't looking for no trouble and we're right guys, Barber. I'll make you a little proposition. You pack up and take the next train back to Chicago and we'll forget about the .32."

"He don't want to go back to Chicago," said Geygan. "He told me."

George walked over to the window and stood there looking down at the street.

"O.K.," he said, "I'll go."

"All right," said the chief. "Buck, you stick with the Chicago boy and see that he gets on the right train."

"All right, chief," said Buck.

Geygan and the chief went out. Buck sat down and began to read a newspaper.

Weinberg was sitting at his desk, smoking a big cigar, when George opened the door. Seeing George, he nearly dropped his cigar.

"Hello, boss," said George.

"By God, I thought you was a ghost," said Weinberg. "What's wrong with your voice?"

"I caught a cold over in Toledo."

"You been to Toledo and back already! Did you go by airplane?"

George grinned.

"No, but I made a quick trip. What a hick town. You ought to go there once, and look it over."

"Chicago suits me," said Weinberg.

George sat down, and Weinberg poured him a drink. George didn't say anything, but just sat there sipping his drink. Pretty soon Weinberg said:

"George, I was hoping you'd stay in Toledo for a while. Rocco was in the other night and he told me that The Spade was telling everybody that your number was up."

George grinned.

"Ain't that funny!"

Weinberg didn't think it was funny, but he laughed and poured himself another drink.

"Yeah," said George, "that's the best one I've heard this year."

RAOUL WHITFIELD
(1898–1945)

Raoul Fauconnier Whitfield was one of the pioneers of the hard-boiled genre. From 1926 to 1934, he wrote around ninety stories for Black Mask alone, twenty of which were about Joe Gar, the Spanish-Filipino detective with the Colt .45 automatic in his back pocket. These stories were penned under the pseudonym Ramon Decolta. In Joseph T. Shaw's groundbreaking anthology The Hard-Boiled Omnibus (1946), Whitfield is the only writer who is honored twice, once as himself and once as Decolta.

Whitfield's maiden novel, Green Ice (1930), was immoderately praised by none other than Dashiell Hammett, who described the work as "280 pages of naked action pounded into tough compactness by staccato, hammerlike writing." Will Cuppy, the influential book critic of the New York Herald Tribune, declared unequivocally that Green Ice was superior to Hammett's own Maltese Falcon, which was published the same year. Despite all this praise, Whitfield is one of the "great uncollecteds" of the hard-boiled genre.

The reason for Whitfield's lack of recognition may be that, like Longfellow's youngest heroine, when he was good, he was very, very good, but when he was bad, he was not very good at all. Much of his non–Black Mask work was churned-out air-war material (he had flown scout-fighters in World War I), written hastily and seemingly without thought, simply for the money. Nonetheless, when one sorts through the abundance of tales for Air Trails, War Stories, Battle Stories, and the like, there is gold to be found amid the dross. Certainly, his Joe Gar tales for Black Mask demand to be collected.

While Shaw described Whitfield as a "hard, patient, determined worker," it appears that his writing often took a back seat. He came from a privileged and moneyed background and was something of a dandy, a far cry from the hard-bitten tough guy that much of his fiction hints he was. When in the money, he preferred to carouse, mostly with Hammett, who was a close friend as well as a major influence.

Whitfield moved to Hollywood in the late 1930s, and after becoming an enormously rich man, he stopped writing altogether. Eventually his money ran out. When he contracted tuberculosis, his old friend Hammett had to lend him $500 to pay for his hospitalization. In January 1945, Raoul Whitfield died.

Despite his production of an abundance of low-quality work, Whitfield was without a doubt one of the founders of hard-boiled fiction. There were times when he created, seemingly without effort, a tough, cold-hearted, thin-lipped piece of fiction; and there were the even rarer occasions when he sat down and wrote a story like "Mistral," which was first published in the December 15, 1931, issue of Adventure and may well be the best story he ever wrote.

J. A.

1931

MISTRAL

It was the way he ate spaghetti that first attracted my attention. I'd put Remmings on the *Conte Grande,* in a more or less sober condition, and the noon sailing vessel had got away from the Genoa docks. I'd been hungry, and I'd wandered along the dock section looking for a restaurant. The one I'd picked had fooled me; it smelled pretty badly and there were thousands of flies. They were persistent and buzzy and they seemed to like Italian food. But the spaghetti was good. As I wound it round my fork I looked around the small, dirty room and saw him. He was eating the stringy stuff, but he was cutting it with a knife. That seemed a bit stiff, in Genoa, and after I'd done two plates of it, smothered with a good Parmesan cheese, I looked him over just out of curiosity.

He was big and dark. He had black eyes and a lean face—very lean for his size. It was a hard face, yet there was softness in his eyes. I caught him once when he was inspecting fly specks on the ceiling, and noticed the scar under his chin. His skin was white and the scar stood out pretty clearly. I'd seen knife scars before, and this looked like one. It was long and slightly curved, and a nasty red color. I got the idea that it wasn't a very old scar.

His suit was of gray material, a quiet cloth. It fit him very well. I decided that he wasn't an Italian. He caught me looking at him, and it seemed to make him nervous. The next time I glanced in his direction I caught him watching me without appearing to do so. His hands were nervous and the muscles of his mouth twitched.

While I was drinking terrible coffee I heard him say—

"Damn flies!"

His voice was thick, but without accent. Two boats had come to Genoa that day from the States—a big one and a small one. I decided that he was an American and that he'd just arrived. He paid his check and went past me as I was trying to think in terms of the lira. I smiled a little, and he started to smile. But something changed his mind. He looked worried and frowned, turning his head away from me. He was better than six feet tall and had very broad shoulders, but his body hunched forward when he walked.

I thought about him several times as I drove toward the border town of Ventimiglia. At St. Remo I got my trunks from the rear of the car and had a swim in the Mediterranean. It was around three in the afternoon and the day was hot. I forgot about the scarred one until I'd driven across the border into France and had reached Monte Carlo. Before the Casino I stopped to light a cigaret, and a great yellow machine pulled up. It was of Italian make—a very expensive type of car. The chauffeur was an Italian. And from the rear of the machine my scarred friend descended. He spoke to the chauffeur and didn't see me, and I turned my back as he went into the Casino. I was very curious about him. That fly filled, dock section eating place, the knifed spaghetti and this expensive machine—there was something strange in the combination.

I followed him into the Casino, and knew at once he had never been there before. He didn't seem to know just what to do, and the ornate reception hall that lay ahead of him didn't offer any solution. I felt that he'd expected to see the gambling tables immediately and he was confused. An attendant approached and spoke to him in French. He merely asked if he could be of service, but the scarred one did not understand.

I was very close to him and I acted on impulse. At his side I smiled.

"You buy an admission ticket in this room on your left," I said, and gestured toward the room with the low counters and the cashiers behind them.

He stared at me with his dark eyes, and then they got very cold. The warmth went from them so suddenly that I started to turn away. But he said—

"Thanks, buddy."

I nodded. Well, I was sure that he was an American and that he didn't speak French and that he was afraid of something. And I was interested. But I knew that showing interest would be about the best way of learning nothing. So I sauntered into the room on my left and reached the *billets de jour* counter. I handed over my passport and ten francs and received the *billet,* after my name and number had been jotted down. It was all done pretty rapidly, and I was turning away when I heard the scarred one say—

"One admission—"

The Frenchman behind the counter smiled and asked for his passport. The scarred one didn't understand, so I said, still helpfully butting in:

"He has to see your passport. Formality here."

The dark eyes widened and his right hand went to the inside pocket of his gray coat. I caught the red color of the passport binding, but that was all. It slipped out of sight again and the scarred one swore.

"Must have left it—at home," he muttered in his thickish voice.

That was a pretty bad one. He wasn't giving me credit for having eyes or brains. But I smiled at him.

"You can still get inside," I said. "Give him your name and the name of your villa or hotel. Tell him you're very anxious to make a little play— you feel lucky. Smile at him."

I expected him to say he couldn't speak French, and to ask me if I would help. And I was prepared to tell him that the man behind the counter could speak five languages quite well, and English was one of them. But I was fooled. The scarred one smiled at the man behind the counter; he said that he'd left his passport in his hotel, and that he felt lucky and would like to try roulette.

The Casino employee smiled back, said that it was not good to leave one's passport behind, and asked him his name. The scarred one said—

"Tom—Thomas Burke."

I knew that he was lying. The man back of the counter continued to smile and asked the hotel and the town where Mr. Burke resided. The scarred one said—

"I stay at Cannes, at the Grand Hotel."

The Grand Hotel was very safe. Practically every French and Italian Riviera town has a Grand Hotel, and I once knew a village that had two for a time. But it happened that the date was August the third, and the Grand Hotel in Cannes had only been opened three days. There were very few persons staying there; it did much better in the Winter season. The proprietor was a friend of mine; I had been at the hotel for a time the night previous and was quite sure no Thomas Burke was staying there.

The scarred one received his *billet,* which ticket entitled him to play roulette, but not baccarat. I went from the room ahead of him and into the large reception hall. The scarred one halted and lighted a cigaret very popular with Americans. I saw the color of the package reflected in the mirrors about the room. Then I passed into the salon and went to a table that was not too crowded.

The ball fell on red numbers four times in succession. I went to a change booth and bought four thousand-franc, oblong chips. Returning to the table, I placed one of the oblongs worth forty dollars on black. The ball rolled against the spin of the wheel, and finally dropped into the groove of a black number. A croupier raked another oblong chip against mine and I picked both of them up and left the table. I had won forty dollars in one play, and that completed *my* particular system for beating the Casino. It was not very often that I won my forty dollars on the first play, but quite often I was one bet ahead of the Casino before I lost my four or five oblongs.

And whenever I was that one bet ahead—I quit. I never attempted to gamble my limited funds against the Casino's almost unlimited ones. And I remembered being told by one of the biggest gamblers of the Riviera that if all those who played at the Casino played as I did, it would be pretty tough for Monte Carlo. It was betting small money against big money, betting that the Casino would go broke before they did, that made it easy for the Casino.

As usual, I was pleased. I cashed in my chips and looked around for the scarred one. In the large salon I failed to see him immediately. When I did see him I strolled over to the table where he had seated himself. He had seven or eight hundred dollars worth of chips before him, and he was playing thousand-franc oblongs on the line between two numbers. He won once while I was watching, and his face was expressionless. The world's greatest gambling casino did not awe him now; he was gambling. And it was easy to see that he was accustomed to gambling.

He won again, just before I left, but he did not smile. The pay-off was eighteen oblongs for his one. Seven hundred and twenty dollars. And it was his second eighteen-for-one win in several minutes.

Outside the Casino I stood for some seconds and thought about the passport I'd seen. I decided that the scarred one was a crook and did not care to take a chance.

Either the passport he had was a bad one and he didn't wish it to get in Monte Carlo records, or it was a good one and he was afraid of a leak somewhere. Or he was afraid of something that might happen in the future, and a checking up at the Casino might follow.

Showing a passport at the border was something else again. And there was just the barest possibility that my scarred friend was a big shot, and might have been recognized and not allowed to play. That has happened at Monte Carlo. The Casino authorities are very careful about some details, and, as every one knows, they are very careless about others.

I forgot about him while driving the Grand Corniche. The day was very hot; there was not a breath of wind. At Nice I stopped at the Frigate bar for a champagne cocktail, and at a little beach between Nice and Cannes I got damp trunks from the rear of my small car and had another swim. Then I drove on again, wondering if Remmings on the way back home from Genoa were sober yet. I decided that he probably was not.

It was a bit cooler when I drove round that point of land to the east of Cannes. The town lay in a semicircle; the waterfront was crescent-shaped before me. On the far side were the Esterel Mountains coming down to the sea. It was a nice sight. A harsh horn from behind caused me to pull to the right of the road along the Croisette, and with a rush and another burst from its horn, a great yellow machine went past. I recognized the machine and the chauffeur, and caught a glimpse of the scarred man in the rear seat. He was grinning broadly, and I guessed that he'd won quite a bit. But why hadn't he stayed on, playing his winning streak to the limit?

The Grand Hotel was along the Croisette a distance beyond the spot where I should have turned off to my small hotel. But I didn't turn off. I drove on slowly, and a square or so from the Grand I passed the big yellow machine, moving slowly. The chauffeur was grinning.

I sat in the car near the Grand and smoked a cigaret. When I went inside there was no sign of the scarred one, but my friend the proprietor was about. We went into his little office and talked about other things and then about the scarred one. Yes, he'd arrived. Traveling very light in a hired car. Just two bags, without many seals. His name was Anthony Senna; he was from New Orleans, in America. He had a room with bath, but not facing the Mediterranean.

I raised my eyebrows and my friend smiled at me.

"It was not a matter of money, I think," he said. "It was a matter of wind."

"Wind?"

My friend the proprietor nodded.

"Monsieur Senna, he does not like the wind," he explained. "It keeps him awake of nights, it annoys him. And when there is a mistral, as you know, there is wind. Much wind."

There was certainly much wind when there was a mistral. For three or six, and on rare occasions for nine days there was the wind. It blew straight in from the Mediterranean, out of a cloudless sky. It spread sand all over the Croisette—the curving road along the beach, with the fashionable bars and shops. It ripped awnings and sent smart yachts behind the concrete seawall to the tiny harbor. It battered ten-foot waves over the sand, and the spray from them was salty on your lips, a square from the Croisette. And all the time the sky was blue.

And the scarred one who had stated in Monte Carlo that his name was Thomas Burke, and in Cannes that it was Anthony Senna, did not like the wind. This one who had cold eyes when spoken to, and who cut spaghetti with a knife in a dirty, waterfront eating place in Genoa, and who played thousand-franc chips at Monte Carlo—the wind kept him awake at night.

"He stays here for some little time?" I asked my friend.

The proprietor shrugged.

"On the Riviera, who can tell how long one stays?" he countered. "But I have given him a room on the top floor, on the corner, facing the rear."

"On the *corner*, facing the rear?" I repeated, puzzled.

I said that because one of the peculiar things about top floor corner rooms at the Grand was that they had only the two windows at the rear. There was no side window. And there was no room next to them, but rather very large linen closets. The rooms were apt to be hot at this time—very hot.

The proprietor nodded, and I said—

"I suppose he looked at some other rooms?"

My friend seemed a little surprised at my interest. But then we talked often of unimportant things—of things that seemed unimportant to us, and yet very important to others.

"Monsieur Senna looked at several rooms and selected the one at the east corner," the proprietor told me.

"Well, in event of a mistral, he will hear only a little wind there," I said.

And my friend agreed.

"The walls are very thick, and the window screens quite tight. He will hear only a little of the mistral," he agreed.

A telegram from Paris took me to St. Raphael the next day. I was searching for a German by the name of Schmidt, who had stolen many marks from a small town bank somewhere near Berlin, and who the Paris office of the agency with which I was connected had heard was in the French Riviera town. The office had heard incorrectly, though the Schmidt at St. Raphael slightly resembled the German thief. He was a good fellow, this Schmidt, and after we had stood each other a few rounds of drinks I left him and drove over the Esterel Mountains toward Cannes. It had started to blow, and when I took my machine over the highest stretch of road, with the Mediterranean almost a thousand feet below, the car rocked from the gusts of wind.

"Mistral," I said. "The beginning of one."

And I thought about my friend with the scar on his chin and the warm eyes that got so suddenly cold. I drove pretty fast and reached Cannes around four. The wind was increasing; awnings were being hauled in and yachts were steaming into the small harbor, behind the concrete breakwater. Sand was swirling in eddies across the Croisette. The two most patronized of the beach bars, the Miramar and the Chatham, were deserted—it was three hours before cocktail time.

I went to my hotel and got the file that held my photographs. It was a big file in a special case, and I'd gone over two hundred photos the night before. I did another fifty and then quit. In the fingers of my right hand I held the likeness of my scarred one. The scar was missing, and the big one was wearing his hair differently. But he was my man. I turned the photo over and read:

Anthony (Tony) Senna. Chicago, September 1926. Jackie Marks' bodyguard until Marks was machine gunned out, in March 1927. Murder suspect. Indicted three times—no convictions. Beer. Mixed up in Spencer Tracy kill. Not indicted. Dropped out of sight for year in early 1928. Turned up in Los Angeles on gambling barge in June, 1930, after standing trial for murder of copper in Chicago in February, 1929. Al Fess murdered on barge three months later. Senna stood trial for murder. No conviction. Used plenty of money to get clear. No record after this.

There was a description of the scarred one that did the trick. I guessed that he'd got heavier, was wearing his hair differently and was only using that Senna tag when he was forced to. He knew that there was the *carte d'identité* business, probably, and that the local police would have his name from the hotel. I decided that his passport was all right, but that he hadn't wanted Senna to get into Monte Carlo records. He'd played safe at the Grand, fearing the police, in event of any sort of accident, might check his passport.

Well, I knew who he was. And I remembered that Al Fess had been a big shot in Chicago, but had been driven out by Capone and had followed Horace Greeley's advice to go West. He'd worked the big gambling barge beyond the three mile limit, and then things had started to go wrong. I remembered that the barge had been blown up once, and set fire another time. And not long after that Fess had been shot to death. My scarred one had been indicted and tried. No conviction. That trial would have taken place along in September or October, I figured. About a year ago.

I shoved the photo back in its proper file and smoked a couple of cigarets. The wind was cutting up now, but I didn't mind it. The screens in my room's three windows rattled, and something loose on a cornice somewhere made a pounding noise at intervals. I thought of the room Senna had selected and smiled a little grimly.

The theory I liked best was that Senna had murdered Al Fess, a year ago. He'd kept out of sight for awhile after his trial. Fess had been pretty big. Perhaps Senna had tried to move around a bit in the States. But it had been too tough. So he'd come across and had landed at Genoa. But he was still worried. He liked rooms with thick walls and without other rooms next to them. He liked them on the top floor. He was lonely and in a strange country, but he was afraid of strangers. In other words, Tony Senna must be a hunted man.

After a little while I had a swim in a sea that was getting rough by the minute. The waves were three and four feet high and, in the manner of the Mediterranean, they pounded to shore very close to each other. When I got back to the hotel after my swim the mistral was still picking up force. I changed into light flannels and slipped a Colt automatic into a deep hip pocket of the trousers. I couldn't quite make up my mind about what I wanted to do with Senna. That is, whether I wanted to talk with him, or try to talk with him. Just out of curiosity—for he wasn't wanted.

A *chasseur* brought in another telegram. After he'd taken my franc tip and had gone, I read it. It was coded simply—from the Paris office. I was to forget about Schmidt for the time. A client in Paris was very anxious to locate one Anthony Senna, who it was thought had landed in Genoa the day before. There was a description of Senna in code, and it included the scar. I was to locate Senna and wire the office. That was all. Except that there were the letters V.I., which meant "very important."

I smoked another cigaret and smiled at the break putting Remmings on the *Conte Grande* had got me. And I felt a little sorry for Senna. My hunch was that Senna hadn't come far enough away, or that he'd come to the wrong place. In any case, business was business. I went to the French telegraph and sent a coded wire to Paris. It was to the effect that one Anthony Senna who answered the required description was staying at the Grand Hotel at Cannes, France.

When I thought of the surprise this speed would cause, in Paris, I decided I rated a drink or two. So I drove against a rising wind and parked near the Chatham. Senna wasn't there. It was after seven and the bar was crowded. The pajamas the women wore were as colorful as usual but had long ceased to startle me. I went outside, having trouble getting the door opened against the mistral wind, and went inside the Miramar.

At first I didn't see my man. This bar was larger and noisier and more crowded. I went toward a small table in a far, dark corner. And then I saw Tony Senna. He was slouched low in one of the big lounging chairs. His big body was slumped, his arms were at his sides. From where he sat he had a view of the whole bar and of the entrance. On the table before him was a glass of beer. His face was twisted; he looked miserable.

When he caught sight of me he straightened a little. He started to smile. I waved a hand carelessly and watched the hard expression come into his eyes. But it went away, and he sort of grinned. He hesitated, then said thickly—

"Alone—have a drink?"

I hesitated. Being an agency man has its Judas moments. This was one of them. I'd sold this man out, and he was asking me to drink with him.

I said—

"All right—sure."

I dropped into the lounge chair across the table from him, leaned forward.

"My name's Benn," I said, lying because I knew he would lie. And he did.

"Mine's Burke," he replied. "Tom Burke. Thanks for that tip at the Casino. I was kinda worried in there, and maybe I didn't act right with you."

I waved that off. A gust of the mistral wind made things sing and rattle outside. The big one shivered.

"Mistral," I said pleasantly. "Just getting into action."

He swore.

"Hate wind. Gets me. Mistral, eh? What in hell's that?"

I ordered a whisky sour.

"Just wind," I told him. "If it's a real mistral it'll last three days, or six—or nine. The nines are pretty rare."

He sat up straight and blinked at me.

"Like *this*—for nine days!" he muttered. "Lord—I'd go crazy."

I nodded.

"Some people do," I said. "There's a sort of unwritten French law— it applies to men and women living together. If one of them murders the other along about the eighth or ninth day, it doesn't count."

Senna stared at me.

"No kiddin'?" he muttered.

"That's what they say—pretty hard to convict in such a case. The wind gets at you after four or five days. I've never seen a nine day affair, but I've been around for a couple of the six day sessions."

He muttered something I didn't catch and sipped his beer. Every few seconds he'd look toward the entrance, and his dark eyes were sharp. No one came in unless he saw him. I thought of the wire I'd just sent, and felt strange about it. The agency game can give you lousy moments.

When the waiter came with my whisky sour I lifted it slowly and said cheerfully—

"Here's to crime!"

He grinned at that and raised his beer glass. I frowned at it.

"Beer's no good here," I told him. "It's a waste of time."

And he said a little grimly, without thinking too much—

"Yeah, but it doesn't hurt my eyes or nerves any."

There was something about the scarred one that I liked. I didn't bother figuring just what it was. Perhaps I felt a little sorry for him. I had a very strong hunch that death was coming his way. His actions didn't hurt my hunch any. He wasn't exactly scared, but he was nervous. I wanted to know something, so I went after it.

"You haven't been over here long, have you?" I asked, and didn't make my voice too anxious.

He looked at me narrowly.

"I'm an engineer," he said. "I've been down in Mexico—alone a lot. Had a couple of months leave due me, and grabbed a freighter for Genoa. Just an idea."

I nodded. I didn't believe that he was an engineer, but I did believe that he'd been in Mexico and that he'd been there alone. He was fed up, and he'd picked the Riviera and Cannes. And it hadn't worked. And he was drinking with the man who had spotted him, turned his name up.

There was a crash of glass, somewhere beyond the bar. The entrance door opened and a group of people came in, laughing and letting the wind carry them along. Senna hunched down in the chair again.

"I hate wind," he muttered. "I gotta get out of this town."

I thought of my wire and didn't like that idea. So I said:

"It'll be blowing all along the Riviera. And you'd have to go pretty far back in the mountains to dodge this breeze. You can't be sure—it may not stick. Tomorrow morning you may not feel a breath of wind."

That was an ironic thought. A fast plane could reach Cannes from Paris in five hours. The regular planes did it in six. If some one wanted to see Senna badly enough, if I wasn't going haywire on my basis and hunches, some one could be at the Grand Hotel around midnight. A good plane could edge into the wind and get down all right.

Senna said—

"You think it may let up, eh?"

I nodded, and finished my whisky sour.

"Sure," I said. "Have one on me?"

He had another beer, and I had another sour. I tried to get him to open up a little, but he didn't want to talk. He kept his eyes on the entrance door and on human faces that passed near our corner. I said—

"You played at the Casino—any luck?"

He grinned, showing white teeth. Then his dark eyes got hard and frowning.

"Yeah—too much, maybe," he stated.

I looked puzzled.

"Too much?" I said.

He got sort of a silly smile on his face only it wasn't all the way silly. After a few seconds of silence he said a little grimly:

"I've only been this lucky a few times in my life. And right after those times—I got unlucky. You know how it is."

I finished my second sour and rose.

"Yes, sure," I said. "I know how it is. See you again."

He didn't seem surprised at the abruptness of my departure.

"Yeah," he said. "So long."

I went out into the wind, got to a phone in the Miramar Hotel and called the office of the small flying field at the end of town. I was known there as Jay Benn, and sometimes I used a ship for a fast hop to Germany or Switzerland or Spain. In Cannes I was thought to be a pretty good American, with enough money but not too much. A fellow who liked that section of the coast.

I got Leon Demoigne on the phone and asked him to ring me if a plane landed around midnight. He said that he would if I wanted him to, but that he could tell me now that one was coming down from Paris. She was a fast monoplane, and there would be two passengers aboard, beside her pilot. I told him that was not the plane I was thinking about, and he said he'd advised by wire against the flight, but that the ship was apparently coming along anyway. He ended up by saying that it was probably bringing along a couple of crazy Americans who had heavy dates.

Even in French his idea didn't sound right to me. I thought it was perfectly right that the plane was bringing along a couple of Americans. But I was quite certain they weren't coming because of the kind of heavy dates Leon anticipated. And I was damned sure they weren't crazy.

I had dinner alone at a small Russian restaurant, and the black bread didn't taste as good as usual. The thing that got me was that I was pretty sure Tony Senna wasn't wanted by the police. I was pretty sure that crooks were using a reputable agency, as they had used agencies before, to trace another crook. I had the feeling that I'd put Senna on the spot, and I didn't like it. He was a killer and probably a lot of things that went with it, but it seemed to me he wasn't going to have much of a chance. I could almost hear guns—and I could almost see the big scarred man going down. I might be all wrong, but the set-up framed things that way.

At ten o'clock I went back to the hotel and found the telegram I expected. It was from McKee, the agency head, and it was brief. I read,

"Fine fast work clients pleased drop further investigation of Senna." It was in code. And it convinced me that death was coming close to the big fellow. I was to drop out, which was not the ordinary method. The clients would handle things themselves. And they were pleased.

I lay on my bed and listened to the mistral wind howl. It was getting on my nerves too. After a half hour or so I made a decision. Business was business, but some of it took away too much self-respect. I drove to the Grand Hotel. Senna was not in. When I got to the Miramar bar he was just where I'd left him. He'd been eating sandwiches, and he was still drinking beer. He grinned at me.

"I couldn't go out in that stuff," he said. "So I just stuck here."

I nodded and pulled a chair close to him. I ordered coffee and *fin*. He was looking at me with his dark eyes narrowed.

"Damn mistral!" he muttered. "You think it'll last three days, maybe six?"

I said:

"You never can tell." Then I went right into it. "Listen, Senna," I said softly and without paying any attention to his start of surprise, "you got a tough break in Genoa. I happened to eat in the same spot and see you. I saw your passport edge, at the Casino in Monte Carlo, and I know some things. My name isn't Benn—and I'm connected with an international detective agency. My office wired me to look for you, and I wired back that you were at the Grand Hotel here. Two Americans are coming down by plane—clients of the Paris office of my agency. They're coming down to see you, and they'll get here about midnight. It took me a little while to figure things out, and when I got them figured out I decided that you were being spotted out for killing Al Fess on his gambling barge, off Santa Monica. I didn't like my part, so I'm warning you. That's all of it."

His big hands were gripping the table edge, and getting white with that grip. His dark eyes were slitted and cold. I kept my right hand on the Colt grip.

"I don't think you're the whitest guy that ever lived, Senna," I said. "And I've got my hand on a rod now. So don't do the wrong thing. What I want to get across is that my hunch is the law isn't coming after you. Not *my* kind of law. You've got a couple of hours, and you don't like wind. *I'm* all right, because I wired you were staying at the Grand, and you were. You can hire a machine—"

I stopped. Senna had taken his whitened knuckles away from the table. He was relaxed in the big chair, and his face held a terrible grin. He chuckled. I stared at him and he shook his head slowly.

"Lord!" he breathed. "Imagine a dick tipping me off! Imagine that!"

I smiled a little. But I didn't say anything. He kept on shaking his head. After awhile he lighted a cigaret.

"I wouldn't waste too much time, Senna," I told him. "This wind may not hold up that plane too much."

He shook his big head.

"I ain't going away, Benn—or whatever your name is," he said slowly, tonelessly. "I've been leaving places for a long time now. Going places—far places. Spots I didn't like, see? They've been after me a long time. I ain't saying I did for Fess, but if ever a guy rated a dose of lead, that rat did, see? But me, I'm staying here."

"Don't be a fool, Senna," I said. "The law doesn't want you—"

He looked suddenly tired.

"These guys are worse than the law, Benn," he said wearily. "I tell you, I'm tired of running away. I'm staying here. Now you—" he raised a big forefinger and pointed it at me—"get the hell out of here!"

I said as I rose slowly:

"Well, I warned you. I may be all wrong—but I tipped you, Senna."

There was irony in his eyes.

"Sure, Benn," he said. "Now you get the hell away from me."

The plane landed at 12:10 by my wristwatch. It landed in a nasty wind, after circling the lighted field three times. She was a small monoplane, cabin type. I had my car on the Frejus road, with the lights out. After about ten minutes a car that had been waiting at the field turned into the main road and moved toward Cannes. I had to drive very fast to follow it. I was several squares behind when it reached the Grand Hotel. The wind was raising the devil with the palms along the Croisette; it seemed to be steadily increasing.

I parked a square away and went into the hotel by a side entrance. When I reached the main lobby no one was about but the *concierge*. He knew me. He said that the two gentlemen had said they didn't want Monsieur Senna disturbed, but was he in his room. And he said that he had told them that Monsieur Senna was at the Blue Frog. And they had thanked him and departed. They had not engaged rooms and they had not brought any baggage into the hotel.

"How do you know Monsieur Senna is at the Blue Frog?" I asked.

The *concierge* shrugged.

"He has told me that he thought he would go there," he returned. "He has asked me for a quiet place to drink, where there is music and yet not a crowd. And where the lights would not hurt his eyes."

"*C'est ça,*" I muttered grimly.

Well, it *was* so. The Blue Frog was a small drinking and dancing place; there was a two-piece orchestra and the lights were dim. It was not smart and it didn't get much of a crowd. I reflected that dim lights would give Senna a better chance, and that a small crowd would mean less chance of humans other than those concerned being hit by stray bullets. I wasn't sure that Senna cared much about other humans, but every man has his particular code of what he calls honor. Senna was no exception.

The Blue Frog was just off the Route d'Antibe, the main business street of Cannes, at the east end of town. It was set back in some palms and there were no buildings very close to it. In my car I drove fast, parked a half square away and hurried on. I went in a side entrance and spotted Senna right away. His eyes were narrowed on mine and he was smiling. He wasn't slumped in any lounging chair this time. He sat on a small, wooden chair. It had no arms. Both hands were in the pockets of his light suit coat, and he was seated slightly to the left of the table. He faced the side entrance directly, and the main entrance to the place was in a line with his big body.

I stood for several seconds looking at him. Then I went to the bar. I ordered Scotch, straight. The two-piece orchestra was playing *"Ay-yi-yi,"* with the guitar dominating the piano. There were only a few people inside; mistrals kept folk at home. And that was good, too.

When I lifted my drink, my fingers were shaking a little. There was a mirror beyond the bar, and I looked into it. I could see the front entrance. The barman saw my shaking fingers and guessed wrong. He said that the mistral was not good, it did bad things with one's nerves. I agreed and downed the Scotch. As I set the glass on the counter my eyes went to the mirror, and I saw a tall, hard faced man come in. I turned and looked toward the side entrance. A shorter, heavier man stepped inside the dimly lighted room, letting a rush of wind in with him. A girl laughed shrilly, and the orchestra continued its swift rhythm.

I think they both saw Senna at the same instant. With so few people in the place that wasn't hard. I saw the shorter one of the two stiffen, and his coat material came up from the bottom. There were two terrific crashes. No Maxim silenced guns, these. There were screams. The short one took one step forward and crashed to the floor.

I swung around and stared at Senna. There was another gun crash and his big body jerked. But his right hand came up. His left battered the table aside and he walked toward the main entrance and toward the tall, hard faced man. There was another gun crash and Senna's left arm hung limp at his side. His gun was up, extended in his right hand. He kept walking, his face twisted in a terrible smile. The tall one was staring at him; he fired again but the bullet went wild. It tore artificial flowers from a wall behind Senna.

And then Senna worked his gun. It crashed again and again. I counted four shots, and then all sound was merged into a terrible roar. When the roar died away, I went toward the two motionless figures on the floor near the door. The tall one was dead. Senna was alive; he said weakly, as I leaned over him:

"The others—done?"

I left him and went to the side entrance door. The thickset one was dead, too. The bullet had ripped upward through his mouth. I went back and kneeled beside Senna.

"Both done," I told him.

He tried to grin, but it was too tough. He said, very weakly:

"Sure—I got—Al Fess." And a few seconds later he said, "Guy—I can't hear—that damn wind—"

"Take it easy, Senna—"

I couldn't think of anything else to say. He closed his eyes and after a few seconds more he said weakly:

"Funny—if it hadn't been for that damn wind—I might have—run again. But it just—made me sore—made me want to—stick here—"

He didn't say any more. He was dead when a very excited gendarme reached my side and asked a dozen questions one after another. I answered one of them and went to the bar for another drink. It was some time before I got it. As I sipped it I decided that it was just as well Senna had had a funny idea about the wind, if he *had* had it. You can't always be running away from things.

The mistral lasted three days, and when it was over the sun was very hot.

The Blue Frog did a big business; the proprietor put a frame around a hole made by one of the bullets that missed Senna. The smart crowd went in for a look, and the French townspeople went in too. The proprietor told me he would have liked to frame one of Tony Senna's bullets, but that couldn't be done. Senna hadn't missed.

FREDERICK NEBEL
(1903–1966)

There were a great many hard-drinking detectives in the pulp magazines and novels of the 1930s. Consumption of alcohol in large amounts not only was a reaction to the demons of poverty and the Depression, but was considered chic in some circles, a badge of honor in others. Nick and Nora Charles, Dashiell Hammett's husband-and-wife team, are crime fiction's champion boozers of that bygone era. A close second is Louis Frederick Nebel's wisecracking newspaperman, Kennedy of the Free Press.

Kennedy is not just a user of alcohol, but an admitted abuser, a serious drunk. In one of his many appearances in the pages of Black Mask, "Bad News" (March 1934), he imbibes so much liquor that he is barely able to function as either a news hawk or a human being. Nevertheless, Kennedy has a wry wit and an unparalleled "nose for news," and his adventures in tandem with Police Captain MacBride of fictitious Richmond City are unfailingly exciting and entertaining pulp fare. The first Black Mask appearance of the popular duo was in "Raw Law" (September 1928), the first of five installments in a series billed as "The Crimes of Richmond City." Thirty-six other tales featuring Kennedy and Mac-Bride in major and minor roles followed over the next eight years, culminating with "Deep Red" in the August 1936 issue. "Backwash" (May 1932) is a novelette concerned with the kidnapping of a governor-elect; it showcases MacBride as typically tough and professional, Kennedy as typically haphazard and sodden, and their relationship as typically adversarial.

Nebel began selling regularly to the pulps when he was in his teens, using his own name as well as such pseudonyms as Eric Lewis and Grimes Hill; detective fiction and northern adventure stories (he once worked in Canada's north woods) were his primary interests. The Kennedy and MacBride stories were one of the two prominent series he created for Joseph T. Shaw during Shaw's ten-year editorial reign at Black Mask. The other starred "Tough Dick" Donahue, an operative for the Inter-State Detective Agency who was not above using illegal methods to achieve his goals. Donahue appeared in fifteen stories between 1930 and 1935, a half-dozen of which were collected in Six Deadly Dames (1950).

Nebel's third major series was published in Dime Detective *from 1931 to 1937. This one concerned another hard-bitten private eye, Cardigan, whose escapades were chronicled in forty-three novelettes, six of which were gathered in book form under the title* The Adventures of Cardigan *(1988).*

In the early 1930s, Nebel wrote his only three novels: two suspense tales, Sleepers East *(1933) and* Fifty Roads to Town *(1936), and a bibulous mainstream story of Depression-era New York City,* But Not the End *(1934). In 1937, he abandoned both novels and the pulps to concentrate on stories for* Collier's, Liberty, *and other slick magazines, a career in fiction at which he was successful for more than twenty years. His last few stories marked a belated return to the mystery field, being published in such genre periodicals as* Ellery Queen's Mystery Magazine *in the late 1950s and early 1960s.*

B. P.

1932

BACKWASH

Kennedy, leaning on the bar with his left elbow and with his chin propped on his left hand, laid his right palm on the top of the siphon, pressed down with the heel of his hand and fizzed seltzer hard into a glass of rye. Rye and seltzer geysered, splashed down on a newspaper George the barman was reading.

George looked up. "Well!" he growled.

"My error," Kennedy said, absently. He raised a hand to his lips to camouflage the disorders of indigestion, then stirred his drink with a glass swizzle stick.

"You're drunk," George said indignantly, patting the despoiled newspaper with a towel.

Kennedy raised his drink. "I say with Dryden, 'Bacchus ever fair and young.' This bootleg is the fairest in color and the youngest in age I've ever guzzled."

"What are you talking about? That there liquor is a month old."

Kennedy's eyes drooped; he opened them with an effort. "What the hell is that radio mumbling about?"

"Dunno." George turned and gave one of the dials a twist. "Police alarms," he said.

"Is there no escape from monotony?"

"Shut up a minute," George growled.

A blunt voice was broadcasting:

"Richmond City Police Headquarters. Attention all cars. All cars attention. Governor-elect Cortland Wayne left his home on Westover Boulevard at seven o'clock this evening. He was driving a black Cadillac coupé; license number six—B as in bottom—four—six; license number six—B as in bottom—forty-six. A black Cadillac coupé. He was to speak at the Foursquare Club at thirty minutes past seven o'clock. He did not arrive there. He is not home. It is now eleven-fifteen o'clock. Foul play is indicated. Stop and investigate any black Cadillac coupé. Report. Again: Attention all cars. All cars attention. Governor-elect Cortland Wayne . . ."

Kennedy stood back on his heels, blinking.

George said: "Cripes, did you hear that?"

Kennedy weaved. "Where's my coat?"

"Over on that hook."

Kennedy wheeled, lost his balance, regained it and lunged towards a wall rack. He unhooked his topcoat, got his right arm into the left sleeve, dropped his hat. George bounded around the bar and straightened him out. Kennedy stepped on his hat. George picked it up and slapped it, battered as it was, on Kennedy's head. Kennedy smashed into the door, got it open and barged out.

Before the door had stopped swinging, it whipped open violently. Kennedy ran headlong into the bar, drained his drink, turned and sloped out again. He hove on to the sidewalk, overran the curb, regained the sidewalk and broke into something between a skip and a hobble. A block farther on he reached a main drag, stood swaying breathless on the corner. He put fingers in his mouth and whistled. A taxi's brakes screeched.

Corinne Wayne was a tall woman of thirty. Her hair was russet and full of unexpected gleams and shimmers. Her eyes were large, luminous, her mouth full and exquisite. She had pale satiny skin touched with a faint glow of damask on the cheeks. Her throat was columnar. At college she had been adjudged the most beautiful girl in her graduating class.

MacBride, appearing in the drawing-room doorway, ducked his spare-boned head.

Corinne, rising from a tapestry wing-chair, said: "I'm so glad you came, Captain."

She extended a hand whose wrist was encircled by a bracelet of hammered silver links. MacBride, carrying his derby in his left hand, crossed the room and took her hand with his right.

"I came right over," he said.

Her eyes were red-rimmed and she held a crumpled damp handkerchief in her left hand. She put the handkerchief to her lips, gestured wearily to a divan, sat down in the wing-chair. MacBride unbuttoned his dark blue Chesterfield, dropped to the divan and held his derby on one knee. His blue suit was neatly pressed, his black shoes shone, his shaven face was ruddy from the cold.

He said: "Cort left here at seven, huhn?"

"Yes."

"Sharp?"

She nodded. "He left at seven. It was Mason's night off, so Cort drove the coupé himself."

"He wasn't nervous, was he?"

"No. He was in the best of spirits."

"When did they call from the Foursquare Club?"

"At eight. I told them he'd left. I began to worry. I called them again at nine and he hadn't arrived. I spoke with Carl Davenport. He told me not to worry. Then they started telephoning a lot of places—where they thought he might have gone. I did also. We didn't want to notify the police and start a hullaballoo until we were sure. At eleven I couldn't stand it any longer. I called Carl Davenport. He hadn't been successful. I told him I was going to report. What do you suppose has happened?"

MacBride said: "We've got all the patrol cars on the lookout. I've ordered out special squads and all the flyers from every precinct. We've notified the authorities in surrounding towns."

"Do—do you suppose it's—abduction?"

MacBride looked at the inside of his hat. "It has the earmarks, Mrs. Wayne."

"Oh!"

He gestured with his hat. "In which case we can rest assured that he's come to no bodily harm."

"But—but it might be political opposition. It might be some gang. You know that as soon he gets in office he's going to push through the Rittenmoore Bill. And if a gang—"

The skipper frowned. "I wouldn't think of that, Mrs. Wayne."

She muffled a sob in her handkerchief.

MacBride said: "If it's a kidnap job, you'll get word by tomorrow. A phone call. Or maybe they'll make Cort write a letter. Whatever it is, let me know right off the bat."

"But if they demand money—and if you interfere . . ."

"Cort's an old friend of mine," MacBride said. "You can bank on it that I'll do whatever I think's best for him. For the time being, try to be calm. You're not going to gain anything by worrying. That's an easy thing for me to say, but try it, anyhow. And do as I say. As soon as you hear, let me know."

She said, haltingly: "And if you're not in the office?"

"When a job like this breaks, I sleep at Headquarters."

There were footsteps on a hardwood floor; they became muffled on a rug; drummed louder again on wood. Corinne looked towards the reception hall. A man came long-legged in through the doorway.

"Corinne—"

Seeing MacBride, his voice stopped and his footsteps slowed down. He was a tall man, darkly handsome; young and with a lean smooth poise. He bowed.

"I didn't mean to interrupt."

Corinne had risen. A hand started towards her breast, fell away back to her side.

"Captain MacBride," she said. "Mr. Figueroa."

MacBride got slowly to his feet.

Figueroa bowed again but remained where he had stopped. "How do you do." And to Corinne: "I just heard over the radio—"

"Yes, yes," she sighed, looking away.

"I came to see if there is anything I might do."

She sighed. "Nothing. Nothing yet. Thank you so much, Manuel."

Figueroa had taken a handkerchief from his breast pocket. He rubbed his palms on it, then patted his temples and shrugged his shoulders at MacBride. "It's quite terrible," he said.

MacBride, thinking of the woman, said: "I wouldn't say that. It's nothing to give a rousing cheer about, but on the other hand there's no sense getting all steamed up."

Corinne sat down, rested her elbow on an arm of the chair and sobbed quietly in her handkerchief.

Figueroa said: "Is there no clue?"

"We only got the report half an hour ago and everything's being done." MacBride buttoned his Chesterfield. "Remember what I told you, Mrs. Wayne. Good-night. Good-night, Mr. Figueroa."

Figueroa's voice was off-key—"I'm glad to have met you, Captain."

"Thanks."

MacBride strode to the door, went across the reception hall towards the front entrance. A maid appeared and opened the latch. MacBride, glancing in an elongated mirror beside the open door, saw Figueroa standing in the drawing-room doorway, watching him. MacBride's step faltered. But he picked it up. He did not look around. He went out. He went down four veranda steps, passed beneath a white porte-cochère and took a pale cement walk that crossed a lawn between blue spruces. He could see the right front cowl-light of the police phaeton. He heard low querulous voices.

Achermann, the driver, was holding a spare figure by the arm and saying: "Nix, I said; nix."

"Hey," MacBride said.

"It's this pest," Achermann complained.

Kennedy said: "It's getting so nowadays that a private citizen takes his life in his hands every time he goes out."

"Yeah?" MacBride muttered. "Who's been picking on you?"

"Achy, here—"

"Oh, yeah?" MacBride muttered. "Well, I told Achy to kick any stray newshawks where it would do good if they clowned around."

"Ah, my pal," Kennedy sighed.

Achermann said: "The reason I'm holding him up, Cap, is that the souse can't stand. He fell out of a taxi, fell over the curb and started crawling up the path there on hands and knees."

Kennedy's tired smile wavered. "I've got to get a statement from Mrs. Wayne."

"Put him in the back, Achy," MacBride said. "Get in, Kennedy! Get in!" Impatient, he took Kennedy away from Achermann, lifted him bodily and piled him into the tonneau. Climbing in, he said: "Shoot, Achy."

The phaeton moved, purred two blocks to an automatic traffic light, made a U-turn on the green and headed back towards midtown. The wind was raw and rowdy. Stars twinkled back of a mackerel sky. The canvas top rat-a-tatted petulantly and the wind whistled in varied keys past lights and braces.

Kennedy was slumped in one corner, his hat still as battered as when he had left George's. Knuckles of his right hand were skinned. There was a ragged tear in his trousers.

"You make me sick," MacBride complained. "What the living hell induced you to take a header off the water wagon again?"

"Well, it was about seven o'clock, and I was off duty, and at the time it bore the hallmark of a swell idea."

"If you were off duty, you gonoph, then what's the idea of this do-or-die monkey business over an interview?"

Kennedy hiccoughed. "I never—uh—thought of that."

MacBride leaned forward and said alongside Achermann's ear: "Twenty-five Olympia Street."

Kennedy went to sleep. Number 25 Olympia Street had an electric sign swung out over the sidewalk. It said: *Turkish Baths.*

MacBride said: "Give me a hand, Achy."

Sergeant Otto Bettdecken was holding down the central room desk. He lowered a half-eaten hamburger from his red jowls when MacBride came in and clamped a half-drunk bottle of Canadian ale between his commodious knees.

"Anything?" MacBride clipped, preoccupied.

"A lady's Pomeranian pup ran away at 10:35 and answers to the name of Goo-goo and—"

"I mean about Wayne."

"Oh, Wayne. Oh, yes. Oh, that Caddy coupé: Sorensen found it parked on Luke Street between Jockey and Havemeyer. It was empty. Jaekel went right down to look for fingerprints."

"Any blood?"

"Sorensen says nope."

"When'd he find it?"

"Just after you left. At twenty minutes past eleven."

MacBride said: "Give Sorensen special mention. That was snappy work. And for crying out loud wipe the beer suds off your chin."

He went down the wide corridor and climbed a flight of stairs. He walked with his hands thrust into his overcoat pockets and his eyes were still preoccupied. He entered his warm neat office, took off his coat, draped it on a hanger and clipped the hanger on a costumer. He absent-mindedly flipped specks of dust from his hat and then put the hat on top of the costumer.

He went to his desk, picked up a charred briar and stuffed it from a glass jar of tobacco. He lit up. He watched the match burn till the flame almost touched his fingers. He popped the match into a glass tray.

Dropping into the swivel-chair with the worn leather cushion, he leaned back and propped his heels on the desk. Thought went round and round in his eyes.

He pressed a button and turned towards a rectangular brown box. A voice said: "Yes, Captain?"

"Did you notify all cars that Cortland Wayne's coupé was found?"

"All them."

"Okey. Broadcast to cars 36 and 38 in the Fourth Precinct to investigate every house in Jockey, Havemeyer and Luke Streets. Vacant houses also. Question residents and report. Broadcast to all cars: Search blind alleys, stop all speeding cars and investigate. Investigate any suspicious character."

He returned to his pipe.

A knock sounded on the door.

"Come in," MacBride said.

Carl Davenport loomed in the doorway. "Glad I found you, Captain."

"Hello, Mr. Davenport. Sit down."

They shook and Davenport took a straight-backed chair, laid one hand on the other atop a silver-knobbed walking stick. He was in evening clothes. A great rock of a man nearing seventy, the rock was crystallizing at the edges. A mane of hair, white and flowing like white silk, swept back from a broad impressive forehead. White thatching for eyebrows. A jaw that still defied loose jowls. Blue eyes like a glacial lake, deep-set and penetrating.

"No word, I understand."

"No," MacBride said. "They found the car."

"Where?"

"Luke Street. Abandoned."

The blue eyes had a touch of frost. "What do you make of it, Captain?"

MacBride puffed. Puffed again. Said: "Offhand, I'd say it's a kidnap. We'll get the shake-down in the morning."

"We?"

"Mrs. Wayne, of course."

Davenport cleared his throat. Latent power was evident in his voice when he said: "I came here to ask you, Captain, in no shape, manner or form to attempt to interfere."

"I don't get you."

"I mean insofar as the safe return of Cortland is concerned. Mrs. Wayne has money. We, his aides, have plenty and we intend putting forth any amount to insure his safe return. This gubernatorial campaign was a stiff one. Cortland won by a fair margin. His inauguration will mark an epic in the history of the state. We who have stood beside him do not want this to have been all in vain. As a boy, I held Cortland on my knee. I saw him grow to be the youngest governor-elect this state has ever known. I coached him. I might say I have been his mentor. Anything I could have done, anything I can do, was and is not too much."

MacBride said, pointing his pipe-stem: "I know. I get you. Well, I've known him too—ten years. I knew him when he was Assistant State's Attorney. I tell you I think he'll be the swellest governor this state's ever had or ever will. Take it from me, I'm just as anxious as you are to get him back safely. When that's done—if it is a kidnap—"

"You don't think it might not be?"

"There's no telling. The Rittenmoore Bill will make carrying a gun without a license a penal offense carrying a minimum sentence of fifteen years. He's sworn to put that bill through. If it is a kidnap, and when he's back safe, I'll go after the guys. My word of honor that there'll be no police interference beforehand."

Davenport stood up. "Captain . . ." His hand was extended.

MacBride rose and gripped it.

Davenport said: "I am infinitely happy that we both realize in Cortland Wayne the man of the hour. I am glad that through the years I have been his guiding light, willing to sacrifice anything in order to put him one notch upward, always. I am not bragging. Forgive me my elation."

"Any idea who's behind this kidnap—if it is a kidnap?"

"None," Davenport said. "You?"

"No-o."

"You say that peculiarly."

MacBride straightened. "I was just thinking. It's nothing. Be seeing you, sir."

Davenport's keen eyes flicked MacBride's spare-boned face. He started to say something. Cleared his throat instead. He went out with a slow sedate step.

MacBride reached for a phone. "Moriarity or Cohen around? . . . Send him up."

It was Cohen. Dapper, well-dressed, one-time a fast lad in the prize ring. "And me holding four kings."

MacBride said, looking at his pipe-bowl, "Name of Manuel Figueroa. Friend of Mrs. Wayne. Find out what he does, where he goes, who he knows. And keep it to yourself until you tell me. Start now."

"Where should I start?"

"That's your job, Ike."

Indefatigable in his haphazard way, Kennedy drifted in at a quarter to one, found MacBride in shirt sleeves over a bowl of chili and a mug of coffee. Kennedy looked refreshed, though weariness was still in his eyes, around his mouth; a droll weariness that seemed more of the soul than of the body.

"Thanks for the bath, skipper."

"Don't mention it. Boy-oh-boy, were you crocked!"

Kennedy expired into a chair, his weathered hat lopped over one ear. "Please omit the post mortems. It was from *Othello:* 'O God, that men should put an enemy into their mouths to steal away their brains.' Remember?"

"How the hell would I remember something I've never read?"

"Ah . . . that leads around to something else again. Something Spanish this time."

"Huh?"

"You read it once. You should remember."

MacBride finished the chili. "Go on, go on."

"Manuel Figueroa."

MacBride choked on a mouthful of coffee, spattered the desk.

Kennedy went on drowsily: "A year ago. A play called *Spanish Bayonet* put on by the Amateur Art Theatre. The feminine lead was played by Corinne Wayne; the male by—you guessed it the first time—Manuel Figueroa. Quite a lot of pawing on the part of the male in the third act. Recollect?"

"No."

"You should."

"All right, then. Now what's the connection?"

"Well, I was pretty whoofled tonight, but not so whoofled that I didn't recognize Manuel hot-foot into the Wayne casa. You were there. Must have seen him."

"I did."

"Two and two make—what?" He laughed. "Or rather, one and one—make what?"

MacBride scowled. "All right. What?"

"Love's a funny thing," Kennedy sighed.

"Are you still drunk?"

Kennedy pushed his hat down over his eyes, bent his head so that only his mouth was visible. His mouth began wearing a droll smile.

MacBride swiveled his chair. His voice dropped to a hard, blunt tone. "Whatever you think, Kennedy, you keep it to your sweet self."

"A crack like that indicates that you think similarly."

"You heard me!"

"Could I help hearing you?"

MacBride glared at the mouth that was wicked and wise—and gentle—and a little weak.

A steam radiator began clanking and went on clanking while neither MacBride nor Kennedy said anything.

The morning papers cut loose. It was something to shout about, the disappearance of a governor-elect. Newsmen arrived from other cities by train, bus, car and plane. They hit Headquarters like a deluge and circulated throughout its chambers. They practically took over two rooms in the building, robbed other offices of chairs and tables.

High pressure special correspondents arrived in baggy coats and carrying portable typewriters. A bootlegger succeeded in delivering a case of gin through a back entrance. Two Boston newshawks drove up with two cases of ginger ale and a gunnysack of ice. An enterprising New York correspondent tried to get the local electric company to wire the room and then tried to get a special wire directly from the room to his home office. MacBride sat on that idea like a ton of brick.

He was pointed, saying to the gang: "Now pipe this, you eggs. I'm on this job—me personally. What I say around this scatter pretty much goes and I'm telling you now, one and all of you, that I'll not stand for any lousy shenanigans. It's only through a kind-hearted commissioner that you're being allowed to stay in these rooms. I don't want any prowling around halls. I don't want to hear raps on doors. I don't want any spitting on the floor or see any bright cartoons on the walls. When there's any news—you'll get it. In the meantime, no monkey shines or you'll get slid on to the pavement."

A wiseacre, winking at a confrère, said: "Any pungent supplement to add to that, Captain?"

"Maybe a punch in the kisser for smart Alecks like you," MacBride said, and went out.

When he strode into his office Ike Cohen was sitting on the desk.

"So you got back," MacBride said. "Well?"

"Figueroa's a young sculptor. Like Mrs. Wayne, he's still a member of the Amateur Art Theatre. He's got a studio on West Walnut Street. He owes two months rent there. He owes his tailor three hundred and ten dollars. Owes his bootlegger a hundred and twenty-five. Has a balance in his bank of eight hundred and six dollars and forty-three cents."

"Where'd you find all this?"

"I went around to art museums first thing this morning. I saw one of his figures. I got his address there. I went over and he wasn't in. I got the door open and fanned his studio. I busted open a trunk—fixed it again—and found six photographs of Mrs. Wayne. He's also modeled a bust of her—from the waist up. It was locked in a closet. I saw letters from an insurance company reminding him he was two hundred bucks in arrears. There was also a letter from an auto finance company reminding him he was four hundred in arrears. I didn't find a bill marked 'paid' in the whole place. I found a lot of photographs, all locked up, of other women with tender sentiments on the backs. I also found—this."

He drew a folded sheet of paper from his pocket, passed it to Mac-Bride. It read:

Dear Manuel,
Please accept this, darling. I hope it will tide you over till better times.
I shan't be able to get over until Thursday afternoon at three. Please
arrange to have no one there. Love, love.
  Corinne

MacBride looked up. "Oh, yeah?"

"Uhuhn."

"Where'd you find this?"

"On the floor back of his desk. It must have fallen down."

MacBride folded the note carefully, tucked it into his wallet, looked keenly at Cohen. "Keep this to yourself, Ike."

"Sure. What do you think?"

"What do you?"

Cohen shrugged. "Maybe I'm naturally bad-minded."

"Well, I'm not. And I think with you."

"That makes Corinne Wayne a nice girl then."

"Yeah, swell."

"And Figueroa a gigolo."

MacBride said: "I've got an old-fashioned word for that guy."

"What's that?"

"Since I joined the Boy Scouts I promised not to swear."

Cohen yawned. "On the eve, so to speak, of the governor-elect's inauguration. And umpteen reporters with their teepees pitched downstairs."

"There's one thing we've got to do, Ike." MacBride squared off in front of Cohen and chewed on his lip. "We've got to keep Cort Wayne's name as clean as we can."

"You're my boss, so what now?"

"Okey, Ike. Pound your ear a while and come up smiling."

Number 48 West Walnut Street was a three-storied stucco building with a broad skylight on the north slanting roof. The broad glass hall-door was open. MacBride climbed the stairs and knocked on the door of the top apartment. Figueroa opened the door. Cigarette smoke made blue-gray skeins across his face.

"Oh, yes—Captain MacBride."

"Hello," MacBride said.

Figueroa let him in, closed the door. A small cubicle served as a reception hall. Off to the left was a living-room. Beyond, a broad airy studio. Figueroa regarded the back of MacBride's bony head as the skipper strode into the living-room.

"Nice place," MacBride offered.

"Won't you sit down?"

"Thanks."

"I have some rather fair Scotch—"

"No thanks. Never touch it till I've had lunch." He crossed his legs, regarded the inside of his derby. "I see you're an artist . . ." He gestured towards the studio.

"Sculptor."

"Busy?"

"Moderately so."

MacBride turned his hat around and looked at the crown. "You act too, don't you?"

"Just as an amateur. I'm a member of the Amateur Art Theatre."

"That's right. You've played with Mrs. Wayne there, haven't you?"

"Quite a bit."

"I take it you're a friend of the family."

"Yes. Yes, indeed."

MacBride nodded. "Yes, I noticed you ran right over to see if you could help Mrs. Wayne. Cort's an old friend of mine. Great guy. I've got a hunch he's very much in love with his wife. She's a very good-looking woman. Should make a swell hostess at the capital. I believe in that. I'm old-fashioned that way. I believe a wife should help her husband in every way she can; stick by him; do nothing that might embarrass him—or even ruin him. It's her duty. Don't you?"

"Why, yes. Why, yes of course."

MacBride had been stuffing his pipe. He lit up. "Have you any other source of income besides what you get out of your profession?"

"No, none."

MacBride puffed. "We've been checking up on all of Cort's friends and so-called friends. We happen to know exactly how much you have in the bank. I hope you don't mind. It's just a sort of precautionary measure. We've done the same on lots of others. You don't, do you?"

"Well—I'd never thought about it. But if—if that comes in line of police routine—why, of course, I can't help minding."

MacBride stood up and looked at the inside of his hat. "You kind of catch on then how tough it would be on you if, say, in a day or a week or a month or so your bank balance jumped a number of thousand dollars."

Figueroa stepped back. "I don't quite see—"

MacBride put on his hat. "Think it over." He walked to the door, opened it. "Good morning, Mr. Figueroa."

He went out.

Corinne's hand shook and that made the plain white sheet of paper shake and rustle. She dropped on to the divan and read the message over again. She looked at the clock on the mantel. It was three o'clock in the afternoon. She sat staring at the message and, after a while, not seeing it. Her eyes filled and a few tears rolled down her cheeks.

She rose with a little outcry followed by a sob which she muffled in her handkerchief. She stood for a moment staring at a sunlit window and sobbing softly. Her tall body shook. She went by fits and starts across the room, into the reception hall. She sat down at a telephone table. She read the message again. She unpronged the receiver and put it to her ear. The hand that held it trembled.

"Please . . . Police Headquarters."

While she waited she blew her nose softly and used the knuckles of her hand to wipe her eyes.

"Captain MacBride, please. . . . Hello—hello. Captain MacBride? . . . This is Mrs. Wayne. Will you come right over?"

The receiver going back into the prong made not a sound.

It took MacBride twenty minutes flat to get over. He came in like a clean blast of wind bringing some of the cold outdoors with him.

"Yes, Mrs. Wayne."

She gave him the letter. He read it:

Dear Mrs. Wayne:

Your husband is safe and sound. To keep him this way and to have him returned safely, you will have to give us $15,000 in $100 bills. On the Old West Road, two miles beyond Sandy Crossing, is the Bullock house that was burned down three months ago. In front, on the road, is an old R. F. D. mailbox. Place the money in this box. Do not come yourself. Send a man who isn't connected with politics or the police. If these orders aren't carried out your husband will be killed. And no tricks, either. The road will be watched a mile on either side of the house. Send it at ten tonight.

There was no name signed.

"How'd it come?" MacBride said.

"Special Delivery."

She showed him the envelope. He folded the letter and inserted it in the envelope, on which name and address had been printed.

"At least," the skipper said, "he's safe. Who'll you send?"

She thought. "All of our friends are one way or another connected with politics. Except Manuel Figueroa."

MacBride blinked.

She looked at him. "Cort thinks so much of him. He'll do anything for me, Manuel will. I'll—call him."

"Wait. Can you get the money?"

"I've a small checking account. But Carl Davenport told me not to worry. He said as soon as I heard I should call him and he'd turn over the proper amount."

MacBride went to the phone and made a call. "Mr. Davenport, this is MacBride. . . . Can you come right over to Wayne's place? . . . Can you bring fifteen thousand in centuries? . . . Good. Yeah, right away."

He hung up and turned to find Corrine regarding him. "Now if you'll call Mr. Figueroa . . ."

She put the call through.

They went back into the drawing-room and she sank exhausted into the divan. "I hope everything will work out."

He could see her profile. His lips drew tightly across his teeth and relaxed when she turned towards him.

He said: "Everything'll be okey."

"Oh, I hope so—I hope so."

Davenport arrived first, breathing heavily. The maid tried to take his overcoat but he detoured around her and went straight into the drawing-room, doffing his hat.

"Mrs. Wayne. Captain."

"The letter came through," MacBride clipped and passed it to Davenport.

Davenport put on pince-nez and read, his lips moving silently. "Well," he said, "it is bitter medicine, but nothing compared with the assurance of Cort's safe return. I trust, Captain, that there will be no interference."

"I gave you my word."

"Who is going?"

There was the sound of footsteps and Figueroa strode quickly into the room, stopped short, made a curt bow.

Corinne was saying: "Manuel, you've got to do something for us, if you will."

"Of course . . ."

His dark eyes shot from MacBride to Davenport.

"Manuel," she went on, "we have a letter from Cort's abductors demanding fifteen thousand. We—Mr. Davenport has the money. Will—will you take it?"

Figueroa squinted. "What?"

"Will you take the money to the place they specify in the letter?"

A flush seemed to creep over his dark cheeks, his eyes appeared to become dazed.

"Manuel, will you?"

"But—but—"

MacBride cut in. "Mrs. Wayne thought you'd be only too glad to do this for her."

Figueroa started to draw his handkerchief from his breast pocket. He didn't. He fussed with the cuffs of his coat, twisted his neck in his collar.

Davenport was leaning back on his heels, looking for all the world like a fat critical prelate. But his eyes were narrow-lidded, his lips a little tight.

Figueroa coughed. "Yes—yes of course. Only too glad to—to do whatever I can."

Davenport beamed and his voice came heavy-timbered: "This is very fine indeed." He drew a long brown envelope from his inside pocket.

MacBride was saying: "You'll take your car, Mr. Figueroa. Hit the Old West Road out of town. Two miles beyond Sandy Crossing, where the railroad's built an underpass—two miles beyond there you'll see the ruins of a farmhouse on the right. Check by your speedometer. In front of the house is one of those old R. F. D. boxes. Slip this package in there and drive on. Don't wait. Drive like hell once you've planted the money."

Figueroa's dark eyes were glazed. "I see. Had I better go armed?"

"No. Absolutely no."

"I see. Will you—will the police cover me?"

MacBride shook his head. "No. We want to get Cortland Wayne back whole. If police followed you there might be a jam and he might get hurt."

Figueroa's voice had become a whisper. "At what time?"

"Reach there at about ten. Leave here at nine-thirty."

Figueroa straightened, moistened his lips. "Of course," his whisper said.

Manuel Figueroa entered his studio apartment, kicked the door shut with his heel, scaled his hat clear across the room, heaved out of his swanky polo coat. Stopping short, he stood erect, very tall; placed a hand at either temple and then drew the hands backward over his ebon hair. His lips were set in a tight ironic line, his dark eyes were alive with crossfires of thought.

"So, Manuel, old fellow!" he said aloud.

He used a key to unlock a closet door. From the closet he drew a bust of Corinne Wayne. He used a hammer to chip away any likeness. He opened a trunk, took out six photographs of Corinne Wayne. In a fire-place where embers still glowed he burned the pictures, knelt and watched the paper become waferlike ashes.

Rising, he stood spread-legged and massaged his palms slowly to-gether. From his inner pocket he drew the long brown envelope. He crossed to his desk, sat down and carefully counted the bills. Exactly fifteen thousand.

He went out and down to a corner drug-store, entered a telephone booth and called the ticket office at Union Station.

"Reserve for—ah—Courtney Blaine a drawing-room on the nine-fifty p. m. train for New York. That reaches New York at eleven-fifty, doesn't it? . . . Yes, I want a reservation on the fast express."

He hung up and thumbed the telephone book. He made a call to a local agent for a transatlantic steamship company. "Can I get a stateroom on the *Magnetic* leaving New York at twelve-thirty tonight? . . . Well, please arrange and see. I shall drop by at four o'clock. . . . Mr. Figueroa."

He caught a taxi outside and went to a luggage store. He carried two suitcases to the Hotel Ardmore and checked in as Louis Massara. He went out again and took a cab to his bank, where he withdrew seven hundred dollars, leaving a hundred and six dollars and forty-three cents.

It took him an hour to buy two new suits, a sports outfit with knickers, shirts, socks, underwear and shoes. He specified that these articles be delivered at his hotel not later than five o'clock. Then he picked up his reservation at Union Station; went to the steamship ticket agency and found he was able to secure a stateroom to Le Havre, France. When he arrived back at his apartment he had eighty dollars in cash—sufficient to get him to New York and aboard the *Magnetic*.

Into a gladstone he threw odds and ends; shaving articles, slippers, a silk robe, his passport. And in one of the compartments he stuffed the packet containing fifteen thousand dollars.

He mused aloud, "And when that is gone there will be women abroad eager to support a handsome young man. Ah, yes, Manuel!" He chuckled liquidly to himself.

He left the paraphernalia of his profession. He left his trunk, a large valise, some objects of art. He left three suits in the closet, and an over-coat. He left four pairs of shoes. Going out with the gladstone, he left the door unlocked. His car was in a garage up the street, but he did not take it. A taxi carried him to the Hotel Ardmore.

Kennedy said: "On the up and up, skipper, hasn't there been any word from Wayne—or about him?"

"Kennedy," MacBride said, "I told you that when there is any news it'll be broadcast. Another thing I'd like to know is, who the hell invited you in my office?"

"Pardon me if I seem not to have been made aware of the fact that you were issuing invitations. Are they engraved 'n' everything?"

"Waltz me around a little more and it'll be engraved on your nice sweet jaw, my son."

Kennedy seemed very comfortable in the armchair. "Captain, I like the atmosphere of your office. The warmth, the genial and abounding good-will exuded by the Department's chiefest exponent of right makes right and wrong, wrong. I carry home with me to my drab hall bedroom a vision of your kindly, smiling face, the tranquil benediction of your smile—"

"Oh, yeah?"

"The feeling of good fellowship, the remembered homilies, the beatific aspect of your profile and, by the way, how is Mrs. Wayne?"

MacBride took his eyes from the clock, which indicated a quarter to nine. "You heard me, sweetheart. Scram."

"And by the way, what do you think of Manuel Figueroa?"

MacBride stood up, darkening. "Kennedy, I'm in no mood to be monkeyed with."

"I was just getting around to telling you, O Captain, that I've found out things about Figueroa. Three years ago he lived in Boston, was supported by Mrs. K.T.P. Weems-Colbrooke, the wife of the president of the Western Ocean Mercantile. Supported for a year. He has no standing as a sculptor anywhere. He's never had a piece exhibited, has never sold—well—not even a miniature of the Washington Monument. The lady's daughter fell for him. He got in Dutch with the girl and lammed. No complaint could be made because he held the whip-hand over mama. This never got in the papers. I remember the name, though—Figueroa. Will Smythe gave me the yarn two years ago. He used to be publicity agent for the Western Ocean Mercantile. I've a good memory.

"It recalls another anecdote from the amours of our hero. At a newspaper club in New York three years ago I met Jim Mapes, late of the Indianapolis Star-Express. Love in the midlands. Mrs. Jennifer Carnes, wife of a potent midland banker, had Figueroa under her wing. One day her husband noticed a twenty-thousand dollar rope of pearls missing from her collection. She said she'd lost them. You figure it out. A month later our hero spreads himself in a Boston studio. Cute?"

MacBride drummed on the desk with his fingers and bored Kennedy with a hard stare. "Kennedy, you spring that in your lousy rag and you're through in this city. You spring that and blow up Cort Wayne's balloon and I'm on you like hell-fire."

"I'm just telling you, old tomato. I'm just trying to suggest, possibly, the X quantity behind this abduction. I'm just trying to give you a faint idea of what kind of a crum this greaseball is."

MacBride sat down. "Thanks, Kennedy. Thanks. I've got ideas about that baby myself. But you give me more. You make me begin to—" He cut himself short and snapped a look at Kennedy. One eye narrowed. He unlocked a drawer and hauled out a bottle of Golden Wedding. He uncorked it, set two glasses side by side.

"This calls for a drink, Kennedy."

"Ah . . . 'drink down all unkindness,' skipper—with the Bard of Avon."

"I still think you're going ga-ga, but what the hell."

They had two more drinks. MacBride rose then, saying, "I'll be back in a minute." He left the bottle on the desk. He went out, locked the door, went down the hall and entered another office. He picked up a phone.

"MacBride. . . . Switch all calls for me to extension twenty-one. Pay no attention to any calls coming from eighteen. . . . That's right. Now try locating Moriarity."

He sat down at the desk, knocked out his dead pipe, restuffed it and lit up. He looked at his watch. Five minutes to nine. Put the watch away in his vest pocket and puffed furiously on his pipe. He got up and paced the room, back and forth, back and forth.

Moriarity came in saying, "Moved?"

"Listen, Mory. I locked Kennedy up in my office with a bottle of rye. It's a dirty trick but I don't want him pulling a tail on me. I'm going places. I may even do things—if I see scenery. Here's the key to my office. You stay in here and take any calls for me. And don't let Kennedy out till you hear from me."

"Oke, Cap."

"If any of these reporters crowd you tell 'em I'm in the building. I'll want to borrow your hat and overcoat."

"Down in my locker. It's open."

"Thanks."

MacBride went downstairs and got into Moriarity's coat. It fit well enough, but the fedora was a little small. It set quaintly on MacBride's bony head, but he pulled the brim down all around and that helped. He took the tunnel to the garage and found the mechanic there.

"The Ford touring with the curtains, Jerry."

"You drivin'?"

"Yeah. But don't tell anybody. I'm supposed to be in the building."

"I gotcha."

The flivver was black, had no police markings. MacBride drove it out of the garage and lit out for the West End. At nine-fifteen he passed Wayne's house, saw Figueroa's roadster parked in front. He drove on and parked at the next block. Traffic plowed past continuously. He twisted around in the seat and kept his eyes on the little cowl-lights that marked Figueroa's roadster.

At exactly nine-thirty the lights moved, were replaced by headlights that swung into westbound traffic. MacBride started the flivver, saw the roadster go by and stop at a red traffic signal beyond. MacBride crawled into the traffic and was the third behind Figueroa when the roadster started again.

Westover Boulevard climbed upward beyond Laurel Street and the traffic ascended like an escalator. It reached a peak, then sloped away westward, going down gradually to the corporation limit, leaving the big houses behind. The flivver ducked around slow moving vehicles, maintained a comparatively equal distance behind the roadster, never approached it too closely.

Traffic thinned out but three cars were still between the roadster and the flivver. Ahead, MacBride saw the white blur of the railroad underpass. He saw the roadster pass beneath it. MacBride passed beneath, and now Westover Boulevard became the Old West Road. Three hundred yards beyond, Riding Pike crossed it north and south.

The roadster made a left turn into Riding Pike. MacBride slapped his foot down on the accelerator, let a southbound sedan head him off and then swung in behind it. He took his gun from its holster and laid it on the seat beside him. A few oaths sizzled on his lips and then his lips clamped tightly shut and he tipped Moriarity's hat lower on his forehead.

The roadster was picking up speed. MacBride had to pass the sedan, and when he did he saw the roadster taking a turn in the Pike fast. The straightaway ended. The Pike became serpentine and MacBride kept his foot jammed down on the throttle. On a moonlit rise ahead he saw the silhouette of the roadster; then it dropped from sight, and when MacBride topped the rise he saw the roadster sweeping ahead and far below. The flivver roared and shook and the wind hammered the loose curtains.

He saw the roadster make a left turn into Black Horse Road. He followed it and had to go a mile before he picked up the red tail-light again. Houses appeared, then a settlement, then a suburb of the city. The roadster shot beneath a raised grade-crossing, turned sharp left, climbed a short hill.

MacBride was going too fast to make the turn. He jammed on the brake and sat tight while the flivver skidded fifty feet. Then he backed up, shifted and swung left hard. He gave the motor the gun to make the short grade and saw Figueroa hauling a bag from the rumble. He went over the hump, jammed on the brake and raised dust skidding past the roadster. On his left was a suburban station of the main line.

He knocked open the door and scooped his gun off the seat as he bounded out. Figueroa saw him and dropped everything but the gladstone. He leaped and ducked beneath the station platform. MacBride went under after him, stumbled over a track and rebounded to his feet.

Figueroa jumped from behind a supporting pillar, scaled the tracks and went under the platform opposite. MacBride followed and crowded him against a stone wall. He walloped his gun against Figueroa's stomach and flattened him upright against the wall.

"Give me that dough, you punk!"

"I—I—"

"You heard me! I've got to get out on the Old West Road and deliver it. Wayne's a friend of mine and if I had the time to pinch you I'd do it. But I'll get you later. Wayne's the only guy matters now. Shake it out, you two-timing so-and-so!"

Far up the line a locomotive whistle hooted.

"I can kill you," MacBride gritted. "I can let you have it in your dirty guts and by —— I will if you don't fork over that money!"

Figueroa's breath was stifled. He shoved his hand into his inside pocket, dragged out the brown envelope. MacBride snatched it and stepped back.

"Remember, greaseball," he said, "I'll be after you inside of an hour. But there's no time now."

He turned and raced across the tracks, beneath the platform. He reached the flivver and as he whipped it down through the underpass he heard the train puff into the station. He hit the Black Horse at sixty miles an hour, wheeled the car into Riding Pike and held the accelerator flat to the boards on the way north. For once he wasn't a cop. He was a friend of governor-elect Wayne. He had to deliver shake-down money to insure the release and safe return of Cortland Wayne. It was against his code, against his principles. It griped him, but a life that mattered was at stake.

He took the turn into Old West Road much too fast. He felt the car heave. He toiled with the wheel, heard the rasp of the rubber, felt the rear end slew, then snap back again. He was off the road. He saw the windows of a filling station rear up in front of him, heard a man's hoarse cry. He hit. Glass exploded and flew. Metal snarled and cracked and the hard stone of the filling station did not budge.

He went through the curtains, did a somersault and landed asprawl on cinders. He lay slightly dazed and blinking while figures ran around him and bent over him. Time seemed to fly, but somehow an ambulance got there and he was still blinking while a white-coated figure ran fingers over his body. Suddenly he made a sweeping motion with his hands and sat up.

"Hey, take it easy," a voice growled.

MacBride saw things clearly. He saw the ambulance, the doctor, a motorcycle cop, and the flivver. The crushed and hardly recognizable flivver.

"Now, now," the doctor was saying.

"I'm MacBride," the skipper declared.

The doctor said: "I don't give a damn—"

"Oh," the motorcycle cop cut in. "That's right! Captain MacBride! This is Enders, Captain; Ninth Precinct."

"Hello, Enders."

MacBride was on his feet. Moriarity's hat was ruined and the seat was completely removed from Moriarity's overcoat. But MacBride slapped the hat on and looked comically pugnacious. He brushed the doctor out of the way and jumped to the wreck of the flivver. From its ruins he drew the brown envelope. But somehow it had been gashed in two. He held the pieces up and looked at them. The envelope had been stuffed with newspaper.

He whipped around. "Enders! Enders, where the hell are you?"

"Here, sir!"

"Lend me your motorcycle."

He forked the machine, gunned it hard, walked it off the cinders and went booming away towards the city.

Enders scratched his head. "The skipper always was wild as a coot."

The maid let MacBride in. He went past her without seeing her. He even forgot to remove his hat. Moriarity's hat was cocked over one eyebrow and the seat of the skipper's pants showed through the ragged hole in Moriarity's coat. His jaw looked teak-hard and a bitter glint was in his eye.

He ran into Davenport. "Mr. Davenport, more dough—and as quick as you can get it. That greaseball pulled the old two-time and Cort—"

"Sh! Sh!"

"Now don't shush me. I figured that guy was a heel and I tailed him. He didn't take the Old West Road. He lit out down Riding Pike and went over Black Horse to the Wentwood main-line station. I took the envelope away from him. I wanted to pinch the sweet double-crosser but I had no time. I wanted to get that dough to the spot. I piled up the car into a filling station—and lucky I did. The envelope contained newspaper. He'd taken out the dough and was on the lam. Come on now—rake up some dough—"

"Not so loud. Not so loud. Cort just came back."

"What!"

"He's in bed. Upstairs. Mrs. Wayne is with him."

"You mean to say—"

"Please, Captain, please!"

MacBride straightened and his jaw set. He clipped: "Okey." He pivoted and walked hard-heeled to the telephone. Davenport heaved after him and grabbed his arm.

"What are you going to do?"

"Get Figueroa. I know what train he's on."

Davenport got between MacBride and the telephone. He shook his white-maned old head. "No, Captain, No."

"What the hell do you mean—no?"

Davenport's blue eyes keened to fine glacial points. "You promised you'd do everything within your power to keep Cort's name clean."

"What's this got to do with Cort? Get away from that phone."

"No. Listen. Figueroa is on his way. Everything has worked out as I hoped. I know where he's going. New York. He's booked on the steamship *Magnetic* for France. I had a secret agent following him. I know just what he did."

MacBride narrowed his eyes. "I don't get you."

Davenport took a deep breath. "You know how I feel about Cort. You know I said that I would do anything to prevent a blemish on his name or his household. I know I can tell you this in strictest confidence. I know or suspect that you already have some knowledge of how things stood.

"In Cort's kidnaping I saw an opportunity to get rid of Figueroa. It was a long chance but I took it. Had not Mrs. Wayne suggested that he go with the money, I should have done so. I wanted him to go. I knew from what I'd heard of this leech that once he got fifteen thousand in his hands he would abscond with it. I wanted just that to happen."

"But—"

"Let me finish. I knew that Figueroa and Mrs. Wayne were more than friends. I was resolved one way or another to get rid of Figueroa without breaking an inch of scandal and without making Cort aware of the fact that this liaison was existent.

"So Figueroa was to take the money to the designated point. A trusted agent of mine followed him. This man also carried an envelope containing fifteen thousand. If Figueroa had gone to the designated point, my agent should have gone on about his business. But we had Figueroa reasoned out. He absconded. My agent, who was only a block behind you when you reached the underpass, carried the money to the rendezvous and shortly afterward Cort walked in that door, haggard and worn but all right otherwise. He had been kept blindfolded all the time. He was helped from a car at a North Side street corner, still blindfolded, and the car had driven away before he got the blindfold off.

"Figueroa is gone. You might say I could have offered him a sum outright, but with bribery there is always backwash, later on. Now he has committed robbery, grand larceny. But no one knows but you and my trusted agent. He will not come back. Leave it that way, Captain."

MacBride rocked on his heels. "What am I going to tell that flock of newshawks? Here I've been clowning all around town, busting up cars and a filling station."

"You could say that you saw a car trailing my agent. You were afraid it contained a newspaperman or perhaps even gangsters who may have found out the identity of the man carrying the ransom. You hailed the car and it started off. You chased it. You noticed it had no rear license plate . . ."

"I get you, Mr. Davenport. In other words, I take the merry razz from the boys and likely a hot calling-down from the chief."

"You like Cort, don't you?"

"Sure."

"And your shoulders are broad, Captain."

MacBride cracked a hard tight grin. His voice was low, saying: "Okey. I'll be the goat then. But just let somebody try riding me! Just let them!"

PAUL CAIN
(1902–1966)

𝔸 great deal of mystery surrounds the life of Paul Cain (George Carrol Sims), including who, precisely, he was and what he did during large slices of his life. He seems to have been one of a kind, a man congenitally at odds with normality. Only very recently has it been established that his birth name was Sims and not Ruric, the latter a surname he used throughout his career. He was George Ruric when he worked as a production assistant on Josef von Sternberg's The Salvation Hunters (1925) and Peter Ruric when he was a successful screenwriter from the late 1930s into the 1940s. As Paul Cain, he wrote almost solely for Black Mask. Of seventeen stories for Black Mask, five were "cannibalized" into his only novel, the extraordinary Fast One (1933), and seven were collected into Seven Slayers (1946).

Cain claimed to have led a colorful, even rackety existence, roaming the globe (South America, North Africa, the Near East, points north, east, south, and west) and posing, among other things, as a tramp-steamer boatswain's mate, a Dadaist painter, and a professional gambler. The last disguise was most likely a true part of Cain's résumé, since, as William F. Nolan has pointed out, the gambling scenes in Fast One were clearly written by someone who had been there.

Fast One was considered by the modern critic E. R. Hagemann to be "one of the toughest . . . and most brutal gangster stories ever written." The anonymous reviewer for the New York Times Book Review described it as "a ceaseless welter of bloodshed and frenzy, a sustained bedlam of killing and fiendishness." While Hagemann's view is clearly positive and the Times critic's negative, both comments seem to be apt. Like all great works of art, Fast One keeps being rediscovered and lauded, worthy of every word of praise that has been showered on it.

"Trouble-Chaser" is as mean and lean as anything Cain ever wrote; it is written in a stripped-down prose style that makes the understatement of Ernest Hemingway look flowery and the minimalism of Andrew Vachss seem somehow overblown. It has not been reprinted anywhere since its first appearance in Black Mask more than sixty years ago.

J. A.

TROUBLE-CHASER

Mae lived at the *Mara Apartments* on Rossmore. It was about nine o'clock when I got there and the party hadn't got going. I mean by that that nobody was falling down and nobody had been smacked over the skull with a bottle. There were six or seven people there besides Mae and Tony—I didn't know any of them, which was just as well. Tony opened the door, and made a pass at introducing me, and Mae came in from the kitchen and we went into a big clinch. She was demonstrative that way when she had two or three fifths of gin under her belt, whoever it might be.

Tony fixed me a drink. I took it because I knew better than to argue about a thing like that; I carried it around with me most of the time I was there and when anybody would ask me if I wanted a drink I'd show them the full glass.

Tony was Italian—from Genoa I think. He was very dark and slim, with shiny blue-black hair, bright black eyes, a swell smile. I'd known him for five or six years—I knew him back in New York when he was trying to build up a bottle business around the *Grant Hotel.* We'd never been particularly friendly but we always liked each other well enough. When he came to California he looked me up and I got him a job running case-stuff for Eddie Garda. I introduced Tony to Mae Jackman when she was a class C extra-girl and not doing so well at it. They'd been living together for about a year. Tony was in business for himself and doing well enough to live at the *Mara.* Mae still worked in pictures occasionally and that helped.

Mae jockeyed me out into the kitchen as soon as she could. She leaned against the sink and sucked up most of a glass of gin and ginger ale and whispered dramatically: "We've got to get rid of Tony."

I am not the most patient person in the world, with drunks. I looked at her with what I hoped would penetrate her gin haze as an extremely disgusted expression.

She went on hurriedly in the stage whisper: "I mean for a minute. I've got something I want to show you an' I don't want him busting in." She finished her drink and then with a very wise and meaning look, said, "Wait," and coasted back into the living-room.

I poured the gin in my glass into the sink and filled the glass with ginger ale and ice.

She came back in a minute. "I sent him up to Cora's to get some ice," she said. Cora was Mae's side-kick; she lived upstairs.

Mae steered me through the short corridor into the bedroom and closed the door behind us. She went to the dresser and dug around in the bottom drawer for a minute and came up with a folded piece of yellow paper and handed it to me. I unfolded it and held it under the light at the head of the bed; it was Louis L. Steinlen's personal check for twenty-five hundred dollars. Steinlen was the executive head of the Astra Motion Picture Company.

I said: "That's swell, Mae." I handed the check back to her and she held it with the light shining down on it and looked at it and then looked up at me.

"It's swell," she said—"an' it's going to be a lot sweller."

She smiled and her face lost its set drunken look for a moment. She was a very pretty girl and when she smiled she was almost beautiful.

I said: "So what?" I wasn't very enthusiastic about staying in the bedroom with her because Tony might come back sooner than she expected and he was a long way from being stone sober—I didn't want him to get any trick ideas.

Mae kept on smiling at me. She said: "So this is the amount"—she bobbed her head at the check—"of your cut for helping me make a deal with Steinlen."

I had a faint idea of what she was getting at, but not enough to help much. I said: "What the hell are you talking about?"

She sat down on the edge of the bed. "We're going to sell Steinlen his two-bit check for twenty-five grand," she said.

I didn't say anything. I felt like laughing but I didn't—I waited.

"This little piece of paper," she went on, "is worth its weight in radium." She glanced down fondly at the check, then back up at me. She was not smiling any more. "Steinlen has been chasing me for months. Last week-end Tony went up to Frisco on business—I went to Arrowhead with Steinlen—on business." She smiled again, slowly. She held the check in one hand and whipped the index finger of her other hand with it. "This is a little token of the deal."

I said: "That's quite a token." I liked Mae at that moment about ninety per cent less than I'd ever liked her, and she'd never been the kind of girl I'd want to take home and introduce to the folks. I didn't tell her I thought she'd been extravagantly overpaid—that was pretty obvious. I waited for her to go on and let me in on what I had to do with it all.

She went into a fast song and dance about what a cinch it was going to be to take Steinlen for the twenty-five grand, about how it wasn't technically blackmail because she was simply exchanging his check—a check that he'd have a hell of a hard time explaining to his wife—for the cash—ten times as much cash. She said the reason she wanted me to come in on it was because she thought I could make the deal better than she could and because we'd have to be careful not to let the twenty-five-hundred-dollar check get out of our hands before we got the cash.

When she finished I grinned at her without any particular warmth and said: "Why don't you have Tony work with you on this?"

She said: "Don't be a sap, Red—if Tony knew about this, or found out about it, he'd cut my throat." Then she went on to cuss Tony out and explain that she was all washed up with him, and had been for a long time—and that she was going to scram to Europe as soon as she got her big dough.

When she got all that out of her system I lit into her and told her that in the first place she was crazy as a bedbug to figure on beating Steinlen out of anything, and in the second place I wouldn't show in a deal of that kind if it was for a million, and a natural—I was getting along too well legitimately—and in the third place she was an awful sucker to finagle around with something that Tony might find out about before she could get away. I finally wound up by explaining to her, with gestures, that my job was keeping people *out* of trouble, not getting them into it.

She took it fairly easy. She said she was sorry I couldn't see it her way, and that she'd have to find somebody else or do it herself. She said that however she worked it it would have to be done quickly because Steinlen's wife, who was Sheila Dale the Astra star, was due back from location the next morning—and Steinlen would be psychologically ripe for the touch with his wife coming in. Mae was a bright girl in some ways. It's too bad she was so full of larceny—bad company I guess.

We went back out into the kitchen and she fixed a drink for herself and started fixing one for me and I showed her my full glass.

She said: "I know I don't have to tell you to keep this under your hat. . . ."

I smiled and shook my head and drank some of the ginger ale in a kind of silent toast to her success. Then I tried to talk her out of it again in a roundabout way but it was no go—she'd made up her mind. A couple drunks weaved out into the kitchen and Mae mixed drinks for them.

Tony came in while they were there, which was just as well because it didn't look like Mae and I had been doing our double act all the time he'd been out.

He said: "Cora made me stay an' have a couple drinks with her. She is very sad and won't come down." He went on to explain to me that Cora's boy-friend had walked out on her, and what a heel he was, and what he, Tony, would do to him if he saw him. Tony's voice was very soft and he spoke each word very quietly, very distinctly, with just a trace of accent.

I glanced at Mae while Tony was telling me in detail what he would do to Cora's boy-friend; she was gargling another drink.

I shoved off pretty soon and went down and got into a cab and went back to the *Derby*. In a little while the fight crowd started drifting in and Franey and Broun and a bookmaker named Connie Hartley came in and we had a few drinks and sat around and told lies. I'd been on the wagon for a couple weeks and I was getting pretty sick of it—I had quite a few drinks. Hartley had some racing-forms and Franey and I picked a few losers for Saturday.

After a while Franey and Hartley and I went out to the *Colony Club* and there was a friend of mine there who was a swell piano player. We listened to him and had a lot more drinks. I got home about four.

I woke sometime around eleven I guess, but I didn't get up right away. I made a couple phone calls and then tried to get back to sleep but that was out. Finally I rolled over to the edge of the bed and looked down at the extra which had been shoved under the door. By twisting my head around I could read the headline:

ACTRESS STRANGLED IN HOLLYWOOD APARTMENT

I got up then, and sat on the bed and read the story. Mae Jackman had been murdered at around three-thirty in the morning, as near as the police could figure, in her apartment at the *Mara*. The body had been discovered at eight-thirty by the maid. The dragnet was out for Tony Aricci.

I had breakfast at a little joint down the street a few doors from the hotel. When I went back up to my room there was a man standing in the dim elbow of the corridor just outside my door. It was Tony. He stepped close to me and jabbed an automatic into my belly. I unlocked the door and we went into my room and closed the door.

I said: "What's it all about?"

Tony's face was something I still dream about when I have too much lobster and cherry brandy. His usually dark swarthy skin was gray; his mouth was a dark gray slit across the lower part of his face, and his eyes were stark crazy.

When he spoke it sounded like the words were coming up out of a well. He said: "You killed Mae." There was no intonation—the words were of exactly the same pitch.

I didn't feel especially good. I edged away from him slowly, sat down very slowly in the chair by the window. While I was doing that I was saying: "For the love of the —— Tony—where did you get such a dumb idea?"

He said: "If you didn't kill her you know who did. She's been calling you for three days. You talked to her alone last night while I was at Cora's—all the time I was away. There is something I do not know. I have known there was something I did not know for a long time. You must tell me what it is. If you do not tell me what it is I am going to kill you."

If I have any gift for figuring whether people mean what they say, he meant it. I stalled, lit a cigarette.

I said: "Sit down, Tony."

He shook his head very sharply.

I went on. "You're on the wrong track, Tony. If that gang of drunks officed you that Mae and I were in the bedroom while you were up-stairs—she took me in to show me the stills on her last picture. We talked about old times. . . ." I leaned forward, shook my head slowly. "I thought *you* had killed her when I read it in the paper just now. I thought you'd had one of your battles and you'd gone a little too far."

He wilted suddenly. He fell down on his knees beside the bed and the automatic clattered to the floor and he put his head in his arms on the bed and sobbed in a terrible dry way like a sick animal. He said brokenly and his voice was muffled by his arms, seemed to come from very far away: "My dear God. My dear God! I kill her!—I kill her who I loved more than anything! Why, my dear God, do they say I killed her? . . ."

It was embarrassing to see a guy like Tony break down like that. I got up and picked up the automatic and dropped it into the pocket of my topcoat and patted Tony's shoulder. I didn't know what else to do and I didn't know what to say, so I went back and sat down and looked out the window.

Pretty soon Tony got up. He said: "I had to go to Long Beach last night. I left Mae about one-thirty. All the gang had gone home. I did not get back until a little while ago. I stopped at *Sardis* for breakfast because I did not want to wake Mae up—and I saw the paper." He cleared his throat. "I am going to Cora. Cora will know something—she will tell me what it is. . . ."

I said: "No. You are not going to do anything like that. You can't stay here because if the Law finds out I came to your place last night they'll come here to ask me a lot of questions, but I'm going to take you to a friend of mine upstairs and I want you to stay with her until I come back. I'm going to see what I can do about getting you in the clear and if I can't do that we will see what we can do about getting you out of town."

He smiled in a way that was not pleasant to see. He said: "I do not care about the clear, and I do not care about getting away. I care about finding the man who killed Mae and cutting his heart out of his body."

I nodded and tried to look as if I felt like doing the same thing. I steered him out of the room and we went up the back stairs to the eighth floor and I knocked at Opal Crane's door. Opal was still in bed; she yelled, "Who is it?" and I told her and in a minute she came to the door and opened it. She was rubbing her eyes and yawning and when I introduced Tony to her and told her I wanted her to let him stay there a little while she didn't look very enthusiastic.

She jerked her head at Tony, who had sat down and was staring out the window, and said: "Hot?"

I nodded.

She looked a little less enthusiastic and I asked her if she thought I'd ask her to do it if I wasn't sure it was all right. She shook her head and yawned some more and went into the bathroom.

I said to Tony: "I'll be back or call you as soon as I can."

He bobbed his head up and down vacantly and then he said: "Give me my gun."

I said: "No. You won't need it, and I might."

I left him sitting by the window staring out into the gray morning and went out softly and closed the door.

Back in my room I called up Danny Scheyer who is a police reporter on the *Post*. I asked him to find out all he could about the inside on the Jackman murder, whether the police were satisfied that it was Tony or were working on any other angles. I asked him particularly to find out if a check that might have some bearing on the case had been found on Mae or in the apartment. Scheyer had a swell in at headquarters and I knew he'd get all the dope there was to get. I told him I'd call him again in a little while.

It was almost twelve-thirty and I figured Steinlen would be at lunch but I called up anyway. He was at lunch and I talked to his secretary. I told her I wanted to make an appointment with Steinlen for around one-thirty and she asked what I wanted to see him about. I told her to tell him that Mister Black, from Arrowhead, would be over at one-thirty and that his business was very personal. Then I went over to the *Derby* and had some more coffee.

I called Scheyer again from the *Derby* and he said they hadn't found anything on Mae or in the apartment that meant anything and that it looked like a cinch for Tony Aricci.

I said: "Maybe not." I told Scheyer he'd get first call on anything I turned up and thanked him.

Steinlen was younger than I'd figured him to be—somewhere between thirty-five and forty. He was a thin, nervous man with a long, bony face, deep-set brown eyes. His hands were always moving.

He said: "What can I do for you, Mister Black?"

I leaned forward and put my cigarette out in a tray on his desk and then leaned back and made myself comfortable. I said: "You can't do anything for me but I can do an awful lot for you."

He smiled a little and moved his head up and down. "People are doing things for me all the time," he said. "That's the reason I'm getting so gray." He scratched his long nose and then put his hand down on the desk and drummed with his fingers. "What are you selling?"

"I sell peace of mind," I said. "They used to call me the Trouble-Chaser back East. I kept people out of jams—and when they got into jams I got them out. I worked at it then—now it's more or less of a hobby."

He was still smiling. He said: "Go on."

The way he kept moving his hands made me jumpy. I still had my topcoat on and I was practically lying down in the chair; I had my hand on Tony's gun in my coat pocket.

I said: "You murdered Mae Jackman."

116

His face didn't change. He stopped drumming on the desk with his fingers and he was entirely still for maybe ten or fifteen seconds. He was looking straight at me and he was still smiling. Then he shook his head very slowly and said: "No."

I said something a little while ago about a gift for figuring whether people mean what they say. Something like fifteen years of intensive study and research into the intricacies of draw and stud poker are pretty fair training for that sort of thing. I mean I'm not exactly a sucker for a liar, and so help me I believed Steinlen.

I said: "Who did?"

Steinlen shook his head again slowly. "Aricci, I suppose."

By that time my sails were flapping. I'd been so sure Steinlen was *it,* and now I was so sure he wasn't—I felt like I'd been double-crossed. Anyway, I wasn't going to let it go at that. My hunch was that Steinlen was telling the truth but I don't play my hunches *that* far. I wanted to know.

I said: "Aricci didn't do it." I said it as if I was sure of it.

Steinlen laughed a little. "You are very sure."

I told him I was very sure and told him why. I told him that if Aricci had killed Mae the check would have figured in it and if Aricci had the check he, Steinlen, wouldn't be alive to be talking about it.

When I mentioned the check Steinlen's expression changed for the first time. His face became almost eager. He said: "Are you sure the police did not find the check?"

I nodded.

He asked: "Who, besides yourself, knew about it?"

"Only you," I said—"and, evidently, whoever has it now." I lit a cigarette and watched Steinlen's face. I said: "As long as that check is in existence it's an axe over your head. If the police get it, it will tie you up with the murder. If Aricci gets it or finds out about it, he'll kill you as sure as the two of us are sitting here."

Steinlen was staring blankly out the window. He nodded slightly.

"I think you'd better tell me all you know about the whole business," I went on. "Maybe I can get an angle."

He swung around in the swivel-chair to face me; he was smiling again. He said: "Did you come here to arrest me?"

I shook my head. "Not necessarily. I wouldn't put the pinch on anyone unless there wasn't anything else left to do. I came here convinced that you did the trick and I intended getting it in writing and then giving you about twenty-four hours' head start. I wasn't especially fond of Mae, and I think her check idea was pretty raw, but I like Tony pretty well and I know he's innocent and I'm not going to have him holding the bag."

He said: "And you are sure of my innocence, too?"

I smiled a little and said: "Pretty sure."

He started drumming on the desk again. He said: "Mae telephoned me about two this morning. She was very drunk. She said that Tony had gone out, that she was alone."

I said: "Uh-huh. Tony went to Long Beach. He left the apartment about one-thirty."

Steinlen scratched his nose. "Can't he establish an alibi in Long Beach?"

"Not with the people he was doing business with. They wouldn't be worth a nickel as an alibi."

Steinlen nodded, went on: "Mae told me what she wanted—twenty-five thousand dollars in cash. She said if I didn't give it to her she was going to Mrs. Steinlen with my check and tell her that I had seduced her and then tried to buy her off for twenty-five hundred. . . ." He smiled crookedly. "Her idea was very sound—the check was irrefutable proof. Picture producers don't give extra-girls twenty-five-hundred-dollar checks as birthday gifts. . . ."

I said: "That was a very chump piece of business for you to do. How come?"

Steinlen laughed shortly, bitterly, shook his head. "I guess we all think we're character sharks," he said. "I thought she was on the level."

One of the phones on his desk rang and he picked it up and told his secretary to put whoever was calling on. While the connection was being made he said, "Pardon me," and then he said, "Hello, Sheila," into the phone. He talked to her for several minutes; he asked her how the location trip had been and whether she had received his last letter. Every fifth word was darling or baby or honey. Finally he asked her if she was coming to the studio and said he'd try to get home early and hung up.

He said: "That was Mrs. Steinlen—she just got back from location in Arizona."

Then he went on about Mae. He said she'd insisted on his meeting her at the corner of Rosewood and Larchmont—she didn't want him to come to the *Mara* because somebody might see him come in. The corner of Rosewood and Larchmont was only a couple blocks from the *Mara*. He explained to her that he couldn't get the money in the middle of the night but she was very drunk; she said he'd *better* get it and hung up on him. He'd decided to meet her and reason with her and talk her out of it until the next day, anyway, so he'd have time to figure out what he was going to do. He went to the corner of Rosewood and Larchmont and waited from two thirty-five until almost four o'clock. She didn't show, so he figured that Tony had come back and she couldn't get away; he went home and tried to sleep. The first thing he knew about the murder was when he read it in the paper after he got to the studio, about ten o'clock.

The more he talked the dizzier I got about the whole layout. It would have been a cinch for Tony to start to Long Beach and then sneak back—he was suspicious of Mae, anyway—and catch her going out to meet Steinlen. He would probably have knocked her down and frisked her and found the check and that would have been that. Tony was a pretty bad boy when he was mad. But if that's the way it had been and Tony had put on that act for me so I'd help him—then Tony was the greatest actor in the world and wasting his time bootlegging. He was not only the greatest actor in the world but I was degenerating into a prize sucker and losing my eyesight.

On the other hand, Steinlen didn't even have the alibi of having been at home. He *said* he'd been on the corner of Rosewood and Larchmont from two thirty-five till almost four. Mae had been killed around three-thirty. Steinlen could have pulled that off very nicely—he didn't have a leg to stand on, except that I thought he was telling the truth. Maybe *Steinlen* was the world's greatest actor. It was a cinch Mae hadn't strangled herself.

I began to think very seriously about chucking the whole thing—after all, it was none of my business—if I wasn't careful I'd be getting myself jammed up.

Steinlen said suddenly: "I'll give five thousand dollars for that check."

That made it my business. I told Steinlen I'd call him later and left the studio.

Tony had gone. Opal said he'd sat at the window for about a half hour without saying anything and then jumped up suddenly and gone.

I went back down to my room and lay down on the bed and tried to figure things out. Tony and Steinlen were both naturals to have put the chill on Mae, but unless I was entirely screwy neither of them had.

It suddenly occurred to me that maybe I'd been overlooking a bet in Cora. Maybe there'd been some kind of jealous play on Tony that I didn't know anything about. I remembered how long he'd stayed with her the night before and how much he'd carried on about her guy walking out on her. That might have been a gag to cover up something else. It was a pretty long shot but I was mixed up enough about the whole business by that time to try anything. I called Cora and she wasn't in. I told the switchboard girl to ask her to call me. Then I lay down again and fell asleep.

When I woke up it was twenty minutes after four and the phone was ringing. It was Bill Fraley; he said Dingo, a horse we'd made a fair-sized bet on the night before, had romped in, we'd won four hundred and thirty dollars apiece. I told him I'd meet him over at the cigar store where Hartley made book and I took a shower and shaved and went downstairs.

When I stopped at the desk for my mail there was a fellow named Gleason—an assistant cameraman that I'd known casually for a year or so—leaning on the counter talking to the clerk. We said hello and I asked him what he'd been doing and he said he'd just got back from location at Phoenix with the Sheila Dale outfit. He said he was living at the hotel and we gave each other the usual song and dance about calling each other up and getting together real soon, then I went over to the cigar store and met Bill and collected my bet from Hartley. Bill and I went into the *Derby* and had something to eat. I called up Cora again but she wasn't in.

After a while I called Steinlen. A man answered the phone in his outer office, instead of the secretary. When he asked who was calling I had a hunch and said Mister Smith and when he asked what I wanted to talk to Steinlen about I said I wanted to talk to him about a bill that was long overdue.

The man said: "Mister Steinlen committed suicide about a half-hour ago," and hung up.

Fraley looked at me and said: "You look like you'd just seen a ghost."

I told him I had.

Steinlen wasn't the kind of guy to bump himself off. It looked very much like Tony to me; it looked like whoever had murdered Mae had reached Tony in some way and let him get a flash of the check. They could have explained having the check by saying that Mae had been afraid Tony would find it and had given it to them for safe keeping. In the state of mind Tony was in he'd go for that. It all fitted in with the Cora angle. She'd killed Mae, and when Tony went to her after he left Opal's she'd shown him the check and told him that that was what Steinlen was after when *he* killed Mae.

I called up Danny Scheyer again. He said, "What about that scoop?" and I told him to hold everything and give me all the details of the Steinlen suicide. He said Steinlen had shot himself at about five o'clock in his office at the Astra Studio. Mrs. Steinlen had been with him at the time and had tried to stop him. She had been unable to give any reason for Steinlen's act, had been taken home in a hysterical condition. I told Scheyer I'd call him back.

Well, that let Tony out—and it looked very much like it stuck Steinlen. It looked like he'd given Mae the works, in spite of my hunch that he hadn't. Maybe he hadn't been able to find the check and was afraid it would turn up, or maybe his wife had found out about the Jackman affair and had figured he murdered her and had faced him with it.

Then Fraley said: "So Steinlen bumped himself off?"

I nodded.

Fraley smiled a little, shook his head. He said: "It's a wonder he didn't do it a long time ago—with that —— wife of his. . . ."

I *took* that a little. I said: "What do you mean?"

"I mean she's the original jealous and vindictive female that all the others are copied from; she's had her spurs in him ever since they were married." Bill finished his coffee. "She was a plenty bad actor when I knew her back in Chi, and she's had her nose full of junk for the last couple years—that makes her three times as bad. . . ."

I said: "Heroin?"

Bill bobbed his head.

I said: "I didn't know about that. . . ."

Bill grinned, said: "You don't get around very much. You're the kind of bug they publish the fan magazines for."

I had an idea. It turned out to be my only good idea for the day, which isn't saying a hell of a lot for it. I went back over to the hotel and called the cameraman Gleason from downstairs. I asked him if Sheila Dale had come back with the rest of the company.

Gleason said: "Huh-uh. We finished all the scenes she was in yesterday—she flew back last night."

I went up to my room and got Tony's automatic. When I went back downstairs Fraley had come over from the *Derby* and was talking to the girl at the cigar counter. I asked him if he had any idea who Dale got her stuff from and he said he supposed it was Mike Gorman, or at least Gorman would have a line on it. I looked up Steinlen's home address in the telephone book and went out and got into a cab.

On the way out to North Hollywood I stopped at the apartment house on Highland Avenue where Gorman lived. A blonde gal in a green kimono came to the door and said Mike was asleep. I said it was important and went past her into the bedroom. Mike was lying on the bed with his clothes on. He was pretty drunk.

The blonde had followed me into the bedroom; I told her I wanted to talk to Mike alone and she made a few nasty remarks and went out.

I sat down on the edge of the bed and asked Mike if he'd been peddling junk to Dale. He laughed as if that was a very wild idea and shook his head and said: "Certainly not."

I said: "Listen, Mike—something big is going to break and you're going to be roped into it. If you'll be on the level about this with me I can fix it."

He shook his head again and said: "I haven't sold any stuff for six months. It's too tough. . . ."

I got up and looked down at him and said: "All right, Mike—I tried to help you."

When I started out of the room he sat up and swung around to sit on the edge of the bed. He said, "Wait a minute," and when I turned around and went back he said: "What's it all about?"

I used a lot of big words and asked him again about Dale and he hemmed and hawed and finally said he wasn't Dale's regular connection but he'd sold her some stuff a few times. He said he'd never done business with Dale personally—it was always through her maid, a German girl named Boehme.

I told Mike I'd see that his name didn't get mixed up with what I referred to mysteriously as the "Case" and went back out to the cab.

On the way out through Cahuenga Pass I had one of those trick hunches that I was being followed but I couldn't spot anybody and I wasn't trusting my hunches very much by that time, anyway.

It was pretty dark. The Steinlen house was lit up like a Christmas tree upstairs. I told the driver to wait and walked up the driveway and around to the back door. A big Negress opened the door.

I said: "I want to see Miss Boehme. It is very important."

The Negress told me to wait and in a minute a very thin, washed-out woman with dull black hair and very light watery blue eyes came to the door, said: "I am Miss Boehme. What do you want?"

I stepped close to her and spoke in a very low voice. I told her I was a friend of Gorman's, that Gorman had been picked up and that his address-book with her name in it as a customer had been found by the police. I told her Gorman had sent word to me to reach all his customers and tell them to get rid of any junk they had around.

She acted like she didn't know what I was talking about for a minute, but I pressed it and she finally said okey and thanked me.

Then I told her I had an idea how she could beat the whole business and get her name out of it and said I wanted to use the phone. I went past her into the kitchen when I asked about the phone because I didn't want to give her a chance to stall out of it. I wanted to get into the house.

She looked pretty scared in the light. She took me through the kitchen, through a dark hall, into a little room that was more a library than anything else. I asked her if there were any servants in the house that might be listening in at any of the other phone extensions and she said only the cook—the Negress. She said Mrs. Steinlen was upstairs lying down.

The phone was on a stand near one of the windows. There was a big chair beside it and I sat down and picked up the phone. There wasn't very much light in the room: there were two big heavily shaded floor lamps and one small table lamp on a desk in one corner. There was enough light though to watch the Boehme woman's face.

I dialed a number and then I pushed the receiver-hook down with my elbow so that the call didn't register and then I let the hook up again. I was turning my body to watch Boehme when I clicked the hook—she didn't see it. She was standing by the table in the middle of the room, staring at me and looking pretty scared.

When I'd waited long enough for somebody to have answered I said: "Hello, Chief. This is Red. I'm out at the Steinlen house—I've got Boehme and it all happened the way we'd figured. . . . Yeah. Mrs. Steinlen flew back from Phoenix last night. She'd had some kind of steer that Steinlen was cheating so she didn't let him know she was coming— she thought she might walk in on something. She did—she walked in on the telephone call from Mae Jackman and listened in on the phone downstairs. She got Mae's address from that and sneaked back out and jumped in her car and went over there. . . . Sure—she killed Mae. . . ."

I was guessing, watching Boehme. She'd turned a very nice shade of nile green; she was leaning against the table and her eyes looked like the eyes of a blind woman.

I went on, into the phone: "Steinlen didn't know anything about it—he went over and waited for Mae on the corner of Rosewood and Larchmont and she didn't show so he came home about four. Mrs. Steinlen hid out some place—probably with a friend or at a trick hotel where she wouldn't be recognized—Steinlen didn't even know she was back from location till this afternoon. Then she went to the studio and either scared Steinlen into his number or killed him herself and made it look like suicide—and I'll lay six, two and even she did it herself. . . . Uh-huh—a nice quiet girl. . . ."

Boehme straightened up and turned slowly and started for the door.

I raised my head from the phone and said: "Wait a minute, baby." I took Tony's gun out of my pocket and held it on my lap.

Boehme stopped and turned and stared at the gun a minute without expression. Then she swayed a little and sank down to her knees, leaned forward and put her hands on the floor. I put the phone down and stood up and took two or three steps towards Boehme.

A woman's voice said: "You're a very smart man, aren't you?" The voice was very soft, with a faint metallic quality underneath, like thin silk tearing.

Boehme toppled over sidewise and lay still.

I turned my head slowly and looked at the doorway on my left. There was a woman there in the semi-darkness of the hallway. As I looked at her she came forward into a little light; she was a very beautiful woman with soft golden hair caught into a big knot at the nape of her neck. Her eyes were large, heavily shadowed; her mouth was very red, very sharply cut. She wore a close-fitting light blue negligée and she held a heavy nickel-plated revolver very steadily in her right hand, its muzzle focused squarely on my stomach.

I was holding Tony's automatic down at my side and I didn't know whether Mrs. Steinlen had seen it or not until she said, still in that gentle, unexcited voice: "Put the gun on the table."

She still moved towards me slowly; she was no more than six or seven feet from me. I looked at her without turning my body towards her or moving; I didn't know whether to make a stab at using the gun or to put it on the table. She was in the full light of one of the floor lamps now and there was an expression in her eyes—the hard glitter of ice—that made me figure I'd lose either way.

I took two steps forward so that I could reach the table, but I didn't put the gun down. I held it down stiff at my side and looked at her and tried to calculate my chances.

She said: "It is too bad so smart a man must die."

She circled slowly until she was on the other side of the table; we were facing each other squarely across the table.

Then a shadow came silently out of the dark hallway behind her—the hallway that led to the kitchen. Tony moved towards her slowly; he walked like a somnambulist with his arms outstretched; his eyes were glazed, fixed in a blank, meaningless stare on the back of her head.

She raised the revolver slowly and I saw the muscles of her hand tense a little. I think she felt there was someone behind her but she did not trust her feeling enough; she raised the revolver and stared at me with cold, glittering eyes.

Then one of Tony's arms went around her white throat and his other arm went smoothly, swiftly out along her arm, his hand grasped her hand and the revolver. They moved like one thing. It was like watching the complex, terribly efficient working of a deadly machine; Tony twisted her arm back slowly, steadily, his arm tightened around her throat slowly. Her eyes widened, the white transparent skin of her face grew dark.

Then suddenly the muzzle of the revolver stopped at her temple and I saw Tony's finger tighten on the trigger. I moved towards them as swiftly as I could around the table and there was a sharp choked roar and I stopped suddenly. Tony released her slowly and she fell forward with the upper half of her body on the table, slid slowly off the table down on to the floor; the revolver with her fingers tightened spasmodically around its butt banged against one of the table legs.

I did not move for several seconds; I stood staring at Tony. He was standing with his legs widespread, looking into space, looking at some place a million miles away. Then, slowly, expression came into his eyes—a curious, almost tender expression. He glanced down at the woman at his feet and smiled a little. She was lying on her back and the small black spot on her temple grew slowly larger.

Tony smiled again and said very softly: "That is for Mae, my beautiful lady."

I went to him very swiftly. I said: "How the hell did you get out here?"

He did not answer; he stood smiling a little, looking down at the dead woman. I shook his shoulder. He raised his smile to me, said: "I have been following you all day. I saw you from the window, from that girl's room when you went to the *Derby*. I went down and got in my car and waited until you came out and followed you to the studio. I have been following you all afternoon—I knew finally you would take me to the one who killed Mae. . . ."

I jerked my head towards the kitchen, asked: "Did the Negro girl see you come in?"

He shook his head. He said: "A woman came out and went upstairs above the garage right after you came in. Maybe that was her—maybe she lives there."

I shoved his gun into his hands. I said: "Get out of here—quick."

He shook his head, shrugged, gestured with one hand towards the woman on the floor.

I repeated: "Get out—quick." I put my hands on his shoulders and shoved him towards the hallway.

He turned his head and stared at me in a puzzled sort of way with his lips pursed. Then he shrugged again and went slowly to the hallway and disappeared into its darkness.

I sat down and called the *Post;* after a minute or so I got Scheyer. I said: "Here's your scoop. Sheila Dale murdered Mae Jackman. I think she murdered Steinlen, too, or at least she bulled him into killing himself—we can check on that. She shot herself about two minutes ago—very dead. I saw her do it but I couldn't stop her. Tell your boss to hold the presses for an extra and grab a load of law and get out here to Steinlen's. I'll give you the details when you get here."

I hung up and went over and looked Mrs. Steinlen over pretty carefully to be sure there weren't any marks on her throat or any chance of Tony's prints being on the revolver. Then I went out to the kitchen and got a glass of water to see what I could do about snapping Boehme out of the swoon.

The Negress came in from outside while I was getting the water. Her eyes were big as banjos. She said: "Didn't ah heah a shot, Mistah?"

I told her she had, that Mrs. Steinlen had shot herself.

Her eyes got bigger. "Daid?"

I said: "Daid."

I went back to the library and worked on Boehme. She came around in a little while and sat up and stared at Mrs. Steinlen and at the revolver in her clenched outstretched hand, then she put her hands up to her mouth and started moaning.

I told her to shut up and asked her if she knew where the check was. She acted like she didn't know what I was talking about and I reminded her that if she'd help me all she could I'd see what I could do about forgetting the junk angle—about her acting as go-between and laying herself open to a bad rap on a narcotic charge.

She looked a lot more intelligent when I mentioned that and when I asked her about the check again she said she thought she could find it.

I was out of cigarettes but I found some in a box on the desk. I found an old edition of Stoddard's Travel Lectures on one of the shelves and I sat down and made myself comfortable and read about Constantinople and waited.

DANIEL MAINWARING
(1902–1977)

During the economically ravaged 1930s, proletarian fiction became a favored form of protest among a small but influential group of young writers. Although widely labeled Communists and rabble-rousers, the majority were not political ideologues but earnest social reformers. Benjamin Appel, in an essay in Tough Guy Writers of the Thirties (1968), refers to them as "mostly middle-class college graduates bemused by a vision of the Noble Worker, exploited by the Wicked Capitalists in Silk Hats, toiling away somewhere in Sweatballs County [who], beaten around the ears, hungry in the belly, somehow would become the savior of America."

A number of factors, in particular World War II and the vehement anti-Communist backlash of the late 1940s and the 1950s, helped to end the proletarian vogue and the careers of such present-day virtual unknowns as Jack Conroy and William Rollins, Jr., who had published a score of nonpolitical crime stories in Black Mask in the 1920s and 1930s. Others, notably John Steinbeck and B. Traven, went on to write other types of fiction with less inflammatory, if no less earnest, subject matter. In the short time that proletarian fiction flourished, it did in fact help bring about some of the social changes championed by its writers. Steinbeck's The Grapes of Wrath (1939) is a notable example.

The plight of migrant farm workers in the West was a topic embraced by other writers besides Steinbeck. Daniel Mainwaring was one of these writers. Born and raised in California's fertile Central Valley, he knew its land, people, and labor struggles as well as Steinbeck knew those of the nearby Salinas Valley. His first (and only mainstream) novel, One Against the Earth (1933), while not proletarian fiction, portrays Depression-era social problems in the Central Valley with a prolet's zeal. "Fruit Tramp," one of Mainwaring's few short stories, first published in Harper's in July 1934, has the same incisive qualities and is proletarian as well as Depression fiction. It is also, given its substance and implication, hard-boiled fiction of the very best kind.

In the mid-1930s, Mainwaring abandoned mainstream stories, with which he had had only limited success, in favor of mysteries. From 1936 to 1946, writing as Geoffrey Homes, he published a dozen first-rate novels *set primarily in the valleys and foothills of north-central California and distinguished by fine dialogue and some of the most evocative descriptive writing to be found anywhere in the genre. He created three series detectives: newspaperman Robin Bishop, whose second case,* The Doctor Died at Dusk *(1936), concerns Central Valley labor strife; unconventional private eye Humphrey Campbell and his fat, lazy, and corrupt partner, Oscar Morgan; and Mexican cop José Manuel Madero. The last and best Homes novel,* Build My Gallows High *(1946), a taut, hard-edged non-series thriller, so firmly established Mainwaring in Hollywood (he had begun writing B movies in 1942) that he produced no more fiction during the last three decades of his life. It was filmed in 1947, from Mainwaring's screenplay, as* Out of the Past—*one of the half-dozen best noir crime films.*

B. P.

1 9 3 4

FRUIT TRAMP

In July the fruit tramps came to Clovis. They put up tents in the eucalyptus grove along the track, and at night you could see them sitting around their little fires.

The Elbertas would be ripening when they drove in battered Fords and Chevrolets along the highway to the hills. Within a week a community would spring up in the grove to stay there until the last peach was in the sweat box and the last raisin had been hauled to the packing shed.

Every year or so, there was talk of turning the grove into a park, but no one did anything about it. Once in a while the townspeople sent Old Tim, the constable, over to make the fruit tramps clean up around the tents that looked like dirty bits of fungus growing against the tree trunks. Tim would hang about for a while talking to the children and telling the women to hang their washing so it could not be seen from the road.

"Them underdrawers now," he would say. "They don't look so good from John Good's store. Better get 'em out of sight." He would grumble a little and then go back to his chair on the porch of his office and sit there for the rest of the day, half asleep, his big hat pulled down over his eyes to keep out the glare of the sun, sucking at his dead pipe and shouting to the people he knew.

Farmers who needed help went to the grove and hired a family, children and all, paying the men so much a day to pick the fruit and the women and children a few cents a box for cutting peaches. Usually one of the little girls stayed at the camp to cook supper and have it ready when the family came back at dusk, and during the day in the fruit season you could see them bending over the pots or washing clothes or making miniature cities out of syrup cans and spools when they had nothing else to do.

For a while, during the War and right after it, fruit prices were good and the tramps made plenty of money. Six dollars a day the men were paid, and the women received as high as four or five cents a box. It wasn't bad being a fruit tramp then.

But people in the cities stopped eating so many peaches and raisins. Prices went way down. The mortgage companies came, took the Lincolns and Cadillacs out of the barns, loaded the furniture the farmers had bought in good times into moving vans and drove away, and the banks foreclosed on the land and took over some of the farms.

Still the fruit tramps came every year when the Elbertas were turning yellow in the shiny leaves. Not so many came, but the grove was pretty well filled with men and women and children who drove along the highway leading to the hills and pitched their camps in the shade of the trees planted there by a man named Cole fifty years before.

When times were bad it wasn't easy to make a living picking peaches and grapes, cutting the peaches in half, laying them in orderly rows on the trays. It was hard, unpleasant work. Out in the orchards the heat waves rose, and when you knelt on the earth to pick the fruit up the sand burned through your overalls. The cutting sheds offered little shelter from the sun, and the fuzz from the peaches crept up the women's arms and down the necks of their dresses. They stood all day on the packed earth of the shed, picking the fruit up with their nimble fingers, jabbing the knife point into the soft flesh and, with a twist, halving the fruit.

The filled trays piled up, and before the stack was thirty high the shorter women and the little girls had to stand on boxes so they could reach. Usually the farmer's youngest son rustled for the cutters, taking the empty boxes away, putting full ones in front of the women, pushing the cars loaded with trays of fruit into the sulphur houses which stood back of the sheds.

When the wind blew from the sulphur houses, the sheds were filled with yellow, choking smoke. In the early morning everyone would be cheerful and the girls would giggle when the rustler pushed against them and the women would shout at the men who drove up in the vineyard trucks. In the afternoon though everyone would be tired and cross and the rustler would growl at the women to hurry. By that time their skins would be covered with peach fuzz and would itch and burn and where they scratched themselves with sticky fingers a rash would break out.

Our family was so big that we didn't have to hire any fruit tramps, but did the work ourselves. Sometimes when the crop was poor we went over to the Jap's and helped him out. Other farmers thought father was lucky because he had so many children to do his work. He used to say, "Well, let them try to feed you for a while and then they'll know who's lucky." Once he offered to trade ranches with John Cadwallader, who had one son. "I'll take your boy. You take my mess of kids," father said. "I'll hire me some tramps to do the work. They feed themselves."

When things got bad we didn't feel it like the other farmers, or maybe it was because we hadn't been used to anything much. It always took all the money father made to feed us, so we never bought a car or new furniture, and father said he couldn't afford a mortgage.

The summer when prices were lowest didn't affect us as it did the others. We were in a position to sit back and watch when the trouble with the fruit tramps started.

It was hot that year. There had been little rain and when June came the mountain tops were bare of snow. From the valley you could see little patches near the ragged crest of the ridge, like bits of paper scattered through the trees. The canals were dry and the river was so low we didn't dare go swimming because they said we'd get typhoid fever. All night the engines throbbed, pulling the water from the deep cool sands, spilling it into the ditches, and sometimes late at night we would go over to the Jap's and lie naked in the little pool near the pump, letting the cold water cover us. We had no pumping plant of our own, so the Jap gave us water when we needed it because we always helped him get his crop in when ours was poor.

The fruit tramps came again that year, more of them than ever. There were new faces in the grove. People who didn't know what a raisin was put up tents and looked round for work. They came from farther away, from Los Angeles and San Francisco where things were bad too and work was hard to find. It was a cheap way to spend a summer, camped in a grove of eucalyptus trees rent free, and I suppose they figured the fruit had to be picked so the farmers would pay them to do it.

Around the first of July, when the Elbertas were coloring up enough so they could be shipped green, Aubrey Bell stopped by the bridge to talk to father.

"What you paying this year?" father asked.

"Don't know. Last year we paid two bits an hour. We can't now."

"You'll make more leaving the peaches on the trees," father said.

"What you going to do?"

"We'll get along," father said, pointing to where we were sitting on the porch with mother stringing capri figs on wires. "I got all the help I need. All I got to do is feed 'em."

"You're lucky," Aubrey said.

"Try it some time," father said. "I'll trade you the whole lot for a pair of mules."

"You won't trade me for a mule," my sister Rose said.

"I couldn't get a mule for you," father said. "Who'd want you?"

"If we pay fifteen cents an hour, we can make a go of it," Aubrey said. "I figure I can make a hundred and fifty bucks off my Elbertas if I pay that."

"They won't take it," father said.

"Let 'em starve then." Aubrey started his Ford and went away along the dusty, rutted road.

We heard no more about it for a week or so. Then father went in to town for some flour and rice and beans and talked for a long time to John Good. At dinner that night he told mother all the farmers had got together and decided to pay fifteen cents an hour to the pickers and a cent a box to the cutters.

"You'd make ten cents a day," he told Rose.

"Not that much," my brother Joe said. "Maybe eight."

Rose threw a book at him and he grabbed her and they rolled over on the porch, almost upsetting the coal oil lamp.

"Stop it. I'll lick you both," mother said.

"That's an awful little bit," father said. "I'd hate to work for that."

"I work for less," mother said.

"Want to quit?"

"Sure," mother said, but when we saw her face we knew she didn't mean it.

"I'm sorry for the farmers," father said. "But it's their own fault. They bought a lot of junk when things were good. They put in electric lights and drove round in cars they couldn't pay for. I guess they'll always be like that though. I'm sorry for those tramps too. That isn't such a nice way to live, camped in the center of town on the dirty ground with everybody looking at your washing hanging on the line, knowing how many holes there are in your undershirt, seeing you eat your dinner every night."

"They don't mind," mother said.

"Some of them do. The new ones. There's people camped in the grove who never was outside a city before. They're going to make trouble, John says. Says some of them are Reds."

"What's Reds?" my sister Nell asked.

"Russians," father said.

"But why Reds? Why not blues or pinks or yellows?" Nell asked.

"Call them anything you like," father said. "I think it's a lot of talk anyway. They don't look bad to me. Only kind of pitiful and white-faced like they didn't have enough to eat. I wanted to take the grub over and give it to them."

"That would have been fine," mother said. "Then you could have felt sorry for us."

I took the wagon in to Clovis next day to have the blacksmith set the tires. I hung round the shop for a while, helping him with the forge, watching him as he spun the steel hoop on the anvil and hit it with his hammer while the sparks flew all around him and dropped in the inch-thick coat of coal dust on the floor. Then I went out into the sun and walked down the main street to John Good's store.

A lot of farmers were hanging about outside, talking. After I listened for a time I found they were having trouble getting pickers. Some of the fruit tramps were willing to work for anything and they had gone out to the farms; but the rest said they'd rather starve than pick peaches for fifteen cents an hour.

Jake Cole came back from the grove pretty soon. "There's a big guy over there who thinks he's running things," Jake said. "He's getting the tramps all together and telling them not to work. He says they should get a living wage."

"He's a damn Communist," Hal Bradley said.

There was a little hunchback in the crowd named Emory Whitfield who lived about a mile from our place. He got pretty excited and began waving his arms and swearing. "Those damn Rooshians," he said, "they ought to go back to their own country. Who in hell do they think they are anyway?" When he talked he kept bobbing his head, and the hump on his back looked like something loose stuck inside of his blue work shirt. He hadn't shaved for a long time and around his lips his red whiskers were brown from tobacco juice.

"He don't look like a Rooshian to me," Jake said. "He's as white as I am."

"You ain't so white," Hal said. "Maybe you would be if you went in the ditch once in a while."

"You can't tell about Communists by their looks," a farmer I didn't know said. "It's the way they talk you can tell by."

"Well, he's always talking about a living wage," Jake said.

"Then he's a Red. They always talk like that," the farmer said.

"Let's all go over and talk to him," Hal said. "Maybe if we put it up to him that we got to live too he'll be reasonable."

"Maybe he won't. I already told him," Jake said.

"It won't do no hurt," Hal said.

"Let's run him out of town," the hunchback said. "We been treating them too good, giving them a place to live and all. I been saying for years we shouldn't let them live in the grove. Look how dirty they keep it."

When I thought about the hunchback's ranch and how dirty the house and yard and outhouses were, I snickered, but no one paid any attention to me. They went across the road and I followed, the hot dust burning my bare feet. I ran across quickly and stood in the shade as close as I could get to the tent where the big man they called a Communist lived. He was sitting on a lug box, cutting a chain out of a piece of white pine with a thin-bladed knife, but when he saw all the farmers he stood up. He was a big man with broad shoulders, bigger even than father, and through the faded blue shirt you could see the muscles on his arms like big lumps. His hair was as pale colored as straw and around his neck and ears it was ragged. Probably his wife cut his hair as mother did mine, with a pair of dull scissors.

Some of the other tramps left their tents and came over and stood behind the big man, and you could see he was different from them because his clothes were clean and his face and hands were clean and when he talked he spoke good English.

"Well, how about it?" Hal asked. "Jake here says you boys won't work for less than two bits an hour."

"That's right," the big man said.

"We can't pay that," Hal said and you could see he was trying to be nice about it. "We don't make much off our farms. Hardly enough to pay the taxes. We can just get by if we pay fifteen cents."

"Would you work for that?" the big man asked.

"If I was hungry I would," Hal said.

"We aren't that hungry," the big man said.

Emory Whitfield pushed up to the front and waved his fist. "You will be before we get through with you," he said.

"Shut up, Emory," Hal said. "Let me do the talking. It won't do no good to get tough about it."

The big man smiled at Hal. "You seem reasonable. Now put yourself in our place. We have to eat too. I feel that it would be better not to work at all than to slave in this hot sun for nothing."

"What do you mean nothing?" the hunchback yelled. "Ain't we willing to pay you fifteen cents an hour and your women folks a cent a box for cutting?"

"You're too kind." The big man wasn't smiling any more. "We won't do it, so there's no use talking about it."

"By God! let's run 'em out of town," the hunchback said.

Hal grabbed Whitfield's arm and told him to shut up. "You think it over," he said to the big man. "We can't pay no more and it ain't because we don't want to. We got to live too."

"I know," the big man said.

The crowd went back to the store. I was going to hang around but then I looked at the clock and remembered about the wagon. I hurried back to the blacksmith shop, hitched up the team, and drove on home. When I told father about the trouble at the grove he said I'd better keep away from the fruit tramps or I'd get hurt.

They didn't give in and the farmers didn't give in, so the Elbertas ripened on the trees, fell on the clods and rotted in the sun. Before the packing sheds, the empty refrigerator cars stood waiting and the crews of women who were to pack the peaches for shipment to the east were laid off. Four families got tired of going hungry and went to work on the Miller ranch. Because the other tramps were mad at them for not holding out, they moved their tents into the willows along Dry Creek.

There had been a couple of fist fights in Clovis already, and some of the tramps were threatening to dump out the fruit that lay on trays in Miller's drying yard down by the river, or so the farmers said. A barn half filled with hay on the Thompson ranch caught fire and burned, and people round us blamed the tramps, though father was sure the Thompson boys had been smoking in the hay loft.

Some of the farmers wanted trouble but the rest were pretty upset about the whole business, feeling sorry for themselves and for the strikers. It wasn't nice to go by the grove and see the women and kids sitting around looking like they needed something to eat. Four or five women in the town got groceries together and took them over to the camp. The big man thanked them and said they didn't need charity, but when he wasn't looking some of the others took the things the women brought. That's what we heard from the farmers who stopped in at dusk to sit on the tank house steps and talk to father.

I saw the big man again two weeks after the strike started. Father and I were spreading trays in the drying yard on the sand, which was burning hot even though the sun was gone. After a while we knocked off to get a drink, and as I brought the cool water from the well I saw him coming through the orchard, carrying a shotgun.

Joe, standing on the porch with his face pressed against the screen, told father to look and pointed at the big man. "He's going to dump our peaches out," Joe whispered.

"Hush," father said and when the man came across the yard, offered him the dipper filled with water.

The big man leaned his gun against the stairs and took the dipper.

"Any luck?" father asked.

The big man shook his head. "Thought I might get a rabbit. Didn't see a single one."

"We don't eat rabbits round here this time of year," father said. "They have sores on their necks."

"They'd be better than nothing, at that."

Father held out his hand. "My name's Bigelow."

"Mine's Martin."

"You don't live around here."

"No. I'm camped in the grove. One of the strikers."

Joe had come out of the porch and stood near the pump. "Are you a Red?" he asked.

"Joe." Father frowned at him.

"Do I look like it, son?" the big man asked and when father started to apologize, he laughed. "I know what they've been saying about us. It doesn't hurt my feelings."

Father rolled a cigarette and gave the papers and tobacco to Martin. "Sit on the steps a while."

Martin sat down, poured the tobacco in a paper, made a cigarette.

"I'm neutral in this business," father said. "I got so many kids I don't hire any help. Couldn't if I wanted to."

"Do you blame us for holding out?"

"They can't pay more."

"Perhaps not. But it seems wrong to me to work for such a little bit. They're taking advantage of our poverty."

"You've never been a farmer, have you?"

"No. This is my first fling at it. Until now I worked in cities."

"You don't see things the way we do then," father said.

"I guess not. I only know I won't work for fifteen cents an hour, and as long as I can control the others, they won't either."

Father didn't say anything more until mother told us supper was ready. "You might as well have supper with us, Mr. Martin."

Martin stood up. "No thanks. They're waiting for me in the grove."

Mother came through the back door. "Please stay. I'll fix some things for you to take home."

"Thanks," the big man said. "I couldn't do that." And he went away from us, down the lane to the bridge toward town. I watched him until his big form was out of sight.

Saturday morning, three weeks after the strike started, Jake Cole came over to borrow our hay wagon. One of his eyes was black and there was a bruise on his jaw.

"Celebrating?" father asked.

Jake shook his head. He was pretty serious. "We had a big fight in town last night. A bunch of us, maybe ten, went over to see if we couldn't knock some sense into those guys."

"Didn't have much luck, did you?"

"We will," Jake said.

"Let them alone," father told him. "You'll just get into trouble and your fruit will rot anyway."

"We're going to fix them to-night," Jake said. "Last night we told 'em. I told that big guy, I said, 'By God, either you pick our fruit for what we'll pay you or get out of our town.' "

Father looked up from hooking the traces. "That sort of stuff gets you nowhere, Jake."

"You talk like you was stringing along with them." Jake sounded angry.

"Be yourself, Jake. I don't want to see you get into trouble."

"All the boys are going to be there. You better show up too."

"Not me."

"You getting yellow? Want us to think that?"

"I don't care what you think," father said. "Go haul your hay and cool off. If I didn't know you so well I'd kick your pants for you."

Jake drove off in our wagon. Father saw me standing around watching and told me to get the hell out in the fields and go to work. I took a shovel and ran out to where Joe was cutting a ditch across the lower end of the patch of Lovells. It would be three weeks yet before they were ripe, and father thought one last soaking would make them a lot bigger.

After supper father hitched the team to the buckboard and climbed to the seat. Joe and I asked if we could go along, but he said no, he had some business to attend to, and the best place for us was home. After he was out of sight we told mother we were going over to the Jap's to swim and lit out on the short cut to Clovis.

We ran for a way, then Joe got out of breath and we lay down in a row of vines and looked at the moon coming up over the hills. It was pretty dark because there was only a piece of moon like a sickle you have just shined up on the grindstone hanging right back of Kings River canyon. The wind was soft and cool to our faces and it moved the arms of the grapevines a little, making a soft whispering sound as though it was trying to tell us something. Joe tugged at my arm. "Let's hurry," he said.

We walked fast along the creek, cut through the Malstar place to the road and then followed the railroad tracks to town.

"Better not let father see us," Joe said. "He'd sure be mad."

There was a packing shed right at the end of the grove, and we climbed on the platform and sat on some lug boxes, waiting. It was pretty quiet at first. Away off a train whistled twice and you could hear the engine puffing, the night was so still. In the grove people were talking and through the trees you could see them sitting around their fires.

A lot of automobiles were parked in front of the stores that faced the main street and up at the end of the line was our buckboard, the only one there, but father wasn't in it.

Someone was talking in a loud voice over by John Good's store. We moved our boxes back so no one could see us, and waited, and then a lot of men were crossing the road to the grove. It was too dark to see who they were, but I knew they were farmers and that father was probably with them. The crowd stopped not far from the tracks, right in front of us. Out of the trees came a bunch of men and the big man was in front.

I looked all through the crowd but couldn't see father, and that made me feel better. Emory Whitfield stepped forward and began to yell, "Get the hell out of our town or we'll run you out, you damned Bolsheviks."

"We're harming no one," the big man said. "We have a right to do as we please."

"Not in this town, you don't." Jake Cole moved toward the tramps beside the hunchback. "Pack up your trash and get out of here."

"We stay here," the big man said.

The farmers moved closer. A couple of them had shotguns under their arms. Others were carrying pitchforks and lumber. The tramps edged backward, all but the big man.

"They won't hurt us," he said.

"Not if you clear out we won't," Jake said.

"Don't let them frighten you," the big man told the other tramps.

The hunchback started to yell again, running back and forth between the crowds of men, yelling at the farmers to run the tramps out of town.

Someone was coming fast across the road. It was father, and Old Tim, the constable, trying to keep up with him.

"Let Tim handle this," father told the farmers. "I routed him out and brought him over here. It's his job. You boys go on home before you get into trouble."

"You keep your nose out of this," Jake said.

The hunchback was jumping up and down in front of father. "You got a mess of kids to do your work," he said. "You don't have to worry none. Come butting in here when it's none of your damn business."

"Send 'em all home, Tim," father said. "To-morrow you can clear the camp out. Old man Galt will give you an order. But hell, they can't move to-night."

Jake stepped up close to father. "I said to keep your nose out of this." Jake was pretty big but my father was a head taller and a lot broader. He grabbed Jake's shoulder, spun him around, and planted his foot in the seat of Jake's pants. "You got that coming to you, Jake," he said. "Run along home."

One of the farmers raised a club.

"Look out, father," I yelled. It didn't do any good. The two by four smashed against his head, he put up his hands, moved around like he was dizzy, and then fell down. Joe jumped off the platform screaming "Father, father" at the top of his voice, and I jumped after him.

And as we ran toward the crowd the big man jumped forward, grabbed Jake, and hurled him at the farmers. I caught Joe and held him because we couldn't do any good. He kept screaming, clawing at my hands to get loose, and over his head I saw the men fighting, the big man hitting at the people I knew with his fists, all alone because the other tramps had run into the grove.

"Red. Bolshevik. Rooshian," the hunchback was yelling. "Kill the bastard Rooshian."

Hal Bradley grappled with the big man, but he was thin, and the tramp picked him up and tossed him out of the way as though he were a little boy. Then the big man stood there, telling them to come on, telling them to drive him out of town.

A gun went off and a red flame pointed at the big man. He put his hands over his belly and started moving backward, very slowly, toward the grove, but he didn't get there. Maybe he tripped over something, I don't know; but he fell down and a woman came running out to him, took his head in her arms, and started to cry.

All of a sudden the farmers were gone and father was sitting up, holding his head and swearing. We went over to him, and Joe held on to him tight and kept asking, "You all right, father, you all right?"

Old Tim helped father up and we all went over and looked at the big man. He wasn't groaning, just lying stretched out with his head in the woman's lap, and she was crying.

In the grove the fruit tramps were tearing the tents down and packing their stuff in automobiles, and inside of an hour there was only one tent left in the grove. That belonged to the big man and he didn't need it any more.

JAMES M. CAIN
(1892–1977)

In the 1930s and 1940s, James M. Cain was the most talked-about writer in the United States. His novels of that period, like the work of Dashiell Hammett a few years earlier, broke new ground in crime fiction. Until the publication of The Postman Always Rings Twice in 1934, sex was a topic handled with kid gloves and almost always peripheral to the central story line. Cain made sex the primary motivating force of his fiction and presented it to his readers frankly, at times steamily.

But Cain was much more than just a purveyor of what one of his critics termed "hard-boiled eroticism." His best works are masterful studies of average people caught up in and often destroyed by passion of one type or another: adultery, incest, hatred, greed, lust. They are also sharp, clear portraits of the times and places in which they were written, especially California during the Depression. As Cain himself said of his work in his preface to Three of a Kind (1942): "I make no conscious effort to be tough, or hard-boiled, or grim, or any of the things I am usually called. I merely try to write as the character would write, and I never forget that the average man, from the fields, the streets, the bars, the offices, and even the gutters of his country, has acquired a vividness of speech that goes beyond anything I could invent."

This is as true of his relatively few short stories as it is of such novels as The Postman Always Rings Twice, Serenade (1937), Love's Lovely Counterfeit (1942), and Double Indemnity (1943). The best of his shorter pieces were collected in The Baby in the Icebox (1981); of these, "Brush Fire" is particularly fine. Its spare, elemental style (which "possesses the sleeve-holding, hypnotic power of an ancient Mariner's tale," in one reviewer's eloquent phrase), sexual motivation, vivid depiction of life during the Depression, and grimly inevitable conclusion give it some of the powerful impact of Postman.

B. P.

1 9 3 6

BRUSH FIRE

He banged sparks with his shovel, coughed smoke, cursed the impulse that had led him to heed that rumor down in the railroad yards that CCC money was to be had by all who wanted to fight this fire the papers were full of, up in the hills. Back home he had always heard them called forest fires, but they seemed to be brush fires here in California. So far, all he had got out of it was a suit of denims, a pair of shoes, and a ration of stew, served in an army mess kit. For that he had ridden twenty miles in a jolting truck out from Los Angeles to these parched hills, stood in line an hour to get his stuff, stood in line another hour for the stew, and then labored all night, the flames singeing his hair, the ground burning his feet through the thick brogans, the smoke searing his lungs, until he thought he would go frantic if he didn't get a whiff of air.

Still the thing went on. Hundreds of them smashed out flames, set backfires, hacked at bramble, while the bitter complaint went around: "Why don't they give us brush hooks if we got to cut down them bushes? What the hell good are these damn shovels?" The shovel became the symbol of their torture. Here and there, through the night, a grotesque figure would throw one down, jump on it, curse at it, then pick it up again as the hysteria subsided.

"Third shift, this way! Third shift, this way. Bring your shovels and turn over to shift number four. Everybody in the third shift, right over here."

It was the voice of the CCC foreman, who, all agreed, knew as much about fighting fires as a monkey did. Had it not been for the state fire wardens, assisting at critical spots, they would have made no progress whatever.

"All right. Answer to your names when I call them. You got to be checked off to get your money. They pay today two o'clock, so yell loud when I call your name."

"Today's Sunday."

"I said they pay today, so speak up when I call your name."

The foreman had a pencil with a little bulb in the end of it which he flashed on and began going down the list.

"Bub Anderson, Lonnie Beal, K. Bernstein, Harry Deever. . . ." As each name was called there was a loud "Yo," so when his name was called, Paul Larkin, he yelled "Yo" too. Then the foreman was calling a name and becoming annoyed because there was no answer. "Ike Pendleton! Ike Pendleton!"

"He's around somewhere."

"Why ain't he here? Don't he know he's got to be checked off?"

"Hey, Ike! Ike Pendleton!"

He came out of his trance with a jolt. He had a sudden recollection of a man who had helped him to clear out a brier patch a little while ago, and whom he hadn't seen since. He raced up the slope and over toward the fire.

Near the brier patch, in a V between the main fire and a backfire that was advancing to meet it, he saw something. He rushed, but a cloud of smoke doubled him back. He retreated a few feet, sucked in a lungful of air, charged through the backfire. There, on his face, was a man. He seized the collar of the denim jacket, started to drag. Then he saw it would be fatal to take this man through the backfire that way. He tried to lift, but his lungful of air was spent: he had to breathe or die. He expelled it, inhaled, screamed at the pain of the smoke in his throat.

He fell on his face beside the man, got a little air there, near the ground. He shoved his arm under the denim jacket, heaved, felt the man roll solidly on his back. He lurched to his feet, ran through the backfire. Two or three came to his aid, helped him with his load to the hollow, where the foreman was, where the air was fresh and cool.

"Where's his shovel? He ought to have turned it over to—"

"His shovel! Give him water!"

"I'm gitting him water; but one thing at a time—"

"Water! Water! Where's that water cart?"

The foreman, realizing belatedly that a life might be more important than the shovel tally, gave orders to "work his arms and legs up and down." Somebody brought a bucket of water, and little by little Ike Pendleton came back to life. He coughed, breathed with long shuddering gasps, gagged, vomited. They wiped his face, fanned him, splashed water on him.

Soon, in spite of efforts to keep him where he was, he fought to his feet, reeled around with the hard, terrible vitality of some kind of animal. "Where's my hat? Who took my hat?" They clapped a hat on his head, he sat down suddenly, then got up and stood swaying. The foreman remembered his responsibility. "All right, men, give him a hand, walk him down to his bunk."

"Check him off!"

"Check the rest of us! You ain't passed the *P*s yet!"

"O.K. Sing out when I call. Gus Ritter!"

"Yo!"

When the names had been checked, Paul took one of Ike's arms and pulled it over his shoulder; somebody else took the other, and they started for the place, a half mile or so away on the main road, where the camp was located. The rest fell in behind. Dawn was just breaking as the little file, two and two, fell into a shambling step.

"Hep! . . . Hep!"

"Hey, cut that out! This ain't no lockstep."

"Who says it ain't?"

When he woke up, in the army tent he shared with five others, he became aware of a tingle of expectancy in the air. Two of his tent mates were shaving; another came in, a towel over his arm, his hair wet and combed.

"Where did you get that wash?"

"They got a shower tent over there."

He got out his safety razor, slipped his feet in the shoes, shaved over one of the other men's shoulders, then started out in his underwear. "Hey!" At the warning, he looked out. Several cars were out there, some of them with women standing around them, talking to figures in blue denim.

"Sunday, bo. Visiting day. This is when the women all comes to say hello to their loved ones. You better put something on."

He slipped on the denims, went over to the shower tent, drew towel and soap, stripped, waited his·turn. It was a real shower, the first he had had in a long time. It was cold, but it felt good. There was a comb there. He washed it, combed his hair, put on his clothes, went back to his tent, put the towel away, made his bunk. Then he fell in line for breakfast— or dinner, as it happened, as it was away past noon. It consisted of corned beef, cabbage, a boiled potato, apricot pie, and coffee.

He wolfed down the food, washed up his kit, began to feel pretty good. He fell into line again, and presently was paid, $4.50 for nine hours' work, at fifty cents an hour. He fingered the bills curiously. They were the first he had had in his hand since that day, two years before, when he had run away from home and begun this dreadful career of riding freights, bumming meals, and sleeping in flophouses.

He realized with a start they were the first bills he had ever earned in his twenty-two years; for the chance to earn bills had long since departed when he graduated from high school and began looking for jobs, never finding any. He shoved them in his pocket, wondered whether he would get the chance that night to earn more of them.

The foreman was standing there, in the space around which the tents were set up, with a little group around him. "It's under control, but we got to watch it, and there'll be another call tonight. Any you guys that want to work, report to me eight o'clock tonight, right here in this spot."

By now the place was alive with people, dust, and excitement. Cars were jammed into every possible place, mostly second-, third-, and ninth-hand, but surrounded by neatly dressed women, children, and old people, come to visit the fire fighters in denim. In a row out front, ice-cream, popcorn, and cold-drink trucks were parked, and the road was gay for half a mile in both directions with pennants stuck on poles, announcing their wares. Newspaper reporters were around too, with photographers, and as soon as the foreman had finished his harangue, they began to ask him questions about the fire, the number of men engaged in fighting it, and the casualties.

"Nobody hurt. Nobody hurt at all. Oh, early this morning, fellow kind of got knocked out by smoke, guy went in and pulled him out, nothing at all."

"What was his name?"

"I forget his name. Here—here's the guy that pulled him out. Maybe he knows his name."

In a second he was surrounded, questions being shouted at him from all sides. He gave them Ike's name and his own, and they began a frantic search for Ike, but couldn't find him. Then they decided he was the main story, not Ike, and directed him to pose for his picture. "Hey, not there; not by the ice-cream truck. We don't give ice cream a free ad in this paper. Over there by the tent."

He stood as directed, and two or three in the third shift told the story all over again in vivid detail. The reporters took notes, the photographers snapped several pictures of him, and a crowd collected. "And will you put it in that I'm from Spokane, Washington? I'd kind of like to have that in, on account of my people back there. Spokane, Washington."

"Sure, we'll put that in."

The reporters left as quickly as they had come, and the crowd began to melt. He turned away, a little sorry that his big moment had passed so quickly. Behind him he half heard a voice: "Well, ain't *that* something to be getting his picture in the paper?" He turned, saw several grins, but nobody was looking at him. Standing with her back to him, dressed in a blue silk Sunday dress, and kicking a pebble, was a girl. It was a girl who had spoken, and by quick elimination he decided it must be she.

The sense of carefree goofiness that had been growing on him since he got his money, since the crowd began to jostle him, since he had become a hero, focused somewhere in his head with dizzy suddenness. "Any objections?"

This got a laugh. She kept her eyes on the pebble but turned red and said: "No."

"You sure?"

"Just so you don't get stuck up."

"Then that's O.K. How about an ice-cream cone?"

"I don't mind."

"Hey, mister, two ice-cream cones."

"Chocolate."

"Both of them chocolate and both of them double."

When they got their cones he led her away from the guffawing gallery which was beginning to be a bit irksome. She looked at him then, and he saw she was pretty. She was small, with blue eyes, dusty blonde hair that blended with the dusty scene around her, and a spray of freckles over her forehead. He judged her to be about his own age. After looking at him, and laughing rather self-consciously and turning red, she concentrated on the cone, which she licked with a precise technique. He suddenly found he had nothing to say, but said it anyhow: "Well, say—what are you doing here?"

"Oh—had to see the fire, you know."

"Have you seen it?"

"Haven't even found out where it is, yet."

"Well, my, my! I see I got to show it to you."

"You know where it is?"

"Sure. Come on."

He didn't lead the way to the fire, though. He took her up the arroyo, through the burned-over area, where the fire had been yesterday. After a mile or so of walking, they came to a little grove of trees beside a spring.

The trees were live oak and quite green and cast a deep shade on the ground. Nobody was in sight, or even in earshot. It was a place the Sunday trippers didn't know about.

"Oh, my! Look at these trees! They didn't get burnt."

"Sometimes it jumps—the fire, I mean. Jumps from one hill straight over to the other hill, leaves places it never touched at all."

"My, but it's pretty."

"Let's sit down."

"If I don't get my dress dirty."

"I'll put this jacket down for you to sit on."

"Yes, that's all right."

They sat down. He put his arm around her, put his mouth against her lips.

It was late afternoon before she decided that her family might be looking for her and that she had better go back. She had an uncle in the camp, it seemed, and they had come as much to see him as to see the fire. She snickered when she remembered she hadn't seen either. They both snickered. They walked slowly back, their little fingers hooked together. He asked if she would like to go with him to one of the places along the road to get something to eat, but she said they had brought lunch with them, and would probably stop along the beach to eat it, going back.

They parted, she to slip into the crowd unobtrusively; he to get his mess kit, for the supper line was already formed. As he watched the blue dress flit between the tents and disappear, a gulp came into his throat; it seemed to him that this girl he had held in his arms, whose name he hadn't even thought to inquire, was almost the sweetest human being he had ever met in his life.

When he had eaten, and washed his mess kit and put it away, he wanted a cigarette. He walked down the road to a Bar-B-Q shack, bought a package, lit up, started back. Across a field, a hundred yards away, was the ocean. He inhaled the cigarette, inhaled the ocean air, enjoyed the languor that was stealing over him, wished he didn't have to go to work. And then, as he approached the camp, he felt something ominous.

Ike Pendleton was there, and in front of him this girl, this same girl he had spent the afternoon with. Ike said something to her, and she backed off. Ike followed, his fists doubled up. The crowd was silent, seemed almost to be holding its breath. Ike cursed at her. She began to cry. One of the state police came running up to them, pushed them apart, began to lecture them. The crowd broke into a buzz of talk. A woman, who seemed to be a relative, began to explain to all and sundry: "What if she *did* go with some guy to look at the fire? He don't live with her no more! *He* don't support her—never *did* support her! She didn't come up here to see *him;* never even knew he was *up* here! My land, can't the poor child have a good time once in a while?"

It dawned on him that this girl was Ike's wife.

He sat down on a truck bumper, sucked nervously at his cigarette. Some of the people who had guffawed at the ice-cream-cone episode in the afternoon looked at him, whispered. The policeman called over the woman who had been explaining things, and she and the girl, together with two children, went hurriedly over to a car and climbed into it. The policeman said a few words to Ike, and then went back to his duties on the road.

Ike walked over, picked up a mess kit, squatted on the ground between tents, and resumed a meal apparently interrupted. He ate sullenly, with his head hulked down between his shoulders. It was almost dark. The lights came on. The camp was not only connected to county water but to county light as well. Two boys went over to Ike, hesitated, then pointed to Paul. "Hey, mister, that's him. Over there, sitting on the truck."

Ike didn't look up. When the boys came closer and repeated their news, he jumped up suddenly and chased them. One of them he hit with a baked potato. When they had run away he went back to his food. He paid no attention to Paul.

In the car, the woman was working feverishly at the starter. It would whine, the engine would start and bark furiously for a moment or two, then die with a series of explosions. Each time it did this, the woman would let in the clutch, the car would rock on its wheels, and then come to rest. This went on for at least five minutes, until Paul thought he would go insane if it didn't stop, and people began to yell: "Get a horse!" "Get that damn oil can out of here and stop that noise!" "Have a heart! This ain't the Fourth of July!"

For the twentieth time it was repeated. Then Ike jumped up and ran over there. People closed in after him. Paul, propelled by some force that seemed completely apart from himself, ran after him. When he had fought his way through the crowd, Ike was on the running board of the car, the children screaming, men trying to pull him back. He had the knife from the mess kit in his hand. "I'm going to kill her! I'm going to kill her! If it's the last thing I do on earth, I'm going to kill her!"

"Oh, yeah!"

He seized Ike by the back of the neck, jerked, and slammed him against the fender. Then something smashed against his face. It was the woman, beating him with her handbag. "Go away! Git away from here!"

Ike faced him, lips writhing, eyes glaring a slaty gray against the deep red of the burns he had received that morning. But his voice was low, even if it broke with the intensity of his emotion. "Get out of my way, you! You got nothing to do with this."

He lunged at Ike with his fist—missed. Ike struck with the knife. He fended with his left arm, felt the steel cut in. With his other hand he struck, and Ike staggered back. There was a pile of shovels beside him, almost tripping him up. He grabbed one, swung, smashed it down on Ike's head. Ike went down. He stood there, waiting for Ike to get up, with that terrible vitality he had shown this morning. Ike didn't move. In the car the girl was sobbing.

The police, the ambulance, the dust, the lights, the doctor working on his arm, all swam before his eyes in a blur. Somewhere far off, an excited voice was yelling: "But I *got* to use your telephone, I *got* to, I tell you! Guy saves a man's life this morning, kills him tonight! It's a *hell* of a story!" He tried to comprehend the point of this; couldn't.

The foreman appeared, summoned the third shift to him in loud tones, began to read names. He heard his own name called, but didn't answer. He was being pushed into the ambulance, handcuffed to one of the policemen.

BRETT HALLIDAY
(1904-1977)

Brett Halliday (Davis Dresser) was the creator of Michael Shayne, a red-haired Miami private detective who was enormously popular in the 1940s and 1950s. Shayne appeared in fifty novels written by Halliday, beginning with Dividend on Death (1939), and, after 1965, in another eighteen written by various ghostwriters under the Halliday byline. He also appeared in a series of seven B films starring Lloyd Nolan, among them Sleepers West (1941, based on Frederick Nebel's Sleepers East [1933]) and Time to Kill (1942, based on Raymond Chandler's High Window [1942]); in five additional B pictures in the late 1940s starring Hugh Beaumont; on the radio from 1944 to 1952 featuring Jeff Chandler, among others; and on television in 1960 and 1961 with Richard Denning. He also lent his name to Mike Shayne Mystery Magazine (1956–1985), one of the longest running crime-fiction periodicals. As critic Art Scott has noted, "Shayne is a tough, direct character, not tricked out with gimmicks, not given to guilt complexes or excessive philosophizing. . . . Mike Shayne is the Generic Private Eye."

Halliday began his writing career with neither Shayne nor crime fiction, but with soft-core sex and Western novels for the lending-library market. Between 1934 and 1942, he published sixteen of the former and ten of the latter under both his own name and various pseudonyms. His first detective novels, Mum's the Word for Murder (1938) and The Kissed Corpse (1939), were published under the name Asa Baker and featured former Texas Ranger Jerry Burke. Even after the success of Shayne, Dresser wrote one mystery under the name Andrew Wayne, two mysteries under the name Hal Debrett (in collaboration with Kathleen Rollins), and three hard-boiled paperback originals under the name Matthew Blood (in collaboration with Ryerson Johnson).

In addition to his prolific output of novels, Halliday found time for an occasional shorter work. "Human Interest Stuff," a nonseries story, is perhaps the strongest of them. Originally published in the pulp magazine Adventure in September 1938, this rough-and-tumble yarn has an offbeat narrative approach, a Mexican railroad-construction-camp setting, and a tight little twist in its tail.

B. P.

1 9 3 8

HUMAN INTEREST STUFF

You want a human interest story for your paper on the execution to-morrow? A guy is slated for a one-way trip to hell in the electric chair, and all you see in it is a front page story!

That's your business, of course. I never blame a man for doing his job. I've kept my mouth shut up to now for Sam's sake, but he won't mind after the juice is turned on in that little gray room.

You're right. There is a whale of a story that hasn't been told. I guess it's what you'd call human interest stuff, all right.

I'm the only person that can give you the real low-down. Me, and one other. But it's a cinch the other fellow isn't going to talk for publication.

All right, if you promise to hold it until after they throw the switch tomorrow morning. I wouldn't want Sam to be sore at me for spilling it.

Yeah. There's a gap of five weeks unaccounted for from the time Bully Bronson's murderer crossed the Rio Grande going south until he came back to fry in the hot seat.

A lot of living can be packed into five weeks. A hell of a lot, Mister.

It's funny the way things worked to bring Sam and me together. It doesn't make a whole lot of sense, but things don't—south of the Border.

I drifted into the railroad construction camp that morning, needing a job bad and not caring what kind of a job it was.

The American engineer, Hobbs, was down with tropical dysentery and was all set for a trip back to a hospital in the States. He had a young assistant he'd planned to leave in charge of the work, but the youngster was new to Mexico and just the night before I hit camp he had gone on a tear and drunk enough *tequila* to make the mistake of insulting a Mexican girl.

The girl's father drained the cactus juice from his belly and left him in bad shape to take charge of a construction job.

With his fever at 105, Hobbs was in a tight spot when I happened along. They were filling the last gap in a railroad line that was to connect St. Louis with the west coast of Mexico and with the Orient by ship, and the rainy season was due in about six weeks.

That meant the fill and culverts had to be in place within six weeks—

or else. The last gap was across that valley south of Terlingua, where plenty of water runs down from the mountains during the rainy season.

And there was more to it, really, than just beating the rainy season. The history of the St. Louis, Mexico & Asiatic Railroad goes back a lot of years to a group of men in St. Louis who dreamed of a direct route from their city to the Orient.

They backed their dream with money and started building the S. L. M. & A. from both ends toward the middle. Something happened— they ran out of money, I guess—and got the American end to within a hundred miles of the Border, and the Mexican end about two hundred miles south of the Border.

For forty years, the line was in a receivership and that three hundred mile gap was the difference between a dream and reality.

Just last year, they got money from somewhere and started filling that gap.

Now, it was narrowed to four miles, and you can't blame Hobbs for jumping at any chance to get the grade finished before the rainy season came along and held them up another six months.

Yeah, that's just what he did. He asked me a couple of questions to see if I knew my stuff, then put me in charge.

They took him north in a Ford ambulance at noon, and his assistant died at four o'clock—the Mexican knife having drained more from his belly than just the over-dose of *tequila.*

That put it strictly up to me. A job I hadn't been formally introduced to, an all-Mexican crew of two hundred mule-skinners, a four-mile fill with drainage culverts to get in place—and the rainy season to beat.

I sat up all night in Hobbs' tent with a gasoline lantern hanging from the ridge-pole, going over the blueprints and field books, trying to get the feel of the job.

We started moving dirt in the morning, and I tried to be all over the job at once.

Mexicans are funny. I'd rather work a job with Mex labor than any other kind, but they do take lots of bossing. The one thing they haven't got is initiative. They'll do anything they're told, and do it well, but they have to be told or they won't do a damn thing.

I was going nuts before the morning was half over. I had a transit set up in the middle of the gap, and a level at each end of the fill that we were working both ways.

Running from one instrument to another; setting a few curve stations with the transit; trotting back to drop in some blue-tops at one end of the fill; then going back to the other end to re-set slope stakes that had been dragged out by careless wheelers—it had me goofy.

With two hundred teams moving dirt all the time, you understand, and I had to keep them moving.

I was standing behind a level, cussing my Mexican rodman who was holding the level rod upside down on a stake, when I heard an American voice behind me:

"You wouldn't be needing a spare engineer, Mister?"

A million dollars wouldn't have sounded as good to me right then. I pushed back my hat and wiped a muddy mixture of sweat and dust from my forehead. The man was sitting a roan mare, looking down at me. He wore white whipcords and a white shirt, but he looked at home in the Texas saddle.

His eyes were blue and there was a flame in them. He didn't blink while I stood there and stared. He was about thirty, and there was red sunburn on his face like a man gets when he comes fresh into the blistering heat south of the Rio Grande.

I couldn't quite figure him out, but I only asked one question:

"Can you run a level?"

He stepped off the roan onto the soft fill and came toward me. There was a bulge under his shirt on the left side. I've seen enough shoulder holsters to know what it was.

The way he stepped up to the level, squinted through the telescope and adjusted the focus to his eye was all the answer my question needed.

You can tell just by the way a man walks up to a tripod whether he knows his stuff or not. It's a trick of seeing the position of the three legs and not stepping close enough to any one of them to throw the instrument out of level. Engineers get so they do it subconsciously, and it's a sure way of spotting a phoney.

He didn't know the Mexican lingo, but you can set grade stakes with arm signals. I gave him the field book showing grade elevations for each station and told him to go to it.

I asked him his name as I started to the other end of the fill.

He gave me a steady look and said: "Just call me Sam."

That was all right with me. I would have called him sweetheart if he'd wanted it that way. I was so damned glad to get some help that I didn't care how many babies he had strangled back in the States.

I took three deep breaths and moved on down the job. Things began to take shape when I had time to study the blueprints and get squared around. With Sam handling one instrument, I felt the job was whipped.

By quitting time that night, everything was going smoothly. I could see it would be a cinch to finish in six weeks if Sam stuck with me.

I told him so after a feed of *frijoles con chile* and *tortillas* that the Mex cook dished up.

We were sitting together in the tent, and Sam nodded. He didn't say anything. He was tired, and the sunburn on his face had deepened to a fiery red. He slouched back on his bunk and seemed to be busy with private thoughts.

I got up and fiddled with the radio, a battery set that Hobbs had left behind. I got it working, and tuned in a news broadcast over a Fort Worth station. The announcer's voice crackled in the quiet that had fallen over camp in the twilight:

"The search for the slayer of Bully Bronson shifts below the Mexican Border tonight. Authorities are convinced that Bronson's assistant engineer, who murdered his chief in cold blood after an argument in a highway construction camp, has slipped through a cordon of officers in the Big Bend section and made his escape across the Rio Grande. This station has been requested by police to broadcast the following description to Mexican authorities who are warned that . . ."

I reached over and snapped the radio off. Sam was sitting up straight, watching me through slitted eyes. Three buttons of his shirt were open and his right arm was crooked at the elbow, gun-hand where it could go inside his shirt in a hurry.

I said: "To hell with that stuff. Everybody in this part of the country knows Bully Bronson needed killing. I hope they never get the guy that did it."

Sam relaxed a little. He reached in his shirt pocket for a cigarette, drew out an empty pack. I tossed him my makings of Bull Durham and brown papers. He tore two papers and spilled half a sack of tobacco before he got a bulging cigarette rolled and licked.

When he had it burning, he said: "But murder is still murder." He clamped his teeth together, like he was having a hard time keeping from saying too much.

"It's not murder when a guy like Bully Bronson gets bumped," I argued. "Hell, I know fifty men that'll sleep easier tonight because Bronson is dead."

"It's murder when a man waits until another is asleep, then blows the top of his head off with a shotgun." Sam's voice was thin and shaky. His cigarette went to pieces in his fingers when he tried to draw on it.

"There's a lot of things that go into a killing like that," I told him. "No one will ever know how much the killer took off Bronson before he got up nerve to do the job. And, from what I know of Bronson, I figure it was smart to wait until the old devil was asleep, and then use a shotgun to make sure of doing a good job."

Sam got another cigarette rolled without tearing the paper. He said, low:

"The law still calls it first degree murder."

I nodded. I was watching his face. "If the law ever gets a chance to say anything about it. If he's across the river, he doesn't have to worry about the law."

"There's such a thing as extradition."

I laughed. "You don't know this country like I do. Extradition is just a big word south of the Rio Grande. What a man has done back in the States doesn't count against him down here. A man leaves his past behind him when he crosses the river."

Sam thought that over, dragging on his brown-paper cigarette. His lips twisted and he asked:

"Can a man ever get away from . . . his past?"

I stood up and yawned. I knew something was going to crack if we kept on along that line. I said:

"Hard work is the best medicine for that kind of thinking. We've got a tough job in front of us here. It's going to take all both of us can do, working together, to put it over."

I turned my back on him to give him time to think it over and get my meaning straight.

There was just enough daylight left to see the end of the railroad fill there in front of camp.

It's an ugly, hard country south of the Big Bend. Nothing will grow in the hot sand except mesquite and cactus, and the only things that can live are lizards and long-eared jack-rabbits.

You forget how ugly it is in the darkness. Even the bare thorny mesquite and the spiny cactus plants look friendly. You're able to take a deep breath again after trying not to breathe all day for fear of burning your lungs.

I remember every little thing as I stood there in the open doorway of the tent waiting for Sam to say something. A mule squealed in the corrals, and some of the Mexicans were singing to a guitar accompaniment.

Did you ever hear Mexicans singing one of their native songs? You've missed something.

A coyote howled on the far rim of the valley while I stood there. I suppose you've never heard a coyote's howl drifting through the darkness across a valley either? That's something else you've missed.

Sam's voice was harsh, close to my ear: "The job isn't my lookout."

I pulled a lot of the cool evening air into my lungs. I knew this was the showdown. I had to make Sam see it my way.

"It's my lookout, Sam. I didn't ask for it, but here it is, dumped in my lap. It's up to us to get the fill in place before water starts running down from the hills and washes it out."

He leaned against the upright supporting pole and looked out over the valley.

I nodded toward the fill. "It's our job, Sam."

There was a twisted funny look on his face. "Engineers are damned fools."

I agreed with him. "They just wouldn't be engineers if they weren't. They'd be ribbon clerks or shoe salesmen."

He laughed, and I know he was thinking about a murdered man across the river:

"Men die and other men run away from the electric chair, but there's always a job to think about."

I turned back into the tent. I knew Sam was going to see me through. I said:

"After we get the grade ready for the track-laying crew will be time enough to talk about other things."

He nodded, came back and sat on his bunk. The twisted look was gone from his face. "I suppose it might help a man . . . to get one more job under his belt."

He took off his shirt, showing a shoulder harness with a .45 automatic in a clip holster.

Neither of us said anything as he unbuckled the harness and hung it over the head of his bunk.

It stayed there until the job was finished.

It wasn't tough, as such jobs go. The usual run of luck you run into on construction work. Rock where you don't expect to find it, and so much sand in the fill that it wouldn't hold a two-to-one slope.

Too much *sotol* in camp on pay nights, grudges settled the Mexican way with knives which left us shorthanded until we could get more teamsters.

Sam was plenty okay. He didn't have an awful lot of experience on dirt work, but he was built out of the stuff that makes engineers. With all the guts in the world, and never trying to get out from under when there was extra work to be done.

Lots of nights those first two weeks we worked until twelve or later under the hot glare of a gasoline lantern, figuring mass diagrams to balance the cut and fill, changing gradients.

Never a word between us about the search for Bully Bronson's murderer—and the radio stayed turned off.

Your mind gets numbed after so long on a rush job that takes everything you've got. There aren't any tomorrows and the yesterdays don't count.

There's only the present—with the heat and the dust, swarms of sandflies, the shouts of teamsters getting their loaded wheelers up the hill, a thick haze rising from the valley with snow-capped mountain peaks showing dimly through it from the southwest, the two ends of a narrow railroad grade creeping toward each other so slowly that you'd swear you were making no progress at all if you didn't have station stakes to tell you different.

Two white men on a job like that are bound to get pretty close, or learn to hate each other's guts.

During those weeks Sam and I got about as close as two men can ever get. Without words, you understand. Neither of us were the kind to shoot off our mouths.

It wasn't the sort of thing you talk about. Working side by side fifteen or twenty hours a day, words get sort of useless.

I quit being the boss after the first couple of days. We were just two engineers pushing a job through.

After it was finished?

Hell, I didn't know.

I didn't waste any time thinking about what would come after it was done. I don't think Sam did, either.

Maybe one of us was a murderer. That didn't count. See what I mean? The job was the only thing that counted.

No. I suppose you don't understand. You're a newspaper reporter. You've spent a lot of years practicing to get cynical. A job, to you, means something to work at eight hours a day and then forget while you go out sporting.

You asked for human interest stuff. I'm giving it to you even if you don't recognize it.

Five weeks dropped out of the lives of two men while time stood still and a construction job went on.

You're going to snort when I tell you how it ended. You're going to say it doesn't make sense and that men don't act that way.

Maybe it won't make sense to you. Maybe your readers won't believe it if you print it.

But it did happen like I'm telling you.

By the end of three weeks I'd forgotten what I'd guessed was his reason for crossing the Border in a hurry. His automatic still hung at the head of his bunk, and neither of us had mentioned Bronson's murder since that first night.

But you can't get away from a thing like that. It was with us all the time.

Sam was right when he said a man can't leave a thing like murder behind him just by crossing a muddy stream of water.

That's why I got a prickly feeling up my spine one afternoon when I saw two riders pushing up a little cloud of dust in the valley between us and the river.

There was that subconscious sense of fear that had been riding me all the time. The feeling that our luck couldn't possibly hold, that there was bound to be a pay-off.

I was running the last bit of center-line with the transit. Sam was on the far end of the fill, staking out a drainage culvert.

I swung the telescope on the riders half a mile away, and it brought them right up to me.

I knew I had guessed right. They spelled trouble. Slouching in the saddle, wearing dust-stained range clothing with cartridge belts slanting across their middles.

They were headed toward camp and I knew I had to keep them away from Sam if the fill was going to get finished.

I left the transit sitting there, and walked back to camp. The two riders were pulling in close when I stepped inside our tent.

One was a heavy man with a gray mustache. The other was long and lanky with a scar on his cheek. Both carried six-shooters in open holsters, and had saddle guns in boots slung beneath their right stirrup leathers.

Cow-country deputies, if I ever saw any.

They pulled up in front of the cook-tent and yelled for the cook. When he came to the door, the heavy one said:

"We heard across the river that you had a new gringo engineer here. Is that right?"

The cook was scared. He bobbed his head, sir: *"Si, si, Senior. Es verdad."*

The scar jumped up and down on the thin man's face. "Where's he at? We've come to take him back."

I waited to hear what the cook would say. He'd seen me pass by on my way to the tent. But Sam was new on the job, too, and he might send them out to Sam.

He didn't. He pointed to the tent and told them I was inside.

I slid back and got hold of Sam's automatic. It was cocked when I met them at the door.

They didn't take time to get a good look at me. They saw the automatic and reached for their guns.

I was lucky. I got one through the hand and broke the other's shoulder.

Then I called to the cook to bring some rope, and made him tie them up while they cussed a blue streak and told me I couldn't do that to the Texas law.

They were still cussing when I loaded them onto their horses and took them to the nearest town; ten miles south.

A ten-dollar bill is talking-money to a *pueblo* chief of police. They had an *adobe* jail that I hoped would hold together until the job was finished. I knew it would be at least that long before they could get a message across the river and any action on it.

That's the whole truth about that affair—the first time it's been told. Sam didn't have a thing to do with it. He didn't even see the deputies. I told the cook to keep his mouth shut, and I told Sam the two shots he heard were me plugging at a coyote. I don't think he believed me, but he didn't ask any questions.

I know the government kicked up a row over the jailing of the two deputies in Mexico, but it happened just like I've told you. They were out of their own back yard, and they got what they were asking for when they crossed the Border.

The job rocked along. We were getting dirt moved and no one else bothered us.

It's a funny country that way. People don't bother you much. Hell, there have been revolutions begun and ended without ever getting into the newspapers. The Mexicans have a queer way of tending strictly to their own business and letting the other guy tend to his.

That is, it'll seem queer to an American newspaper man. You make a living sticking your nose into other people's affairs and you wouldn't understand a Mexican's lack of curiosity.

But that's the way they are. It was as though our construction camp was in a vacuum, and we slept and worked and ate in that vacuum with no contact with the outside world.

There was a feeling of tensity between Sam and me as we began to see the end of the job coming up. We were going to finish a week ahead of schedule, but neither of us was any too happy about it.

When the last wheeler-load was dumped in place on the fill it was going to mark more than just the end of another job. It had been swell going while it lasted, but everything has to end.

I didn't know what Sam was thinking when I'd catch him looking at me queerly those last few days as the two ends of the fill came together, and I didn't want to know.

After that last load was dumped to grade would be time enough to find out what Sam was thinking.

We were going on stolen time and we both knew it. But neither one of us slowed up to make the job last longer. Not even the extra week we might have taken before there was danger of rains.

It's something you can't do much about—the pressure to put a job on through when the end is in sight.

I knew Sam pretty well by that time, better than I've ever known another man, but his private thoughts still remained a secret to me.

I guess no man ever wholly knows what's in another's mind. There's a certain barrier that you can't quite squeeze past. No matter how hard both of you try.

Know what I mean?

You're married, aren't you? All right. Take an honest look at your own thoughts. How well does your wife know them?

Don't kid yourself. Make an honest-to-God checkup on the secrets you keep in your mind from her.

That's what I'm talking about.

There's a part of you that's *you*. Which is probably as close to a definition of the human soul as anyone will ever get.

That's the difference between a man and an animal. You can pretty well figure what an animal will do under a given set of circumstances. Only God ever knows what a man is going to do.

Which pretty well brings us up to the morning Sam and I stood and looked at the completed railroad fill. It was ten o'clock in the morning and the last yard of dirt had been dumped and spread to grade.

Sam had been to the tent, and he came back to see it ended with me. It was in the cards.

All at once, it was over. Teams were standing idle, and the Mexicans were squatting on their heels, sucking on *cigarillos*.

The sun was searing down and there was a heat haze hanging over the valley and everything was pretty much like it had been for weeks— except that our job was done.

The track-laying crew would be coming along with cross-ties and steel. Trains would soon be running on schedule over the grade we had sweated out our guts on, and no one would think a damned thing about it.

The job didn't seem so important after all.

I looked at Sam and I saw the same bulge inside his shirt that had been there when he first rode up on a roan mare. He had gone back to the tent to buckle on his .45.

That gave me an idea what to expect, but I still wasn't sure what he had on his mind. I said:

"I don't know why it makes any difference, Sam, but I would have hated to quit before this was finished."

He said: "I know how you feel," and we both stood there without saying anything for a little.

I didn't look at him when I said: "There's other jobs waiting to be done, south of here."

"I know. It's too bad we can't do them together."

"Can't we?" Hell, I was so choked up that's all I could trust myself to say.

Sam wasn't choked up. His voice was clearer, harder, than I had heard it before:

"I'm afraid not. They're still looking for Bronson's murderer across the Rio Grande."

"Do we have to worry about that?"

"Haven't you known all along that it was *my* worry?"

I had, of course. There wasn't any use trying to lie to Sam. I saw that same gleam in his blue eyes that had been there the first time I saw him.

My lips were parched. I wet them with a tongue that felt like a dry sponge.

"What are you figuring on doing, Sam?"

"I've got to go back across the Border where I belong."

Well, there it was. Things had been building toward that ever since he stepped off the roan and took hold of the level.

I had known it was coming all along. Sam was that kind of an hombre.

Enough of an engineer to stay and see the job through, but too much of a man to take the easy way and go on down into the tropics with me, where they don't give a damn how many men you've murdered.

I said: "I'm ready whenever you are. It's been swell knowing you, Sam."

And we shook hands.

There, Mister, is your human interest yarn. You know the rest of it. The newspapers gave the story a heavy play when we crossed the Border together. There were headlines about the lone American who had gone into Mexico and brought out Bronson's murderer single-handed.

The feature writers did a lot of guessing about what happened during those five weeks.

Your paper will be the first to carry the straight story.

Am I sore at Sam?

No. Not even when I sit down in that chair tomorrow to pay the price for killing Bronson.

You see, Mister, I know how Sam felt about finishing *his* job. They picked him to go after me because he'd studied engineering in college.

But his real job was with the Texas Rangers.

WILLIAM COLE

(fl. late 1930s)

Waiting for Rusty" originally appeared in the October 1939 issue of Black Mask, which, strangely enough, published only this one story by William Cole. What is even more astonishing, given the tale's excellence, is that Cole published no other story anywhere, according to Michael Cook and Stephen Miller's exhaustive Mystery, Detective, and Espionage Fiction: A Checklist of Fiction in U.S. Pulp Magazines, 1915–1974 (1988). Of course, it is possible that Cole wrote extensively for the pulps, but under another name or even a variety of other names. Or perhaps he was just a lowly editor assigned to fill some space in the magazine. Still, Cole's true identity remains a mystery.

At barely 1,400 words, "Waiting for Rusty" is one of the shortest stories in this collection, yet it is also one of the most remarkable. While it is a masterpiece of concision, it contains enough plot for a full-length novel. From the moment the fluffy-haired girl in the blue slicker enters the little roadhouse with her sawed-off-shotgun-wielding cohorts, it is at once clear that they are all on an undeviating path toward catastrophe. In so few words, Cole is able to transform his chief character into a tragic heroine of truly epic proportions.

"Waiting for Rusty" is a character piece, a story built along softer, more objective, more emotional lines than the vivid and often brutal hard-boiled tales of Joseph T. Shaw's era at Black Mask. This was the era of Fanny Ellsworth, an accomplished yet different type of editor (of Ranch Romances fame) who, according to the writer Frank Gruber, "knew what she wanted." What she wanted, as the writer Dwight Babcock learned from his agent once Ellsworth had taken over Black Mask's editorial chair, was "a bit more emotion . . . leads played up in a more sympathetic manner. . . . " Ellsworth brought into the Black Mask fold such moody noir talents as Steve Fisher and Cornell Woolrich, both of whom seem to epitomize her approach to the genre. All this leads one to wonder whether Ellsworth herself took a shot at writing a Black Mask story, with "Waiting for Rusty" as the result.

J. A.

WAITING FOR RUSTY

One of these days I'm going to tell the sheriff. One of these days he's going to blow his mouth off once too often and I'm going to take him out there and show him. I may get on the wrong side of him but it'll be worth it. . . .

I'm just closing up my little roadside place for the night when they come in. Dotty and three guys. One of the men has a sawed-off shotgun and he stands by the window. Dotty and the others come up to the bar.

"Evenin', professor," Dotty says, looking around. "You here alone?"

"Yeah," I says, when I'm able to talk. "Yeah, but—"

"Good," Dotty says. "Lock that back door and then start pourin' rye."

She's wearing a blue slicker turned up at the neck and no hat. Her light hair is a little fluffed from the wind. She looks about the same as I remember she did when she went to the high school at Milbrook, only now you can't look long at her eyes.

"Listen, Miss," I says, "listen, you don't want to stay here. They're surrounding the whole county. I just got it over the radio."

"He's right," the man at the window says. "We gotta keep movin', Dot. We gotta keep movin'—and fast, or we'll wake up in the morgue."

"Get outside," Dotty tells him, "and keep your eyes open or you'll wake up there anyway."

She goes over and turns on the radio. The other two men keep walking around. They're all smoking cigarettes, one right after the other.

I know enough to do what I'm told.

There's nothing on the radio but some dance music. The two men look at each other; then the shorter one goes over to Dotty.

"I know how you feel, Dot," he says. "But they're right on our tail. We gotta—"

"I told you boys once," Dot says, "and I'm not tellin' you again. We wait here for Rusty."

"But supposin' he don't come?" the man says. He has a way of rubbing his wrist. "Supposin' . . . supposin' he can't make it? Supposin'—"

"Supposin' you dry up," Dotty says. "Rusty said he'll be here and when Rusty says something. . . ."

The music breaks off and she whirls to listen to the press-radio flash.

It's about the same as the last. The police have thrown a drag-net around the entire northern part of the State and are confident of capturing Rusty Nelson and his mob at any hour. Dotty don't think much of this but when she is called Rusty's girl and Gun Moll, No. 1, she smiles and takes a bow.

"After the bank hold-up yesterday," the announcer says, "Rusty and Dotty split up, one car going north, the other northwest. The State Trooper who tried to stop Dotty at Preston this afternoon died on the way to the hospital."

"Too bad," Dotty says. "He had the nicest blue eyes."

A car goes by on the highway outside and they all stand still for a second. Then the music comes back loud and the men jump to tune it down low. The taller one is swearing under his breath.

"Canada ain't big enough," he says sarcastic-like. "We gotta meet here."

Dotty don't say anything.

In no time at all, they finish the bottle of rye. I open another.

"Maybe he couldn't get through," the shorter man says. "Maybe he tried to but couldn't."

There's another radio flash. The cops have traced Rusty to Gatesville.

This makes Dotty feel a lot better. She laughs. "He's near Gatesville," she says, "like we're near Siberia."

She gets feeling pretty good, thinking of Rusty. She don't mind the music now, the way the men do. She asks me if it comes from the Pavilion and I tell her yes.

"I was there once," she says. "I went there with Rusty. They were havin' a dance and he took me." The men aren't interested and she tells it to me. "I had to wear an old dress because that's all I had, but Rusty, he sees me and says, 'Gee, kid, where'd you get the new dress?' and we hop in his boiler and roll down there."

She has stopped walking around now and her eyes are all different.

"They have the whole place fixed up . . . those colored lights on a string and the tables under the trees and two bands on the platform. As soon as one stops, the other one starts. And there's a guy goes around in a white coat with those little sandwiches and you can take all you want."

There's the scream of a siren in the distance. The men take out guns.

"The girls all wear flowers," Dotty says. "And I don't have none. But Rusty says, 'You just wait here,' and soon he's back with a big bunch of flowers, all colors and kinds. Only I can't wear half of them, there's too many. And then we dance and drink punch until the cops come. And then we have to lam out of there; they say Rusty bust in the glass in the town florist shop."

The siren is much louder now. The man with the shotgun runs in.

"A patrol car just passed!" he says. "Come on, let's blow!"

Dotty don't seem to hear. "Get back out there," she tells him.

The man's face goes even whiter. He looks at Dotty and then at the others. "I say we move," he says. "Rusty or no Rusty. We'll be knocked off here sure."

The other men try to stop him but can't.

"And we don't even know that he'll show. He might've turned south, or kept west. All the time we're waitin' here he might even be—"

Dotty has put her back to the bar. She waves a gun at the man.

"Get away from that door," she says. She leans back on her elbows. "Drop that rattle and get over there. We don't want to have to step over you."

It takes the man a minute to get it. Then his knees begin to give. He opens his mouth a few times but nothing comes out.

Then there's that static on the radio and the announcer telling how Rusty was nabbed down in Talbot. Dotty stands there and listens, resting back on the bar.

"Not a single shot was fired," the announcer says. "The gangster was completely surprised by the raid. Alone in the hide-out with Nelson was a pretty dark-haired, unidentified girl."

Then there's that static and the music again.

Nobody looks at Dotty for a while. Then the man with the shotgun bolts for the door. No sooner he's opened it, he shuts it again. "There's a guy comin' up the road," he says. "He's got on a badge."

For what seems a long time, Dotty don't move. Then she reaches out and snaps off the radio. "Let him come," she says. "You guys get out in the car."

The men don't argue. They go out the back.

Dotty walks slowly to the door. When she speaks, her voice isn't flat any more.

"You know," she tells me, "it was funny about those flowers. They just wouldn't stay put. Every minute I'd fix them and the next minute they'd slip. One of the girls said the pin was too big."

She steps out on the porch, and I drop flat in back of the bar.

"Hello, copper," I hear her say. The rest is all noise. . . .

One of these days I'm going to show the sheriff. One of these days he's going to tell once too often how he got Dotty and I'm going to take him out on the porch and show him. . . .

Sure, she might have missed him, even Dotty might have missed him twice in a row. But she would never have put those two slugs in the ceiling. Not Dotty. Not unless she had reason to. Not unless she wanted to die.

RAYMOND CHANDLER
(1888–1959)

Raymond Chandler brought to the hard-boiled genre the unique perspective of an American whose formative years had been spent in England. He was educated at Dulwich College, a liberal, classics-oriented school only a few notches down from Eton and other top-echelon institutions. In his five years there, Chandler gained a code of behavior, a moral tone, a sense of honor and public service, a broad knowledge of literary allusion, and an immense understanding of the precise workings of the English language. The last was a skill that stayed with him all his life. Even when he deliberately adopted colloquial American English (southern California variety), it became the most powerful weapon in his writing armory.

In his unpublished essay "Notes . . . on English and American Style," Chandler justifies his own Anglophilic influences by arguing that "all the best American writing has been done by . . . cosmopolitans. They found [in the United States] . . . freedom of expression, . . . richness of vocabulary, . . . wideness of interest. But they had to have European taste to use the material." Whether this assertion is true or not, Chandler's sharp colloquialisms, vivid use of metaphor and allusion, trenchant wisecracks, and extraordinarily evocative scene-setting combine into a style that is distinct, memorable, and, on occasion, richly comic.

While Dashiell Hammett (whom Chandler admired up to a point) wrote from close experience about life at the tough end as a former Pinkerton operative, Chandler created his own world, in which villains are vicious, cops are corrupt, and women are (mostly) decadent. Chandler's most famous character, Philip Marlowe, more than most detectives of his kind, is a righter of wrongs as well as a defender of values and moral precepts. He believes in justice, honesty, and faithfulness; he loathes injustice, dishonesty, and faithlessness. He is a "verray parfit gentil" gumshoe in a savage, threatening, neon-lit concrete jungle.

Marlowe is rather fond of taking his licks from thugs and sadistic cops, but this may be explained as a hangover from Chandler's own school days. What cannot so easily be excused is the sentimentality that at times seeps into the stories like a northern California fog. It is Chandler's worst and at the same time most curious fault. He knew perfectly well that his is a created and frequently melodramatized world, while his hero, for all his wisecracking toughness, is an impossible eternal Galahad. "The real-life private eye," Chandler once wrote, "is a sleazy little drudge . . . [who] has about as much moral stature as a stop and go sign." But Marlowe is different, and for this reason, Chandler seems to have been almost in love with him, in much the same way that Dorothy L. Sayers famously exhibited a distinct tendresse for her creation, Lord Peter Wimsey. Perhaps it is this very love for his hero that has made his books so good and enduring.

Chandler wrote seven complete novels, three of which—Farewell, My Lovely (1940), The Little Sister (1949), and The Long Goodbye (1953)— are considered masterpieces by some. The Long Goodbye was arguably the first book since Hammett's The Glass Key, published more than twenty years earlier, to qualify as a serious and significant mainstream novel that just happened to possess elements of mystery.

Chandler was a perceptive critic of others' work, although less so of his own. He did not care for "I'll Be Waiting," which he wrote in 1939 for the Saturday Evening Post. Perhaps the large sum of money he received for the story engendered a fit of guilt. To his friend the novelist William Campbell Gault he wrote in 1957: "It was too studied, too careful. . . . I could have written it much better, without trying to be smooth and polished." As though to demonstrate his less than acute judgment concerning his own talents, he went on: "I'm an improviser." But, of course, this is precisely what Chandler was not. What he was was a painstaking rewriter and polisher, whose diligence made "I'll Be Waiting" a superbly atmospheric night-piece.

J. A.

1 9 3 9

I'LL BE WAITING

At one o'clock in the morning, Carl, the night porter, turned down the last of three table lamps in the main lobby of the Windermere Hotel. The blue carpet darkened a shade or two and the walls drew back into remoteness. The chairs filled with shadowy loungers. In the corners were memories like cobwebs.

Tony Reseck yawned. He put his head on one side and listened to the frail, twittery music from the radio room beyond a dim arch at the far side of the lobby. He frowned. That should be his radio room after one a.m. Nobody should be in it. That red-haired girl was spoiling his nights.

The frown passed and a miniature of a smile quirked at the corners of his lips. He sat relaxed, a short, pale, paunchy, middle-aged man with long, delicate fingers clasped on the elk's tooth on his watch chain; the long delicate fingers of a sleight-of-hand artist, fingers with shiny, moulded nails and tapering first joints, fingers a little spatulate at the ends. Handsome fingers. Tony Reseck rubbed them gently together and there was peace in his quiet sea-grey eyes.

The frown came back on his face. The music annoyed him. He got up with a curious litheness, all in one piece, without moving his clasped hands from the watch chain. At one moment he was leaning back re- laxed, and the next he was standing balanced on his feet, perfectly still, so that the movement of rising seemed to be a thing imperfectly per- ceived, an error of vision.

He walked with small, polished shoes delicately across the blue car- pet and under the arch. The music was louder. It contained the hot, acid blare, the frenetic, jittering runs of a jam session. It was too loud. The red-haired girl sat there and stared silently at the fretted part of the big radio cabinet as though she could see the band with its fixed professional grin and the sweat running down its back. She was curled up with her feet under her on a davenport which seemed to contain most of the cush- ions in the room. She was tucked among them carefully, like a corsage in the florist's tissue paper.

She didn't turn her head. She leaned there, one hand in a small fist on her peach-colored knee. She was wearing lounging pyjamas of heavy ribbed silk embroidered with black lotus buds.

"You like Goodman, Miss Cressy?" Tony Reseck asked.

The girl moved her eyes slowly. The light in there was dim, but the violet of her eyes almost hurt. They were large, deep eyes without a trace of thought in them. Her face was classical and without expression.

She said nothing.

Tony smiled and moved his fingers at his sides, one by one, feeling them move. "You like Goodman, Miss Cressy?" he repeated gently.

"Not to cry over," the girl said tonelessly.

Tony rocked back on his heels and looked at her eyes. Large, deep, empty eyes. Or were they? He reached down and muted the radio.

"Don't get me wrong," the girl said. "Goodman makes money, and a lad that makes legitimate money these days is a lad you have to respect. But this jitterbug music gives me the backdrop of a beer flat. I like something with roses in it."

"Maybe you like Mozart," Tony said.

"Go on, kid me," the girl said.

"I wasn't kidding you, Miss Cressy. I think Mozart was the greatest man that ever lived—and Toscanini is his prophet."

"I thought you were the house dick." She put her head back on a pillow and stared at him through her lashes. "Make me some of that Mozart," she added.

"It's too late," Tony sighed. "You can't get it now."

She gave him another long lucid glance. "Got the eye on me, haven't you, flatfoot?" She laughed a little, almost under her breath. "What did I do wrong?"

Tony smiled his toy smile. "Nothing, Miss Cressy. Nothing at all. But you need some fresh air. You've been five days in this hotel and you haven't been outdoors. And you have a tower room."

She laughed again. "Make me a story about it. I'm bored."

"There was a girl here once had your suite. She stayed in the hotel a whole week, like you. Without going out at all, I mean. She didn't speak to anybody hardly. What do you think she did then?"

The girl eyed him gravely. "She jumped her bill."

He put his long delicate hand out and turned it slowly, fluttering the fingers, with an effect almost like a lazy wave breaking. "Uh-uh. She sent down for her bill and paid it. Then she told the hop to be back in half an hour for her suitcases. Then she went out on her balcony."

The girl leaned forward a little, her eyes still grave, one hand capping her peach-colored knee. "What did you say your name was?"

"Tony Reseck."

"Sounds like a hunky."

"Yeah," Tony said. "Polish."

"Go on, Tony."

"All the tower suites have private balconies, Miss Cressy. The walls of them are too low for fourteen storeys above the street. It was a dark night, that night, high clouds." He dropped his hand with a final gesture, a farewell gesture. "Nobody saw her jump. But when she hit, it was like a big gun going off."

"You're making it up, Tony." Her voice was a clean dry whisper of sound.

He smiled his toy smile. His quiet sea-grey eyes seemed almost to be smoothing the long waves of her hair. "Eve Cressy," he said musingly. "A name waiting for lights to be in."

"Waiting for a tall dark guy that's no good, Tony. You wouldn't care why. I was married to him once. I might be married to him again. You can make a lot of mistakes in just one lifetime." The hand on her knee opened slowly until the fingers were strained back as far as they would go. Then they closed quickly and tightly, and even in that dim light the knuckles shone like little polished bones. "I played him a low trick once. I put him in a bad place—without meaning to. You wouldn't care about that either. It's just that I owe him something."

He leaned over softly and turned the knob on the radio. A waltz formed itself dimly on the air. A tinsel waltz, but a waltz. He turned the volume up. The music gushed from the loud-speaker in a swirl of shadowed melody. Since Vienna died, all waltzes are shadowed.

The girl put her head on one side and hummed three or four bars and stopped with a sudden tightening of her mouth.

"Eve Cressy," she said. "It was in lights once. At a bum night club. A dive. They raided it and the lights went out."

He smiled at her almost mockingly. "It was no dive while you were there, Miss Cressy . . . That's the waltz the orchestra always played when the old porter walked up and down in front of the hotel entrance, all swelled up with his medals on his chest. *The Last Laugh.* Emil Jannings. You wouldn't remember that one, Miss Cressy."

"Spring, Beautiful Spring," she said. "No, I never saw it."

He walked three steps away from her and turned. "I have to go upstairs and palm doorknobs. I hope I didn't bother you. You ought to go to bed now. It's pretty late."

The tinsel waltz stopped and a voice began to talk. The girl spoke through the voice. "You really thought something like that—about the balcony?"

He nodded. "I might have," he said softly. "I don't any more."

"No chance, Tony." Her smile was a dim lost leaf. "Come and talk to me some more. Redheads don't jump, Tony. They hang on—and wither."

He looked at her gravely for a moment and then moved away over the carpet. The porter was standing in the archway that led to the main lobby. Tony hadn't looked that way yet, but he knew somebody was there. He always knew if anybody was close to him. He could hear the grass grow, like the donkey in *The Blue Bird.*

The porter jerked his chin at him urgently. His broad face above the uniform collar looked sweaty and excited. Tony stepped up close to him and they went together through the arch and out to the middle of the dim lobby.

"Trouble?" Tony asked wearily.

"There's a guy outside to see you, Tony. He won't come in. I'm doing a wipe-off on the plate glass of the doors and he comes up beside me, a tall guy. 'Get Tony,' he says, out of the side of his mouth."

Tony said: "Uh-huh," and looked at the porter's pale blue eyes. "Who was it?"

"Al, he said to say he was."

Tony's face became as expressionless as dough. "Okay." He started to move off.

The porter caught his sleeve. "Listen, Tony. You got any enemies?"

Tony laughed politely, his face still like dough.

"Listen, Tony." The porter held his sleeve tightly. "There's a big black car down the block, the other way from the hacks. There's a guy standing beside it with his foot on the running board. This guy that spoke to me, he wears a dark-colored, wrap-around overcoat with a high collar turned up against his ears. His hat's way low. You can't hardly see his face. He says, 'Get Tony,' out of the side of his mouth. You ain't got any enemies, have you, Tony?"

"Only the finance company," Tony said. "Beat it."

He walked slowly and a little stiffly across the blue carpet, up the three shallow steps to the entrance lobby with the three elevators on one side and the desk on the other. Only one elevator was working. Beside the open doors, his arms folded, the night operator stood silent in a neat blue uniform with silver facings. A lean, dark Mexican named Gomez. A new boy, breaking in on the night shift.

The other side was the desk, rose marble, with the night clerk leaning on it delicately. A small neat man with a wispy reddish mustache and cheeks so rosy they looked rouged. He stared at Tony and poked a nail at his mustache.

Tony pointed a stiff index finger at him, folded the other three fingers tight to his palm, and flicked his thumb up and down on the stiff finger. The clerk touched the other side of his mustache and looked bored.

Tony went on past the closed and darkened news-stand and the side entrance to the drugstore, out to the brass-bound plate-glass doors. He stopped just inside them and took a deep, hard breath. He squared his shoulders, pushed the doors open and stepped out into the cold, damp night air.

The street was dark, silent. The rumble of traffic on Wilshire, two blocks away, had no body, no meaning. To the left were two taxis. Their drivers leaned against a fender, side by side, smoking. Tony walked the other way. The big dark car was a third of a block from the hotel entrance. Its lights were dimmed and it was only when he was almost up to it that he heard the gentle sound of its engine turning over.

A tall figure detached itself from the body of the car and strolled towards him, both hands in the pockets of the dark overcoat with the high collar. From the man's mouth a cigarette tip glowed faintly, a rusty pearl.

They stopped two feet from each other.

The tall man said: "Hi, Tony. Long time no see."

"Hello, Al. How's it going?"

"Can't complain." The tall man started to take his right hand out of his overcoat pocket, then stopped and laughed quietly. "I forgot. Guess you don't want to shake hands."

"That don't mean anything," Tony said. "Shaking hands. Monkeys can shake hands. What's on your mind, Al?"

"Still the funny little fat guy, eh, Tony?"

"I guess," Tony winked his eyes tight. His throat felt tight.

"You like your job back there?"

"It's a job."

Al laughed his quiet laugh again. "You take it slow, Tony. I'll take it fast. So it's a job and you want to hold it. Oke. There's a girl named Eve Cressy flopping in your quiet hotel. Get her out. Fast and right now."

"What's the trouble?"

The tall man looked up and down the street. A man behind in the car coughed lightly. "She's hooked with a wrong number. Nothing against her personal, but she'll lead trouble to you. Get her out, Tony. You got maybe an hour."

"Sure," Tony said aimlessly, without meaning.

Al took his hand out of his pocket and stretched it against Tony's chest. He gave him a light, lazy push. "I wouldn't be telling you just for the hell of it, little fat brother. Get her out of there."

"Okay," Tony said, without any tone in his voice.

The tall man took back his hand and reached for the car door. He opened it and started to slip in like a lean black shadow.

174

Then he stopped and said something to the men in the car and got out again. He came back to where Tony stood silent, his pale eyes catching a little dim light from the street.

"Listen, Tony. You always kept your nose clean. You're a good brother, Tony."

Tony didn't speak.

Al leaned towards him, a long urgent shadow, the high collar almost touching his ears. "It's trouble business, Tony. The boys won't like it, but I'm telling you just the same. This Cressy was married to a lad named Johnny Ralls. Ralls is out of Quentin two, three days, or a week. He did a three-spot for manslaughter. The girl put him there. He ran down an old man one night when he was drunk, and she was with him. He wouldn't stop. She told him to go in and tell it or else. He didn't go in. So the Johns come for him."

Tony said, "That's too bad."

"It's kosher, kid. It's my business to know. This Ralls flapped his mouth in stir about how the girl would be waiting for him when he got out, all set to forgive and forget, and he was going straight to her."

Tony said: "What's he to you?" His voice had a dry, stiff crackle, like thick paper.

Al laughed. "The trouble boys want to see him. He ran a table at a spot on the Strip and figured out a scheme. He and another guy took the house for fifty grand. The other lad coughed up, but we still need Johnny's twenty-five. The trouble boys don't get paid to forget."

Tony looked up and down the dark street. One of the taxi drivers flicked a cigarette stub in a long arc over the top of one of the cabs. Tony watched it fall and spark on the pavement. He listened to the quiet sound of the big car's motor.

"I don't want any part of it," he said. "I'll get her out."

Al backed away from him, nodding. "Wise kid. How's mom these days?"

"Okay," Tony said.

"Tell her I was asking for her."

"Asking for her isn't anything," Tony said.

Al turned quickly and got into the car. The car curved lazily in the middle of the block and drifted back toward the corner. Its lights went up and sprayed on a wall. It turned a corner and was gone. The lingering smell of its exhaust drifted past Tony's nose. He turned and walked back to the hotel, and into it. He went along to the radio room.

The radio still muttered, but the girl was gone from the davenport in front of it. The pressed cushions were hollowed out by her body. Tony reached down and touched them. He thought they were still warm. He turned the radio off and stood there, turning a thumb slowly in front of his body, his hand flat against his stomach. Then he went back through the lobby toward the elevator bank and stood beside a majolica jar of white sand. The clerk fussed behind a pebbled-glass screen at one end of the desk. The air was dead.

The elevator bank was dark. Tony looked at the indicator of the middle car and saw that it was at 14.

"Gone to bed," he said under his breath.

The door of the porter's room beside the elevators opened and the little Mexican night operator came out in street clothes. He looked at Tony with a quiet sidewise look out of eyes the colour of dried-out chestnuts.

"Good night, boss."

"Yeah," Tony said absently.

He took a thin dappled cigar out of his vest pocket and smelled it. He examined it slowly, turning it around in his neat fingers. There was a small tear along the side. He frowned at that and put the cigar away.

There was a distant sound and the hand on the indicator began to steal around the bronze dial. Light glittered up in the shaft and the straight line of the car floor dissolved the darkness below. The car stopped and the doors opened, and Carl came out of it.

His eyes caught Tony's with a kind of jump and he walked over to him, his head on one side, a thin shine along his pink upper lip.

"Listen, Tony."

Tony took his arm in a hard swift hand and turned him. He pushed him quickly, yet somehow casually, down the steps to the dim main lobby and steered him into a corner. He let go of the arm. His throat tightened again, for no reason he could think of.

"Well?" he said darkly. "Listen to what?"

The porter reached into a pocket and hauled out a dollar bill. "He gimme this," he said loosely. His glittering eyes looked past Tony's shoulder at nothing. They winked rapidly. "Ice and ginger ale."

"Don't stall," Tony growled.

"Guy in 14B," the porter said.

"Lemme smell your breath."

The porter leaned toward him obediently.

"Liquor," Tony said harshly.

"He gimme a drink."

Tony looked down at the dollar bill. "Nobody's in 14B. Not on my list," he said.

"Yeah. There is," The porter licked his lips and his eyes opened and shut several times. "Tall dark guy."

"All right," Tony said crossly. "All right. There's a tall dark guy in 14B and he gave you a buck and a drink. Then what?"

"Gat under his arm," Carl said, and blinked.

Tony smiled, but his eyes had taken on the lifeless glitter of thick ice. "You take Miss Cressy up to her room?"

Carl shook his head. "Gomez. I saw her go up."

"Get away from me," Tony said between his teeth. "And don't accept any more drinks from the guests."

He didn't move until Carl had gone back into his cubby-hole by the elevators and shut the door. Then he moved silently up the three steps and stood in front of the desk, looking at the veined rose marble, the onyx pen set, the fresh registration card in its leather frame. He lifted a hand and smacked it down hard on the marble. The clerk popped out from behind the glass screen like a chipmunk coming out of its hole.

Tony took a flimsy out of his breast pocket and spread it on the desk. "No 14B on this," he said in a bitter voice.

The clerk wisped politely at his mustache. "So sorry. You must have been out to supper when he checked in."

"Who?"

"Registered as James Watterson, San Diego." The clerk yawned.

"Ask for anybody?"

The clerk stopped in the middle of the yawn and looked at the top of Tony's head. "Why, yes. He asked for a swing band. Why?"

"Smart, fast and funny," Tony said. "If you like 'em that way." He wrote on his flimsy and stuffed it back into his pocket. "I'm going upstairs and palm doorknobs. There's four tower rooms you ain't rented yet. Get up on your toes, son. You're slipping."

"I make out," the clerk drawled, and completed his yawn. "Hurry back, pop. I don't know how I'll get through the time."

"You could shave that pink fuzz off your lip," Tony said, and went across to the elevators.

He opened up a dark one and lit the dome light and shot the car up to fourteen. He darkened it again, stepped out and closed the doors. This lobby was smaller than any other, except the one immediately below it. It had a single blue-panelled door in each of the walls other than the elevator wall. On each door was a gold number and letter with a gold wreath around it. Tony walked over to 14A and put his ear to the panel.

He heard nothing. Eve Cressy might be in bed asleep, or in the bathroom, or out on the balcony. Or she might be sitting there in the room, a few feet from the door, looking at the wall. Well, he wouldn't expect to be able to hear her sit and look at the wall. He went over to 14B and put his ear to that panel. This was different. There was a sound in there. A man coughed. It sounded somehow like a solitary cough. There were no voices. Tony pressed the small nacre button beside the door.

Steps came without hurry. A thickened voice spoke through the panel. Tony made no answer, no sound. The thickened voice repeated the question. Lightly, maliciously, Tony pressed the bell again.

Mr. James Watterson, of San Diego, should now open the door and give forth noise. He didn't. A silence fell beyond that door that was like the silence of a glacier. Once more Tony put his ear to the wood. Silence utterly.

He got out a master key on a chain and pushed it delicately into the lock of the door. He turned it, pushed the door inward three inches and withdrew the key. Then he waited.

"All right," the voice said harshly. "Come in and get it."

Tony pushed the door wide and stood there, framed against the light from the lobby. The man was tall, black-haired, angular and white-faced. He held a gun. He held it as though he knew about guns.

"Step right in," he drawled.

Tony went in through the door and pushed it shut with his shoulder. He kept his hands a little out from his sides, the clever fingers curled and slack. He smiled his quiet little smile.

"Mr. Watterson?"

"And after that what?"

"I'm the house detective here."

"It slays me."

The tall, white-faced, somehow handsome and somehow not handsome man backed slowly into the room. It was a large room with a low balcony around two sides of it. French doors opened out on the little, private, open-air balcony that each of the tower rooms had. There was a grate set for a log fire behind a paneled screen in front of a cheerful davenport. A tall misted glass stood on a hotel tray beside a deep, cozy chair. The man backed toward this and stood in front of it. The large, glistening gun drooped and pointed at the floor.

"It slays me," he said. "I'm in the dump an hour and the house copper gives me the buzz. Okay, sweetheart, look in the closet and bathroom. But she just left."

"You didn't see her yet," Tony said.

The man's bleached face filled with unexpected lines. His thickened voice edged toward a snarl. "Yeah? Who didn't I see yet?"

"A girl named Eve Cressy."

The man swallowed. He put his gun down on the table beside the tray. He let himself down into the chair backwards, stiffly, like a man with a touch of lumbago. Then he leaned forward and put his hands on his kneecaps and smiled brightly between his teeth. "So she got here, huh? I didn't ask about her yet. I'm a careful guy. I didn't ask yet."

"She's been here five days," Tony said. "Waiting for you. She hasn't left the hotel a minute."

The man's mouth worked a little. His smile had a knowing tilt to it. "I got delayed a little up north," he said smoothly. "You know how it is. Visiting old friends. You seem to know a lot about my business, copper."

"That's right, Mr. Ralls."

The man lunged to his feet and his hand snapped at the gun. He stood leaning over, holding it on the table, staring. "Dames talk too much," he said with a muffled sound in his voice, as though he held something soft between his teeth and talked through it.

"Not dames, Mr. Ralls."

"Huh?" The gun slithered on the hard wood of the table. "Talk it up, copper. My mind reader just quit."

"Not dames. Guys. Guys with guns."

The glacier silence fell between them again. The man straightened his body slowly. His face was washed clean of expression, but his eyes were haunted. Tony leaned in front of him, a shortish plump man with a quiet, pale, friendly face and eyes as simple as forest water.

"They never run out of gas—those boys," Johnny Ralls said, and licked at his lip. "Early and late, they work. The old firm never sleeps."

"You know who they are?" Tony said softly.

"I could maybe give nine guesses. And twelve of them would be right."

"The trouble boys," Tony said, and smiled a brittle smile.

"Where is she?" Johnny Ralls asked harshly.

"Right next door to you."

The man walked to the wall and left his gun lying on the table. He stood in front of the wall, studying it. He reached up and gripped the grillwork of the balcony railing. When he dropped his hand and turned, his face had lost some of its lines. His eyes had a quieter glint. He moved back to Tony and stood over him.

"I've got a stake," he said. "Eve sent me some dough and I built it up with a touch I made up north. Case dough, what I mean. The trouble boys talk about twenty-five grand." He smiled crookedly. "Five C's I can count. I'd have a lot of fun making them believe that, I would."

"What did you do with it?" Tony asked indifferently.

"I never had it, copper. Leave that lay. I'm the only guy in the world that believes it. It was a little deal I got suckered on."

"I'll believe it," Tony said.

"They don't kill often. But they can be awful tough."

"Mugs," Tony said with a sudden bitter contempt. "Guys with guns. Just mugs."

Johnny Ralls reached for his glass and drained it empty. The ice cubes tinkled softly as he put it down. He picked his gun up, danced it on his palm, then tucked it, nose down, into an inner breast pocket. He stared at the carpet.

"How come you're telling me this, copper?"

"I thought maybe you'd give her a break."

"And if I wouldn't?"

"I kind of think you will," Tony said.

Johnny Ralls nodded quietly. "Can I get out of here?"

"You could take the service elevator to the garage. You could rent a car. I can give you a card to the garage-man."

"You're a funny little guy," Johnny Ralls said.

Tony took out a worn ostrich-skin billfold and scribbled on a printed card. Johnny Ralls read it, and stood holding it, tapping it against a thumbnail.

"I could take her with me," he said, his eyes narrow.

"You could take a ride in a basket too," Tony said. "She's been here five days, I told you. She's been spotted. A guy I know called me up and told me to get her out of here. Told me what it was all about. So I'm getting you out instead."

"They'll love that," Johnny Ralls said. "They'll send you violets."

"I'll weep about it on my day off."

Johnny Ralls turned his hand over and stared at the palm. "I could see her, anyway. Before I blow. Next door to here, you said?"

Tony turned on his heel and started for the door. He said over his shoulder, "Don't waste a lot of time, handsome. I might change my mind."

The man said, almost gently: "You might be spotting me right now, for all I know."

Tony didn't turn his head. "That's a chance you have to take."

He went on to the door and passed out of the room. He shut it carefully, silently, looked once at the door of 14A and got into his dark elevator. He rode it down to the linen-room floor and got out to remove the basket that held the service elevator open at that floor. The door slid quietly shut. He held it so that it made no noise. Down the corridor, light came from the open door of the housekeeper's office. Tony got back into his elevator and went on down to the lobby.

The little clerk was out of sight behind his pebbled-glass screen, auditing accounts. Tony went through the main lobby and turned into the radio room. The radio was on again, soft. She was there, curled on the davenport again. The speaker hummed to her, a vague sound so low that what it said was as wordless as the murmur of trees. She turned her head slowly and smiled at him.

"Finished palming doorknobs? I couldn't sleep worth a nickel. So I came down again. Okay?"

He smiled and nodded. He sat down in a green chair and patted the plump brocade arms of it. "Sure, Miss Cressy."

"Waiting is the hardest kind of work, isn't it? I wish you'd talk to that radio. It sounds like a pretzel being bent."

Tony fiddled with it, got nothing he liked, set it back where it had been.

"Beer-parlour drunks are all the customers now."

She smiled at him again.

"I don't bother you being here, Miss Cressy?"

"I like it. You're a sweet little guy, Tony."

He looked stiffly at the floor and a ripple touched his spine. He waited for it to go away. It went slowly. Then he sat back, relaxed again, his neat fingers clasped on his elk's tooth. He listened. Not to the radio—to far-off, uncertain things, menacing things. And perhaps to just the safe whir of wheels going away into a strange night.

"Nobody's all bad," he said out loud.

The girl looked at him lazily. "I've met two or three I was wrong on, then."

He nodded. "Yeah," he admitted judiciously. "I guess there's some that are."

The girl yawned and her deep violet eyes half closed. She nestled back into the cushions. "Sit there a while, Tony. Maybe I could nap."

"Sure. Not a thing for me to do. Don't know why they pay me."

She slept quickly and with complete stillness, like a child. Tony hardly breathed for ten minutes. He just watched her, his mouth a little open. There was a quiet fascination in his limpid eyes as if he was looking at an altar.

Then he stood up with infinite care and padded away under the arch to the entrance lobby and the desk. He stood at the desk listening for a little while. He heard a pen rustling out of sight. He went around the corner to the row of house phones in little glass cubbyholes. He lifted one and asked the night operator for the garage.

It rang three or four times and then a boyish voice answered: "Windermere Hotel. Garage speaking."

"This is Tony Reseck. That guy Watterson I gave a card to. He leave?"

"Sure, Tony. Half an hour almost. Is it your charge?"

"Yeah," Tony said. "My party. Thanks. Be seein' you."

He hung up and scratched his neck. He went back to the desk and slapped a hand on it. The clerk wafted himself around the screen with his greeter's smile in place. It dropped when he saw Tony.

"Can't a guy catch up on his work?" he grumbled.

"What's the professional rate on 14B?"

The clerk stared morosely. "There's no professional rate in the tower."

"Make one. The fellow left already. Was there only an hour."

"Well, well," the clerk said airily. "So the personality didn't click tonight. We get a skip-out."

"Will five bucks satisfy you?"

"Friend of yours?"

"No. Just a drunk with delusions of grandeur and no dough."

"Guess we'll have to let it ride, Tony. How did he get out?"

"I took him down the service elevator. You was asleep. Will five bucks satisfy you?"

"Why?"

The worn ostrich-skin wallet came out and a weedy five slipped across the marble. "All I could shake him for," Tony said loosely.

The clerk took the five and looked puzzled. "You're the boss," he said, and shrugged. The phone shrilled on the desk and he reached for it. He listened and then pushed it toward Tony. "For you."

Tony took the phone and cuddled it close to his chest. He put his mouth close to the transmitter. The voice was strange to him. It had a metallic sound. Its syllables were meticulously anonymous.

"Tony? Tony Reseck?"

"Talking."

"A message from Al. Shoot?"

Tony looked at the clerk. "Be a pal," he said over the mouthpiece. The clerk flicked a narrow smile at him and went away. "Shoot," Tony said into the phone.

"We had a little business with a guy in your place. Picked him up scramming. Al had a hunch you'd run him out. Tailed him and took him to the kerb. Not so good. Backfire."

Tony held the phone very tight and his temples chilled with the evaporation of moisture. "Go on," he said. "I guess there's more."

"A little. The guy stopped the big one. Cold. Al—Al said to tell you good-bye."

Tony leaned hard against the desk. His mouth made a sound that was not speech.

"Get it?" The metallic voice sounded impatient, a little bored. "This guy had him a rod. He used it. Al won't be phoning anybody anymore."

Tony lurched at the phone, and the base of it shook on the rose marble. His mouth was a hard dry knot.

The voice said: "That's as far as we go, bud. G'night." The phone clicked dryly, like a pebble hitting a wall.

Tony put the phone down in its cradle very carefully, so as not to make any sound. He looked at the clenched palm of his left hand. He took a handkerchief out and rubbed the palm softly and straightened the fingers out with his other hand. Then he wiped his forehead. The clerk came around the screen again and looked at him with glinting eyes.

"I'm off Friday. How about lending me that phone number?"

Tony nodded at the clerk and smiled a minute frail smile. He put his handkerchief away and patted the pocket he had put it in. He turned and walked away from the desk, across the entrance lobby, down the three shallow steps, along the shadowy reaches of the main lobby, and so in through the arch to the radio room once more. He walked softly, like a man moving in a room where somebody is very sick. He reached the chair he had sat in before and lowered himself into it inch by inch. The girl slept on, motionless, in that curled-up looseness achieved by some women and all cats. Her breath made no slightest sound against the vague murmur of the radio.

Tony Reseck leaned back in the chair and clasped his hands on his elk's tooth and quietly closed his eyes.

CHESTER HIMES
(1909–1984)

For most of his life, Chester Bomar Himes was a driven man. It is arguable that the only time he stayed still for any appreciable period was during the seven years, from 1928 to 1936, that he served in the Ohio State Penitentiary for armed robbery.

While he was serving his time, Himes began to write short stories and try to get them published. His models were Ring Lardner, Ernest Hemingway, Damon Runyon, and the Black Mask writers, particularly Dashiell Hammett. He swiftly graduated from black weekly newspapers such as the Atlanta Daily World to Esquire, a magazine with a relatively progressive attitude toward race at that time (Esquire also published the clever cartoons of the black artist Campbell Simms).

Himes's first sale to Esquire in 1934 was two stories: "Crazy in the Stir" and "To What Red Hell," the latter an extraordinary mélange of savagery and hilarious farce set in a top-security hoosegow that is burning to the ground. This potent mix of black farce and violence, recounted in a deadpan style, became Himes's hallmark. His one real financial success, though, was a sexual satire dealing with black–white relations called Pinktoes (1961), written for Maurice Girodias's notorious Olympia Press in Paris. Other than that one great success, Himes was in many ways a prophet in his own country, almost entirely without honor. Even his famous series of Harlem police procedurals, featuring the characters Grave Digger Jones and Coffin Ed Johnson, started and continued as a commission from the French publisher Gallimard for its Serie Noire, the celebrated line of hard-boiled thrillers with a distinctly existential edge.

Himes was often surprisingly modest about his own achievements. "I haven't created anything," he once said, "just made the faces black, that's all." But almost everyone who reads Himes would certainly disagree. Whereas most writers of the period, however gifted as stylists or character delineators, hardly did more than trot out insulting, stereotypical characters such as "dinge" sexual predators or Cab Callowayesque tap-dancing jesters, Himes let the reader in on the ethnic secret, with humor, vigor, and a faint but always discernible underscoring of anger.

His depiction of life at the rough end was unfailingly accurate and involving, most of all because he had been there and seen it all. This is

no better experienced than in the sixty superb tales in his posthumous
Collected Stories: 1933–1978 *(1990).*

On a first reading, it may seem as though "Marijuana and a Pistol,"
which first appeared in Esquire *in 1940, comes straight from the school*
of didactic "anti" propaganda, written by one who had never experi-
enced the effects of marijuana at first hand but was simply writing from
a government handout. Nothing could have been further from the truth.
What Himes describes so graphically is precisely the effect of extremely
strong "grass" going straight into the bloodstream. At fewer than 2,000
words, "Marijuana and a Pistol" is a little noir masterpiece of needle-
sharp observation.

J. A.

1940

MARIJUANA AND A PISTOL

Red Caldwell bought two "weeds" and went to the room where he lived
and where he kept his pearl handled blue-steel .38 revolver in the dresser
drawer and smoked them. Red was despondent because his girl friend
had quit him when he didn't have any more money to spend on her. But
at the height of his jag, despondency became solid to the touch and attained weight which rested so heavily upon his head and shoulders that
he forgot his girl friend in the feeling of the weight.

As night came on it grew dark in the room; but the darkness was
filled with colors of dazzling hue and grotesque pattern in which he
abruptly lost his despondency and focused instead on the sudden, bril-
liant idea of light.

In standing up to turn on the light, his hand gripped the rough back
of the chair. He snatched his hand away, receiving the sensation of a
bruise. But the light bulb, which needed twisting, was cool and smooth
and velvety and pleasing to the touch so that he lingered a while to caress
it. He did not turn it on because the idea of turning it on was gone, but
he returned slowly to the middle of the floor and stood there absorbed
in vacancy until the second idea came to him.

He started giggling and then began to laugh and laugh and laugh until
his guts retched because it was such a swell idea, so amazingly simple
and logical and perfect that it was excruciatingly funny that he had never
thought of it before—he would stick up the main offices of the Cleveland

Trust Company at Euclid and Ninth with two beer bottles stuck in his pockets.

His mind was not aware that the thought had come from any desire for money to win back his girl friend. In fact it was an absolutely novel idea and the completely detailed execution of it exploded in his mind like a flare, showing with a stark, livid clarity his every action from the moment of his entrance into the bank until he left it with the money from the vault. But in reviewing it, the detailed plan of execution eluded him so that in the next phase it contained a pistol and the Trust Company had turned into a theatre.

Perhaps ten minutes more passed in aimless wanderings about the two-by-four room before he came upon a pistol, a pearl handled blue-steel .38. But it didn't mean anything other than a pistol, cold and sinister to the touch, and he was extremely puzzled by the suggestion it presented that he go out into the street. Already he had lost the thought of committing a robbery.

Walking down the street was difficult because his body was so light, and he became angry and annoyed because he could not get his feet down properly. As he passed the confectionery store his hand was tightly gripping the butt of the pistol and he felt its sinister coldness. All of a sudden the idea came back to him complete in every detail. He could remember the idea coming before, but he could not remember it as ever containing anything but the thought of robbing a confectionery store.

He opened the door and went inside, but by that time the idea was gone again and he stood there without knowing what for. The sensation of coldness produced by the gun made him think of his finger on the trigger, and all of a sudden the scope of the fascinating possibilities opened up before him, inspired by the feeling of his finger on the trigger of the pistol. He could shoot a man—or even two, or three, or he could hunt and kill everybody.

He felt a dread fascination of horror growing on him. He felt on the brink of a powerful sensation which he kept trying to capture but which kept eluding him. His mind kept returning again and again to his finger on the trigger of the pistol, so that by the time the store keeper asked him what he wanted, he was frantic and he pulled the trigger five startling times, feeling the pressure on his finger and the kick of the gun and then becoming engulfed with the stark, sheer terror of sound.

His hands flew up, dropping the pistol on the floor. The pistol made a clanking sound, attracting his attention, and he looked down at it, recognizing it as a pistol and wondering who would drop a pistol.

A pistol on a store floor. It was funny and he began to giggle, thinking, *a pistol on a store floor,* and then he began to laugh, louder and louder and harder, abruptly stopping at sight of the long pink and white sticks of peppermint candy behind the showcase.

They looked huge and desirable and delicious beyond expression and he would have died for one; and then he was eating one, and then two, reveling in the sweetish mint taste like a hog in slop, and then he was eating three, and then four, and then he was gorged and the deliciousness was gone and the taste in his mouth was bitter and brackish and sickening. He spat it out. He felt like vomiting.

In bending over to vomit he saw the body of an old man lying in a puddle of blood and it so shocked him that he jumped up and ran out of the store and down the street.

He was still running when the police caught him but by that time he did not know what he was running for.

NORBERT DAVIS
(1909-1949)

Although a relatively prolific contributor to the pulps of the 1930s and 1940s, Norbert Harrison Davis was cursed with a sense of humor, the fatal flaw that some believed was ultimately responsible for keeping him from being published more regularly. His friend and collaborator W. T. Ballard explained that Davis could write "the best 'writer to editor' letter of anyone in the business," but his main work was simply "too whimsical to fit well into the action pattern." For this reason, Davis managed to squeeze only six stories past Joseph T. Shaw during his editorship at Black Mask. It seems that Shaw's enthusiasm for Davis's work was qualified, even though he did include Davis's story "Red Goose" (1934) in his seminal Hard-Boiled Omnibus (1946). It appears that most of the stories by Davis that Shaw did publish were thoroughly worked over with the editor's blue pencil.

Davis sold his first stories to Argosy and Black Mask while studying law at Stanford University. He never practiced law, but became a professional fiction writer instead, selling mainly detective and mystery stories as well as Westerns, adventure yarns, and the odd terror tale. The blurb for his "Idiot's Coffin Keepsake," which he sold to Strange Detective Mysteries in 1937, reads: "Trapped in that horror mansion, Wade fought for a tortured child and a woman's sanity—his only ally a hacked-off dead man's hand, the jealous prize of a hopeless fool!" When one reads the story itself, it is difficult to believe that Davis's tongue was anywhere but planted firmly in his cheek as he hammered away at his typewriter.

Probably his best and funniest characters are Doan and Carstairs, the latter a Great Dane that Doan won in a poker game and cannot, try as he might, get rid of. These two appear in Davis's only solo novels, The Mouse in the Mountains (1943), Sally's in the Alley (1943), and Oh Murderer Mine (1946), the second a glorious comic classic with a clever and workable plot—a real feat, considering that many of Davis's plots became so entangled that even he lost track. Other fine creations include Max Latin, who operates out of a restaurant where the chef hates and insults his customers, and William "Bail-Bond" Dodd, who appears here, in a typically screwball story with a typically screwball title: "Who Said I Was Dead?"

Davis seems to have enjoyed his work; he found a good deal of success in his chosen markets and was well paid for his efforts. His stories appeared regularly in the Saturday Evening Post, *whose payment for just one story would probably have kept an Okie family in clover for six months. But it appears that Davis's private life was a bit less charmed, and at a certain point, things took a turn for the worse. Editors began to turn him down. In the end, Davis took his own life; as in most tragedies of this sort, no one was ever able to produce a satisfactory explanation.*

J. A.

1942

WHO SAID I WAS DEAD?

It was a very nice casket—all shiny black with bronze handles—and it sat on a bier at the end of the chapel under the long somber sweep of dark blue drapes that hung from the arched ceiling. There were flowers banked around it with loving care, blended artistically for shading, and their scent was cloying in the still, heavy air.

Dodd felt very bad about it all. He sat at the back of the chapel and blinked gloomily in the softly shaded light that came through one of the colored glass window panels. He was a tall man with a long, homely face that normally carried an expression of cynical and wary belligerence. He usually looked like he expected the worst. Now he looked like it had happened. He wore a pair of horn-rimmed glasses that had been patched across the bridge with a piece of adhesive tape.

He was all alone in the chapel except for Mr. Miltgreen, and Mr. Miltgreen didn't count as a mourner because he was there for business and not for sorrow, unless you could say that sorrow was his business. He was the representative of the Valley Vale Cemetery. He was a stooped, cadaverous man with black hair slicked in scanty parallel lines across the top of his bald skull. He had a sadly benign, a patient, long suffering smile.

A concealed pipe organ played notes that lingered and sobbed softly, and now a liquid tenor voice picked up the thread of melody and sang it with beautiful, modulated feeling.

Dodd turned around and beckoned to Mr. Miltgreen.

Mr. Miltgreen tiptoed noiselessly forward. "Yes?"

"Who's that singing?" Dodd asked.

"That's our Mr. Pillsbury. He's part of the service."

"Oh," said Dodd.

He listened until the song was ended and the music faded to a humming monotone.

Mr. Miltgreen leaned over him. "That's the end of the chapel service, Mr. Dodd."

"What?" said Dodd. "Oh. All right."

He got up and followed Mr. Miltgreen down the thickly carpeted aisle and out through the wide front doors. The sunlight was so bright after the dimness inside the chapel that it hurt his eyes.

"You're sure you don't want to see the interment?" Mr. Miltgreen inquired sympathetically.

"No," said Dodd.

"Perhaps it is better," Mr. Miltgreen soothed. "It is sometimes distressing."

"How much?" Dodd asked.

Mr. Miltgreen stared at him. "I beg your pardon?"

"How much do I owe you?"

"Oh," said Mr. Miltgreen. "Well, it's very difficult for us to keep within the limitations of an exact figure such as you set, Mr. Dodd. I'm sorry, but in this case it ran sixteen dollars and some odd cents over. There are certain charges and fees that vary . . ."

"That's O.K.," Dodd said glumly. "Who do I pay?"

"If you'll step this way, I'll take care of the matter."

They went the length of the stone-paved chapel porch and down stone steps. Lawns swept away from them in beautiful undulating waves, and the grass was so green and smooth it was incredible. A sprinkler threw water in a glistening circle. A bird sang in a subdued way.

Mr. Miltgreen led the way along a mathematically curved white gravel path to a low building masked in shrubbery that looked like an early Norman cottage. He eased one of the side doors open and motioned Dodd into a small luxuriously furnished office.

"Sit down at the desk here, Mr. Dodd."

Dodd sat down in a spindle-legged chair and took his check book from his hip pocket.

"You don't mind taking a check?"

"Of course not," said Miltgreen, offended. He found a slip of paper at hand in a drawer of the antique desk. "The exact sum is five hundred and sixteen dollars and eighty-six cents. Here is a pen, Mr. Dodd."

Dodd wrote the check and tore it out of the book. Mr. Miltgreen appropriated the pen and wrote carefully and precisely on the slip of paper.

"Be sure you put his name on that receipt," Dodd requested.

Mr. Miltgreen nodded. "Elwin Tooper. I've written it out carefully. There you are, Mr. Dodd. Thank you."

Dodd read the receipt—all of it—and then read it over the second time to make sure. It was in order, and he folded it up and stowed it away in his wallet.

"The deceased—Mr. Tooper—was a relative of yours?" Mr. Miltgreen asked gently.

"He was not."

"A very dear friend, perhaps?"

Dodd leaned forward. "It's a damned good thing he was dead in that coffin, because if he hadn't been I'd have hauled him out and slit his fat throat for him."

"What?" Mr. Miltgreen gasped.

"You bet," said Dodd. "That dirty rat. When you get him buried, I'm going to come around and dance on his grave."

Mr. Miltgreen indicated the check timidly. "B-but—"

"You know what he did?" Dodd demanded. "I'll tell you. I'm a bail bondsman. When guys get thrown in jail for this and that, I bail them out, if it's possible, for a percentage of the bail I have to put up."

Mr. Miltgreen nodded uncertainly. "Yes. But—"

"This guy Tooper," said Dodd, "was a blue-sky salesman who doubled in forgery and other little stunts like that. Blinky Tooper, they called him, and he was a very smooth article. So he got slung in the hopper here in Bay City a couple of times, and he had references from other bondsmen I know from out-of-state, so I bailed him out. He squawked like hell about paying up both times, but I finally shook it out of him. So it got too hot for him here after a while, and he went away, which was just dandy by me. I never liked him."

"But—but—"

"I'm coming to the payoff. The first of last week I get a telegram from an undertaker in Sparkling Falls, South Dakota, informing me that Blinky Tooper had just blown his head off with a shotgun there and that he had left a farewell note in which he said that he had deposited five hundred dollars with me for his funeral expenses and that he wanted to be shipped back and buried here."

"And he hadn't deposited the money with you?" Mr. Miltgreen asked, wide-eyed.

"No!" said Dodd violently. "Not a dime!"

"But you paid for his funeral."

"Look," said Dodd. "A lot of the guys I deal with are slightly on the dishonest side. And I'll give you a tip about crooks. They go in heavy for funerals. They think funerals are very important. Now supposing my clients got the idea that I was trying to gyp Blinky out of his after he had laid the money by with me to take care of it. They'd treat me like I had the bubonic plague. My business would go ker-floo right about now."

"But you could have denied that he left the money with you."

"I'll tell you something else about crooks," said Dodd. "They think everybody is just as dishonest—if not more so—as they are. Nobody would have believed me for a second. They'd just have thought I was trying to hook Blinky's five hundred now that the poor guy was dead and couldn't beef about it. No. I had to pay. That's why I was so particular about that receipt. I want to be able to show that I did."

"It seems very strange," Mr. Miltgreen observed vaguely, "and very hard on you. Of course, we appreciate your business, and if ever we can serve you again . . ."

"I'll remember," said Dodd.

When Dodd came in the front room of his office, he found Meekins, his runner, curled up in the big leather chair in the corner dozing peacefully. Meekins was a wispy little man with a sadly cynical face. He might have been almost any age, but he was young enough to be sensitive about his baldness, and he never removed his hat unless it was absolutely necessary. He had it on now, brim turned up front and back, collegiate style. He opened one eye and squinted at Dodd.

"Have a nice time?"

"Lovely," said Dodd. "Why aren't you over to the station tending to business?"

Meekins yawned. "Things are dead today. Hennessey will take care of anybody that comes in."

"Hennessey is the desk sergeant," Dodd said. "If they ever catch him writing bail bonds for us, they'll give him the old heave-ho right off the police force."

"They won't catch him—not Hennessey."

"I hope not," said Dodd. "Give me a drink."

Meekins leaned over and fumbled around under the big chair. "I wish you'd buy your own whiskey or else raise my wages." He found a flat pint bottle and handed it over.

Dodd got a paper cup from the water cooler and poured himself a drink. He threw it down and grunted appreciatively as it hit bottom.

"The mail just came," Meekins said. "It's over there on the table."

Dodd picked up the envelopes and riffled through them absent-mindedly. There were several bills, and he dropped them on the floor. The one remaining letter had his name and address written in neat print-script in green ink. Dodd opened it and unfolded the paper inside and read:

> *Dear Dodd: Thanks for the swell funeral. I never enjoyed anything so much in my life.*
>   *Your pal,*
>   *Blinky*

Dodd made a strangling sound.

Meekins looked at him in an injured way. "My whiskey ain't that bad."

"Read this!" Dodd choked. "Read it!"

Meekins took the letter and glanced through it and said, "Well," in a mildly surprised voice and then read it again with dawning unbelief.

Dodd was pacing back and forth across the room. His eyes were narrowed, dangerously gleaming slits behind his glasses.

"Well," said Meekins again, "I knew they had all the modern conveniences at Valley Vale Cemetery, but I never figured they'd put mail boxes in the graves."

Dodd said things to himself in an undertone.

"It's Blinky's writing, all right." Meekins observed. "I remember it well. He used to be a chemical engineer before he got to fooling around with phoney stocks and stuff, and it seems lots of engineers write in this sort of print style on account of lettering so many graphs and junk like that. Blinky used to curl his *h*'s like this here, too. Yup, Blinky sure wrote this."

"Shut up," said Dodd.

Meekins got out of the chair and picked up the envelope the letter

194

had been in. "Yeah, and it was mailed at ten forty-five. Funeral was at ten, wasn't it? This is sure mighty funny."

"Oh, you think so, do you?" Dodd said. "I don't. That damned Blinky not only gypped me out of five hundred berries to pay for his funeral, but then he didn't even die!"

"You figure Blinky ain't dead?" Meekins asked.

Dodd just glared at him.

"Well," said Meekins defensively, "it seems like it's a mighty funny—I mean, peculiar—thing to do. What would he want to make you put out for his funeral for if he ain't dead?"

"I don't know," said Dodd grimly, "but you can just bet I'm going to find out."

He stalked into his private office, sat down on the edge of his cluttered desk and picked up the telephone. He dialed long distance, and when the operator answered, he said: "I want to put in a call to the police department of Sparkling Falls, South Dakota."

"Yes, sir. Your number, sir?"

Dodd told her and said: "I'll hold the line. Make it as snappy as you can."

Meekins came in from the front room carrying the pint bottle of whiskey and sat down in the chair behind Dodd's desk. "It don't seem reasonable—"

"Shut up," said Dodd.

Meekins shrugged and took a drink. Dodd waited, swinging one long leg and muttering profanely under his breath.

The operator said in his ear: "Your party is not there now, sir. Shall I try again later?"

"What?" said Dodd. "Wait a minute. I'm not calling any particular party. Just the police department."

"There is no answer, sir."

"You mean the police department doesn't answer?" Dodd demanded incredulously. "Well, why not?"

"Just one moment, sir."

Meekins said: "You didn't try to reverse the charges on 'em, did you?"

"No," Dodd answered. "Shut up."

The operator said: "Do you wish to talk to his wife, sir?"

"What's that?" Dodd said. "Look here, operator. I just want the police department of Sparkling Falls, that's all. How can a police department have a wife?"

"Wait just one moment, sir."

"You want another drink?" Meekins asked.

"No," said Dodd.

The operator spoke again: "The police department of Sparkling Falls consists of one officer only—a constable. His name is Harold Stacy. He is not available now, sir. Do you wish to speak to Mrs. Stacy?"

"O.K.," Dodd said. "All right. Put her on."

The line clicked and clicked again, and then a tinny, raw-edged voice shouted: "Hello hello hello hello hello—"

"Hello!" Dodd said loudly. "I want to speak to Harold Stacy!"

"Where is he?"

"I don't *know* where he is!" Dodd shouted. "That's what I'm trying to find out."

"Oh, you liar! You dirty, filthy liar!"

"What?" said Dodd, startled.

The tinny voice screeched fiercely: "Oh, you can't fool me! I know that miserable little wretch is sitting right there beside you grinning and gloating. Oh, you just wait until he gets back home, and I'll make him regret the very day he was born! You tell him that! You tell him I'll—"

"Hey!" Dodd interrupted. "Your husband isn't here. I'm calling long distance from Bay City—"

"You're lying! He didn't have enough money to get that far! You tell him—"

"He—isn't—here! I'm trying to find him because I want to find out—"

"Oh, you can't get around me with your smooth talk! I know you're one of his vicious, drunken friends trying to cover up for him! You tell him I'll make him pay tenfold for all the suffering and disgrace he's caused me! And don't you dare have the impudence to call me again, or I'll have you arrested and sent to jail for life! And Harold with you!"

The line clicked and then hummed emptily.

The operator said: "Just a moment, sir. There seems to be some difficulty. . . ."

Dodd nodded at Meekins. "I'll have that drink now." He took it out of the bottle, holding the receiver to his ear.

The operator said suddenly: "Is this an official call, sir?"

"Oh, sure," Dodd answered. "This is Lieutenant Bartlett of the Homicide detail. The message is very vital—a matter of life and death, you might say."

"The operator at Sparkling Falls would like to speak to you. Shall I put her on?"

"Go ahead," Dodd invited. "Why not?"

"Hello," said a soft, shyly feminine voice.

"Hello," Dodd said. "How are you?"

"Fine, thank you. My name is Elsie Bailey."

"I'll write it down," Dodd promised. "I hear you want to talk to me, Elsie."

"Yes, I guess I do. I mean, I think I ought to. I heard you speaking to Mrs. Stacy. I couldn't help it because she started yelling at you before I had time to see if the connection was clear."

"Think nothing of it, Elsie. I have no secrets."

"Hah!" Meekins observed skeptically. "Say, what kind of game is this?"

Elsie was saying earnestly: "I knew you weren't fooling about Harold Stacy, because I knew you were really calling from Bay City, and of course he would never go that far."

"Of course," Dodd agreed. "But why not?"

"He only gets a hundred and nineteen dollars and fifty-three cents a month."

"That's as good a reason as any, I guess," Dodd said. "Elsie, did you have anything in particular you wanted to talk to me about?"

"I am! About Harold Stacy. He's married."

"I gathered that," Dodd admitted.

"His wife is really terribly strict with him, and sometimes he—he sort of has to blow up steam."

"Blow off steam," Dodd corrected. "Elsie, about this matter you wanted to tell me—"

"I *am* telling you! Harold Stacy got paid yesterday—he gets paid every two weeks—and he's off somewhere now blowing up steam. What did you want to ask him? Maybe I can help you."

"I wanted to talk to him about the suicide of a man by the name of Elwin Tooper."

"Oh, wasn't that awful!"

"Not nearly awful enough to suit me. That's why I'm calling. Do you know how it happened?"

"He just shot himself. Blew his brains all over!"

"Who identified him?"

"Identified him? Why, everyone knew him! He'd lived here for months."

"Do you know if Stacy printed him afterwards?"

"What?" Elsie said blankly.

"Took his fingerprints."

"Why, of course not! What on earth for?"

"I wouldn't know," Dodd admitted wearily. "Did you see him after he was dead?"

"Why, what an awful thing to suggest! Of course I didn't! They wouldn't let anyone see him, because his head was all blown to pieces. Isn't it too bad? He was such an awfully nice little man. We all liked him. I suppose Harold Stacy could tell you more about his death, if you really want to know."

"I really do," Dodd assured her. "How long do you think it will be before Harold gets through blowing up steam?"

"Well. . . . If I tell you something will you promise not to tell anybody?"

"Cross my heart," said Dodd.

"Sometimes," said Elsie carefully, "sometimes when Harold wants to blow up steam he goes to see a friend of his by the name of Doctor Herman Ramsey, who lives outside of Milesville, South Dakota. They fish and drink beer and play pinochle together. You might try to get him there, but you can't call because there is no telephone."

"A doctor with no telephone?" Dodd said skeptically.

"He's a horse doctor."

"O.K.," said Dodd, giving it up. "Thanks a lot, Elsie. By the way, do you know what Blinky—I mean, Tooper—was doing in Sparkling Falls?"

"Why, he ran the paper."

"He what?" said Dodd.

"He ran our newspaper. It comes out twice a week."

"Oh," said Dodd. "Thanks again, Elsie. If I ever come to Sparkling Falls—God forbid—I'll look you up." He put the telephone back on its cradle and looked at Meekins. "Blinky was running the newspaper in Sparkling Falls."

"I don't believe it," Meekins said flatly. "Even Blinky wouldn't be low enough to publish a paper. He was a high-class liar. What would he go clear out there and do it for, anyway?"

"That reminds me," said Dodd. He found a telephone directory in the drawer of the desk and thumbed through it rapidly. He found the number he wanted and dialed it.

"Greater Pacific Railroad," a voice answered.

"Have you got a complaint department?" Dodd asked. "I've got a beef with your railroad."

"One moment, please. I'll connect you with our Mr. Carter. He's in charge of complaints."

The line snapped, and then a smoothly polite voice said: "Yes? Carter speaking."

"My name is Dodd—William Dodd. Day before yesterday you delivered a body to me. I mean, a corpse. I want to make a complaint on that."

"Wait a second, Mr. Dodd, and I'll look up our records on the matter. Hold the line."

Dodd waited, and Carter finally came back on the phone again: "Yes, Mr. Dodd. I have the record here now. The body was consigned from Sparkling Falls, South Dakota, to you here in Bay City. Is there some trouble about it?"

"Trouble!" Dodd echoed. "Hah! You shipped the wrong body, and I'm not going to pay for it. I want my money back."

"What?" said Carter blankly.

"You shipped me the wrong body. I'm not going to pay the fare for just any old corpse."

Carter said frigidly: "Now just a minute. It happens to be the law that if a body is shipped in interstate commerce, the coffin in which it is shipped must be sealed and it cannot be opened at its destination. That coffin consigned to you was sealed before it left Sparkling Falls. Did you open it?"

"No," said Dodd.

"Then how do you know the proper body isn't inside?"

"The guy is writing me letters!" Dodd snarled. "You don't claim he's doing that inside a sealed coffin, do you?"

"If this is a joke, Mr. Dodd, it is in very poor taste."

"It's no joke! Not unless you can laugh off seven hundred and fifty odd dollars. If you don't refund that fare to me I'm going to sue you."

"Now look here, Mr. Dodd. You have no claim whatsoever against this railroad. We accepted the body at Sparkling Falls and delivered it to you as per our instructions and obligations as a common carrier and bailee. We didn't guarantee the identity of the corpse. Both tickets have

199

been validated and receipted, and we certainly are not going to return you your money."

"What did you say about both tickets?" Dodd demanded. "Were there two?"

"Of course. It is a rule of railroads everywhere that if we accept a body for shipment, you must buy an extra regular passenger fare. And that's what you did."

"This is the first I've heard about it. Who used that extra ticket?"

"A woman who signed herself as Blanche Trilby."

"I don't know any Blanche Trilby!" Dodd said. "I've never even heard of her!"

"That's quite possible, Mr. Dodd. If the deceased has no relatives who wish to accompany the body, then it is customary to make arrangements with some local person who will do so. It's often just a formality."

"A very peculiar one," Dodd commented. "I have to pay for a funeral for a guy who isn't dead and the fare for a corpse I don't want, and on top of that I get nicked for another ticket for somebody I don't even know!"

"You have no claim against this railroad, Mr. Dodd. If you think you have, I would suggest you take the matter up in court. We have an extensive legal staff. Good-bye."

Dodd slammed the telephone back on its stand.

"Say," said Meekins. "I just happened to think—why didn't you take the railroad fare out of the five hundred bucks and give Blinky a cheaper funeral?"

"Because," said Dodd bitterly, "there are a lot of guys like you, who are so dumb they don't know you can't ship a corpse by parcel post. They'd have all thought—when I showed them the funeral receipt—that I was cheating on a dead guy who trusted me."

"I guess maybe so," Meekins admitted. "There's something wrong about all this, Dodd. It don't look a bit good to me."

Dodd turned his head slowly. "Say, what the hell do you mean by sitting around here and drinking yourself dumb? Get over to the police station and get to work!"

"Sure, sure," Meekins soothed. "I'm going in a minute. Don't get in an uproar. What are you going to do yourself?"

"Send telegrams to a horse doctor," Dodd said.

Dodd walked past the long, glistening plate glass window and went through the door into the telegraph office. It was a narrow, deep room with a waist-high counter running across it about twenty feet back from the front.

Dodd found a pad of blanks and composed a message to Doctor Herman Ramsey and then tapped on the high counter with the pencil. A mousy little girl with dark, smooth hair and thick-lensed spectacles came forward. She accepted the blank and counted the words.

"Can you read it?" Dodd asked.

She quoted mechanically: " 'To Doctor Herman Ramsey Milesville South Dakota if Harold Stacy is there have him telegraph me collect a telephone number at which I can get in touch with him at once matter is urgent signed William Dodd.' "

"That's right," said Dodd. "How long will it take to get there?"

"The message will reach Milesville in about a half-hour. How soon it reaches your party after that will depend on the delivery service there."

Dodd sighed. "All right. I'll wait. Is there a bar near here anywhere?"

The girl looked up. "A what?"

"A bar. A grog-shop. A saloon."

"There's a place called Coon's Cafe down the street a block and to your right on Sixth," the girl said disapprovingly.

"I'll be back in a little while," Dodd promised.

Coon's Cafe was down six steps from the street level. It was a dim, shadowy little place acrid with the sharp smell of ammonia from beer coils, and dust motes danced lazily in front of the horizontal slits that served as windows.

When Dodd came in, it was deserted except for a wizened little man with a long, drooping yellow mustache who was standing behind the bar.

"Hello," he said in a discouraged voice. "You don't look very good."

"Well, thanks," Dodd answered. "I don't feel very good, either."

"What you need," said the bartender, "is a sherry flip. There's nothing like a sherry flip to put you right. It's tasty and nutritious and—"

"Bourbon," Dodd said. "Straight. Leave the bottle."

The bartender produced a bottle and a glass. "I'm telling you this for your own good. Whiskey is very bad for you when you have the megrims."

Dodd ignored him. He poured a drink and swallowed it and shuddered.

"You see?" said the bartender, nodding gravely.

Dodd poured another drink, propped his elbows on the bar, and stared down at it gloomily.

"You sure you wouldn't like a sherry flip?" the bartender asked.

"No!" Dodd said violently.

There was silence for about ten minutes, and then the telephone rang stridently.

"That'll be me," said Dodd.

The telephone was in a booth at the back of the room, and Dodd crowded inside and lifted the receiver.

"How did you know where to find me?" he asked.

"Hah!" said Meekins. "Deduction, that's what. I just remembered what a sourpuss you had on you, and I started looking in the directory for the bar that was nearest the telegraph office and—"

"All right. So you're smart. What do you want?"

"Well, listen, boss, do you remember that office you used to have in the Booth Building?"

"What do you mean—used to have?" Dodd demanded. "That's where I have my office now."

"No," said Meekins. "Not now."

"What?" Dodd shouted. "What are you saying?"

"Well, I pulled out of there about five minutes after you did. I got about a block down the street, and I heard a big boom. I thought maybe Hitler or Hirohito had dropped in to call, and I looked around quick-like, and I saw a lot of smoke and stuff coming out of a window, and it was the window of your office."

"Go on, go on!" Dodd ordered tensely. "What was it? What happened?"

"Somebody chucked a bomb through the door, boss, and blew everything all to hell."

"A bomb?" Dodd yelled. "A bomb! Are you crazy?"

"Not me. It wasn't a very big bomb, they tell me, but it sure scrambled things around, and if we'd have been in there it would have spread us out like strawberry jam. Dodd, do you know a tall, skinny dame with thick ankles who wears a wide-brimmed hat and a black veil and a moth-eaten fur coat?"

"No! Who's she?"

"I wish I knew. She's the one that chucked the bomb, I think. I snooted around and found out that the elevator guy carried such a party up to our floor, and she didn't go to any other office on that floor or in the building, even. She was there about the right time, and she sort of disappeared about the time of the explosion. So what do you think?"

"I don't know," Dodd said in a stunned voice. "I can't figure. . . . Where are you now?"

"I'll tell you where I am. I'm in the locker room at police headquarters. There are about twenty cops here with me and more coming and going all the time, and this is right where I'm going to stay. I didn't hire out to catch bombs, and I'm not going to do it."

"Our files!" Dodd said in sudden agony. "Our confidential files! You didn't go away and leave—"

"Oh, I took care of that. I had Hennessey send a couple of flatfeet over to watch the joint."

"Cops!" Dodd shouted. "You want cops to read what's in those files, you half-wit?"

"I thought of that, too. I had Hennessey send Broderick and Mason over there. They'll steal any bric-a-brac like fountain pens and stamps and stuff that ain't blown up, but they won't bother the files, on account they can't read."

"Are you punch-drunk?" Dodd asked. "You can't be a cop unless you can read. You have to take a written examination before you can be appointed."

"Naw. Broderick and Mason hired substitutes to take the examination for 'em. They pay Hennessey ten bucks a week apiece to write out their reports for 'em. It's a fact. Now look here, boss, that was a very dirty trick somebody played on you when they hooked you for Blinky's phoney funeral, but heaving bombs around is something else again. People ain't fooling when they do things like that. You better lay off, or they'll be scraping you off the walls."

"The hell with that," said Dodd bitterly. "Blinky can't pull this kind of a stunt on me and walk off laughing. Take me for seven hundred odd bucks and give me the bird and then blow up my office on top of it. Just wait until I find him. I'll give him a funeral, but I'll make damned sure he's in the coffin this time!"

"What do you want to act like that for? You'll just buy yourself a big bag of trouble."

"Don't be so dumb," Dodd said savagely. "Blinky or whoever did this wants to be cute about it—like he was in that letter. I'm supposed to be halfway smart. What will I look like when the guy starts spreading this story around?"

"It's better to be dumb than dead," Meekins warned. "There's something more behind this than just somebody's sense of humor. That bomb wasn't funny at all, and remember that there was *someone* in that coffin. Somebody already got his brains spattered. You wouldn't want to be next on the list, would you?"

"Phooey!" said Dodd. He hung up the receiver and went back to the bar.

"Did you get some bad news?" the bartender asked hopefully.

Dodd drank his whiskey in eloquent silence, flipped a half-dollar on the bar, and went out.

The mousy little girl with the thick glasses was still behind the high counter when Dodd came back in the telegraph office. She looked him over in a critical way and then sniffed twice pointedly.

"It's whiskey you smell," Dodd informed her. "Bourbon whiskey. Not very good. Did I get an answer to my telegram?"

The girl nodded. "It came through very rapidly, indeed. The charge is one dollar and sixty-three cents."

Dodd paid her, and she gave him the telegram reluctantly. It was addressed to Dodd in care of the telegraph company's branch office, and it said:

> HAROLD STACY NOT HERE
> BUT YOU CAN REACH HIM AT
> PARMLEE 4142 IN BAY CITY.

It was signed "Ramsey." Dodd stared at the telephone number, scratching his head.

"That number sounds awfully familiar," he said absently to himself. His head jerked up suddenly. "That's *my* number! That's the number of my office!"

"I beg your pardon?" said the mousy girl, watching him suspiciously.

"Never mind," Dodd said, scowling at the telegram.

A telephone buzzed softly, and the mousy girl looked toward the clerks busy at the machines in the back of the office and then reached down and took the instrument from its shelf under the desk.

"Postal Union," she said. "What? Who? . . . Oh, yes. He's right here."

She pushed the telephone across the desk with an annoyed gesture. "It's for you."

Dodd picked up the receiver. "What do you want now?" he demanded.

But it wasn't Meekins this time. It was a softly guttural voice that spoke very slowly, making a pause between words, but it was so indistinct that Dodd could hardly understand what it was saying.

"Is this Mr. William Dodd?"

"What?" said Dodd. "Oh, yeah. I'm Dodd. Who is speaking?"

"I can not give you my name yet, Mr. Dodd. Not until I talk to you personally. I am in trouble with the authorities. I wish to surrender myself, but I wish to make arrangements for my bail before I do so."

"O.K.," said Dodd. "I'll have my man at the police station whenever you say."

"No, no! *You!* I must talk to you personally about our arrangement. I wish to talk to you now. I am calling from a store just across the street from you. If you will step closer to the window, you can see me."

The telephone had a long cord on it, and Dodd stepped toward the big plate glass window carrying the instrument with him. "Where are you?" he asked.

"Come just a little closer to the window, Mr. Dodd."

Dodd took another couple of steps. "I don't see any store where you could be."

"Just a little closer. . . ."

Dodd dropped the telephone and fell flat on his face. "Get down!" he yelled at the mousy girl.

There was a series of light snaps, and the big piece of plate glass quivered and jumped and groaned in its frame. Bits of broken glass sang lethally through the air, and the flat, fluttering sound of revolver shots rattled faintly from the street outside. From the back of the office, a clerk yelled indignantly.

The silence seemed to stretch like a thin, taut thread. Finally Dodd turned over and looked up at the window. There were four ragged, starred holes through the thick glass, all in a line, just about on the level of Dodd's chest, had he still been standing.

He pushed himself up to his hands and knees and, heedless of splinters, crawled across the floor and through under the flap-gate of the counter. The mousy girl was crouched into a shivering ball, and she stared at him with fascinated horror.

"Got a gun?" Dodd demanded.

"Wh-wh-what?" she blubbered.

From the back, the clerk said angrily: "Say, what do you think—"

"Stay out of sight!" Dodd ordered. "Somebody's gunning for me. Have you got anything to shoot with back there?"

"No!" said the clerk in a voice suddenly shaky. "Are—are you sure—"

"If I was any surer, I'd be dead," Dodd answered.

Out in the street, a woman screamed and screamed again. Somebody shouted furiously, and then a police whistle trilled.

Dodd crawled out through the gate again, across the floor to the front door. He put his head out cautiously. On the opposite side of the street a yelling, gesticulating group of people milled around the solid blue core of a stocky policeman.

Dodd waited for a moment, looking all around, and then got up and ran for the crowd. He ducked into the edge of it and pushed himself forward toward its center.

A woman in a pink housecoat, her face smeared with cold cream until it looked like a weird Halloween mask and her hair screwed tight into scores of metal curlers, was screeching furiously at the policeman.

"Right in my apartment! Right up there!"

The policeman was trying to fend off the gaping crowd. "What, lady? What was it? What happened?"

"A woman in my apartment, I tell you! I was in the bathroom, and she opened the door and came right in! With a gun!"

"Get back," said the policeman to the crowd. "Stand back there, can't you? Yes, lady. What happened?"

"She told me to shut up! Right in my own bathroom! She pointed her gun at me! And she used my telephone! And then she fired shots right out of my window!"

"Stand *back!*" the policeman ordered. "Quit shovin'! Yes, lady. Did she rob you? Did she steal anything?"

"No! She came right in my bathroom and—"

"Yes, lady. But where is she now?"

The woman shook both fists at him. "I don't *know* where she is, you big dummy! She ran out and slammed the door! What are you standing here asking questions for? Why don't you find her and arrest her? What am I paying taxes for?"

"Yes, lady," the policeman said in a pained voice. "But what did she look like?"

"She was a big, tall woman, and she had an awful old floppy hat and a black veil and an imitation fur coat that never cost more than nineteen dollars—"

Dodd wormed back through the crowd. He went down the block at a fast walk, turned the corner into Sixth, and trotted down the stairs into the Coon Cafe.

The wizened bartender with the drooping mustache was still the sole occupant of the place. "Now you sure do feel bad, don't you?" he asked knowingly. "I told you so. You got the shakes, ain't you?"

Dodd sat down on a bar stool and took out his handkerchief and wiped his forehead. He breathed in deeply, trying to quiet the pounding of his heart.

"If you'd just take a sherry flip—" said the bartender.

"Bourbon," Dodd said hoarsely. "The bottle."

"You're gonna be a nervous wreck," the bartender warned.

"Go away," Dodd requested.

He poured himself a drink and then wiped his forehead with his handkerchief again. He took out the telegram from Ramsey and read it three times, but there was no doubt about it. It said Harold Stacy could be reached at Parmlee 4142, and Parmlee 4142 was the telephone number of Dodd's office. He shook his head uncomprehendingly. Finally he got up and went to the booth at the back of the room and dialed the number.

The instrument at the other end rang only once, and then a voice said cheerily: "This here is the Dodd Bail-Bond Company. Service any old time, any old place! What can we do for you, chum?"

"Who are you?" Dodd asked incredulously.

"What's it to you, bud?"

"I'm Dodd!"

"Oh hello, Dodd, old pal. This is Broderick. Me and Mason is keeping tabs on what's left of your joint for you. I'm takin' care of the phone calls. How am I doin'?"

"Just dandy," Dodd said bitterly. "I was hoping that telephone was out of order."

"Oh, no. It got knocked around some, but it still talks good. I can even talk to my old man in Memphis, Tennessee, on it and hear him just as plain as if he was across the road. Say, Dodd, what is this about Blinky Tooper, anyway?"

"I'll bite," Dodd said warily. "What about him?"

"Well, I thought you buried him. What is he doing calling up your office, then?"

Dodd stiffened. "Blinky Tooper called me up?"

"Yup. He didn't sound so very healthy, but on the other hand he didn't sound so very dead, either."

"What did he say?"

"He says, are you here. And I say, no. And then he says, where are you. I say, I ain't got no idea. Then he says, can he leave a message. I say, sure. So he does."

"Well, what was it?" Dodd demanded tensely.

"He says, it's very important you should call him right away quick if not sooner."

"Where?" Dodd yelled.

"Huh? Oh, wait a minute. Mason, what was that number I give you a while back—just before we ordered the second bottle? . . . Oh, yeah. I remember, Dodd, it was Garden 2212."

"All right," said Dodd.

"Now don't go gettin' worried about your business, Dodd. We got everything under control here, and we're takin' care of your customers like you wouldn't hardly believe."

"Good-bye," said Dodd sourly.

He hung up and put another nickel in the slot and dialed the Garden number. He could hear the steady buzz that indicated the instrument at the other end was ringing, but there was no answer. After a while, he hung up, retrieved his nickel and dialed another number.

"Police department," a voice said.

"Give me the locker room," Dodd requested.

There was a pause, and then Meekins' voice stated importantly: "This is the locker room."

"Dodd speaking."

"Hi, boss," said Meekins. "I was just wondering where you were. Do you know how much money you've got in the bank—in your personal account?"

"Not exactly," Dodd answered, puzzled. "Why?"

"You ain't got enough."

"Enough for what?"

"To cover that check you wrote for Blinky's funeral. It bounced."

"It couldn't!" Dodd exploded. "I'm sure I have enough to cover it, and anyway it hasn't had time to bounce yet."

"It did. There was a guy by the name of Miltgreen just over here crying to me about it. It seems he maybe didn't think you looked so honest, so instead of sending the check through in the regular way, he takes it right over to your bank personally and tries to cash it. They tell him it's no soap. You ain't got enough in your account to pay it."

Dodd said: "Why, I can't understand. . . . What did you tell Miltgreen?"

"I didn't know hardly what to tell him, boss. I thought maybe you might have bounced the check on purpose or stopped payment on it or something. I gave him the brush-off by telling him I didn't know anything about it and that he'd have to talk to you. I told him to go over to your office and wait for you. I figured I could tip you off if you didn't want to see him, but you better had because he's puttin' out a hell of a squawk. He says he's got to make the check good unless you do, and he's got a wife and sixteen starvin' kids. He nearly had me cryin' before he got through."

"I'll go over to the office now," Dodd decided, "and catch him there. I want you to—"

"Wait a minute," Meekins requested. "I got something else to tell you. Did you ever think how Tooper was a very funny name for a guy to have?"

"Oh, very funny," said Dodd.

"Yeah. Well anyway, me and Hennessey was talking about it, and he got to thinking that maybe he had seen a name that was something like it and just as funny somewhere kinda recently. You know them wanted posters they send out—with a guy's picture and description and fingerprints and stuff on 'em?"

"Yes," Dodd said patiently.

"Well, they get 'em by the bale here because the cops in Bay City is supposed to distribute them around to the other departments in the north end of the state, but of course they don't."

"Of course not," Dodd agreed.

"Hennessey just turns 'em over to the junkman for wastepaper as they come in. He nets himself five-six dollars a month that way. Well, he had an idea he had seen this name on one of them wanted posters, and so we started calling up other police departments in New York and Chicago and Miami and places and sure enough we run it down."

"What?" Dodd asked.

"Get this. A guy by the name of Colonel Hans E. Van Tooper of Batavia, Netherlands East Indies, married a rich widow by the name of Blanche Trilby in Lansing, Michigan, last August."

Dodd jumped. "Blanche Trilby!"

"Yeah. Ain't that the name you spoke when you was beefing with the railroad guy about gettin' your dough back?"

"Yes!" Dodd exclaimed. "She's the one who used the extra ticket—the one who came here with Blinky's alleged body."

"No, she ain't."

"What?" said Dodd.

"She ain't the one, because she's dead. Colonel Van Tooper went and cut her throat while they was on their honeymoon and walked off with all her jewelry and dough. He was very smart and didn't leave no fingerprints behind him, but they got a good description of him on the poster, and it sure sounds an awful lot like Blinky Tooper to me."

Dodd swore softly to himself.

Meekins said: "This looks worse and worse to me, Dodd. There's altogether too many people running around here that are dead and don't stay that way. Maybe they can get buried and still percolate, but I can't. And another thing: You know Lieutenant Kastner?"

"I know him, all right," Dodd stated.

"Yeah. Well, he's the one that's supposed to be investigating that bomb blast in our office. He's been around here laughing like hell. He says he ain't going to do nothing until that old gal makes a better job of wiping you out because if he started now it might discourage her."

"That's very thoughtful of him," Dodd said grimly. "He may have to start sooner than he thinks. I've got a telephone number here—Garden 2212. Find out the name and the address of the party for me right away."

"O.K. I'll have Hennessey check it."

"Call me at the office. I'm going over there now."

"Take it easy, boss," Meekins warned. "Somebody is mad at you, I think."

It was dusk when Dodd drove his battered coupe slowly along the street past his office. He made a U-turn at the end of the block and came back again, watching closed store fronts and shadowy doorways warily. Now, after business hours, the street had a sinisterly deserted appearance that made him feel very uncomfortable.

He stopped near the corner and whistled to the newsboy who was sitting on the curb. The newsboy strolled over and put his head in the window.

"Hi, guy. What's it?"

Dodd said: "I'm looking for a dame. I wondered if you'd seen her around here."

"Seen lots of 'em. What kind you want?"

"This is an old dame," Dodd explained. "She's tall and skinny and she wears a ratty old fur coat and she's got thick ankles."

"Oh, that one," said the newsboy. "I seen her just a minute or so ago. She was hangin' around like she was waitin' for somebody."

A voice said softly: "Hello, Mr. Dodd."

Dodd jumped so violently that his head hit the roof of the coupe and smashed his hat down over his eyes. He pushed the brim up shakily and stared into the round, dour face of Lieutenant Kastner.

"Well, if you ain't the jumpy one," Kastner observed. "You ain't really scared of just a screwy old dame, are you?"

"You haven't run into her yet, pop-off," Dodd said angrily. "Just wait till you do. She may be screwy, but she knows how to make bombs and guns work."

"Never mind. I'll protect you."

"That relieves my mind a lot," Dodd told him. "Who's going to protect you?"

Kastner opened the door of the coupe. "Tut-tut. Don't get overwrought. Come on along up to your office. Hang on to mama's hand."

Dodd got out and slammed the door. He stalked across the pavement toward the darkened entrance of the office building with Kastner strolling along behind, chuckling to himself.

Dodd pushed through the heavy door. There was only one dim light burning in the lobby, over the elevators, and Dodd started in that direction. Kastner came in the door.

There was quick, furtive movement in the shadows of the stairs to Dodd's left.

"Look out!" Kastner yelled. He whirled around and dove back out the door into the street.

Dodd was caught in the middle of the lobby with nowhere to go. He stood rigid, his pulse hammering a hard drumbeat in his throat. Nothing happened. After a minute that dragged like a century, Dodd swallowed and said thickly: "Who's there?"

"Oh, Mr. Dodd!" a voice gasped. "Oh. Oh, Mr. Dodd!"

Slowly a head wavered into view above the railing on the staircase.

"Miltgreen!" Dodd exclaimed. "What are you doing there? What's the matter with you?"

"Oh, Mr. Dodd," said Miltgreen in helpless agony.

"Are you hurt?" Dodd demanded.

"Mr. Dodd," Miltgreen sobbed, "I haven't got any trousers!"

"No what?" Dodd asked, advancing.

The front door squeaked open a cautious foot, and Kastner said: "Dodd! Hey, Dodd! Has she got another bomb?"

"Come on in, superman," Dodd told him. "Everything's under control. Miltgreen, have you turned nudist on us?"

Miltgreen was crouched woefully on the stairs, trying to pull his shirt-tails down far enough to hide green shorts and long, skinny legs.

"Mr. Dodd, I've never, never had anything as horrible as this happen to me before! She—she took my trousers!"

"Who did?"

"That awful woman. That awful, immodest creature. That Blanche Trilby. She pointed a gun at me and made—made me take off my trousers and give them to her."

"Blanche Trilby!" Dodd repeated. "Do you know her?"

"Why, yes," said Miltgreen. "That is, I've met her. She was at the station when I went to get Mr. Tooper's body. She introduced herself to me."

"That's the bomb dame, huh?" said Kastner eagerly. "What does she look like?"

Miltgreen stared at him blankly. "Why, I don't know. I mean, she's middle-aged and thin and tall for a woman. She comes up to about here on me." He indicated the level of his nose. "She's very hard-looking, and she has a rough, hoarse way of speaking."

"What do you care?" Dodd asked Kastner. "Or do you figure on spotting her a long ways away and getting a headstart? Miltgreen, what happened? Why did she take your pants?"

"To—to keep me from following her, she said. I told her I didn't *want* to follow her, but she took them anyway. I had just come in the building, and I was over there by the elevator trying to figure out how it worked, and she jumped out of somewhere and put a gun right against my chest. She marched me down that hallway and—and made me undress. Mr. Dodd, what will I *do*?"

"Relax," Dodd advised absently. "What did she do after she got your pants?"

"Just went out the front door."

"Why didn't you run out and yell for a cop?"

"Without any trousers on?" Miltgreen gasped. "Right out in the street where people could see me? Oh, *no!*"

"Say," said Kastner uneasily, "you don't suppose she planted a time bomb around here, do you?"

"We'll find out," Dodd informed him, "sooner or later. Look, Miltgreen, I'm sorry about that bum check for the funeral. There must be some mistake, but don't worry about it."

"Well, Mr. Dodd," Miltgreen said grievously, "I just can't help worrying. I'm not *used* to things like have been happening recently. I just don't understand how people can—can act like you and the people you know do. It isn't right at all."

"Yes, yes," said Dodd. He went to the door and whistled to the newsboy again. "Hey, Sam. Flag me a taxi, will you?" He came back to the stairs. "Now you take a taxi home, Mr. Miltgreen, and get some other pants and compose yourself. Everything is going to be all right, I assure you."

"But that check—"

"I'll take care of that. It's too late to get into the bank now. After you get your pants, you go on down to Siegal's Restaurant on Cable Street and wait there for me. Joe Siegal will cash a check for me, but he won't do it for that amount unless I present it personally. I've got some other things to do right now, but I'll be down just as soon as I can. Have dinner on me while you wait."

A taxi pulled up in front of the building.

Miltgreen gathered his shirt-tails around him like a skimpy skirt. "I'm sorry, but I don't feel very hungry. Oh, this is awful! What will my wife think . . . And my poor children. . . . Mr. Dodd, I hope—I sincerely hope—that you can make a satisfactory settlement of this matter at once. I wouldn't like to resort to legal action—"

"It'll be O.K.," said Dodd.

Miltgreen craned his neck, trying to see both ways along the street, and then hopped across the sidewalk like some weirdly elongated bird. He ducked into the taxi, and the door slammed emphatically behind him.

"I think," said Kastner, watching the taxi pull away, "that maybe I better scout around outside a little. That old dame might be hanging around—"

Dodd grinned at him wryly. "All right. If I find any bombs, I'll yell so you can run."

"It ain't that I'm afraid—" said Kastner.

"Oh, no!" said Dodd.

He got in the elevator and punched the button for his floor. The elevator moaned and groaned and carried him up. He was halfway there when he heard the singing. Two voices were making very heavy weather of "The Old Mill Stream." They were not in harmony.

Swearing to himself, Dodd got out of the elevator and went down the hall. There was a great jag-edged hole blown through the frosted glass panel of his door. The singing came from his office.

Dodd opened the door and stepped inside on glass that grated and crunched under his feet. The place looked like a newsreel shot from London. The walls were scarred in livid streaks, the water cooler lay shattered on its side, and papers and letters were drifted all over the floor in charred, sodden piles. One chair lacked its legs and another its seat. The center table was battered but still intact, and a policeman lay full length on his back on top of it.

He stopped singing and said cheerfully: "Hi, Dodd, you old fuddy-duddy. Here's our host, Mason."

Mason was seated in what remained of Meekins' favorite leather lounging chair. It was tilted over sideways, and the stuffing was oozing out of the back cushion. Mason fixed his eyes on a point six feet to Dodd's left and nodded solemnly.

"Glad to meet you."

"You're drunk," Dodd accused, looking from one to the other.

"You hear that, Mason?" said Broderick, the policeman on the table. "He says we're drunk. That's the kind of a greeting he gives us after all our work and worry."

"He's just envious," said Mason. "Pay no attention to him, Broderick. Ignore him."

"Where'd you get the whiskey?" Dodd demanded.

"At the drugstore on the corner," Broderick told him. "You know you got credit there, Dodd? It's a fact. You ought to use the joint more. All you do is call 'em up and say you're Dodd and tell 'em what you want, and they send it right up. Want I should show you how?"

"No," said Dodd. "Thanks just the same."

The telephone rang stridently.

Broderick said: "It's your turn to answer it, Mason. I answered it last time."

"Nuts," said Mason grumpily. "Let it ring. See if I care."

Dodd went into the shambles of his private office. The telephone was sitting on the floor where his desk had been. He picked it up. "Yes?" he said.

"Hello, boss," Meekins said. "The address on that telephone number is 1702 Cottage Grove Avenue. The name is Peterson. They just had the phone put in last week."

"O.K."

"Wait a minute," Meekins requested. "There's another little matter."

"My God!" Dodd shouted. "What next?"

"Well, it ain't my fault. Long distance has been calling the station here looking for Lieutenant Bartlett of the homicide detail."

"Well, so what?"

"*You're* Lieutenant Bartlett," Meekins said patiently. "At least that's what you told the dame over the telephone this afternoon."

"Oh, hell!" Dodd exclaimed, remembering. "I did, at that."

"Yeah. There ain't no particular party tryin' to get you, as far as I could find out. It's just long distance. You don't suppose the telephone company is after you for impersonating an officer, do you, Dodd?"

"No," said Dodd. "I think I know who it is. I'll take care of it." He depressed the breaker bar on the telephone, let it up again, and dialed long distance. When he got the operator, he said: "This is Lieutenant Bartlett of the homicide detail. I understand you've been trying to locate me."

"One moment, please . . . Oh yes, Lieutenant. The operator at Sparkling Falls, South Dakota, wants to get in touch with you at once. Shall I call her?"

"Do that," Dodd agreed. "I'll hold the line."

He waited through a long series of clicks and snaps, and then Elsie Bailey's shy voice said: "Hello, Lieutenant Bartlett."

"Hello, Elsie," said Dodd. "How are you?"

"I'm fine. I got your name from the operator at Bay City. I hope you don't mind."

"Not at all, Elsie. What can I do for you?"

"I thought maybe you ought to know that Mr. Gillispie has had a nervous breakdown."

"Who has had a what?" Dodd asked incredulously.

"Mr. Gillispie is the undertaker here at Sparkling Falls, and he has just had a nervous breakdown and is in the hospital and can't see anyone—not anyone at all."

"When did this happen?"

"Just this afternoon. Right after I talked to him."

"Oh," said Dodd. "You talked to him, eh? What about, Elsie?"

"Why, about you. I told him you had called up and inquired about Elwin Tooper, and right away he had a nervous breakdown."

"I see," said Dodd slowly. "I'm very grateful for this, Elsie. I wish I could do something for you."

"Well—you can. I'm coming to Bay City next month on my vacation, and—and you could thank me personally."

"Yeah," said Dodd. "But I don't think my wife would like that. I'll tell you, though. I've got a friend. His name is Dodd. He's a swell fellow. He's got money, brains, personality, looks—the works. You'll love him."

"I'd rather—see you. You have such a nice voice."

"Dodd has one just like it," said Dodd. "You send me a telegram in care of Dodd—his address is in the Bay City directory—and I'll have him meet your train. Good-bye now, Elsie dear."

He hung up the receiver and put the telephone back on the floor. "Why didn't I think of the undertaker?" he muttered to himself. "I must be getting feeble-minded."

He went back into the front office. Mason was singing in a blurred, gentle monotone, keeping time with an empty bottle. Broderick was asleep on the table.

Dodd nudged him. "Give me your gun."

"Sure," said Broderick, without opening his eyes. He fumbled it out of the holster and extended it blindly.

Dodd looked to make sure it was loaded and then slipped it in the waistband of his trousers and buttoned his coat to conceal it.

"Take care of things," he said sarcastically, going to the door.

"You can rely on us," Broderick answered, his eyes still tightly shut.

Cottage Grove Avenue straggled off into the outskirts of the city north of the bay and petered out in a dead-end halfway to the summit of a steep hill. Someone had popped out the last street light, and Dodd parked his coupe at the end of the pavement and felt his way up a stony, weed-lined path in the darkness.

He had gone only about fifty yards when another car, its lights out, stole cautiously up behind his coupe and parked there.

Dodd had been looking for just that, and he stopped and watched a shadowy, furtive figure climb out of the second car, scout around for a moment, and then start up the path.

Dodd stepped into the weeds and waited until the figure was even with him and then said harshly: "Halt! Hands up!"

"*Wah!*" Kastner yipped in sheer terror. He raised his arms so violently his heels left the ground.

"Look who's jumpy now," said Dodd.

"Oh!" Kastner gasped. "You—you—What'd you wanta do that for? What's the idea?"

"You tell me."

"Well," said Kastner defensively, "I just thought I'd follow you just in case—"

"Just in case I'd uncover something you could hog the credit for," Dodd finished. "Now you're here, you might as well tag along. I'm headed for number 1702. It must be that bungalow right ahead."

He pointed to a darkened, spindly building that was crushed in against the side of the hill and braced there precariously with long timbers.

"What—what's in there?" Kastner asked warily. "Not that dame with bombs?"

"I hope so. I'm going in the front. You dodge around in back and catch anything I scare out."

"Well," said Kastner reluctantly. "All right."

Dodd went on up the path to the bungalow. He went quietly, but he made no effort to conceal himself. No slightest ray of light showed from the windows, and the whole place had a slatternly, decayed air that hinted at long vacancy.

Dodd climbed the long flight of steps up to the front porch, and the braced structure trembled uneasily under his weight. He felt around until he found the door knob. The door was unlocked. Dodd flipped it open and flattened himself against the wall beside it, Broderick's gun held loosely in his right hand.

"Want to come out?" he asked conversationally. "Or do you want me to come in?"

There was no answer. The silence was so deep that it hummed in Dodd's ears. He took a long breath and then whirled around away from the wall and jumped through the door. The air felt still and sticky against his face. He crouched tensely, alert for the slightest sound.

After a long moment, he straightened a little and groped along the wall behind him with his left hand. The light switch snapped under his fingers, and a dusty globe swung down from the ceiling on a long green cord suddenly jumped into brilliance.

Dodd gulped, swallowing hard against the pressure in his throat. Blinky Tooper was lying flat on the bare floor not six feet away. He was a fat, smooth little man, and the bulge of his paunch looked like a half-deflated balloon now. He was dead enough this time. His throat had been cut from ear to ear, and he had bled in a great semi-circular glistening pool.

Dodd took a step forward, and then the door on the opposite side of the room opened. Dodd caught a glimpse of the white sheen of a face under a black, floppy-brimmed woman's hat, and then the mouth in the face opened and shrieked crazily at him, and the door slammed.

Dodd shot through it twice, aiming at the middle of the panels. Another shriek and a jangling crash answered the bellow of the reports. Dodd hit the door with his shoulder and knocked it open and half-fell into a scummy, stale-smelling kitchen. The dull oblong of another door loomed at his right. Dodd jumped for it.

He stumbled down two shallow wooden steps, and then he saw a grotesque, skirted figure flopping and stumbling through the brush twenty yards away up the hill. He aimed the revolver at it and then, suddenly changing his mind, pointed the gun up in the air and fired.

The skirted figure fell down. It screeched and rolled over and over and slapped at the weeds madly. Dodd approached it, circling warily, the revolver leveled. "Here, you!" he said loudly.

The figure sat up and looked at him. Then it screamed and fell over backwards and lay still.

"Hey, Dodd," Kastner's voice called cautiously from the corner of the house. "Are you all right?"

"Yeah," said Dodd absently.

Kastner came up to him. "What were you shooting—Hey! It's the bomb dame! But—but she ain't a dame at all!"

It was true. Trousered legs extended out from under the wrecked tangle of skirt on the prone figure.

"What's the matter with her—him?" Kastner demanded. "Did you kill him?"

"No," said Dodd. "He's just so stinking drunk he couldn't hit the ground with his hat. He's passed out."

"Who is he?"

"His name is Harold Stacy. He's the police force of Sparkling Falls, South Dakota. That is, he was. Blinky Tooper is up in the bungalow. He's dead."

"Blinky Tooper," Kastner repeated stupidly. "Dead. Police force."

"Never mind," Dodd said. "I'll explain it to you later. Go in the bungalow and call the wagon. There's a telephone somewhere."

"But I don't *want* to eat!" Kastner said complainingly.

"I do," Dodd told him. "Come on."

Kastner got out of the coupe and tagged him across the sidewalk. "I gotta write a report, Dodd. I gotta know what this is all about."

"Later," said Dodd.

He pushed through glass and chrome swinging doors into the immense brightly white cavern of Siegal's Restaurant. It was crowded now with workers going on night-shift, and the rattle and bang of crockery echoed like gun-fire.

Jack Siegal sat like a fat, bland Buddha behind his cash register beside the door. He nodded gravely at Dodd.

Dodd stopped to look around, and Miltgreen jumped up from behind one of the tables. "Mr. Dodd!" he called eagerly.

Dodd jerked his head at Kastner and walked over to the table.

"You remember Miltgreen, Kastner," he said casually. "He's the guy who lost his pants. He's also the guy who bombed my office, took a few shots at me this afternoon, and cut Blinky Tooper's throat."

Miltgreen struck like a snake. He picked up the catsup bottle off the table and hit Kastner between the eyes with it. The bottle broke, and Kastner went sprawling in a welter of artificial gore.

Dodd kneed the table out of his way with a jangling crash and lunged forward in a driving tackle. Miltgreen tried to draw a gun from his hip pocket and sidestep at the same time, and one of Dodd's swinging arms caught him and brought him down, but it didn't keep him down.

Miltgreen was as lithely muscled as a snake. He squirmed out of Dodd's grasp, hit him three times with a bony, rock-hard fist and then stuck his thumb in Dodd's eye.

Dodd yelled in agony and rolled away, trying to draw his own gun. Miltgreen came up to his feet and ran for the door. He didn't get far. A waiter behind the short order counter picked up a filled water carafe and threw it with force.

The carafe hit Miltgreen in the back of the head and burst like a bomb. Miltgreen slid ten feet on his face and hit the wall and stayed there in a crumpled pile.

Dodd got up, feeling his eye tenderly. "I'm sorry, Jack," he said. "I had no idea this monkey would start a riot like that. I figured he'd just wilt on us."

"You'll pay for the damage," said Siegal, and it wasn't a question.

"Sure," Dodd agreed.

"It's O.K., then," said Siegal. "Meekins wants you to call him. You can do that when you call the cops." He raised his voice. "Everything is all over, folks. Just sit down and mind your own business. Wash that catsup off Kastner before he comes to, Joe."

Dodd dialed the number of the police station on the phone beside the cash register. "Send a radio car to Siegal's Restaurant," he said, when a voice answered. "And give me the locker room."

"This is the locker room," said Meekins.

"What do you want?" Dodd asked.

"Dodd!" Meekins yelped. "Where you been? I tried every place in town. Look, I got something red-hot for you! Me and Hennessey was talkin' about this deal, and he remembered that Blinky Tooper was once hauled in for selling phoney lots in a phoney cemetery and he had a partner then that looked something like this bird Miltgreen."

"Hennessey!" Dodd shouted. "That fat lame-brained rum-dumb! And you too! Why don't either one of you get your smart ideas before I have to bat my brains out figuring the answers myself?"

"Well, we didn't know . . . What? Did you say you had the answers? What are they, boss? I'm going nuts here with nobody but cops to talk to."

Dodd said: "It all goes back to Sparkling Falls, South Dakota. Blinky Tooper holed up there after he knocked off the rich widow, Blanche Trilby. He had dough from her jewelry, so he bought the town paper. What would you think he would do if he had a printing press and a knowledge of chemistry?"

"I dunno, but he'd make himself some crooked dough if it was possible."

"That's what he did. Cooked up some counterfeit money—and the plates to make it with, I figure. The printing press should have tipped me off right away. He also made friends with this constable, Harold Stacy. Stacy got the same reward poster Hennessey did. He'd be just dope enough to notice the resemblance to his old pal Elwin Tooper and take the notice around and show it to him for a laugh. Blinky knew then that things were getting a little warm. He figured to check out—permanently. If people thought he was dead, no one would be looking for him."

"Blinky was always a smart one," Meekins observed.

"Yeah. So he went to work on Harold Stacy. Blinky could toss out a very smooth line when he wanted to. He told Harold Stacy how Blinky and I were great pals—always clowning and playing elaborate practical jokes on each other. They got the undertaker in with them and faked a suicide for Blinky. Blinky probably paid off heavy—in funny money. The idea was that they were going to ship the non-existent body to me and Blinky was going to ride along disguised as a woman and then hand me a hearty laugh.

"Blinky used the name of Blanche Trilby because he wanted to be connected with her—after he was supposed to be dead. Then the police would stop stirring around on her murder."

"Well, what was in the coffin?"

"All the counterfeit money he could pack in there and the plates to make more. He picked Miltgreen to handle things at the cemetery—figuring to pick up the coffin from Miltgreen, after I had paid for the funeral, give Miltgreen a couple of bucks and a pat on the back and walk off whistling. But Miltgreen didn't think so. Some way he found out what was in the coffin—probably opened it. He wanted a cut—about ninety-five per cent. He had Blinky right behind the eight-ball. Blinky couldn't squawk even a little bit or all his elaborate scheme for dying and disappearing would blow off in his face.

"So now Smarty Blinky was struck with Miltgreen. But Blinky's brain was still hitting on all cylinders. He wrote me that note. He knew that would make me hop like a flea on a griddle. He knew, also, I would start something, and Blinky hoped that would scare Miltgreen into a more reasonable frame of mind.

"But friend Miltgreen didn't care. He's a lot tougher character than he looks or acts normally. He dressed up in Blinky's phoney woman's outfit and chucked that bomb into the office to scare *me* into a more reasonable frame of mind."

"He ain't got no wife or kids, by the way," Meekins put in.

"Lucky for them. In the meantime, back in Sparkling Falls, this Harold Stacy, dumb as he is, began to realize that he had bitten off something with a pretty sour taste. He headed for Bay City, leaving my number with a friend of his. He intended to get in touch with me and find out about this joke. But he went to the cemetery first and Blinky or Miltgreen found him and carted him off to the joint Blinky had prepared as a hideout. They told him he was in this with them, and he couldn't get out. He drank himself dumb trying to figure what to do. And then you, you fat-head, told Miltgreen where I was when I was telegraphing."

"No, I didn't!"

"So," said Dodd. "Then I've got another bone to pick with that butterfly-brained Hennessey. Miltgreen found out, anyway, and took a couple of shots at me. He missed, so he went over to my office to try again.

"He waited in the lobby, dressed in his woman's outfit. Then he saw me pick up Kastner outside. Kastner looks so much like a cop nobody could miss.

"Miltgreen chucked his woman's clothes into the alley. Only he didn't have any pants on under the skirt, so he had to make up a story about Blanche Trilby holding *him* up. He did it well, too. I took it in— then. I was still after Blinky. I'll have to give the guy one thing. He tried to call me and warn me when he found out Miltgreen was really after me. Miltgreen found that out, too. Anyway, he was tired of me running around. So he framed up a nice ending by killing Blinky and dressing Harold Stacy in the woman's clothes and leaving him in the joint with Blinky's body. Harold Stacy was one step off the D.T.s, and he could take the rap."

Suddenly Meekins said: "Dodd, I just remembered something. I heard a while back that the Postal Union Telegraph Company slapped a suit on you today for malicious mischief."

A waiter tapped Dodd on the shoulder. "Here's a paper you dropped."

"Thanks," Dodd said absently, taking it. "Meekins! Did you say malicious—?"

"Yeah. They claim you caused one of their plate glass windows to be busted. The guy that's got the process to serve on you is too lazy to go hunting for people. He just dresses like a waiter and hangs around Siegal's Restaurant—"

"Oh!" Dodd moaned. "Oh-oh!" He looked reluctantly down at the paper the waiter had given him and read: "You are herewith informed that you have been named defendant in a suit instituted. . . ."

"Dodd!" Meekins said. "When am I going to see you again?"

"At ten A.M. on May 7th," Dodd answered bitterly. "In Department A of the Superior Court."

JOHN D. MACDONALD
(1916–1986)

Ask any aficionado of hard-boiled and noir fiction to compile a list of its best writers in the 1940s and 1950s, and chances are that John D. MacDonald's name will not be on it. Despite his pulp origins and the numerous paperback originals he wrote, MacDonald's work is generally considered to be upscale and literary, rather than wholly in the mean-streets tradition. Yet many of his stories for Black Mask, Dime Detective, Detective Tales, and other pulps are distinctly hard-edged, peopled with men and women who are anything but upscale. Two-thirds of the contents of The Good Old Stuff (1982) and More Good Old Stuff (1984), his two collections of pulp stories, fall into this category. His first novel, The Brass Cupcake (1950), is nothing if not a noir tale, as are The Damned (1952), Soft Touch (1958), One Monday We Killed Them All (1961), and several other nonseries novels; so are the early Travis McGee novels, most notably the first, The Deep Blue Goodbye (1963), and Darker Than Amber (1966). The latter title, in fact, has one of crime fiction's hardest and most evocative opening sentences: "We were about to give up and call it a night when somebody dropped the girl off the bridge."

"Nor Iron Bars" is vintage MacDonald in more ways than one: the story was bought in 1946 by his first editorial mentor, Babette Rosmond, shortly after MacDonald returned from his World War II military duty, and it appeared in the March–April 1947 issue of Doc Savage. Brief though it is, it is hard as nails; and it would be difficult to find a tougher—or more human—character in any pulp story of the period than Sheriff Commer.

B. P.

1947

NOR IRON BARS

The appearance of Sheriff Commer's hand as he sat in the office of the jail told as much about him as most people who had lived in that little Southern city all their lives had learned. It was a square heavy hand with a thatch of brown curling hair on the back and short knobbed powerful fingers, tanned by the sun and wind, yellowed by the constant cigarette. He sat listening to the angry crowd noises, yelling for Burton, roaring from the park across from the jail, his thumb and first finger clenched so tightly on the short butt of his cigarette that the damp end of it was only a thin brown line.

He glanced down at his hand propped against the side of the oak desk and marveled that his fingers didn't tremble; secretly he always wondered at it. He respected and admired the independent nerveless-ness of his body, the way his brain could whirl in a mad haze of fear, his throat knotted, his heart thumping, and still his body, huge, ponder-ous and powerful, would go about its appointed tasks, with steady hands, calm eyes, quiet voice.

He kept safely tucked back on a secret shelf of his mind the thought that one day the body would break, the frenzied mind would have its way; and he would collapse into a quivering hulk, moaning over the imminence of pain and death.

The swelling roar of the lynching crowd faded from his conscious mind as he remembered the bright afternoon long ago when he had walked out of the group surrounding the Otis barn, walked steadily across the dark timbered floor, climbed slowly and heavily up the ladder until his head was above the floor of the loft, turned slowly and looked with chill impassivity into the crazed eyes of Danny Reneta. The only objects he saw in the dim hay-fragrant loft were those two shining eyes and the round vacant eye of the rifle which stared at him with infinite menace.

The room seemed to swing around him in a dizzy cycle of remem-bered fear as he recalled how he had calmly said, "Now, Danny. Better give me the gun," had slowly reached out with a hand as firm as a rock and grasped the muzzle of the rifle.

The two insane eyes had stared into the two calm ones for measure-less silent seconds until Commer thought he would drop screaming down the ladder.

Then a great rasping sob had come from Danny's throat and Commer had pulled the rifle out of the nerveless fingers.

Now he dropped his cigarette butt on the stained floor and ground it out with his heavy heel while that incident faded with the others from the dark place in his soul.

He rose slowly to his feet, walked over to the window, stood and looked out into the park, saw dimly the shifting, growing crowd, heard the increased roar as they saw his bulky silhouette against the office light. He half-sneered as he realized who they must be: The drug-store commandos. The pool room Lotharios. The city's amateur Cagneys.

But he felt also the slow certain growth of fear, an ember threatening to ignite the ready tinder of his mind. He realized what a lynching would mean to him and to the city. It would kill his pride and self-respect more certainly than the impact of lead would kill his stubborn body.

He sighed, trying to shrug off his fear, walked to the desk and brought out two large official thirty-eights. He held one in each hand and looked at them then tossed them back into the drawer, slamming it shut with his chunky knee. He fumbled in the wall locker and brought out a submachine gun. He held it and looked down at it, looked at its shining, oiled efficiency, fingered the compensator, tested the slide and then stood silently, testing his strength against the smoldering ember of fear.

He grunted as he stooped and hauled two heavy drums of fifty shells each out of the bottom of the locker. He snapped one onto the gun and then walked back toward the cells, the gun dangling from one blunt hand, the drum clenched in the other.

At the door of Burton's cell he laid the gun and drum on the floor, unlocked the cell and walked in. The hanging bulb made harsh light and blocky shadows in the cell. Burton slid off the cot and made quick short steps backward until he was pressed against the far wall, his huge black hands pressed palm-flat, fingers spread, against the whitewashed concrete, his face a shining impassive mask except for the wide eyes, dark iris rimmed with white. He was straight and tall, broad-shouldered and slim-hipped, a graceful and living creature, shocked and helpless under the pressure of the threat of sudden, violent death.

Commer stood for a few minutes looking at him, expression calm, eyes friendly. "Got a feeling you didn't do it, Burton," he said. "You look like a good boy to me."

Burton licked his lips, the glaze of fear fading slightly from his eyes as he answered, "I swear to God, Sheriff, I didn't do it. I ain't a killin' man. I hear 'em yellin' out there like they goin' to come in and get me any minute. Don't let 'em do it. Don't let 'em do it!" The last few words were a sob.

"Whether they come in or not depends on you, Burton."

"On me, sir? On me?" His tone was incredulous.

"That's right. Can I trust you?"

"Yes, sir. I do anything you tell me."

"Would you run away if you had the chance and knew I didn't want you to?"

Burton stood silently. Then he said, "No, sir." Commer believed him, believed him because of the pause, the weighing of loyalty against the fear that he could almost see in Burton's eyes. The man hadn't answered too fast.

Commer walked out, picked up the gun and drum and went back into the cell. He threw the drum onto the cot and poked the gun toward Burton. The big man stared in silent wonder and then reached out and took the gun in shaking hands.

"Careful, now! This-here thing is the safety. I've set the gun so that each time you pull the trigger you get a shot. The drum comes off like this. See? When it's empty the slide stays back and then you stick on the other drum like this."

"Yessir, but . . ."

"Now I'm going to leave you with your cell door open so you can sight down the hall here. If they come in, they'll come through that door there, the door to my office. Shoot first into the ceiling. If they keep coming put a few in the floor. If they still keep coming, lock yourself in quick. Here's the key. Then drop behind the corner of the cot and shoot low through the bars at their legs. Understand?"

"Yessir." Burton stood holding the gun, a glow of hope in his eyes, his face full of a gratitude so deep that tears formed along his lower lids. "I'll do just like you tell me, sir. I couldn't let you down after this, Sheriff." And he held the gun out, cradled in his arms as though it were the present of kings.

Commer grunted, turned on his heel and walked out, leaving the cell door open, walking steadily and slowly down the corridor, through his office, out the front door and onto the porch. There he stopped and watched the crowd, listening to their animal growling, every fiber of his mind screaming to him to turn and run for shelter. But he stood and held his arms up, a travesty of a benediction, calling for silence. For long minutes there was no response, then the shouting died to a murmuring. He heard a few last shouts of "We want Burton" and "Bring him out or we're a-comin' in after him!"

In his deep slow voice Commer bellowed into the darkness, "You all can come in after him right now. I just give him a submachine gun and plenty of ammunition. He's in there a-waitin' for you. Come ahead, boys! He's all yours!"

There was an angry mutter from the crowd. Commer imagined that those who had bolstered their frail courage with corn liquor now felt a sudden sobering chill. He was glad that he had always backed up his statements, never bluffed. Yet he could hardly see because of the dizzy spin of fear in his head.

Then a top-heavy man with a shock of light hair came striding out of the shadows into the dim glow of the street lamp. Commer walked heavily down the steps to meet him, recognizing him as Ham Alberts, itinerant handyman, loud-mouth and trouble-maker. But he was a bull in the strength of his youth.

They stared at each other. Commer saw through his film of fear that Ham was quivering with outraged righteous indignation. The offended honor of a taxpayer who had never paid a tax.

"Commer," he said hoarsely, "you got no call to arm a killer. You're paid to stay on the side of the law. What the hell you doin'?"

"Just saving a man from a bunch of corner loafers. Why?" Commer's voice sounded flat and disinterested, but he wondered if Alberts could hear the beating of his heart.

"If any of us gets kilt goin' in after him, it's gonna be your fault!"

"Do I looked worried, sonny? I do my duty my own way. No call for you to try to tell me how to do it. Now go on in and get him. What you waiting for? Yellow maybe?"

"Why, you tin-shield copper . . ." and Alberts lifted a beefy fist back and poised it two feet from Commer's jaw. In spite of the roaring in his ears, Commer looked calmly at the fist and then into Alberts' narrowed eyes.

"Don't know as that there is one of your best ideas, sonny. I'm going down to the corner for some coffee while you boys take care a this little matter." He turned away from Alberts, jiggling a cigarette out of a crumpled pack as he walked away.

Inside he writhed with terror, but there was room in his mind to wonder at the sober, quiet way his thick legs carried him along down the street. He stopped at the corner and lit his cigarette, his fingers strong and steady, the flare of the wooden match lighting up his stolid cheek bones, his mild brow.

Then he glanced back and saw Ham Alberts under the light, hollering into the shadows, his arms spread wide in a beseeching gesture. Commer couldn't hear the words, but he could see in the distance the vague forms of the men who had been clustered in the park melting back away from the jail, away from the deadly Burton, ignoring the furious Alberts.

Then Alberts dropped his arms helplessly and wandered after them.

Commer sucked in a deep lungful of smoke and expelled it in a long, blue column into the soft night air. He turned and headed for his coffee, knowing in his heart that the strong body had defeated the fear demons of the mind, this time.

But the next time. . . .

BENJAMIN APPEL
(1907–1977)

The New York World Telegram *said of Benjamin Appel after the publication of his first novel,* Brain Guy *(1934): "Jimmy Cain hasn't even a running chance as dean of tellers of hard-boiled stories. He is completely outpointed, outsocked, outslugged, and outcursed by Benjamin Appel." Nelson Algren said of Appel's first collection of short stories,* Hell's Kitchen *(1952): "[His] stories have never been prettied up for the parlor. Their forthrightness will do more than leave the reader feeling that he has read an honest story: he will feel as well that he has met an honest man."*

The slum streets and back alleys of New York City were Appel's primary fictional domain. Gangsters, whores, grifters, dope dealers and addicts, corrupt political and union officials, cops good and bad, and honest citizens trapped in poverty were the people he wrote about most convincingly. The comparison with Cain is valid enough; but whereas Cain's prose is controlled, sparse, and strongly dependent on dialogue for its effects, Appel's is raw, harsh, and sprawling, and it relies more on exposition and quick shifts of scene and viewpoint for its power.

About half of the substantial number of novels and stories produced by Appel can legitimately be termed hard-boiled. Brain Guy, *a savage tale of the New York underworld, is darkly reminiscent of W. R. Burnett's* Little Caesar *(1929) without in any way being imitative.* The Power-House *(1939),* The Dark Stain *(1943), and a paperback original,* Sweet Money Girl *(1954), are likewise tough and uncompromising studies of urban crime and corruption.* The Raw Edge *(1958) exposes the greed, graft, and violent struggle for power on the New York waterfront—the same theme, with a different slant, as that of the novelette that follows. Mordant and memorable, "Dock Walloper" was written expressly for, and became the title story of, Appel's second collection,* Dock Walloper *(1953).*

B. P.

DOCK WALLOPER

Johnny Blue Jaw Gibbons offered Willy Toth the chance to get himself connected right on the waterfront—and not the first time either that opportunity has come knocking on a prison door.

Those two could have become buddies only in a clink, for they were about as different as a pearl-handled .38 is from a piece of lead pipe. Johnny Blue Jaw was a power on the New York waterfront where the steamship lines paid more for insurance against pilferage than for the rent of their piers. Willy Toth was a stickup man from Utica, working the upstate towns. A nobody who'd drawn a fifteen to twenty year sentence for a two hundred and eight dollar armed robbery in Schenectady. Willy thought he was lucky getting out the first week in March after serving only seven years. Johnny Blue Jaw, with a two year sentence for manslaughter, expected to be free in the summer after doing nineteen months. Was he satisfied? Not Johnny Blue Jaw. "My God damn lawyers!" he griped. "What'm I payin' 'em for?"

They were different any way you took them. The New Yorker was the dark smoky Irish type. "I gotta shave every day, three times on Sunday," Johnny Blue Jaw kidded himself. He was built small, except for his outsize dock walloper's hands. Years ago he'd carried a hook himself. "The hook's in my head now," he explained once to Willy. Maybe it was at that. For his eyes were a metal-blue under his black hair. "I own a piece of the docks," was how the ex–dock walloper described his present occupation. In fact, being an owner'd fouled him up with the law. "This bandit Nolan owns the Chelsea docks, see, and he tried to grab up my piece, too. I got the guy he sent after me. Self defense, see. Where they get off with manslaughter, I dunno. Just politics."

Willy was blondish and he was big, almost six feet. Big and dumb, Johnny Blue Jaw thought with the razor-edged contempt of a small smart man for a big not-too-smart one. Willy never wisecracked like the tough little mobster; Willy was a great listener. And maybe that was why they were buddies. They were that different.

A few days before Willy hit the outside, Johnny Blue Jaw said, "You see this Clancy first thing. Clancy runs the union and he'll take care of you 'til I get out."

"Thanks," Willy said gratefully. "That's all I want. A job and no trouble." He meant it with all his heart. Seven long years in Sing Sing'd given the stickup man the chance to do a little one-plus-two. Willy wasn't really dumb. He was just another drifter—a drifter with a gun—and stickups were one way to make a living. But when a guy added seven years in Sing Sing to the four and a half at Wallkill, to the three years in the reforms, it was just too God damned much for one lifetime. If he broke parole, he'd have the rest of his fifteen-to-twenty to sweat out, another eight or thirteen years. The thought gave Willy the creeps. "The cat's out of me," he said to Johnny Blue Jaw. "I'm forty-three. All I want's no more trouble."

"There's no trouble down the waterfront I can't fix."

"That's all I want."

Johnny Blue Jaw, who was only thirty, grinned. "The No More Trouble Kid himself! Maybe you even wanna go straight, Willy?"

"That's okay with me too."

"Yeh? Well, for a while it won't kill you."

Willy Toth arrived in New York on a bright blowy March day—an ex-con in a gray hat, a gray topcoat and a blue suit, the parting gifts of the institution where he'd finally learned something about the terrible arithmetic of time.

He walked along Ninth Avenue into a red brick neighborhood not too unlike the upstate slums where he'd lived between stretches in prison. Trucks rolled west towards Tenth and Eleventh and Twelfth Avenues, towards the piers and the deep green water where the big ships of the Cunard and French lines berthed when in port. The address he had from Johnny Blue Jaw was a two-story building between Eleventh and Twelfth Avenues, a tinsmith on the street, the union headquarters above. Up on the second floor, a blonde secretary led Willy into a private office. There behind a beat-up desk sat a big man in his fifties who looked like an ad for a soft life. Thomas E. Clancy, president of the union local, wearing an expensive suit. The Thomas E. Clancy jowl hung over a silk necktie shining orange and yellow against a light blue shirt, the color of the sky outside. The Thomas E. Clancy voice boomed. "I been expectin' you, Willy."

Willy stammered through his story.

"Any friend of Johnny's a friend of mine. We'll go out to the girl and get you a union book."

The outer office was a dead ringer for Clancy's private office. The same cheap buff paint was slapped on the walls, the same American flag covered with dust, and near the windows, a duplicate of the lithograph of the president—with the motto OUR PRESIDENT—that hung behind Clancy's desk.

"Sign this man up, Alice," Clancy said to the blonde. "Skip the initiation fee and monthly dues and send him to see Ray."

"The monthly dues, too, Mr. Clancy?" she asked.

"We're givin' this man special consideration." Clancy smiled at Willy. "When I started onna docks I only made thirty-three cents an hour," Clancy said with a quick look down memory-lane. "I worked on the docks in my underwear."

He turned his fat broad back covered with fine cloth and returned to his own office. The blonde reached for a pencil and pad. "What's your name?"

It was seven years since Willy'd been alone in a room with a woman, and this one was ripe as only a blonde past thirty can be. Willy hadn't heard her questions. He was staring at her round breasts as if they were lit up with neon. Her dress was made of some green shiny material so that her body, too, seemed to be shining at him, bursting with light and sex like the women he'd dreamed about in prison. A jailbird's dream—woman come alive. Her pale golden hair, cut in a bang across her forehead, gleaming yellower than yellow, her lips redder than red.

"Through having a look?" the blonde asked him. She wasn't angry. She was just asking, and besides she was used to dock wallopers. Once a month, more than two thousand of them tramped up into this office with their three dollar dues.

Willy was blushing like a kid, his jaw muscles tight. The blonde's red lips showed a smile thin as the blade of a knife. She thrust that knife-edged smile into him and mockingly arched her breasts a little, for she was thirty-two and beginning to fade and she was out to get even with all the men who hadn't married her.

The next day one of the dock wallopers in Willy's work-gang answered his question. "Go to Florence's. She'll give yuh credit on yer union book."

Florence's was a side-street joint on 49th Street between Tenth and Eleventh, with two girls, a redhead and a blonde who'd once been a brunette. You noticed Florence who had the bulging eyes of a peke and was always taking cough medicine more than you did her girls. But the redhead Gloria and the blonde Lulu weren't bad, Willy decided.

He wasn't hard to please. He became a regular, and as March breezed into April, he kind of settled on Lulu. Lulu got to like him, too. One night she sat on his lap, just talking. Her lips, as hard under their lipstick as the cracked sidewalks down in the street, softened. "Wanna know my nickname, Willy?"

"Sure."

"It's Babe. I don't tell that to all the boys. Oney those I like. You gotta nickname, Willy?"

He laughed and then as a tug boat whistle sounded from the waterfront, he remembered Johnny Blue Jaw's wisecrack. "The No More Trouble Kid—that's me, Lulu. Or should I call you Babe from now on?"

He wasn't joking about being the No More Trouble Kid. After seven years in stir, Willy Toth, a dock walloper at the age of forty-three, didn't want to make any more noise than a mouse. He worked when the ships were in, drank a whiskey or two at Reagan's, the union hangout on the corner of 47th and Eleventh, and in the spring tenement night after a visit to Babe he'd walk home. On the stoops, the men sat smoking and in the gutters a few last kids like phantoms in sneakers raced their shadows. He lived in a Hotel for Men Only on the corner of 42nd Street and Tenth, in a room not much bigger than his cell at Sing Sing. But there were no bars in the single window.

Sometimes he wasn't sure. Sometimes he'd wake in the dead hours, moaning with fear, and only when he hurried to the window, sticking his head and shoulders outside, could he relax. Down below, in the moonlight, down below, in the rain, Tenth Avenue stretched before him. Not heaven maybe. But pretty close. The stillness of the Avenue in the hours after midnight, a stillness that wasn't really still, but beating ever so slowly, would fold about him like some huge and peaceful wing.

Another wing covered the waterfront: the racket. A wing with many feathers. Kickback and shape-up. Phoney charity raffle and whiskey tax.

At 7:30 each morning, Willy stepped into Pete's Shoe Repairs on Eleventh to pay his kickback buck. Pete was only the collector for the hiring boss. But there was always some sorehead in the crowd of dock wallopers smoking their stogies and belching after their three fried-egg breakfasts, who'd let off steam against the kickback racket by cursing Pete. "Lousy ginzo!" the sorehead'd jabber. "He's gonna buy a yacht with our bucks!"

At 7:40 Willy and his work-gang were loafing at the head of the pier where the shape was coming off. They knew they were going to work, but hundreds of other dock wallopers were there on the off-chance. Dock wallopers in caps that looked as if they'd been fished off a rag pile. Dock wallopers in two sweater combinations. Dock wallopers with lucky scarves around their necks. "I never get hurted when I wear it." Maybe the *Queen Mary* or the *United States* would be towering up to the sky, immense and iron-walled and yet somehow human as all ships are somehow human.

At 7:55 the hiring boss, Red Rizzo, showed up, a short bulky man who looked like a light heavyweight whose legs'd been cut down. Red Rizzo blew a whistle. The dock wallopers shaped-up around him in a semi-circle. This particular hiring boss liked to stare up into the sky. "Mickey's gang," he called, his eyes on a little cloud. As Mickey's gang stepped out of the shape-up, he fixed his eye on a wheeling seagull. "Fat Tony's gang . . . Ray's gang . . ."

Willy was one of the boys in Ray's gang. He worked steady even when the steadies were s. o. l. Willy developed into a pretty good man with a hook. He was husky to start with and up in Sing Sing he'd been in the metal shop five years. Ray taught him how to use a sling. Pete Harris, an ex-con like himself, demonstrated a few tricks of the trade. "The load's like a woman. She's gonna give if you work her right." Out on the piers jutting into the sparkling river, Willy's face tanned and he began to feel good. Even when he climbed down into the holds of the great ships, he didn't feel closed in as in prison where the bars somehow threw their shadows into the sunniest of yards.

Kickback? Shape-up? So what, Willy thought. Every morning he saw the beaten-hound look in the eyes of the men Red Rizzo hadn't called. Some of those men'd been members of the union for twenty years and were still catch-ons. They could drag their tails home. Or if they were lucky, the hiring boss might let them treat him to a shot of whiskey at Reagan's. Or even buy him a pint or a fifth.

No man in Clancy's local drank anywhere else but Reagan's. The rumble was that Johnny Blue Jaw was Reagan's silent partner. And it was a fact that in the back-room at Reagan's, the mob hung its hat. "Between you an' me an' the crapper," a blarneying dock walloper by the name of Paddy Lynch said to Willy one night over a beer at Reagan's brawling bar, "I'd like to be in the boots of the boyo who's always needin' a shave to mention no names. There's the kickback king, himself."

"Yeh?" Willy led him on. "That so?"

"Reagan kicks back to him, Red Rizzo kicks back to him."

Willy asked himself if Paddy Lynch was one of the secret followers of Father Bannon. He'd heard of this Father Bannon, a waterfront priest always talking up Jesus Christ and reform. About Father Bannon, the dock wallopers said, "The father's a nut. Nobody's ever seen Jesus Christ down the waterfront, and nobody ever will."

"Red Rizzo gets paid by the steamship an' stevedore comp'nies," Paddy Lynch was saying. "But who picked him for the job? The boyo who's always needin' a shave."

"Lynch, you're a God damned troublemaker!" Willy said and picking up his beer, he walked away. Before that night was over, Delaney, sec-retary-treasurer of the union, had soaked him for a raffle ticket. "You might win a Chevvy and ride to work," Delaney'd smiled. But every dock walloper stuck with a ticket knew the only riding they would do'd be inside their double-soled shoes.

"Everything's a racket," the ex–stickup man and ex-con would have said if anybody'd asked his opinion. And if this particular racket worked both sides of the street, Willy Toth for one couldn't get excited. It was a racket that scrounged every loose buck it could out of the dock walloper's pay. And it just about used a winch helping itself to steamship cargo. "That Johnny Blue Jaw deserves a lot of credit," Willy used to say in a voice full of genuine admiration to Pete Harris. And that ex-con would answer with an admiration gone just a little sour. "Yeh. He's a wonder, a cock-eyed wonder."

Working the 5 P.M. or midnight shapes, the two best shapes for stealing, Willy had marveled at the operations of Al Linn, one of Johnny Blue Jaw's top men. Al Linn was a gray-faced mobster, a sick man who couldn't drink or chase women whom the dock wallopers called "Vice President of the Stealing Department." All Al Linn had left were his brains. The rumble was that Johnny Blue Jaw listened to Al Linn when he wouldn't listen to anybody else in his mob. One night Willy'd seen an Al Linn truck, loaded with ship's cargo, almost run over a pier watchman. "Pete," he said later over pancakes and cof-fee. "That watchman'd jumped out of the way like a rabbit and kept on jumping."

"What'd you want him to do? If he ratted to the dock super he'd've had himself an accident."

The huge ships were floating department stores full of Christmas presents all the year round—Christmas presents for the taking. And the "Vice President of the Stealing Department" took. And the dock wallopers said, "We gotta right to a lil honest stealin' ourself. We're entitle' too!"

Down in the hold of the *Ile de France,* Ray's gang broke open a box of perfume, stuffing the bottles under their shirts.

"I know a guy'll gimme a buck apiece," they said.

"Not for me. I want my ole woman to smell nice."

"Yeh," a wisecracker said. "Put this parley voo stuff onna tits and you won't smell the cabbage and diapers."

"So long *I* put it on her tits okay."

Only Willy felt uneasy. He was stuffing perfume, too, but he couldn't help muttering, "Our luck to have the watchman grab us."

They gave him the horse laugh. "Hell," Willy argued, "I don't care how crooked they are, they have to make an arrest once in a while for the record." He'd had his experience with crooked coppers.

Ray, the gang-boss, agreed. "Willy's got something. There was a dumb mick Lacey once, something wrong with his head. Well, one night on a Queen ship, he stuffed a bunch of them soft wooly limey sweaters into his pants. Stuffed so damn many he looked like a clown in the circus. When Lacey walked out on that pier in broad daylight, the watchman just had to arrest him. They took that dumb mick Lacey to the judge and the judge says, 'You plead guilty or not guilty.' Lacey was so mixed up he says, 'Guilty.' The judge didn't believe his ears. 'Guilty?' he says. 'Guilty!' says Lacey. 'Six months,' says the judge. 'Sentence suspended.' "

Babe or Lulu couldn't believe it when Willy gave her a bottle of French perfume. "Gee!" she exclaimed happily. "You're a sweetie. I oney wished you hadda nickname, Willy. Suppose—" doubtfully—"do you like Big Boy, Willy?"

"Nope. Everybody calls me that. I told you once, Babe—No More Trouble suits me fine."

Johnny Blue Jaw Gibbons came outside in July and spent a busy week or so picking up what he termed "the loose strings" and organizing new ones. Nights, he was dashing around like a terrier in a kennel of bitches. Then he sent for Willy. He was sitting in the back-room at Reagan's with Al Linn and Red Rizzo when Willy came in. Johnny Blue Jaw shook hands with Willy, pounded him on the back, and invited him to have a double shot of the best whiskey in the house. "You know these guys?" he asked, jabbing his thumb at Al Linn and Red Rizzo.

Willy knew them all right. He knew also that he was just another face to them, if that. He felt as if he didn't know Johnny Blue Jaw either. Johnny, the jailbird, yes. This big-shot Johnny, no.

The mob leader was dressed like a gigolo in the money—of a couple well-heeled dames. His gray summerweight suit was brand new, his dark gray shirt and maroon necktie out of a box, and on his right hand a huge diamond glittered. When Willy's eyes shifted to the diamond, Johnny Blue Jaw raised his right fist. "How do you like it?" he said with a cocky grin. "The latest style in brass knucks."

They all laughed and Willy said, "I heard a rumble you were out, Johnny."

"Ask the girls that, Willy. Ask the girls. Clancy tells me you're doin' okay as a dock walloper."

Al Linn sneered. "How would fatso know? He hasn't been on a dock since the year one."

"That blondie up there at Clancy's—" Johnny Blue Jaw whistled between his teeth, his blue eyes shining. He seemed to've forgotten all about Willy. "I'm takin' her out tomorrow."

"She's a hot piece," Red Rizzo said in a flat voice as if talking about the morning's shape-up, no more expression in his face than on a bulkhead. "That blonde likes to go out with big-shots."

"That what you are?" Johnny Blue Jaw wanted to know.

"How do you spell big-shot?" Al Linn joined the kidding. "With an *o* or two *i*'s?"

Johnny Blue Jaw leaned across the table and pinched Willy's cheek. "My old buddy. Aw, Willy, nineteen months a helluva time." He shook his black-haired head. "Willy put in seven years!"

"I put in two, three years myself," Red Rizzo volunteered.

Al Linn shrugged. "Okay, okay, we all put in time and we all had the clap. That's supposed to've made men out of us."

Johnny Blue Jaw laughed. "How do you like that Al? Hey, Willy, no more runnin' around with a hook for you. When you hit the docks again, you'll have yourself a lil cigar box."

"A cigar box?"

"For the numbers."

"What numbers?"

"Don't you love them hicks?" Johnny Blue Jaw said delightedly to Red Rizzo and Al Linn. "What numbers, Willy, you shoulda give yourself back to the Indians. You're gonna be a number collector, see." Numbers was one of the new strings Johnny Blue Jaw'd promoted since his return to town.

"Oh!" Willy said. He wasn't much of a newspaper reader. But lately the boys'd been chopping up a lot of words about an investigation into the gambling rackets. "I'm satisfied with what I'm doing, Johnny," he said in a rush.

"You don't want it?" Johnny Blue Jaw asked him unbelievingly.

"No, Johnny. Honest—"

"I'll be damned! Here he is, guys! You can hunt high and low and up Mabel's crotch and you won't find another. The one guy who don't want you should do him a favor! Willy, you dumb lug, you crazy?"

"I'm satisfied longshoring, Johnny. Honest—"

"You dumb sonovabitch, you'll get your full day's pay as a long-shoreman and only work a coupla hours for it."

"Johnny, I'm satisfied. I don't need much to get along."

The three mobsters stared at him as if what he really needed was a straitjacket.

"I know what's eatin' the poor guy," Johnny Blue Jaw announced. "He's got the balance of twenty years over his dumb head if he breaks parole. Willy," Johnny said softly as if he were talking to a baby, "don't sing them parole blues to me. Whatta you think I got protection for down the waterfront? The Big Mob's behind this numbers deal. Who do you think kept my piece of the docks for me when I was up the river?"

That week Willy started to collect numbers. What else could a guy do? You did what you were told with Johnny Blue Jaw. What else was there? Stickups? He was finished with that. And besides there was Lulu whose nickname was Babe whom he'd gotten used to and Babe didn't come free. "I'm carrying my cross these days," he said to her when she asked him why all the worry.

"What is it, sweetie? You tell Babe."

"It's the numbers, the damn numbers. I smell trouble ahead," he said with a sigh.

Every morning Willy put on his dock walloper's clothes and ate a solid dock walloper's breakfast; oatmeal, three eggs and bacon, rolls and two cups of coffee. "I got to force myself to eat," he was complaining to Babe. Then he walked to his pier, and in the July sun, hot even in the early mornings, prepared for business. This was simple. He set his cigar box down on top of a barrel. He was ready. The dock wallopers, hanging around for the shape, came over to make their bets. They kidded him as they picked their lucky numbers, but Willy felt they were on different sides of the fence now. The men with the hook had a name for the guys like him—"the ex-cons' club." Even Pete Harris, an ex-con himself who was always softsoaping Willy in hopes of Willy putting in a word for him for a collecting job, was on the other side now. You were either in the club or you were out. With a double triple out.

The club met in the back-room at Reagan's. Number collectors from every pier between 42nd and 57th Streets. Stealers from the Stealing Department. Gunmen whom Johnny Blue Jaw tagged "the Sullivan boys" or "the Sullivans" because they carried guns in violation of the New York State Sullivan Law.

That back-room was a parolee's nightmare.

"Got to allow for what the boys put under their shirts," Al Linn might be saying when he felt mellow and in a mood to chew the fat about the secrets of his trade. "Got to allow for what the company expects to be lifted. You can't steal the anchors off the anchor chains. You got to leave 'em the eyes in their heads."

Buyers of stolen goods, fences and middlemen dickered with Al about shipments of Swiss watches or Scotch whiskey. Loan sharks who wanted an exclusive on the two thousand members of the union local showed up to get things straight with Johnny Blue Jaw. Gamblers with floating crap games, pimps, sure-thing operators, and always a character or two about whom Willy didn't want to know more than he had to. Maybe a sailor or a steward off a ship whose specialty was thinking up new ways to outsmart the Narcotics Squad. Willy always felt better after he got rid of his policy slips and could beat it out.

And when some newspaper featured a series of articles on the waterfront rackets, Willy only wished that Johnny Blue Jaw'd never come back to town. For not only was he collecting numbers for Johnny. He'd also been elected to his old job of number-one listener.

As Johnny Blue Jaw was the number-one collector. Collecting from number collectors and number players both, from dope smugglers and loan sharks, from Al Linn and his Stealing Department and from the steamship lines for keeping something called "Labor Peace" while he collected a thousand a month of the union dues from Clancy the representative of the laboring man.

Willy just didn't want to know the details about Johnny Blue Jaw's different collections. But practically every week, usually on a Tuesday or Wednesday night, "my take-it-easy night," Johnny'd have him up to his hotel suite. It was a hotel in a sidestreet opposite Madison Square Garden. There with the fans blowing and a bellhop bringing in the gin and ice and lemons, it was like the old days up the river with Johnny doing all the talking, and Willy all the listening. "Know why I trust you, Willy," Johnny Blue Jaw liked to say when he was tanked up. "S'because, Willy, you're the one guy who don' wanna damn thing outa me. You're okay, Willy, even if you're a hick." Stripped down to a pair of red or green silk shorts, Johnny Blue Jaw could've been a lightweight boxer himself escaped from the Garden. And the black-haired blue-eyed little mobster was in a fight sure enough. He was fighting a non-stop decision against the other big collectors.

Mainly, he was worried by his old enemy Nolan who owned the Chelsea docks, Nolan who had the Grace and U.S. lines in his pocket. "That bandit ain't gonna feel good 'til he sees me inna silver coffin wi' golden handles." Johnny was worried, too, by the Big Mob. "See, Willy, I'm in good wi' them. They kept Nolan from grabbin' up my piece o' the docks when I was in stir. Didn' do it for nothin' though. Hadda give 'em a fifty-fifty split on everything I make. I'm in good with 'em but you never can tell from one day t' the next. Aw, let's have another Tom Collins, Willy." He had the drinking capacity of a big man. And Willy, his head reeling, would reach for his refilled glass and wish to God he was at Reagan's where the drinks weren't free, but where at least a guy could get stewed without filling his brain with another guy's griefs. With another guy's schemes, another guy's secrets. And it was a guy who was about as hot as they come . . .

He was leaving Reagan's back-room one August day when Johnny Blue Jaw caught up with him. "Cmon, Willy, I'll give you a ride in my new boat." The new boat was a cream-colored Cadillac upholstered in dark green leather. As they drove uptown, Johnny Blue Jaw smiled. "A car's not broken in right 'til it's had dames in it. Bring a dame to the hotel tonight, Willy. We'll do the town. Know any classy dames?"

Willy thought of Babe down at Florence's. "Only whores," he admitted.

"Whores!" Johnny Blue Jaw said disgustedly. "Whores is out! I'll have a dame for you."

The dame was Clancy's office girl, the blonde whom Willy'd last seen in March. He didn't recognize her until Johnny Blue Jaw said. "Imagine a beaut like this workin' in an office with only fat Clancy to look at her. Alice, I want you to meet Willy, a good pal of mine."

The blonde smiled a come-on smile at him. Willy thought excitedly she didn't remember him, and the hell with that. What counted was that he rated now. He was Johnny Blue Jaw's pal.

They were all Johnny Blue Jaw's pals; Willy his listening pal, and Alice his old bed-time pal and Dolores the new one. Dolores was a blonde, too, but she couldn't have been more than seventeen, long-legged, thin-armed, slender and fresh as new grass with a KEEP OFF sign on it. There wasn't a wrinkle or a line under her gray slanted eyes or at the corners of her lips. Next to her, Alice looked old, her body on the heavyish side, with only her white summer dress blooming like a fresh flower.

They had cocktails in the hotel bar, and then they drove north out of the city in the new Cadillac to a club where they had dinner and high-balls until they were all floating. Johnny Blue Jaw listened to the blues singer, a tall girl naked except for three glittering metallic patches. "I might buy that," he smiled. "If I do I'll gi' you Dolores, too, Willy. S'all inna fam'ly."

Alice smiled at Dolores, a smile that was too sweet. "We'll have a hotel for all the girls Johnny-boy's played around with."

Dolores giggled drunkenly, "He thinks he's so great. Bet Big Boy can show him plenty. Can't you, Big Boy?"

"Yeh! His arm pits!" Johnny Blue Jaw hooted.

"Let's dance, Big Boy," Dolores said.

Willy hadn't said much all night; he'd concentrated on hoisting the drinks. But now he grinned foolishly. "First, I got to dance with Alice here, Dolores."

"Dance with botha the tomatoes!" Johnny Blue Jaw yawned.

Out on the elbow-poking, packed dance floor, Alice pushed her body close to Willy. She smiled up at him and in the dim light, her eyes seemed as bright and fresh as Dolores'. Willy breathed in her perfume, and an unbelieving smile touched his lips.

"How long do you know Johnny-boy?" she asked him.

"I'm prackally his best friend," Willy mumbled drunk and happy. "You're somethin', you know that, Alice? What Johnny sees in a bag of bones like Dolores, robbing the cradle, aw—"

"You down the waterfront, Willy?"

"With Johnny," he said cagily. Willy was drunk and he wasn't extra smart even when he was sober, but nobody had to explain some things to him. "I'm a big-shot on the waterfront you wanna know," he said with all the delicacy of a dock walloper leaning on his hook.

He slept with Alice that night.

He began dating her, and towards the end of August, he rented a furnished apartment on West 23rd Street and she moved in with him. Johnny Blue Jaw grinned when he heard. "Willy, you're gettin' to be a great lover for an old guy."

"Great lover, my foot! She knows you're behind me."

"Well, I am!" Johnny Blue Jaw stated. "You're one guy I like. That's why I'm a lil worried about this dame. She's no bargain."

But Willy thought Alice the best little bargain he'd ever made. And Babe agreed with him. He'd gone to see her for the last time to explain things all fair and square. "The girl's got a steady job," Babe said as she sat on Willy's lap. "She cooks for you. And a girl over thirty ain't burnin' up like a young kid which is okay for you, Willy. For a ball of fire you ain't no more neither." Babe nodded, a philosopher in a red silk robe. "Nothin' like home-cooked eats, I say." Babe thought for a second. "She got a nickname?"

"No."

Babe stroked Willy's cheek with a hand whose nails were a brighter red than her robe. "If you wanna, for old times sake, you can call her Babe."

The No More Trouble Kid gave her a big hug. He said sincerely, "Babe, you're a good girl."

"I did you a lot of good and you don't appreciate it. I ask you to do something and you won't do anything. Gwan back to where you came from. And take that fat-ass blonde with you."

Willy was still too stunned by what Johnny Blue Jaw'd asked him to do to think of a good answer. Besides there were no good answers. It was either yes or no and neither of them was any good. Willy glanced at the bandage on Johnny's neck. Then, at the gunman smoking a butt over on the couch.

The bandage and the gunman went together somehow like black crepe and an undertaker. The gunman's name was Mack, one of "the Sullivan boys" from Reagan's back-room. He was a narrow-built guy with blue eyes like any other blue eyes. If his mouth was tight and thin, so were the mouths of half the town, a town where everybody was hustling to make a buck. He looked like a shoe salesman or a junior executive. Only he happened to be a gunman and a killer.

"Beat it, you yellow bum!" Johnny Blue Jaw said to Willy.

"You got no right to call me that."

"Why not?"

"You know why not."

"Don't start in on them parole blues again. I thought we were pals. Some pal! Soon's I get in a spot, he turns yellow!"

"I'm not letting you down," Willy said quietly.

Johnny Blue Jaw sighed. "I didn't think you would." He fingered the bandage. "You're one guy I trust. You and Mack there." But he had also trusted the man who'd slashed at his throat that morning—Bugs Dennis, one of the Sullivan boys, on his payroll for years. Johnny Blue Jaw'd come out of Reagan's and Dennis was there waiting for him. With a knife. "A lil closer and he'd've cut through my juggler vein," Johnny said gloomily. "Nolan reached him. Nolan maybe reached some of my other boys. You two guys—" He didn't finish his sentence.

Willy peered over at Mack. They were the two guys Johnny Blue Jaw trusted most.

"We're gonna knock down that Nolan bastid once and for all," Johnny Blue Jaw said. "Nolan, we'll let alone a while. Nolan expects us so we'll let'm alone a while. There's others . . ."

The next few weeks, for Willy, went off like an endless bad dream. One night with the fog in from the waterfront, he was at the wheel of a car, piloting it into a sidestreet below 14th. Burnham's block, it was. Burnham, the third or fourth biggest guy in the Nolan mob. The fog swirled around the big yellow street lamp and Willy thought giddily that only a few blocks away on 23rd, Alice was sitting cozy in their apartment. "Wait here," Mack said. There were just the two of them. Willy watched Mack ease out of the car, cross the sidewalk and climb the stoop of a brownstone.

When the shots burst out, they sounded far away, muffled, as if the walls of the house had also turned into layers of blanketing fog.

Down the stoop, Mack came on the double. Into the car! Willy stepped on the gas while from behind them the muffled screaming of a woman tore at all his strained nerves.

It was Burnham's wife who had roused the neighborhood.

"An easy mark," Johnny Blue Jaw said grimly a couple hours later. "That Burnham never figured we'd want him."

The next day Willy read the newspaper headlines WATERFRONT WAR . . . Following instructions, he stayed in his apartment. At night when Alice came home from her job he was drunk. He couldn't eat supper. He couldn't sleep. After a few hours, he awoke and began to curse his luck. She poured him a shot of whiskey like a mother feeding a baby medicine. And as he lay there in bed with his big head between her breasts, she whispered soft as a mother with a sick child. "It's a ratrace, honey, so what can you do? Walk out on Johnny? No sense in that. Always been shootings on the waterfront. The cops never convict nobody. It blows over and things're like before. It'll blow over, you'll see. And you'll be set."

Clancy's secretary had latched onto the big numbers collector with the desperation of a woman whose mirror has begun to show the first silver hairs among the touched-up beauty-parlor gold.

"You'll be set," she repeated. "That's one thing about Johnny. He don't let his friends down. Look at Red Rizzo. Look at Al Linn—"

"Why don't he have them gunning at Nolan's mob?"

"They're in it!" she assured him, stroking his hot forehead. "The whole organization's in it one way or another. That is, everybody he trusts."

"Yeh, but who gets the dirty work? Me and Mack. That Blue Jaw's just trouble," he said miserably.

He awoke in the morning, a hangover grinding inside his head like hundreds of raking little wheels. The newspapers Alice brought up only made those little wheels spin faster. The police had questioned a lot of characters, including Johnny Blue Jaw Gibbons and Nolan. But nobody could explain the Burnham killing. Nobody at all. "See!" Alice said triumphantly. "It'll blow over."

Towards the end of the second week, at supper-time, Mack called on them. He sniffed at the platter of pork chops and French fries on the table. "I'll wait'll you eat," Mack said and sat down in his dark brown top coat, his brown felt hat balanced on his knees.

"What's up?" Willy asked, pushing his plate away.

"Better eat," Mack advised him and turned his eyes on the woman. He seemed to be sniffing all her curves over as he had the food. She smiled and brought him a cup of coffee. "Thanks," said Mack.

It was drizzling when the two men walked downstairs. The lights of the stores on 23rd shone brightly from the wet black sidewalks. They walked east and Mack, who wouldn't answer Willy upstairs, began to speak. "It's Nolan, Willy. He's out in Brooklyn in his sister's house. With the flu. He wouldn't lay up in his own place or go to the hospital. Had to go to his sister's house. He's got two of his boys with him."

He's out in Brooklyn in his sister's house . . . Willy thought over and over again, riding the BMT subway. Johnny Blue Jaw's stool-pigeons hadn't missed a trick. That Johnny had himself an organization. An organization and a half. His heart thudded heavily. "Mack, what do I do? You haven't told me."

Mack eyed him. Reaching into his pocket he silently passed Willy a slice of gum.

"Well?"

"What's the rush, Willy?" Mack said.

It wasn't drizzling or raining in Brooklyn when they stepped out at their subway station, elevated here, and walked down to the street. In front of a stationery store, a car was waiting for them. Inside they saw four men. As Willy squeezed into the front seat, glancing at the two pale blobs of faces there, he wondered why he was needed tonight. That damn Blue Jaw'd just gotten into the habit, he thought.

As if reading his mind, Mack said, "Willy, the boys Nolan got with him maybe know us. They don't know you. You'll ring the door bell. You'll say you're from Cunningham's. That's the drugstore they've been getting Nolan's medicine from—"

"What am I? The clay pigeon!"

"Nobody's going to pop at you. You're from this Cunningham drugstore and we'll be right behind you. That's all you do! Ring the bell and get back into the car—to the wheel."

The car cut into a quiet neighborhood of two-story brick houses, each sitting snug and solid behind its lawn.

"Okay," Mack said to the driver. "Here's good enough." They all piled out on the sidewalk. "It's the corner house. Willy, you go ahead!"

Willy walked up three stone steps to a door with two triangular panes of glass set in the wood. The panes shone yellow from a lamp inside the foyer. He rang the bell, saw a woman, followed by a man, come to the door. Their faces were framed in the yellow glass triangles, the woman fat and middle-aged, the man dark and slab-chinned, a face not too different from the faces of the mobsters who'd come to Brooklyn this night.

"I'm from Cunningham's, Cunningham's drugstore," Willy said in a quick jittery patter. And miraculously, for he didn't believe his own eyes, the door was opening. Wider and wider it opened, as Willy felt his heart turn into an empty hole. His nerves were laced across that empty hole, stretched tighter and tighter. What were they waiting for, his nerves shrieked. For the Nolan boy to pull his gun. And then in a rush, they weren't waiting any more, hurling past Willy into the foyer. "Don't try nothin' or I'll kill you!" Mack was warning the woman and the man.

Frantically, Willy dashed down towards the car. The woman shrilled, "No, no!" and then her voice suddenly vanished, the house door closing.

Willy sat at the wheel of the car: a car in another world.

He learned later that the Nolan bodyguard, seeing five gunmen, had folded like a folding chair, with only the woman having the guts to yell and warn her brother. A gun butt'd floored her. Johnny Blue Jaw's Sullivans had moved fast. Two of them'd rounded up the woman's husband and son and daughter listening to the radio in the living-room, while Mack and the others marched the disarmed bodyguard up to Nolan's room. Up the stairs they raced, the radio blaring downstairs. Nolan's second bodyguard had run out onto the landing, gun in fist. He'd hesitated a second because the first man coming up was his side. While he hesitated, one of the Sullivans'd plugged him through the head. They stepped over his body and finished off Nolan. The whole thing'd taken maybe ten minutes.

There were more headlines. Some editorialist wrote that the port of New York was more corrupt than Port Said, and over in Reagan's back-room, Al Linn said, "If Port Said's that crooked what're we wasting our time here for?"

A few days after Nolan was buried, Fassetti, the number-two Nolan man who was now both number one and number three, sent his mouth-piece to meet with Johnny's mouthpiece. A settlement was worked out. Fassetti promised to stay on his own docks, to deliver Dennis, and to pay ten thousand in cash for Johnny Blue Jaw's slashed throat. Dennis was tortured before he was killed, and Johnny, completely satisfied, turned the ten thousand over to his boys. "I don't want the lousy money," he grandly said. "It's the principle o' the thing. Them Chelsea sonova-bitches should be satisfied with their own docks."

Mack, the brain, got five of the ten. The four gunmen who'd driven out to Brooklyn split thirty-five hundred between them and Willy got the remaining fifteen hundred.

When the winter winds began to blow the old newspapers with the old headlines of unsolved murders down the waterfront streets—when all good dock wallopers treated themselves to a rye fortifier before shaping up—Johnny Blue Jaw thought of his pal Willy collecting numbers on the bitter cold piers. One day when Willy, coughing and red-faced, entered Reagan's back-room, Johnny called him over to where he was sitting with Al Linn. "It must be raw as an oyster down there, Willy. I'm thinkin' of pullin' you off 'til spring. How'd you like to work with Al here?"

"Let me think about it. Huh, Johnny?"

"There he goes again! Ain't he a corker, Al! The one guy who never wants a favor. Okay, freeze 'em off. You're so old you don't need 'em anyway."

Alice was excited when Willy told her. "Johnny-boy's ready to pay off! That fifteen hundred wasn't so much—"

"But who wants that Stealing Department," Willy said uneasily as if he hadn't been in on the business with Burnham and Nolan. "That Al Linn's too damn wise. One of these days he'll find himself in the clink. One of these investigators'll mean something."

"How about hitting Johnny up for something in the union then," she said suddenly.

"The union? Clancy?"

"Things're quiet at Clancy's. Like an old age home!" She laughed out of sheer excitement: money excitement.

"What could I do there?"

"What they all do. Make some easy graft."

The next day in the back-room, Johnny Blue Jaw laughed his sides off when Willy said, could he get into the union somewhere. But Al Linn only smiled. "Willy's got an idea," he said.

"You mean, his girl friend's got an idea. That blonde's one connivin' dame!"

"Johnny, Clancy's been operating all by his lonesome for years now," Al argued. "We can put Willy in to keep an eye on him. You can't trust those union crooks further than you can see them."

"They're entitled to a lil somethin' outa the pot, Al."

"Right, Johnny. But it's a good thing to shake the pot once in a while. Willy can take Delaney's job and Delaney can work for me."

"Aw right," Johnny Blue Jaw gave in. "We'll shake the pot real good. Willy, your girl friend's through at the office!" He grinned. "That'll show Blondy to mind her own damn business, pal!"

Delaney had been the local's secretary-treasurer, a job, as Willy learned, that was wearing mostly on the eyes. Sometimes as he read a little murder, a little sex, a little sports in the *News,* with Mary the new office girl reading her love magazine, he'd think he was getting three grand a year for belonging to a library.

Once a month though, for a couple of days there was some action. The dock wallopers'd come trooping into the office with their three dollar dues. They'd line up at Mary's desk, whistling and wolf calling. Sometimes in the crowd, some trouble-maker, maybe a Father Bannon man, might stage-whisper, "Where do the rats go when the ship sinks? To the waterfront!" But Willy never let on he heard. Bunch of suckers, he thought.

There were no receipts, no books. "We'll let them boondogglin' Screw Dealers down there in Washington pile up the paperwork!" fat Clancy said slyly to his new secretary-treasurer as they cut up a pair of (union expense account) steaks at White's Restaurant.

The local had over two thousand members and they paid in more than six thousand in cash every month. "I know where every nickel goes," Alice said to Willy, "and don't let Clancy double-talk you. A thousand goes for salaries, yours, Clancy's and Mallet's, the absentee vice-president. You'll never see him in the office 'cause he's always with the politicians. A thousand covers the office girl, the rent and such. Two thousand every month goes to ILA headquarters for general assessments and the per capita tax on the local membership. Clancy always holds out a couple hundred members on headquarters, Willy," Alice tipped him off. "Be sure to get cut in on that graft. Johnny-boy's graft is a thousand a month. He don't need it but he takes it to keep Clancy from forgetting who owns the union. That leaves a thousand to be split up between Clancy, Mallet and you. Delaney used to get two fifty of it. Willy," she said smiling. "You're making enough to support a wife."

"What!" he exclaimed, astonished.

She kissed him. "Honey, don't faint. Just a lil idea. We're set now, aren't we, and whose idea was it about the union?"

In April, Clancy threw a quickie strike on two piers where the Mathews Stevedoring Company had contracts. Within twenty-four hours a messenger arrived with three gold Swiss watches. Clancy kept one and gave the others to his vice-president and secretary-treasurer. "Now we'll go see old Dan Mathews and negotiate."

"Don't they get sore when you shake them down?" Willy asked.

"Shakedown's a mobster word," Clancy corrected him. "You better learn some union words, my friend. On the waterfront there's the mob and there's the union. You're a union man now. As to Old Dan Mathews, he don't expect nothin' for nothin'. He'd be the first to tell you, Willy, that only tough leaders can keep the men in line."

Willy shook his head. This union was a pie where you could come back for all kinds of helpings. And all of it legit! Like the raffle tickets he was selling to the dock wallopers over at Reagan's bar. What a racket, Willy thought blissfully. He saw Johnny Blue Jaw less and less, traveling more with Clancy and Mallet. There were banquets and political balls where he took Alice. At a benefit for the benevolent order of firemen, between the chicken à la king and the ice cream, Alice pressed his hand under the table. "All these men with their wives, Willy. Why not you and me?" She was wearing a soft rose dress and her eyes were suddenly warm and even a little uncertain as if she were really worried Willy wouldn't marry her after all. He was a big-shot in the union now.

"I never thought of it," he admitted.

"Think of it, Willy."

He laughed. "Maybe I will."

They got married at City Hall. When Johnny Blue Jaw heard the news he said to Al Linn, "Only a hick'd marry a dame fadin' like a funeral parlor lily. We were pals, but leave it to a dame!" He was bitter but when he saw Willy he poked him in the ribs. "Hi, stranger. No wonder I never see you no more. Remember who introduced you! Hey, the three of us could sleep in one bed. I'll come around some night, Willy, okay?"

They grinned at each other. But both of them felt the difference. "Leave it to a dame to put the ring in the guy's nose," Johnny Blue Jaw jeered.

By summer, Willy'd put on fifteen pounds. His pants wouldn't close and his jackets screamed at the shoulders. Alice laughed and said he deserved some new clothes anyway. In a new gray suit, his feet in fifteen dollar shoes, Willy attended the Union Convention at the Hotel Commodore. He sat between Clancy and Mallet and listened to a lot of speeches that made him yawn. *Improve union conditions . . . A longshoreman's lucky if he works half the year . . .* He got more of a bang when Clancy arose to second some resolution and boom out a little speech of his own. "I started as a wagon boy on a one-horse team, a member of the teamster union! When I joined the longshoreman's union I worked on the docks in my underwear! For thirty-three cents an hour! I worked all my life and I ain't got a cent in the bank and I ain't got a cent at home! Nobody gives the workingman a five cent piece . . .''

Later that night, in a suite of rooms over on the West Side, eight or nine delegates sat around smoking cigars and drinking whiskey, while they waited for the girls. Three call girls were en route. "Fifty bucks a lay stuff but t'night it's free," Clancy said to Willy. "You don't tell my wife and I don't tell yours. One of these girl's not seventeen, Willy."

"Who pays for them? The rank-and-file?" Willy smiled. It looked to him as if he'd got on that gravy train for keeps.

In the fall, at an election rally, Clancy introduced Willy to a man by the name of King who was in the contracting business. At a bar downstairs, King got to the point right away. "You boys run your local and your local unloads the biggest steamships that come into this port. Have you boys thought of getting into the stevedoring business yourself? Sure, you're union men, but what's to stop you from being silent partners? I'll put up the capital but capital's nothing. The big thing's the in. With the in we can get our share of contracts from the lines."

Nobody mentioned Johnny Blue Jaw, but he was the fourth man at that bar. The fourth man and the big man. Johnny Blue Jaw, who had picked Red Rizzo as hiring boss for the steamship and stevedoring companies, could also give the nod to an up-and-coming brand-new stevedore outfit out to make an honest dollar. King, Clancy and Willy met again, agreed on the details. King would get a third, Clancy and Willy between them a third, and a third for Johnny Blue Jaw. "You see him, Willy," Clancy said later. "You've got the in with him. It's a fair deal all around."

Willy went up to Johnny Blue Jaw's hotel room on a cool cloudy night. The sky was tinted pinkish from the bright lights on Broadway. Johnny fixed him a drink and Willy said, "I came to see you about a deal . . ."

When he finished Johnny Blue Jaw smiled. "You've got somethin' there."

"It's okay then?" Willy said, beginning to smile, too.

"Sure, it's okay. Okay for me. I don't need this King! I don't need nobody!"

Willy'd gained fifteen pounds or more, but now he almost seemed to sag inside his suit. His meaty cheeks went pale. He stared dumbly at Johnny Blue Jaw.

"For Christ sake, Willy! Don't you put the cryin' towel on with me!" Johnny Blue Jaw snapped at him.

"I thought—"

"Thought what? That I'd bite?"

"Bite? You'd be getting a third, Johnny—"

"Wouldn't I be a sucker to take it when I can get it all?"

"But, Johnny—"

"But what? What the hell you beefin' for! Ain't I done enough for you?"

"Sure but—"

"Sure but," Johnny Blue Jaw mimicked him. "You're pullin' down eight G's a year at the union. Not to mention extras. So now you wanna be a stevedore boss."

"What's wrong with that, Johnny?" Willy pleaded, wiping his sweaty face. "What's so wrong with that?"

"You're what's wrong! I send you to watch this Clancy crook and you turn crook yourself."

"That's a damn lie!" the big man shouted.

The little man whipped out of his chair and rushed to within a foot of where Willy was sitting. "Don't you back-talk me!" His dark bluish lips had lifted over his teeth. "Where'd you be if not for me? Who connected you? Who made a walkin' delegate outa you? What was you but a dumb heister?"

"Maybe I was but I'm no crook and you called me a crook."

"What d'you call this stevedorin' racket you and Clancy've rigged up?"

"You'd be getting a third!" Willy protested hoarsely as if Johnny Blue Jaw had only to be reminded of that detail and everything'd be okay.

"Ain't that white of you and Clancy?" the mob leader yelled, the veins cording on his temples. "Whose docks're they? Whose docks'd you be stevedorin'? The Chelsea docks or Brooklyn, or my damn docks! My docks!" he raged and lifted both his clenched fists over his head.

For a second he stood there and he no longer seemed small but big with ownership. He'd paid for his docks, all right. Paid with every kind of coin there was. With the blood-red coin of murder and the slimy thin one of treachery, with the fat coins that make no sound as they drop into the tin boxes of the politicians. Mouthpiece money, he'd paid that too. There wasn't any kind of money that he hadn't paid.

He stood there, not seeing Willy. Then he walked to his chair, again becoming a small black-haired man, not much bigger than a big jockey. He sat down, put a cigarette in his mouth and said flatly, "Nobody's pullin' a fast one on me."

"Nobody's trying to, Johnny—"

"Nobody will!" He had himself under control now. He was silent for a long second. "I had a hunch you shouldn't've been in the union. You wanted it, I give it to you. So now you come 'round with this stevedore proposition."

"For God's sake, what's so wrong with that, Johnny. Tell me, will you!" Willy pleaded.

"I think up the propositions on my docks—that's what's wrong with it! This King guy's another thing wrong with it!"

"Why?"

"Who's behind him? How do I know the Chelsea mob ain't behind him? Burnham—hell, he's gotta right to hate my guts. How do I know Fassetti's not behind King? I made the wop shell out ten G's, didn't I? How do I know it's not some kind of a scheme to muscle in on my docks?"

Willy said quietly, "I wouldn't have any part of a scheme like that, Johnny."

"You wouldn't. But what about Clancy? That bum don't love me." His voice lifted. "What about Alice? Why was she so hot to get you into the union? She and Clancy—" His eyes narrowed with a hard-bitten pity. "You and me were buddies 'til you let her talk you into marryin' her— fat-ass connivin' whore!"

As Willy lurched up from the couch, Johnny Blue Jaw sprang to his feet and quick as a cat picked up a chair, ready for anything. But Willy was on his way out. He had his hand on the door knob when Johnny Blue Jaw hollered. "Where you goin'?"

Willy's head pivoted on his thick neck. "No use talking to you, Johnny," he said bitterly. "You don't believe nobody, you don't trust nobody! You're crazy, that's what you are. Crazy!"

"I'm crazy like a fox. And wait a minnit before you go! You're through bein' a walkin' delegate, Willy! Clancy's through! The rank-and-file, they can elect some new bums." He became conscious of the chair in his hands for he lowered it to the floor. "You tell Clancy, I'll give him a job in *my* stevedore firm. And you, you dumb heister, you'll go back to collectin' numbers. Tell that to your missus!"

In the apartment over on 23rd Street, Willy went over the whole thing again for Alice, while Clancy listened for the second time.

The first time, Clancy'd cried like a baby. Three straight shots of whiskey in a bar weren't enough to straighten him out. The bottle of whiskey on the table around which they were sitting now hadn't helped Clancy much either. "That bastid don't trust you and he don't trust me no more," Clancy said when Willy stopped talking. "That bastid's got to feel he owns you a hundred percent or nothin'. It's nothin' for us, Willy! All that stuff about you collectin' and me workin' for him's just a lotta crap. We're through!"

"Clancy's right," the woman said, her eyes like stones in her blonde pale face. Clancy's face was twice the size of hers, big and jowly like an old-fashioned bartender's. But now they seemed to look strangely alike: the face of the big town itself, the town of the whore's mouth and the bought-and-paid-for heart, with the waterfront like a gleaming band around its forehead.

"Clancy's right," she repeated.

"I guess so," Willy mumbled. The newspapers called the docks a jungle where there were no rules. But Willy knew better than that now. He was slow but he learned, and he'd learned the big lesson tonight. It was a jungle all right, but a jungle with rules. Rules galore. And all the rules made by Johnny Blue Jaw Gibbons.

"Funny," he mumbled. "Funny how I was going to steer clear of trouble working in the union. Should've gone to work for Al Linn. Should never've bucked him."

"You should never've breathed!" the woman shouted. "You make me sick! Clancy, what're we going to do?"

Clancy shrugged hopelessly. He was an old and broken man, his jowls hanging like balloons with the air out of them. "I might've known it," he groaned. "A third wouldn't satisfy him. Has to hog it all. This King's a gentleman and that bastid of a hog—"

"You men make me sick!" she burst out. "Clancy, what're we going to do? Sit here and have a wake?"

Clancy lifted his head. "What can we do? Nothin'."

"We can go to the guy who's taken Nolan's place, to this Fassetti—"

They stared at Alice as if something extraordinary had happened to her between one breath and the next. As if she'd exploded into light or crumpled into dust before their very eyes.

"What else?" she continued, obsessed. "We might do something with them—"

"Forget them ideas!" Clancy nodded at the whiskey on the table. "They come straight outa that bottle. I'm goin' home."

He took his hat and coat and left.

Willy poured himself another shot. His hand was trembling. "You shouldn't have said that about Nolan."

"Nolan's dead, you dope!" she said in a fury.

"You know what I mean."

"Yeh," she said dejectedly. "I gave Clancy my head on a silver platter." She shut her eyes so tight they crinkled at the corners.

"Alice," he said in alarm.

Her breasts lifted convulsively, her eyelids sprang wide open. "Clancy left in an awful hurry, didn't he? He on his way, I wonder—"

He guessed her meaning but he had to ask the question anyway. "On his way where?"

"To Johnny!"

"He wouldn't do that!"

"How do you know?"

"I know!"

"You don't know Clancy then! Didn't he leave Mallet out in this stevedore deal, a guy he's been with for years. He'd leave Jesus Christ out if he had to! Willy, you think Clancy's going to let Johnny throw him out of his union without trying to save himself—just because you're the secretary-treasurer and I'm your damn fool wife shooting off her fool mouth about Nolan? Nolan!" she spat out in terror. She stood there paralyzed for a second and then her arm swung and her hand pointed to the telephone. "Willy, call him up before Clancy gets there, Willy!"

Willy's shoulders smacked against the back of the chair where he was sitting as if something'd leaped at him. Something that hadn't been there a second ago, something wet and bloated and evil like a drowned waterfront rat come alive.

"Willy, don't waste time."

He didn't move. She ran to him. "Willy, we got no time to lose!" Her hands moved feverishly across his slumped shoulders, gripping at his heavy body.

"Lemme alone," he muttered. "I got enough trouble—"

"Let Clancy have the trouble!" she cried pulling at him. "Willy, c'mon! What do you care about Clancy. Let him have the trouble! Let 'em all have it, the whole damn world!"

It was as if she'd forgotten about Clancy as a person. Was Clancy on his way home or on his way to Johnny Blue Jaw's hotel? It didn't matter any more. All that mattered was holding onto what they had. It was dog eat dog, and rat eat rat, down the waterfront. That was all that mattered now or ever.

She walked away from Willy, cursing him, and dialed the phone number of Johnny Blue Jaw's hotel herself, and when she had it, and Johnny answered, she said. "Here Willy comes!" She clapped her free hand over the mouthpiece. "Willy!" She called him savagely, her teeth like fangs. "Willy! Willy!"

He shambled over, his eyes glazed, as reluctant as any man about to deliver another man to his death. But he came. Because he didn't want any trouble.

ELMORE LEONARD
(b. 1925)

The traditional Western story and the hard-boiled crime story are more closely allied than might be apparent at a glance. As is pointed out in the Introduction, hard-boiled fiction can be traced back to the early days of nineteenth-century American life and letters. Viewed in that context, the justice-seeking twentieth-century private eye is a direct descendant not only of James Fenimore Cooper's Natty Bumppo, but of the frontier lawman and the hard-nosed Pinkerton detective of the last century. The subject matter of the Western story and the contemporary noir story is similar: murder, murder for hire, bank and other types of robbery, kidnapping, extortion. Even such Western-fiction staples as cattle rustling and range wars have present-day counterparts and have been utilized in hard-boiled fiction.

The fundamental kinship between the two genres is one reason that so many writers have worked in both. Carroll John Daly was one of the first "crossovers"; Two-Gun Gerta (1926), written in collaboration with C. C. Waddell, chronicles the Mexican border adventures of silent-movie cowboy Red Connors. In the 1920s, when Black Mask regularly featured frontier fiction, Erle Stanley Gardner published several short stories about adventurer Bob Larkin that may be classified as Western; and in the 1930s, he wrote a series of Western-style stories set in the deserts of the Southwest. W. T. Ballard, Norbert Davis, John D. MacDonald, Fredric Brown, and Cornell Woolrich are just a few of the early crossover writers. Contemporary crossovers include Ed Gorman, Loren D. Estleman, Robert J. Randisi, Bill Crider, and Bill Pronzini.

No one, however, has been more successful in both genres than Elmore Leonard. Before he turned to the production of such outstanding urban crime thrillers as Fifty-Two Pickup (1974), Unknown Man No. 89 (1977), and City Primeval (1980), Leonard's fictional output was confined to Westerns. His early pulp stories, which began appearing in the late 1940s in such magazines as Dime Western, Zane Grey's Western Magazine, and Argosy, are of uniformly high quality. One of his frontier novels, Hombre (1961), can be found on numerous lists of the best traditional Westerns. Almost as fine are The Bounty Hunters (1953) and Valdez Is Coming (1970). Indeed, and despite the critical acclaim and *bestseller status that his later crime novels have brought him, a strong case can be made that his most accomplished and memorable works are Westerns.*

Certainly, "Three-Ten to Yuma," which appeared in Dime Western *in March 1953, is Leonard at his best and ranks with* Hombre *as a Western classic. (The 1957 film version, starring Van Heflin and Glenn Ford, is likewise considered by many to be a classic of its type.) But this tense account of a deputy marshal who undertakes the deadly task of delivering a killer to the Yuma penitentiary is also a distinguished noir story, with all the elements of character, plot, incident, and suspense of the best contemporary thriller. With a few alterations, it might well have been written and published as a tale of the 1990s rather than the 1890s.*

B. P.

1953

THREE-TEN TO YUMA

He had picked up his prisoner at Fort Huachuca shortly after midnight and now, in a silent early morning mist, they approached Contention. The two riders moved slowly, one behind the other.

Entering Stockman Street, Paul Scallen glanced back at the open country with the wet haze blanketing its flatness, thinking of the long night ride from Huachuca, relieved that this much was over. When his body turned again, his hand moved over the sawed-off shotgun that was across his lap and he kept his eyes on the man ahead of him until they were near the end of the second block, opposite the side entrance of the Republic Hotel.

He said just above a whisper, though it was clear in the silence, "End of the line."

The man turned in his saddle, looking at Scallen curiously. "The jail's around on Commercial."

"I want you to be comfortable."

Scallen stepped out of the saddle, lifting a Winchester from the boot, and walked toward the hotel's side door. A figure stood in the gloom of the doorway, behind the screen, and as Scallen reached the steps the screen door opened.

"Are you the marshal?"

"Yes, sir." Scallen's voice was soft and without emotion. "Deputy, from Bisbee."

"We're ready for you. Two-oh-seven. A corner . . . fronts on Commercial." He sounded proud of the accommodation.

"You're Mr. Timpey?"

The man in the doorway looked surprised. "Yeah, Wells Fargo. Who'd you expect?"

"You might have got a back room, Mr. Timpey. One with no windows." He swung the shotgun on the man still mounted. "Step down easy, Jim."

The man, who was in his early twenties, a few years younger than Scallen, sat with one hand over the other on the saddle horn. Now he gripped the horn and swung down. When he was on the ground his hands were still close together, iron manacles holding them three chain lengths apart. Scallen motioned him toward the door with the stubby barrel of the shotgun.

"Anyone in the lobby?"

"The desk clerk," Timpey answered him, "and a man in a chair by the front door."

"Who is he?"

"I don't know. He's asleep . . . got his brim down over his eyes."

"Did you see anyone out on Commercial?"

"No . . . I haven't been out there." At first he had seemed nervous, but now he was irritated, and a frown made his face pout childishly.

Scallen said calmly, "Mr. Timpey, it was your line this man robbed. You want to see him go all the way to Yuma, don't you?"

"Certainly I do." His eyes went to the outlaw, Jim Kidd, then back to Scallen hurriedly. "But why all the melodrama? The man's under arrest—already been sentenced."

"But he's not in jail till he walks through the gates at Yuma," Scallen said. "I'm only one man, Mr. Timpey, and I've got to get him there."

"Well, dammit . . . I'm not the law! Why didn't you bring men with you? All I know is I got a wire from our Bisbee office to get a hotel room and meet you here the morning of November third. There weren't any instructions that I had to get myself deputized a marshal. That's your job."

"I know it is, Mr. Timpey," Scallen said, and smiled, though it was an effort. "But I want to make sure no one knows Jim Kidd's in Contention until after train time this afternoon."

Jim Kidd had been looking from one to the other with a faintly amused grin. Now he said to Timpey, "He means he's afraid somebody's going to jump him." He smiled at Scallen. "That marshal must've really sold you a bill of goods."

"What's he talking about?" Timpey said.

Kidd went on before Scallen could answer. "They hid me in the Huachuca lock-up 'cause they knew nobody could get at me there . . . and finally the Bisbee marshal gets a plan. He and some others hopped the train in Benson last night, heading for Yuma with an army prisoner passed off as me." Kidd laughed, as if the idea were ridiculous.

"Is that right?" Timpey said.

Scallen nodded. "Pretty much right."

"How does he know all about it?"

"He's got ears and ten fingers to add with."

"I don't like it. Why just one man?"

"Every deputy from here down to Bisbee is out trying to scare up the rest of them. Jim here's the only one we caught," Scallen explained—then added, "Alive."

Timpey shot a glance at the outlaw. "Is he the one who killed Dick Moons?"

"One of the passengers swears he saw who did it . . . and he didn't identify Kidd at the trial."

Timpey shook his head. "Dick drove for us a long time. You know his brother lives here in Contention. When he heard about it he almost went crazy." He hesitated, and then said again, "I don't like it."

Scallen felt his patience wearing away, but he kept his voice even when he said, "Maybe I don't either . . . but what you like and what I like aren't going to matter a whole lot, with the marshal past Tucson by now. You can grumble about it all you want, Mr. Timpey, as long as you keep it under your breath. Jim's got friends . . . and since I have to haul him clear across the territory, I'd just as soon they didn't know about it."

Timpey fidgeted nervously. "I don't see why I have to get dragged into this. My job's got nothing to do with law enforcement . . ."

"You have the room key?"

"In the door. All I'm responsible for is the stage run between here and Tucson—"

Scallen shoved the Winchester at him. "If you'll take care of this and the horses till I get back, I'll be obliged to you . . . and I know I don't have to ask you not to mention we're at the hotel."

He waved the shotgun and nodded and Jim Kidd went ahead of him through the side door into the hotel lobby. Scallen was a stride behind him, holding the stubby shotgun close to his leg. "Up the stairs on the right, Jim."

Kidd started up, but Scallen paused to glance at the figure in the arm chair near the front. He was sitting on his spine with limp hands folded on his stomach and, as Timpey had described, his hat low over the upper part of his face. *You've seen people sleeping in hotel lobbies before,* Scallen told himself, and followed Kidd up the stairs. He couldn't stand and wonder about it.

Room 207 was narrow and high-ceilinged, with a single window looking down on Commercial Street. An iron bed was placed the long way against one wall and extended to the right side of the window, and along the opposite wall was a dresser with wash basin and pitcher and next to it a rough-board wardrobe. An unpainted table and two straight chairs took up most of the remaining space.

"Lay down on the bed if you want to," Scallen said.

"Why don't you sleep?" Kidd asked. "I'll hold the shotgun."

The deputy moved one of the straight chairs near to the door and the other to the side of the table opposite the bed. Then he sat down, resting the shotgun on the table so that it pointed directly at Jim Kidd sitting on the edge of the bed near the window.

He gazed vacantly outside. A patch of dismal sky showed above the frame buildings across the way, but he was not sitting close enough to look directly down onto the street. He said, indifferently, "I think it's going to rain."

There was a silence, and then Scallen said, "Jim, I don't have anything against you personally . . . this is what I get paid for, but I just want it understood that if you start across the seven feet between us, I'm going to pull both triggers at once—without first asking you to stop. That clear?"

Kidd looked at the deputy marshal, then his eyes drifted out the window again. "It's kinda cold, too." He rubbed his hands together and the three chain links rattled against each other. "The window's open a crack. Can I close it?"

Scallen's grip tightened on the shotgun and he brought the barrel up, though he wasn't aware of it. "If you can reach it from where you're sitting."

Kidd looked at the window sill and said without reaching toward it, "Too far."

"All right," Scallen said, rising. "Lay back on the bed." He worked his gun belt around so that now the Colt was on his left hip.

Kidd went back slowly, smiling. "You don't take any chances, do you? Where's your sporting blood?"

"Down in Bisbee with my wife and three youngsters," Scallen told him without smiling, and moved around the table.

There were no grips on the window frame. Standing with his side to the window, facing the man on the bed, he put the heel of his hand on the bottom ledge of the frame and shoved down hard. The window banged shut and with the slam he saw Jim Kidd kicking up off of his back, his body straining to rise without his hands to help. Momentarily, Scallen hesitated and his finger tensed on the triggers. Kidd's feet were on the floor, his body swinging up and his head down to lunge from the bed. Scallen took one step and brought his knee up hard against Kidd's face.

The outlaw went back across the bed, his head striking the wall. He lay there with his eyes open looking at Scallen.

"Feel better now, Jim?"

Kidd brought his hands up to his mouth, working the jaw around. "Well, I had to try you out," he said. "I didn't think you'd shoot."

"But you know I will the next time."

For a few minutes Kidd remained motionless. Then he began to pull himself straight. "I just want to sit up."

Behind the table, Scallen said, "Help yourself." He watched Kidd stare out the window.

Then, "How much do you make, Marshal?" Kidd asked the question abruptly.

"I don't think it's any of your business."

"What difference does it make?"

Scallen hesitated. "A hundred and fifty a month," he said, finally, "some expenses, and a dollar bounty for every arrest against a Bisbee ordinance in the town limits."

Kidd shook his head sympathetically. "And you got a wife and three kids."

"Well, it's more than a cowhand makes."

"But you're not a cowhand."

"I've worked my share of beef."

"Forty a month and keep, huh?" Kidd laughed.

"That's right, forty a month," Scallen said. He felt awkward. "How much do you make?"

Kidd grinned. When he smiled he looked very young, hardly out of his teens. "Name a month," he said. "It varies."

"But you've made a lot of money."

"Enough. I can buy what I want."

"What are you going to be wanting the next five years?"

"You're pretty sure we're going to Yuma."

"And you're pretty sure we're not," Scallen said. "Well, I've got two train passes and a shotgun that says we are. What've you got?"

Kidd smiled. "You'll see." Then he said right after it, his tone changing, "What made you join the law?"

"The money," Scallen answered, and felt foolish as he said it. But he went on, "I was working for a spread over by the Pantano Wash when Old Nana broke loose and raised hell up the Santa Rosa Valley. The army was going around in circles, so the Pima County marshal got up a bunch to help out and we tracked Apaches almost all spring. The marshal and I got along fine, so he offered me a deputy job if I wanted it." He wanted to say that he had started for seventy-five and worked up to the one hundred and fifty, but he didn't.

"And then someday you'll get to be marshal and make two hundred."

"Maybe."

"And then one night a drunk cowhand you've never seen will be tearing up somebody's saloon and you'll go in to arrest him and he'll drill you with a lucky shot before you get your gun out."

"So you're telling me I'm crazy."

"If you don't already know it."

Scallen took his hand off the shotgun and pulled tobacco and paper from his shirt pocket and began rolling a cigarette. "Have you figured out yet what my price is?"

Kidd looked startled, momentarily, but the grin returned. "No, I haven't. Maybe you come higher than I thought."

Scallen scratched a match across the table, lighted the cigarette, then threw it to the floor, between Kidd's boots. "You don't have enough money, Jim."

Kidd shrugged, then reached down for the cigarette. "You've treated me pretty good. I just wanted to make it easy on you."

The sun came into the room after a while. Weakly at first, cold and hazy. Then it warmed and brightened and cast an oblong patch of light between the bed and the table. The morning wore on slowly because there was nothing to do and each man sat restlessly thinking about somewhere else, though it was a restlessness within and it showed on neither of them.

The deputy rolled cigarettes for the outlaw and himself and most of the time they smoked in silence. Once Kidd asked him what time the train left. He told him shortly after three, but Kidd made no comment.

Scallen went to the window and looked out at the narrow rutted road that was Commercial Street. He pulled a watch from his vest pocket and looked at it. It was almost noon, yet there were few people about. He wondered about this and asked himself if it was unnaturally quiet for a Saturday noon in Contention . . . or if it were just his nerves . . .

He studied the man standing under the wooden awning across the street, leaning idly against a support post with his thumbs hooked in his belt and his flat-crowned hat on the back of his head. There was something familiar about him. And each time Scallen had gone to the window—a few times during the past hour—the man had been there.

He glanced at Jim Kidd lying across the bed, then looked out the window in time to see another man moving up next to the one at the post. They stood together for the space of a minute before the second man turned a horse from the tie rail, swung up and rode off down the street.

The man at the post watched him go and tilted his hat against the sun glare. And then it registered. With the hat low on his forehead Scallen saw him again as he had that morning. The man lying in the arm chair . . . as if asleep.

He saw his wife, then, and the three youngsters and he could almost feel the little girl sitting on his lap where she had climbed up to kiss him good-bye, and he had promised to bring her something from Tucson. He didn't know why they had come to him all of a sudden. And after he had put them out of his mind, since there was no room now, there was an upset feeling inside as if he had swallowed something that would not go down all the way. It made his heart beat a little faster.

Jim Kidd was smiling up at him. "Anybody I know?"

"I didn't think it showed."

"Like the sun going down."

Scallen glanced at the man across the street and then to Jim Kidd.

"Come here." He nodded to the window. "Tell me who your friend is over there."

Kidd half rose and leaned over looking out the window, then sat down again. "Charlie Prince."

"Somebody else just went for help."

"Charlie doesn't need help."

"How did you know you were going to be in Contention?"

"You told that Wells Fargo man I had friends . . . and about the posses chasing around in the hills. Figure it out for yourself. You could be looking out a window in Benson and seeing the same thing."

"They're not going to do you any good."

"I don't know any man who'd get himself killed for a hundred and fifty dollars." Kidd paused. "Especially a man with a wife and young ones . . ."

Men rode to town in something less than an hour later. Scallen heard the horses coming up Commercial, and went to the window to see the six riders pull to a stop and range themselves in a line in the middle of the street facing the hotel. Charlie Prince stood behind them, leaning against the post.

Then he moved away from it, leisurely, and stepped down into the street. He walked between the horses and stopped in front of them just below the window. He cupped his hands to his mouth and shouted, *"Jim!"*

In the quiet street it was like a pistol shot.

Scallen looked at Kidd, seeing the smile that softened his face and was even in his eyes. Confidence. It was all over him. And even with the manacles on, you would believe that it was Jim Kidd who was holding the shotgun.

"What do you want me to tell him?" Kidd said.

"Tell him you'll write every day."

Kidd laughed and went to the window, pushing it up by the top of the frame. It raised a few inches. Then he moved his hands under the window and it slid up all the way.

"Charlie, you go buy the boys a drink. We'll be down shortly."

"Are you all right?"

"Sure I'm all right."

Charlie Prince hesitated. "What if you don't come down? He could kill you and say you tried to break . . . Jim, you tell him what'll happen if we hear a gun go off."

"He knows," Kidd said, and closed the window. He looked at Scallen standing motionless with the shotgun under his arm. "Your turn, Marshal."

"What do you expect me to say?"

"Something that makes sense. You said before I didn't mean a thing to you personally—what you're doing is just a job. Well, you figure out if it's worth getting killed for. All you have to do is throw your guns on the bed and let me walk out the door and you can go back to Bisbee and arrest all the drunks you want. Nobody's going to blame you with the odds stacked seven to one. You know your wife's not going to complain . . ."

"You should have been a lawyer, Jim."

The smile began to fade from Kidd's face. "Come on—what's it going to be?"

The door rattled with three knocks in quick succession. Abruptly the room was silent. The two men looked at each other and now the smile disappeared from Kidd's face completely.

Scallen moved to the side of the door, tip-toeing in his high-heeled boots, then pointed his shotgun toward the bed. Kidd sat down.

"Who is it?"

For a moment there was no answer. Then he heard, "Timpey."

He glanced at Kidd who was watching him. "What do you want?"

"I've got a pot of coffee for you."

Scallen hesitated. "You alone?"

"Of course I am. Hurry up, it's hot!"

He drew the key from his coat pocket, then held the shotgun in the crook of his arm as he inserted the key with one hand and turned the knob with the other. The door opened—and slammed against him, knocking him back against the dresser. He went off balance, sliding into the wardrobe, going down on his hands and knees, and the shotgun clattered across the floor to the window. He saw Jim Kidd drop to the floor for the gun . . .

"Hold it!"

A heavyset man stood in the doorway with a Colt pointing out past the thick bulge of his stomach. "Leave that shotgun where it is." Timpey stood next to him with the coffeepot in his hand. There was coffee down the front of his suit, on the door and on the flooring. He brushed at the front of his coat feebly, looking from Scallen to the man with the pistol.

"I couldn't help it, Marshal—he made me do it. He threatened to do something to me if I didn't."

"Who is he?"

"Bob Moons . . . you know, Dick's brother . . ."

The heavyset man glanced at Timpey angrily. "Shut your damn whining." His eyes went to Jim Kidd and held there. "You know who I am, don't you?"

Kidd looked uninterested. "You don't resemble anybody I know."

"You didn't have to know Dick to shoot him!"

"I didn't shoot that messenger."

Scallen got to his feet, looking at Timpey. "What the hell's wrong with you?"

"I couldn't help it. He forced me."

"How did he know we were here?"

"He came in this morning talking about Dick and I felt he needed some cheering up, so I told him Jim Kidd had been tried and was being taken to Yuma and was here in town . . . on his way. Bob didn't say anything and went out, and a little later he came back with the gun."

"You damn fool." Scallen shook his head wearily.

"Never mind all the talk." Moons kept the pistol on Kidd. "I would've found him sooner or later. This way, everybody gets saved a long train ride."

"You pull that trigger," Scallen said, "and you'll hang for murder."

"Like he did for killing Dick . . ."

"A jury said he didn't do it." Scallen took a step toward the big man. "And I'm damned if I'm going to let you pass another sentence."

"You stay put or I'll pass sentence on you!"

Scallen moved a slow step nearer. "Hand me the gun, Bob."

"I'm warning you—get the hell out of the way and let me do what I came for."

"Bob, hand me the gun or I swear I'll beat you through that wall."

Scallen tensed to take another step, another slow one. He saw Moons' eyes dart from him to Kidd and in that instant he knew it would be his only chance. He lunged, swinging his coat aside with his hand and when the hand came up it was holding a Colt. All in one motion. The pistol went up and chopped an arc across Moons' head before the big man could bring his own gun around. His hat flew off as the barrel swiped his skull and he went back against the wall heavily, then sank to the floor.

Scallen wheeled to face the window, thumbing the hammer back. But Kidd was still sitting on the edge of the bed with the shotgun at his feet.

The deputy relaxed, letting the hammer ease down. "You might have made it, that time."

Kidd shook his head. "I wouldn't have got off the bed." There was a note of surprise in his voice. "You know, you're pretty good . . ."

At two-fifteen Scallen looked at his watch, then stood up, pushing the chair back. The shotgun was under his arm. In less than an hour they would leave the hotel, walk over Commercial to Stockman and then up Stockman to the station. Three blocks. He wanted to go all the way. He wanted to get Jim Kidd on that train . . . but he was afraid.

He was afraid of what he might do once they were on the street. Even now his breath was short and occasionally he would inhale and let the air out slowly to calm himself. And he kept asking himself if it was worth it.

People would be in the windows and the doors though you wouldn't see them. They'd have their own feelings and most of their hearts would be pounding . . . and they'd edge back of the door frames a little more. The man out on the street was something without a human nature or a personality of its own. He was on a stage. The street was another world.

Timpey sat on the chair in front of the door and next to him, squatting on the floor with his back against the wall, was Moons. Scallen had unloaded Moons' pistol and placed it in the pitcher behind him. Kidd was on the bed.

Most of the time he stared at Scallen. His face bore a puzzled expression, making his eyes frown, and sometimes he would cock his head as if studying the deputy from a different angle.

Scallen stepped to the window now. Charlie Prince and another man were under the awning. The others were not in sight.

"You haven't changed your mind?" Kidd asked him seriously.

Scallen shook his head.

"I don't understand you. You risk your neck to save my life, now you'll risk it again to send me to prison."

Scallen looked at Kidd and suddenly felt closer to him than any man he knew. "Don't ask me, Jim," he said, and sat down again.

After that he looked at his watch every few minutes.

At five minutes to three he walked to the door, motioning Timpey aside, and turned the key in the lock. "Let's go, Jim." When Kidd was next to him he prodded Moons with the gun barrel. "Over on the bed.

Mister, if I see or hear about you on the street before train time, you'll face an attempted murder charge." He motioned Kidd past him, then stepped into the hall and locked the door.

They went down the stairs and crossed the lobby to the front door, Scallen a stride behind with the shotgun barrel almost touching Kidd's back. Passing through the doorway he said as calmly as he could, "Turn left on Stockman and keep walking. No matter what you hear, keep walking."

As they stepped out into Commercial, Scallen glanced at the ramada where Charlie Prince had been standing, but now the saloon porch was an empty shadow. Near the corner, two horses stood under a sign that said *Eat,* in red letters; and on the other side of Stockman the signs continued, lining the rutted main street to make it seem narrower. And beneath the signs, in the shadows, nothing moved. There was a whisper of wind along the ramadas. It whipped sand specks from the street and rattled them against clapboard, and the sound was hollow and lifeless. Somewhere a screen door banged, far away.

They passed the cafe, turning onto Stockman. Ahead, the deserted street narrowed with distance to a dead end at the rail station—a single-story building standing by itself, low and sprawling with most of the platform in shadow. The westbound was there, along the platform, but the engine and most of the cars were hidden by the station house. White steam lifted above the roof to be lost in the sun's glare.

They were almost to the platform when Kidd said over his shoulder, "Run like hell while you're still able."

"Where are they?"

Kidd grinned, because he knew Scallen was afraid. "How should I know?"

"Tell them to come out in the open!"

"Tell them yourself."

"Dammit, *tell* them!" Scallen clenched his jaw and jabbed the short barrel into Kidd's back. "I'm not fooling. If they don't come out, I'll kill you!"

Kidd felt the gun barrel hard against his spine and suddenly he shouted, "Charlie!"

It echoed in the street, but after there was only the silence. Kidd's eyes darted over the shadowed porches. "Dammit, Charlie—hold on!"

Scallen prodded him up the warped plank steps to the shade of the platform and suddenly he could feel them near. "Tell him again!"

"Don't shoot, Charlie!" Kidd screamed the words.

From the other side of the station they heard the trainman's call trailing off, ". . . Gila Bend, Sentinel, Yuma!"

The whistle sounded loud, wailing, as they passed into the shade of the platform, then out again to the naked glare of the open side. Scallen squinted, glancing toward the station office, but the train dispatcher was not in sight. Nor was anyone. "It's the mail car," he said to Kidd. "The second to last one." Steam hissed from the iron cylinder of the engine, clouding that end of the platform. "Hurry it up!" he snapped, pushing Kidd along.

Then, from behind, hurried footsteps sounded on the planking, and, as the hiss of steam died away—"Stand where you are!"

The locomotive's main rods strained back, rising like the legs of a grotesque grasshopper, and the wheels moved. The connecting rods stopped on an upward swing and couplings clanged down the line of cars.

"Throw the gun away, brother!"

Charlie Prince stood at the corner of the station house with a pistol in each hand. Then he moved around carefully between the two men and the train. "Throw it far away, and unhitch your belt," he said.

"Do what he says," Kidd said. "They've got you."

The others, six of them, were strung out in the dimness of the platform shed. Grim-faced, stubbles of beard, hat brims low. The man nearest Prince spat tobacco lazily.

Scallen knew fear at that moment as fear had never gripped him before; but he kept the shotgun hard against Kidd's spine. He said, just above a whisper, "Jim—I'll cut you in half!"

Kidd's body was stiff, his shoulders drawn up tightly. "Wait a minute . . ." he said. He held his palms out to Charlie Prince, though he could have been speaking to Scallen.

Suddenly Prince shouted, "Go down!"

There was a fraction of a moment of dead silence that seemed longer. Kidd hesitated. Scallen was looking at the gunman over Kidd's shoulder, seeing the two pistols. Then Kidd was gone, rolling on the planking, and the pistols were coming up, one ahead of the other. Without moving, Scallen squeezed both triggers of the scatter gun.

Charlie Prince was going down, holding his hands tight to his chest, as Scallen dropped the shotgun and swung around drawing his Colt. He fired hurriedly. *Wait for a target!* Words in his mind. He saw the men under the platform shed, three of them breaking for the station office, two going full length to the planks . . . one crouched, his pistol up. *That one! Get him quick!* Scallen aimed and squeezed the heavy revolver and the man went down. *Now get the hell out!*

Charlie Prince was face down. Kidd was crawling, crawling frantically and coming to his feet when Scallen reached him. He grabbed Kidd by the collar savagely, pushing him on and dug the pistol into his back. "Run, damn you!"

Gunfire erupted from the shed and thudded into the wooden caboose as they ran past it. The train was moving slowly. Just in front of them a bullet smashed a window of the mail car. Someone screamed, "You'll hit Jim!" There was another shot, then it was too late. Scallen and Kidd leaped up on the car platform and were in the mail car as it rumbled past the end of the station platform.

Kidd was on the floor, stretched out along a row of mail sacks. He rubbed his shoulder awkwardly with his manacled hands and watched Scallen who stood against the wall next to the open door.

Kidd studied the deputy for some minutes. Finally he said, "You know, you really earn your hundred and a half."

Scallen heard him, though the iron rhythm of the train wheels and his breathing were loud in his temples. He felt as if all his strength had been sapped, but he couldn't help smiling at Jim Kidd. He was thinking pretty much the same thing.

JONATHAN CRAIG
(1919-1984)

Jonathan Craig (Frank E. Smith) was a staple of Manhunt during its best and most influential years, the mid-1950s. He was variously described in the magazine's editorial column, "Mugged and Printed," as a "former night-club pianist," an "ex-trombonist," an "erstwhile bartender," a "carnival man," and a "sailor." The third edition of Lesley Henderson's Twentieth Century Crime and Mystery Writers (1991) presents a quite different and rather less rackety curriculum vitae, one that sits somewhat uneasily with his alleged Bohemian and freewheeling lifestyle. There Craig is said to have been "head research analyst for the U.S. navy, the Pentagon and the Joint Chiefs of Staff during World War II," a startlingly mature role for a man who was barely twenty-five years old at the time of the Normandy landings in 1944. Later he is reported to have been "adviser to President Truman at the Potsdam Conference, 1945."

Given that the editor of Manhunt was keen to have his authors be seen as leading colorful, even mildly gamey lives, it is difficult to ascertain the truth about Craig's history. But without a doubt, Craig clearly had more than enough experience of the hard end of life to become one of the leading chroniclers of the "JD" (juvenile delinquent), or "juvie," genre, which was so popular with editors and readers in the "rebel without a cause" era of the mid-1950s. He combined a gritty realism with a sardonic outlook and mastered a style that was spare while at times hinting at lushness and moral decay. In his early novels, especially So Young, So Wicked (1957), young women are depicted as sly and knowing, concupiscently old for their years, and all too aware of their own sexual power. Yet in their greed lies the seed of their inevitable downfall. A palpable undercurrent of misogyny can be found in many of Craig's stories, "The Bobby-Soxer" in particular. The theme was always power without responsibility, a hoary plot line that Craig hauled into the 1950s again and again, freshening it up each time.

Craig began his Sixth Precinct police-procedural series set in Manhattan with The Dead Darling in 1955, beating the first of Ed McBain's famous Eighty-seventh Precinct books, Cop Hater, by a year. But whereas McBain began his long-running saga in paperbacks before graduating to *prestigious hardcover houses, Craig worked on an altogether less epic scale, beginning and ending in paperback.*

J. A.

1953

THE BOBBY-SOXER

It was almost ten o'clock on a sultry August night when Donna Taylor turned the corner at Howard Street and started walking west toward Center Avenue. She was seventeen, but without make-up and dressed as she was now, in white blouse and plaid skirt and saddle shoes, she could have passed for a year or so younger than that.

She was a remarkably pretty girl, with slim tapering legs that were tanned to almost the same dark-gold color of the hair caught at the nape of her neck in a pony tail, but she seemed completely unaware of the appreciative glances following her.

She was humming to herself as she walked. Just before she reached the avenue, she paused to look at the display in a store window. A tall, middle-aged man in a pin-striped suit was looking at the display, too. When he saw Donna, he kept his face toward the window, but his eyes stayed on her. They were funny eyes, shifty and sort of wild.

She hesitated a moment, then moved around him, walking in the direction of the avenue again.

Just as she reached the mouth of the alley beside the store building, she heard a quick step behind her. A hand went over her mouth, and a man's arm whipped around her body in such a way that her arms were pinioned to her sides. She felt herself being lifted off her feet, and then she was being dragged into the blackness of the alley.

She struggled against him, but it was useless. The man carried her as easily as if she had been a doll.

When he had taken her a dozen yards into the alley, he stopped and forced her down to the pavement.

Terror sickened through her. And then she felt the man's sweaty palm across her mouth slip a half inch to one side, and she jerked her head violently in the other direction. For just an instant her mouth was uncovered, and she screamed. She knew, instinctively, that the man would be afraid after it was over and would try to kill her, and she screamed so loudly that her ears rang.

273

The man cursed and jumped to his feet, and his heels echoed hollowly on the pavement as he ran toward the mouth of the alley.

Then, out in the street, she heard the pounding of other feet, and men yelling, and she got up and steadied herself against the wall. Then she began to walk toward the mouth of the alley, very slowly, trying to catch her breath.

She came out on the street just as two shirt-sleeved men started into the alley.

"You all right?" one of the men asked.

She nodded. Across the street she caught sight of the man in the pin-striped suit. He was being held by three other men, one of whom had grabbed his hair and jerked his head back. He was trying to fight his way loose, but a man had hold of each of his arms, and they were standing slightly in back of him so that he couldn't kick at them.

One of the men in shirt-sleeves put his arm around Donna and led her over to the man who had attacked her. She looked at him, and then looked down at the sidewalk.

The other shirt-sleeved man said, "Exactly what happened, Miss—not that I can't guess."

Donna didn't look up. "He pulled me into the alley," she said. "He—tried to . . ." Her voice trailed off.

"For God's sake, Ed!" one of the men said. "Aren't you bright enough to know what happened, without making her talk about it?" He stepped close to the man in the pin-striped suit and hit him flush in the mouth. "You son of a bitch," he said softly.

Donna glanced about her. A crowd was forming now. She didn't know any of the men and women who were pressing in close. The man in shirt-sleeves still had his arm around her, gently and protectively, the way her father sometimes held her. She heard the newcomers asking questions, and the indignant, angry replies they made when they learned what had happened.

She looked at the man in the pin-striped suit again. There was blood at the corner of his mouth and his eyes were sick with fear.

A woman stepped up to him and shook her fist in his face. "You ought to hang!" she said. "A little girl like that! Why, she's hardly more than a baby!" She spat in the man's face.

"Anybody call the cops?" someone asked.

"Joe's just run back to his candy store to call," someone else said.

The man in the pin-striped suit made a sudden, violent lunge and broke free from the men who had been holding him. He stumbled and went to one knee, then righted himself and started to run. A foot went out to trip him, and he sprawled headlong on the cement. Before he could get up again, a man in a flowered sport shirt leaped upon him and pulled his arm up behind his back in a hammerlock.

Another man drew back his foot and kicked the fallen man in the ribs. The attacker screamed, but the foot sank into his ribs again and again.

The woman who had spit at him said, "That's the way, George! Kick him in the face!"

Donna turned away. She felt as if she might be sick at her stomach.

The man who had his arm around her said, "You poor little kid . . ." Then the man on the ground screamed again, and Donna heard the meaty impact of a shoe-toe meeting his face.

"Kick his damn head off, George!" the woman yelled.

"You better stop," someone said. "You'll kill him if you aren't careful."

A police siren keened on the heavy night air, rising and falling, coming fast.

The police cruiser turned the corner and squealed to a stop. The crowd moved back, and suddenly there was no sound other than the sobbing moans of the man on the sidewalk. He was lying on his back now, motionless, his face battered to a swollen, bleeding pulp. One wrist had been broken, and two inches of bone shard had pushed through the skin.

Fifteen minutes later, Donna sat on a wooden bench at the station house, talking to Sergeant Clinton. The police had taken her attacker to a hospital under guard.

"You sure you wouldn't rather we took you home in a squad car?" Clinton asked.

She shook her head. "My folks, they would . . ."

"All right, then," Clinton said gently. "But make sure you bring them right back here with you. We got to get your statement, and we got to have your folks here on account of you're a minor."

Donna turned and walked slowly out of the station house and along the street until she reached the corner. Then she quickened her pace, and another five minutes brought her to Center Avenue, the main drag along which she walked every evening, and for which she had been heading when she had paused to look in the store window. She was still shaken from her experience, but rapidly beginning to return to normal.

Half a block farther on, she stopped before another store window. And at this window too a man was looking at the display. He was about the same age and size as her attacker had been, but *he* looked all right, not funny and wild-eyed like the other one, This man, she knew, would be okay.

She glanced both ways along the avenue, and then she said softly, "You want to have a party, mister?"

The man looked at her, first with surprise and then with interest.

"What would it cost me?" he asked.

She smiled at him. "A fiver," she said.

DAVID GOODIS
(1917–1967)

In the mid-1940s, David Goodis seemed to be on the brink of monumental success. A busy, published writer since 1939, he was the author of a reasonably well received first novel, Retreat from Oblivion (1939). He had discovered the pulp magazines and found he had a knack for combat fiction, especially in the air-war genre. Throughout the war, he provided a host of colorfully titled novelettes ("Sky-Coffins for Nazis," "Doom for the Hawks of Nippon," "The High-Hat Squadron from Hell") for pulps such as Battle Birds, Air War, and Dare-Devil Aces. Under his own name as well as the pseudonyms Ray P. Shotwell and David Crewe, and the house name Lance Kermit, he contributed stories to such detective pulps as New Detective and Big-Book Detective. It is said that he also wrote torrentially, although pseudonymously, for the principal "shudder" pulps—Terror Tales, Horror Stories, and Dime Mystery—until their demise in 1941, although no one has yet cracked his pseudonyms for these markets. There is no doubt that he wrote radio scripts for Superman as well as Hop Harrigan: America's Ace of the Airways (for which he became associate producer in 1945).

Goodis's annus mirabilis was 1946. His novel Dark Passage (about an innocent man on the run) was sold to the Saturday Evening Post for $25,000, and the Warner Brothers film studio picked it up for the same, then-staggering sum. Humphrey Bogart and Lauren Bacall starred. A promotional photograph shows a grinning Bogart with his arm through Goodis's and Goodis's other arm around Bacall. At that time, this was a portrait of triumph and fame. A six-year contract with Warner Brothers followed, its first fruit being a Goodis co-script (with James Gunn) for The Unfaithful, which, along with Dark Passage, was a huge success. There followed three years of unsensational script tinkering before Warner's dropped him completely.

Goodis fled home to Philadelphia and sat in his room, day after day writing archetypical noir paperback originals about small and hopeless lives. His first paperback original, the bestselling Cassidy's Girl, was published in 1951. Both his writing and his life during the 1950s were obsessive to the point of madness. He wrote short, bleak sagas of lives lived at the edge of common decency, often tumbling over into a stew of al-

coholism, paranoia, debilitating poverty, and failure. His own lifestyle could also be described as seriously eccentric, and for the last fifteen years of his life, he lived as a virtual recluse with his parents in Philadelphia.

First published in Manhunt *in December 1953, Goodis's "Black Pudding" is a tale of violence, hatred, and revenge—with the unusual addition of a modicum of hope.*

J. A.

1 9 5 3

BLACK PUDDING

They spotted him on Race Street between Ninth and Tenth. It was Chinatown in the tenderloin of Philadelphia and he stood gazing into the window of the Wong Ho restaurant and wishing he had the cash to buy himself some egg-foo-yung. The menu in the window priced egg-foo-yung at eighty cents an order and he had exactly thirty-one cents in his pocket. He shrugged and started to turn away from the window and just then he heard them coming.

It was their footsteps that told him who they were. There was the squeaky sound of Oscar's brand-new shoes. And the clumping noise of Coley's heavy feet. It was nine years since he'd heard their footsteps but he remembered that Oscar had a weakness for new shoes and Coley always walked heavily.

He faced them. They were smiling at him, their features somewhat greenish under the green neon glow that drifted through after-midnight blackness. He saw the weasel eyes and buzzard nose of little Oscar. He transferred his gaze to the thick lips and puffed-out cheeks of tall, obese Coley.

"Hello, Ken." It was Oscar's purring voice, Oscar's lips scarcely moving.

"Hello," he said to both of them. He blinked a few times. Now the shock was coming. He could feel the waves of shock surging toward him.

"We been looking for you," Coley said. He flipped his thick thumb over his shoulder to indicate the black Olds 88 parked across the street. "We've driven that car clear across the country."

Ken blinked again. The shock had hit him and now it was past and he was blinking from worry. He knew why they'd been looking for him and he was very worried.

He said quietly, "How'd you know I was in Philly?"

"Grapevine," Oscar said. "It's strictly coast-to-coast. It starts from San Quentin and we get tipped-off in Los Angeles. It's a letter telling the Boss you been paroled. That's three weeks ago. Then we get letters from Denver and Omaha and a wire from Chicago. And then a phone call from Detroit. We wait to see how far east you'll travel. Finally we get the call from Philly, and the man tells us you're on the bum around Skid Row."

Ken shrugged. He tried to sound casual as he said, "Three thousand miles is a long trip. You must have been anxious to see me."

Oscar nodded. "Very anxious." He sort of floated closer to Ken. And Coley also moved in. It was slow and quiet and it didn't seem like menace but they were crowding him and finally they had him backed up against the restaurant window.

He said to himself, *They've got you, they've found you and they've got you and you're finished.*

He shrugged again. "You can't do it here."

"Can't we?" Oscar purred.

"It's a crowded street," Ken said. He turned his head to look at the lazy parade of tenderloin citizens on both sides of the street. He saw the bums and the beggars, the winos and the ginheads, the yellow faces of middle-aged opium smokers and the grey faces of two-bit scufflers and hustlers.

"Don't look at them," Oscar said. "They can't help you. Even if they could, they wouldn't."

Ken's smile was sad and resigned. "You're so right," he said. His shoulders drooped and his head went down and he saw Oscar reaching into a jacket pocket and taking out the silver-handled tool that had a button on it to release a five-inch blade. He knew there would be no further talk, only action, and it would happen within the next split-second.

In that tiny fraction of time, some gears clanged to shift from low to high in Ken's brain. His senses and reflexes, dulled from nine years in prison, were suddenly keen and acutely technical and there was no emotion on his face as he moved. He moved very fast, his arms crossing to shape an X, the left hand flat and rigid and banging against Oscar's wrist, the right hand a fist that caught Coley in the mouth. It sent the two of them staggering backward and gave him the space he wanted and he darted through the gap, sprinting east on Race Street toward Ninth.

As he turned the corner to head north on Ninth, he glanced backward and saw them getting into the Olds. He took a deep breath and continued running up Ninth. He ran straight ahead for approximately fifteen yards and then turned again to make a dash down a narrow alley. In the middle of the alley he hopped a fence, ran across a backyard, hopped another fence, then a few more backyards with more fence-hopping, and then the opened window of a tenement cellar. He lunged at the window, went in head-first, groped for a handhold, couldn't find any, and plunged through eight feet of blackness onto a pile of empty boxes and tin cans. He landed on his side, his thigh taking most of the impact, so that it didn't hurt too much. He rolled over and hit the floor and lay there flat on his belly. From a few feet away a pair of green eyes stared at him and he stared back, and then he grinned as though to say, *Don't be afraid, pussy, stay here and keep me company, it's a tough life and an evil world and us alleycats got to stick together.*

But the cat wasn't trusting any living soul. It let out a soft meow and scampered away. Ken sighed and his grin faded and he felt the pressure of the blackness and the quiet and the loneliness. His mind reached slowly for the road going backward nine years . . .

It was Los Angeles, and they were a small outfit operating from a first-floor apartment near Figueroa and Jefferson. Their business was armed robbery and their work-area included Beverly Hills and Bel-Air and the wealthy residential districts of Pasadena. They concentrated on expensive jewelry and wouldn't touch any job that offered less than a ten-grand haul.

There were five of them, Ken and Oscar and Coley and Ken's wife and the Boss. The name of the Boss was Riker and he was very kind to Ken until the face and body of Ken's wife became a need and then a craving and finally an obsession. It showed in Riker's eyes whenever he looked at her. She was a platinum blonde dazzler, a former burlesque dancer named Hilda. She'd been married to Ken for seven months when Riker reached the point where he couldn't stand it any longer and during a job in Bel-Air he banged Ken's skull with the butt end of a revolver. When the police arrived, Ken was unconscious on the floor and later in the hospital they asked him questions but he wouldn't answer. In the courtroom he sat with his head bandaged and they asked him more questions and he wouldn't answer. They gave him five-to-twenty and during his first month in San Quentin he learned from his lawyer that Hilda had obtained a Reno divorce and was married to Riker. He went more or less insane and couldn't be handled and they put him in solitary.

Later they had him in the infirmary, chained to the bed, and they tried some psychology. They told him he'd regain his emotional health if he'd talk and name some names. He laughed at them. Whenever they coaxed him to talk, he laughed in their faces and presently they'd shrug and walk away.

His first few years in Quentin were spent either in solitary or the infirmary, or under special guard. Then, gradually, he quieted down. He became very quiet and in the laundry-room he worked very hard and was extremely cooperative. During the fifth year he was up for parole and they asked him about the Bel-Air job and he replied quite reasonably that he couldn't remember, he was afraid to remember, he wanted to forget all about it and arrange a new life for himself. They told him he'd talk or he'd do the limit. He said he was sorry but he couldn't give them the information they wanted. He explained that he was trying to get straight with himself and be clean inside and he wouldn't feel clean if he earned his freedom that way.

So then it was nine years and they were convinced he'd finally paid his debt to the people of California. They gave him a suit of clothes and a ten-dollar bill and told him he was a free man.

In a Sacramento hash-house he worked as a dishwasher just long enough to earn the bus-fare for a trip across the country. He was thinking in terms of the town where he'd been born and raised, telling himself he'd made a wrong start in Philadelphia and the thing to do was go back there and start again and make it right this time, really legitimate. The parole board okayed the job he'd been promised. That was a healthy thought and it made the bus-trip very enjoyable. But the nicest thing about the bus was its fast engine that took him away from California, far away from certain faces he didn't want to see.

Yet now, as he rested on the floor of the tenement cellar, he could see the faces again. The faces were worried and frightened and he saw them in his brain and heard their trembling voices. He heard Riker saying, "They've released him from Quentin. We'll have to do something." And Hilda saying, "What can we do?" And Riker replying, "We'll get him before he gets us."

He sat up, colliding with an empty tin can that rolled across the floor and made a clatter. For some moments there was quiet and then he heard a shuffling sound and a voice saying, "Who's there?"

It was a female voice, sort of a cracked whisper. It had a touch of asthma in it, some alcohol, and something else that had no connection with health or happiness.

Ken didn't say anything. He hoped she'd go away. Maybe she'd figure it was a rat that had knocked over the tin can and she wouldn't bother to investigate.

But he heard the shuffling footsteps approaching through the blackness. He focused directly ahead and saw the silhouette coming toward him. She was on the slender side, neatly constructed. It was a very interesting silhouette. Her height was approximately five-five and he estimated her weight in the neighborhood of one-ten. He sat up straighter. He was very anxious to get a look at her face.

She came closer and there was the scratchy sound of a match against a matchbook. The match flared and he saw her face. She had medium-brown eyes that matched the color of her hair, and her nose and lips were nicely sculptured, somewhat delicate but blending prettily with the shape of her head. He told himself she was a very pretty girl. But just then he saw the scar.

It was a wide jagged scar that started high on her forehead and crawled down the side of her face and ended less than an inch above her upper lip. The color of it was a livid purple with lateral streaks of pink and white. It was a terrible scar, really hideous.

She saw that he was wincing, but it didn't seem to bother her. The lit match stayed lit and she was sizing him up. She saw a man of medium height and weight, about thirty-six years old, with yellow hair that needed cutting, a face that needed shaving, and sad lonely grey eyes that needed someone's smile.

She tried to smile for him. But only one side of her mouth could manage it. On the other side the scar was like a hook that pulled at her flesh and caused a grimace that was more anguish than physical pain. He told himself it was a damn shame. Such a pretty girl. And so young. She couldn't be more than twenty-five. Well, some people had all the luck. All the rotten luck.

The match was burned halfway down when she reached into the pocket of a tattered dress and took out a candle. She went through the process of lighting the candle and melting the base of it. The softened wax adhered to the cement floor of the cellar and she sat down facing him and said quietly, "All right, let's have it. What's the pitch?"

He pointed backward to the opened window to indicate the November night. He said, "It's chilly out there. I came in to get warm."

She leaned forward just a little to peer at his eyes. Then, shaking her head slowly, she murmured, "No sale."

He shrugged. He didn't say anything.

"Come on," she urged gently. "Let's try it again."

"All right." He grinned at her. And then it came out easily. "I'm hiding."

"From the Law?"

"No," he said. "From trouble."

He started to tell her about it. He couldn't understand why he was telling her. It didn't make sense that he should be spilling the story to someone he'd just met in a dark cellar, someone out of nowhere. But she was company and he needed company. He went on telling her.

It took more than an hour. He was providing all the details of events stretched across nine years. The candlelight showed her sitting there, not moving, her eyes riveted to his face as he spoke in low tones. Sometimes there were pauses, some of them long, some very long, but she never interrupted, she waited patiently while he groped for the words to make the meaning clear.

Finally he said, "—It's a cinch they won't stop, they'll get me sooner or later."

"If they find you," she said.

"They'll find me."

"Not here."

He stared at the flickering candle. "They'll spend money to get information. There's more than one big mouth in this neighborhood. And the biggest mouths of all belong to the landlords."

"There's no landlord here," she told him. "There's no tenants except me and you."

"Nobody upstairs?"

"Only mice and rats and roaches. It's a condemned house and City Hall calls it a firetrap and from the first floor up the windows are boarded. You can't get up because there's no stairs. One of these days the City'll tear down this dump but I'll worry about that when it happens."

He looked at her. "You live here in the cellar?"

She nodded. "It's a good place to play solitaire."

He smiled and murmured, "Some people like to be alone."

"I don't like it," she said. Then, with a shrug, she pointed to the scar on her face. "What man would live with me?"

He stopped smiling. He didn't say anything.

She said, "It's a long drop when you're tossed out of a third-story window. Most folks are lucky and they land on their feet or their fanny. I came down head first, cracked my collar-bone and got a fractured skull, and split my face wide open."

He took a closer look at the livid scar. For some moments he was quiet and then he frowned thoughtfully and said, "Maybe it won't be there for long. It's not as deep as I thought it was. If you had it treated—"

"No," she said. "The hell with it."

"You wouldn't need much cash," he urged quietly. "You could go to a clinic. They're doing fancy tricks with plastic surgery these days."

"Yeah, I know." Her voice was toneless. She wasn't looking at him. "The point is, I want the scar to stay there. It keeps me away from men. I've had too many problems with men and now, whenever they see my face, they turn their heads the other way. And that's fine with me. That's just how I want it."

He frowned again. This time it was a deeper frown and it wasn't just thoughtful. He said, "Who threw you out of the window?"

"My husband." She laughed without sound. "My wonderful husband."

"Where is he now?"

"In the cemetery," she said. She shrugged again, and her tone was matter-of-fact. "It happened while I was in the hospital. I think he got to the point where he couldn't stand to live with himself. Or maybe he just did it for kicks, I don't know. Anyway, he got hold of a meat-cleaver and chopped his own throat. When they found him, he damn near didn't have a head."

"Well, that's one way of ending a marriage."

Again she uttered the soundless laugh. "It was a fine marriage while it lasted. I was drunk most of the time. I had to get drunk to take what he dished out. He had some weird notions about wedding vows."

"He went with other women?"

"No," she said. "He made me go with other men."

For some moments it was quiet.

And then she went on, "We lived here in this neighborhood. It's a perfect neighborhood for that sort of deal. He had me out on the street looking for customers and bringing the money home to him, and when I came in with excuses instead of cash he'd throw me on the floor and kick me. I'd beg him to stop and he'd laugh and go on kicking me. Some nights I have bad dreams and he's kicking me. So then I need the sweet dreams, and that's when I reach for the pipe."

"The pipe?"

"Opium," she said. She said it with fondness and affection. "Opium." There was tenderness in her eyes. "That's my new husband."

He nodded understandingly.

She said, "I get it from a Chinaman on Ninth Street. He's a user himself and he's more than eighty years old and still in there pitching, so I guess with O it's like anything else, it's all a matter of how you use it." Her voice dropped off just a little and her eyes were dull and sort of dismal as she added, "I wish I didn't need so much of it. It takes most of my weekly salary."

"What kind of work you do?"

"I scrub floors," she said. "In night-clubs and dance-halls. All day long I scrub the floors to make them clean and shiny for the night-time customers. Some nights I sit here and think of the pretty girls dancing on them polished floors. The pretty girls with flowers in their hair and no scars on their faces—" She broke it off abruptly, her hand making a brushing gesture as though to disparage the self-pity. She stood up and said, "I gotta go out to do some shopping. You wanna wait here till I come back?"

Without waiting for his answer, she moved across the cellar toward a battered door leading to the backyard. As she opened the door, she turned and looked at him. "Make yourself comfortable," she said. "There's a mattress in the next room. It ain't the Ritz Carlton exactly, but it's better than nothing."

He was asking himself whether he should stay there.

He heard her saying, "Incidentally, my name is Tillie."

She stood there waiting.

"Kenneth," he said. "Kenneth Rockland."

But that wasn't what she was waiting for. Several moments passed, and then somehow he knew what she wanted him to say.

He said, "I'll be here when you come back."

"Good." The candlelight showed her crooked grin, a grimace on the scarred face. But what he saw was a gentle smile. It seemed to drift toward him like a soothing caress. And then he heard her saying, "Maybe I'll come back with some news. You told me it was two men. There's a chance I can check on them if you'll tell me what they look like."

He shook his head. "You better stay out of it. You might get hurt."

"Nothing can hurt me," she said. She pointed her finger at the wreckage of her face. Her tone was almost pleading as she said, "Come on, tell me what they look like."

He shrugged. He gave a brief description of Oscar and Coley. And the Olds 88.

"Check," Tillie said. "I don't have 20-20 but I'll keep them open and see what's happening."

She turned and walked out and the door closed. Ken lifted himself from the floor and picked up the candle. He walked across the cement floor and the candle showed him a small space off to one side, a former coal-bin arranged with a mattress against the wall, a splintered chair and a splintered bureau and a table stacked with books. There was a candle-holder on the table and he set the candle on it and then he had a look at the books.

It was an odd mixture of literature. There were books dealing with idyllic romance, strictly from fluttering hearts and soft moonlight and violins. And there were books that probed much deeper, explaining the scientific side of sex, with drawings and photos to show what it was all about. There was one book in particular that looked as though she'd been concentrating on it. The pages were considerably thumbed and she'd used a pencil to underline certain paragraphs. The title was *The Sex Problem of the Single Woman.*

He shook his head slowly. He thought, *It's a damn shame . . .*

And then, for some unaccountable reason, he thought of Hilda. She flowed into his mind with a rustling of silk that sheathed the exquisite contours of her slender torso and legs. Her platinum blonde hair was glimmering and her long-lashed green eyes were beckoning to say, Come on, take my hand and we'll go down Memory Lane.

He shut his eyes tightly. He wondered why he was thinking about her. A long time ago he'd managed to get her out of his mind and he couldn't understand what brought her back again. He begged himself to get rid of the thought, but now it was more than a thought, it was the white-hot memory of tasting that mouth and possessing that elegant body. Without sound he said, *Goddamn her.*

And suddenly he realized why he was thinking of Hilda. It was like

a curtain lifted to reveal the hidden channels of his brain. He was com-
paring Hilda's physical perfection with the scarred face of Tillie. His eyes
were open and he gazed down at the mattress on the floor and for a
moment he saw Hilda naked on the mattress. She smiled teasingly and
then she shook her head and said, *Nothing doing.* So then she vanished
and in the next moment it was Tillie on the mattress but somehow he
didn't feel bitter or disappointed; he had the feeling that the perfection
was all on Tillie's side.

He took off his shoes and lowered himself to the mattress. He yawned
a few times and then he fell asleep.

A voice said, "Kenneth—"

He was instantly awake. He looked up and saw Tillie. He smiled at
her and said, "What time is it?"

"Half-past five." She had a paper bag in her hand and she was taking
things out of the bag and putting them on the table. There was some
dried fish and a package of tea leaves and some cold fried noodles. She
reached deeper into the bag and took out a bottle containing colorless
liquid.

"Rice wine," she said. She set the bottle on the table. Then again she
reached into the bag and her hand came out holding a cardboard box.

"Opium?" he murmured.

She nodded. "I got some cigarettes, too." She took a pack of Luckies
from her pocket, opened the pack and extended it to him.

He sat up and put a cigarette in his mouth and used the candle to
light it. He said, "You going to smoke the opium?"

"No, I'll smoke what you're smoking."

He put another cigarette in his mouth and lit it and handed it to her.

She took a few drags and then she said quietly, "I didn't want to wake
you up, but I thought you'd want to hear the news."

He blinked a few times. "What news?"

"I saw them," she said.

He blinked again. "Where?"

"On Tenth Street." She took more smoke into her mouth and let it
come out of her nose. "It was a couple hours ago, after I come out of the
Chinaman's."

He sat up straighter. "You been watching them for two hours?"

"Watching them? I been with them. They took me for a ride."

He stared at her. His mouth was open but no sound came out.

Tillie grinned. "They didn't know I was in the car."

He took a deep breath. "How'd you manage it?"

She shrugged. "It was easy. I saw them sitting in the car and then they got out and I followed them. They were taking a stroll around the block and peeping into alleys and finally I heard the little one saying they might as well powder and come back tomorrow. The big one said they should keep on searching the neighborhood. They got into an argument and I had a feeling the little one would win. So I walked back to the car. The door was open and I climbed in the back and got flat on the floor. About five minutes later they're up front and the car starts and we're riding."

His eyes were narrow. "Where?"

"Downtown," she said. "It wasn't much of a ride. It only took a few minutes. They parked in front of a house on Spruce near Eleventh. I watched them go in. Then I got out of the car—"

"And walked back here?"

"Not right away," she said. "First I cased the house."

Silly Tillie, he thought. *If they'd seen her they'd have dragged her in and killed her.*

She said, "It's one of them little old-fashioned houses. There's a vacant lot on one side and on the other side there's an alley. I went down the alley and came up on the back porch and peeped through the window. They were in the kitchen, the four of them."

He made no sound, but his lips shaped the word. "Four?" And then, with sound, "Who were the other two?"

"A man and a woman."

He stiffened. He tried to get up from the mattress and couldn't move. His eyes aimed past Tillie as he said tightly, "Describe them."

"The man was about five-ten and sort of beefy. I figure about two hundred. He looked about forty or so. Had a suntan and wore expensive clothes. Brown wavy hair and brown eyes and—"

"That's Riker," he murmured. He managed to lift himself from the mattress. His voice was a whisper as he said, "Now let's have the woman."

"She was something," Tillie said. "She was really something."

"Blonde?" And with both hands he made a gesture begging Tillie to speed the reply.

"Platinum blonde," Tillie said. "With the kind of a face that makes men sweat in the wintertime. That kind of a face, and a shape that goes along with it. She was wearing—"

"Pearls," he said. "She always had a weakness for pearls."

Tillie didn't say anything.

He moved past Tillie. He stood facing the dark wall of the cellar and seeing the yellow-black play of candlelight and shadow on the cracked plaster. "Hilda," he said. "Hilda."

It was quiet for some moments. He told himself it was wintertime and he wondered if he was sweating.

Then very slowly he turned and looked at Tillie. She was sitting on the edge of the mattress and drinking from the bottle of rice-wine. She took it in short, measured gulps, taking it down slowly to get the full effect of it. When the bottle was half-empty she raised her head and grinned at him and said, "Have some?"

He nodded. She handed him the bottle and he drank. The Chinese wine was mostly fire and it burned all the way going down and when it hit his belly it was electric-hot. But the climate it sent to his brain was cool and mild and the mildness showed in his eyes. His voice was quiet and relaxed as he said, "I thought Oscar and Coley made the trip alone. It didn't figure that Riker and Hilda would come with them. But now it adds. I can see the way it adds."

"It's a long ride from Los Angeles," Tillie said.

"They didn't mind. They enjoyed the ride."

"The scenery?"

"No," he said. "They weren't looking at the scenery. They were thinking of the setup here in Philly. With Oscar putting the blade in me and then the funeral and Riker seeing me in the coffin and telling himself his worries were over."

"And Hilda?"

"The same," he said. "She's been worried just as much as Riker. Maybe more."

Tillie nodded slowly. "From the story you told me, she's got more reason to worry."

He laughed lightly. He liked the sound of it and went on with it. He said, through the easy laughter, "They really don't need to worry. They're making it a big thing and it's nothing at all. I forgot all about them a long time ago. But they couldn't forget about me."

Tillie had her head inclined and she seemed to be studying the sound of his laughter. Some moments passed and then she said quietly, "You don't like black pudding?"

He didn't get the drift of that. He stopped laughing and his eyes were asking what she meant.

"There's an old saying," she said. "Revenge is black pudding."

He laughed again.

"Don't pull away from it," Tillie said. "Just listen to it. Let it hit you and sink in. Revenge is black pudding."

He went on laughing, shaking his head and saying, "I'm not in the market."

"You sure?"

"Positive," he said. Then, with a grin, "Only pudding I like is vanilla."

"The black tastes better," Tillie said. "I've had some, and I know. I had it when they told me what he did to himself with the meat-cleaver."

He winced slightly. He saw Tillie getting up from the mattress and moving toward him. He heard her saying, "That black pudding has a wonderful flavor. You ought to try a spoonful."

"No," he said. "No, Tillie."

She came closer. She spoke very slowly and there was a slight hissing in her voice. "They put you in prison for nine years. They cheated you and robbed you and tortured you."

"That's all past," he said. "That's from yesterday."

"It's from now." She stood very close to him. "They're itching to hit you again and see you dead. They won't stop until you're dead. That puts a poison label on them. And there's only one way to deal with poison. Get rid of it."

"No," he said. "I'll let it stay the way it is."

"You can't," Tillie said. "It's a choice you have to make. Either you'll drink bitter poison or you'll taste that sweet black pudding."

He grinned again. "There's a third choice."

"Like what?"

"This." And he pointed to the bottle of rice-wine. "I like the taste of this. Let's stay with it until it's empty."

"That won't solve the problem," Tillie said.

"The hell with the problem." His grin was wide. It was very wide and he didn't realize that it was forced.

"You fool," Tillie said.

He had the bottle raised and he was taking a drink.

"You poor fool," she said. Then she shrugged and turned away from him and lowered herself to the mattress.

The forced grin stayed on his face as he went on drinking. Now he was drinking slowly because the rice-wine dulled the action in his brain and he had difficulty lifting the bottle to his mouth. Gradually he became aware of a change taking place in the air of the cellar; it was thicker, sort of smoky. His eyes tried to focus and there was too much wine in him and he couldn't see straight. But then the smoke came up in front of his eyes and into his eyes. He looked down and saw the white clay pipe in Tillie's hand. She was sitting on the mattress with her legs crossed, Buddha-like, puffing at the opium, taking it in very slowly, the smoke coming out past the corners of her lips.

The grin faded from his face. And somehow the alcohol-mist was drifting away from his brain. He thought, *She smokes it because she's been kicked around.* But there was no pity in his eyes, just the level look of clear thinking. He said to himself, *There's only two kinds of people in this world, the ones who get kicked around and the ones who do the kicking.*

He lowered the bottle to the table. He turned and took a few steps going away and then heard Tillie saying, "Moving out?"

"No," he said. "Just taking a walk."

"Where?"

"Spruce Street," he said.

"Good," she said. "I'll go with you."

He shook his head. He faced her and saw that she'd put the pipe aside. She was getting up from the mattress. He went on shaking his head and saying, "It can't be played that way. I gotta do this alone."

She moved toward him. "Maybe it's good-bye."

"If it is," he said, "there's only one way to say it."

His eyes told her to come closer. He put his arms around her and held her with a tenderness and a feeling of not wanting to let her go. He kissed her. He knew she felt the meaning of the kiss, she was returning it and as her breath went into him it was sweet and pure and somehow like nectar.

Then, very gently, she pulled away from him. She said, "Go now. It's still dark outside. It'll be another hour before the sun comes up."

He grinned. It was a soft grin that wasn't forced. "This job won't take more than an hour," he said. "Whichever way it goes, it'll be a matter of minutes. Either I'll get them or they'll get me."

He turned away and walked across the cellar toward the splintered door. Tillie stood there watching him as he opened the door and went out.

It was less than three minutes later and they had him. He was walking south on Ninth, between Race Street and Arch, and the black Olds 88 was cruising on Arch and he didn't see them but they saw him, with Oscar grinning at Coley and saying, "There's our boy."

Oscar drove the car past the intersection and parked it on the north side of Arch about twenty feet away from the corner. They got out and walked toward the corner and stayed close to the brick wall of the corner building. They listened to the approaching footsteps and grinned at each other and a few moments later he arrived on the corner and they grabbed him.

He felt Coley's thick arm wrapped tight around his throat, pulling his head back. He saw the glimmer of the five-inch blade in Oscar's hand. He told himself to think fast and he thought very fast and managed to say, "You'll be the losers. I made a connection."

Oscar hesitated. He blinked puzzledly. "What connection?"

He smiled at Oscar. Then he waited for Coley to loosen the armhold on his throat. Coley loosened it, then lowered it to his chest, using both arms to clamp him and prevent him from moving.

He made no attempt to move. He went on smiling at Oscar, and saying, "An important connection. It's important enough to louse you up."

"Prove it," Oscar said.

"You're traced." He narrowed the smile just a little. "If anything happens to me, they know where to get you."

"He's faking," Coley said. Then urgently, "Go on, Oscar, give him the knife."

"Not yet," Oscar murmured. He was studying Ken's eyes and his own eyes were somewhat worried. He said to Ken, "Who did the tracing?"

"I'll tell that to Riker."

Oscar laughed without sound. "Riker's in Los Angeles."

"No he isn't," Ken said. "He's here in Philly."

Oscar stopped laughing. The worry deepened in his eyes. He stared past Ken, focusing on Coley.

"He's here with Hilda," Ken said.

"It's just a guess," Coley said. "It's gotta be a guess." He tightened his bear-hug on Ken. "Do it, Oscar. Don't let him stall you. Put the knife in him."

Oscar looked at Ken and said, "You making this a quiz game?"

Ken shrugged. "It's more like stud poker."

"Maybe," Oscar admitted. "But you're not the dealer."

Ken shrugged again. He didn't say anything.

Oscar said, "You're not the dealer and all you can do is hope for the right card."

"I got it already," Ken said. "It fills an inside straight."

Oscar bit the edge of his lip. "All right, I'll take a look." He had the knife aiming at Ken's chest, and then he lowered it and moved in closer and the tip of the blade was touching Ken's belly. "Let's see your hole-card, sonny. All you gotta do is name the street and the house."

"Spruce Street," Ken said. "Near Eleventh."

Oscar's face became pale. Again he was staring at Coley.

Ken said, "It's an old house, detached. On one side there's a vacant lot and on the other side there's an alley."

It was quiet for some moments and then Oscar was talking aloud to himself, saying, "He knows, he really knows."

"What's the move?" Coley asked. He sounded somewhat unhappy.

"We gotta think," Oscar said. "This makes it complicated and we gotta think it through very careful."

Coley muttered a four-letter word. He said, "We ain't getting paid to do our own thinking. Riker gave us orders to find him and bump him."

"We can't bump him now," Oscar said. "Not under these conditions. The way it stacks up, it's Riker's play. We'll have to take him to Riker."

"Riker won't like that," Coley said.

Oscar didn't reply. Again he was biting his lip and it went on that way for some moments and then he made a gesture toward the parked car. He told Coley to take the wheel and said he'd sit in the back with Rockland. As he opened the rear door he had the blade touching Ken's side, gently urging Ken to get in first. Coley was up front behind the wheel and then Oscar and Ken occupied the rear seat and the knife in Oscar's hand was aimed at Ken's abdomen.

The engine started and the Olds 88 moved east on Arch and went past Eighth and turned south on Seventh. There was no talk in the car as they passed Market and Chestnut and Walnut. They had a red light on Locust but Coley ignored it and went through at forty-five.

"Slow down," Oscar said.

Coley was hunched low over the wheel and the speedometer went up to fifty and Oscar yelled, "For Christ's sake, slow down. You wanna be stopped by a red car?"

"There's one now," Ken said, and he pointed toward the side window that showed only the front of a grocery store. But Oscar thought it might really be a side-street with a police car approaching, and the thought was in his brain for a tiny fraction of a second. In that segment of time he turned his head to have a look. Ken's hand moved automatically to grab Oscar's wrist and twist hard. The knife fell away from Oscar's fingers and Ken's other hand caught it. Oscar let out a screech and Ken put the knife in Oscar's throat and had it in there deep just under the ear, pulled it out and put it in again. The car was skidding to a stop as Ken stabbed Oscar a third time to finish him. Coley was screaming curses and trying to hurl himself sideways and backward toward the rear seat and Ken showed him the knife and it didn't stop him. Ken ducked as Coley came vaulting over the top of the front seat, the knife slashing upward to catch Coley in the belly, slashing sideways to rip from navel to kidney, then across again to the other kidney, then up to the ribs to hit bone with Coley gurgling and trying to sob, doubled over with his knees on the floor and his chin on the edge of the back seat, his arms flung over the sprawled corpse of Oscar.

"I'm dying," Coley gurgled. "I'm—" That was his final sound. His eyes opened very wide and his head snapped sideways and he was through for this night and all nights.

Ken opened the rear door and got out. He had the knife in his pocket as he walked with medium-fast stride going south on Seventh to Spruce. Then he turned west on Spruce and walked just a bit faster. Every now and then he glanced backward to see if there were any red cars but all he saw was the empty street and some alley cats mooching around under the street lamps.

In the blackness above the rooftops the bright yellow face of the City Hall clock showed ten minutes past six. He estimated the sky would be dark for another half-hour. It wasn't much time, but it was time enough for what he intended to do. He told himself he wouldn't enjoy the action, and yet somehow his mouth was watering, almost like anticipating a tasty dish. Something on the order of pudding, and the color of it was black.

He quickened his pace just a little, crossed Eighth Street and Ninth,

and walked faster as he passed Tenth. There were no lit windows on
Spruce Street but as he neared Eleventh the moonlight blended with the
glow of a street lamp and showed him the vacant lot. He gazed across
the empty space to the wall of the old-fashioned house.

Then he was on the vacant lot and moving slowly and quietly toward
the rear of the house. He worked his way to the sagging steps of the back
porch, saw a light in the kitchen window, climbed two steps and three
and four and then he was on the porch and peering through the window
and seeing Hilda.

She was alone in the kitchen, sitting at a white-topped table and
smoking a cigarette. There was a cup and saucer on the table, the saucer
littered with coffee-stained cigarette butts. As he watched, she got up
from the table and went to the stove to lift a percolator off the fire and
pour another cup of coffee.

She moved with a slow weaving of her shoulders and a flow of her
hips that was more drifting than walking. He thought, *She still has it,
that certain way of moving around, using that body like a long-
stemmed lily in a quiet breeze. That's what got you the first time you
laid eyes on her. The way she moves. And one time very long ago you
said to her, "To set me on fire, all you have to do is walk across a
room." You couldn't believe you were actually married to that hot-
house-prize, that platinum blonde hair like melted eighteen-karat, that
face, she still has it, that body, she still has it. It's been nine years, and
she still has it.*

She was wearing bottle-green velvet that set off the pale green of her
eyes. The dress was cut low, went in tight around her very narrow waist
and stayed tight going down all the way past her knees. She featured
pearls around her throat and in her ears and on her wrists. He thought,
*You gave her pearls for her birthday and Christmas and you wanted to
give her more for the first wedding anniversary. But they don't sell pearls
in San Quentin. All they sell is plans for getting out. Like lessons in how
to crawl through a pipe, or how to conceal certain tools, or how to disguise the voice. The lessons never paid off, but maybe now's the time to
use what you learned. Let's try Coley's voice.*

His knuckles rapped the kitchen door, and his mouth opened to let
out Coley's thick, low-pitched voice saying, "It's me and Oscar."

He stood there counting off the seconds. It was four seconds and then
the door opened. It opened wide and Hilda's mouth opened wider. Then
she had her hand to her mouth and she was stepping backward.

"Hello, Hilda." He came into the kitchen and closed the door behind him.

She took another backward step. She shook her head and spoke through the trembling fingers that pressed against her lips. "It isn't—"

"Yes," he said. "It is."

Her hand fell away from her mouth. The moment was too much for her and it seemed she was going to collapse. But somehow she managed to stay on her feet. Then her eyes were shut tightly and she went on shaking her head.

"Look at me," he said. "Take a good look."

She opened her eyes. She looked him up and down and up again. Then, very slowly, she summoned air into her lungs and he knew she was going to let out a scream. His hand moved fast to his coat pocket and he took out Oscar's knife and said quietly, "No noise, Hilda."

She stared at the knife. The air went out of her without sound. Her arms were limp at her sides. She spoke in a half-whisper, talking to herself. "I don't believe it. Just can't believe it—"

"Why not?" His tone was mild. "It figures, doesn't it? You came to Philly to look for me. And here I am."

For some moments she stayed limp. Then, gradually, her shoulders straightened. She seemed to be getting a grip on herself. Her eyes narrowed just a little, as she went on looking at the silver-handled switchblade in his hand. She said, "That's Oscar's knife—?"

He nodded.

"Where is Oscar?" she asked. "Where's Coley?"

"They're dead." He pressed the button on the handle and the blade flicked out. It glimmered red with Oscar's blood and Coley's blood. He said, "It's a damn shame. They wouldn't be dead if they'd let me alone."

Hilda didn't say anything. She gave a little shrug, as though to indicate there was nothing she could say. He told himself it didn't make sense to wait any longer and the thing to do was put the knife in her heart. He wondered if the knife was sharp enough to cut through ice.

He took a forward step, then stopped. He wondered what was holding him back. Maybe he was waiting for her to break, to fall on her knees and beg for mercy.

But she didn't kneel and she didn't plead. Her voice was matter-of-fact as she said, "I'm wondering if we can make a deal."

It caught him off balance. He frowned slightly. "What kind of deal?"

"Fair trade," she said. "You give me a break and I'll give you Riker."

He changed the frown to a dim smile. "I've got him anyway. It's a cinch he's upstairs sound asleep."

"That's fifty percent right," she said. "He's a very light sleeper. Especially lately, since he heard you were out of Quentin."

He widened the smile. "In Quentin I learned to walk on tip-toe. There won't be any noise."

"There's always noise when you break down a door."

The frown came back. "You playing it shrewd?"

"I'm playing it straight," she said. "He keeps the door locked. Another thing he keeps is a .38 under his pillow."

He slanted his head just a little. "You expect me to buy that?"

"You don't have to buy it. I'm giving it to you."

He began to see what she was getting at. He said, "All right, thanks for the freebee. Now tell me what you're selling."

"A key," she said. "The key to his room. He has one and I have one. I'll sell you mine at bargain rates. All I want is your promise."

He didn't say anything.

She shrugged and said, "It's a gamble on both sides. I'll take a chance that you'll keep your word and let me stay alive. You'll be betting even-money that I'm telling the truth."

He smiled again. He saw she was looking past him, at the kitchen door. He said, "So the deal is, you give me the key to his room and I let you walk out that door."

"That's it." She was gazing hungrily at the door. Her lips scarcely moved as she murmured, "Fair enough?"

"No," he said. "It needs a tighter contract."

Her face was expressionless. She held her breath.

He let her hold it for awhile, and then he said, "Let's do it so there's no gamble. You get the key and I'll follow you upstairs. I'll be right in back of you when you walk into the room. I'll have the blade touching your spine."

She blinked a few times.

"Well?" he said.

She reached into a flap of the bottle-green velvet and took out a door-key. Then she turned slowly and started out of the kitchen. He moved in close behind her and followed the platinum blonde hair and elegant torso going through the small dining-room and the parlor and toward the dimly lit stairway. He came up at her side as they climbed the stairs, the knife-blade scarcely an inch away from the shimmering velvet that covered her ribs.

They reached the top of the stairs and she pointed to the door of the front bedroom. He let the blade touch the velvet and his voice was a whisper saying, "Slow and quiet. Very quiet."

Then again he moved behind her. They walked slowly toward the bedroom door. The blade kissed the velvet and it told her to use the key with a minimum of sound. She put the key in the lock and there was no sound as she turned the key. There was only a slight clicking sound as the lock opened. Then no sound while she opened the door.

They entered the room and he saw Riker in the bed. He saw the brown wavy hair and there was some grey in it along the temples. In the sun-tanned face there were wrinkles and lines of dissipation and other lines that told of too much worry. Riker's eyes were shut tightly and it was the kind of slumber that rests the limbs but not the brain.

Ken thought, *He's aged a lot in nine years; it used to be mostly muscle and now it's mostly fat.*

Riker was curled up, his knees close to his paunch. He had his shoes off but otherwise he was fully dressed. He wore a silk shirt and a hand-painted necktie, his jacket was dark grey cashmere and his slacks were pale grey high-grade flannel. He had on a pair of argyle socks that must have set him back at least twenty dollars. On the wrist of his left hand there was a platinum watch to match the large star-emerald he wore on his little finger. On the third finger of his left hand he had a three-karat diamond. Ken was looking at the expensive clothes and the jewelry and thinking, *He travels first-class, he really rides the gravy train.*

It was a bitter thought and it bit deeper into Ken's brain. He said to himself, *Nine years ago this man of distinction pistol-whipped your skull and left you for dead. You've had nine years in Quentin and he's had the sunshine, the peaches-and-cream, the thousands of nights with the extra-lovely Mrs. Riker while you slept alone in a cell—*

He looked at the extra-lovely Mrs. Riker. She stood motionless at the side of the bed and he stood beside her with the switchblade aiming at her velvet-sheathed flesh. She was looking at the blade and waiting for him to aim it at Riker, to put it in the sleeping man and send it in deep.

But that wasn't the play. He smiled dimly to let her know he had something else in mind.

Riker's left hand dangled over the side of the bed and his right hand rested on the pillow. Ken kept the knife aimed at Hilda as he reached toward the pillow and then under the pillow. His fingers touched metal. It was the barrel of a revolver and he got a two-finger hold on it and eased it out from under the pillow. The butt came into his palm and his middle finger went through the trigger-guard and nestled against the back of the guard, not touching the trigger.

He closed the switchblade and put it in his pocket. He stepped back and away from the bed and said, "Now you can wake up your husband."

She was staring at the muzzle of the .38. It wasn't aiming at anything in particular.

"Wake him up," Ken murmured. "I want him to see his gun in my hand. I want him to know how I got it."

Hilda gasped and it became a sob and then a wail and it was a hook of sound that awakened Riker. At first he was looking at Hilda. Then he saw Ken and he sat up very slowly, as though he was something made of stone and ropes were pulling him up. His eyes were riveted to Ken's face and he hadn't yet noticed the .38. His hand crept down along the side of the pillow and then under the pillow.

There was no noise in the room as Riker's hand groped for the gun. Some moments passed and then there was sweat on Riker's forehead and under his lip and he went on searching for the gun and suddenly he seemed to realize it wasn't there. He focused on the weapon in Ken's hand and his body began to quiver. His lips scarcely moved as he said, "The gun—the gun—"

"It's yours," Ken said. "Mind if I borrow it?"

Riker went on staring at the revolver. Then very slowly his head turned and he was staring at Hilda. "You," he said. "You gave it to him."

"Not exactly," Ken said. "All she did was tell me where it was."

Riker shut his eyes very tightly, as though he was tied to a rack and it was pulling him apart.

Hilda's face was expressionless. She was looking at Ken and saying, "You promised to let me walk out—"

"I'm not stopping you," he said. Then, with a shrug and a dim smile, "I'm not stopping anyone from doing what they want to do." And he slipped the gun into his pocket.

Hilda started for the door. Riker was up from the bed and lunging at her, grabbing her wrist and hurling her across the room. Then Riker lunged again and his hands reached for her throat as she tried to get up from the floor. Hilda began to make gurgling sounds but the noise was drowned in the torrent of insane screaming that came from Riker's lips. Riker choked her until she died. When Riker realized she was dead his screaming became louder and he went on choking her.

Ken stood there, watching it happen. He saw the corpse flapping like a rag-doll in the clutching hands of the screaming madman. He thought, *Well, they wanted each other, and now they got each other.*

He walked out of the room and down the hall and down the stairs. As he went out of the house he could still hear the screaming. On Spruce, walking toward Eleventh, he glanced back and saw a crowd gathering outside the house and then he heard the sound of approaching sirens. He waited there and saw the police-cars stopping in front of the house, the policemen rushing in with drawn guns. Some moments later he heard the shots and he knew that the screaming man was trying to make a getaway. There was more shooting and suddenly there was no sound at all. He knew they'd be carrying two corpses out of the house.

He turned away from what was happening back there, walked along the curb toward the sewer-hole on the corner, took Riker's gun from his pocket and threw it into the sewer. In the instant that he did it, there was a warm sweet taste in his mouth. He smiled, knowing what it was. Again he could hear Tillie saying, "Revenge is black pudding."

Tillie, he thought. And the smile stayed on his face as he walked north on Eleventh. He was remembering the feeling he'd had when he'd kissed her. It was the feeling of wanting to take her out of that dark cellar, away from the loneliness and the opium. To carry her upward toward the world where they had such things as clinics, with plastic specialists who repaired scarred faces.

The feeling hit him again and he was anxious to be with Tillie and he walked faster.

ROSS MACDONALD
(1915–1983)

Ross Macdonald (Kenneth Millar) has been widely acclaimed as the most important successor to the tradition epitomized by the work of Dashiell Hammett and Raymond Chandler, as well as the writer who elevated the hard-boiled private-eye novel to a "literary" art form (although it can be argued that Hammett and Chandler had in their own ways already done so.) In Macdonald's case, the claim is based partly on the fact that his fiction sparkles with simile and metaphor; his descriptions of California, his adopted state, are poetic and bring its places and people vividly alive. In fact, however, it is the addition of deep psychological characterization and complex thematic content that is Macdonald's primary contribution both to the hard-boiled genre and to the noir detective story.

Lew Archer, the narrator of most of Macdonald's fiction, is more an observer than a fully fleshed-out human being. Indeed, it was the author's stated intent that Archer be a camera recording events and the people involved in those events. This is both a strength and a weakness of the series, for Archer comes alive for the reader only in terms of his professional life. As he himself states in The Instant Enemy (1968): "I had to admit that I lived for nights like these, moving across the city's great broken body, making connections among its millions of cells. I had a crazy wish or fantasy that some day before I died, if I made all the right neural connections, the city would come all the way alive." The reader often has a similar wish or fantasy where Archer is concerned.

Some aficionados feel that the best Archer novels were written between 1949 and 1958, particularly those that appeared under the name John Ross Macdonald. (The "John" was dropped when John D. MacDonald complained that the similarity to his name confused readers.) These early works include The Moving Target (1949), The Way Some People Die (1951), and The Ivory Grin (1952). Others prefer such middle-period titles as The Galton Case (1959), The Chill (1964), and Black Money (1966), which have denser plots and larger themes. This middle group is also more consciously (sometimes self-consciously) literary than the early novels and is less deeply rooted in the hard-boiled tradition.

The few Archer short stories sparkle almost as brilliantly as the full-

length works; the best, in fact, are miniature novels honed to the sharpest essentials of plot, character, and incident. Seven were published between 1946 and 1954 in Ellery Queen's Mystery Magazine, Manhunt, *and* American Magazine, *and were then collected in* The Name Is Archer *(1955). Two additional stories were written and published in the 1960s, and in 1977 all nine were collected under the title* Lew Archer, Private Investigator. *"Guilt-Edged Blonde" originally appeared in* Manhunt *in January 1954. Despite the author's claim that the first seven Archer stories were written to "show my debt to other writers, especially Hammett and Chandler, and in fact did not aim at any striking originality," all are first-rate, and "Guilt-Edged Blonde" is original enough to satisfy any discerning reader.*

B. P.

1 9 5 4

GUILT-EDGED BLONDE

A man was waiting for me at the gate at the edge of the runway. He didn't look like the man I expected to meet. He wore a stained tan windbreaker, baggy slacks, a hat as squashed and dubious as his face. He must have been forty years old, to judge by the grey in his hair and the lines around his eyes. His eyes were dark and evasive, moving here and there as if to avoid getting hurt. He had been hurt often and badly, I guessed.

"You Archer?"

I said I was. I offered him my hand. He didn't know what to do with it. He regarded it suspiciously, as if I was planning to try a judo hold on him. He kept his hands in the pockets of his windbreaker.

"I'm Harry Nemo." His voice was a grudging whine. It cost him an effort to give his name away. "My brother told me to come and pick you up. You ready to go?"

"As soon as I get my luggage."

I collected my overnight bag at the counter in the empty waiting room. The bag was very heavy for its size. It contained, besides a toothbrush and spare linen, two guns and the ammunition for them. A .38 special for sudden work, and a .32 automatic as a spare.

Harry Nemo took me outside to his car. It was a new seven-passenger custom job, as long and black as death. The windshield and side windows were very thick, and they had the yellowish tinge of bulletproof glass.

"Are you expecting to be shot at?"

"Not me." His smile was dismal. "This is Nick's car."

"Why didn't Nick come himself?"

He looked around the deserted field. The plane I had arrived on was a flashing speck in the sky above the red sun. The only human being in sight was the operator in the control tower. But Nemo leaned towards me in the seat, and spoke in a whisper:

"Nick's a scared pigeon. He's scared to leave the house. Ever since this morning."

"What happened this morning?"

"Didn't he tell you? You talked to him on the phone."

"He didn't say very much. He told me he wanted to hire a bodyguard for six days, until his boat sails. He didn't tell me why."

"They're gunning for him, that's why. He went to the beach this morning. He has a private beach along the back of his ranch, and he went down there by himself for his morning dip. Somebody took a shot at him from the top of the bluff. Five or six shots. He was in the water, see, with no gun handy. He told me the slugs were splashing around him like hailstones. He ducked and swam under water out to sea. Lucky for him he's a good swimmer, or he wouldn't of got away. It's no wonder he's scared. It means they caught up with him, see."

"Who are 'they,' or is that a family secret?"

Nemo turned from the wheel to peer into my face. His breath was sour, his look incredulous. "Christ, don't you know who Nick is? Didn't he tell you?"

"He's a lemon-grower, isn't he?"

"He is now."

"What did he used to be?"

The bitter beaten face closed on itself. "I oughtn't to be flapping at the mouth. He can tell you himself if he wants to."

Two hundred horses yanked us away from the curb. I rode with my heavy leather bag on my knees. Nemo drove as if driving was the one thing in life he enjoyed, rapt in silent communion with the engine. It whisked us along the highway, then down a gradual incline between geometrically planted lemon groves. The sunset sea glimmered red at the foot of the slope.

Before we reached it, we turned off the blacktop into a private lane which ran like a straight hair-parting between the dark green trees. Straight for half-a-mile or more to a low house in a clearing.

The house was flat-roofed, made of concrete and fieldstone, with an attached garage. All of its windows were blinded with heavy drapes. It was surrounded with well-kept shrubbery and lawn, the lawn with ten-foot wire fence surmounted by barbed wire.

Nemo stopped in front of the closed and padlocked gate, and honked the horn. There was no response. He honked the horn again.

About halfway between the house and the gate, a crawling thing came out of the shrubbery. It was a man, moving very slowly on hands and knees. His head hung down almost to the ground. One side of his head was bright red, as if he had fallen in paint. He left a jagged red trail in the gravel of the driveway.

Harry Nemo said, "Nick!" He scrambled out of the car. "What happened, Nick?"

The crawling man lifted his heavy head and looked at us. Cumbrously, he rose to his feet. He came forward with his legs spraddled and loose like a huge infant learning to walk. He breathed loudly and horribly, looking at us with a dreadful hopefulness. Then died on his feet, still walking. I saw the change in his face before it struck the gravel.

Harry Nemo went over the fence like a weary monkey, snagging his slacks on the barbed wire. He knelt beside his brother and turned him over and palmed his chest. He stood up shaking his head.

I had my bag unzipped and my hand on the revolver. I went to the gate. "Open up, Harry."

Harry was saying, "They got him," over and over. He crossed himself several times. "The dirty bastards."

"Open up," I said.

He found a keyring in the dead man's pocket and opened the padlocked gate. Our dragging footsteps crunched the gravel. I looked down at the specks of gravel in Nicky Nemo's eyes, the bullet-hole in his temple.

"Who got him, Harry?"

"I dunno. Fats Jordan, or Artie Castola, or Faronese. It must have been one of them."

"The Purple Gang."

"You called it. Nicky was their treasurer back in the thirties. He was the one that didn't get into the papers. He handled the payoff, see. When the heat went on and the gang got busted up, he had some money in a safe deposit box. He was the only one that got away."

"How much money?"

"Nicky never told me. All I know, he come out here before the war and bought a thousand acres of lemon land. It took them fifteen years to catch up with him. He always knew they were gonna, though. He knew it."

"Artie Castola got off the Rock last Spring."

"You're telling me. That's when Nicky bought himself the bulletproof car and put up the fence."

"Are they gunning for you,?"

He looked around at the darkening groves and the sky. The sky was streaked with running red, as if the sun had died a violent death.

"I dunno," he answered nervously. "They got no reason to. I'm as clean as soap. I never been in the rackets. Not since I was young, anyway. The wife made me go straight, see?"

I said: "We better get into the house and call the police."

The front door was standing a few inches ajar. I could see at the edge that it was sheathed with quarter-inch steel plate. Harry put my thoughts into words:

"Why in hell would he go outside? He was safe as houses as long as he stayed inside."

"Did he live alone?"

"More or less alone."

"What does that mean?"

He pretended not to hear me, but I got some kind of an answer. Looking through the doorless arch into the living room, I saw a leopardskin coat folded across the back of the chesterfield. There were redtipped cigarette butts mingled with cigar butts in the ashtrays.

"Nicky was married?"

"Not exactly."

"You know the woman?"

"Naw." But he was lying.

Somewhere behind the thick walls of the house, there was a creak of springs, a crashing bump, the broken roar of a cold engine, grinding of tires in gravel. I got to the door in time to see a cerise convertible hurtling down the driveway. The top was down, and a yellow-haired girl was small and intent at the wheel. She swerved around Nick's body and got through the gate somehow, with her tires screaming. I aimed at the right rear tire, and missed. Harry came up behind me. He pushed my gun-arm down before I could fire again. The convertible disappeared in the direction of the highway.

"Let her go," he said.

"Who is she?"

He thought about it, his slow brain clicking almost audibly. "I dunno. Some pig that Nicky picked up some place. Her name is Flossie or Florrie or something. She didn't shoot him, if that's what you're worried about."

"You know her pretty well, do you?"

"The hell I do. I don't mess with Nicky's dames." He tried to work up a rage to go with the strong words, but he didn't have the makings. The best he could produce was petulance: "Listen, mister, why should you hang around? The guy that hired you is dead."

"I haven't been paid, for one thing."

"I'll fix that."

He trotted across the lawn to the body and came back with an alligator billfold. It was thick with money.

"How much?"

"A hundred will do it."

He handed me a hundred-dollar bill. "Now how about you amscray, bud, before the law gets here?"

"I need transportation."

"Take Nicky's car. He won't be using it. You can park it at the airport and leave the key with the agent."

"I can, eh?"

"Sure. I'm telling you you can."

"Aren't you getting a little free with your brother's property?"

"It's my property now, bud." A bright thought struck him, disorganizing his face. "Incidentally, how would you like to get off of my land?"

"I'm staying, Harry. I like this place. I always say it's people that make a place."

The gun was still in my hand. He looked down at it.

"Get on the telephone, Harry. Call the police."

"Who do you think you are, ordering me around? I took my last order from anybody, see?" He glanced over his shoulder at the dark and shapeless object on the gravel, and spat venomously.

"I'm a citizen, working for Nicky. Not for you."

He changed his tune very suddenly. "How much to go to work for me?"

"Depends on the line of work."

He manipulated the alligator wallet. "Here's another hundred. If you got to hang around, keep the lip buttoned down about the dame, eh? Is it a deal?"

I didn't answer, but I took the money. I put it in a separate pocket by itself. Harry telephoned the county sheriff.

He emptied the ashtrays before the sheriff's men arrived, and stuffed the leopardskin coat into the wood-box. I sat and watched him.

We spent the next two hours with loud-mouthed deputies. They were angry with the dead man for having the kind of past that attracted bullets. They were angry with Harry for being his brother. They were secretly angry with themselves for being inexperienced and incompetent. They didn't even uncover the leopardskin coat.

Harry Nemo left the courthouse first. I waited for him to leave, and tailed him home, on foot.

Where a leaning palm-tree reared its ragged head above the pavements, there was a court lined with jerry-built frame cottages. Harry turned up the walk between them and entered the first cottage. Light flashed on his face from inside. I heard a woman's voice say something to him. Then light and sound were cut off by the closing door.

An old gabled house with boarded-up windows stood opposite the court. I crossed the street and settled down in the shadows of its verandah to watch Harry Nemo's cottage. Three cigarettes later, a tall woman in a dark hat and a light coat came out of the cottage and walked briskly to the corner and out of sight. Two cigarettes after that, she reappeared at the corner on my side of the street, still walking briskly. I noticed that she had a large straw handbag under her arm. Her face was long and stony under the streetlight.

Leaving the street, she marched up the broken sidewalk to the verandah where I was leaning against the shadowed wall. The stairs groaned under her decisive footsteps. I put my hand on the gun in my pocket, and waited. With the rigid assurance of a WAC corporal marching at the head of her platoon, she crossed the verandah to me, a thin high-shouldered silhouette against the light from the corner. Her hand was in her straw bag, and the end of the bag was pointed at my stomach. Her shadowed face was a gleam of eyes, a glint of teeth.

"I wouldn't try it if I were you," she said. "I have a gun here, and the safety is off, and I know how to shoot it, mister."

"Good for you."

"I'm not joking." Her deep contralto rose a notch. "Rapid fire used to be my specialty. So you better take your hands out of your pockets."

I showed her my hands, empty. Moving very quickly, she relieved my pocket of the weight of my gun, and frisked me for other weapons.

"Who are you, mister?" she said as she stepped back. "You can't be Arturo Castola, you're not old enough."

"Are you a policewoman?"

"I'll ask the questions. What are you doing here?"

"Waiting for a friend."

"You're a liar. You've been watching my house for an hour and a half. I tabbed you through the window."

"So you went and bought yourself a gun?"

"I did. You followed Harry home. I'm Mrs. Nemo, and I want to know why."

"Harry's the friend I'm waiting for."

"You're a double liar. Harry's afraid of you. You're no friend of his."

"That depends on Harry. I'm a detective."

She snorted. "Very likely. Where's your buzzer?"

"I'm a private detective," I said. "I have identification in my wallet."

"Show me. And don't try any tricks."

I produced my photostat. She held it up to the light from the street, and handed it back to me. "So you're a detective. You better do something about your tailing technique. It's obvious."

"I didn't know I was dealing with a cop."

"I was a cop," she said. "Not any more."

"Then give me back my .38. It cost me seventy dollars."

"First tell me, what's your interest in my husband? Who hired you?"

"Nick, your brother-in-law. He called me in Los Angeles today, said he needed a bodyguard for a week. Didn't Harry tell you?"

She didn't answer.

"By the time I got to Nick, he didn't need a bodyguard, or anything. But I thought I'd stick around and see what I could find out about his death. He was a client, after all."

"You should pick your clients more carefully."

"What about picking brothers-in-law?"

She shook her head stiffly. The hair that escaped from under her hat was almost white. "I'm not responsible for Nick or anything about him. Harry is my responsibility. I met him in line of duty and I straightened him out, understand? I tore him loose from Detroit and the rackets, and I brought him out here. I couldn't cut him off from his brother entirely. But he hasn't been in trouble since I married him. Not once."

"Until now."

"Harry isn't in trouble now."

"Not yet. Not officially."

"What do you mean?"

"Give me my gun, and put yours down. I can't talk into iron."

She hesitated, a grim and anxious woman under pressure. I wondered what quirk of fate or psychology had married her to a hood, and decided it must have been love. Only love would send a woman across a dark street to face down an unknown gunman. Mrs. Nemo was horsefaced and aging and not pretty, but she had courage.

She handed me my gun. Its butt was soothing to the palm of my hand. I dropped it into my pocket. A gang of Negro boys at loose ends went by in the street, hooting and whistling purposelessly.

She leaned towards me, almost as tall as I was. Her voice was a low sibilance forced between her teeth.

"Harry had nothing to do with his brother's death. You're crazy if you think so."

"What makes you so sure, Mrs. Nemo?"

"Harry couldn't, that's all. I know Harry, I can read him like a book. Even if he had the guts, which he hasn't, he wouldn't dare to think of killing Nick. Nick was his older brother, understand, the successful one in the family." Her voice rasped contemptuously. "In spite of everything I could do or say, Harry worshipped Nick right up to the end."

"Those brotherly feelings sometimes cut two ways. And Harry had a lot to gain."

"Not a cent. Nothing."

"He's Nick's heir, isn't he?"

"Not as long as he stays married to me. I wouldn't let him touch a cent of Nick Nemo's filthy money. Is that clear?"

"It's clear to me. But is it clear to Harry?"

"I made it clear to him, many times. Anyway, this is ridiculous. Harry wouldn't lay a finger on that precious brother of his."

"Maybe he didn't do it himself. He could have had it done for him. I know he's covering for somebody."

"Who?"

"A blonde girl left the house after we arrived. She got away in a cherry-colored convertible. Harry recognized her."

"A cherry-colored convertible?"

"Yes. Does that mean something to you?"

"No, nothing in particular. She must have been one of Nick's girls. He always had girls."

"Why would Harry cover for her?"

"What do you mean, cover for her?"

"She left a leopardskin coat behind. Harry hid it, and paid me not to tell the police."

"Harry did that?"

"Unless I'm having delusions."

"Maybe you are at that. If you think that Harry paid that girl to shoot Nick, or had anything—"

"I know. Don't say it. I'm crazy."

Mrs. Nemo laid a thin hand on my arm. "Anyway, lay off Harry. Please. I have a hard enough time handling him as it is. He's worse than my first husband. The first one was a drunk, believe it or not." She glanced at the lighted cottage across the street, and I saw one half of her bitter smile. "I wonder what makes a woman go for the lame ducks the way I did."

"I wouldn't know, Mrs. Nemo. Okay. I lay off Harry."

But I had no intentions of laying off Harry. When she went back to her cottage, I walked around three-quarters of the block and took up a new position in the doorway of a dry-cleaning establishment. This time I didn't smoke. I didn't even move, except to look at my watch from time to time.

Around eleven o'clock, the lights went out behind the blinds in the Nemo cottage. Shortly before midnight the front door opened and Harry slipped out. He looked up and down the street and began to walk. He passed within six feet of my dark doorway, hustling along in a kind of furtive shuffle.

Working very cautiously, at a distance, I tailed him downtown. He disappeared into the lighted cavern of an all-night garage. He came out of the garage a few minutes later, driving a prewar Chevrolet.

My money also talked to the attendant. I drew a prewar Buick which would still do seventy-five. I proved that it would, as soon as I hit the

310

highway. I reached the entrance to Nick Nemo's private lane in time to see Harry's lights approaching the dark ranch-house.

I cut my lights and parked at the roadside a hundred yards below the entrance to the lane, and facing it. The Chevrolet reappeared in a few minutes. Harry was still alone in the front seat. I followed it blind as far as the highway before I risked my lights. Then down the highway to the edge of town.

In the middle of the motel and drive-in district he turned off onto a side road and in under a neon sign which spelled out TRAILER COURT across the darkness. The trailers stood along the bank of a dry creek. The Chevrolet stopped in front of one of them, which had a light in the window. Harry got out with a spotted bundle under his arm. He knocked on the door of the trailer.

I U-turned at the next corner and put in more waiting time. The Chevrolet rolled out under the neon sign and turned towards the highway. I let it go.

Leaving my car, I walked along the creek bank to the lighted trailer. The windows were curtained. The cerise convertible was parked on its far side. I tapped on the aluminum door.

"Harry?" a girl's voice said. "Is that you, Harry?"

I muttered something indistinguishable. The door opened, and the yellow-haired girl looked out. She was very young, but her round blue eyes were heavy and sick with hangover, or remorse. She had on a nylon slip, nothing else.

"What is this?"

She tried to shut the door. I held it open.

"Get away from here. Leave me alone. I'll scream."

"All right. Scream."

She opened her mouth. No sound came out. She closed her mouth again. It was small and fleshy and defiant. "Who are you? Law?"

"Close enough. I'm coming in."

"Come in then, damn you. I got nothing to hide."

"I can see that."

I brushed in past her. There were dead Martinis on her breath. The little room was a jumble of feminine clothes, silk and cashmere and tweed and gossamer nylon, some of them flung on the floor, others hung up to dry. The leopardskin coat lay on the bunk bed, staring with innumerable bold eyes. She picked it up and covered her shoulders with it. Unconsciously, her nervous hands began to pick the wood-chips out of the fur. I said:

"Harry did you a favor, didn't he?"

"Maybe he did."

"Have you been doing any favors for Harry?"

"Such as?"

"Such as knocking off his brother."

"You're way off the beam, mister. I was very fond of Uncle Nick."

"Why run out on the killing then?"

"I panicked," she said. "It could happen to any girl. I was asleep when he got it, see, passed out if you want the truth. I heard the gun go off. It woke me up, but it took me quite a while to bring myself to and sober up enough to put my clothes on. By the time I made it to the bedroom window, Harry was back, with some guy." She peered into my face. "Were you the guy?"

I nodded.

"I thought so. I thought you were law at the time. I saw Nick lying there in the driveway, all bloody, and I put two and two together and got trouble. Bad trouble for me, unless I got out. So I got out. It wasn't nice to do, after what Nick meant to me, but it was the only sensible thing. I got my career to think of."

"What career is that?"

"Modeling. Acting. Uncle Nick was gonna send me to school."

"Unless you talk, you'll finish your education at Tehachapi. Who shot Nick?"

A thin edge of terror entered her voice. "I don't know, I tell you. I was passed out in the bedroom. I didn't see nothing."

"Why did Harry bring you your coat?"

"He didn't want me to get involved. He's my father, after all."

"Harry Nemo is your father?"

"Yes."

"You'll have to do better than that. What's your name?"

"Jeannine. Jeannine Larue."

"Why isn't your name Nemo if Harry is your father? Why do you call him Harry?"

"He's my stepfather, I mean."

"Sure," I said. "And Nick was really your uncle, and you were having a family reunion with him."

312

"He wasn't any blood relation to me. I always called him uncle, though."

"If Harry's your father, why don't you live with him?"

"I used to. Honest. This is the truth I'm telling you. I had to get out on account of the old lady. The old lady hates my guts. She's a real creep, a square. She can't stand for a girl to have any fun. Just because my old man was a rummy—"

"What's your idea of fun, Jeannine?"

She shook her feathercut hair at me. It exhaled a heavy perfume which was worth its weight in blood. She bared one pearly shoulder and smiled an artificial hustler's smile. "What's yours? Maybe we can get together."

"You mean the way you got together with Nick?"

"You're prettier than him."

"I'm also smarter. I hope. Is Harry really your stepfather?"

"Ask him if you don't believe me. Ask him. He lives in a place on Tule Street—I don't remember the number."

"I know where he lives."

But Harry wasn't at home. I knocked on the door of the frame cottage and got no answer. I turned the knob, and found that the door was unlocked. There was a light behind it. The other cottages in the court were dark. It was long past midnight, and the street was deserted. I went into the cottage, preceded by my gun.

A ceiling bulb glared down on sparse and threadbare furniture, a time-eaten rug. Besides the living-room, the house contained a cubbyhole of a bedroom and a closet kitchenette. Everything in the poverty-stricken place was pathetically clean. There were moral mottoes on the walls, and one picture. It was a photograph of a tow-headed girl in a teen-age party dress. Jeannine, before she learned that a pretty face and a sleek body could buy her the things she wanted. The things she thought she wanted.

For some reason, I felt sick. I went outside. Somewhere out of sight, an old car-engine muttered. Its muttering grew on the night. Harry Nemo's rented Chevrolet turned the corner under the streetlight. Its front wheels were weaving. One of the wheels climbed the curb in front of the cottage. The Chevrolet came to a halt at a drunken angle.

I crossed the sidewalk and opened the car door. Harry was at the wheel, clinging to it desperately as if he needed it to hold him up. His chest was bloody. His mouth was bright with blood. He spoke through it thickly:

"She got me."

"Who got you, Harry? Jeannine?"

His mouth grinned, ghastly red like a clown's. "No. Not her. She was the reason for it, though. We had it coming."

Those were his final words. I caught his body as it fell sideways out of the seat. Laid it out on the sidewalk and left it for the cop on the beat to find.

I drove across town to the trailer court. Jeannine's trailer still had light in it, filtered through the curtains over the windows. I pushed the door open.

The girl was packing a suitcase on the bunk bed. She looked at me over her shoulder, and froze. Her blonde head was cocked like a frightened bird's, hypnotized by my gun.

"Where are you off to, kid?"

"Out of this town. I'm getting out."

"You have some talking to do first."

She straightened up. "I told you all I know. You didn't believe me. What's the matter, didn't you get to see Harry?"

"I saw him. Harry's dead. Your whole family is dying like flies."

She half-turned and sat down limply on the disordered bed. "Dead? You think I did it?"

"I think you know who did. Harry said before he died that you were the reason for it all."

"Me the reason for it?" Her eyes widened in false naiveté, but there was thought behind them, quick and desperate thought. "You mean that Harry got killed on account of me?"

"Harry and Nick both. It was a woman who shot them."

"God," she said. The desperate thought behind her eyes crystallized into knowledge. Which I shared.

The aching silence was broken by a big diesel rolling by on the highway. She said above its roar:

"That crazy old bat. So *she* killed Nick."

"You're talking about your mother. Mrs. Nemo."

"Yeah."

"Did you see her shoot him?"

"No, I was blotto like I told you. But I saw her out there this week, keeping an eye on the house. She's always watched me like a hawk."

"Is that why you were getting out of town? Because you knew she killed Nick?"

"Maybe it was. I don't know. I wouldn't let myself think about it."

Her blue gaze shifted from my face to something behind me. I turned. Mrs. Nemo was in the doorway. She was hugging the straw bag to her thin chest.

Her right hand dove into the bag. I shot her in the right arm. She leaned against the door-frame and held her dangling arm with her left hand. Her face was granite in whose crevices her eyes were like live things caught.

The gun she dropped was a cheap .32 revolver, its nickel plating worn and corroded. I spun the cylinder. One shot had been fired from it.

"This accounts for Harry," I said. "You didn't shoot Nick with this gun, not at that distance."

"No." She was looking down at her dripping hand. "I used my old police gun on Nick Nemo. After I killed him, I threw the gun into the sea. I didn't know I'd have further use for a gun. I bought that little suicide gun tonight."

"To use on Harry?"

"To use on you. I thought you were on to me. I didn't know until you told me that Harry knew about Nick and Jeannine."

"Jeannine is your daughter by your first husband?"

"My only daughter." She said to the girl: "I did it for you, Jeannine. I've seen too much—the awful things that can happen."

The girl didn't answer. I said:

"I can understand why you shot Nick. But why did Harry have to die?"

"Nick paid him," she said. "Nick paid him for Jeannine. I found Harry in a bar an hour ago, and he admitted it. I hope I killed him."

"You killed him, Mrs. Nemo. What brought you here? Was Jeannine the third on your list?"

"No. No. She's my own girl. I came to tell her what I did for her. I wanted her to know."

She looked at the girl on the bed. Her eyes were terrible with pain and love. The girl said in a stunned voice:

"Mother. You're hurt. I'm sorry."

"Let's go, Mrs. Nemo," I said.

DAVID ALEXANDER
(1907–1973)

Perhaps it was because David Alexander started writing late in life that his talent was so often overlooked. His first book was not published until 1951, when he was forty-four years old; but he went on to write fifteen novels and a volume of short stories entitled Hangman's Dozen (1961). Alexander's ten-year stint in the 1930s as managing editor of New York's then-oldest sports and theater paper, the Morning Telegraph, gave him what many described as his unique insight into Broadway's seamy side. He saw "the Great White Way" as an elongated carny midway—"the world's most blatant." Its theaters, movie houses, boxing booths, flea circuses, brothels, shops, hotels, and bars were glorified sideshows from which he delightedly extracted the raw material for his sardonic tales. Alexander believed that the only true individual left in the United States was the Bowery bum.

While Alexander's novels are clearly hard-boiled, they are written in an idiosyncratic, sometimes self-consciously poetic and mannered style that some readers find off-putting. This is most likely the reason that his work is not more highly regarded. Alexander wrote three series of mysteries, the most prominent of which features Bart Hardin, a columnist for the Broadway Times, a sporting newspaper modeled after the Morning Telegraph. Most notable among the Hardin series are Paint the Town Black (1954) and Shoot a Sitting Duck (1957). One of his two earlier series stars the duo of Tommy Twotoes, an eccentric penguin fancier, and private eye Terry Rooke; the other features Broadway lawyer Marty Land.

After having become involved in television during the 1950s, Alexander was chosen to join the U.S. Academy of Television Arts and Sciences in 1957, along with Brett Halliday, Dorothy Salisbury Davis, and Mignon G. Eberhart. Their mission was to save "live" television, but Alexander had such a dim view of the medium, finding it difficult to take it entirely seriously, that the mission was doomed to failure.

At that time, television's two primary taboos were sexual perversion and antireligious sentiment. Any synopsis submitted that incorporated even a whiff of such goings-on would likely be given a muscular rejection. The first story Alexander submitted concerned a sex-crazed religious fa-

316

natic who doubled as a serial killer of young girls. While he did sell this proposal, Alexander was considered anything but television's savior.

A long-time fan of horse racing, Alexander was publicity director for the California Jockey Club before joining the armed forces during World War II. When he retired from mystery and suspense writing, he rekindled his passion for the horses by publishing The History and Romance of the Horse *(1963) and* A Sound of Horses *(1966).*

Originally published in the May 1955 issue of Manhunt, *"Mama's Boy," the story of a vicious psychotic, is a fine example not only of Alexander's hard-edged style and faintly amoral outlook, but also of his seemingly innate understanding of characters whose moral and social awareness is fast disintegrating.*

J. A.

1 9 5 5

MAMA'S BOY

He awakened at noon. That was his usual hour unless there'd been something special the night before. If there'd been something special, he slept later. He was scrupulous about having eight hours of sleep. He yawned and rubbed his big hand over the blue briar patch on his jowls that always grew overnight no matter how late and how closely he shaved. The sandpapery touch of his beard gave him a sense of assurance. His beard was rough, rough like he was, he thought. A man's beard, not just fuzzy female down that some men called whiskers.

He lowered his hand and fondled his chest. The hair was thick and matted, like an animal's. He liked that, too. He was always seeking a sense of assurance from observing and touching his own powerful body. He liked to flex his biceps and square his shoulders and throw short, wicked punches at imaginary adversaries when he was alone.

As always, when he first awakened, he kicked off the covers and lay still in bed, regarding himself in the full-length mirror on the door of the closet across the little room. That was the only thing he liked about this flea trap—the big mirror. He guessed they had the mirrors in the rooms because the cheap hotel appealed to Broadway dolls, night club chorines and hustlers. There were also a few grifters like himself who roomed there.

He slept without pajamas, summer and winter. He lay there and admired himself in the mirror. He was six feet tall and had the bulging, hourglass build of a professional weight-lifter. His body was always bronzed. One whole corner of the little room was filled by an enormous sun lamp. He'd stolen it from the apartment of a middle-aged woman he'd picked up in a bar once. It was the biggest thing he'd ever stolen. He'd intended to hock it with a fence he knew on Sixth Avenue, but he'd decided to keep it. It made him look as if he'd just stepped off a train from Florida, and he liked that.

He suddenly realized it was Friday. That meant he'd have to be on the prowl again tonight. The room rent was due again tomorrow and there was less than ten bucks in cash strewn over the dresser-top. He hadn't paid the rent for two weeks. By tomorrow the bill would be thirty-four dollars and they wouldn't let it ride any longer. They'd lock him out tomorrow night if he hadn't settled up at the desk. They'd hold his clothes and his sun lamp and his toilet articles and even his stack of magazines. Tonight he had to go down to one of those traps in Greenwich Village that were patronized by unaccompanied middle-aged women. He'd have to pick a well-dressed one with jewelry, one that looked like ready money. Usually they didn't carry much cash in their pocketbooks, of course. Just enough for the drinks. But they almost always had cash and jewelry and other valuables in their apartments. All you had to do was get them to take you home. He knew where to look for cash and valuables. The old dolls all hid them in the same places, like the medicine cabinets in their fancy bathrooms. Sometimes, if you couldn't find what you were looking for, you had to smack them around a little.

He liked that. That was the real kick, beating them up. That was what he liked. It was a bigger kick than finding a shoe box full of hundred-dollar bills and diamond rings in their apartments.

He got up and posed in front of the mirror, flexing his muscles, throwing short jabs and uppercuts at his image. Then for ten minutes he did sitting-up exercises, bends and pushups. There was a pile of magazines and paperback novels on the glass-topped table that served him as a desk. The magazines were all physical culture publications. The ones he'd saved, a dozen or so, all had his picture in them. He often made a few bucks hiring out as a photographer's model. The soft-cover books were all murder stories with lurid covers. They concerned the adventures of guys who spend most of their time beating hell out of naked blondes who were on the make for them. Usually they wound up putting a forty-five slug into the blondes.

He lifted a magazine off the top of the pile and admired his picture on the cover. "Buck Crowley, a Leading Mr. America Candidate," the caption read. In the cover photograph he was wearing only a loincloth. He was standing spraddle-legged and holding aloft a bar bell that wasn't as heavy as it looked.

He put the magazine down and picked up a letter from Moira, who was living at some place down in Florida now. Moira was one of the middle-aged women he'd picked up in a Village trap one night, and she'd been a good source of income for him for months. She was always giving him little presents that could be converted into cash. Moira was a widow, but she had married this rich old man who was retired and she had gone down to Florida to take care of him. Moira was cagey. She'd given him only a post office box for an address. He took the letter out of the envelope, read it again, and threw it down angrily.

Jesus, what mush, he thought. Could you imagine the dumb woman putting stuff like that on paper? That was really leading with the chin. He grinned and read his own scrawled writing on another sheet of paper he hadn't mailed yet.

Dear Moira,

I got the 25. It's not enough. I got to have a lot more, at least a couple hundred. If you havn't got it you can get it from that rich old man you married alright. You better. If you don't I'll find out how to write to him and tell him some things about you and me maybe.

Your friend,

Buck

He went into the connecting bath he shared with the tenant of the next room. He tried the door of the neighbor's room. It was locked from the other side. He didn't bother to bolt it from his side. He never did. There was a puny little guy lived in the next room. Crowley was always halfway hoping the puny little guy would blunder into the bath while he was there so he could show him what a real man who took good care of his body looked like. There wasn't any use in fooling around with the puny little guy, though. He couldn't have any dough or he wouldn't be living in a trap like this, in the Forties west of Eighth.

Crowley used almost a whole cake of wafer-thin hotel soap in lathering his shaggy body under a warm shower. Then he turned the cold water on full-blast. His teeth chattered and his body shook, but he endured the icy torture for two full minutes. That was part of his daily regimen. He dried himself with the last of the three sleazy bath towels the hotel issued to its guests in the course of a week. Then he slapped rubbing alcohol on his body, kneading the muscles as he applied the pungent stuff. What he really needed was a good rubdown, he reflected. But in his present financial state he couldn't afford a gym or a Turkish bath. As he shaved, he thought: Maybe after tonight I can afford a few little luxuries. A Broadway haberdasher was displaying a new line of tight-fitting pink sports shirts, but they cost $8.95 a copy. Moira used to give him presents of expensive haberdashery from time to time, he recalled. He'd got twenty bucks from a hock shop for a gold tie clasp with twin hearts on it that Moira had given him. What the hell did he need with a tie clasp? He seldom wore a tie. He liked open-throated shirts that showed the hair on his chest.

Crowley returned to his room. He pulled the sun lamp apparatus over to the bed and turned on the current. He lay down on the bed, letting the lamp toast his body. The warm rays from the big bulb flowed over him and made him feel pleasantly relaxed. For minutes he let his mind dwell comfortingly on his strong, perfect body. The feeling of surging power inside him was almost sensual. But then he got to thinking about Moira and he became bitter about the tiny crumb she'd sent him when he'd appealed to her for a little financial help.

When Crowley had baked his front for ten minutes, he turned over and baked his back. When another ten minutes had elapsed, his daily regimen was finished. He'd had his sitting-up exercises, his cold shower, his sun-ray treatment. It was time to dress and get breakfast.

Crowley led a very orderly life. A good, clean life.

2.

He dressed very carefully because this was his night to prowl and he wanted to look his best. He'd discovered the Village traps, where the middle-aged, unaccompanied women hung out, quite by accident. Often, when the need for sheer physical exertion asserted itself, he would walk at a rapid pace from one end of Manhattan Island to another, with no destination at all in mind. One such walk had carried him to the Village and he had arrived there physically exhausted. He did not like to drink. Drinking was not part of the good clean life he led. But a bar had seemed the only place where he might pause and rest for a moment.

There had been an aging woman with a painted face at the bar and she had been a little drunk, and that was the start of it. He had learned that there were many such women, well-heeled women who had lost their men through death or divorce and who had lost their youth through the inexorable flow of time, and who were frantically determined to recapture the excitements of the past by bribing some young man with liquor or food or money or little luxuries. They came to these places in the Village because here they could find husky young men who were painters and sculptors and writers and didn't have a dime and the aging women could retain some shred of respectability by pretending an interest in the young men's work instead of the young men themselves and by calling them their protégés instead of their gigolos. Crowley was not a painter or a writer or a sculptor but his abundant physical assets made him attractive to such women, even without this thin coat of respectability.

Crowley took Moira's letter and put it under a pile of shirts in his drawer, to hide it from the maid. He'd mail his own letter, but he could hardly expect Moira to come through in time for the rent, so he had to prowl tonight. He kept several things hidden from the maid under the shirts. He took out a small jar of cream deodorant and a bottle of rose hair oil. He glanced over his shoulder guiltily, as if he expected someone to be spying on him, before he rubbed the cream deodorant in his armpits. He poured several drops of the fragrant oil into his black, curly hair and massaged his scalp vigorously. He combed his hair, letting one curl spill down over his forehead. Moira had liked the way the curl hung down. She said it made him look like a mischievous little boy. He glanced again behind him, as if he were making sure he was alone in the tiny room, and then put a drop of the perfumed oil on his fingertip and rubbed it into his thick eyebrows. His eyebrows grew together in a straight line over his nose.

He replaced the hair oil and cream deodorant beneath the shirts. He put on a pair of shorts and chose a tight-fitting knit rayon gaucho shirt. It was white and showed off the deep bronze of his skin. He had almost as much trouble forcing his big upper torso into the shirt as a plump woman has squeezing her thick body into a latex girdle. He selected a pair of slim-legged, fawn-colored slacks with a pleated waist. He wore a wide leather belt with a Western buckle. His socks were soft wool argyle and his shoes were saddle leather with thick crepe soles. As a final adornment, he hooked on a slave bracelet with heavy sterling silver links that Moira had given him. His wrist watch was in hock.

He preened himself in front of the mirror and nodded with satisfaction. He'd qualify. The tight shirt and slim-legged trousers showed off his fine body to perfection.

He had to get a stamp for his letter to Moira, but he wouldn't get it at the desk. He always avoided the desk when his rent was overdue. He went down the back stairs and crossed a yard of lobby at one long step and entered the lunch room which was connected with the hotel.

It was around two o'clock as usual before he breakfasted. He sat on a stool and he was a long time getting served because the girl behind the counter knew he never tipped. His breakfast was a very light one, considering the lateness of the hour and the fact he was a large, athletic-looking young man. He always ordered a certain brand of cereal because he believed implicitly in the ads which stated it was a breakfast of champions which furnished the principal nourishment for the most publicized heroes of the sports world. He never drank tea or coffee. He had milk, two boiled eggs and dry toast.

He handed the girl a dollar bill and showed her his strong white teeth in a smile. She didn't react. As usual, she glared at him when he pocketed his thirty-five cents change. The tramp, he thought. They're all alike, even the young ones.

He walked to Eighth Avenue and found a stationery store and stamp machine. He stamped the letter to Moira. As he dropped the letter into the mailbox he thought: I'll show her. Going off and leaving me all alone like that, without even enough money to eat on. I should have asked for five Cs instead of two.

He walked to Broadway.

3.

The world's most blatant midway was alive with women, it seemed. He hated them all. He especially hated the aging women, the old actresses with the thick paint on their withered faces who dashed from agent to agent desperately seeking a job. I'd like to smash them, he thought. God, how I'd like to smash them. But he couldn't afford kicks. He was in this business purely for money, he reminded himself. Broadway wasn't his beat. His beat was the Village. That's where the ones with the gold hung out. The wealthy ones. The ones worth fooling with.

Trouble was the old dolls didn't start hitting the Village bars until late afternoon and usually there wasn't any real business to be done until after midnight. Sometimes you didn't get picked up until almost closing hour. That bothered Crowley, having to hang around the bars so long. You couldn't hang around unless you had a drink in front of you and he didn't approve of alcoholic beverages. He didn't think a clean-living man like him should drink at all. But he had to sip beer in the Village bars. He always took as long as he could over a bottle. A lousy bottle of beer cost half a buck in those dives. After half an hour or so of nursing your beer, the bartender started looking crosseyed at you and you had to buy another bottle—or go to another bar. It could be expensive if there wasn't some bag around giving you the eye and paying for your drinks. What was worse, drinking beer ruined your health. If he started getting a waistline, his career as a model would be over and he wouldn't stand a chance in the Mr. America contest.

Crowley loafed around Broadway for a couple of hours, and then dropped by a photographic agency to see if there were any calls for muscle models. When he found there weren't, he turned up Jacobs Beach and went to Stillman's Gym. He didn't like to spend the half a buck they charged to watch the sparring, but he went in anyway. Boxers were men, rough guys like himself. They had hairy chests and hairy hands and they knew how to hit and cut and hurt.

He watched the sparring in several rings, watched heavy-shouldered men with broken faces pound their gloved fists into weighty bags. That's what I want, he thought. I want to smash. I take care of myself. I lead a good, clean life. My body's made for smashing.

He remained in the gym for several hours, breathing in the mingled odors of stale sweat and stale smoke and rubbing alcohol and liniment, hearing the steady thud of cushioned fists that plummeted into leather bags and human flesh with the peculiarly rhythmic and insistent sound of dark hands beating jungle drums.

It was late afternoon when he reached the street. He decided to have an early dinner. He went to a Riker's Restaurant and sat at a counter and paid a dollar sixty-five for a T-bone steak, potatoes, salad and milk. His money was rapidly disappearing, but he thought he needed the steak. Steak gave you strength. Fighters always had a steak a few hours before they went into the ring, he'd heard.

He was restless as he left the restaurant. He was quivering inside with a kind of excited anticipation. It was almost evening now. Soon he would go down to the Village and find the woman who would supply the money to pay the rent. But he hardly thought about the money or the rent he owed. He thought about what he was going to do to the woman.

He was breathing heavily when he went into his stuffy little room. He raised the window that the maid had lowered. He paced the floor, hearing the animal sound of his own breathing and the screech and hum of the city outside the window.

He picked up one of the paperback books and lay down on the bed. He skipped a good deal of it because he'd read it before, but he read the part about a guy branding a girl with a red-hot poker. He branded her with a double-cross because she'd framed a pal of his for murder. The story excited Crowley. He read the part again, his lips moving. There was a picture of the girl on the jacket of the book. She was young and red-mouthed and full-bosomed. But Crowley thought of her as being middle-aged, an old bag trying to find a strong young man. I could do that, he kept telling himself. That stuff with the hot poker. I could do that.

The room was cool but he was sweating. There's something inside me, he thought. It's got to break. He caught a glimpse of himself in the full-length mirror. His big fists were clenched tight. He was biting his lower lip. His body was rigid.

Jesus, he thought, I've got to smash.

He began to tremble with excitement. When he'd started out this afternoon it had been strictly business, solely a matter of dollars and cents. But now it was something different. I've got to get one tonight, he told himself. It's not just the money. I've got to pound one with my fists. He kept thinking about the guy branding the woman. It would be a hell of a kick, he thought. I could brand my initials on one of 'em. I could do it easy.

4.

It was after eight o'clock when Crowley finally walked out into the night to start his prowl. He started downtown on foot. It took him nearly an hour to reach the Village, walking fast. The first bar he went into was on Sheridan Square. There was nothing there for him. Collegiate-looking kids, laughing too loudly, a few characters in beards and berets to give atmosphere to the place.

He stopped in two bars on West Fourth Street. Each was crowded and filled with raucous sound and swirling smoke. Their patrons were the self-conscious bohemians, the men in corduroy jackets and baggy pants, the girls in smocks or blue jeans, chattering about matters Crowley did not understand.

He tried a bar on Sixth Avenue, and then another. He hardly paused in either place. They were filled with working-class men.

His eagerness was mounting unbearably now. It had never been like this before, he thought.

He passed a brownstone walk-up, saw the girl a few steps back in the dimly-lighted foyer, and almost passed on before he realized what she was doing. She was standing with her back to the door, leaning over, adjusting her stockings. A small purse lay on the floor beside her feet.

Crowley moved almost without conscious thought. He looked both ways, saw that no one was watching him, glanced again into the foyer to make certain the girl was alone, and then opened the door silently and crossed the floor to her in three noiseless steps. Just as he reached her, she dropped her skirt and straightened up and started to turn. His fist caught her just beneath the ear.

The girl went down without a sound and lay there, jerking a little. Crowley studied her for a second, and then, certain she was out, dumped the contents of her purse on the floor and picked up the man's billfold. He flipped it open. It contained two one-dollar bills. He shoved the bills in his pocket and threw the billfold at the girl's face as hard as he could. "Two lousy bucks," he said aloud. "For Christ's sake."

Thirty seconds after he had first spotted the girl, he was on the street again, walking rapidly, but not rapidly enough to interest anyone. The girl he'd robbed was almost forgotten. Even the vague regret he'd felt because there hadn't been time to do a job on her was nothing more than a memory now. It could have been last night that he'd slugged the girl in the foyer, or last week. His last thought of her was that she had been just an appetizer. Hell, he'd hardly slugged her at all. What he needed was somebody like Moira, and a place where he could really take his time. He began to think about how it would be to brand one of them, and now he had forgotten the girl in the foyer completely.

Finally he headed through the Minetta for Macdougal Street. He walked toward Bleecker and went into Ernesto's. This was the place. This was where he had met Moira and many of the others. This was where the wealthy uptown ladies of uncertain age came to pick up their "protégés."

But there was no Moira at the bar, no one who resembled her even slightly. He felt wildly angry. He'd been cheated. But this was the last chance. He had to stay here. There was no place else to look.

He pushed his way to the crowded bar and ordered a beer he did not want.

The bartender said, "Weekends we serve only bottle beer, fifty cents a copy. You can get a shot for the same price. We gotta keep the sippers out. The place gets crowded weekends."

"Beer," said Crowley righteously. "I never drink hard liquor."

There was a mixed crowd of Villagers and "tourists" from uptown in Ernesto's. The Villagers, who were elaborately casual in their attire to mark them as artistic souls, seemed mainly occupied in cadging drinks from the well-dressed visitors. Tourists were fair game every weekend for the regulars of such taverns.

Crowley sipped his beer slowly and urgent restlessness grew inside him. The crowd shifted every few minutes. A party would leave and another would come through the door to replace it at the long bar. But the one Crowley was looking for did not arrive. He became sullen and angry. He was in a crowd, but he was alone again.

A pair of street musicians entered the bar. One carried a violin, the other a piano accordion. They took a stance away from the crowded bar and began to play an old tune. And immediately afterward she came in. Crowley knew at once that she was the one he had been waiting for.

She was about Moira's age, he judged, past her middle forties, pushing fifty. She wore a beautifully tailored suit of grayish lavender. There was a clip of sparkling stones at her lapel and Crowley thought the stones were diamonds. Her hat was small and smart with a jaunty feather. Her face was expertly made up to hide the lines and crowsfeet of middle age. A high, ruffled collar concealed the sagging flesh of her throat. She wore glasses, but they were very special glasses, harlequin-shaped, the rims twinkling with gold work and tiny stones. She was alone.

Crowley shifted his position, used his weight to make a place at the bar. As she passed him, he called to her, "You can get in here, lady. There's quite a crowd tonight."

She nodded to him coolly, murmured thanks. She took the place beside him, but seemed unimpressed by the muscular young man. She's playing it cagey, Crowley thought. She's like Moira. The well-dressed woman ordered a dry martini and Crowley exulted. Moira had drunk dry martinis. Dry martinis worked on them fast. This was going to be easy. Crowley looked speculatively at the alligator bag the woman carried. It was a large bag. It must have cost at least a hundred dollars. It would hold a lot of money and a lot of expensive gadgets like gold cigarette cases and lighters and jeweled compacts.

The woman finally looked at Crowley. There was neither great interest nor distaste in the look she gave him. It was just a look of calm appraisal. She said, "Since you were good enough to make a place for me, the least I can do is offer you a drink."

Crowley decided his little-boy act was best for this situation. "I'd appreciate it, ma'am," he said. "I'm kind of broke tonight. I've just been locked out of my room, in fact."

A shadow of suspicion flickered on the woman's face, but she ordered Crowley's beer. She handled her martini like an experienced drinker. She didn't gulp and she didn't sip. She drank. She was out to get a lift, obviously, and she was going to.

She finished her martini before she spoke again. She said, "You're a husky young man. I'd think you could get a job that would pay enough for your room rent. Don't tell me you're one of these artists who like to starve in attics. You hardly look the type."

Crowley said, "I'm kind of a model. I pose for photographers mostly, but I pose for artists, too, now and then. Artists say I've got a good body. I come down here to the Village to see if maybe some artist would pay me to pose."

The woman gave a short laugh that was almost a contemptuous snort. "Artists don't look for models in saloons at ten o'clock at night."

Crowley thought, The stinking phony. A goddamn know-it-all. Just wait till I get my hands on you, you phony. He said, "Are you a painter, ma'am?"

She ordered another drink and took a swallow from it before she answered. She said, "As a matter of fact, I do paint, and I paint rather well in an academic way. But with me it's strictly a hobby. And don't get ideas, young man. I've done some portraits and figure studies, but since my husband died three years ago I've concentrated on still life. A bowl of fruit can't get you in any trouble. A living model can, sometimes, especially if he's a muscular young man like you."

Crowley said, "I didn't mean anything. I'm only trying to get a little honest work, that's all."

The woman turned toward Crowley, drank from her glass, regarded him squarely for the first time. The bright brown eyes behind the harlequin glasses studied his face, wandered over his big body. She said,

"You're a rather strange young man. You have a queer look. It's even rather frightening. With your build, you should be driving a trailer truck or playing professional football. But all you want to do is make a few miserable dollars displaying your body for a photographer or an artist. It must be some kind of complex. A Narcissus complex, maybe. You want something, I can tell that. You want something rather terribly. Everyone does, I guess."

Crowley said, "Maybe all I want is a little friendship."

She nodded slowly. "You know, that could be true. I've learned to understand loneliness since my husband died. This is a lonely city. The loneliest in the world. I'm well enough off and I have friends, but it's not the same. Are you married?"

Crowley shook his head. "No," he said. "Maybe we're both lonesome. Maybe we could be friends."

Her regard was speculative now. At length she said, "Friends? I suppose we could be that. But don't get wrong ideas. You're an extraordinarily attractive young male animal and I'm a woman. But I don't kid myself. I'm forty-eight and I admit it. I'm old enough to be your mother."

God, Crowley thought, she just had to say that. How many times had he heard that line? They just had to say it. All of them did. He smiled sadly, "I never had a real mother. My mother died when I was born. I was brought up in an orphanage."

The woman said, "Maybe that's what you're looking for. A mother. Well, it's a new role for me. My husband and I never had children. So maybe I'm looking for a son." She smiled wryly. "Maybe I can be a mother instead of a sister to you. Let's have a drink on it. My name's Kate Maynard."

Crowley said, "My name's Joe Harvey." He never gave them his right name the first time. If he merely robbed them and beat them and left, they wouldn't know his name in case they hollered copper. If he decided it was more profitable to play them along for a while—the way he had Moira—he could always give them his right name later. But there wouldn't be any more nights for Kate Maynard. She was going to get the big treatment tonight. The works.

Kate laughed. "Harvey," she said. "Harvey, the rabbit. You're a hell of a big rabbit, Harvey."

They had another drink. And another. The beer was choking Crowley. He hated it and stalled her when her own glass was empty and she signaled the bartender, telling her he'd finish the beer in his bottle. He kept trying to get her out of the bar, to make her take him home with her, but she was cagey, even though the martinis were creeping up on her. Damn her, Crowley thought. I'll make her pay for stalling me. She'll pay for making me beg like this. Just wait till she pokes that face of hers up against a mirror in the morning, if she's able to get off the floor by then. Jesus, Crowley thought, I'll go crazy if I can't start soon.

He'd never before been so impatient for the conclusion of an affair like this. He knew somehow that this would be different from all the others.

By midnight Kate Maynard was tight and she admitted it. She wasn't a messy female drunk. She held her liquor like a lady. Her legs were under her and her tongue wasn't thick. But she was laughing too loudly and her bright eyes had a glazed look in them. She said, "The party's over for little Kate. Get me a cab, Harvey. Get me a cab, son, like a nice little boy."

Crowley said, "I'll take you home."

She shook her head stubbornly. "Just take me to a cab," she said.

When Crowley finally found a cab, he climbed in after her. She didn't protest too much. She said, "Now I'll have to pay your cab fare back. But I guess it's worth it. I live in a supposedly exclusive neighborhood, but the young hoods wander into it at this time of night and the doormen in the big apartment houses are usually snoozing."

5.

Kate Maynard's house was a remodeled private dwelling overlooking the East River in mid-Manhattan. There were three apartments in the house, one to a floor. The brick façade had been painted charcoal black. The door and the shutters were enameled bright red. There was a big ornamental brass knocker made in the shape of a spread eagle on the door. It was class. Rich people lived in houses like this, Crowley gloated. This one was really the payoff.

Kate Maynard protested again when Crowley insisted on going in with her. "I have to get up early tomorrow, Harvey. My sister's picking me up at nine."

"Look," he said. "I'm lonesome. Can't you understand? I just want to sit around and talk a little while. I'm not in a hurry to sleep on a park bench. I got no place else to go."

She hesitated before she put her key in the lock, but in the end alcohol overcame her natural caution. She said, "All right, Harvey. You come up with me for just a little while. I'll give you enough money for a hotel tonight. And maybe I could inquire around about a job for you next week." She lingered just a little longer in the doorway. Finally she said, "I guess it's all right, really. I confess I'm a little afraid to go in alone. This is a co-op with no night man. And I'm alone in the house. My neighbors haven't come back from their summer vacations yet. I can't really flatter myself into believing you have designs on me."

She opened the door to him.

Crowley walked through it stiffly, his fists clenched tight, hardly daring to say anything. Now that the thing he'd brooded about all day was about to happen, he was like a lecher sweating out the last few minutes before his tryst with the woman he desires.

Kate's apartment was on the second floor. The living room was large. It was furnished with traditional English pieces and it shone with polished wood and bright upholstery fabrics and brocaded damask drapes. Kate's oils, in gold frames, hung on the walls. There were still lifes, landscapes, a portrait or two done with sure brush work and a competent sense of balance. It wasn't like Moira's place had been at all, Crowley thought. Moira had gone in for that low-slung modernistic stuff, a lot of divans and ottomans and coffee tables a foot or so off the floor, and her walls had been decorated mainly by pictures of naked young men with bulging muscles.

Crowley stood quite still in the middle of the room. Kate Maynard took off the hat with the jaunty feather and tossed it carelessly on a divan. "I've had it," she said. "No nightcaps for me. I don't have any beer, but there's Scotch and gin and stuff if you need a drink."

"I never drink hard liquor," Crowley told her. "I got to take care of my body."

Kate regarded him quizzically. "Yes," she said thoughtfully, "I guess your body is important to you. It's about the only thing you're proud of, isn't it?" When Crowley didn't answer, she said, "There might be something in the ice box if you're hungry."

"I'll have a glass of milk," Crowley said. "It's not good for the stomach to eat late at night."

He wanted to get the woman out of the room so he could appraise any portable assets that might be lying around. There was a silver table lighter that might be worth something and a gold-mounted desk set, he noted hurriedly. He was opening one of the desk drawers and looking for a bankbook when Kate came into the room.

Kate set the glass of milk down on a library table. She said, "Look here, I don't like people prying into my things. What are you looking for?"

Crowley turned slowly toward her. "That's too bad," he said. "Now let's get down to it. Why'd you bring me up here? You didn't just want to watch me drink milk, did you, sweetheart?" He moved toward her deliberately, grinning. "I want some money, Katie. I want all you've got in that fancy handbag. And I want what you've got hid around the house, too. You better be a sweet girl and give it to me, Katie, or I might get nasty. If I got to look for it, I might wreck the joint."

Kate stood her ground. She said, "You told me you wanted to talk a while. That's why I brought you here. I was lonesome myself, I guess, and I was trying to be kind. You'd better get out now. I won't give you any money."

Crowley was moving slowly toward the woman, still grinning. His eyes were slitted and crazy and, most terrifyingly, he had begun to sing, very softly, the same song the street musicians had played at the Village bar.

Jesus, he thought. This is the one. This is the one I've been waiting for. I always knew I'd kill one of them some day. This is the one. I'm going to kill you, Katie.

Kate stood still, gaping at Crowley, fascinated by the panther grace, the mad and evil look on his face and the song he was singing.

Oh, sweet Jesus, this is good, thought Crowley. She's the one. She's the one I've been waiting for all my life. I'm going to kill you with my fists, Katie. I'm going to show you how a real man kills. He doesn't need a gun. I'm going to smash and break and keep on pounding until you're dead.

Crowley was a couple of feet from Kate now, and Kate didn't back away. Crowley's left flew straight and hard like a mallet that is hurled. Kate's harlequin glasses flew off and shattered against a television console. She staggered back, almost fell, braced herself against a heavy table. Crowley had begun to laugh. His laughter was a treble giggle like a girl's.

Amazingly, Kate Maynard fought back. None of the other women had fought back. But Kate hurled her frail body forward, her small fists flailing ridiculously against Crowley's solid body.

It didn't do her any good, of course.

Crowley simply ignored her blows. Crowley was busy.

Finally he sank into a chair, looking down at her, entranced.

He said aloud, "You see, Katie? I didn't need a gun."

But Kate Maynard didn't hear. Kate had been dead for quite a while.

6.

There was nearly a hundred dollars in Kate's alligator bag. Kate hadn't wised up like the others. She carried her cash right on her. Crowley had some trouble getting the rings off Kate's fingers. He took Kate's wrist watch and the silver lighter and the gold-mounted desk set and a gold pencil and a jeweled cigarette case. Then he searched the apartment thoroughly. In an envelope, hidden beneath a pile of lingerie in one of Kate's dresser drawers, he found another sixty dollars, all in fives, and two diamond rings.

Then he went into the bathroom to wash up. He let the cold water run over his bleeding knuckles for a long time. There wasn't any hurry. He felt as calm and relaxed as a man could feel.

Crowley was closing the door when he remembered something. He re-entered the apartment and drank the glass of milk that was still sitting on the table.

He always had a glass of milk before he went to bed.

It made him sleep good.

7.

When Crowley hit the street he started walking west, looking for a taxi. The knuckles of his right hand were beginning to bleed again, and he took out his handkerchief and wrapped it around them. The knuckles of his left hand were swollen and raw, but the bleeding had stopped.

He had walked almost a block when the police car came by. It crawled past him, and Crowley looked after it and laughed softly. The bastards, he thought. You take their guns away from them and they wouldn't know what the hell to do. They'd kill you with a gun fast enough, but they'd never have the guts to beat you to death with their fists.

The police car slowed, then drew to the curb and stopped.

Crowley kept walking, but there was tightness in his chest now, as if he'd run too long and too fast. As he came abreast of the police car, one of the patrolmen got out and moved toward him.

"You have an accident, son?" he asked.

Crowley glanced down at the handkerchief around his knuckles. He shook his head. He wanted to say something, but somehow the words wouldn't come.

"Maybe you had a fight," the patrolman said. He moved a little closer to Crowley.

"No," Crowley said. He couldn't take his eyes from the revolver on the policeman's belt. "I—I tripped on a curb," he said. "I fell down and scraped my knuckles."

The patrolman stared at him. "You're lucky you didn't hurt your clothes any, aren't you?"

The other patrolman had moved over in the seat to watch, and now he got out and walked up beside the first one. He looked Crowley over slowly. "You been down in the Village tonight, boy?" he asked. He said it the same way he would ask someone the time of day.

The goddam New York coppers, Crowley thought. You never know what the hell's going on in their mind. He shook his head again. "No. I haven't been downtown at all."

One of the patrolmen looked at the other. "That assault and robbery we got on the radio about nine o'clock," he said. "The guy was dressed just like this." He looked back at Crowley. "And the physical description matches up, too."

"Listen—" Crowley began.

"Suppose you just step over to the car there," the patrolman said. "Just lean up against it with your hands flat on the top."

"You got no right to search me," Crowley said. "Just because I fell and hurt myself don't mean—"

"Up against the car," the patrolman said, almost pleasantly. "We don't like to do it this way, son. But there's an alarm out for a guy could be your twin. He slugged a girl down in the Village earlier tonight and took two whole bucks off her. She—"

Crowley whirled and began to run. And almost instantly he heard the two fast warning shots which meant that if he took another step a third shot would kill him. He stopped.

8.

In the police car, on the way to the station house, one of the patrolmen said, "Where'd you get all that junk in your pockets, son?"

The other patrolman said, "That girl you slugged in the Village. She was a cool one. You didn't knock her out, but she was smart enough to make you think you had. She gave the precinct detectives a damn good description of you."

But Crowley wasn't thinking about the girl he'd slugged in the foyer. He was thinking about Kate Maynard, and remembering she'd said her sister was coming by the apartment at nine o'clock in the morning. She'd find Kate, and she'd know exactly what was missing from the apartment. And when the police matched the list up with the things they'd taken off him a few moments ago . . .

"You got that girl's mad money," one of the patrolmen said. "She was waiting for her date, and she'd just stepped into that foyer for a minute."

It was just a kind of appetizer, Crowley thought. Just a little warmup. And all I got was two bucks. Two stinking, lousy bucks. Her mad money, for Christ's sake.

"Stop the car," he said suddenly. "I'm going to be sick at my stomach."

MICKEY SPILLANE
(b. 1918)

Few readers of crime ficiton are indifferent when it comes to the merits of Mickey Spillane and his creation, Mike Hammer. They either love or hate the pair, and with considerable passion in either case. Max Allen Collins, co-author of a book about Spillane and his work, One Lonely Knight (1984), considers him "one of the most remarkable literary artists ever to confine himself to a popular genre." In a 1955 Good Housekeeping article on Spillane's work, Philip Wylie concluded that "if millions of people are reading [his books] voluntarily the public must be losing its senses." Anthony Boucher, who would later develop a grudging admiration for Spillane's accomplishments, in 1951 reviewed The Big Kill as "the ultimate degradation of the [hard-boiled] school."

The first Mike Hammer novel, I, the Jury (1947), sold 8 million copies in its various U.S. paperback editions; the five that followed it in the early 1950s were likewise multimillion-copy sellers. (Aggregate sales for all of Spillane's novels were estimated in 1984 to be an amazing 160 million copies.) The Hammer books inspired ten theatrical and television films (in one of which, The Girl Hunters [1963], Spillane himself played Hammer), a radio show, two television series (with a third in the works at the time of this writing), and a syndicated comic strip.

Spillane's influence began to wane in the 1960s. Mike Hammer was properly a child of the postwar 1940s and the Red Scare–dominated 1950s, and the tactics of a violent, vigilante private eye grew less appealing to readers and writers in later decades. Recognizing this, Spillane at first considered turning Hammer into a secret agent, so as to make his brand of justice more contemporary and therefore more palatable. He abandoned the idea, however, in favor of creating a new character, Tiger Mann, his American "answer" to James Bond. Mann is an agent in the employ of Martin Grady, an ultra-right-wing billionaire whose "Group" is his own privately financed personal espionage organization. In such novels as Day of the Guns (1964) and Bloody Sunrise (1965), Mann with impunity slaughters Russian assassins and other villains bent on destroying America's democratic freedom. His adventures have neither the power nor the passion of even the minor Hammers; they are imitations rather than the real thing.

Spillane's output of short fiction is relatively small and was produced for the most part between 1953 and 1960. A few of his stories appeared in Manhunt, *notably a four-part serial, "Everybody's Watching Me," in the magazine's first four issues; most of the rest were published in such men's magazines as* Cavalier *and* Male, *and featured a variety of tough cops and criminals. None of his short stories or novelettes, significantly, has as its protagonist Mike Hammer or any other private detective. "The Screen Test of Mike Hammer," which originally appeared in* Male *in July 1955 and was reprinted with the title "Killer's Alley," is as close as Spillane came to writing a Hammer short story (with one exception, an even shorter vignette for the cover of a radio-show-style record album entitled* Mickey Spillane's Mike Hammer Story, *also produced in the mid-1950s). The playlet was written for a test film directed and produced by Spillane, in the abortive hope of casting a friend, actor Jack Stang, in the film version of* Kiss Me, Deadly *(1955). In microcosm, "The Screen Test of Mike Hammer" has all the hard-boiled elements and all the intensity of a Hammer novel.*

B. P.

1 9 5 5

THE SCREEN TEST OF MIKE HAMMER

SCENE: MIKE *in near darkness in narrow passageway between two buildings. Lighting from low left only, focusing on face.* MIKE *smoking. He does not come in until he lights his cigarette, then the light holds. From outside camera range come feet running, pause, heavy breathing.* BUM *comes stumbling up, sees* MIKE, *is terrified.*

BUM *(breathlessly)*: Mike . . . Mike! *(Then fast.)* They're closing in. The cops got everything covered. There ain't no place that kill-happy maniac can get out. He's trapped on the street, Mike. *(Pause.)* Mike . . . he's around here someplace. Already he shot up two more. Like he said, he's gonna wipe out the whole street, piece by piece.

MIKE *looks at him, lifts lip in a snarl that fades into a cold smile.*

MIKE *(softly)*: Beat it. *(Then drags on cigarette.)*

336

BUM: Yeah. . . . The great Mike Hammer. Nothing bothers him. Not even a maniac with a gun, or blood all over the street he grew up on. *(Pause.)* Maybe this'll bother you. Maybe you'll shake now. Maybe those eyes of yours will get alive for just once instead of being all dead inside. *(Pause.)* They're using your girl for bait!

Here MIKE *looks at him slowly, coldly, as if he doesn't care.*

Your girl, Mike. Your Miss Rich-Britches who grew up on the street, too, and is marked same as us. Carmen hates her worst of all for what she's got and now the cops are using her for bait. They're smart, the cops. All the way from Park Avenue they call her in because they know how Carmen hates her. She's the bait, friend. You won't be marrying no dead woman, Mike. How do your eyes feel now, big boy?

MIKE *(looks at him cautiously)*: Scram.

SOUND FROM BACKGROUND: *Siren and police whistles.*

BUM: They'll get Carmen tonight. But he'll get her first. Maybe you, too!

MIKE *cracks him one and stands there smoking.*

SOUND: *Girl's heels clicking. Fast. Faster. Stop, then on again. Suddenly* HELEN *steps into camera range. Sees* MIKE. *Eyes go wide, then happy, and she collapses on his shoulder.*

HELEN *(crying)*: Mike! *(Head goes down,* MIKE *holds her, then head up.)*

MIKE: Easy, kitten.

HELEN: Mike . . . you know what I've done?

MIKE: I know. You're nuts. Why, Helen?

HELEN: Mike . . . oh, Mike . . . the police asked me to. Mike . . . I thought you'd be proud of me if . . . if . . .

MIKE *(overlap)*: If you baited a homicidal maniac into bullet range?

HELEN *nods, jerkily, frightened.*

I grew up on the street too, kid. I'm one of those he wants, too. Didn't you think I'd be in on it?

HELEN: I—thought you would . . . but I wanted to . . . help. Oh, Mike, I wanted you to be proud of me and now I'm scared. *(Pause. She looks up, bites lip.)* Mike . . . you don't know what it is to be scared. You . . .

MIKE: Don't I, kid?

HELEN: No . . . not like this. He's trapped here on the street someplace, Mike.

MIKE *(looks over her head into the darkness)*: The street. Putrid Avenue. Killer's Alley. They've called it everything. Just one street that isn't even alive and it can make murderers out of some people and millionaires out of others. One street, Helen. *(Long pause.* MIKE *looks over her head.)* I can hear them, kid. They're closing in now. There's no place for the maniac to go now. *(Looks at her.)* Can you imagine a mind filled with a crazy obsession for a whole lifetime? Imagine hating a street so hard you wanted to kill everybody on it. One stinking street that makes up your whole background that you can never escape from. Can you imagine that, Helen?

HELEN: No, Mike . . . it's incredible. It's almost . . . impossible!

MIKE: Is it?

Now he gives her the cold look.

HELEN: Your eyes . . . aren't looking at me anymore.

MIKE: That's right, Helen. They're watching you.

HELEN *(eyes widen—softly)*: Mike!

MIKE: You're a great girl to love, Helen. A beautiful, talented louse. *(Here* HELEN *injects a note of incredible curiosity into her look.)* Beautiful enough to marry a playboy and leave the street. But the street was still there. You couldn't escape it, kid. It kept coming back, didn't it? It came back until it showed on you and the playboy couldn't stand it so he gave you the heave. *(Pause.)* How you must have hated it. *(Slowly.)* Imagine hating one street so much you work a crazy man out of an asylum and have him try to kill off the whole street for you! It took talent to do that, kid. Enough talent to almost fool me.

HELEN: Mike . . . please. You don't realize . . . Carmen is still killing. Ten minutes ago he killed Gus and now . . .

MIKE: Nah. *(Pause.)* Helen . . . he wasn't the maniac. *(Pause.)* You were.

HELEN: *(scared stiff; crying)*: Mike . . . no . . . you . . . loved me. We were going to . . . be married. You . . .

MIKE: So we were in love. Should it make a difference? Fourteen dead people. Should it make a difference? So because I loved you I'll do you a favor, Helen. Nobody will ever know. They'll have to think Carmen got you and I got Carmen. Like it that way, Helen?

HELEN: *No!* Carmen is the . . .

MIKE: He wasn't, Helen. Thirty minutes ago Carmen was dead . . . before the last murders. I shot him right here . . .

> *Camera goes to body on ground behind* MIKE.

HELEN'S VOICE: Mike . . . you can't . . . *(Suddenly choked off.)*

MIKE'S VOICE: Don't pull your gun on me. So long, kid.

> *Camera catches* HELEN, *her neck in* MIKE's *hand,*
> *sinking . . . slowly on top of Carmen.* MIKE *lets her fall,*
> *then flips cigarette on her back. Gun falls from her hand.*

> *Music up and out.*

GIL BREWER
(1922–1983)

$\mathbb{B}$lacks, Mexicans, Asians, and other minorities and foreigners received rough treatment in popular fiction during the first forty-odd years of this century. If ethnic characters were not portrayed as villains or dragged into stories for dubious comic relief, they were all too often shown as inferior to American-born whites—and were almost always made to behave in stereotypical fashion and to speak in atrocious dialect. Even the best writers of crime fiction, along with such generally progressive magazines as Black Mask, were guilty of racism in one form or another. But the grim years of World War II, and the new awareness and compassion that came out of that intense time of global strife, put an end to the worst offenses and helped to bring about a more honest and intelligent depiction of ethnic groups.

Still, relatively few realistic crime stories in the postwar years utilized race relations as a central theme. The ones that were written are for the most part excellent: Hal Ellson's series of sociological novels, including Duke (1949) and The Golden Spike (1952), as well as his short stories for Manhunt and other magazines, about Harlem teenagers; Runaway Black, a 1954 paperback original by Evan Hunter (writing as Richard Marsten), which also has a New York street setting; and Gil Brewer's "Home," first published in the short-lived (four issues) Manhunt clone, Accused, in March 1956. This brief but angry condemnation of bigotry and racial violence is set in the Deep South, its message made all the more powerful by the brutal nature of its final paragraph.

Gil Brewer began writing after his army service in France and Belgium during World War II, and with the help of former Black Mask editor Joseph T. Shaw, he sold his first short story in 1949 and his first novel in 1950. His debut novel, 13 French Street, was a million-copy bestseller. Brewer's prose is distinguished by a lean, Hemingwayesque style and by raw emotion genuinely portrayed and felt. His strongest work is A Killer Is Loose (1954), a truly harrowing portrait of a psychopath that comes close to rivaling the nightmare visions of Jim Thompson; it also contains elements of surrealism and an existentialist sense of doom.

B. P.

HOME

Already he was wishing he hadn't come home for this visit. He would not admit to the real reason, either. It was a bit past dawn now, and lying on the bed, he could see the room in the old mottled leaning mirror above the dresser. He could see himself and parts of his brothers and sisters, all in the same room. Three brothers and three sisters and two beds. In all, seven kinky black heads and parts of black bodies; arms and legs and here and there a foot. He closed his eyes.

He had lain here on his share of the bed since before dawn, listening to the mouth noises, the swallowings, the snores and careful turnings. The beds were small and creaky and the slightest movement brought a groan from somebody.

He'd forgotten how it was. He'd come home yesterday to spend a week and now he was remembering little things and he had to swallow against the shame that had become a ghost inside him since being away at school. The ghost was stirring, too.

He heard his mother in the kitchen, heard the stove.

He suddenly wanted to be out of the house.

"Chandler, Chandler," his mother had said yesterday. "You set and tell me. How's everything up there?"

"Fine, Ma."

"Is the people nice?"

"Sure."

"Reckon you learning something?"

"You bet, Ma."

With her hands twisting in the old apron. She didn't know what to do, what to say. Neither did he. And his brothers and sisters standing and leaning around, watching, not saying a thing. He was welcome. They wanted to see him. They were happy he was home, but they couldn't tell him.

His mother was singing softly to herself in the kitchen and he heard one of his sisters stir with wakefulness. He wanted to get out. Fast.

He rolled carefully off the bed to the floor and found his socks and shoes and sat on the floor, putting them on. He didn't want to wake them. He crept across the floor and got the dungarees he'd brought down and the clean T-shirt and slipped them on and rose quietly and went into the kitchen.

"You up already?" his mother said. "Ain't you going to sleep in on your holiday?"

"I never sleep late."

"But this is your holiday, son."

She was standing over by the black stove. The wood was smoking. He could smell the pone. His mother wore a shapeless once blue dress, patched with pink cloth. Coffee water was already boiling in a black kettle. The same kettle.

"I gave you money, Ma," he said. "Why don't you fix bacon and eggs and grits for breakfast? That's what it was for."

"You used to that?"

"Well, I just thought it'd be a treat. Something."

"We ain't used to that, Chandler."

He looked at his mother.

"Set down," she said. "I'll have breakfast ready for you, Chandler. You like pone."

"I don't think I want any breakfast."

They watched each other and she did not move, her eyes getting that veiled look. They kept watching each other and he heard somebody speak in the bedroom and the years turned inside out, rushing backward.

"Think I'll take a little walk around town," he said.

His mother nodded. "I see."

"All right, then. You go ahead and eat, Ma. I won't be long. We'll do something—maybe this afternoon."

"Chandler."

"Yes, Ma?"

"You got a chip, boy. I can see it plain. Big old axe chip, setting on your shoulder." She folded her hands across the apron and clasped the long worn fingers. "Knock it off, boy!"

"Ma."

She started to turn away, then turned back. "They a circus in town," she said. "Maybe they'll let you in and see it."

"Sure."

She sighed and turned to the stove. He went out, fast. He stepped into the alley and closed the door. An accordion-ribbed cat crawled under the house. A bird flew. There was no paint on the house. The boards were old and bare, with a kind of patina-like character of their own. Rich whites tried to achieve the effect of those old boards on their country places, their summer cottages, with chemicals. A raggy honeysuckle vine sprawled over the tiny porch roof. It looked hungry.

He started down the alley, walking fast past the short row of shacks which were homes like the one he'd just left. He felt to make sure he had his wallet with him. He'd put it in his jeans the night before and he realized now that he'd known what he was going to do.

He would have to come home slowly, meet them again. It would take more than a week and he only had a week, so he wouldn't meet them again.

Why did I come home? he thought. It's bad enough up there, but Christ, Christ!

He reached the street beyond the alley and stomped his shoes on the sidewalk. Tiny round rims of gray dusty earth marked the cement where he stomped. Dirt from the alley; the front yards. He had tried not to acknowledge the smell, the tin cans, the broken bottles.

It was very early and the sun was up and it possessed that quality of bright white light that could put you right back to sleep if you stared at it for a few seconds.

He remembered, that was how he'd lost the job at the car-wash place. He'd sat down early in the morning in the boss' chair and looked into the sun. The boss knocked him out of the chair.

"You goddamned snoring black bastard," the boss said. "Get out of here!"

Funny, remembering that. It had happened a long while ago.

He quit thinking with sudden familiar panic. It was bad to think. Right away all the recollections of agony rushed in.

He started along the street. It hadn't changed much. Early cars swept past and the morning hadn't as yet done away with the night. As he walked along, he began to feel hungry. He thought momentarily of the corn pone, then shut it all off. He made his mind a blank.

He passed a drunk leaning against the front of a bar. The drunk looked very pale and sick. The sidewalk was wet where the drunk stood.

He crossed the tracks and turned left, walking slowly. He passed a couple of men hurrying to work. They didn't look at him. He walked on, saw the all night restaurant sign and turned in the door.

The cashier stared at him. He smiled at her and moved toward a booth.

"Wait," the cashier said.

He turned and looked at her. Two men and a woman were drinking coffee at a nearby table. The woman looked at him, then stared.

"Jesus, will you look at that," the woman said.

"What is it?" he said to the cashier.

A large man wearing a dirty white shirt came from the back of the restaurant, walking fast, saying, "What is this? What is this?"

He looked at the man.

"Get out of here," the man said.

He couldn't think for a minute. Then he realized what it was. He'd made a mistake. He turned toward the door, but the man had caught up with him, saying it low and harsh into his ear.

"You lousy black! What the hell you reckon you're doing, coming in here?"

"I was just—"

"Sure!" the man said, shoving him through the door. "You cockeyed black-faced bastard!"

The man followed him through the door. He turned and looked at the man. The man shook with rage and began to curse until he was out of breath. Chandler kept watching the man, the fat jiggling jowls, and the man stepped up close, still cursing, gasping for breath, his eyes popping a little.

Chandler turned away and started back down the street.

He recrossed the tracks, keeping his mind shut tight up.

He started along the empty street, walking more slowly now. Suddenly, up there a white man ran from an alley. He came running by, panting and staggering and grinning and, as he passed Chandler, Chandler smelled gin trailing on the air.

He walked on down toward the alley.

Three men were coming up the street, about a block away, and two cars went by, tires hissing. A window rattled up across the street.

He reached the alley and started past the entrance, looking in there. He saw a girl and half paused. She didn't see him. She was struggling, trying to put on a red dress, but she was drunk and couldn't keep her balance. She reeled around, trying to pull the dress on over her head. Then she laughed to herself, and tried stepping into the dress. She didn't see Chandler at first. She was naked, except for rolled stockings with a hole in one knee, her full white body stark against the alley dirt, the charred walls. She was standing on a broken cardboard box that was spread like a pallet on the alley floor. A stack of boxes in front of the cardboard half-hid the little nook from view.

He started moving on. This was no place to be.

She saw him. She lifted her eyes and chuckled and let the dress fall away onto the ground. Her long blonde hair swung across her face. Her lipstick was smeared down on her chin.

"Hello, black boy," she said softly. She took a step toward him, staggered back and leaned against the wall. She moved her body for him. "Wait," she said. "Come here, black boy. Come and fix me. You want some? Huh?"

He turned away, going on down the street.

"Come on, black boy. Don't be bashful."

He continued walking and passed the three men he'd seen coming along before.

A woman screamed. Chandler stopped and turned and looked back there. The woman was at the alley entrance, on her hands and knees, with the red dress trailing from one ankle. She sprawled out on the sidewalk, then sat up and got on her knees and began crawling again.

Chandler looked at her, thinking about the restaurant, and he wondered how he could have been so dumb as to forget? Forgetting a simple thing like that! He was home! And he kept looking back there at the girl with a kind of numbness, standing perfectly still.

The three men began running toward the girl.

"Help," she called. "Help me, for God's sake!"

As she crawled on hands and knees, one knee left a spongy pattern of blood on the cement. Her breasts slung loose and large under her arms. Her blonde hair straggled down over her wailing face.

"It was him!" she yelled. "Get him!"

She fell on her back and lay there writhing and screaming it into the morning, yelling it at the open blue sky, and windows rattled up on both sides of the street. She kept banging her head back against the sidewalk. A car horn began to blat. The three men bent over her, staring.

"Help!" she yelled.

One of the men pointed back at Chandler.

"Yes!" she yelled. "Him. That black!"

Two of the men turned and started to run at Chandler and he heard the sound of tires shrieking on the street and the soft moan of a tripped siren.

"I called the cops, you black bastard!" a man yelled from across the street in an open window directly opposite the alley. "I seen you! I called the cops!"

She rolled on the sidewalk, rolling back and forth, slamming her naked white body against the cement. She lay still on her back and wailed it.

"That black boy!"

Chandler turned and ran. The two men were very close to him. He kept calling back over his shoulder, running as fast as he could, "No. It's a mistake. I didn't do it. She's drunk. Can't you see?"

He heard the wild gunning of a car's engine. He turned into the first alley at hand and ran down that. At the far entrance, he looked back. The two men were in front of the car. It was a police car, for Jesus Christ, and they had got in its way. They stopped running and the police car stopped and they began talking, waving their arms.

He turned and ran again. He ran across the street and down the other side, and up another alley. He got out of that alley, and turned straight up the street. Then he saw this was the wrong way. That was the way toward the center of town. He turned back the other way. He crossed the street, feet pounding, running with the panic inside him, his lungs burning.

Why had he stopped to look? Why hadn't he stayed home?

Why had he forgotten all the things?

He turned into another alley, completely out of breath and dodged and huddled by a cellar door, hunkered down. He began to tremble, then shake all over. His head, his legs, his arms. He looked at his hands, trying to get his breath, gasping, watching the way his hands shook with a kind of detached wonder.

They shouldn't do this. He was studying to be a doctor. He was going to college. He was just home visiting for a week, and he'd forgotten certain things.

He hunkered shaking by the cellar door.

His mind was already taken up with a certainty.

That girl. For spite, she'd done that. Or was it because she'd been ashamed to be seen naked and like she was by three white men? What reason was there? No reason. What if he'd gone in there with her?

He clamped his eyes shut, fighting a kind of craziness that seeped up into him.

He thought of his school, but it wouldn't hold in his mind.

Only this. The great big booming now.

He didn't want to be afraid. But he was. And he knew he had to get away from this section of town. He got up and staggered and ran again. Maybe he could get home and get his clothes and take a train out. A plane. Go back where he belonged.

Where did he belong?

He made himself run hard, out and across the street and into another alley. He saw the gray police car coming down the street. Somebody yelled at him. He saw still another car pass the police car, careening.

Halfway down the alley, he turned wildly and looked back there. A car slammed into the alley, engine roaring.

He stood there, watching it.

It wasn't the police. Everybody was after him; they all believed that girl, because they wanted to. The whole world believed her. Then he saw the police car enter the alley behind the other car.

He turned and ran. He couldn't run very fast now.

The car speeded up and smashed into him from behind, crushing his back and he screamed and went down, whipped. The car passed over him and brakes squealed as it stopped a few yards beyond.

"We get him?" a man shouted.

"We got him!"

He lay there on the alley floor, then pushed himself to one elbow. He could not see very well and he was broken and split with pain.

He heard the police car stop back there, siren softly moaning.

"Back her up," the man said, from inside the car that had struck him. "Quick, back her up and make sure!"

He watched, unable to move, as the car gunned viciously backward. Steel bumpers smashed him in the face.

LEIGH BRACKETT
(1915–1978)

Until the runaway popularity of the female private eye in recent years, few women wrote hard-boiled and noir fiction. Most women authors seem to have preferred their crimes and misdemeanors to take place in surroundings more genteel than Raymond Chandler's mean streets and to be couched in less graphic and violent prose. But a few women did enter what was perceived as a "man's world" in the 1940s and 1950s, and some of them had significant careers. One was Georgiana Ann Randolph Craig, who (under the pseudonym Craig Rice) created Chicago lawyer John J. Malone. Other notables were Helen Nielsen, M. V. Heberden, and Dolores Hitchens. But the woman with the most impressive body of work, whose achievements rank her as one of the top hard-boiled-fiction writers of all time, was Leigh Brackett.

Brackett was an avowed admirer of Chandler and the Black Mask school, and her novel No Good from a Corpse (1944), a southern California tale featuring private detective Edmond Clive, is so Chandleresque in style and approach that it might have been written by Chandler. Indeed, Brackett was one of the co-authors of the screenplay of The Big Sleep in 1946, and twenty-five years later she wrote the script for the Robert Altman–Elliot Gould film version of The Long Goodbye (1973). The Tiger Among Us and An Eye for an Eye, her two 1957 suspense novels, are also powerful noir stories set against midwestern backdrops.

Oddly, 1957 was the only year in the 1950s in which Brackett published crime fiction; the balance of her output during that decade consisted of science fiction and screenplays. "So Pale, So Cold, So Fair," a gripping tale of political corruption and murder in a small Ohio town where "sin is organized, functional, and realistic," first appeared in the men's magazine Argosy in July 1957. Like the best of her handful of crime shorts published in the 1940s, this story contains echoes not only of Chandler, but of both Dashiell Hammett and Paul Cain. It might well have been featured in Black Mask one or two decades earlier—a magazine in which Brackett did not appear even once.

B. P.

SO PALE, SO COLD, SO FAIR

She was the last person in the world I expected to see. But she was there, in the moonlight, lying across the porch of my rented cabin.

She wore a black evening dress, and little sandals with very high heels. At her throat was a gleam of dim fire that even by moonlight you knew had to be made by nothing less than diamonds. She was very beautiful. Her name was Marjorie, and once upon a time, a thousand years ago, she had been engaged to me.

That was a thousand years ago. If you checked the calendar it would only say eight and a half, but it seemed like a thousand to me. She hadn't married me. She married Brian Ingraham, and she was still married to him, and I had to admit she had probably been right, because he could buy her the diamonds and I was still just a reporter for the Fordstown *Herald*.

I didn't know what Marjorie Ingraham was doing on my porch at two-thirty-five of a Sunday morning. I stood still on the graveled path and tried to figure it out.

The poker game was going strong in Dave Schuman's cabin next door. I had just left it. The cards had not been running my way, and the whiskey had, and about five minutes ago I had decided to call it a night. I had walked along the lake shore, looking with a sort of vague pleasure at the water and the sky, thinking that I still had eight whole days of vacation before I had to get back to my typewriter again.

And now here was Marjorie, lying across my porch.

I couldn't figure it out.

She had not moved. There was a heavy dew, and the drops glistened on her cheeks like tears. Her eyes were closed. She seemed to be sleeping.

"Marjorie?" I said. "Marjorie—"

There wasn't any answer.

I went up to the low step and reached across it and touched her bare shoulder. It was not really cold. It only felt that way because of the dew that was on it.

I laid my fingers on her throat, above the diamonds. I waited and waited, but there was no pulse. Her throat was faintly warm, too. It felt like marble that has been for a time in the sun. I could see the two dark, curved lines of her brows and the shadows of her lashes. I could see her mouth, slightly parted. I held my hand over it and there was nothing, no slightest breath. All of her was still, as still and remote as the face of the moon.

She was not sleeping. She was dead.

I stood there, hanging onto the porch rail, feeling sick as the whiskey turned in me and the glow went out. A lot of thoughts went through my mind about Marjorie, and now suddenly she was gone, and I would not have believed it could hit me so hard. The night and the world rocked around me, and then, when they steadied down again, I began to feel another emotion.

Alarm.

Marjorie was dead. She was on my porch, laid out with her skirt neat and her eyes closed, and her hands folded across her waist. I didn't think it was likely she had come there by herself and then suddenly died in just that position. Someone had brought her and put her there, on purpose.

But who? And why?

I ran back to Dave Schuman's.

I must have looked like calamity, because the minute I came in the door they forgot the cards and stared at me, and Dave got up and said, "Greg, what is it?"

"I think you better come with me," I said, meaning all of them. "I want witnesses."

I told them why. Dave's face tightened, and he said, "Marge Ingraham? My God." Dave, who is in the circulation department of the *Herald*, went to school with me and Marjorie and knows the whole story.

He grabbed a flashlight and went out the door, and the local physician, our old poker pal Doc Evers, asked me, "Are you sure she's dead?"

"I think so. But I want you to check it."

He was already on his way. There were three other guys beside Dave Schuman and Doc Evers and me: another member of the *Herald* gang; Hughie Brown, who ran Brown's Boat Livery on the lake; and a young fellow who was a visiting relation or something of Hughie's. We hurried back along the lake shore and up the gravel path.

Marjorie had not gone away.

Somebody turned on the porch light. The hard, harsh glare beat down, more cruel but more honest than the moonlight.

Hughie Brown's young relative said, in a startled kind of way, "But she can't be dead, look at the color in her skin."

Doc Evers grunted and bent over her. "She's dead, all right. At a rough guess, three or four hours."

"How?" I asked.

"As the boy says, look at the color of her skin. That usually indicates carbon-monoxide poisoning."

Dave said, in a curiously hesitant voice, "Suicide?"

Doc Evers shrugged. "It usually is."

"It could have been accidental," I said.

"Possibly."

"Either way," I said, "She couldn't have died here."

"No," said Doc, "hardly. Monoxide poisoning presupposes a closed space."

"All right," I said. "Why was she brought here and left on my door-step?"

Doc Evers said, "Well, in any case, you're in the clear. You've been with us since before six last evening."

Hughie Brown's young relative was staring at me. I realized what I was doing and shoved my hands in my pockets. I had been running my fingers over the scars that still show on my face, a nervous trick I haven't quite been able to shake.

"Sure," said Dave. "That's right. You're in the clear, Greg. No matter what."

"That comforts me," I said. "But not greatly."

I went back to fingering the scars.

I had enemies in Fordstown. I went out of my way to make them, with a batch of articles I was brainless enough to write about how things were being run in the city. The people involved had used a simple and direct method of convincing me that I had made a serious error in judgment. I turned again to look at poor Marjorie, and I wondered.

A man named Joe Justinian was my chief and unassailable enemy. Chief because he was the control center of Fordstown's considerable vice rackets, and unassailable because he owned the city administration, hoof, horns and hide.

A uniformed cop and a city detective of the Fordstown force had stood by and watched while Justinian's boys had their fun, bouncing me up and down on the old brick paving of the alley where they cornered me. The detective had had to move his feet to keep from getting my blood on his shoes. Afterward neither he nor the cop could remember a single identifying feature about the men.

Justinian had two right-hand bowers. One was Eddie Sego, an alert and sprightly young hood who saw to it that everything ran smoothly. The other was Marjorie's husband—now widower—Brian Ingraham. Brian was the respectable one, the lawyer who maintained in the world the polite fiction that Mr. Joseph Justinian was an honest businessman who operated a night club known as the Roman Garden, and who had various "investments."

Brian himself was one of Justinian's best investments. From a small lawyer with several clients he had become a big lawyer with one client.

And now his wife was dead on my doorstep.

Any way I looked at it, I couldn't see that this night was going to bring me anything but trouble.

Hughie Brown came back with a folded sheet fresh from the laundry. Doc Evers unfolded it, crisp and white, and that was the last I ever saw of Marjorie.

Doc said, "Where's the nearest phone?"

CHAPTER TWO

On Monday afternoon I was in Fordstown, in the office of Wade Hickey, our current chief of police.

Brian Ingraham was there, too. He was sitting in the opposite corner, his head bowed, not looking at me or Hickey. He seemed all shrunken together and gray-faced, and his fingers twitched so that it was an effort to hold the cigarettes he was chain-smoking. I kept glancing at him, fascinated.

This was a new role for Brian. I had never seen him before when he didn't radiate perfect confidence in his ability to outsmart the whole world and everybody in it.

Hickey was speaking. He was a big, thick-necked man with curly gray hair and one of those coarse, ruddy, jovial faces that can fool some of the people all of the time, but others for only the first five minutes.

"The reports are all complete now," he said, placing one large hand on a file folder in front of him on the desk. "Poor Marjorie took her own life. What her reasons may have been are known only to herself and God—"

Suddenly, viciously, Ingraham said, "You're not making a speech now, Wade. You don't have to ham it up."

His face was drawn like something on a rack. Hickey gave him a pitying glance.

"I'm sorry, Brian," he said, "but these facts have to be made perfectly clear. Mr. Carver is in a peculiar position here, and he has a right to know." He turned to me and went on.

"Marjorie's car was found in a patch of woods off Beaver Run Road, maybe ten miles out of town. There's an old logging cut there, and she had driven in on it about a quarter of a mile, where she wasn't likely to be disturbed. As it happened, of course, somebody did find her, too late to be of any help—"

"Somebody," I said, "with a fine sense of humor."

"Or someone wanting to make trouble for you," said Hickey. "Let's not forget that possibility. You do have enemies, you know."

"Yes," I said. "What a pity they were all complete strangers."

Hickey's eyes got cold. "Look, Carver," he said, "I'm trying to be decent about this. Don't make it hard for me."

"It seems to me," I said, "that I've been shamefully co-operative."

"Cooperation," said Hickey, "is how we all get along in this world. You oughtn't to be ashamed of it. Now then." He turned a page over in the folder. "Whoever found her and removed her body left the front door open, but all the windows were tight shut except the wind-wing on the right side. That was open sufficiently to admit a hose running from the exhaust pipe. The autopsy findings agree with the preliminary reports made by the doctor up at Lakelands—"

"Doctor Evers."

"That's right, Doctor Evers—and the police doctor who accompanied the ambulance. Carbon-monoxide poisoning." He closed the folder. "There's only one possible conclusion."

"Suicide," I said.

Hickey spread his hands and nodded solemnly.

I looked at Brian Ingraham. "You knew her better than anybody. What do you think?"

"What is there to think?" he said, in an old, dry, helpless voice that hardly carried across the room. "She did it. That's all." He ran the back of his hand across his eyes. He was crying.

"Now," said Hickey, "as to why her body was removed from the car, transported approximately twenty miles and left on your porch, Carver,

I don't suppose we'll ever know. A ghoulish joke, an act of malice—a body can be an embarrassing thing to explain away—or simply the act of a nut, with no real motive behind it at all. Whatever the explanation, it isn't important. And we certainly can't connect you in any way with Marjorie's death. So if I were you, I'd go home and forget about it."

"Yes," I said. "I guess that's the thing to do. Brian—"

"Yes."

"Do you know of any reason? Was she sick, or unhappy?"

He looked at me, through me, beyond me, into some dark well of misery. "No, I don't know of any reason. According to the autopsy she was in perfect health. As far as I knew"—he faltered, and then went on, in that curiously dead voice—"as far as I knew, she was happy."

"It's always a cruel thing to accept," said Hickey, "when someone we love takes that way out. But we have to realize—"

"We," said Ingraham, getting up. "What the hell have you got to do with it, you greedy, grubbing, boot-licking slob? And how would you know, anyway? You've never loved anything but yourself and money since the day you were born." .

He went past me and out the door.

Hickey shook his fine, big, leonine head. "Poor Brian. He's taking this mighty hard."

"Yes," I said.

"Well," said Hickey, "it's no wonder. Marjorie was a mighty fine girl."

"Yes," I said. I got up. "I take it that's all?"

Hickey nodded. He picked up the file and shoved it in a drawer. He shut the drawer. Symbol of completion.

I went to the *Herald* and did a nice, neat, factual follow-up on the story I had already filed. Then I stopped at the State Store and picked up a bottle, and returned to the bachelor apartment I inhabit for fifty weeks of the year.

So I was home, as Hickey had recommended, but I did not forget it. I forgot to go out for food, and I forgot later to turn the lights on, but I couldn't forget Marjorie. I kept seeing her face turned toward me in the moonlight, with the dew on her cheeks and her lips parted. After a while it seemed to me that she had been trying to speak, to tell me something. And I got angry.

"That's just like you," I said. "Make a mess of things, and then come running to me for help. Well, this time I can't help you."

I thought of her sitting all alone in her car in the old logging cut, listening to the motor throb, feeling death with every breath she breathed, and I wondered if she had thought that at the end. I wondered if she had thought of me at all.

"Such a waste, Marjorie. You could have left Brian. You could have done a million other things. Why did you have to go and kill yourself?"

It was hot and dark in the room. The Marjorie-image receded slowly into a thickening haze.

"That's it," I said. "Go away."

The haze got thicker. It enveloped me, too. It was restful. Marjorie was gone. Everything was gone. It was very nice.

Then the noise began.

It was a sharp, insistent noise. A ringing. It had a definite significance, one I tried hard to ignore. But I couldn't, quite. It was the doorbell, and in the end I didn't have any choice. I fought my way partly out of the fog and answered it.

She was standing in the hall, looking in at me.

"Oh, God," I said. "No. I told you. You can't come back to me now. You're dead."

Her voice reached me out of an enormous and terrible void.

"Please," it said. "Mr. Carver, please! My name is Sheila Harding. I want to talk to you."

She was shorter than Marjorie, and not so handsome. This girl's hair was brown and her eyes were blue.

I hung onto the door jamb. "I don't know you," I said, too far gone to be polite.

"I was a friend of Marjorie's." She stepped forward. "Please, I must talk to you."

She pushed by me, and I let her. I switched the light on and closed the door. There was a chair beside the door. I sat in it.

She didn't look like her at all, really. She didn't move the same way, and the whole shape and outline of her was different. She kept glancing at me, and it dawned on me that she hadn't counted on finding me drunk.

"I can still hear you," I said. "What's on your mind?"

She hesitated. "Maybe I'd better—"

"I plan to be drunk all the rest of this week. So unless it's something that can wait—"

"All right," she said rather sharply. "It's about Marjorie."

I waited.

"She was a very unhappy person," Sheila Harding said.

"That's not what Brian said. He said she was happy."

"He knows better than that," she said bitterly. "He must know. He just doesn't want to admit it. Of course, I knew Marjorie quite a long while before I realized it, but that's different. We both belonged to the League."

"Oh," I said. "You're one of those society dolls. Now wait." The name Harding clicked over in my dim brain with a sound of falling coins. "Gilbert Harding, Harding Steel, umpteen millions. I don't remember a daughter."

"There wasn't one. I'm his niece."

"Marjorie enjoyed belonging to the League," I said. "She was born and raised on the South Side, right where I was. Her biggest ambition was to grow up to be a snob."

I was annoying Miss Harding, who said, "That isn't important, Mr. Carver. The important thing is that she needed a friend very badly, and for some reason she picked me."

"You look the friendly type."

Her mouth tightened another notch. But she went on. "Marjorie was worried about Brian. About what he was doing, the people he was mixed up with."

I laughed. I got up and went over to the window, in search of air. "Brian was working for Justinian when she married him. She knew it. She thought it was just splendid of him to be so ambitious."

"Nine years ago," said Sheila quietly, "Justinian was a lot more careful what he did."

She sounded so sensible and so grim that I turned around and looked at her with considerably more interest.

"That's true," I said. "But I still think it was late in the day for Marjorie to get upset. I told her at the beginning just what the score was. She didn't give a damn, as long as it paid."

"She did later. I told you she was an unhappy person. She had made some bad mistakes, and she knew it."

"They weren't that bad," I said. "They weren't so bad she had to kill herself."

Her eyes met mine, blue, compelling, strangely hard.

"Marjorie didn't kill herself," she said.

CHAPTER THREE

I let that hang there in the hot, still air while I looked at it.

Marjorie didn't kill herself.

There were two sides to it. One: Of course she killed herself; the evidence is as clear as day. Two: I'm not surprised; I never thought she did.

I said carefully, "I was in the office of the chief of police this afternoon. I heard all the evidence, the autopsy report, the works. Furthermore, I saw the body, and a doctor friend of mine saw it. Monoxide poisoning, self-administered, in her own car. Period."

"I read the papers," said Sheila. "I know all about that. I know all about you, too."

"Do you?"

"Marjorie told me."

"Girlish confidences, eh?"

"Something a little more than that, Mr. Carver. It was when you were beaten so badly, a year or so back, that Marjorie began to feel—well, to put it honestly—guilty."

"I'm sorry. I'm not at my best tonight. Go on."

"Then," said Sheila, "my brother was killed, just after New Year's."

"Your brother?" I sat down again, this time on the edge of the bed, facing her.

"He was in the personnel department of Harding Steel, a very junior executive. He told me the numbers racket—the bug, he called it—was taking thousands of dollars out of the men's pay checks every month. I guess that goes on in all the mills, more or less."

"Around here it does. And more, not less."

"Well, Bill thought he'd found a way to catch the people who were doing it, and clean up Harding Steel. He was ambitious. He wanted to do something big and startling. He was all excited about it. And then a load of steel rods dropped on him, and that was that. Just a plant accident. Everybody was sorry."

I remembered, now that she told me. I hadn't covered the story myself, and there was no reason in particular why it should stick in my mind. But there hadn't been any suspicion of foul play at the time. I said so.

"Of course not. They were very careful about it. But Bill had told me the night before that his life had been threatened. He almost bragged about it. He said they couldn't stop him now; he had the men he wanted—Justinian's men, naturally—right here." She held out her hand and closed the fingers. "He was murdered."

"And you told this to Marjorie."

"Yes. We were very good friends, Mr. Carver. Very close. She didn't think I was hysterical. She knew Bill, and liked him. She became terribly angry and upset. She said she would find out everything she could, and if it was really murder she was going to make Brian quit Justinian."

"Go on."

"It took her a long time. But last Saturday afternoon, late, she stopped by. She said she was pretty sure she had the full story, and it was murder, and she was going to face Brian with it that night. I asked her for details. She wouldn't tell me anything because she didn't think Brian was personally involved, and she was in duty bound to give him his chance to get clear of Justinian before she told.

"Then she was going to give the whole story to my Uncle Gilbert. She said he was big enough to fight Justinian."

And he was, plenty big enough. If he had even reasonable proof that his nephew had been murdered, he could go right over the heads of the local law, to where the Emperor Justinian of Fordstown had no influence at all. He could smash him into little pieces.

Reason enough for Justinian to silence Marjorie. Reason enough. But . . .

Sheila was still talking. "Marjorie did tell me one thing, Mr. Carver."

"What?"

"If Brian still insisted on sticking with Justinian, she was going to leave him. She said, 'I'll go back to Greg, if he still wants me.' "

That turned me cold all over. "And she did. No, what am I saying? She didn't come, somebody brought her. Somebody. Who? Why?"

"Surely you must have guessed that by now, Mr. Carver."

"You tell me."

"Who it was exactly, of course, I don't know. But it was somebody who knows Marjorie's suicide was a lie. It was somebody who liked her and wanted the truth known. Somebody who thought that if he brought her to you, you would understand and do something about it."

Yes. I could see that.

"But why me? Why not lay her on Brian's doorstep? He was her husband."

"They probably felt that he would be too shocked and grieved to understand. Or perhaps they didn't trust him to fight Justinian. You wouldn't be involved either way. And you already have a grudge against Justinian."

Oh yes, I had a grudge, all right. But who was this thoughtful someone? One of the killers? An accidental witness? And why did he have to pass the thing along to anyone? Why didn't he just come out and tell the truth himself?

That last one was easy. He was afraid.

Well, so was I.

Sheila was waiting. She was looking at me, expectant, confident. She was a pretty girl. She seemed like a nice girl, a loyal friend, a loving sister. She had had her troubles. I hated to let her down.

I said, "No sale. Marjorie killed herself. Let's just accept that and forget it."

She stared at me with a slowly dawning astonishment. "After what I've just told you—you can still say that?"

"Yes," I said. "I can. In the first place, how would Marjorie find it out even if your brother was really murdered? Eddie Sego plans those things, and Eddie is not the babbling type. Not to anybody, including the boss's lawyer's wife."

"Eddie Sego had nothing to do with it. He was in the hospital then with a burst appendix. That's one thing that made it harder for Marjorie, because she didn't know where to start." She added, with angry certainty, "She did find out, somehow."

"Okay then. She found out. Maybe she found out even more. Maybe she discovered that Brian was so deeply involved that she couldn't tell. Maybe she was in such a mess that there wasn't any other way out of it but suicide. You don't know what happened after she left you." I got up and opened the door. "Go home, Miss Harding. Forget about it. Lead a long and happy life."

She didn't go. She continued to look at me. "I understand," she said. "You're scared."

"Miss Harding," I said, "have you ever been set upon by large men with brass knuckles? Have you ever spent weeks in a hospital getting your face put back together again?"

"No. But I imagine it wasn't pleasant. I imagine they warned you that the next time it would be worse."

"A society doll with brains," I said. "You have the whole picture. Good night."

"I don't think you have the whole picture yet, Mr. Carver. If you could find the man who brought Marjorie's body to you, you would have a witness who could break Justinian."

"All right," I said, "we'll get right down to bedrock. I don't like Justinian any better than you do, but it's going to take somebody or something bigger than me to break him. I tried to once, and he did the breaking. As far as I'm concerned, that's it."

"I don't suppose," she said slowly, "that I have any right to call you a coward."

"No. You haven't."

"Very well. I won't."

And this time she went.

I closed the door and turned off the lights. Then I went to the window and looked down at the street, three floors below. I saw her come out of the building and get into a black-and-white convertible parked at the curb. She drove away. Before she was out of sight a man got out of a car across the street and then the car went off after her. The man who had been left behind loitered along the street, where he could watch the front of the building and my window.

Somebody was keeping tabs on what I did and who came to see me. Wade Hickey? Justinian? And why?

I began to think about Brian Ingraham, and wonder how deeply he might be involved. I began to think about Joe Justinian, and what might be done about him. The Marjorie-image came back into my mind, and it was smiling.

Then I thought of the brass knuckles and the taste of blood and oil on the old brick paving. I looked down at the loitering man. "The hell with it," I said, and I went and lay down on my bed.

But I couldn't sleep.

About midnight I quit trying. I smoked a couple of cigarettes, sitting by the window. I did not turn the lights on. I don't remember that I came to any conscious and reasoned decision, either. After a certain length of time I just got up and went.

I didn't go near my car. I knew they would be watching that, expecting me to use it. I slipped out the back entrance into the alley and across it to an areaway that ran alongside another apartment house to the next street. I was careful. I didn't see anybody. I didn't want anybody to see me. I still thought I could quit on this thing any time it got too risky.

At my age, and with my experience, I should have known better.

CHAPTER FOUR

There were still honest cops on the force, plenty of them. It wasn't their fault if they were hamstrung. As things stood, they had two choices. They could resign and go to farming or selling shoes, or they could sweat it out, hoping for better days. One who was sweating it out was an old friend of mine, a detective named Carmen Prioletti.

His house was pitch-dark when I got to it, after a twenty-minute hike. I rang the bell, and pretty soon a light came on, and then Carmen, frowsy with sleep, stuck his head out the door and demanded to know what the hell.

"Oh," he said. "It's you."

He let me in and we stood talking in low voices in the hall, so as not to wake the family.

"I want to borrow your car," I said. "No questions asked, and back in an hour. Okay?"

He looked at me narrowly. Then he said, "Okay." He got the keys and gave them to me.

"I'll need a flashlight, too," I said.

"There's one in the car." He added, "I'll wait up."

I drove through quiet streets to the northern edge of town, and beyond it, into the country, where the air was cool and the dark roads were overhung with trees, and the summer mist lay white and heavy in the bottoms. I drove fast until I came to Beaver Run Road, and then I went slower, looking for the logging cut. Beaver Run was a secondary road, unpaved, washboarded and full of potholes. Dust had coated the trees and brush on either side, so they showed up bleached and grayish.

I found the cut and turned into it, and stopped the motor. It became suddenly very still. I picked up the flashlight and got out. I walked down the rutted track.

They had taken Marjorie's car away, of course, and the comings and goings of men and tow trucks had pretty well flattened everything in sight. But I found where the car had been. I looked all around at the crushed brambles, the rank weeds and the Queen Anne's lace. Then I walked a little farther down the track where no one had been. I walked slowly, watching my feet. I circled around to the side of the track, as one would in walking around a car. My trouser legs were wet to the knees with dew. The briars caught in them and scratched my shins. I went back to Prioletti's car and sat sideways, with the door open, picking a batch of prickly green beggar's lice out of my socks. The socks, and my shoes, were wet.

I backed out of the cut and drove into town again, to Prioletti's.

He was waiting up for me, as he had promised. We sat in the kitchen, smoking, and all the time he watched me with his bright dark eyes.

"Carmen," I said, "suppose you're a girl. You're wearing an evening dress, sheer stockings, high-heeled shoes. You decide to kill yourself. You drive to a nice quiet spot, an old logging cut off a back road. You have brought a hose with you—"

Carmen's eyes were fairly glittering now, but wary. "Continue."

"You wish to attach that hose to the exhaust pipe, and then run it in through the front window. Now, to do this you have to get out of the car. You have to walk around it to the back, and then around it again to the front. Right?"

"Indubitably."

"All right. There are briar thickets, weeds, beggar's lice, unavoidable, and all soaked with dew. What happens to your nylons and your fancy shoes?"

"They're pretty much of a wreck."

"Hers were not."

"I see," said Carmen slowly. "You're sure of that? Absolutely sure."

"When I found her on my porch she was neat and pretty as a pin. Carmen, she never got out of that car until she was carried out, dead."

I filled him in on Sheila Harding, and what she had told me. Then we were both through talking for awhile. The electric clock on the wall touched two and went past it. Carmen smoked and brooded.

"What did you have in mind?" he asked finally.

"That depends," I said. "How much are you willing to risk? The minute certain people around Headquarters realize you're suspicious, you'll be in trouble."

"Leave that to me. I used to be proud of my job, Greg. Now I tell my kids I'm not really a cop, I play piano in a disorderly house." He clenched his hands together on the table top, and shivered all over. "This might be it. This might just by the grace of God be it."

"You'll have to play it mighty close to the vest. Now, what I would like to know is whether the autopsy report mentioned any external marks, no matter how slight, around the wrists and ankles, and maybe the mouth. Or a bruise on the head, under the hair."

"I'll see what I can find out. We'd better not be seen meeting. How about north of the lake in Mill Creek Park, around three?"

I nodded and got up.

I walked home. I didn't meet anyone along the way. When I got within a block or so of my apartment house I took extra pains to stay in the shadows. I figured to come in the way I had gone out, across the alley and through the back door. I figured the boys out front would never know I had been away.

I was happy in that thought right up to the minute I actually opened the door. Inside, in the narrow well of the service stairs, a dim light was burning, and I saw a man there. A large man, with a crushed hat pulled down over his eyes. I saw him in the act of leaping toward me, and I let go of the door and turned to run, and there was another man in back of me. He hit me as I turned, and then the man in the stairwell came out and banged me across the nape of the neck. I went down on my hands and knees in the alley, onto the uneven bricks, and there we were again. A visit with old friends. Justinian's boys.

One of them pulled me up and wrenched my head back, and the other one gave me a fast chop over the Adam's apple. That was to stop me yelling.

Then he said, "Where were you?"

I coughed and choked. Nameless, who was holding my arm doubled up behind me, gave it an upward twist. I winced, and Faceless, who was in front of me, with his hat still pulled down so that nothing much showed in the dark of night, asked again, "Where were you?"

I whispered, "Out for a walk."

"Yeah," said Faceless, "I know that. You didn't take your car. So where'd you walk to?"

"Around. No place."

He hit me twice, once on the left cheekbone, once on the right.

"I'm asking you," he said. "Me. The dame came to see you, and right away you went sneaking out. I want to know why."

"No connection," I said. "She just dropped by. And it wasn't right away. I was restless and couldn't sleep. I went for a walk. So sue me."

Nameless said conversationally, "I could break your arm."

He showed me how easy it would be. I went down on my knees again. There was a taste of blood in my mouth. I thought my face was bleeding. I thought I could feel it running down my cheeks, hot and wet, to spatter on the bricks.

"If it hadn't been," said Faceless, "that we could hear your phone ringing and ringing through the open window, and you didn't answer it, we wouldn't never have known you'd gone. Now, that kind of thing can lead to trouble." He kicked me. "Get up, buddy. I don't like to have to bend over when I'm talking."

I got up. I couldn't stand the feeling of blood on my face. I got up fast. I threw myself backward, butting Nameless as hard as I could with my head. It must have been hard enough, because he grunted and let go. He fell, and I fell on top of him, whipped around with my feet under me, and went for Faceless. He looked very queer. He was cloud-shaped, huge and looming, and the alley and the building walls were all twisted and quivering as though I was seeing them through dark water. I hit him full on and he went over backward, floating, slow-motion, like something in a dream. The blood ran down my face, filling my eyes, my nose, my mouth. I thought, *This is what it feels like to be crazy.* I knocked his hat off and got hold of his head and beat it up and down, up and down, hard, hard on the alley bricks.

It was nice, but it didn't last long. It hardly lasted at all. Nameless got up. He was mad. He hit me with something much harder than a fist, and pretty soon Faceless got up, and he was mad, too. They let me know it. I heard one of them wanting to kill me right now, but the other one said, "Not yet, not till we get the order." He shook me. "You get that, buddy? The order. It can come any minute. And when it does, you got nothing left to hope for."

He threw me down and they went away, down a long black tunnel that lengthened until I got dizzy watching and shut my eyes. When I opened them again I was lying in the alley, alone. It was still dark. I wanted to go to my apartment. I know I started and I know I must have made it up two flights of the service stairs, because I was lying on the landing when Shelia found me . . .

"I'm sorry, I'm so sorry," she said and helped me up, and we walked together up the rest of the steps and down the hall to the apartment. I told her to pull the blind shut.

"They're watching the place," I said.

"I know it," she said. "Somebody followed me home."

She took me into the bathroom and went to work.

"It's not bad at all," she said. "Just ordinary cuts and bruises. But why did they do this to you? What were you doing?"

"I went out on an errand," I said. "They'd never have known I was gone, but some clown had to call me on the telephone. They could hear it ringing and they knew I wasn't here. What's the matter?"

She was already pretty white and tense. Now she put her hand over her mouth and her eyes got big and full of tears.

"Oh Lord," she said. "Oh, Lord, that was me."

"You?"

"I got to thinking after I got home. I didn't have any right to expect you to do anything. I didn't have any right to reproach you. I wanted to tell you that. And I thought I ought to warn you that you were being watched. So I called. When you didn't answer I thought at first you'd—"

She hesitated, and I said, "Passed out," and she nodded.

"Then I began to get really worried. I called again, and again, and then finally I had to come back to see if you were all right." She began to cry. "And it was my fault."

"You didn't mean it," I said. "You were trying to help." My first impulse was to kill her, but she looked so miserable. "Please, stop crying."

"I can't," she whispered, and looked at the bloody washrag she had in her other hand. "I think I'm going to faint."

She looked as though she might. I put my arm around her and took her into the other room, and we sat together on the edge of the bed, with her face buried on my shoulder. I wound up kissing her.

I think both of us were surprised to find we liked it.

"You're a nice kid," I said. "If you weren't so rich—"

She said quickly, "Didn't you know? My side of the family doesn't have a million to its name. We're the poor Hardings. That's one reason my brother was so anxious to show off."

"You may be in danger yourself," I said, suddenly alarmed for her. "They're already curious about you."

"Since you're not going to do anything about Marjorie, I can't see that it matters," she said.

"Well—" I said.

"You *have* done something! What? Please tell me."

"No. You're in trouble enough already. Anyway, it isn't much." It wasn't, either, unless Prioletti could turn up something on that autopsy report. And even that would only be a first step, an opening wedge. "One thing I'd give a lot to know," I told her, "is where Brian Ingraham was the night his wife was killed."

"You don't think," she said, her face reflecting horror, "that Brian had anything to do with it."

"He's Justinian's man. Body and bank account."

"But his own wife!"

"This is a hard world we live in."

She shivered. "And Marjorie said she'd given the maid the night off, so they'd be alone, and she was going to make herself beautiful so Brian would have to choose her instead of Justinian. She was vain, poor Marjorie. I just can't believe— Well, it doesn't matter what I believe, does it? Anyway, I know where Brian was that night, or at least where Marjorie thought he was. She was going to have to wait until he got home to talk to him."

"Go ahead," I said. "Where was he?"

"At the Roman Garden, with Justinian."

CHAPTER FIVE

Sin in a middle-western steel town is organized, functional, and realistic. It is not like in the movies. The necessary furniture is there, and nothing more. No velvet drapes, no gilt mirrors, no ultramodernistic salons, no unbelievably beautiful females. The houses are just houses, and the whores are just whores. Numbers slips can be bought in almost any dingy little sandwich shop, pool hall, or corner grocery, and anyone can play, even the kids with as little as a penny. The night clubs and gambling palaces, like the Roman Garden, are businesslike structures wasting no time on the fancy junk. There's a bar, and there are the gambling layouts, and that's that. Food, entertainment, and decor are haphazard. The bosses don't figure that's what you came for.

At nine o'clock on a hot morning the Roman Garden looked downright dreary. It was primarily a big, barny, old two-and-a-half-story frame house, with a new front tacked on it, yellow glazed brick with glass-brick insets and a neon sign. There was a parking lot around back. A couple of cars were already in it. The sports car I knew was Eddie Sego's.

I went in through the back door. No one followed me. No one had followed me since the two musclemen left me in the alley. I had escorted Sheila to her apartment, making her promise that she would go to her uncle's first thing in the morning, and there had not been a sign of a tail, nor was there now. I wished I knew why.

I walked down the hall and pushed open the door that said OFFICE.

A thoroughly respectable-looking, middle-aged female was sitting at a desk, writing busily. I went past her to the door marked PRIVATE and went through it before she could do more than squawk.

Eddie Sego was in the inner office. He was busy, too. There's a lot of paper work in any business, and he had a stack of it. He was wearing a magnificent silk sports shirt, and a pair of hornrimmed glasses. With his hairy forearms and thick, low-growing black hair, the glasses made him look like a studious gorilla.

He leaped up, startled. Then he saw who it was and sat down again, and swore. He took his glasses off.

"You ought to know better than that, Carver," he said. "Bursting in without warning. I might have thought it was a heist and shot you." He looked at me with his head on one side. "What are you doing here, anyway? And what hit you?"

"You know damn well what hit me," I said. "Eddie, it isn't fair. I've played ball. The Emperor wanted me to shut up, and I did. What more does he want?"

"Look," said Eddie, "I'm no mind reader. What's this all about?"

"Of course," I said, "you're not going to admit you know. Okay, I'll spell it out. Last night a girl came to visit me. A mutual friend just died, and she was looking for sympathetic conversation. Everything was going fine with us until she went home. Then I found out my place was being watched. A big goon followed her and scared the wits out of her, and then when I left my room for a breath of air two guys jumped me. They wanted to know where I was going and why, and then they threatened to kill me, when they got the order. And I haven't done a damned thing. Everybody's got a limit, even me. And I'm pretty close to it."

"Are you?" said Eddie. He got up and came around the desk to me. he looked at me for a moment, close to. Then he hit me, fast as a coiled snake, in the pit of the belly. He watched me double up and move back, and his lip curled. He stood there with his hands at his sides, almost as though he was giving me an invitation.

I didn't take it, and Eddie said, "Limit! You've got no limit. You haven't got anything." He turned his back on me. "You don't even have a reason to come whining to me. I didn't send anybody around. I don't care what dames you see, and I can't imagine Justinian does, either."

He sounded as though he really had not sent anybody. In the small corner of my mind that was not concerned with the pain in my gut, I wondered if Justinian was playing this one over Eddie's head. It was possible.

I managed to say, "They were his boys, just the same. The same two that beat me before."

Eddie didn't even bother to answer that. He picked up the phone and dialed a number. I started to go, and he gave me a black look and said, "Stick around."

"Why? What are you doing?"

"I'm calling the cops."

I stared at him, feeling my face go wide open and foolish. "You're what?"

"Calling the cops. They're looking for you—didn't you know that? I got the word just a few minutes ago."

I stopped holding my belly. I turned and went out of there, paying no attention to Eddie's shouts. I burned rubber going away.

So the cops were after me. This was a switch. This I had not looked for. I thought now that that was why the musclemen had been withdrawn. Justinian liked to keep his right hand and his left from getting tangled up. But I couldn't figure what possible charge they could have against me.

Of course, under the present setup, they didn't really need one . . .

I thought it was about time somebody did something about cleaning up this town.

I decided to go across the line into Pennsylvania for the rest of the day, until it was time to meet Prioletti. From Fordstown, Pennsylvania is less than thirty miles. I had a lot of time to kill, and nothing to do but hug my bruises and think. I thought of Marjorie, and of young Harding. I thought of the way Justinian's corporation was set up. Two main branches, gambling and prostitution, under separate heads, with separate organizations. Gambling subdivided into three—regular layouts like the Roman Garden, horse rooms, and the bug. The bug, day in and day out, probably brought in more money than all the rest put together. I thought of Eddie Sego, who was almost boss of all the gambling rackets, next under Justinian himself.

When it was time, I went back over the state line, using the farm roads, dusty and quiet in the heat of the afternoon. At three o'clock I was in Mill Creek Park, in a grove of trees north of the little lake with the swans on it. Prioletti was already there.

"I didn't know if you'd make it," he said. He looked haggard and excited. "You know I'm supposed to be looking for you?"

"Yeah," I said. "But what for?"

"Investigation. That's a big word. It can cover a lot of things. It can keep you out of circulation for a while, and it can demand answers to questions."

He peered around nervously. "I got a look at that report."

"Any luck?"

"Minor contused area on the scalp, minor abrasions at the mouth corners and cuts on the inside of the lips. There were also bruises and other minor abrasions on both wrists. No explanation."

"What would you say, Carmen?"

"Coupled with your other evidence, I would say it indicates that the girl was hit on the head, gagged and bound to prevent any outcry, and then driven to the logging cut, where her car was rigged for the fake suicide."

I felt a qualm of sickness. I had known that was how it must have been, but put into words that way it sounded so much more brutal.

"Poor kid," I said. "I hope she never came to."

"Yeah," said Carmen. "But we've almost got it, Greg. Brian Ingraham is the key. If he knew that Justinian—"

He broke off, looking over my shoulder. "I was afraid of that," he said. He reached out and grabbed me fiercely. "Hit me. Hit me hard and then run. Hickey's cops."

He said that as though it was a dirty word, and it was. I hit him, and he let go, and I ran. Hickey's cops ran after me, but they were still a long way back, and I knew the park intimately from boyhood days. They shouted and one of them fired a shot, but it was in the air. I guess the order hadn't come yet. Anyway, I shook them and got back to my car. For the second time that day I burned rubber, going away.

I headed for the Country Club section, and Brian Ingraham's home.

What Carmen had started to say was that if Brian, believing his wife a suicide, were to find out that Justinian had had her killed, he could be expected to turn on Justinian.

What Carmen had not said was that if Brian already knew it, and was co-operating with Justinian, his reaction would be quite different.

I went in the long drive to the house, set far back among trees. I rang the bell, and Brian opened the door, and I walked in after him down the hall.

Brian looked like a ghost. He seemed neither pleased nor displeased to see me. He didn't even ask me why I had come. He led me into the living room and then just stood there, as though he had already forgotten me.

"Brian, I've come about Marjorie."

He looked at me, in the same queer, twisted, other-dimensional way he had in Hickey's office that day.

"You didn't have to," he said. "I know."

And I thought, *Well, here it is, and I'm finished, and so is the case.* But something about his face made me ask him, "What do you know?"

"Why she killed herself. It was me." He said it simply, honestly, almost as though I was his conscience and he was trying to get straight with me. "I said she was happy, but she wasn't. For a long time she wanted me to quit and go back into regular practice, but I wouldn't. I laughed at her. Kindly, Greg. Kindly, as you would laugh at a child. But she wasn't a child. She could see me quite clearly. As I have been seeing myself since Sunday morning."

He paused. Then, still in that heartbreakingly simple way, he said, "I loved her. And I killed her."

He couldn't be lying. Not with that face and manner. It wasn't possible. I felt weak in the knees with relief.

"You had nothing to do with it," I said. "Justinian killed her, to save his neck."

He stood still, and his eyes became very wide and strange. "Justinian? Killed her?"

"Sit down," I said, "and I'll tell you how it was done."

We sat in the quiet house, with the hot afternoon outside the French windows, and I talked. And Brian listened.

When I was all through he said, "I see." Then he was silent a long time. His face had altered, becoming stony and hard, and there was a dim, cold spark at the back of his eyes.

"I remember Sheila Harding. I didn't know about her brother. That side of Justinian's business is in Eddie Sego's hands, and Eddie is not talkative."

"No," I said. "But Eddie was in the hospital then. Justinian had to attend to that emergency himself. And somehow Marjorie found out."

"Marjorie was my wife," said Brian softly. "He had no right to touch her." He stood up, and his voice became suddenly very loud. "He had no right. Marjorie. My wife."

I thought I heard a car, coming up the long drive and coming fast, but Brian was shouting so I couldn't be sure. I tried to shut him up, but he was coming apart at the seams in a way that couldn't be stopped. I couldn't blame him, but I wished he would make sense. I put my hands on his shoulders and shook him.

"For God's sake, Brian! We don't have all year—"

We didn't even have the rest of the afternoon. Two big men came in through the French windows, with guns in their hands. My old friends of the alley. Between them came a third man, with no gun. He never carried a gun. He didn't need one. He was Justinian, the Emperor of Fordstown.

Brian saw him. Instantly he became silent, poised, his eyes shining like the eyes of an animal I once saw, mangled by dogs and dying. He sprang at Justinian.

It was Eddie Sego, entering through the door behind us, who slugged Brian on the back of the head and put him down.

CHAPTER SIX

The long, full draperies were drawn across the French windows. The doors were locked. The cars, mine and Justinian's, had been taken around to the back, out of sight of any chance caller. The house itself stood in the middle of two wooded acres, and so did the houses on either side. In this section you paid for seclusion, and you got it.

Justinian was talking. He was a tall man, gray at the temples, distinguished-looking, dressed by the best tailors. He had immense charm. Women fell over fainting when he smiled at them, and then were always astonished to discover that the underlying ruthlessness in his steel-trap mouth and bird-of-prey eyes was the real Justinian.

He was not bothering now to be charming. He was entirely the business man, cerebral, efficient.

"It's a pity I didn't get here a little sooner," he said. "I might have stopped Carver. As it is—" He shrugged.

Brian looked up at him from the chair where he was sitting, with Eddie Sego behind him. "Then you admit you killed Marjorie."

Justinian shook his head. "I haven't admitted anything, and I don't intend to. The thing is, you believe I killed her, or that I might have killed her. The doubt has been planted. I could go to a lot of trouble to convince you you're wrong, but I couldn't make you stop wondering. I could never trust you again, Brian, any more than you would trust me. So your usefulness to me is ended.''

He turned to glare at me. "That's all *you've* accomplished, Carver."

"Oh, I understand," said Brian. "I've understood all along. Why else was all the business done in your office, and all records kept in your safe? You wanted to be able to eliminate me at any time, with no danger of incriminating papers lying around where you couldn't get at them. So that angle is covered. But I'm a pretty important man, Joe. Won't there be some curiosity?''

"If the bereaved husband takes his own life? I don't think so."

"I see," said Brian. "Just like Marjorie."

"And what about me?" I asked.

Justinian shrugged. "We planned that on the way. It will appear that Brian shot you first, before killing himself. You see? The old lover, accusing the husband of having driven his wife to . . .''

Brian whimpered and rose up, and Eddie Sego knocked him down again.

"All right," Justinian said. "He keeps his gun in the desk in the next room. Go get it.''

Eddie nodded. "Cover him," he said to Faceless. He went out.

I said, "There's a couple of things wrong with your plan, Joe."

"I'm listening."

"Other people know the whole story. You can't kill off everybody in town.''

"If you mean Miss Harding, she doesn't know anything, not at first-hand. Suspicions are a dime a dozen. If you mean Prioletti, he'll forget. He has a family to consider.''

"You're overlooking the most important person of all," I said.

"Who's that?"

"The guy who brought me Marjorie's body. He knows."

Justinian's face tightened ominously. "A crank, that's all. Doesn't mean a thing.''

Eddie Sego had come back from the next room. He was holding Brian's gun. Brian was hunched over in his chair, but he was staring at me intently. The two large men stood still and listened.

"You don't believe that, Joe," I said. "You're saying it because you haven't been able to find out who the man is, and you don't want your underlings to get panicky about it.''

"If he'd had anything to tell he'd have told it by now," said Justinian. "Anyway, I'll find him. One thing at a time."

"You'd better find him fast, Joe," I said, "because he belongs to you. You've got a traitor in your own camp."

Justinian said, "Hold it a minute, Eddie." He moved a step or two closer to me. "That's an interesting thought. Go on with it."

"Well," I said, "a casual crank would have had to just accidentally stumble on the car with Marjorie's body in it. He would also have had to know who she was, and that she had once been engaged to me. He would have had to know I was on vacation, and where. Now, does all that seem likely?"

He shook his head impatiently. "Go on."

"I'm just laying it out for you. Okay, we forget the crank. We say instead it was somebody who was fond of Marjorie and wanted her avenged, but was afraid to come out and tell the truth. So he figured that handing me the body would sic me on to what really happened to her."

"This sounds better."

"But still not good enough. If he was just a friend of Marjorie's, how did he know about the murder? Guess at it, stumble on it, happen to follow the cars into the logging cut and then wait around unseen while the thing was being done, when he could have been calling for help? Not likely. If it was one of the killers suddenly getting conscience-stricken, that fills all the requirements except one. Would he deliberately sic someone onto himself, to get himself hanged?"

Very briefly, Justinian's eyes flicked from Nameless to Faceless and back again to me. "No. This I can tell you."

"So what does that leave? It leaves a man who knew about Marjorie's murder, but was personally clear of it. A man who was clear on the Harding murder, too—so clear he could afford to talk about it. A man who wanted the murderer brought to justice, but who didn't want to appear in the business himself. Too dangerous, if something went wrong. So he handed the job on to me. Not to Brian, because he was too close to it, but to me. See? If I got killed, he hadn't lost anything but this chance, and there'd be another some day. But if I succeeded in pulling you down, he—"

Nameless fired, past Justinian.

The noise was earsplitting. Justinian, with the instinct of an old campaigner, dropped flat on the floor. Eddie Sego, behind him and across the room, was already down and rolling for the shelter of a sofa. He wasn't hit. He did not intend to be hit, either.

"He was gonna shoot you in the back, Boss," said Nameless, on a note of stunned surprise. "He was gonna—"

I tipped my chair over onto him, and we went staggering down together, with my hands on his wrist. I wanted his gun. I wanted it bad.

He wasn't going to give it up without a struggle. We got tangled in the furniture and when I got a look around again I saw Justinian, kneeling behind a big armchair. He was paying no attention to us. He had bigger things on his mind, like the gun he was too proud to carry. Faceless was crouched over in an attitude of indecision, his gun wavering between me and Eddie Sego. He couldn't see Eddie, and he couldn't shoot me without very likely killing his friend. Eddie solved his problem for him. He fired from the opposite end of the sofa and Faceless fell over with a sort of heavy finality.

Brian Ingraham sat where he was, in the middle of it, watching with the blank gaze of a stupid child.

I saw a heavy glass ashtray on the floor where we had knocked it off an end table. I let go with one hand and grabbed it and hit Nameless with it. He relaxed, and then the gun was quite easy to take out of his fingers. I took it and whirled around.

Justinian was moving his armchair shield, inch by inch, toward the gun that Faceless had dropped.

I said, "Hold it, Joe."

He gave me a hot, blind look of feral rage, but he held it, and I picked up the gun. Justinian looked from me to where Eddie Sego was, and he cursed him in a short, violent burst, and then grew calm again.

"That was a crummy way to do it, Eddie. You didn't have guts enough to face up to me yourself."

Eddie stood up now. He shrugged. "Why should I commit suicide? I figured Carver ought to be mad enough to do something." He glanced at me. "I just about gave you up this morning. I was really going to turn you in."

"How did you find out?" asked Justinian. "I didn't tell you anything. The Harding job, yes. But about Marjorie. I didn't tell anybody."

"A guy like me," said Eddie, "can find out an awful lot if he sets his mind to it. Besides, I'd been feeding Marjorie what she wanted to know about Harding."

"Sure," I said. "How else could she have found out? You've been taken, Joe. You're through."

I motioned him to get up. And then Brian remembered who Justinian was, and what he had just admitted he had done, and he got up and rushed in between us and flung himself on Justinian, and I was helpless.

They rolled together, making ugly sounds. They rolled out from the shelter of the chair into the open center of the room. And I saw Eddie Sego raise his gun.

"Eddie," I said. "Let them alone."

"What the hell," he said, "now he knows what I did I have to get him, or he'll drag me right along with him. I'm clean on those killings, but there's plenty else."

"Eddie," I said. "No."

He said, "I can do without you, too," and I saw the black, cold glitter come in his eyes.

I shot him in the right elbow.

He spun around and dropped the gun. He doubled up for a minute, and then he began to whimper and claw with his left hand for his own gun, in a holster under his left shoulder. I went closer to him and shot him again, carefully, through the left arm.

He crumbled down onto the floor and sat there, looking at me with big tears in his eyes. "What did you have to do that for?" he said. "You wanted him dead, too."

"Not that way. And not Brian, too."

"What do you care about Brian?" He rocked back and forth on the floor, hugging his arms against his sides and crying.

"You make me sick," I said.

I went to where Justinian and Brian were in the center of the room, locked together, quiet now with deadly effort. I didn't look to see who was killing who. "You make me sick," I said. "All of you make me sick." I kicked them until they broke apart.

I felt sorry for Brian, but he still made me sick. "Get up. Brian, you get on the phone and call the police. Prioletti and the decent cops, not Hickey's. They've been waiting a long time for this. Go on!"

He went, and I told Justinian to sit down, and he sat. He looked at Eddie Sego and laughed.

"Empires aren't so easy to inherit after all, are they, Eddie?" he said.

Eddie was still looking at me. "I just don't see why you did it."

"I'll tell you," I said. "Because I want to see you hang right along with the others. Did you think I was going to do your dirty work for you, for free?"

I turned to Justinian. "How did you find out Marjorie was so close to you on the Harding thing?"

"Why," he said, "I guess it was a remark Eddie made that got me worried."

"A remark that got Marjorie killed. But you didn't care, did you, Eddie? What's another life, more or less, to you?"

His face had turned white, with fear instead of pain. Justinian was looking at me with a sort of astonishment. And then Brian came and took my arm, and I stepped back and shook my head, and we sat down and waited until Prioletti came.

When they were all gone and the house was empty and quiet again, I stood for a minute looking around at all the things that had been Marjorie's, and there was a peacefulness about them now. I went out softly and closed the door, and drove away down the long drive.

HELEN NIELSEN
(b. 1918)

From 1955 to 1958, Helen Berniece Nielsen wrote just six short stories for the seminal hard-boiled digest, Manhunt. Yet these stories add up to some of the toughest tales of the mid-century, written by an author who was unusually gifted in a number of fields.

A newspaper and commercial artist before World War II, Nielsen transferred from illustration to aeronautical draftsmanship during the conflict, working on the U.S. Defense Engineering Program. From her mid-twenties until her sixtieth year, she owned an apartment building. Managing this caravanserai, with its ever-shifting population, gave her a unique, invaluable view of her fellow humans—their foibles, their passions, their outlooks, and their obsessions. This insight later proved useful in such books as A Killer in the Street (1967), which begins in an apartment house in New York, and The Woman on the Roof (1954), in which murder takes place in the bungalow court owned by the heroine's brother.

Nielsen was also adept at most subgenres in the mystery field, from the pursuit thriller (the superb and claustrophobic Detour [1953], for instance, in which a man finds a whole community ranged against him) to the novel of bafflement. A good example of the latter is Nielsen's second book, Gold Coast Nocturne (1951), in which the hero cannot even remember his own marriage because he was drunk at the time. Her later books generally concern the resolution of situations that threaten either career or life.

Nielsen seems to be appreciated most by British aficionados, and her last two books, The Severed Key (1973) and The Brink of Murder (1976), were published only in England. By the mid-1970s, Nielsen had virtually ceased writing, and her remaining work moved well away from her hard-boiled, Manhunt period. One of her last stories, "The Room at the End of the Hall," written for Alfred Hitchcock's Mystery Magazine in 1973, is an out-and-out ghost story, familiarly set in a residential hotel.

Chameleonlike, Nielsen could subtly alter her style with each new direction she took, each new subgenre she conquered. But none of her later work can compete with the early stories, celebrated in her one paperback-original collection, Woman Missing (1961). "A Piece of

Ground" is a bleak and uncompromising noir tale that first appeared in 1957 in Manhunt.

J. A.

1 9 5 7

A PIECE OF GROUND

They called him the farmer. He had a name the same as any man; but it was seldom spoken. Names weren't important in the city. A number on a badge, a number on a time card, a number on the front of a rooming house—that's all anyone needed. Names were for people who got into the newspapers; and, down around the warehouses that backed up against the river, a man didn't get into the newspapers unless he was found with his throat cut or his head bashed in. Even then he rarely had a name. He was just another unidentified body.

He was a tall man. He stooped when he went through doorways, out of habit. He had long arms with big hands stuck on the ends of them—calloused and splinter-cut from handling the rough pine crates of produce; and he had large feet that hurt from walking and standing all the time on cement and not ever feeling the earth under them any more. He had a large-boned face and sad eyes, and he never laughed and seldom smiled unless he was alone, to himself, and thinking of something remembered. He worked hard and took his pay to the bank, except for the few dollars he needed for the landlady at the rooming house, the little food he ate, and some pipe tobacco. He never spent money for liquor or women. It was a joke all along the river-front.

"The farmer ain't give up yet. He's saving to buy out the corporation that took over his farm."

It was a big joke, but it wasn't true. Not quite. Once a week he wrote home:

> *Well, I put another thirty dollars in the bank this week. It's beginning to add up. I hope Uncle Matt don't get tired of having you and the kids around the place. You make them help out now. We don't want to be beholding to anybody. It looks like I might get in some overtime next week and that will sure help. Don't forget to keep an eye open for any small farms put up for sale. It shouldn't take me long to get enough for a down payment, and I know if we can get a little piece*

of ground somewhere everything will work out this time. We just had
some bad luck before.

I am fine and hope you are the same,
Your loving husband

The letters were pretty much the same every week, and the answers were pretty much the same, too, because he and Amy had never had to write letters to one another before and didn't really know how. If he missed her, and he did, he couldn't put it down on paper without feeling foolish; and if he hated every minute in the city, and he did, he didn't want her to know it and worry. It was just one of the hard things that happened in life, like the kids getting whooping cough or the hail stripping the corn when it was ready to tassel. It was just one of the things that had to be endured.

The winter months were bad, but, when the last of the snows had melted and the first rains came, it was harder than ever. Spring was planting time. Even in a back room of the rooming house he could smell the earth around him. He took to walking out nights, smoking his pipe and looking for a plot of grass at his feet, or for a star in the strip of sky showing above the rooftops. The city wasn't quite so ugly at night. The dirt didn't show in the shadows. He walked slowly, and he never spoke to anyone until the night he met Blanche.

It was a Saturday night and warm. Spring came early along the river. There had been a shower earlier, and pools of water still stood in the street. When he came to the corner, he looked down and saw a star reflected in the puddle. It seemed strange. He'd looked for stars in the sky and never found them, and here was a star at his feet. He hesitated a moment thinking about it, and while he stood there a woman came and stood beside him. He knew it was a woman by the smell of her powder and perfume.

"It sure is warm tonight," she said.

He didn't answer or look around. The neighborhood was full of women of her kind, and he didn't like to look at them. He hadn't had any woman but Amy for the seventeen years of their marriage, and he missed her too much to dare look at a woman now.

But she didn't go away.

"Lose something in the puddle?" she asked.

"The star—"

The words slipped out. He didn't want to talk to her about anything, but especially not the star. That was crazy. Only she didn't think so.

"Oh, I see it! It's pretty, ain't it?" She crowded closer to him. He could feel her body next to his. "You don't see many stars in the city," she added. "It's because of all the lights, I guess."

Her voice wasn't the way he expected it to be. It had a kind of wonder—something almost childish in it. He looked at her then and was surprised at what he saw. She was young, not much more than a schoolgirl. She did wear powder, but not very much, and she had a soft look about her. She was small and dark and wore a plain blue sweater over a cotton dress.

"Are you—" He struggled with words. He hadn't used them much for many months. "—from the country?"

She nodded. "A long time ago—when I was a little girl. I was born on a farm on the other side of the river."

"Now that's funny," he said. "I was born on a farm, too, only I come from the other way—back towards Jefferson City. I only been here a few months."

"Alone?" she asked.

"Yes, alone. That is, I got a wife and two girls, but they didn't come. I didn't think this was any place—" He caught back the words. He'd started to say that he didn't think this was any place to bring up his girls, but he didn't want to insult her. "I just came to make a little money and go back," he explained.

It was hard to be sure with her face ducked down and only the street lamp to see by, but she seemed to be smiling. Not a happy smile, but a kind of twisted one. Then she looked up, and for a moment he looked straight into her eyes and saw that they weren't young at all.

But it was a warm spring night, and he hadn't talked to a woman for a long time.

"I was just going down to the corner for a beer," she said. "Maybe you were going the same place. We could walk together."

He wasn't; but he did. Some of the faces that peered at them as they walked past the bar to the booths in the rear were familiar. He could see the grins and the heads wagging. The farmer had a woman. The farmer was going to spend some money. By this time he wished he hadn't come; but the woman sat down in the last booth and he sat down across from her. They ordered two beers and he put a fifty-cent piece on the table.

"I didn't mean that you had to pay for mine," she said.

She didn't seem at all like what he knew she was; and he did know. There was never any doubt about that. They talked a little more about the country, and about the weather, and then one of the men who had been drinking at the bar—one he didn't recognize from the warehouse—came back to the booth and stood looking down at them. He was a little man compared to the farmer; but his suit had wide shoulders, and he wore his roll-brimmed hat at a cocky angle as if he were the biggest man on the river-front.

"Well, if Blanche ain't got herself a new friend!" he said.

"Knock it off, Morrell," she answered.

Her voice had turned hard; but Morrell didn't go away. Instead, he sat down beside her in the booth. He looked straight at the farmer.

"I heard about you," he said, after studying him for a few seconds. "You're the one they call 'the farmer'—the one who saves all his money."

"I got a reason," the farmer said.

"Who needs a reason? You think I'm like those stupid bums over at the bar? You think I make fun of a guy who saves his money? Look at me, I got a few put away myself. Only trouble is, Blanche don't seem to like the color of my money. How do you figure that, farmer?"

"I said knock it off," Blanche repeated.

"I guess there just ain't no accounting for tastes," Morrell added. "I guess a woman can have it for one guy and not for another."

Morrell grinned at Blanche, but she didn't even look at him. It was hard to know what to do or what to say. Maybe there was something between these two, and the farmer didn't want to get mixed up in anything. He finished his beer and came to his feet.

"Leaving so soon?"

Blanche looked disappointed.

"I've got to get back to my room," he said. "I've got to write a letter."

"But it's early."

Morrell laughed.

"Leave him alone, Blanche. Can't you see he don't want any? Leave him be smart and save his money. It's a good thing somebody has sense. Go ahead, farmer. I'll buy Blanche another beer. Go write your letter."

He didn't like to go then. He didn't like the way Blanche looked up at him, or the way she edged away from Morrell. But he still didn't want to get mixed up in anything. He walked out, trying to not to hear the laughter behind him, and went back to the rooming house to write the longest letter he'd ever written.

It was a full week before he went out for a walk again. He didn't pay any attention to the cracks made around the warehouse about him buying a beer for Blanche, and he tried not to listen to the things they said about her. He just made up his mind not to be so foolish again. When Saturday night came, he sat down and started his letter:

Dear Amy,
Well, I got in that overtime like I said, and put forty dollars in the bank this week. It's adding up, and it can't add up too soon . . .

It was hot in the room. A bunch of kids were playing handball in the alley, and their screaming was in his ears until he could hardly think. He started to write again.

. . . I sure don't like the city. It's noisy and hot, and there isn't anybody to talk to. It's not like back home. You can't hardly meet anybody . . .

He put down his pencil and looked at the words. They were true. Everything was different in the city, but people were still people. They still got lonely and knew hunger. If a starving man stole a loaf of bread it wasn't the same as stealing for profit. Everything was different in the city.

The ball kept bouncing against the wall, and now it was as if it were bouncing against his head. He wrinkled up the letter and threw it on the floor. It was too hot to write. He couldn't sit in a hot room forever . . .

He met Blanche about three houses down the street. He never asked, but she might have been waiting for him.

"I'm going down to the corner for a beer," he said. "Maybe you'd like to come with me."

She wasn't wearing the blue sweater. It was too warm for that. Spring and summer had a way of running together this time of year. She wore the cotton dress and that soft look that came sometimes when the shadows were kind.

"A friend of mine got generous and gave me a whole case of beer," she answered. "Why don't we go to my place? I don't like the corner much any more."

Her words were as good as any. He went along with her for a couple of blocks to a rooming house the duplicate of his own. She lived on the second floor. He stooped when he went through the doorway.

"You're big," she said, closing the door behind them. "Golly, you're big—you know?" Then she ran her hand up his back and around his shoulders. "But you're so skinny I can feel the bones through your shirt. I bet you don't eat half enough."

"I don't like restaurant cooking," he said.

"I don't either! I tell you what you should do. I've got a hot plate, see?"

He saw. He saw a room no larger than his own, but with a hot plate and a sink and a yellowed enamel refrigerator in one corner. He looked for a chair, but the only one he could find had laundry on it. He sat down on the edge of the bed. By this time, she'd taken the beer out of the refrigerator, opened the cans, and handed one to him. All the time she kept talking.

"I do most of my own cooking, so if there's something you'd like—something you're hungry for—you just buy it and bring it here. Those restaurants can kill you."

She took a couple of pulls at the beer.

"God, it's hot!" she said.

She pulled off her dress. She didn't wear anything underneath except a slip as thin as a silk curtain. She was thin, too, her thighs, her stomach, her small breasts poking at the slip. She finished her beer and tossed the can into the sink, and then reached down for the hem of her slip. Then she looked at the window. The shade was rolled up to let in the night breeze in case one ever came, so she turned out the light.

Afterwards, he lay with her a while, staring at the ceiling and listening to his heart beat. Finally he spoke.

"That man at the bar last week—Morrell. Is he the friend who gave you the beer?"

It wasn't that he had to make conversation. It was that he felt guilty and wanted to be reassured that it was nothing to her.

"What of it?" she answered. "I work for him sometimes. I entertain his customers."

"He's got some kind of business, then?"

"Morrell? He's got all kinds of business."

"I guess some people know how to make money. I wish I knew."

"Morrell knows, all right. That's one thing he knows."

Blanche sounded sleepy. He waited a while, thinking she might speak again; but she didn't and he left her that way. He wasn't sure what to do, so he left two dollars on the refrigerator.

He didn't intend to go back; but he did, of course. After a few more Saturdays it didn't bother him. He'd give her a few dollars for groceries, and she'd have supper waiting when he got off work. The rest of his pay went into the bank the same as before, and he wrote home every week as usual. One night Blanche wanted to go out, so they went back to the bar on the corner and had a couple of beers and listened to the music in the record machine. Then Morrell came back to their booth.

"Well, it's been a long time," he said. "You don't come around much any more, Blanche. What's the matter? Got somebody keeping you busy?"

He had an obscene smile. He sat down beside Blanche again, and she edged over toward the wall.

"Still saving your money, farmer? Still going to buy back that farm?"

He shook his head. "I don't aim to buy back anything," he said. "All I want is a few acres for a truck garden and a house. Just a little piece of ground."

Morrell nodded, still smiling.

"That's what I like to hear—a man with ambition. But the trouble is, farmer, you're going to be an old man before you get that piece of ground doing it the hard way."

Morrell's teeth were like pearls, and a diamond ring on his finger shot fire. The farmer listened.

"Is there an easy way?" he asked.

"Look at me," Morrell said. "Six years ago I was broke—hoisting crates at the warehouse the same as you. But I got smart. I saved my dough, too, and then I did what the big boys do. I invested my dough."

"In a business?"

"In the market, chum. Ain't you ever heard?"

"But I don't know anything about the market."

"So who knows? I got me a broker—one of those young sharpies out of college. He studies all the time—tells me what to buy and when to sell. Not this six and seven percent old lady stuff, but the sweet stuff. You got to gamble to get anywhere in this world."

Blanche was restless. She shoved her half-finished beer away from her.

"You talk big, Morrell," she said, "but talk don't do the farmer any good."

"So why should I do the farmer good?"

"Why should you blow your mouth off?"

The farmer didn't want any part of the argument. He would just as soon have dropped the subject; but Blanche's taunt only made Morrell talk more.

"You think I talk big and that's all?" he said. "You think I'm bluffing? Okay. I'll show you how I'm bluffing. You want me to cut you in, farmer? It happens I've got a sweet thing going right now. Give me a hundred dollars and I'll double it for you. Go ahead, try me and see."

The farmer hesitated. He looked at Blanche and caught a glimpse of that twisted smile again.

"My money's in the bank," he said.

"Okay, so the bank opens Monday morning, don't it? One hundred dollars, that's all I'll cut you in for. I know you've got it. You've got plenty."

One hundred dollars. Monday noon he went to the bank on his lunch hour, and Monday night he gave the money to Morrell. He knew that he was a fool and never expected to see the money again; but Blanche had set it up for him and he didn't want to back out.

It was exactly three weeks later that Morrell gave him two hundred dollars.

"You got lucky," Blanche said.

"Luck?" Morrell laughed. "Using your head ain't luck, honey. Any time you want to get smart again, farmer, let me know. Any time . . ."

It nagged at his mind. For the next few weeks everything went on as usual. He still went to Blanche every Saturday, and he still wrote home; but now the time seemed to pass more slowly because in the back of his mind he carried Morrell's words. Only one thing about them bothered him.

And then one week the letter from Amy had news:

. . . It's just a little place, but it has water on it and the house could be fixed up nice. Uncle Matt thinks we could get it for two thousand down, and he'll go our note for the rest . . .

He read the letter over several times, and each time he could see the place more clearly and almost smell the earth and the water. Finally, he went to see Morrell.

"There's just one thing I want to know," he told him. "Why did you cut me in, and why did you say 'any time'? You ain't a man to give anything away."

Morrell grinned.

"That's right, farmer. You're smart enough to think of that, but how come you ain't smart enough to think of the answer? Don't you know what I want? I want you to get that little piece of ground and clear the hell out of here!"

"Because of Blanche?"

"What do you think?"

"But she's nothing to me."

"It ain't what she is to you that bothers me, farmer. It's what she is to me—or could be with you out of the way. Now, what's on your mind?"

"I need two thousand dollars," he said.

"How much have you got to invest?"

He handed Morrell his bank book. All the months of saving had gone into it—the winter, the spring, the summer, and autumn on the way; but it was still only a little over a thousand dollars.

"Okay," Morrell said. "I'll meet you at the bank tomorrow—no, better make it tomorrow night at my office. You know where that is?"

The farmer nodded. He passed it every day going down to the warehouse.

"Make it about nine o'clock. That'll give me time to see my broker and have him find something good for you. And don't tell anybody what I'm doing. I'll have every bum on the river-front trying to cut in."

The next day at noon, he went to the bank and drew out everything. He kept it in an envelope pinned to the inside of his shirt until he was through work. After work he was too nervous to eat. He sat alone in his room until it was time to put the envelope in his pocket and start for Morrell's office. Out on the street, he met Blanche. She was looking for him.

"I thought you might come over tonight," she said. "I bought some pork chops."

She clung to his arm, leaning against him. He pulled away.

"Maybe later," he said. "I've got to see somebody first."

"Morrell?"

"Just somebody. I'll tell you about it later."

He was lying. He walked off down the street knowing that he'd never go to Blanche again. That kind of life was over. He was going to go home and get clean.

After a time, he came to Morrell's office. He opened the door and saw no one, but the door banged shut behind him and Morrell laughed once as he stepped forward. The farmer felt a gun cold against the back of his neck.

Even then he didn't know what had happened or what had gone wrong; he wasn't thinking at all. He felt terror and panic creep slowly up his body, but he made no move, not even when the door opened again and Blanche came in and walked past him.

"Has he got it with him?" Morrell asked from behind him.

"He's got it," Blanche said. "I felt it in his pocket."

"Good. I'll be up later with your cut. In the meantime, you don't have to stay here. You might look around for another farmer who's saving his money. You've got a real technique with the country boys, and there's plenty of them around."

Now the farmer knew that it was all over. He was finished. Fear remained, but the panic was gone; there was nothing for him to do. He felt only sick, and dirty, and he waited for Morrell to fire the gun and cleanse him.

"At least he'll get what he wanted," Blanche said, far away in the distance. "At least he'll get a little piece of ground."

EVAN HUNTER
(b. 1926)

A prodigious worker with a prodigious talent, Evan Hunter was multi-talented from the very start of his writing career. Hunter was a prolific contributor to Manhunt during its most influential period, the early to middle 1950s. Although considered a mainstay of the digest, he had in fact only just made it into the last of the pulps: his earliest stories, written under the name Hunt Collins, had appeared in Robert Lowndes's Smashing Detective and Famous Detective. In Manhunt, he ran a series featuring the tormented former private eye Matt Cordell, and he penned tough, shock-ending stories as Richard Marsten, a name he also used for his science fiction. Quite often, pieces by Marsten and Hunter sat next to each other in the same issue.

While writing hard-boiled short stories and novels for magazines such as Manhunt and for action-oriented paperback-original houses, Hunter was also producing thoughtful and engrossing science fiction for young people. He worked with the John C. Winston Company's superior and influential "Adventures in Science Fiction" line, together with writers of the caliber of Arthur C. Clarke, Poul Anderson, and the anthropologist Chad Oliver. He wrote "JD" (juvenile delinquent) stories and novels, pulp science fiction, and private-eye tales before producing the novel that transformed him from a journeyman genre writer into a respected and world-famous figure.

Set in a New York City public high school, The Blackboard Jungle (1954) is still a compelling and intelligent novel forty years later. It was immediately recognized as a major work, having been serialized for the prestigious Ladies' Home Journal, published to great critical acclaim, and bought for the then-record sum of $95,000 by a major film studio. This windfall freed Hunter from the tyranny of editors and publishers and enabled him to write only what he wanted to write. This included such fine mainstream novels as Strangers When We Meet (1958, filmed to Hunter's own script two years later), Buddwing (1964), and the impressive Mothers and Daughters (1961).

Hunter's greatest triumph, however, was undoubtedly the Eighty-seventh Precinct novels, a series of police-procedural stories set in a fictional, although far from imaginary, New York City. Using his pseudonym

Ed McBain, he created the series in 1956 for a paperback house, later graduating to hardcover. It is said that his model was Sidney Kingsley's celebrated 1949 play Detective Story, which was later filmed by William Wyler in a self-conscious pseudo-documentary style. The series consists of nearly fifty books, including one collection of novelettes. Perhaps only Georges Simenon's Inspector Maigret series comes anywhere near Hunter's epic achievement in terms of consistency and quality.

"The Merry, Merry Christmas" appeared in Manhunt in 1957 and is one of Hunter's later stories; it was not a part of any series. While the tone seems sentimental, it is not at all a comfortable story. Rather, it is a superbly written tale about the randomness, the appalling arbitrariness, of violence.

J. A.

1957

THE MERRY, MERRY CHRISTMAS

Sitting at the bar, Pete Charpens looked at his own reflection in the mirror, grinned, and said, "Merry Christmas."

It was not Christmas yet, true enough, but he said it anyway, and the words sounded good, and he grinned foolishly and lifted his drink and sipped a little of it and said again, "Merry Christmas," feeling very good, feeling very warm, feeling in excellent high spirits. Tonight, the city was his. Tonight, for the first time since he'd arrived from Whiting Center eight months ago, he felt like a part of the city. Tonight, the city enveloped him like a warm bath, and he lounged back and allowed the undulating waters to cover him. It was Christmas Eve, and all was right with the world, and Pete Charpens loved every mother's son who roamed the face of the earth because he felt as if he'd finally come home, finally found the place, finally found himself.

It was a good feeling.

This afternoon, as soon as the office party was over, he'd gone into the streets. The shop windows had gleamed like pot-bellied stoves, cherry hot against the sharp bite of the air. There was a promise of snow in the sky, and Pete had walked the tinseled streets of New York with his tweed coat collar against the back of his neck, and he had felt warm and happy. There were shoppers in the streets, and Santa Clauses with bells, and giant wreaths and giant trees, and music coming from speakers, the timeless carols of the holiday season. But more than that, he had felt the pulse beat of the city. For the first time in eight months, he had felt the pulse beat of the city, the people, the noise, the clutter, the rush, and above all the warmth. The warmth had engulfed him, surprising him. He had watched it with the foolish smile of a spectator and then, with sudden realization, he had known he was a part of it. In the short space of eight months, he had become a part of the city—and the city had become a part of him. He had found a home.

"Bartender," he said.

The bartender ambled over. He was a big red-headed man with freckles all over his face. He moved with economy and grace. He seemed like a very nice guy who probably had a very nice wife and family decorating a Christmas tree somewhere in Queens.

"Yes, sir?" he asked.

"Pete. Call me Pete."

"Okay, Pete."

"I'm not drunk," Pete said, "believe me. I know all drunks say that, but I mean it. I'm just so damn happy I could bust. Did you ever feel that way?"

"Sure," the bartender said, smiling.

"Let me buy you a drink."

"I don't drink."

"Bartenders never drink, I know, but let me buy you one. Please. Look, I want to thank people, you know? I want to thank everybody in this city. I want to thank them for being here, for making it a city. Do I sound nuts?"

"Yes," the bartender said.

"Okay. Okay then, I'm nuts. But I'm a hick, do you know? I came here from Whiting Center eight months ago. Straw sticking out of my ears. The confusion here almost killed me. But I got a job, a good job, and I met a lot of wonderful people, and I learned how to dress, and I . . . I found a home. That's corny. I know it. That's the hick in me talking. But I love this damn city, I *love* it. I want to go around kissing girls in the streets. I want to shake hands with every guy I meet. I want to tell them I feel like a person, a human being, I'm alive, alive! For Christ's sake, I'm alive!"

"That's a good way to be," the bartender agreed.

"I know it. Oh, my friend, do I know it! I was dead in Whiting Center, and now I'm here and alive and . . . look, let me buy you a drink, huh?"

"I don't drink," the bartender insisted.

"Okay. Okay, I won't argue. I wouldn't argue with anyone tonight. Gee, it's gonna be a great Christmas, do you know? Gee, I'm so damn happy I could bust." He laughed aloud, and the bartender laughed with him. The laugh trailed off into a chuckle, and then a smile. Pete looked into the mirror, lifted his glass again, and again said, "Merry Christmas. Merry Christmas."

He was still smiling when the man came into the bar and sat down next to him. The man was very tall, his body bulging with power beneath the suit he wore. Coatless, hatless, he came into the bar and sat alongside Pete, signaling for the bartender with a slight flick of his hand. The bartender walked over.

"Rye neat," the man said.

The bartender nodded and walked away. The man reached for his wallet.

"Let me pay for it." Pete said.

The man turned. He had a wide face with a thick nose and small brown eyes. The eyes came as a surprise in his otherwise large body. He studied Pete for a moment and then said, "You a queer or something?"

Pete laughed. "Hell, no," he said. "I'm just happy. It's Christmas Eve, and I feel like buying you a drink."

The man pulled out his wallet, put a five dollar bill on the bar top and said, "I'll buy my own drink." He paused. "What's the matter? Don't I look as if I can afford a drink?"

"Sure you do," Pete said. "I just wanted to . . . look, I'm happy. I want to share it, that's all."

The man grunted and said nothing. The bartender brought his drink. He tossed off the shot and asked for another.

"My name's Pete Charpens," Pete said, extending his hand.

"So what?" the man said.

"Well . . . what's your name?"

"Frank."

"Glad to know you, Frank." He thrust his hand closer to the man.

"Get lost, Happy," Frank said.

Pete grinned, undismayed. "You ought to relax," he said, "I mean it. You know, you've got to stop . . ."

"Don't tell me what I've got to stop. Who the hell are you, anyway?"

"Pete Charpens. I told you."

"Take a walk, Pete Charpens. I got worries of my own."

"Want to tell me about them?"

"No, I don't want to tell you about them."

"Why not? Make you feel better."

"Go to hell, and stop bothering me," Frank said.

The bartender brought the second drink. He sipped at it, and then put the shot glass on the bar top.

"Do I look like a hick?" Pete asked.

"You look like a goddamn queer," Frank said.

"No, I mean it."

"You asked me, and I told you."

"What's troubling you, Frank?"

"You a priest or something?"

"No, but I thought . . ."

"Look, I come in here to have a drink. I didn't come to see the chaplain."

"You an ex-Army man?"

"Yeah."

"I was in the Navy," Pete said. "Glad to be out of that, all right. Glad to be right here where I am, in the most wonderful city in the whole damn world."

"Go down to Union Square and get a soap box," Frank said.

"Can't I help you, Frank?" Pete asked. "Can't I buy you a drink, lend you an ear, do something? You're so damn sad, I feel like . . ."

"I'm not sad."

"You sure look sad. What happened? Did you lose your job?"

"No, I didn't lose my job."

"What do you do, Frank?"

"Right now, I'm a truck driver. I used to be a fighter."

"Really? You mean a boxer? No kidding?"

"Why would I kid you?"

"What's your last name?"

"Blake."

"Frank Blake? I don't think I've heard it before. Of course, I didn't follow the fights much."

"Tiger Blake, they called me. That was my ring name."

"Tiger Blake. Well, we didn't have fights in Whiting Center. Had to go over to Waterloo if we wanted to see a bout. I guess that's why I never heard of you."

"Sure," Frank said.

"Why'd you quit fighting?"

"They made me."

"Why?"

"I killed a guy in 1947."

Pete's eyes widened. "In the ring?"

"Of course in the ring. What the hell kind of a moron are you, any-way? You think I'd be walking around if it wasn't in the ring? Jesus!"

"Is that what's troubling you?"

"There ain't nothing troubling me. I'm fine."

"Are you going home for Christmas?"

"I got no home."

"You must have a home," Pete said gently. "*Everybody's* got a home."

"Yeah? Where's your home? Whiting Center or wherever the hell you said?"

"Nope. This is my home now. New York City. New York, New York. The greatest goddamn city in the whole world."

"Sure," Frank said sourly.

"My folks are dead," Pete said. "I'm an only child. Nothing for me in Whiting Center anymore. But in New York, well, I get the feeling that I'm here to stay. That I'll meet a nice girl here, and marry her, and raise a family here and . . . and this'll be home."

"Great," Frank said sourly.

"How'd you happen to kill this fellow?" Pete asked suddenly.

"I hit him."

"And killed him?"

"I hit him on the Adam's apple. Accidentally."

"Were you sore at him?"

"We were in the ring. I already told you that."

"Sure, but were you sore?"

"A fighter don't have to be sore. He's paid to fight."

"Did you like fighting?"

"I loved it," Frank said flatly.

"How about the night you killed that fellow?"

Frank was silent for a long time. Then he said, "Get lost, huh?"

"I could never fight for money," Pete said. "I got a quick temper, and I get mad as hell, but I could never do it for money. Besides, I'm too happy right now to . . . ."

"Get lost," Frank said again, and he turned his back. Pete sat silently for a moment.

"Frank?" he said at last.

"You back again?"

"I'm sorry. I shouldn't have talked to you about something that's painful to you. Look, it's Christmas Eve. Let's . . ."

"Forget it."

"Can I buy you a drink?"

"No. I told you no a hundred times. I buy my own damn drinks!"

"This is Christmas E . . ."

"I don't care what it is. You happy jokers give me the creeps. Get off my back, will you?"

"I'm sorry. I just . . ."

"Happy, happy, happy. Grinning like a damn fool. What the hell is there to be so happy about? You got an oil well someplace? A gold mine? What is it with you?"

"I'm just . . ."

"You're just a jerk! I probably pegged you right the minute I laid eyes on you. You're probably a damn queer."

"No, no," Pete said mildly. "You're mistaken, Frank. Honestly, I just feel . . ."

"Your old man was probably a queer, too. Your old lady probably took on every sailor in town."

The smile left Pete's face, and then tentatively reappeared. "You don't mean that, Frank," he said.

"I mean everything I ever say," Frank said. There was a strange gleam in his eyes. He studied Pete carefully.

"About my mother, I meant," Pete said.

"I know what you're talking about. And I'll say it again. She probably took on every sailor in town."

"Don't say that, Frank," Pete said, the smile gone now, a perplexed frown teasing his forehead, appearing, vanishing, reappearing.

"You're a queer, and your old lady was a . . ."

"Stop it, Frank."

"Stop what? If your old lady was . . ."

Pete leaped off the bar stool. "Cut it out!" he yelled.

From the end of the bar, the bartender turned. Frank caught the movement with the corner of his eye. In a cold whisper, he said, "Your mother was a slut," and Pete swung at him.

Frank ducked, and the blow grazed the top of his head. The bartender was coming towards them now. He could not see the strange light in Frank's eyes, nor did he hear Frank whisper again, "A slut, a slut."

Pete pushed himself off the bar wildly. He saw the beer bottle then, picked it up, and lunged at Frank.

The patrolman knelt near his body.

"He's dead, all right," he said. He stood up and dusted off his trousers. "What happened?"

Frank looked bewildered and dazed. "He went berserk," he said. "We were sitting and talking. Quiet. All of a sudden, he swings at me." He turned to the bartender. "Am I right?"

"He was drinking," the bartender said. "Maybe he was drunk."

"I didn't even swing back," Frank said, "not until he picked up the beer bottle. Hell, this is Christmas Eve. I didn't want no trouble."

"What happened when he picked up the bottle?"

"He swung it at me. So I . . . I put up my hands to defend myself. I only gave him a push, so help me."

"Where'd you hit him?"

Frank paused. "In . . . in the throat, I think." He paused again. "It was self-defense, believe me. This guy just went berserk. He musta been a maniac."

"He *was* talking kind of queer," the bartender agreed.

The patrolman nodded sympathetically. "There's more nuts outside than there is in," he said. He turned to Frank. "Don't take this so bad, Mac. You'll get off. It looks open and shut to me. Just tell them the story downtown, that's all."

"Berserk," Frank said. "He just went berserk."

"Well . . ." The patrolman shrugged. "My partner'll take care of the meat wagon when it gets here. You and me better get downtown. I'm sorry I got to ruin your Christmas, but . . ."

"It's *him* that ruined it," Frank said, shaking his head and looking down at the body on the floor.

Together, they started out of the bar. At the door, the patrolman waved to the bartender and said, "Merry Christmas, Mac."

JIM THOMPSON
(1906-1977)

As a chronicler of madness and gratuitous viciousness, James Myers (Jim) Thompson was one of the great nihilists of the hard-boiled genre. Most of his protagonists live their lives as candle flames—now leaping, now falling, now dying. His heroes are starkly unheroic: psychopaths for the most part, congenital liars, killers, escapees from mental institutions, and sometimes even men in positions of power and trust. Usually these are deputies rather than sheriffs, underlings whose bland features or innocent chuckling hides seriously demented psyches. More than any other noir writer of the 1940s and 1950s, Thompson honed to perfection the "narrator-as-psychopath" approach. He did this brilliantly, not letting the reader in on the secret all at once, but gradually, artfully dropping hints of madness in the middle of the narrators' sly and ingratiating soliloquies.

All of Thompson's output during the 1950s and 1960s was published as paperback originals. In 1953 and 1954, he wrote ten books, including some of his best-known titles: A Hell of a Woman, A Swell-Looking Babe, and Savage Night. Perhaps the most representative of Thompson's style is The Killer Inside Me (1952), which tells of the dark odyssey of Deputy Lou Ford, the cheerful and brutal psychopath who slays humans like others swat flies and who, in the end, believes that he must be sacrificed as humanity's savior. Much later, in Pop. 1280 (1964), Thompson refined this plot so that the protagonist imagines himself actually to be the son of God.

Much of Thompson's work constitutes a bitter salute to American success, his novels being bleak parables of postwar desolation and despair. His spiritual nihilism was admired by French intellectuals and literary types, and although his books went out of print and out of favor in his own country, his reputation flourished in Europe.

The 1972 film version of Thompson's hard-boiled heist thriller, The Getaway, starring Ali MacGraw and Steve McQueen, gave a final boost to his career, even though the ending was sanitized. Thompson was no stranger to the world of film, having worked on Stanley Kubrick's antiwar masterpiece Paths of Glory (1957), and he wrote scripts for the hugely successful Dr. Kildare television series. In addition, Thompson was not *averse to the odd journeyman job when times were hard, having written a novelization of one of the popular* Ironside *teleplays. Short stories, however, do not appear to have attracted him as a genre. His small output of shorts and novelettes was collected in* Fireworks *(1988), along with several unpublished novel excerpts, true-crime pieces, and autobiographical sketches.*

"Forever After" is another matter altogether. It is absolutely hardboiled, absolutely noir, and, like Elmore Leonard's "Three-Ten to Yuma," a story that extends the boundaries of the genre in an utterly shocking yet satisfying way.

J. A.

1960

FOREVER AFTER

It was a few minutes before five o'clock when Ardis Clinton unlocked the rear door of her apartment, and admitted her lover. He was a cow-eyed young man with a wild mass of curly black hair. He worked as a dishwasher at Joe's Diner, which was directly across the alley.

They embraced passionately. Her body pressed against the meat cleaver, concealed inside his shirt, and Ardis shivered with delicious anticipation. Very soon now, it would all be over. That stupid ox, her husband, would be dead. He and his stupid cracks—all the dullness and boredom would be gone forever. And with the twenty thousand insurance money, ten thousand dollars double-indemnity . . .

"We're going to be so happy, Tony," she whispered. "You'll have your own place, a real swank little restaurant with what they call one of those intimate bars. And you'll just manage it, just kind of saunter around in a dress suit, and—"

"And we'll live happily ever after," Tony said. "Just me and you, baby, walking down life's highway together."

Ardis let out a gasp. She shoved him away from her, glaring up into his handsome empty face. "Don't!" she snapped. "Don't say things like that! I've told you and told you not to do it, and if I have to tell you again, I'll—!"

"But what'd I say?" he protested. "I didn't say nothin'."

"Well . . ." She got control of herself, forcing a smile. "Never mind,

397

darling. You haven't had any opportunities and we've never really had a chance to know each other, so—so never mind. Things will be different after we're married." She patted his cheek, kissed him again. "You got away from the diner, all right? No one saw you leave?"

"Huh-uh. I already took the stuff up to the steam-table for Joe, and the waitress was up front too, y'know, filling the sugar bowls and the salt and pepper shakers like she always does just before dinner. And—"

"Good. Now, suppose someone comes back to the kitchen and finds out you're not there. What's your story going to be?"

"Well . . . I was out in the alley dumping some garbage. I mean—" he corrected himself hastily, "maybe I was. Or maybe I was down in the basement, getting some supplies. Or maybe I was in the john—the lavatory, I mean—or—"

"Fine," Ardis said approvingly. "You don't say where you were, so they can't prove you weren't there. You just don't remember where you were, understand, darling? You might have been any number of places."

Tony nodded. Looking over her shoulder into the bedroom, he frowned worriedly. "Why'd you do that now, honey? I know this has got to look like a robbery. But tearin' up the room now, before he gets here—"

"There won't be time afterwards. Don't worry, Tony. I'll keep the door closed."

"But he might open it and look in. And if he sees all them dresser drawers dumped around, and—"

"He won't. He won't look into the bedroom. I know exactly what he'll do, exactly what he'll say, the same things that he's always done and said ever since we've been married. All the stupid, maddening, dull, tiresome—!" She broke off abruptly, conscious that her voice was rising. "Well, forget it," she said, forcing another smile. "He won't give us any trouble."

"Whatever you say," Tony nodded docilely. "If you say so, that's the way it is, Ardis."

"But there'll be trouble—from the cops. I know I've already warned you about it, darling. But it'll be pretty bad, worse than anything you've ever gone through. They won't have any proof, but they're bound to be suspicious, and if you ever start talking, admitting anything—"

"I won't. They won't get anything out of me."

"You're sure? They'll try to trick you. They'll probably tell you that

I've confessed. They may even slap you around. So if you're not absolutely sure . . ."

"They won't get anything out of me," he repeated stolidly. "I won't talk."

And studying him, Ardis knew that he wouldn't.

She led the way down the hall to the bathroom. He parted the shower curtains, and stepped into the tub. Drawing a pair of gloves from his pocket, he pulled them onto his hands. Awkwardly, he fumbled the meat cleaver from beneath his shirt.

"Ardis. Uh—look, honey."

"Yes?"

"Do I have to hit you? Couldn't I just maybe give you a little shove, or—"

"No, darling," she said gently. "You have to hit me. This is supposed to be a robbery. If you killed my husband without doing anything to me, well, you know how it would look."

"But I never hit no woman—any woman—before. I might hit you too hard, and—"

"Tony!"

"Well, all right," he said sullenly. "I don't like it, but all right."

Ardis murmured soothing endearments. Then, brushing his lips quickly with her own, she returned to the living room. It was a quarter after five, exactly five minutes—but *exactly*—until her husband, Bill, would come home. Closing the bedroom door, she lay down on the lounge. Her negligee fell open, and she left it that way, grinning meanly as she studied the curving length of her thighs.

Give the dope a treat for a change, she thought. Let him get one last good look before he gets his.

Her expression changed. Wearily, resentfully, she pulled the material of the negligee over her legs. Because, of course, Bill would never notice. She could wear a ring in her nose, paint a bull's eye around her navel, and he'd never notice.

If he had ever noticed, just once paid her a pretty compliment . . .

If he had ever done anything different, ever said or done anything different at all—even the teensiest little bit . . .

But he hadn't. Maybe he couldn't. So what else could she do but what she was doing? She could get a divorce, sure, but that was all she'd get. No money; nothing with which to build a new life. Nothing to make up for those fifteen years of slowly being driven mad.

It's his own fault, she thought bitterly. I can't take any more. If I had to put up with him for just one more night, even one more hour . . . !

She heard heavy footsteps in the hallway. Then, a key turned in the doorlatch, and Bill came in. He was a master machinist, a solidly built man of about forty-five. The old-fashioned gold-rimmed glasses on his pudgy nose gave him a look of owlish solemnity.

"Well," he said, setting down his lunch bucket. "Another day, another dollar."

Ardis grimaced. He plodded across to the lounge, stooped, and gave her a half-hearted peck on the cheek.

"Long time no see," he said. "What we havin' for supper?"

Ardis gritted her teeth. It shouldn't matter, now; in a few minutes it would all be over. Yet somehow it *did* matter. He was as maddening to her as he had ever been.

"Bill . . ." She managed a seductive smile, slowly drawing the negligee apart. "How do I look, Bill?"

"Okay," he yawned. "Got a little hole in your drawers, though. What'd you say we was havin' for supper?"

"Slop," she said. "Garbage. Trash salad with dirt dressing."

"Sounds good. We got any hot water?"

Ardis sucked in her breath. She let it out again in a kind of infuriated moan. "Of course, we've got hot water! Don't we always have? Well, don't we? Why do you have to ask every night?"

"So what's to get excited about?" he shrugged. "Well, guess I'll go splash the chassis."

He plodded off down the hall. Ardis heard the bathroom door open, and close. She got up, stood waiting by the telephone. The door banged open again, and Tony came racing up the hall.

He had washed off the cleaver. While he hastily tucked it back inside his shirt, Ardis dialed the operator. "Help," she cried weakly. "Help . . . police . . . murder!"

She let the receiver drop to the floor, spoke to Tony in a whisper. "He's dead? You're sure of it?"

"Yeah, yeah, sure I'm sure. What do you think?"

"All right. Now, there's just one more thing . . ."

"I can't, Ardis. I don't want to. I—"

"Hit me," she commanded, and thrust out her chin. "Tony, I said to hit me!"

He hit her. A thousand stars blazed through her brain, and disappeared. And she crumpled silently to the floor.

. . . When she regained consciousness, she was lying on the lounge. A heavy-set man, a detective obviously, was seated at her side, and a white-jacketed young man with a stethoscope draped around his neck hovered nearby.

She had never felt better in her life. Even the lower part of her face, where Tony had smashed her, was surprisingly free of pain. Still, because it was what she should do, she moaned softly; spoke in a weak, hazy voice.

"Where am I?" she said. "What happened?"

"Lieutenant Powers," the detective said. "Suppose you tell me what happened, Mrs. Clinton."

"I . . . I don't remember. I mean, well, my husband had just come home, and gone back to the bathroom. And there was a knock on the door, and I supposed it was the paper-boy or someone like that. So—"

"You opened the door and he rushed in and slugged you, right? Then what happened?"

"Well, then he rushed into the bedroom and started searching it. Yanking out the dresser drawers, and—"

"What was he searching for, Mrs. Clinton? You don't have any considerable amount of money around do you? Or any jewelry aside from what you're wearing? And it wasn't your husband's payday, was it?"

"Well, no. But—"

"Yes?"

"I don't know. Maybe he was crazy. All I know is what he did."

"I see. He must have made quite a racket, seems to me. How come your husband didn't hear it?"

"He couldn't have. He had the shower running, and—"

She caught herself, fear constricting her throat. Lieutenant Powers grinned grimly.

"Missed a bet, huh, Mrs. Clinton?"

"I—I don't know what you're—"

"Come off of it! The bathtub's dry as an oven. The shower was never turned on, and you know why it wasn't. Because there was a guy standing inside of it."

"B-but—but I don't know anything. I was unconscious, and—"

"Then, how do you know what happened? How do you know this

guy went into the bedroom and started tearing it apart? And how did you make that telephone call?"

"Well, I . . . I wasn't completely unconscious. I sort of knew what was going on without really—"

"Now, you listen to me," he said harshly. "You made that fake call of yours—yes, I said *fake*—to the operator at twenty-three minutes after five. There happened to be a prowl car right here in the neighborhood, so two minutes later, at five-twenty-five, there were cops here in your apartment. You were unconscious then, more than an hour ago. You've been unconscious until just now."

Ardis' brain whirled. Then, it cleared suddenly, and a great calm came over her.

"I don't see quite what you're hinting at, lieutenant. If you're saying that I was confused, mixed up—that I must have dreamed or imagined some of the things I told you—I'll admit it."

"You know what I'm saying! I'm saying that no guy could have got in and out of this place, and done what this one did, in any two minutes!"

"Then the telephone operator must have been mistaken about the time," Ardis said brightly. "I don't know how else to explain it."

Powers grunted. He said he could give her a better explanation—and he gave it to her. The right one. Ardis listened to it placidly, murmuring polite objections.

"That's ridiculous, lieutenant. Regardless of any gossip you may have heard, I don't know this, uh, Tony person. And I most certainly did not plot with him or anyone else to kill my husband. Why—"

"He says you did. We got a signed confession from him."

"Have you?" But of course they didn't have. They might have found out about Tony, but he would never have talked. "That hardly proves anything, does it?"

"Now, you listen to me, Mrs. Clinton! Maybe you think that—"

"How is my husband, anyway? I do hope he wasn't seriously hurt."

"How *is* he?" the lieutenant snarled. "How would he be after gettin' worked over with—" He broke off, his eyes flickering. "As a matter of fact," he said heavily, "he's going to be all right. He was pretty badly injured, but he was able to give us a statement and—"

"I'm so glad. But why are you questioning me, then?" It was another trick. Bill had to be dead. "If he gave you a statement, then you must know that everything happened just like I said."

She waited, looked at him quizzically. Powers scowled, his stern face wrinkling with exasperation.

"All right," he said, at last. "All right, Mrs. Clinton. Your husband is dead. We don't have any statement from him, and we don't have any confession from Tony."

"Yes?"

"But we know that you're guilty, and you know that you are. And you'd better get it off your conscience while you still can."

"While I still can?"

"Doc"—Powers jerked his head at the doctor. At the man, that is, who appeared to be a doctor. "Lay it on the line, doc. Tell her that her boy friend hit her a little too hard."

The man came forward hesitantly. He said, "I'm sorry, Mrs. Clinton. You have a—uh—you've sustained a very serious injury."

"Have I?" Ardis smiled. "I feel fine."

"I don't think," the doctor said judiciously, "that that's quite true. What you mean is that you don't feel anything at all. You couldn't. You see, with an injury such as yours—"

"Get out," Ardis said. "Both of you get out."

"Please, Mrs. Clinton. Believe me, this isn't a trick. I haven't wanted to alarm you, but—"

"And you haven't," she said. "You haven't scared me even a little bit, mister. Now, clear out!"

She closed her eyes, kept them closed firmly. When, at last, she re-opened them, Powers and the doctor—if he really had been a doctor—were gone. And the room was in darkness.

She lay smiling to herself, congratulating herself. In the corridor outside, she heard heavy footsteps approaching; and she tensed for a moment. Then, remembering, she relaxed again.

Not Bill, of course. She was through with that jerk forever. He'd driven her half out of her mind, got her to the point where she couldn't have taken another minute of him if her life depended on it. But now . . .

The footsteps stopped in front of her door. A key turned in the lock, the door opened and closed.

There was a clatter of a lunchpail being set down; then a familiar voice—maddeningly familiar words:

"Well. Another day, another dollar."

Ardis' mouth tightened; it twisted slowly, in a malicious grin. So they hadn't given up yet! They were pulling this one last trick. Well, let them; she'd play along with the gag.

The man plodded across the room, stooped, and gave her a half-hearted peck on the cheek. "Long time no see," he said. "What we havin' for supper?"

"Bill . . ." Ardis said. "How do I look, Bill?"

"Okay. Got your lipstick smeared, though. What'd you say we was having for supper?"

"Stewed owls! Now, look, mister. I don't know who you—"

"Sounds good. We got any hot water?"

"Of course, we've got hot water! Don't we always have? Why do you always have to ask if—if—"

She couldn't go through with it. Even as a gag—even someone who merely sounded and acted like he did—it was too much to bear.

"Y-you get out of here!" she quavered. "I don't have to stand for this! I *c-can't* stand it! I did it for fifteen years, and—"

"So what's to get excited about?" he said. "Well, guess I'll go splash the chassis."

"Stop it! *STOP IT!*" Her screams filled the room . . . silent screams ripping through silence. "He's—you're dead! I know you are! You're dead, and I don't have to put up with you for another minute. And—and—!"

"Wouldn't take no bets on that if I was you," he said mildly. "Not with a broken neck like yours."

He trudged off toward the bathroom, wherever the bathroom is in Eternity.

H. A. DEROSSO
(1917-1960)

Henry Andrew DeRosso was primarily a writer of grim, objectively realistic Western fiction, a genre in which he produced hundreds of short
stories and novelettes as well as five novels over a twenty-year span. His
output was not limited to Westerns, however. He also published some
forty dark-suspense tales, in such pulps as Street & Smith's Detective
Story Magazine and Thrilling Detective, and in such digest-size periodicals as Manhunt, Hunted, Mystery Tales, Alfred Hitchcock's Mystery
Magazine, and Mike Shayne Mystery Magazine.

Like his Western stories, DeRosso's crime fiction is offbeat and
character-oriented, with more depth of feeling—and substance—than
the typical magazine fare of its time. "The Old Pro," which first appeared
in Manhunt in December 1960, is a prime example.

In many respects, DeRosso's life and vision approximate those of Cornell Woolrich. Both men were loners, DeRosso having spent his entire
life in a small town in the remote iron-mining country of northeastern
Wisconsin. Both wrote introspective, sometimes crude, often violent, and
predominately visceral prose unlike that produced by any of their peers.
Both were obsessed with what they perceived to be the ultimate futility
of human existence and yet, paradoxically, with a man's constant need
to strive for some sense of meaning and salvation in his own existence.
And both understood and wrote feelingly about unrequited love, lost
innocence, and loneliness.

B. P.

1960

THE OLD PRO

It seemed rather strange and chilling to him because he had never contracted for another man's death before. But it was something that had to
be done and he could not do it himself because he wanted to remain
clean. Direct involvement, if discovered, would destroy all that he had
built these past few years. He might even lose Loretta and she meant too
much to him to risk that. So he made a long distance call and entered
into the contract.

"Mike? This is Burn. Remember me?"

"Burn?" Sargasso's voice over the phone sounded as coarse and rasping as it had always been. "Oh, yes. It's been a long time. Four years, isn't that right?"

"About that."

"How's retirement?"

"Good. Never had it better. Until something came up."

"Oh? Is that why you're calling?"

"Yes. I was wondering if you couldn't refer someone to me, a—an engineer experienced in removing obstructions. It's a ticklish matter and I need a good man. You know of someone like that around?"

There was a short silence. Then from Sargasso's end of the line there came a soft, grating chuckle.

"Is something funny?" he asked with a touch of anger in his tone.

"In a way, yes," Sargasso said. "I mean, you of all people—" The chuckle sounded again.

He flushed in the privacy of the phone booth. "Well, do you have the man?" he asked testily.

"Sure, Burn, sure." Amusement still lingered in Sargasso's voice. "You were always the hasty one. Take it easy. When do you want the engineer?"

"This weekend. Sometime Saturday. At my place out at Walton Lake. I'll have the job all set up for him. Can you get him up here in that time?"

"Now, Burn, you know I always guarantee results." The humor still teased in Sargasso's tone. "Well, luck."

"Thanks, Mike. So long."

The line clicked dead at Sargasso's end before he had even started to hang up . . .

The name on his mailbox spelled Ralph Whitburn. He had a comfortable home here on the edge of the small town with a nice view of the curving river that was the boundary between Wisconsin and the Upper Peninsula of Michigan. Beyond the river stretched the vast, second-growth forest. He had fallen in love with the view the first time he had seen it. He enjoyed the cool green colors of summer and the tartan hues of autumn, he even enjoyed the bleak look of winter with the trees standing dark and dead among the silent snow. It was so far removed from the squalor and stench of all the cities he had once known.

This was the good life. He could hear Loretta humming in the kitchen. The aroma of cooking was pleasant in his nostrils. He stood on the lawn and watched some swallows wheeling and darting not far overhead in their swift pursuit of summer insects. Yes, this was the good life and he was not going to let anything destroy it. That was why he had contracted for a man's death.

"Chow's ready, Ralph."

His eyes feasted on Loretta as he sat down at the table in the dining nook. She was tall and red-headed with a pert, saucy face spattered with freckles that also spread over her bare shoulders and arms. She was wearing halter and shorts that set off her good figure, which was high-breasted, lean-hipped and long-legged. Once he had thought that love was an emotion he would never experience but that had been before he had met Loretta.

This was the good life, this was true contentment.

"Is something wrong, Ralph?"

He looked up with a start, surprised that he had revealed anything. Loretta was watching him with a half-frown, half-smile, green eyes clouded with puzzlement and concern.

His lips twisted into a smile that felt awkward and forced to him. "Why do you say that?"

"You look—preoccupied."

"Do I?" He laughed. "The approach of middle age when muscles grow flabby and the skin sags and—"

"Oh, stop it, Ralph. I'm serious." The frown was very pronounced on her forehead now. "Something's been eating you lately. What is it?"

He sobered and the great solemnness came over him again and the needling of a dark and futile anger. "It's nothing, Loretta. I swear it's nothing."

"Well, if this is how 'nothing' affects you, I'd hate to think how you'd be when something big and serious pops up."

"I've been thinking. You know, about expanding the plant. Wood products are selling very well. I've been trying to decide between enlarging the existing plant and building a new one, maybe over in Michigan."

She was staring at him in a strange, examining way. "Funny you never mentioned this to me before. Are you starting to keep things from me, Ralph?" She tried to say the last lightly but it did not quite come off. There had been a catch in her throat.

He got up and bent over her and kissed her cheek. "I'm just a little down. Kind of tired. A weekend at the lake will fix me up."

She hugged his arm and looked up at him with shining eyes. "I was just going to suggest that. Why don't we go out there tonight? You can stay away from the plant tomorrow. It's Friday and the business will get along without you for one day. I'll start getting ready now."

She rose to her feet but he put a detaining hand on her arm. "Saturday's soon enough. And, Loretta, this weekend I'm going out there alone."

She gave him a long look. Then her mouth smiled but the eyes said she was just pretending. "You mean what the Hollywood people call a trial separation?"

"No, no," he said hurriedly, "nothing like that." He took her in his arms and held her very tightly, thinking that this was something he would never allow anyone to break up. "There's something I've got to thrash out alone. I wish I could explain to you, Loretta, but it's something I've got to do by myself. I'll miss you every minute I'm at the lake. Believe me."

"Ralph," she gasped, "I can't breathe." She leaned back in his relaxing arms and caressed his cheek while she smiled up at him. "Old and flabby?" she teased. "Another minute of that and I'd have had to go see a chiropractor."

"Then you don't mind my going alone?"

"Of course I mind, but I bow to your will, master." She kissed him fervently. "I'll miss you, too, you big lug. Very, very much."

He buried his face in her hair. This was the good life, he thought. Nothing, no one was going to take it from him . . .

He had always liked the solemnity and quiet of the forest. There was something restful and soothing in the isolation, the lack of the sounds of machinery and motors, the absence of the hurry and bustle of the cities. The only intrusion from the outside world was the occasional snarl of an outboard motor out on the lake but even this was not overdone for he had selected a far end of Walton Lake on which to build his cottage. There were no immediate neighbors. He had come to these north woods for seclusion and here at the lake he had it.

He found the waiting hard to take and this was unusual for he had always been a patient man. The thing he disliked most about the waiting was that so many doubts and uncertainties were forming in his mind. He realized these were foolish fears for the man Sargasso sent would be efficient and capable. He knew how these killers operated. They entered a town or city as strangers, studied the habits of their quarry, decided on the best means of liquidation, did so and departed. They were the professionals who very seldom were apprehended and if they were never named their employers. He knew that very well but still he could not keep a feeling of anxiety from creeping over him. There was too much at stake, he had too much to lose, that was the reason he worried so endlessly.

He tried fishing to while away the time. He got his boat and went out to the center of the lake by the island and on his third cast hooked a wall-eye. But his heart was not in it and he played the big fish carelessly and impatiently and lost it. He started the motor again, intending to cruise about the lake, and with his mind on other matters almost wrecked the craft on the treacherous rocks that lurked just beneath the surface of the water at the south end of the island. He swerved the boat barely in time and as he looked back over his shoulder at the place where he could have torn the bottom out of the craft the idea was born.

He could feel his heart begin to pound with an old excitement. Then he remembered that Sargasso was sending someone and that whoever it was he would have his own ideas. So Whitburn filed the thought away, somewhat regretfully, telling himself he could not become involved directly. He had to stay clean.

Heading back to the cottage, he saw the car parked beside his convertible. A strange tightness gathered in his throat, a sensation of uneasiness almost akin to panic, and he wondered at this for he had always prided himself on his iron nerve. He told himself to relax. The matter would be in capable hands. No one was ever delegated by Sargasso unless he were thoroughly competent.

The stranger was standing on the small dock, watching the boat come in. He was on the short and chunky side. He wore a gay sport shirt and tan slacks. The head was round, the face chubby with small, hard eyes staring out of thick pouches. The graying hair was clipped short, giving him a Teutonic appearance.

"Burn?" he asked. The voice was soft, almost gentle.

"Whitburn. Been waiting long?"

"Maybe five minutes."

Whitburn tied the boat to the dock and stepped ashore. The other was watching him with a patent curiosity.

"I didn't catch your name," Whitburn said.

"Mace." There was a silence while the small, granitic eyes went on measuring Whitburn. "I understand you have a—an engineering problem."

"Come inside," Whitburn said. "I've got some cold beer."

This was rather unusual, Whitburn was thinking. It was a new experience for him, this outlining the matter and arranging a man's death. It had never been quite like this before.

"I don't know how to begin," Whitburn said.

Mace smiled thinly. It was an expression of patience as well as amusement. "Take your time. Tell it any way you like."

Whitburn took a sip of beer. It seemed without taste, he found no pleasure in it, and told himself angrily to stop acting so damned childish. He had seen his share. Why should this appall him? And he told himself it was because he had never trusted anyone, only himself. That was his creed. To that he attributed survival and the good life he was now enjoying.

"There's a man—" he began and then had to pause, searching for words that were not there. Mace watched him, smile widening slightly, and Whitburn knew a touch of resentment. He remembered Sargasso's amusement over the phone. Was this the same? It couldn't be. Mace seemed to sense his thoughts and the small smile vanished. Mace took a deep swallow of beer.

"He'll be coming here this evening," Whitburn went on after a while. "After dark. Not exactly here but to the island. You noticed it, didn't you, the island? He comes there every Saturday night. I want this to be the last time."

"Blackmail?" Mace asked in his quiet voice.

Whitburn leaned forward in his chair, somewhat angered. "What did Mike tell you?"

"Mike? Oh, you mean— Nothing, Whitburn. You know how it is. He just acts as an agent. You know, like agents who book actors? He sends us where there's work for us. You know that."

"Why did you say blackmail?"

"You mentioned a man you don't want coming around any more. I've found it's almost always blackmail. Something else, a guy can run to the cops. Blackmail, a guy has something to hide, he can't have the cops nosing around. Anyway, that's what I've found. Don't you agree?"

"You know the man?"

Mace spread his hands. "How would I? Brief me."

Whitburn could hear the leaden thumping of his heart. That sense of anxiety would not leave him. If he could only be sure that there would be no slip up. Mace looked competent. All of Sargasso's men were competent. Failure sealed their doom, there was no such thing as a second chance. But if something did go wrong and he was implicated, there would be small comfort in knowing that Mace would pay for his bungling. The good life would be gone, most likely lost forever.

"His name is Cullenbine, Earl Cullenbine," Whitburn said. In his ears his voice sounded dull and flat. "He used to be a police reporter with underworld connections. Blackmail had always been a sideline with him. The last couple of years he's been giving it his full time. He came up north last November to hunt deer and recognized me. At the time he didn't let on but he came back this spring and hasn't let me alone since."

He looked down at his hands and saw that they were clenched tight. He forced them open and became aware that a trickle of sweat ran down each cheek. It was warm outside and some of the heat had penetrated into the cottage. Still he cursed silently and asked what had happened to his iron nerve?

He glanced at Mace and thought he caught the vanishing of a look of amusement on the man's face. But it could have been only imagination. He was as jumpy as a wino after a month long binge.

"You want it on the island?" Mace asked.

"That's as good a place as any. It'll be night and there shouldn't be anyone around. There's no one living on the island, not even a shack. During the day sometimes fishermen pass by there but very seldom at night."

"Fine," Mace said, nodding. "Fine."

"I don't want you to think I'm trying to tell you how to do your job but would it be possible somehow to make it look like an accident?"

Mace smiled the amused smile. "I imagine it could be arranged."

"I mean, without a weapon. That is, without something like a gun or a knife. It would be a dead giveaway otherwise. I don't want you to think I'm trying to tell you just what to do but I don't want to be connected with it in any way. You see, I'm alone at this end of the lake. If a weapon is used, naturally I'll be questioned on whether I saw or heard something. Perhaps I might even come under suspicion. I don't want that."

He felt a little foolish talking like this. It was so strange for him to be the one saying these words.

"Relax," Mace said, the smile still on his face. "I'll fix it just the way you want it."

"I suppose I better describe Cullenbine to you."

"I've just thought of something better," Mace said. "Why don't you come to the island with me? You can make sure it's Cullenbine then. No chance for a mistake that way."

Whitburn was silent, unable to find anything to say. The feeling of anxiety was stronger than ever in him and he could not understand why it should be. Tension and suspense had never bothered him before.

Mace laughed softly. "If you're squeamish, I'll wait until you've left the island. After all, you do want to make sure it's Cullenbine and not someone else I might mistake, don't you? This way there's no chance for error. Like I said, I'll wait until after you've gone from the island. You won't have to watch anything."

Whitburn remained silent, thinking.

"You said you're the only one at this end of the lake. So who's to see you going to the island with me? You do want to make sure it's Cullenbine, don't you? Chances are he'll be the only one to show up on the island tonight but you never can tell. I just thought, you worrying so much about something going wrong and all that, you'd want to be positive it's Cullenbine."

Whitburn sighed. "All right, Mace."

Mace glanced at his wristwatch. "What time do you expect him on the island?"

"About ten."

"Good. Is there a place I can catch some sleep here? . . ."

Frogs had their choral groups scattered along the shore of the lake and in the ponds in the nearby forest. Something flew past not far overhead on softly flapping wings. Stars glittered brightly. The surface of the lake looked black, like the underground river of the dead.

They got into the boat and Whitburn used an oar to push the craft away from the dock and into deeper water so that he could drop the outboard. The motor caught on the first try and he kept the throttle barely open, easing the boat toward the island with as little sound as he could manage.

"This how you make your payoffs?" Mace asked. "On the island?"

"Every Saturday night."

"Didn't your wife ever get suspicious?"

"Sometimes I'd fish off shore in the afternoon and then cruise around to the other side where she couldn't see me go ashore. We had a place where I'd leave the money. Sometimes I'd come here at night, like now, and hand it to him in person. I'd vary it from time to time. Loretta never caught on."

Saying her name put a tightness in Whitburn's throat. For you, Loretta, he thought, I'm doing all this for you and the good life we have together. I'd never have got into this otherwise.

"Why didn't you ever take care of Cullenbine yourself?"

"I— That's not my line."

Mace laughed, a sound barely heard above the purr of the outboard.

The island loomed dark and brooding in the starlight. An owl hooted softly. Whitburn eased the boat in to shore, cutting the motor and letting the craft drift the last few yards. The prow grated gently against gravel and he stepped out into several inches of water and with Mace's help pulled the boat halfway up on the beach.

He stood for a few moments, staring out over the lake, wondering if anyone had seen him and Mace crossing to the island. Only the black water appeared. There were no sounds other than the glee-clubbing of the frogs and the soft lapping of the lake against the shore.

"He'll be on the other side of the island," Whitburn said to Mace and started walking.

He led the way with Mace several steps behind him. They took a roundabout route, following the shore line for this was easier going than plunging through the timber that was choked with thick underbrush. Even so, Mace, who was more accustomed to walking the uncluttered and smooth cement and asphalt of the cities, stumbled a couple of times over the uneven earth and spongelike ground littered with debris that had been washed ashore. His curses were angry and vicious.

Mace was breathing hard by the time they reached the southern end of the island. Whitburn's breath, too, had quickened, from his exertions and a strange, uneasy excitement that he could not quite fathom. Mace caught up with Whitburn as he paused to study the darkness ahead. Finally Whitburn saw it, the faint, pink glow of a cigarette as the smoker inhaled on it.

He started ahead again, aware that Mace once more trailed him. He could understand Mace's difficult progress for he himself tripped and all but fell over a piece of driftwood. Then he made out the tall shadow standing there, watching them approach.

He should have known how it was when Cullenbine evinced no surprise that Whitburn was not alone. Cullenbine stood there quite calmly, inhaling on his cigarette. The night concealed whatever expression there was on his lean, sallow face.

"I see you got here, Burn," Cullenbine said.

Whitburn felt his throat constrict. Something shrieked a warning in his brain but he realized that the alarm had come too late. Like an amateur he had let Mace stay behind him all the while. He turned and saw Mace standing a few feet away. Even in the darkness he could make out the black shape of the pistol in Mace's hand.

Cullenbine chuckled. "Have you finally got it, Burn?"

It was too late for recriminations and reproach. He had grown soft these past four years, he had lost that fine edge, that intuitive sense that had always served him well. He had lost all that and his life in the bargain.

Loretta, he thought, and for the first time since he had been a child he could have wept. Once more he said her name to himself and then put all his mind to what was at hand.

"I guess I read you just in the nick of time," Cullenbine was saying. "I didn't realize how fine I had drawn it until Mace told me that you had called Sargasso, too, but only after I'd done so. Mike has a sense of humor, don't you think, Burn? I mean, sending Mace up here to both of us?"

Whitburn became aware of the calm, hard beat of his heart. This was more like it had once been. He was beginning to feel some of the coolness, the detachment he used to experience. Maybe it was coming back. Maybe he had not lost it after all.

"Who did Mike tell you to serve, Mace?" he asked.

He sensed Mace's shrug. "Mike said it was up to me. He told me to figure out if you'd gone soft, if there was nothing worth salvaging about you. I never knew you when you were one of Mike's boys, I was with another organization then, but he said you'd been his best. But then you got married and went in hiding up here in these woods. He said if you'd gone soft to take you and you are soft, Burn, like a creampuff."

"I have the priority, Burn," Cullenbine put in. "After all, I called Sargasso first. You were a mite too late. I figured you were tired of paying me and were about to do something about it. But I thought you'd do it personally. After all, I wouldn't have been the first man you'd have killed. But like Mace says, you went soft and called Sargasso, just after

I did. I figured I wouldn't have a chance against a professional like you which is the reason I got in touch with Sargasso. Anything else you'd like to know?''

Whitburn stood there, silent. It was as though he were already hearing the earth thudding down upon his coffin.

"Good," Cullenbine said. "No sense in dragging it out, is there? Mace. Do me a favor. I'd rather not watch."

"You're the boss," Mace said. He motioned with the pistol. "Start moving, Burn. Back the way we come. I told you I was going to do it like you wanted it. An accident, you said? That's how it'll be."

He walked on wooden legs, hardly conscious of the pain when he barked his shin against a piece of driftwood. He walked like a beaten man, shoulders slumped, feet dragging. Mace stepped in close once and jabbed Whitburn hard in the back with the pistol.

"Faster, damn you," Mace snarled.

Whitburn's pace quickened then, after a while, began to slow and drag again. They were well away from Cullenbine now. Only the night was there, and the inanimateness of the island, and the frogs chorusing and the water lapping against the beach.

Whitburn had angled close to the edge of the water. He paused when he felt a stick of driftwood and stood with one heel poised against it. Mace's curse sounded softly and Whitburn sensed the man moving in to jab him again with the pistol. Whitburn kicked back with his heel, sending the piece of driftwood hard against Mace's shins. Mace swore as his feet tangled and tripped him. He fell heavily, cursing sharp and loud. The pistol roared as he dropped but the bullet went wild.

Whitburn was on Mace instantly. A hard toe against Mace's wrist sent the pistol flying out of numbed fingers. They grappled, rolling into the water. With a fury he had never known, Whitburn got a hold on Mace, forcing him face down into the water. Whitburn's knees dug into the small of Mace's back, his hands never for an instant relaxed their iron grip.

Mace thrashed and kicked and tried to roll, he tried swiveling his head to get his mouth out of the water but it was just deep enough to thwart his efforts. Whitburn held him until Mace's movements weakened and finally slackened and were still. He stayed as he was on Mace until he was sure Mace would breathe no more.

He had never known rage and hate when killing until now. The realization came to him as he was walking back to Cullenbine. But then,

Whitburn told himself, this was the first time he had ever been personally involved with his victims. All the others had been detached objects for whom he'd had no feelings. They had merely represented a job he had to do. They had never been a question of survival.

He had Mace's pistol in his hand as he came up to Cullenbine who was waiting, smoking calmly. It was not until Whitburn was almost on him that recognition, shock, then horror came to Cullenbine.

"Burn," he cried, voice harsh with surprise and terror.

Whitburn motioned with the pistol. "Start walking, Cullenbine. You're going to join Mace . . ."

He had the good life again, without the worry and fear of being exposed for what he had been. It was never better than it was now with Loretta. He bought her a Thunderbird for her birthday and in return she became more affectionate and satisfying than ever before. Yes, he had the good life again.

The deaths of Cullenbine and Mace had not created too much of a stir. They had been found drowned at the south end of the island, among the treacherous rocks. Cullenbine's boat had been found there, too, with the bottom smashed in where Whitburn had run it onto the rocks. The deaths were officially written off as accidental.

One day his phone rang and all the joy ran out of him and he was just a shell, hollow and empty, as he heard the coarse, rasping voice from the other end of the long distance line.

"Burn? Mike. How goes it?"

He had to run his tongue over his lips and swallow before he could speak. "All right," he managed.

"You handled yourself very well," Sargasso said. "They never tumbled, did they? Accidental drowning." Sargasso chuckled. "I always said you were the best. That's why I hated to see you go into retirement. Didn't a taste of it make you hungry for more? You want to come back, Burn?"

"No, damn you, and listen to me. What was the big—"

"You listen to me, Burn," Sargasso snapped. "I just wanted to know if you still had it. If you couldn't handle Mace you weren't worth taking back."

"I'm not coming back. I—"

"Listen, Burn. Listen good. You got a wife, huh? Good looker, huh? She wouldn't be such a pretty sight after she'd caught acid in her face. Get what I mean, Burn?"

Something sickening formed in his stomach. He could see the good years begin to fade.

"There's something in Vegas," Sargasso went on when Whitburn didn't answer. "Something real touchy. It needs the best. That's you, Burn."

"No." He tried to shout it but it came out as a barely audible whisper. He was not sure whether Sargasso had heard it.

"Maybe you'd like to think it over," Sargasso was saying. "I can give you twenty-four hours. No more."

"All right," he said in a dull voice, "I'll think about it."

"Fine. See you, Burn." The line went dead at Sargasso's end.

He stood there with the receiver in his hand, staring with unseeing eyes at the view he had once enjoyed so much. He could think it over but there was only one answer Sargasso would accept. And the Vegas thing would not be the last. There would be another and another and another until he eventually bungled and had to pay the penalty.

Finally he stirred and placed the phone back on its cradle. The sound that made was the requiem for the good life . . .

MICHAEL KERR
(b. 1933)

Although gifted and imaginative enough to be able to turn his typewriter to a variety of popular-fiction genres, Michael Kerr (Robert Hoskins) seems never to have fully utilized this talent. His identifiable output is not extensive. As Kerr, he wrote a good deal of science fiction during the mid-1970s, appearing in many of the leading magazines as well as writing a paperback original, The Gemini Run (1979). Under his real name, he edited the anthology series Infinity (1970–1973), whose five volumes regularly featured new material from the best science-fiction writers, including Robert Silverberg, Arthur C. Clarke, and Poul Anderson.

Kerr began his novel-writing career by penning modern Gothics. A Place on Dark Island (1971) was the first of seven titles to appear under the pseudonym Grace Corren. As Susan Jennifer, he wrote two Gothics, the first of which, The House of Counted Hatreds (1973), was reissued in 1980 under the Corren name. During the 1980s, he turned to the action-adventure field, contributing such titles as Argentine Deadline (1982) and The Fury Bombs (1983) to the Mack Bolan spinoff series, Phoenix Force, under the house name Gar Wilson. According to certain reference books, Kerr appears to have ceased writing altogether in the mid-1980s.

Under his real name, Kerr wrote only a handful of mystery shorts, all more or less hard-boiled in concept and execution. "The Saturday Night Deaths," a fine, moody shocker, appeared in the July 1976 issue of Mystery Monthly; a second story, "Candy Man," was published in the same issue as by Robert Hoskins.

J. A.

1976

THE SATURDAY NIGHT DEATHS

Dolan was the first: he died at 5:48 P.M.

Technically it wasn't yet Saturday night, for just like the traffic council, counting usually starts at 6 P.M. And it was early for a family-triangle blowup. But Dolan was known as a morning drinker and an any-time skirt chaser, and when the police finally picked through the blood painted throughout all three rooms of the floosie's apartment, it was fairly obvious that Mrs. Dolan had reached the point where she could take no more. They figured she took care of her husband first, ripping him open from groin to breastbone, then used the blonde for a pincushion. It's amazing how much strength an aging woman can have: the Medical Examiner counted over one hundred stab wounds on the girl. But it looked as if Mrs. Dolan was neatest with herself—one slash on each wrist, letting her life run out and soak the cushions of the sex-stained sofa.

7:07 P.M.: Lettoli was next to die.

They found him in the alley behind one of his own cheap hotels, ordinarily a place Lettoli avoided like the plague. They found him with his wallet ripped open and the credit card section missing. The gun was a .32 and most probably a Special—good enough to do the job.

According to Mrs. Lettoli the thief didn't get much besides the credit cards, for her husband did not believe in carrying cash—twenty bucks at the most, maybe only four or five, in case he decided to pick up a newspaper or if he ran out of cigars. Of course, in a way it was his own fault, wearing that three-hundred-dollar suit in an area where cops went only in pairs. Still, nobody—not his wife, his lawyer, even his boys—could figure out what brought him to that alley on that particular night. He didn't make his own collections. Of the hotel staff, the only one to see him that Saturday was the janitor, who came out into the alley to dump garbage into the already overflowing cans, and thus discovered the body.

It wasn't a bad night for murder in one sense—at least as far as the cops were concerned. The weather was cooperative, almost warm, the temperature just breaking through the fifty mark and the smell of spring in the air. There was no drowning rain to blur the vision of men bending over the chalked outline of Lettoli's body, no water running in the streets or brown slush to slop over the side of one's shoes. Of course, they still had to breathe in the stink of violent death, but that goes with the job.

7:55 P.M.: Huegens was number three, only forty-eight minutes after Lettoli.

His wife was screaming hysterically while the cop rode with her in the ambulance to the hospital. Although the intern tried to sedate her against the pain of the broken arm and ribs, the officer did manage to gather that some maniac had forced them off the road after first riding their tail so closely that Huegens had sped up in fear of being rammed. He was pushing eighty on the old parkway with its treacherous curves when the guy behind cut out on the worst curve on the whole damn road—cut too close. The red paint of the other car was deep in the scratch that went from Huegens' rear fender halfway across his door. It was at that point that Huegens lost control of the Cadillac: the car went through the low stone fence and knocked over a dozen hundred-year-old gravestones before it came to a stop fifty feet inside the cemetery.

Death by violence is not something unknown in a city the size of this one—the average annual rate of murders since 1960 comes out to just over seventeen. That's enough to justify maintaining a homicide division at detective central, although in slack periods some of the four men assigned there go on loan to divisions cut short by the economy-minded, tight-fisted city council.

August can be a bad month most years, particularly during a summer of drought. The city sizzles then, for days and sometimes for weeks under the relentless sun, the heat captured by the concrete streets and concrete buildings. Christmas can be bad for murder too, as can any other holiday season—when the pressures to achieve can seem the heaviest, and those who are failing—at least in their own eyes—can easily break. But the average rate for murder means that over the course of a year there will be no more than one death by violence every three weeks.

And so three times in one evening was definitely unusual. Not yet a record, but certainly bringing this day to the top of the list of deadly days.

9:50 P.M.: Pelk was number four. He tied the record.

He got it coming back from the candy store two blocks from his house with the early edition of the Sunday paper. He always took the dog out for a walk at that time of the evening, and his habits were well known in the neighborhood and among his friends and business acquaintances. All of the cops agreed that this death was deliberate. Why else would a car coming from no farther than the stop sign at the end of the block not have time to slow down, not be able to swerve to avoid him? But there had been no unusual traffic noises noted by the neighbors, and certainly no squeal of brakes just before the impact.

The retired captain showed up at the investigation of what was still officially being called the hit-and-run death of Pelk, arriving perhaps twenty minutes after the boys from downtown. Peter Lorgos was in charge, one of the up-and-coming bright young men of the department. When he saw the captain, he moved away from the cluster of reporters.

"Cap, what are you doing here?"

"I caught the squeal, Pete, thought maybe I could help out—direct traffic or something. You boys seem to be having a busy night."

Lorgos was embarrassed. "I thought you had taken off for California."

"I leave tomorrow. If I don't change my mind. I haven't seen my sister for seventeen years, another week or month won't make that much difference."

"Well, Cap, we have things pretty well in hand. . . ."

The retired captain understood his feelings, knew before he came that he would be in the way. Besides, he hadn't worked the street end of an investigation for almost twenty years, and even when he was chief of detectives—up until six weeks ago—he always had the feeling that Pete and a few of his contemporaries were only tolerating him, would rather not have to put up with him. Now that the captain was out of the way some of the other old-timers would be clearing out soon, and then Pete and the others would have their chance at running things.

Not that the retirement was the captain's idea at all—it was the regulations: sixty-five and out. The pension was generous enough, and he had put some money aside the last twenty-five years. It was just that he wasn't ready to quit.

A patrolman came up to Pete, one of the new kids out of the last class. For a minute the captain couldn't think of his name. Then it came to him—Minetti.

"Sergeant, they've just located a vehicle, abandoned behind the high school about six blocks from here. The headlight is smashed, and it looks like it's the car that hit Pelk. But it's black—it's definitely not the car involved in the Huegens crash."

"Scenting conspiracy, Pete?" the captain asked.

He shrugged. "You never know, Cap. Wouldn't you check out all angles when four of the city's biggest hoods get it on the same night?"

"Pelk has been out of the rackets and clean for over twenty years," the captain said mildly.

"Maybe someone has a long memory. He and Dolan started out together on the streets, and for a long time Huegens did his legal dirty work. . . ."

His voice trailed off; he seemed to feel awkward to be lecturing the older man on the history of the power structure of the city. He was glad suddenly to have the opportunity to shout orders at a too pushy television cameraman. The captain stood there for another two or three minutes, watching from the sidelines, then finally walked back to his own car.

He heard the low murmur of the police radio—he should have turned it in the day he retired, but somehow he forgot. Maybe it was because the day before the sergeant in charge of the supply office had told him that for some strange reason he couldn't find the paperwork charging the captain for the thing.

He sat in his car for perhaps another ten minutes, until the meat wagon came to claim Pelk. After that the television crew left, and then most of the gawkers as well. He watched Pete moving around for another couple of minutes, and then he started the car and pulled away from the curb, cutting around the barricades blocking off the scene of the accident.

Midnight: Chelton broke the record. He was number five.

They found him with a gun in his hand, the smell of scorched flesh coming from the hole under his chin where the bullet had entered. There was another hole the size of a fist in the top of his head and a half-kilo of uncut heroin under the front seat of his car.

It didn't figure: Chelton wasn't under pressure, apart from the usual surveillance by the federal, state, and city narcotics boys. Everyone knew that he was the number one man in the city drugstore, but he was too smart to be caught with so much as an aspirin in his machine-turned gold cigarette case—unless there was a doctor's prescription folded around the tablet. There were plenty of others to take the risks, to do the holding. Chelton himself was on top of his world, respected among his fellow syndicate associates, living in a fantastic riverfront mansion, built during the Thirties by a famous movie queen for three hundred thousand dollars. Chelton enjoyed a happy family life; his kids were educated in the most exclusive private schools, where never was heard a discouraging word or intimation as to the source of Papa's wealth and the nature of his business.

Why should Chelton stick a gun under his face and pull the trigger?

But the gun was in his hand.

And the only other prints on or in the car belonged to members of his family.

About then somebody in the department came up with the bright idea that since all of the deaths except Dolan's were connected with cars, maybe there was something worth looking into. The genius blabbed to a television newsman, and he got to make his first public appearance on the one o'clock news roundup, just a few minutes after Sellinger walked off the balcony of his penthouse on the twenty-third floor.

12:53 A.M.: Sellinger was number six. He landed on the hood of a car pulling out of the building garage, almost adding the car's four passengers to the death list. They would have been the first extraneous victims since the death of Dolan's wife and girl friend.

By now there were a great many nervous people in town, almost everyone who was still awake. The ones with criminal connections were perhaps justified in their worries, but the police switchboard was besieged with distraught callers of the little-old-lady variety, who were certain that a mad killer was lurking in the hydrangea bushes below their bedroom. There was no way such calls could be checked out, for every available man had been called in to duty and the city was being saturated with patrols—but someone got the bright idea of bringing in some of the volunteers from the drug and suicide centers, and letting them talk to the nervous grandmas. They did a pretty good job of calming the old ladies.

After that the pace seemed to pick up:

1:21 A.M.: someone poured a glass of household lye solution down Bergen's throat. It was possible the man was unconscious at the moment of assault, as there was no sign of struggle. But it made no difference, for he would have been just as dead if he had struggled.

2:02 A.M.: Wentworth's north-side house went up in a shower of flames that reminded one late-pacing neighbor of a giant Roman candle. The cause was later determined to be an exploding gas line.

2:43 A.M.: someone entered Korman's bedroom without waking his wife. He was strangled with one of her stockings, also without waking his wife. His body was not discovered until morning, at which time his servants also found the dead bodies of three guard dogs, struck down by poisoned tranquilizer darts.

At 3:50 the captain arrived home to find Pete Lorgos' city sedan in his driveway. Pete was sitting in the porch swing that the captain had never gotten around to taking down, with Ellie no longer there to nag him about such matters. He knew there was a three-inch rip in the window screen behind Lorgos as well, although this new nylon screening didn't rust like the old stuff did. The storm windows were still stacked in the garage behind the house.

"Pete," the captain said, speaking to the spark of the other's cigarette as he got out of his car. He walked up to the porch. "Come on in and I'll fix coffee, if you can stand instant."

"That'll be fine, Cap."

Lorgos said nothing as he followed him through the clutter of the living room, even when he saw the dust coating the tables and the pile of unwashed dishes in the kitchen sink. The captain found two mugs in the cupboard and set the teakettle on the gas range to boil, then pulled out a chair at the kitchen table.

"Sit down, Pete."

Pete stared at him a minute before doing so.

"It doesn't look as though you've done much packing, Cap."

"Oh, I'm ready to go—what I'm taking will fit in three suitcases. No sense burdening yourself when you strike out for a whole new life, Pete."

"That makes sense. Are you planning to come back for a visit?"

"There's nothing to bring me back here now—I'm letting the real estate people handle everything, including the cleaning up. I won't even have to come back to sign the papers."

He glanced towards the living room, closed his eyes suddenly as he saw it the way it had been before Ellie died last summer. She was with him in that instant, her old rose fragrance strong in the air, her firm hand touching his shoulder to reassure him. He almost lifted his hand to hers, before he opened his eyes again.

"Nothing personal, Pete—but I don't expect to miss you people a bit."

The teakettle whistled, and he got up to spoon crystals into the mugs and pour in the water. He found milk in the refrigerator, brought it out, and found a spoon for the cracked sugar bowl on the table. Then he sat down again and stirred his coffee.

Pete sipped from his mug and stared at the captain over the lip. At last he set it down again and sighed, scratching his nose.

"I still don't know how you did the Dolan job, Cap—the neighbors heard nothing, although the walls are paper thin. I'm almost ready to concede that you had nothing to do with that one, that it was just as it seemed."

The captain's face was carefully blank.

"The others all check out—you made it easy, although you must be tired now. Everybody knows what a hard-nose you are, Cap. For forty years this has been one of the crookedest cities in the country, but you won't even pick a nickel off the sidewalk if there's anybody to see you. Every other top cop to retire from the department walked away with enough to make him comfortable for life, but look at you—planning to drive to California to stay with your old-maid schoolteacher sister. How much money do you have, Cap?"

"More than most people think, thanks to Ellie. But every penny of it came honest, Pete—most of it because my wife was smart enough to scrimp out a few dollars and put them in mutual funds right from the beginning of our marriage. A few years ago she believed some psychic's prediction that the market was headed for trouble and switched everything into government securities."

"It must have been tough, Cap, watching the world fall into a sewer and not be able to do anything about it. A lot of old sins were expunged from the record tonight. I'm glad you're leaving tomorrow."

He got up then, leaving his cup half full. The captain followed him back through the house, stood on the porch as he opened the door to his car.

"If I could connect you to Dolan, Cap, I wouldn't be walking away now. But I don't really think you'd kill innocent bystanders. Send us a postcard from California—something to put up on the bulletin board."

The captain stood on the porch watching the taillights of Lorgos' car winking until they turned the corner, not wanting to go back into the house, to be reminded again of Ellie's absence. Ellie had always been proud of him, even during the bad years when some of the mobsters had leaned hard—he still bore the scars of the beating that put him in the hospital for three months. It was rough for her then, with only him to worry about, but he was glad they never had kids. He hated to think what might have happened if there had been kids. . . .

He went back in the house, stopped in the kitchen to pick up the mugs and place them in the sink with the other dishes. For a moment he was tempted to clean up, then decided no. He went upstairs to the bedroom, found the laundry bag stuffed with the clothes he had been wearing earlier in the evening. They were all the old things from the bottom drawer, threadbare pants and worn shirts that Ellie had stuck away to give to a charity that never came calling.

He stripped off the things he had on now, adding them to the bag, and went in the closet to find something more decent. Then he came back to the dresser and noticed the pile of mail that had been sitting there for days now. He flipped through the stack, saw that one of the letters was from the real estate company that had wanted to list the house. He dropped them all back unopened.

Then he picked up the silver-framed photo of Ellie as she had been when they first met, just after the war. She was smiling—it seemed to him now that she had always been smiling, no matter what her real feelings, trying to make it easier for him. He put the picture back down, went downstairs to check over the house.

The feeling of clutter, of mess, was pervasive. In the kitchen the captain leaned against the counter again, staring at the pile of dishes in the sink. Again he was tempted to start cleaning up, but instead he went into the living room, went to the little smoking stand that he had before he married Ellie. For the last three months the copper-lined compartment had been full, what with the heroin that he planted on Chelton to make sure the newsmen played up his drug connections, and the various guns he had used. They were gone now, of course, except for the one he left with Chelton, even the tranquilizing gun he had used on Dolan's girl friend, on Chelton, and on all of them after that. The only things left in the cabinet were a few of his old pipes and a half a can of tobacco, stale now; he hadn't touched them since Ellie's death. In the back corner was the collection of lighters he had accumulated over the years.

Now he brought out a pipe and the tobacco, stuffed the bowl carefully, and picked up one of the lighters. It was dry, as were the next two, and then he spotted a butane job that had been given to him as a Christmas present by someone two or three years ago. As he flicked the wheel orange flame leaped up; the fuel had not leaked.

He sat down in his chair now, lighting his pipe and then reaching to turn off the lights, wanting to sit in the darkness for a time. He closed his eyes, thinking back over the evening, remembering now the excitement that had stabbed at his heart as he rode up on Huegens, forced him from the road. The captain had been so intent on checking out his plates that he had not realized his wife was in the car until the moment of impact. Afterwards he was relieved to learn she had survived. It had been a close thing for the captain, but he managed to bring the car back under control and leave the parkway at the next exit, as he had planned.

He flicked the wheel of the lighter again, watching the flame shoot up nearly four inches as he adjusted the little wheel. It was a pretty thing.

In a way he felt sorry for Dolan's women, although he was not so unaware of their involvement in Dolan's operation as Pete Lorgos was— neither of them could be called an innocent bystander, and there were those who thought his wife was the actual brains of the organization. The thought of killing them had been distasteful, had been what had taken the captain so many weeks to work up to this night. That's why he made them the first to die, to have it done with.

The girl friend came first. She was the first human being he had ever killed—in all his thirty-eight years on the force he never once fired his gun at anything other than a target on the range. He must have lost control when he started driving the knife into her, for he could not remember hitting her so many more times after the first stroke.

By the time Dolan's wife arrived the captain was composed, waiting for her behind the door; he got his hand over her mouth before she had a chance to spot the body. It had been a long time since he learned about pressure points, but they worked just like the book said they would. Once she was unconscious it was easier to use the knife and slash her wrists. And it was no trouble at all to take Dolan when he walked through the door a few minutes later. The knife was in his gut and ripping up before he even realized that something had happened to the women, before he could ask the captain why he had summoned him to this meeting.

The hardest part of all was getting the knife back into the woman's fingers. . . .

Suddenly he was trembling, cold sweat pouring from his face as he remembered them dying, remembered the way in which they had all died. It seemed easy at the time, but now the truth was catching up to him.

He shivered, forced his back stiff, bit down on his lip. He thought, "Why should I feel sorry for them?" For thirty-eight years he had been forced to watch Dolan and Lettoli and Huegens and the others, watch them ride over the bodies of the people of this city, unable to touch them; forced even to hold their car doors for them. Until Ellie died the captain had swallowed the hate he felt for himself because of them, accepted the dirt that they threw at him even as he turned down their money. He was Mr. Clean of the department, the one incorruptible cop—the one who turned his back and washed his hands of the affair, refusing to be involved.

Maybe, he thought, maybe he should have quit the job right at the beginning, even though he would never have met Ellie. . . .

But he hung on, tried to do his best within the strictures placed on him by the men who really ran the city. He started the list early, though, even before he knew Ellie. It began with a dozen names, and over the years there had been many additions and deletions, until tonight only the nine men had remained.

Now they were all dead.

The captain's pipe was out. He flicked the wheel once more, but he did not relight it. Instead, he got up and went into the kitchen, bent to blow out the pilot lights on the gas stove, then turned all the burners on full. Then he went back to the living room, sat down in his chair again, thinking of California. . . .

But there was nothing for him there. He had lost touch with his sister years ago, except for the Christmas cards that Ellie sent with both of their names on them. His sister had sent him one from California this year, but he had not bothered to send one back.

Everything he wanted was in the past, everything he needed to do finished. He looked at the lighter in one hand, placed his pipe back in his mouth now, sucking on the cold bowl.

The smell of gas was very strong now.

He spun the wheel of the lighter, over and over, watching the dance of the beautiful flames. . . .

JAMES M. REASONER
(b. 1953)

With the demise of Manhunt in the late 1960s, the only consistent magazine market for short noir fiction over the next fifteen years was Mike Shayne Mystery Magazine. Founded by pulp maven Leo Margulies, and edited for twenty years by his wife, Cylvia Kleinman, and then by Sam Merwin, Jr., and Charles E. Fritch, MSMM often was a showcase for hardboiled tales by established writers of the period. But the magazine also published new writers whose careers subsequently blossomed in the fields of suspense and horror fiction, including George Chesbro, Margaret Maron, Joe R. Lansdale, Gary Brandner, Robert J. Randisi, Richard Laymon, and James M. Reasoner.

Reasoner, a Texan, published his first story in MSMM in 1976, following up with some seventy-five others in the mystery-detective genre. His only crime novel, Texas Wind (1980), which features a Fort Worth private eye named Cody, is considered a minor paperback classic by those fortunate enough to have found a copy. Only a small number were published, and just a fraction of those were distributed to retail outlets. Under pseudonyms, Reasoner has also produced dozens of Western novels and historical sagas, alone and in collaboration with his wife, award-winning novelist L. J. Washburn.

"Graveyard Shift," which was published in Mike Shayne Mystery Magazine in November 1978 under the name M. R. James, is one of the first stories to address the ultramodern issues of the convenience store as a target for small-time armed robbers bent on a quick score, and the many kinds of violence that stem from such an establishment's vulnerability. Like James Hannah's "Junior Jackson's Parable," it is a trenchant parable for our time.

B. P.

GRAVEYARD SHIFT

Graveyard shifts are all alike. I know too well the emotions that fill the long nights: boredom and fear. Boredom because nothing different ever happens, fear that sometime it might.

Convenience stores are all alike, too. Boxy little buildings filled with junk food and a few staples like bread and milk. The prices are too high, but where else can you buy things after midnight?

The little KwikStop store wasn't the first one in which I had worked. I've been traveling the country, trying to see some of that I haven't seen, now that I'm a widower and don't have any reason to stay in one place. The convenience stores always need help, and I have experience. Getting a job is no problem.

Neither is the fact that I'm usually assigned the all-night shift. It gives me the days free to do anything I want.

You see the same type of customers, no matter where the store is. Before midnight, you get teenagers buying cokes and college kids buying beer and potato chips. A lot of young couples come in to buy milk and diapers. Sometimes you get a drunk who wants to buy beer after hours. Sometimes they get nasty when you refuse.

And sometimes you get one like the man who stepped in earlier tonight. That's where the fear comes in.

He was thin and had a pinched, beard-stubbled face, with too-wide eyes that never stopped moving. His clothes were shabby and his hands were pushed deep in the pockets of his windbreaker. I knew the type right away.

I've been working in the little stores long enough that attempted robberies are nothing new to me. Most stores have a policy about robberies that emphasizes cooperation and observation. They tell the clerks to do whatever the robber says. It's supposed to be safer that way.

But as I looked at this guy, I felt an ache in my belly and the palms of my hands began to sweat. This might be one of those times. The hammer of my pulse began to accelerate.

The man picked up a sack of Fritos and came toward the cash register. His other hand was still in his pocket.

The doors opened and two men and a young boy came in, heading for the soft drink case.

The man in the windbreaker looked hard at the newcomers and then dropped a quarter and a penny on the counter to pay for the Fritos. I rang up the sale and began to breathe again as he pushed through the doors on his way out.

It wasn't long afterward that George and Eddie pulled up in their patrol car and came inside for coffee, like they do every night.

"Hello, fellas," I said. "You should have been here a little earlier."

George poured himself a cup of the always-ready coffee and asked, "What happened, Frank?"

"Maybe I'm being paranoid, but there was a guy in here I think was going to rob the place. Some customers came in and he changed his mind."

"Did he pull a gun on you?"

"No, I didn't see a gun. It was just a gut feeling. Like I said, maybe I'm paranoid."

"Gut feelings are the best ones," Eddie said. "What did he look like?"

"Thin, maybe one-forty or fifty, about five-nine, sandy hair, probably about thirty years old. He was wearing blue jeans and a brown windbreaker."

Eddie wrote it all down in his notebook while George asked, "Did you see what he was driving?"

"He walked in. He might've had a car parked out of the lights, but if he did, I didn't see it."

"Okay, we'll keep an eye out for him. He probably won't be back, though, at least not tonight."

Business picked up not long after they left, and I was too busy to worry about the man who had been in earlier. I had quite a few customers in and out until three o'clock, when traffic tapered off. It would be slow now until a little after four, when the early morning workers would start coming in.

It was 3:37 when the man returned. I hadn't even seen a car drive by outside for over ten minutes, and I knew he wouldn't have to back out this time. I nodded to him and tried not to look scared as he stepped up to the counter.

"Pack of Camels," he said shortly. I put the cigarets on the counter between us. "Too late to buy beer?"

"I'm afraid so," I answered. I could feel sweat breaking out on me, dampening the red and white smock all the clerks wore. "Midnight is the latest you can buy it except on Saturdays."

He rocked back on his heels, then forward. His teeth were yellowed and I could see old acne scars on his face. I knew I would never forget the way he looked as he sneered and said, "I guess that'll do it then."

I began to work the cash register. When it popped open, he said, "You come out from behind there. There's a gun in my pocket."

I knew it was silly, but I couldn't help asking, "Is this a hold-up?"

"That's right, jackass. Now you get out from behind that counter like I told you. *Move!*"

I swallowed the huge lump in my throat and began to do like he told me, moving down around the microwave oven and the popcorn machine. The machines shielded me from his view momentarily, and I don't think he even saw my hand go behind my back, under the long smock, to the clip-on holster.

I stepped out, bringing the little pistol up and aiming it at the bridge of his nose. Surprise and fear leaped into his eyes.

The same emotions that must have been on my wife Becky's face when she walked into a little store far away and surprised a man just like this one, a man who had gotten away clean, leaving my world bleeding to death on a dirty tile floor . . .

I pulled the trigger and shattered the expression on his face. He didn't even have time to fire his own gun.

I put the gun on the counter and went to the pay phone to call the police. As I did, I thought about where I would go next. No one would be surprised when I quit this job, not after something like this.

That meant a new town, a new name, a new job. I wouldn't have any trouble finding work.

Like I said, convenience stores are all alike. And I've got plenty of experience.

MARGARET MARON
(b. 1938)

Truckers, that hardy breed of men (and in recent years, women) who push the big rigs across America's highways, have been the subject of noir fiction and films for more than a half-century. A. I. Bezzerides's 1938 novel of wildcat produce carriers in northern California, Long Haul *(filmed in 1940 as* They Drive by Night, *starring Humphrey Bogart), was the first major work with a trucking theme. A second Bezzerides novel,* Thieves' Market *(1949), explores the lives of postwar independent freighters and was a near bestseller. In recent years, the CB-radio craze and the enormously successful Burt Reynolds film* Smokey and the Bandit *(1977) inspired a plethora of big-rig novels; notable among these is Phillip Finch's* Haulin' *(1979).*

Two of the best crime shorts about the lives of road jockeys are Robert Reeves's Black Mask *novelette, "Murder in High Gear" (1941), a rollicking action yarn featuring tough "highway detective" Bookie Barnes, and Margaret Maron's dark fable "Deadhead Coming Down," which first appeared in* Mike Shayne Mystery Magazine *in April 1978.*

Maron began writing short fiction in the late 1960s. More than a dozen of her stories appeared between 1968 and 1980 in a variety of digest periodicals, most prominently Alfred Hitchcock's Mystery Magazine, *nine of them under the byline Margaret E. Brown. Her first novel,* One Coffee With *(1981), began a critically acclaimed series featuring police lieutenant Sigrid Harald. A second series character, attorney Deborah Knott, made her debut in* Bootlegger's Daughter, *a haunting tale of old and new crimes in the tobacco country of North Carolina, which received the Mystery Writers of America Edgar award for best novel of 1992.*

B. P.

1978

DEADHEAD COMING DOWN

Funny thing about this CB craze—all these years we trucking men've been going along doing our job, just making a living as best we could, and people in cars didn't pay us much mind after everything got four-

433

laned because they didn't get caught behind us so much going uphill, so they quit cursing us for being on the roads we was paying taxes for too and sort of ignored us for a few years.

Then those big camper vans started messing around with CB, tuning in on us, and first thing you know even VWs are running up and down the cloverleafs cluttering up the air with garbage and all of a sudden there's songs about us, calling us culture heroes and knights of the road.

Bull!

There's not one damn thing romantic about driving an 18-wheeler. Next to standing on a assembly line and screwing Bolt A into Hole C like my no-account brother-in-law, driving a truck's got to be the dullest way under God's red sun to make a living. 'Specially if it's just up and down the eastern seaboard like me.

Maybe it's different driving cross-country, but I work for this Jerry outfit—Eastline Truckers—and brother, they're just that. Contract trucking up and down the coastal states. Peaches from Georgia, grapefruit from northern Florida, yams and blueberries from the Carolinas—whatever's in season, we haul it. I-95 to the Delaware Memorial Bridge, up the Jersey Turnpike, across the river and right over to Hunt's Point.

Fruit basket going up, deadhead coming down and if you think that's not boring, think again. Once you're on I-95, it's the same road from Florida to New Jersey. You could pick up a mile stretch in Georgia and stick it down somewhere in Maryland and nobody'd even notice the difference—same motels, same gas stations, same billboards.

There's laws put out by those Keep America Pretty people to try and keep billboards off the interstates, but I'm of two minds about them. You can get awful tired of trees and fields and cows with nothing to break 'em up, but then again, reading the same sign over and over four or five times a week's a real drag, too.

Even those Burma Shave signs they used to have when I was driving with Lucky. We'd laugh our heads off every time they put up new ones, but you can't laugh at the same things more'n once or twice, so we'd make up our own poems. Raunchy ones and funnier'n hell some of 'em.

Those were the good old days. Right after the war. I was a hick kid just out of the tobacco fields and Lucky seemed older'n Moses, though I reckon he was only about 35. His real name was Henry Driver, but everybody naturally called him Lucky because he got away with things nobody else ever could. During the blackouts, he once drove a load of TNT across the Great Smokies with no headlights. All them twisty mountain roads and just a three-quarter moon. I'd like to see these bragging hot-shots around today try that!

Back then it took a real man to truck 'cause them rigs would fight you. Just like horses, they were. They knew when you couldn't handle them. Today—hell! Everything's so automatic and hydraulic, even a 90-pound woman can do it.

Guess I shouldn't knock it though. I'll be able to keep driving these creampuffs till I'm 70. Not like Lucky. Hardly a dent and then his luck ran out on a stretch of 301 in Virginia. A blowout near a bridge and the wheel must've got away from him.

Ten years ago that was, and the company'd quit doubling us before that, but I still miss him. Things were never dull driving with Lucky. We was a lot alike. He used to tell me things he never told nobody else. Not just the things a man brags about when he's drinking and slinging bull, but other stuff.

I remember once we were laying over in Philly, him going, me coming down, and he says, "Guess what I saw me today coming through Baltimore? A red-tailed hawk. Right smack in the middle of town!"

Can you feature a tough guy like him getting all excited about seeing a back-country bird in town? And telling another guy about it? Well, that's the way it was with me and him.

I was thinking about Lucky last week coming down and wishing I had him to talk to again. Ninety-five was wall-to-wall vacation traffic. I thumbed my CB and it was full of ratchet jaws trying to sound like they knew what the hell they were saying. It was *Good Buddy* this and *Smokey* that and *10-4* on the side, so I cut right out again.

I'd just passed this Hot Shoppe sign when the road commenced to unwind in my head like a movie picture. I knew that next would come a Howard Johnson and a Holiday Inn and then a white barn and a meadow full of black cows and then a Texaco sign and every single mile all the way back home. I just couldn't take it no more and pulled off at the next cloverleaf.

"For every mile of thruway, there's ten miles on either side going the same way," Lucky used to say and, like him, I've got this skinny map stuck up over my windshield across the whole width of the cab with I-95 snaking right down the middle. Whenever that old snake gets to crawling under my skin, I look for a side road heading south. There's little Xs scattered all up and down my map to keep track of which roads I'd been on before. I hadn't never been through this particular stretch, so I had my choice.

Twenty minutes off the interstate's a whole different country. The road I finally picked was only two lanes, but wide enough so I wouldn't crowd anybody, not that there was much traffic. I almost had the road to myself and I want to tell you it was as pretty as a postcard, with trees and bushes growing right to the ditches and patches of them orangy flowers mixed in.

It was late afternoon, the sun just going down and I was perking up and feeling good about this road. It was the kind Lucky used to look for. Everything perfect.

I was coasting down this little hill and around a curve and suddenly there was a old geezer walking right up the middle of my lane. I hit the brakes and left rubber, but by the time I got her stopped and ran back to where he was laying all crumpled up in orange flowers, I knew he was a sure goner, so I walked back to my rig, broke on Channel 9 and about ten minutes later, there was a black-and-white flashing its blue lights and a ambulance with red ones.

Everybody was awful nice about it. They could see how I'd braked and swerved across the line. "I tried to miss him," I said. "But he went and jumped the same way."

"It wasn't your fault, so don't you worry," said the young cop when I'd followed him into the little town to fill out his report. "If I warned Mr. Jasper once, I told him a hundred times he was going to get himself killed out walking like that and him half-deaf."

The old guy's son-in-law was there by that time and he nodded. "I told Mavis he ought to be in a old folks' home where they'd look after him, but he was dead set against it and she wouldn't make him. Poor old Pop! Well, at least he didn't suffer."

The way he said it, I guessed he wasn't going to suffer too much himself over the old man's death.

I was free to go by 9 o'clock and as I was leaving, the cop happened to say, "How come you were this far off the interstate?"

I explained about how boring it got every now and then and he sort of laughed and said, "I reckon you won't get bored again any time soon."

"I reckon not," I said, remembering how that old guy had scrambled, the way his eyes had bugged when he knew he couldn't get out of the way.

Just west of 95, I stopped at a Exxon station and while they were filling me up, I reached up over the windshield and made another little X on my road-map. Seventeen Xs now. Two more and I'd tie Lucky.

I pulled out onto 95 right in front of a Datsun that had to sit on his brakes to keep from creaming himself. Even at night it was all still the same—same gas stations, same motels, same billboards.

I don't know—maybe it's different driving cross-country.

ROBERT SAMPSON
(1927–1992)

Robert Sampson was fascinated by pulp magazines. He published seven books on the subject and wrote countless articles for various "fanzines," "prozines," and mainstream periodicals. He was also a collector of pulp fiction—yet not a collector, for rather than storing his rare finds in plastic bags and locking them away from the sun, he read and enjoyed them, using them as they were meant to be used.

Sampson's ultimate aim was not to legitimize pulp fiction, for part of its charm had always been its illicitness. Rather, he wished to celebrate its color, its wild invention, its absurd luridness, its exhausting pace, its glorious vitality. He was interested in both American and British versions of popular fiction, the kind of subliterary stuff that George Eliot once referred to as "spiritual gin." Above all, he was intrigued by the mental and emotional processes that go into making an author a super-seller, such as the British phenomenon Edgar Wallace, who wrote a quarter of all books sold in Great Britain from 1927 to 1932.

Sampson envisaged a multivolume study dealing with all aspects of the pulps: the different genres (crime fiction, fantasy, science fiction, air-war, war, adventure, mystery, weird menace, Western, history) as well as the writers, editors, and publishers, many of whom were still alive in the early 1970s, when Sampson began his project. He called the series Yesterday's Faces, and in 1991, the year before he died, the fifth (and penultimate) volume was published. As a monumental survey and critique of twentieth-century popular fiction, it is unique and invaluable. Other critical works include The Night Master (1982), on the superhero the Shadow; Spider (1987); and Deadly Excitements: Shadows and Phantoms (1989), which doubles as a nonseries commentary on pulp magazines and a volume of memoirs.

In his early years as a radio continuity writer, Sampson cracked one or two fiction markets, including Planet Stories and the digest Science Fiction Adventures. His story "Rain in Pinton County" appeared in New Black Mask in 1986 and won that year's Edgar award for best short story from the Mystery Writers of America. Other stories appeared in A Matter of Crime, Weird Tales, Spectrum, Spectrum II, and The Year's Best Science Fiction (1989).

"To Florida" concerns a man headed straight for hell and is a masterpiece of contemporary nihilism.

J. A.

1 9 8 7

TO FLORIDA

Music blared as a ton of pink rocks flattened the orange bear. He sat up bonelessly, rubbing mauve stars from his head, and marched off the television screen, aggressive and undaunted.

Teller, not watching the bear's problem, started recounting the money. His fingers danced through the stack of twenties like hunger in motion, like a love song, caressing.

A purple boxing glove belted the bear across a yellow room. Laughter screamed.

Teller glanced up, then down. His face was insolently wary, the face of a kid grown up to find out it was all a lie. He wore heavy sideburns, very black, and a lot of undisciplined mustache. He was on the short side of thirty, and looked soiled and a little crazy.

The apartment door bumped open. A girl's voice said apologetically, "Whoops, slipped, I guess." She backed into the room, angular and ugly, almost twenty. She wore blue jeans and a dirty pink sweatshirt. A big gray yarn purse, striped blue-yellow-green, had slipped to the crook of her arm. She clutched two sacks of groceries.

"Jerry, can you grab a sack?"

"Dump 'em on the table."

"They're slipping." She sidled crabwise across the room, showing too many teeth in a mouth like a frog's. She thumped the sacks on a green painted table holding an air conditioner and the remains of last night's Kwik-Karry Chicken. The window behind the table puffed cold air at her.

Jerry said to his hands, "You know what? I'm fixing to take me down to good old Florida and have a time." He stroked the money. "I'm gonna drink me some beer and soak up some of that sun."

"Yea, Florida," she said. And speaking saw the money in his hands. All the expression flattened out of her face. "Is that yours?"

"Mine." Their eyes met. "What you think, Sue Ann? Want to run down to Florida?"

439

She eyed the money, wary, surprised. "You got enough maybe we could give Mr. Davidson some? For the rent. He keeps calling."

"He gave me this." His quick fingers doubled over the bills, thrust them into the pocket of his shirt.

"He didn't."

"Go look in the kitchen and see. But don't squeal, now. Don't you squeal."

"He wants we should pay him something."

"Look there in the kitchen."

She looked into the kitchen and her shoulders lifted slowly and slowly settled.

"Is he dead?"

"Naw."

"I mean, really, is he dead?"

"I told you no. I just tapped him. Not even hard."

"His one eye's open."

"So he sleeps with one eye open."

She swung around to look at him. Apprehension twisted in her face like a snake in a bottle. "If you hurt him, we better not let anybody know."

"We're gonna be gone. I got his car keys. I'm cuttin' out." He waited for her enthusiasm and his face hardened when it did not come. "I figured you were so hot to run down to Florida."

"To Florida. Well, I guess . . . sure . . ."

He heaved up from the recliner, boot heels cracking on the uncarpeted floor. "You get yourself together." He grinned, watching her mind stumble after his words. "I want to go get me some of that good beer."

"Jerry, you're sure Mr. Davidson's all right, aren't you?"

"I said he was OK. Get packed."

"Should I put a blanket over him?"

"You just let him be, now." He pulled her to him with one arm, pressing hard, but that didn't reassure her much.

She went into the bedroom and began opening and closing drawers. He shook his head and, grinning, went to the table, and heaved up the air conditioner. It was a small window model, the simulated wooden front very new. Through the open window he could see out along Holmes Avenue, glowing with spring dogwood, white and pink. Above the flowering branches spread a pale blue sky, featureless as painted wood.

He carried the air conditioner out into the hallway. From the back apartment, a radio hammered rock, violent and forlorn, into the dim air. He used two fingers to open the front door, carried the air conditioner across the porch, along a cracked brown concrete walk, to the light blue Toyota parked by the curb in the bright morning sunlight. He dumped the conditioner into the backseat and straightened up, working his fingers.

"Jesus is Lord, and salvation is at hand," said a voice at his right ear.

Behind him on the sidewalk stood a hook-nosed old ruin, all bone and wrinkles, holding out a printed tract. "Let me give you the Lord's word, brother. It ain't too late for the word."

"Ain't that nice." He stepped around the scarecrow, who smelled sourly of upset stomach. As he climbed the porch steps, the old voice called, "All sins forgiven in the bosom of Jesus, brother."

In the apartment bedroom, she had pulled out all their clothing. The bed was piled with stuff that looked and smelled like specials at the Saturday flea-market.

She told him, "I don't know what to take."

"All of it."

"All of it?" She snatched up a pair of shoes.

"You think we're coming back here?"

Confusion blurred her face. "You got to open the filling station to-morrow, Jerry."

"You think so, huh?"

He loaded two cardboard boxes of his own clothing into the Toyota's trunk. The old boy with the wet eyes was talking Jesus at a house up the street. When he reentered the apartment, she was still staring at the clothing, jerking her arms. Impatience twisted his mouth.

"You ready?"

"Not yet. Not yet." She blundered into uncoordinated motion.

"Like a scared blind hen," he muttered, stepping into the kitchen.

It was a long, dirty room painted pink. A narrow window spilled sunshine across unwashed dishes, paper sacks, fruit peelings, empty cans, a squadron of flies. The room stunk sourly of garbage and cigarettes. Old Man Davidson lay on the floor by the sink, his head in a jumble of beer cans. One eye glimmered palely under a sagging lid. He was a sharp-nosed runt with reddish hair. His mouth lolled open and a fly tilted and curved above the lard-colored lips.

"Show you to bad-mouth me," Jerry said to the figure on the floor.

In half an hour, he hustled her out the door, her arms dripping loose clothing. He put on a wide-brimmed brown hat, banded with pheasant feathers, and a shabby leather coat with the hunting knife tucked down in one pocket. It was tough that the television was too big to load into the car. "Hell with you," he said and closed the door.

No one called good-bye. He fed the Toyota gas and they eased off between the exuberant dogwoods.

Half a block down the street, she clutched his arm. "I forgot the groceries."

"Let 'em sit."

"They'll spoil."

"So what?"

Thin brown fingers slipped across her mouth. "I used all our food stamps on them. Got some ribs for you."

"Now, that was nice."

"They were for you."

He said in a flat, rapid voice, "Look, if we drive back, maybe somebody sees us in his car. You ever think of that? Then what you going to tell them?"

She stared at him, brown eyes blankly confused.

"What you going to say?"

"I . . . Well . . ."

"You got to think about that."

She said faintly, "I just didn't want them to spoil."

"Well, OK. We'll just go on."

"I'm sorry, Jerry. I didn't think about the car and—and all."

"Shoot, you don't have to think. You just sit there and have you a good time. We're going to Florida."

The Toyota shot around a yellow truck and picked up speed past rows of Victorian houses built close together, painted in shades of green and brown. They looked orderly and neat, like old women waiting for relatives on visiting day.

At the Friendly station, they stopped for gas and he bought a six-pack of Old Jack beer at the carryout. They drove north, then, along streets of grimy stores, small and set far apart with dust-gray windows and trash spilled along the sidewalk. The stores were replaced by narrow fields, still brown, stippled with weed stalks and bordered by trees blurred with new green. Beyond the trees, small hills humped up, dark with cedar, dappled by the dull rose and white of flowering trees.

"It's just so beautiful," Sue Ann said.

"Here we are," he said.

He slewed the Toyota onto a gravel apron, jerked to a stop before a building the shape and color of a dirty sugar cube. Above the open door slanted a hand-painted sign:

STAFFORD'S PARTS AND HOUSE APPLENCES

In the doorway under the sign leaned a fat man without much hair, his circular face tarnished red-brown by years of sun. He watched Jerry work the air conditioner off the backseat.

"You jus' come in here right now," the fat man said.

Jerry plunged past him, banged the air conditioner onto a scarred wooden counter. The little room was hot, smelling disagreeably of rubber and cardboard. Orange boxes of auto parts packed the wall shelves. The floor was patched with flattened coffee cans, blue and red against silver-gray wood.

Jerry said, "Wanna sell me this air conditioner."

The fat man worked his belly behind the counter. "It works, does it?"

"You give it a feel. Probably still cold."

Thick brown hands deftly unfastened the grill. "She looks nice and clean."

A door opened in back and a big old man, gone to bone and loose gray skin, limped into the room. The effort of moving thickened his breath. He inched over to a wooden chair by the counter, lowered himself into it joint by joint, said in a remote voice, "She's getting cold out there, Dandy."

Jerry said, "How much you fixing to give me for this beauty? Worth three hundred dollars, easy."

"Oh, now, then," Dandy said. He grinned at his fat hands. "It's early for air conditioners."

The old man grunted, spit at a blue can, looked at the air conditioner with sour suspicion.

Jerry said, "I got to get rid of it. They broke my lease."

Fat fingers snapped the grill into place. "What do you think, Mr. Stafford?"

The old man sniffed, grunted, painfully extended his legs. "Expect she's stole."

"Like hell," Jerry said, jerking his head. "What's with you?"

"Couldn't be nothin' like that," Dandy said. "I know this young fellow. He's been in here before."

"You know it," Jerry said. Back stiff, hands jammed into his pockets, he stood without moving, watching them, grinning very slightly.

"Tell you what," Dandy said. "You maybe got the bill of sale, I could give you, like, say fifty dollars."

Stafford said in his sick old voice. "We don't need no stole stuff."

"Why don't you shut up your mouth?" Jerry said to him.

Dandy said, very quickly, "No need to holler, son."

"You want this or not?"

"Fifty dollar the best I can do."

"No way, man. Hell with that." White light leaped into his eyes. "I wouldn't carry this thing across the street for fifty dollars."

"We don't hold none with thieving," Stafford said, loudly triumphant.

"It's worth one hundred dollars, easy," Jerry said.

Dandy shook his head. "Not to me."

Stafford yelped, "Get that stole thing out of here right now."

Jerry made a small, bitter sound. He put his chin down on his chest, and a tremor, beginning at his hips, shook upward through his chest, shoulders, neck. His eyes became not quite human.

In a soft voice, he said, "Who asking you?" Then, very loudly, "Who asking you?" The sides of his mouth grew wet. "And so damn what?"

He jerked the air conditioner up from the counter. Held it poised. Wheeled left and flung the machine into the old man's lap. Stafford shrieked as the chair legs snapped off. He slapped against the counter screaming and pitched heavily onto the floor, hands clawing his legs. "They's broke."

Jerry flipped the hunting knife from his jacket pocket and slashed backhand at Dandy. The fat man banged himself back against the shelves. Orange boxes slipped thumping into the aisle.

Jerry leaned across the counter, his eyes intent, yellow-tan teeth showing under his mustache. He whipped the knife around, splitting Dandy's tan shirt. As he slashed, he made a thick, grunting sound. Dandy squealed frantically as a thin, red line ran across the top of his shoulder.

Jerry got over the counter, fell into the aisle. His body felt hot and slow. Hunched over, he moved toward Dandy, knife blade out in front of him, a bright splinter.

Dandy said in a voice full of wonder, "Oh, this is a terrible thing." His eyes were round. As Jerry moved toward him, he jerked a rack of cans thunderously into the aisle.

Jerry stumbled over a can, fell, hitting one knee. Taking small, quick steps, Dandy shuffled back from the knife. He got to the rear door. His eyes, round in a round pale face, stared past the edge of the door as it whacked shut.

"You better watch," Jerry yelled. Jerking around, still holding the knife out before him, he darted back along the littered aisle, snatched the cash box from under the counter.

The box, chained to the shelf, snapped out of his hands. Change sprayed into the aisle among boxes and cans and broken glass. He clawed up a five, a one, another one. Dimes glinted among orange boxes. He found a quarter, a ten, two nickels. Urgency choked him.

He swung over the counter in one hard twist. The old man lay contorted against the counter, eyes rolled up, mouth open exposing his dull yellow tongue. He breathed like a compressor. The air conditioner canted across one leg.

Two steps to the door and out. Seven steps long across the crunching gravel, fury in his legs, rage lifting his shoulders. He felt laughter like hot fat boiling in his chest and throat.

He slid behind the wheel. Sue Ann gaped at him, excited, "What's the matter? What's the matter?"

"No damn thing."

The Toyota leaped away spewing gravel. "They tried to cheat me."

As the car skidded onto the highway, Dandy appeared at the side of the building. His arms were extended and from hands clenched before his face projected the dark snout of a revolver. Then a screen of bushes lashed past, hiding him.

"Cheated me, by God." His boot rammed the accelerator.

Gray-shaded clouds skated sedately across a pale sky. Beneath the clouds spread calm fields, furred with new light green. From Stafford's dirty sugar-cube the road was a lean gray strip stretched north past a small housing development, a small store. Beyond the fields rose a sudden hill studded with the brick buildings of A & M College, sober, dull red blocks following the hill's contours like bird nests along a cliff. Hill and buildings looked neatly peaceful as a European travel poster.

The Toyota hammered north, eighty miles an hour. Wheels jittered on the road. Fields reeled past. The pedestrian overpass swelled toward them, was over them, shrank behind. The car leaped, floated above a small rise, light as blowing leaves.

"Oh, my God, Jerry, what is it?"

Down the road by the lumber yard, a fat yellow truck wallowed onto the highway.

"Oh, Jerry!"

He tapped the brakes, cut left, cut back across an oncoming pickup, the driver's face shocked.

"Cheated me," he yelled. Tapped the brakes. They slid through a four-way stop, jerked left. Accelerated past shabby apartments screened by vivid forsythia. On the main highway, he slowed, turned south.

"Jerry, what happened?"

He said, "I made them remember me."

His eyes were white stones.

Five miles down the road, rolling west at thirty-five miles an hour through streets lined endlessly with small houses. Each had its own yard, its own driveway, its own bush. He yawned, as dull-headed as if he had slept. A black child in a red cap waved at them.

"I was so scared," she told him. "You looked so funny."

"How'd I look funny?"

"You just did."

He gulped beer from a can. "You're OK, Lu Ann. You're nuts, but you're OK. I think you're fine, you know that?"

"You scared me."

She looked like no one he had ever seen before. The lumpy face shone with tear smears. The big teeth, the loose dull hair belonged to a stranger. Only her voice was familiar, stumbling, hesitating, the voice of a confused child.

". . . please don't say that. It's what Daddy said."

"What?" he asked her.

"He looked at me. He looked at Momma. He said . . ." The thin voice faltered and shook, unsteady with shame. "Said, 'You take that dumbnut brat with you, too.' He said that. My daddy. 'Take your ugly brat with you.' He's in Saint Louis now. I won't forget him saying that."

His empty beer can clattered behind the seat. "Open me another one."

"Am I ugly?"

"You?"

"Yes, am I ugly?"

"Shoot," he said, "where's that beer?"

"You don't have to say I'm pretty. I know I'm not pretty. I know what pretty is, like on television, all shiny like there's sun on them."

"You're all right," he said, sucking beer.

"But he didn't ought to say that. Was your daddy nice?"

At last, Jerry said, "He played him some games with us."

"What like?"

"Held up his two fists all closed together. Says, 'Which hand's the candy in, kid?' So you guessed. You guess wrong—bamo! He fetch you one up the side of the head."

"That's awful."

"Never was any candy. Not in either hand. He tells me, 'Don't expect nothing cause that's what you're going to get.' " He clattered the empty can into the rear. "That's right, too. You better know it. Both hands empty, all the time."

"That's terrible."

Her face disgusted him. It was brainless, narrow, and brown, shapeless, the teeth ledged in a loose pale mouth. Now, at last, he remembered her name. "Give me one of them beers, Sue Ann."

Twenty miles west of Huntsville the highway intersected I-65 South. Between ploughed fields a broad concrete strip undulated beneath a filmy white sky. The Toyota began to eat miles.

"Now we're going down to Florida," he said.

"Yea, Florida." She leaned toward him, fingers closing over his right arm, a disagreeable soft pressure. "You glad you're taking me to Florida, Jerry?"

"Oh, God, yes."

"I'm sorry they cheated you."

"Took that air conditioner in and they say, 'Why this looks like you stole it, we're gonna call the police.' Said, 'You better leave that old air conditioner here, we'll call the police.' "

"You showed them."

"I showed them good. I messed them up good." In his mind the old man screamed as the pale highway flowed toward them. "You bet I did."

"You didn't hurt them?"

"Damn right I did."

"You shouldn't do that, Jerry. That isn't right."

"OK for them to hurt me, though," he said, stiff-voiced.

"No, no. I mean . . ." She struggled with the soft stuff of her mind. "It's in the Bible. Don't be mean, that's what it says."

"Your tongue's sure bubbling."

"Well, you shouldn't. I don't think people are really mean. Like my daddy. He just yells. When he's drunk, he's sweet."

He burst into laughter. "You're somebody, you sure are, Sue Ann."

She pulled back from him. "Now don't you laugh at me."

"Listen," he said, "nobody's got candy in their hands. You just remember that."

"I'd give you some candy."

"I guess you'd try, wouldn't you?"

"You know I would."

Under their wheels, the road down Alabama pulsed like a concrete heart.

"This thing's a gas hog," he said. "We better pull her in and fill up."

They pulled off the highway and wound through a complicated series of small roads to a combination filling station, restaurant, and general store, spreading out under a bright orange roof. He gave her five dollars and she went inside, among the strange voices, and bought crackers, two large coffees, and four comic books with shiny girls wet-faced on the glowing covers. As she came out, he hurried up to her, white-faced and tight-lipped as if he had just smelled hell.

"You come on here."

They drove around back of the restaurant and parked by a big square trash container. "That damn Dandy," he said. "Look here."

Two bullet holes punched the light blue metal, one above the license plate, the other over a taillight. Impact had dimpled the metal and the edges showed raw and clean. There was a strong smell of gasoline.

He said savagely, "Just creased the tank. Put a big old crack in it. It's been slopping out gas all this time."

She goggled at him, making inconsequential sounds.

"That Dandy fellow. I didn't even hear him shooting."

"Can—can we fix it?"

"Shoot. Can't run along showing bullet holes. Turn on the lights at night, maybe blow the whole back out of her."

Fingers crept over her teeth. "Who's Dandy?" she asked faintly.

"Might tape it. Probably work right loose. Tank'll hold maybe four gallon. But shoot—I'm not going to drive all over Florida sticking gas in this sucker every hour."

"Can't we go to Florida?"

"Will you shut up?"

"Please don't be mad, Jerry."

"Don't you start whining. Give me a hand."

They unloaded the trunk, piling reeking cardboard boxes by the side of the car. Under the floor mat shone a pungent skin of gasoline.

"Better not chance it," he said at last. "Give her a spark, she'll flare up like the sun in a sack."

As they stared into the trunk, a dirty station wagon rolled past behind them, packed to the windows with staring children and luggage.

"I gotta get me another car," Jerry said. Briefly his long arms beat at his sides, a furious sudden violence.

In their inconspicuous place behind the road stop, they waited in a numb paralysis of time, the journey compromised. From out front engines sounded, voices rose, and doors slammed and reslammed, a purposeful outcry of activity emphasizing their inactivity and isolation. Limp in the Toyota, Sue Ann fingered through a comic book. Alone by the dumpster, Jerry fidgeted, a wolf watching empty plains, glancing impatiently off toward the main parking area.

After a long time, a black Lincoln, arrogantly polished, rolled past with three people inside. It was followed by a red Ford with a young woman driving.

"Hey, can you give me a hand?" he called.

She drove slowly by, not looking around. He snarled after her and waited. After another ten minutes, a truck full of ropes eased past.

"Hey, can you give me a hand? Just need a second."

Then a small tan station wagon drew to a stop and a thin-faced young man with glasses and neat dark hair leaned out and asked, "Trouble?" in a cheerful voice.

"Look," Jerry said, "I need three hands for a second and I only got two."

The young man elevated his eyebrows and, grinning, pushed open the car door. "Like the way you said that." He was long-legged, long-armed, and walked with shoulders bent forward, as if being tall bothered him. He left the engine of the wagon running.

"This is a problem," Jerry said.

The tall man said, "You sure got a gas leak." And then, in an interested voice, "Those bullet holes?"

Jerry took a blackjack out of his hip pocket and hit the tall man hard on the side of the head above the right ear. The blow made a solid, single sound. His glasses flew off. Long legs buckled, folding him over the edge of the trunk. His head and shoulders dropped inside. Jerry shuffled sideways, struck twice more. He placed the blows carefully, leaning into them. He tried to heave the tall man into the trunk, could not turn the body. Legs dangled.

Grunting with the effort, he hauled the tall man out and wrapped both arms around his body. He lugged the limp figure along the side of the Toyota. Sue Ann stared at him, face convulsed.

"Get out of there," he snarled at her.

She leaped away, scattering comic books on the cement.

He stuffed the body onto the seat, fought the long legs into the compartment. The head flopped over to expose an ear webbed with blood. From the rear, he jerked out a gray blanket, threw it over the body, pulled the head right, hiding the scarlet ear.

She was crowded against him, breath loud. "Is he dead? Is he dead, Jerry?"

"No, no."

"Oh, Jerry."

"Get that car loaded."

"Oh, Jerry."

He came at her, furious and tall, shoved her violently against the Toyota. She yelped as her head cracked against the glass. "Listen to me. Move."

They tumbled boxes into the station wagon. They jerked their possessions from the backseat, rushing between the cars, stuffing sacks, armloads of coats, shoes, fishing rods blindly into any unfilled space.

A Volkswagen pulled in behind the wagon, blasted its horn. "Get this thing outta the street, buddy."

"Go on around."

"Dumb jerks parking in the road."

The Volkswagen snarled around the wagon and was gone. Sweat iced his body; his fingers were lengths of marble.

"Let's go," he said to her.

"Oh, no," she said, backing away. "No no no."

He said in a soft distant voice, "Sue Ann, get in that car or I am going to have to hurt you bad."

Her mouth fell open. She went back from him, taking small uneven steps as if moving ankle-deep through a marsh. She tottered around the car, got in. He darted back to the Toyota and, leaning in the driver's side, fumbled under the gray blanket until he found the tall man's wallet. He locked all the doors. Stuffing the wallet into his pocket, he swung into the station wagon, eased it away from the building, down the road, turned left, moving with precise care, went down the clipped access road to I-65. The wagon handled fine. Sue Ann, staring and white, slumped in the corner.

The fingers of his right hand felt greasy. Making a fist, he saw the back of his hand smeared darkly with blood.

From the car radio a slow voice whined the lyrics of "Whiskey Woman."

Behind the voice pulsed guitar, bass, drums, filling the interior of the automobile with urgent pressure. Over that sound their intense voices went back and forth, birds riding a heavy wind.

"You did. You beat on him."

"I had to."

"Oh, you didn't have to. Take away your hand. It's bloody."

He clenched the fist, lifted it, rotated it before her face. "You see blood? You tell me, you see blood?"

"You beat on him and beat and beat. I heard you."

He said thick-voiced, "You shut up and hear me. I had to get us a car. Us with a shot-up old bomb, the police maybe lookin'."

"Police?"

In the southwest, mouse-gray clouds ledged in the silver sky.

"You don't know anything at all, do you? You sit there like a dummy, big grin on your dummy face, don't know a thing."

Fear came between them and she strained away from him, her back against the door, feet jamming the floor.

451

"We need a car, I took us a car. Nobody going to give us a car. Nobody going to give us anything. You need it, you go and get it."

"You was always so nice."

"I'm same as I always was."

"No, you're not." She stared at him and it was like looking into a long tunnel with a fire burning in it, far back. "You're glad you hit him."

"I didn't and you wouldn't be in this car right now, going to Florida, going to have you some fun."

She began to cry. Country rock poured from the radio. They were building in the fields beyond the highway, orange iron skeletons rising in the sun, with trucks shuttling back and forth and men small among the shining beams.

Eyes on the fields, she said, "You don't like me any more."

"I don't want to hear that. I'm not going to listen to that all the way to Florida."

"It isn't right."

He felt the shaking begin then, the glorious deep trembling that would build and rise, wave on rich wave, half fear, half joy, a terrible exhilaration lifting him out of himself to tower gigantic, invincible, striding, and magnificent.

"It's what I do."

Her voice, muffled, wept. "But you hurt them, Jerry."

"Shoot," he said, feeling his body stretch and grow. "I busted their heads. Didn't hurt them. Didn't feel a thing. Old Davidson, too."

"Mr. Davidson?"

He said, with cold satisfaction, "I knocked his head loose of his shoulders. Him with his mouth—'Gimmie, gimmie, you pay.' Him with a big fat wallet and a nice blue car."

"He's a nice man."

"He's nothing now. He's dead on the floor with his head cracked."

"Dead?" she asked. "Dead?" Her mouth went quite square and bloodless.

He began to laugh. "You wanting to put a blanket on a dead man."

"I want to go home. I want to go home, Jerry."

He laughed.

"You let me out."

She was across the seat then, snatching at the wheel, jerking it toward her. The car reeled right. He smashed her hand away as the metallic shriek of tires cut above the music. The world outside weaved and bobbed. He drove the back of his hand against her face, wrenched the wheel, accelerated, felt the skidding berme under the tires and the pop of stones flung against the body, felt the sheering lurch back onto the highway. Fought the wheel, tapped the brakes as the station wagon steadied. Struck past her snatching arms.

He slammed her forehead, her ear, drove her back, hands up before her face, smashing the hands back into her face. Awkward blows, slow and deliberate as if he were pounding nails.

She made a thin, high sound, like tearing flesh.

Steady on the road, the wagon lost speed as he pumped the brakes. They swerved to a stop on the shoulder.

"You get out," he said.

She squealed thinly, without sense, brown eyes rolling.

"Don't hurt me, Jerry."

He showed her the point of the knife. It glittered unsteadily in the sunlight, the hot tip jittering in arcs and circles, trembling with a dreadful eagerness. She grew quite still.

"Out that door, Sue Ann."

"Please please please please."

He yelled at her. "I'll do it if you make me. I don't want to."

The door opened. She sprawled out onto the shoulder, one hand before her face, palm out. She slipped and fell heavily, crying out.

Leaning across the seat he said, along the length of the knife, "Now you stay gone."

"Jerry, dear."

The door slammed. The station wagon leaped forward, kicking up dirt. It picked up speed, rushing south, full of towering mindless power. In the rear mirror he saw her staring after him, her figure dwindling, hidden by a gentle rise, reappearing smaller as the road rose again, still motionless, a huddle of pink by the white highway. Perhaps looking after him.

Five miles down the road, he saw her gray yarn purse on the floor. He cranked down the window. After a moment's hesitation, he opened the purse, opened the worn brown wallet inside. It contained a dime, a nickel, seven pennies. He shook the change onto the seat, dropped the wallet into the purse. Then he hurled the purse from the window. It bounded among the road weeds, leaping flying twisting.

The sun was low now. It was hard to see where the purse had gone. He drove in silence for ten miles, listening to the radio.

At last he said, "She could have come on to Florida if she wanted to."

He began to sing softly with the music. He had a pleasant baritone voice, warm and with a sort of lilt to it.

ANDREW VACHSS
(b. 1942)

Andrew Henry Vachss writes of a dark—indeed, pitch-black—world, one that he not only has visited, but still inhabits. In his early years, Vachss's work experience was wide-ranging and intensive. He was a case worker for New York City's Department of Social Services, a special investigator for Save the Children in Biafra during its bloody civil war, and director of a maximum-security institution for juveniles. All these occupations, as well as his current work as a lawyer in New York City, seem to reflect the subject that has absorbed Vachss for more than fifteen years—the saving of children from neglect, dispossession, victimization, physical and sexual abuse, and all the attendant horrors that can be inflicted on them by adults.

An angry man, Vachss writes to make others angry, to make them sit up and sweat. His fury is relentless and unforgiving; in his public pronouncements on the subject of sexual abuse, there is an Old Testament thunder to his disgust. In Vachss's writing, old-fashioned vengeance is often a trigger to the action. In his novels, his chief weapon against the fearsome dark forces is the character Burke, a renegade who lives in New York and has no papers, no Social Security number, no official identity. Technically, he does not exist; yet he lives, furiously in fact, righting wrongs with savage abandon. He is aided by a group of similarly dissentient outcasts, including former madam Mama Wong (who serviced the military at Fort Bragg during the Korean War), the midget Prof, the Mole, Max the Silent, and Michelle the transsexual hooker, who all bear an uncanny resemblance to the 1930s pulp hero Doc Savage and his disparate and bizarre team.

Vachss started his novel-writing career with Flood (1985), a weighty tome about the search for an unhinged rapist-murderer. Gradually, over the years, his style has been pared down to the bone and become distinctly minimalist. His books hurtle along at white-knuckle pace. "It's a Hard World" is his earliest crime short. The protagonist is not Burke, although he demonstrates all of Burke's ingenuity in staying ahead of the game—in staying alive.

J. A.

1 9 8 7

IT'S A HARD WORLD

I pulled into the parking lot at LaGuardia around noon and sat in the car running my fingers over the newly-tightened skin on my face, trying to think through my next move. I couldn't count on the plastic surgery to do the job. I had to get out of New York at least long enough to see if DellaCroce's people still were looking for me.

I sat there for an hour or so thinking it through, but nothing came to me. Time to move. I left the car where it was—let Hertz pick it up in a week or so when I didn't turn it in.

The Delta terminal was all by itself in a corner of the airport. I had a ticket for Augusta, Georgia, by way of Atlanta. Canada was where I had to go if I wanted to get out of the country, but Atlanta gave me a lot of options. The airport there is the size of a small city; it picks up traffic from all over the country.

I waited until the last minute to board, but it was quiet and peaceful. They didn't have anybody on the plane with me. Plenty of time to think; maybe too much time. A running man sticks out too much. I had to find a way out of this soon or DellaCroce would nail me when I ran out of places to hide.

Atlanta Airport was the usual mess: travelers running through the tunnels, locals selling everything from shoe shines to salvation. I had a couple of hours until the connecting flight to Augusta, so I found a pay phone and called the Blind Man in New York.

"What's the story?" I asked, not identifying myself.

"Good news and bad news, pal," came back the Blind Man's harsh whisper. He'd spent so much time in solitary back when we did time together that his eyes were bad and his voice had rusted from lack of practice. "They got the name that's on your ticket, but no pictures."

"Damn! How did they get on the ticket so fast?"

"What's the difference, pal? Dump the ticket and get the hell out of there."

"And do what?"

"You got me, brother. But be quick or be dead," said the Blind Man, breaking the connection.

The first thing I did was get out of the Delta area. I went to the United counter and booked a flight to Chicago, leaving in three hours. You have to stay away from borders when you're paying cash for an airline ticket, but I didn't see any obvious DEA agents lurking around and, anyway, I wasn't carrying luggage.

With the Chicago ticket tucked safely away in my pocket, I drifted slowly back toward the boarding area for the Augusta flight. It was getting near to departure time. I found myself a seat in the waiting area, lit a cigarette, and kept an eye on the people at the ticketing desk. There was a short walkway to the plane, with a pretty little blonde standing there checking off the boarding passes. Still peaceful, the silence routinely interrupted by the usual airport announcements, but no tension. It felt right to me. Maybe I'd try for Augusta after all; I hate Chicago when it's cold.

And then I spotted the hunters: two flat-faced men sitting in a corner of the waiting area. Sitting so close their shoulders were touching, they both had their eyes pinned on the little blonde, not sweeping the room like I would have expected. But I knew who they were. You don't survive a dozen years behind the walls if you can't tell the hunters from the herd.

They wouldn't be carrying; bringing handguns into an airport was too much of a risk. Besides, their job was to point the finger, not pull the trigger. I saw how they planned to work it; they had the walkway boxed in. But I didn't see what good it would do them if they couldn't put a face on their target.

The desk man announced the boarding of Flight 884 to Augusta. I sat there like it was none of my business, not moving. One by one, the passengers filed into the narrow area. The sweet southern voice of the blonde piped up, "Pleased to have you with us today, Mr. Wilson," and my eyes flashed over to the hunters. Sure enough, they were riveted to the blonde's voice. She called off the name of each male passenger as he filed past her. If the women passengers felt slighted at the lack of recognition, they kept quiet about it. A perfect trap: if I put my body through that walkway, the little blonde would brand the name they already had to my new face, and I'd be dead meat as soon as the plane landed.

I got up to get away from there just as the desk man called out, "Last call for Flight 884." They couldn't have watchers at all the boarding areas. I'd just have to get to Chicago, call the Blind Man, and try and work something out. As I walked past the desk, a guy slammed into me. He bounced back a few feet, put a nasty expression on his face, and then dropped it when he saw mine. A clown in his late thirties, trying to pass for a much younger guy: hair carefully styled forward to cover a receding hairline, silk shirt open to mid-chest, fancy sunglasses dangling from a gold chain around his neck. I moved away slowly and watched as he approached the desk.

"I got a ticket for this flight," he barked out, like he was used to being obeyed.

"Of course, sir. May I see your boarding pass?"

"I don't have a goddamn pass. Can't I get one here?"

"I'm sorry, sir," the desk man told him, "the flight is all boarded at this time. We have four more boarding passes outstanding. We can certainly issue one to you, but it has to be on what we call the 'modified standby' basis. If the people holding boarding passes don't show up five minutes before flight time, we will call your name and give you the pass."

"What kind of crap is this?" the clown demanded. "I paid good money for this ticket."

"I'm sure you did, sir. But that's the procedure. I'm sure you won't have any trouble boarding. This happens all the time on these short flights. Just give us your ticket, and we'll call you by name just before the flight leaves, all right?"

I guess it wasn't all right, but the clown had no choice. He slammed his ticket down on the counter, tossed his leather jacket casually over one shoulder, and took a seat near the desk.

It wasn't a great shot, but it was the best one I'd had in a while. I waited a couple of heartbeats and followed the clown to the desk. I listened patiently to their explanation, left my ticket, and was told that they would call me by name when my turn came.

I didn't have much time. I walked over to where the clown was sitting, smoking a cigarette like he'd invented it. "Look," I told him, "I need to get on that flight to Augusta. It's important to me. Business reasons."

"So what's that to me?" he smirked, shrugging his shoulders.

"I know you got ahead of me on the list, okay? It's worth a hundred to me to change places with you. Let me go when your name is called, and you can go when they call mine, if they do," I told him, taking out a pair of fifties and holding them out to him.

His eyes lit up. I could see the wheels turning in his head. He knew a sucker when he saw one. "What if we both get on?" he wanted to know.

"That's my tough luck," I said. "I need to do everything possible to get on the flight. It's important to me."

He appeared to hesitate, but it was no contest. "My name's Morrison," he said, taking the fifties from my hand. "Steele," I said, and walked toward the desk.

The watchers hadn't looked at us. A couple of minutes passed. I gently worked myself away from the clown, watching the watchers. The desk man piped up: "Mr. Morrison, Mr. Albert Morrison, we have your boarding pass." I shot up from my seat, grabbed the pass, and hit the walkway. The little blonde sang out, "Have a pleasant flight, Mr. Morrison," as I passed. I could feel the heat of the hunters' eyes on my back.

I wasn't fifty feet into the runway when I heard, "Mr. Steele, Mr. Henry Steele, we have your boarding pass." I kept going and found my seat in the front of the plane.

I watched the aisle and, sure enough, the clown passed me by, heading for the smoking section in the rear. I thought he winked at me, but I couldn't be sure.

The flight to Augusta was only half an hour, but the plane couldn't outrun a phone call. The airport was a tiny thing, just one building, with a short walk to the cabs outside. The clown passed by me as I was heading outside, bumped me with his shoulder, held up my two fifties in his hand, and gave me a greasy smile. "It's a hard world," he said, moving out ahead of me.

I watched as two men swung in behind him. One was carrying a golf bag; the other had his hands free.

JAMES HANNAH
(b. 1951)

Readers of hard-boiled and dark-suspense fiction are unlikely to be familiar with James Hannah's name. A Texan who earned a Master of Fine Arts degree from the Iowa Writers' Workshop, Hannah is a short-story writer whose small but impressive output has appeared exclusively in such literary magazines as Cimarron Review, Crazyhorse, Florida Review, and Quarterly West. His first collection, Desperate Measures (1988), includes ten stories about "desperate people, desperate solutions," in the words of his publisher, in which "there is no god but chance, and life's surprises are seldom sources of joy." Noir writer James Crumley called them "stories for brave readers," and indeed they are.

It would be inaccurate to pin a "hard-boiled" label on Hannah's fiction; nevertheless, the best of his tales have all the elements of style, characterization, insight, and social commentary of the classic hard-boiled story. Junior Jackson, the narrator of "Junior Jackson's Parable," is the most desperate of all of Hannah's desperate people, and a true noir creation: it is difficult to imagine a more completely disaffected and dissatisfied individual, or a world more disordered than the one in which he exists. His parable is a dark and cautionary one about life and wasted lives in the American Southwest as the twentieth century lurches headlong toward its final days.

B. P.

1988

JUNIOR JACKSON'S PARABLE

I tore out to Mama's. Punched the old Chevy pickup and slung gravel halfway down Papermill Drive. I'd left the goddamned phone out in the service bay at the Firestone store dangling after the bitch'd hung up on me.

I flew past the Sonic. Luckless sonofabitch, I kept saying. Luckless, worthless, sorry stupid sonofabitch. And pushed down harder on the accelerator, rattling the shitty unleaded through the carb.

I guess I'd had enough. Roger Blake, my court-appointed lawyer, said that later a hundred times. He painted all sorts of pictures of me and her and him—mostly true—but some I couldn't quite make out. Wondered who the hell he was talking about exactly. But the fucking D.A.! What a peckerhead he was. When he called his surprise witness a couple of days before the trial ended and grinned down at me, all three of us knew I'd really fucked the duck. I dropped my stare to my ugly worthless hands.

But I didn't only have the shotgun on my mind. That's what the peckerhead kept harping on. The shotgun. Twelve-gauge. Buckshot, ladies and gentlemen of the jury. I mean, it passed through my mind, sure, but I'd had enough, you know. I guess I was mainly just going to Mama's and leaving everything behind—the Firestone store, our mobile home over in Regency Gardens behind Wal-Mart, the Casbah Club. Daddy's gun came to me somewhere on the farm-to-market road. Came and went. Came back some more. Sitting in his closet behind boxes of coveralls he'd saved from the mill, old broken Emerson fans. In my mind maybe I even crammed the gun back deeper, covered it with clothes.

Remember, you'd had enough, Roger Blake reminded me. And he wasn't lying; I'd had all the shit a man can take. Luckless bastard.

Mr. Stroud had yelled from the front of the Firestone store, over some cutouts of Richard Petty. The two women customers behind him and to his left open-mouthed. Ed, the other underpaid employee, standing up under a car on the rack as I skidded past, burning rubber. His eyes bugged out. Where I have a limp, he has a twisted, smaller-than-a-twig right forearm. He tucks tools in the bony crook. Together we hobble, gimp around the place. That story another example of my luck. Up under a car at Walker's Sinclair over by the tracks when I was just sixteen and the jack decides to let down. Simply spews out fluid in a long spurt and drops the fucking Buick across my shin. Sixteen and the makings of a gimp. Some quack at the county hospital working by the hour patched me up. A couple of okay years and then it starts hurting like a bastard right after I get in the Navy.

I'm driving past the road to the dump, gimpy leg aching, and I reach down to rub it. What do you think it all means? I'm asking. First I keep reeling it around over and over. Then I blurt it out to the noisy Chevy cab—coffee cups rattling, cigarette packs slithering from side to side on the dash. But I don't even smoke. I don't take the time to light up. Now that shows you the state I'm in.

"Why that day? That particular time?" Roger Blake asked me on the stand. But I don't know. I'd had enough bad luck. But I didn't mention luck. I kept that to myself. "You'd been married a little over two years?"

"Yes sir." "She'd been Bud Frazer's girlfriend before your marriage?" "Yes sir." Marriage, I'd thought. Shit on that.

"Hey, come on by for a beer when you get off, okay?" she'd said as soon as I'd answered the phone. I'd tucked the greasy receiver under my chin.

Ed had scuttled past, edged by me, his little arm clenching a ratchet and some extensions. Me and Mary Louise had been up late the night before fighting. She'd been high on something. Some pills he'd gotten her. She'd come in at three. But just a week before, she'd sworn no later than nine or ten from now on. Just a few free hours, she'd said, after she finished work at the Catfish Castle. Free hours, she called them. Shit on that too.

"You're takin' those pills again! Don't lie to me, Mary Louise." I raised my voice and Ed looked away, scampered back up under the Cougar; he was used to all this. "Goddammit, you promised you'd stop. You said you'd leave him alone!" I swallowed to stifle a whine.

The house was always a mess. We'd argue and then drink. Bud would drop by to talk. He was from South Carolina and he'd served time for murder and assault and other shit. Mary Louise told me about his tattoos once. Even about the one on his dick—a dozen arrows that swelled into rockets. She'd laughed and snuggled up to me and said she was all mine now but those tattoos of his are hilarious. Are, I kept thinking. She'd said *are*.

The prosecution wanted to take out the part about the arrows but the judge decided not to. Twenty-four eyes batted when Roger Blake said *penis* over and over.

"Hey, boy." She'd given Bud the phone or he'd taken it. I heard her laughing in the background. Some band was warming up at the Casbah Club.

"Come on by and I'll buy you a couple. We're havin' a fine time already."

"Sounds like it."

"Huh?"

"I thought you were going to leave her alone."

He was big and moved like a bear or one of them sloths at the zoo. He went to sheriff department picnics. He drove a truck for Gulf Freight Lines. And he scared everybody shitless.

"Come on by and we'll party. Come on."

"You said you'd leave her alone. You said you would."

The band tuned up some more and Mary Louise buzzed something into the receiver. Bud laughed right into it for a minute. Then I listened to the band playing "Blue Eyes Crying in the Rain" out of key and awful-sounding on the phone.

"Suit yourself, you little motherfucker."

"Let me talk to her, Bud. Put her on."

"Oh, Bud," she laughed, and then, "Come on, you old asshole. We'll have a good time. Bud'll buy."

Remember all them examples in church? I'd come into Big Church, as Mama called it, from Sunday School and there were these stories the preacher'd tell. The very same plane this guy missed crashed not ten minutes after he'd missed it. Somebody'd gone from whiskey to heroin, his life on the skids. But one afternoon, as he'd laid dirty and lonely and sick on an overdose, he'd watched a trail of ants on the floor. Helping share the burden of a breadcrumb. And he'd seen his own need for other people's help.

Everybody always understood something. Everything fit together and made sense at the end. Explained the car wreck, the alcoholic's whipping his wife, the sparrow falling from the sky. That and them parables. The Good Samaritan finally helped that hurt guy; the prodigal son's daddy fixed a feast for him. Everything sorted itself out. A whole lifetime of sin, uselessness, bad luck was cleared up, explained, paid for, worked out in a minute flat.

A man came to sing once. His face eaten totally away by acid from an exploding battery. Not till that explosion had he really valued life. And later, faceless, he'd praised God for the moment of revelation. He'd warbled out "Oh, why not tonight?" his skin plastic and tight.

"Mary Louise, you leave there right now. You hear me?"

"But Bud brought me."

"Don't argue, dammit! You get someone else to take you home. You promised . . ."

She hung up. Or Bud did. She testified he did. But who knows about that? She's back heavy into drugs already. And I got a letter from her lawyer yesterday talking about divorce, getting the mobile home and everything else. Sure, why not? *What* everything else?

I sort of lied. What else could I do? I said I was in a blind rage. Yeah, he'd been tearing my home apart. Yeah, he'd been supplying my wife with drugs. Yeah, I did suspect they'd been having sex. Shit, she soaked her underwear every night in the kitchen sink. I smelled him on her skin. Yeah, yeah, yeah, I was afraid of him. That's the whole truth there. He was a scary fucker. Solid. Big. Tattooed. Somehow friends of the cops. Dangerous. Fill in the blank about him. And only use bad words.

But it wasn't blind rage. It was too jumbled up for just that simple answer. But I knew the peckerhead wanted the maximum he could get—thirty years, or so Roger Blake had said. I knew I had to play up the passionate rage part, leave out the stuff about bad luck.

I drove up to Mama's gate and turned off the engine. I caught my breath for the first time. But I didn't leap out and up the steps. Nope. I settled back and shook out a Winston and lit it and sucked it deep.

Junior Jackson. That's me. Junior luckless, meaningless Jackson. Crippled by a falling car. What'd Mama used to say . . . ? "Jun'er, don't hold them magazines over your eyes to read, somethin'll drop out and blind you . . . stick right in your eyeball." Good start, huh? "Don't lean back in the chair, Jun'er, it'll break and ram a piece up your spine. Damaged for life."

Oh sure, blame your mama and daddy, right? But how about the old man? Fell off a log truck at thirty, crushed a shoulder, spends the rest of his life in a little pain, sitting in front of the TV in his vinyl lounger saying "It's ever' dog eat a dog out there." "The world's a fucking mess, Jun'er." And later even more fuel. "What's that shit about them Arabs and Jews?" Arabs and Jews. Nigras on the dole. Mama'd hobble in, her knees locked from arthritis—Arthur, Daddy called it—and they'd shake their heads over TV (when I was little it had been the radio; neither could read much). And when things got real bad they'd both sleep. Take to their beds if the car broke down, the well pump needed new packing, something had eaten her pullets. Living at home, I'd do the same. Until finally, after twelve, fourteen hours of silence with only the faucets dripping, the wind blowing across the eaves, one of us would crawl out of bed, make a pot of coffee, force his thoughts on the problem, wake the others up.

The first year with Mary Louise, I slept most of the weekends until I decided I might ought to go out with her and try keeping up.

They met me at the back door; Wolf, the old black-and-tan, as slow as Mama.

"Surgery's the only thing, the doctor says. They'll cut along here," she bends gingerly to slide a finger over her kneecap, "and lift it out. Put in a plastic one."

"Plastic . . . shee-it." Daddy's leaning over the table pecking at a bought apple pie they've picked to pieces.

"He was a wild man," Mama said on the stand. I didn't look at her then or later. The old man broke down in tears. I think he thought he was on trial for something himself. The Jews, Arabs, nigras had finally finagled him out of his lounger to humiliate him.

"Want some pie?" she'd asked.

Somewhere along the way it had dawned on me that maybe all this would become the moment of revelation like the ends of those parables. Do all this in order to get to the sense of things.

Hmmm, I thought. And went in to take the shotgun, check the shells, walk straight through the house to the front door.

That's sort of how I went in the Navy. Then the goddamned leg gets worse and worse from all that marching and exercise and fighting them practice oil fires. So this Navy doctor says it'll be fine and dandy after he opens it up and unpinches something and rotates something else. Shit, I don't believe in doctors like Mama and I'm already homesick, so I'm out of there in a minute. All the way to Quartzite, Arizona, before they pick me up AWOL. Of course they didn't just give me a medical. The monkey-suited bastards process me out with a D.D. Junior Jackson, D.D. So I finally did get to come home to work at Beasley's Shell station, though it was a pretty crooked route.

The peckerhead brought up my run-ins with the law. But it was just the usual kid stuff and I'd never served any time for it. Just warnings and a couple of J.P. fines. Stealing a couple of tires, a tape player—that sort of thing. We'd drink, go to the high school games in town, drink some more and smoke some dope. End up smashing a window and taking tapes, radios, fuzzbusters. Everybody did it. It was more a sport—like hunting deer out of season—than something bad. We stole from each other most of the time.

But I quit it. When I got the job changing flats and mounting tires at the Firestone place, I went cold turkey. Some of the guys said me and Ed was sitting on top a gold mine, but I said no. Besides, I was the one who always got caught—figures—and this job was my only way to stay out of jail.

"She's trouble," Daddy'd said, his head level with his toes, looking between them at "Gunsmoke."

Mama'd shook her head as Mary Louise'd drove off in her Camaro after her first visit.

It'd turn out bad. Trouble. Misery. Out of luck. First the Navy business and a dishonorable discharge. Then coming back to steal. What'd we teach you anyway? Then they'd troop to bed to recharge their last sparks into a smolder.

They were right. I was right, too—I'd thought the same thing when I saw her first inhale dope for a new world's record. Saw the first boyfriend, Bud, she'd had since moving down from Norman.

But when she opened those long, brown legs what can I say? Nobody asked about that at the trial.

"He was like a wild animal I'm tellin' you. All tussled hair, eyes wild, bugged out."

"I don't know. I can't rightly say," the old man kept saying. They must have done some Olympic sleeping the first couple of weeks. I know I did. They'd take me back up—who the fuck did I know who'd make bail?—and the nigras would catcall, thump burning butts at me, jeer. And I'd lay down and sleep and dream luckless dreams. A vacuum that sucked the hours up, shortened my life without refreshing me one bit.

All the shit at the Casbah's a mess. It wasn't like the movies. Not in regular motion or slow motion like them Peckinpah flicks. It was in fast motion; more like old Keystone Kop movies or WWI where doughboys scurry past, their legs pumping nine to nothing.

I sat and cried most of the first week of the trial. I was shocked by what had happened at the club. And it was so fast it could replay itself in my head fifty times a minute.

So I thought it over and over while the peckerhead D.A. trotted out everything about my life he could find. The theft charges they'd dropped; Mary Louise's drug problem. Her and Bud. Poor old Bud Frazer, he'd say, a victim of us sorry white trash—that's what he'd meant, anyway. And I'd think about it and couldn't help crying. But not for Bud, you see. Fuck him. Though I was sorry about it all and pretty damned confused. I was crying for Mary Louise, who I glanced at now and then, who sat blank-eyed resting her clean shiny brown hair against the oak paneling. And I cried about my bad luck.

Toward the end of the week, Roger Blake began putting on people who knew Bud; people from South Carolina even, and they had some stories to tell. Bad-assed wasn't the half of it.

"You'd seen him at the Casbah Club before?"

Old decrepit Mickey Cotter'd drank with us a hundred nights there. "Yes sir."

"How'd he act in there? How'd he treat people?"

"Shit!"

The judge leaned over quickly and spoke to Cotter.

"Sorry, your honor." He scratched his fuzzy chin and talked on.

I replayed the scene.

All the way back into town I'd argued with myself like them angels sitting on your shoulder—the good one and the bad one.

Way back in my mind I kept thinking that this would end it all somehow. I'd take her home, wash her face with a cold washrag like I'd done before, and put her to bed. Maybe I'd pull up her t-shirt and run a finger over her wide pink nipples.

The twelve-gauge shotgun bounced on the seat but I only heard it. I didn't look at it at all. It was really for protection. Just in case, that's all. I sweated and the air rushing in the rolled-down window only made me stickier. Dried in a film on my greasy face. I smelled myself, my body odor strong from the day's work. But stronger than that by now.

But all this went fast as I rolled up in the parking lot at dusk, jumped out, went in and sat down at their table, ordered a beer and looked away for a time before I jerked my head around and told Bud to take his arm from her neck, the fingers of his left hand—crowded with nugget rings— squeezing her tight nipple. Houston Oilers, the t-shirt said, and I stared at the message.

Objections would interrupt me a little, you know. The peckerhead kept harping about me going all the way to Mama's to get the gun. He wanted thirty years at least, Roger Blake kept saying. But my witnesses just talked about Bud. Someone said you'd need a couple of shotguns for him. You couldn't find a single friend. None of his sheriff buddies talked. Homewrecker, ruined lives, tattooed penis, belligerent.

Belligerent, shit. I'd wipe my eyes, glance at Mary Louise who sat staring straight at the space just over the white-faced clock. Here like the TV shows. Perry Mason. Except this was less real. Everything seemed too soft. The tabletop gave a little. I sank too deep into the oak chair. The paper tissue the hardest surface anywhere around.

"Oh, I seen him do awful things to people at the bar. Cuss'em. Taunt 'em. Shove 'em around like he owned the place. Beat the . . . hell out of 'em in the parking lot."

There were cars parked every which way as usual. I towed her through the door. She seemed dead weight, like dragging something that weighed a lot more than it looked. I shoved her in the pickup but going around to my door I stopped.

Bud moved like a bear from the door of his den to a car right in front of my Chevy. He grinned, rested a huge hip on the rear fender. The sheet metal dipped in.

"Let her out now, Jun'er. Be a good boy and let her come out to play with old Buddy boy. Okay, Jun'er?"

And this all quick motion too, sped up, the film sprockets rattling like mad, the machine clattering. I'm terrified, smell myself suddenly, but I'm all scrambled up with the need to do something final to free us for the feast, the happy ending. Something that makes good sense.

I jerked the gun out from under Mary Louise and through the window. I had come to kill him. The frames snapping faster, breakneck speed.

He cussed me, sitting idly on the fender. Then in his bear's movement he lifted his hip off. Turned to see the people gathered at the door. I looked to see them all open-mouthed. A few took quick swallows of beer. The silver cans caught the parking lot lights.

I said something. Bud moved like a wall, or train, gliding easily toward me, his left hand out. Everything quick and full of things at the same time. Mary Louise blew the horn, held it down until minutes after I'd aimed for his head and then, finally, shot at his·legs, the dust coming up to tangle with his shredded khaki pants. I saw how I'd riddled the car's fender. A tire hissed. Mary Louise let up on the horn and the people in front of the bar took a couple of steps and stopped again.

I couldn't look at his face. I couldn't kill him. I didn't even pump in another shell. All I could think of was how much I hoped this ended it all. Though it didn't seem much of an ending to anything important.

When Mary Louise screamed I stared in the dark window in surprise. Her finger jabbed at the windshield and I looked at Bud for the first time just to see him cough and spit in my direction and fall, bounce off my hood, land like a boulder in the floating dust. The single ricocheted pellet. Off the bumper and up through his left temple.

There were color slides. The peckerhead brought them. The bailiff set up the projector and screen. The shiny pointer circled the stuff like chewed newspaper that had dribbled from his head onto the hospital sheet. And I cried.

I lied too. I'd gone to kill him, not just scare him, and I'd chickened out. Junior Jackson, the chickenshit sonofabitch who'd shot at the ground and missed. He'd got two superficial leg wounds, but one of the pellets had come up off the bumper and into his brain. Off the heavy chrome bumper of a blue and white '57 Ford. Everything since made from shitty metal or plastic. But let's talk luck, huh? That's why I cried. Slept in the cell as if I'd died too. Mary Louise didn't come by. I asked Roger Blake to talk to her for me. The D.A. wanted thirty fucking years. All I wanted was them to brick up the rusty bars and window and let me sleep. In my luckless dreams the shooting expanded so I could try to cram meaning in a thousand pockets of air where nothing happened. In the pickup. At Daddy's closet door. Between the gun barrel and Mary Louise's ass. Unlucky stupid bastard. I think only Bud came out prepared. I'm fucked up. Fucked over. She's stoned shitless. Bud's the man with his hand out, sliding along the fender. The dented metal popping out without a sound.

But this is the part that lays me out like you'd smacked me with a shovel.

About six days into the trial I'd cried myself pretty dry. After a shitty breakfast and kicking the huge water roaches I'd smashed that night into a pile, I'd change into the blue seersucker Roger Blake had brought me and they'd lead me down. I'd sit but not listen now, the courtroom breezeless, the suit hot, sweat dripping down the small of my back. They put everybody on: the police, the coroner with his lousy slides, everybody else in the Casbah parking lot. Mary Louise, me, the whole nine yards.

But Wednesday afternoon after a supper of hash browns and those link sausages Daddy called donkey dicks, I stretched out, used to the loud racket of the place. Nigras bullshitting one another with a vengeance. Cell doors clanging. The pile of roaches still there and big enough to give you the creeps.

Then Blake shows up and sits on the cot with me. He opens his fat battered briefcase full of legal pads and folders and rolls of Lifesavers and offers me a wintergreen and sits back, his hands across his stomach.

Mostly I'm numb by now. I think that's why the noise doesn't bother me anymore. Four weeks in here and I'm numb like a catfish you'd thumped on the head. Waiting for the cold knife up the asshole.

But Blake fidgets and shifts away from the light through my window and edges close to me, his breath a burst of mint the smell of Pepto-Bismol. He's a good man, I've decided. But the busted veins that start on his nose and flare out across his cheeks say he's got problems, too. I don't think he's any too lucky either and that figures in like everything else.

But he whispers something and reaches out to give my knee a tremendous whack and squeeze and then he bellylaughs and I have to sit up closer to get his drift. He talks on now, fumbling through the briefcase, but instead of another mint, he takes out some folders.

"Just be quiet about it. Keep your head down in there a few more days. It's looking real fine." And he goes on and on, fidgeting with happiness.

After he leaves I lay down in a state. "You haven't been listening, paying good attention, looking at the jury like I have, that's all. I didn't want to say anything sooner though I noticed it after the business about the penis. Didn't want to get your hopes up too much." And he'd whacked me again a couple of times. "We'll walk on this. Bud Frazer was a sorry bastard. It was almost a community service. Him a snitch for the sheriff, too. Some protection there. I'd guess five years probated. Probated, Junior." He'd whacked me again, leaned back and crossed his arms over his stomach.

I'll walk, I keep saying over and over. And toward morning—the moon flying across my high small window—I nodded and stood up for the millionth time. Goddammit, maybe it was all going to work out. I'd shot him by accident and that'll walk me out of here and with that bastard gone me and Mary Louise'll do fine. Now I'd feel the kick of the gun and hear the splatter of pellets against the fender and dirt but I'd shrug it off. God works in mysterious ways, Mama'd say.

I paced. Then I'd lay down. I felt light-headed, the man in the story, my stupid fucking life making some sense. If I'd shot the fucker down, they'd toss me in the pen for thirty years. But I had cried real tears too, and pity and mercy and all that stuff was being leveled at me, Junior Jackson. Junior Jackson, not guilty or maybe guilty but probated. He was sure and by full daybreak so was I.

It was a miracle. I ain't no Pentecostal like Mama but that morning I almost shook with the Holy Ghost and spoke in tongues.

The trial was almost over. Maybe another three days. But that Thursday I didn't care about anything. I listened more and saw how right he was. The jurors looked kind and sympathetic. I could see all this had been hard on them too. Once I started doodling on a spare yellow pad but like a hawk Blake's hand swept over and took the pen away. I'd written my name down one side and next to it Mary Louise Jackson. I'd glanced around at her in the corner. All that dope didn't do much for her wanting sex, but after seeing her there, her hair shiny and long, the light brown of acorns, my dick nudged the hell out of the seersucker.

After supper I listened to the bullshit. I reached around the wall of my cell and took a Kool from the guy next door. Willy'd been in about two weeks charged with car theft. We knew some guys in common, so we talked all sorts of shit. He smoked my Winstons and I smoked his Kools.

Almost dark Friday night, they took me down to their dirty little reception room where I'd gone to talk to Mama a couple of times.

Friday had looked even better for me. By Tuesday it could all be over, Roger Blake had said. I smiled at the fat fucker of a guard. He stood by the door and inhaled Pall Malls, gabbed to himself, waved his cigarette.

Mary Louise slumped at the filthy cheap table, her hair hiding most of her face.

My face lit up and I reached across the table to take her hands. This time my pecker rubbed rough twill.

"Hey, you okay?"

She looked up and nodded. Her eyes were flat as slate. Like looking into a blackboard for some emotions. She was high. It was in the slope of her shoulders too, and the way her head lolled a bit too loose.

"Shit, Mary Louise, you're fucked up. I thought you were staying at Mama's?"

She nodded. Her hands under mine were ice-cold, the coldest thing I'd touched in weeks.

But I was too happy to let her get me down for long. So I squeezed her hands, ran my forefinger up and down her palm. My zipper close to busting.

"Roger Blake says I can walk on this. He told you that, didn't he?" She nodded. Mumbled something. "Honey, I love you, you know that. I only wanted us together. With him gone we'll have a good chance now. Hell, we'll move to Norman or somewhere. Houston's booming, they say. Okay? I'll borrow some money and rent my own station. Shit, I'll sell a million tires. I'm good at that. Okay?"

And on I went until the guard had a pile of butts to match my cockroaches and he slung himself over to cough out a "Let's go, asshole."

I stopped at the door and watched her stand and look at me and then she grinned like she used to when we'd go to a high school game together and yell till we were hoarse.

I almost leapt up the cement steps, gimpy leg and all, and swung the door shut behind me. If I'd believed a lot in God, like Mama, I'd have got on my knees. Then again, I thought about how everybody really does believe. They have to, specially when things start going right. So maybe I mumbled something and went to the wall to jerk a thumb up to Willy Devereaux, the car thief. He passed over a Kool and I traded him a Winston. And we hung our hands out and inhaled deep as we could and blew smoke towards the bullshitting nigras.

His old lady'd come by with some cookies. They were store-bought but we ate a dozen apiece. And I told him about seeing Mary Louise and how we'd move to Norman. He said he knew of a closed Conoco station in town, out past the loop. We wondered about the rent.

"But you'll have to put all that good stuff off, huh?"

"Not a bit."

"Shee-it, man, you're gonna do some ser'us time in them Walls."

I took a deep breath and blew puffs of Kool toward the babbling nigras. "My lawyer's gonna walk me right out of here. And then I'll open up that station. Batteries, tires—look at the price of gas. Hell, station owners must be putting back a fortune." And we talked on. He shook my hand a couple of times. Told me he could use a job someday, knew a hell of a lot about cars. "I'll bet," I said. And we laughed and later I laid down but didn't sleep. Instead I jerked off twice, one right after the other, while trying to forget Mary Louise's cold hands.

I'm Junior Jackson, remember? Remember me? So you can guess the rest.

Sure enough. Monday morning bright and early the peckerhead brings Willy Devereaux out dressed in a lime-green seersucker suit. I guess maybe lawyers have some sort of deal at Weiner's. And Roger Blake looks at me sharply, his veins like black ink lines across his face, and I just stare at him and then back at Willy.

Willy lies like a sonofabitch of course. Has me strutting and cocky, a stone-cold murderer. The court buzzes, the old blue-haired ladies in the audience whispering hard. Blake objects and objects but the judge makes him sit down. Later Blake tears into Willy about the deal he'd struck with the D.A. All that sort of shit. But when he comes back and sits in the oak chair, he doesn't look at me at all. Instead he takes a roll of Lifesavers from his shirt pocket and bites off one end.

And I don't look up at the jury because I know they're staring at me with jaws locked tight, fingers squeezing each other. I don't look at Mary

Louise because I'm afraid she's just looking at the clock. Instead I look straight ahead at a spot about a foot under the short flagpole the American flag's on. There's a crack in the plaster and it looks like a river from up in a plane. A river cutting through snow. I let it carry Junior Jackson off because it's pretty fucking plain to see that this story don't end like old Job getting a bunch of new sheep and camels, a wife and kids. Or with the prodigal son's homecoming feast. Or even old Jonah spit up on the beach with a new line of work.

I've been here six months. Roger Blake says I'll only serve three years max. "It could have been a lot worse," he says. He don't need to mention it could have been a whole lot better.

Here's what I've learned so far: You call nigras blacks; you can make a mean shiv out of a sharpened tablespoon; if you drop the soap in the showers, don't bend down to pick it up.

Now there's some revelations to take to the bank. There's the lessons. Maybe when I get out I'll make my living going from revival to revival. I'll stand up at the pulpit and give the bastards my story. At the end I'll raise my arms high over my head, my face sweating, and deliver the meaning of it all. Won't it be fine to see their faces before the organ starts up.

FAYE KELLERMAN
(b. 1952)

Much of the work of Faye Kellerman explores the traditions of Judaism and Jewish orthodoxy as set against the vast secular society that is the United States (particularly southern California, which Raymond Chandler once defined as a foreign land). Her novels detail the alienation that is experienced even though assimilation was supposed to have taken place two or three generations back. Her characters are often bigoted and unforgiving, unable or simply unwilling to jump off the doomed roller coaster of their own hatreds once they are launched into a course of action.

Kellerman is fascinated by the plot possibilities inherent in the interplay between characters, an interest strongly demonstrated in her main series featuring Los Angeles police sergeant Pete Decker and the young widow Rina Lazarus. In Kellerman's debut novel, The Ritual Bath (1985), Lazarus is attracted to Decker, but cannot fully fall in love with him because he is a gentile. It is then miraculously disclosed that Decker was adopted as a young child and is, in fact, a Jew. While this rather suspect, "carried-off-by-gypsies-as-a-child" plot line obviates a good deal of future character conflict in the series, it does clear the ground for other, perhaps more complex, religious conflict.

A foray into the past, The Quality of Mercy (1988), proves that Kellerman can easily handle other fictional structures. The book concerns Elizabeth I's personal physician, Dr. Roderigo López, and his daughter, Rebecca. López, who was ultimately hanged, drawn, and quartered for allegedly trying to poison his employer, may have been the template for Shakespeare's Shylock. The finely delineated scenes of torture and violence in this book are certainly not for the squeamish. In fact, there is much that is deliberately, and necessarily, gruesome in most of Kellerman's modern novels.

"Bonding" is quite unlike anything else Kellerman has written. It is not particularly violent, but rather an extraordinary mix of noir and sheer hopelessness, featuring a teenage heroine who is far outside the sphere of normal morality. On the surface, the girl seems to be a murderous monster with no redeeming features, yet Kellerman portrays her with such profound insight and humanity, and even humor, that the reader *cannot help but understand her point of view. Nevertheless, both story and heroine are so hard-boiled they could break your teeth.*

J. A.

1989

BONDING

I became a prostitute because I was bored. Let me tell you about it. My mother is a greedy, self-centered egotist and a pill-popper. I don't think we exchange more than a sentence worth of words a week. Our house is very big—one of these fake-o hacienda types on an acre of flat land in prime Gucciland Beverly Hills—so it's real easy to avoid each other. She doesn't know what I do and wouldn't care if she did know. My father doesn't hassle me 'cause he's never around. I mean, *never* around. He rarely sleeps at home anymore, and I don't know why my parents stay married. Just laziness, I guess. So when my friend came around one day and suggested we hustle for kicks, I said sure, why not.

Our first night was on a Saturday. I dressed up in a black mini with fishnet stockings, the garter lower than the hem of my dress. I painted my lips bright red, slapped on layers of makeup, and took a couple of downers. I looked the way I felt—like something brought up from the dead. We boogied on down to the Strip, my friend supplying the skins, and made a bet: who could earn the most in three hours. I won easily; I didn't even bother to screw any of the johns—just went down on them in a back alley or right in their cars. I hustled seven washed-out old guys at sixty bucks a pop. Can't say it was a bundle of yucks, but it was different. Jesus, anything's better than the boredom.

The following day, after school, me and my friend got buzzed and went shopping at the mall. I took my hustle money and bought this real neat blouse accented with white and blue rhinestones and sequins. I also saw this fabulous belt made of silver and turquoise, but it was over a hundred and fifty dollars and I didn't want to spend *that* much money on just a belt. So I lifted it. Even with the new electronic gizmos and the security guards, stealing isn't very hard, not much of a challenge.

Let me tell you a little about myself. I was born fifteen years ago, the "love child" of a biker and his teenage babe. I think my real mother was like twelve or thirteen at the time. I once asked my bitch of a mother about her, and she got *reaaallly* agitated. Her face got red and she began to talk in that hysterical way of hers. The whole thing was like too threatening for her to deal with. Anyway, I was adopted as an infant. And I never remember being happy. I remember crying at my sixth birthday party 'cause Billy Freed poked his fingers in my Cookie Monster cake. Mom went bonkers—we hadn't photographed the cake yet—and started screaming at Billy. Then he started crying. God, I was mad at Billy, but after Mom lit into him, I almost felt sorry for the kid. I mean, it was only a cake, you know.

Once, when I was around the same age, my mom picked me up and we looked in the mirror together. She put her cheek against mine as we stared at our reflections. I remember the feel of her skin—soft and warm, the sweet smell of her perfume. I didn't know what I'd done to deserve such attention, and that frustrated me. Whatever I did, I wanted to do it again so Mom would hold me like this. But of course, I didn't do anything. Mom just stared at us, then clucked her tongue and lowered me back onto my feet with an announcement: I'd never make it on my looks.

Well, what the hell did she expect? Beggars shouldn't be choosers. It's not like someone forced her to adopt me. The bitch. Always blaming me for things out of my control.

Did I tell you Mom is beautiful? Must have slipped my mind. We forget what we want to, right? Mom is a natural blonde with large blue eyes and perfect cheekbones. I've got ordinary brown hair—thin, at that—and dull green eyes. It's been a real bitch growing up as her daughter. Mom turned forty last year, and she treated herself to a face-lift—smoothing out imaginary wrinkles. Now her face is so goddamn tight, it looks wrapped in Saran. Her body is wonderful—long and sleek. I'm the original blimpo—the kind of woman that those old artists liked to paint. I'm not fat but just really developed. Big boobs, big round ass. My mother used to put me on all these diets, and none of them ever worked. I finally told her to fuck herself and gorged on Oreo cookies. Ate the whole package right in front of her, and boy, did that burn her ass.

She gave me this little smirk and said: "You're only hurting yourself, Kristie."

"I'm not hurting myself," I said. "In fact, I'm enjoying myself!"

Then she walked away with the same smirk on her face.

She once went to bed with this guy *I* was sleeping with. Can you believe that? Happened last summer at our beach house. I caught the two of them together. Mom got all red-faced, the guy was embarrassed, too, but I just laughed. Inside, though, I felt lousy. I felt lousy 'cause I knew that the guy really wanted to fuck her all along and was just using me as a stepping-stone.

You might ask where the hell was my dad when all this went down? I told you. He's never around.

My friend and co-hooker came down with strep throat today and asked if I could service her regular johns. I said sure. So I go to the room she rents. It's a typical sleazebucket of a place—broken-down bed, filthy floor, and a cracked mirror. Who should I see in it but my *father?* I turn my face away before he sees me. To tell you the truth, I barely recognize his face. Then I realize that he must have gotten a lift like Mom, 'cause his skin is also like stretched to the max.

I'm shaking—half with fear, half with disgust. That dirty son of a bitch. Doing it with teenage hookers. Then I remember a few years ago. How he eyed my friends when we sat around the pool. How he strutted out of the cabana wearing red bikini briefs and shot a half-gainer off the diving board. My friends were impressed. He popped through the water's surface, a strange expression on his face.

It was lust.

I sneak another glance in the mirror.

He holds the same look in his eyes now.

What the hell do I do?

I think about running away, but I know my friend will be real pissed. Jesus.

My dad.

I can't screw my dad!

Then I think to myself, My mom screwed *my* guy. . . .

But this is something different. He's my dad.

'Course, he's isn't my dad by blood. . . .

And it's been a long time since I've seen him. . . .

The thought starts to excite me. Yeah, I know it's real perverse, but my whole family is perverse.

And at least it isn't boring.

I take a quick hit of some snow from the vial I wear around my neck. Man, I need to be buzzed to pull this one off.

I'm real excited by now.

I drop my voice an octave—I can do that 'cause I have a great range— and tell him to can the lights. He starts bitching and moaning that he likes to do it with the lights on, and where the fuck is my friend. I tell him my friend has strep and it's hard to give head with your throat all red and raw, and if he doesn't want me, fine, he just won't get laid tonight.

He cans the lights. The only illumination in the room comes from a neon sign outside that highlights his semi. It's a good-looking one, and it turns me on even further. But I stay well hidden in the shadows of the room.

I wonder what he'll think of my body after laying Mom all these years. Maybe he'll think I'm too fat, but the minute he touches my boobs, his you-know-what becomes ramrod-straight. I let him bury his head in my chest, kiss my nipples. I give him a line of coke, then I take another snort. My face is always hidden.

I ask him what kinds of things he wants to do, and he says everything. I say it will cost him a hundred and fifty, and he gets suddenly outraged. A real bad acting job. I know what he makes, and he could buy all of Hollywood if he wanted to. Anyway, by now he's too excited to argue, and three fifty-dollar bills are slapped into my wet hand. I do whatever he wants as long as he can't see my face.

When it's over, I tell him I have a surprise for him. He's lying in bed now, smoking a joint. Still naked, I saunter over to the light switch, then suddenly flip it on. The cheesy room is flooded with bright yellow light. We both squint, then he sees me. It takes him a moment, then I see his tanned, tight face drain of all its color. His eyes pop out and he begins to pant. His skin takes on a greenish hue and he runs for the toilet. I hear him throw up.

Afterward he cries in my arms. But we both know it's not over.

Dad came home at eleven tonight. Mom and he start fighting. They always fight, did I tell you that? Probably why Dad started staying away. Anyway, it's the first time I ever remember Dad coming home in like twenty years or something. I'm no dummy. I know what the sucker has in mind, and that's okay by me. After all, I'm not really his daughter by blood, you know.

He comes into my room at around two o'clock. I make him pay, and no shit, he agrees. Man, I know you're gonna think I'm sick, but I gotta tell you. My dad's all right in the sack.

This goes on for the next month. If Mom suspects anything, she doesn't say a word. Then a strange thing happens. Life is weird—very weird. A real strange thing happens.

We fall in love.

Or something like it.

We consider all the options. The first is running away and giving me a new identity so that we can marry. The idea is discussed, then tossed in the circular file. Dad makes a couple a million buckeroos as a TV producer, and no way he could make that kind of money outside of L.A. Neither of us likes poverty.

We consider having Dad and Mom divorce and I'd live with Dad. That's out. California has stiff community-property laws, and the bitch would get half of *everything!*

There's only one option left.

First off, I gotta tell you that neither one of us really feel guilty about our decision 'cause: A, I'm not my dad's real daughter; and B, Mom has had this coming for a long time.

Way overdue.

We plan to do it next Saturday right after she comes home from one of her parties. She's usually pretty sauced and hyped and has to pop some downers to get to sleep. We figure we'll help her along.

She comes in at two A.M., surprised that I'm still up. I say I was having trouble sleeping and offer to make her some hot coffee. She nods and dismisses me with a wave of her hand. Like I'm a servant, instead of her daughter doing her a favor. I lace the java with Seconal. Halfway through the drink, her lids begin to close. But she knows something is wrong. She tells me she's having trouble breathing and asks me to call the doctor. I act like I'm real worried and place the phony call. By the time I hang up, she's out.

Both Dad and I are worried. She only drank half a cup, and we wonder if it's enough dope to do her in. Dad feels her pulse. It's weak but steady. A half hour later her heartbeat is even stronger. Dad says, "What the hell do we do now?" I think and think and think, then come up with a really rad brainstorm.

I get ten tablets full of Seconal, crush them in water, and suck the mixture into my old syringe. Did I tell you I shoot up occasionally? When the boredom is just too much. I haven't done it for a while, but I keep the syringe—you know, just in case the mood hits me. I shoot the dope under her tongue. It's absorbed fast that way and doesn't leave any marks. A friend of mine told me that.

Dad feels her pulse for a third time. Squeezes her wrist hard. Nothing. *Nada!* We celebrate with a big hug and a wet kiss, then wash the cup and wipe the place clean of fingerprints.

A half hour later Dad places a panic call to the paramedics.

God, I'm a great actress, carrying on like Mom and I were like bosom buddies.

"Mommmeeeee," I wail at the funeral.

Everyone feels sorry for me, but I don't accept their comfort.

My dad has his arm around me. He pulls me aside later on.

"You're overdoing it," he tells me.

"Hell, Paul." I call him Paul now. "I lost my fucking mother. I'm supposed to be upset."

"Just cool it a little, Kristie," Paul says. "Act withdrawn. Like someone took away your Black Sabbath records."

I sulk for a moment, then say what the hell. He's older. Maybe he knows best. I crawl into this shell and don't answer people when they talk to me. They give me pitying looks.

The detective shows up at our door unannounced. He's a big guy with black hair, old-fashioned sideburns, and acne scars. My heart begins to take off, and I say I don't answer any questions without my dad around.

"Why?" he asks.

"I don't know," I respond. Then I ask him if he has a warrant.

He laughs and says no.

"I'm sorry," I say. "I can't help you."

"Aren't you supposed to be in school?" he asks.

"God, are you crazy?" I say. "I mean, with all that happened? I can't concentrate on school right now. I mean, I lost my *mother!*"

"You two were pretty close, then."

"Real close."

"You don't look much like her," he remarks.

I feel my face changing its expression and get mad at myself. I say, "I'm adopted."

"Oh," the detective says. His face is all red now. "That would explain it."

Then he says, "I'm sorry to get personal."

"That's okay," I say, real generous.

There's a pause. Then the detective says, "You know we got the official autopsy report back for your mother."

I feel short of breath. I try to keep the crack out of my voice. "What's it say?" I ask.

"Your mother died of acute toxicity," he says. "Drug OD."

"Figures," I say calmly. "She had lots of problems and was on and off all sorts of drugs."

He nods, then asks, "What kind of drugs did she take?"

Then all of a sudden I realize I'm talking too much. I tell him I don't know.

"I thought you two were close."

I feel my face go hot again.

"We were," I say. "I mean, I knew she took prescribed drugs to help her cope, but I don't know *which* drugs. Our relationship wasn't like that, you know."

"Why don't we just peek inside the medicine cabinet of your house?" he says.

I shake my head slowly, then say, "Come back tonight, when my dad is home. Around eight, okay?"

He agrees.

Paul has a shit-fit, but I assure him I handled it well. By the time the detective shows up, we're both pretty calm. I mean, all the drugs found in her stomach came from her own pills. And then there was the party she went to. I'm sure at least a half dozen people remember her guzzling a bottle or two of white wine. She loved white wine—Riesling or Chardonnay.

My mother was an alcoholic. Did I tell you that?

The detective has on a disgusting suit that smells of mothballs. It hangs on him. He scratches his nose and says a couple of bullshitty words to Paul about how sorry he is that he had to intrude on us like this. Paul has on his best hound-dog face and says it's okay. Now I understand what he meant by not overdoing it. Man, is he good. *I* almost believe him.

"Sure," Paul says to the detective. "Take a look around the house."

I think about saying we've got nothing to hide, but don't. The detective goes over some details with Paul. My mom had gone to a party by herself. Paul didn't go 'cause he wasn't feeling well. At around three in the morning he got up to make himself a cup of milk. I was asleep, of course. He went downstairs and found my mother dead.

"Where'd you find your wife?" the detective asks.

"On that chair right there."

Paul points to the Chippendale.

The detective walks over to the chair but doesn't touch it. He asks, "What'd you do when you found her?"

Paul is confused. He says, "What do you mean? I called the paramedics, of course."

"Yeah," the detective says. "I know that. Did you touch her at all?"

"Touch her?" Paul asks.

The detective says, "Yeah, feel if the skin was cold . . . see if she was breathing."

Paul shakes his head. "I don't know anything about CPR. I figured the smart thing to do was to leave her alone and wait for the paramedics."

"How'd you know she was dead?" the detective asks.

"I didn't *know* she was dead," Paul says back. His voice is getting loud. "I just saw her slumped in the chair and knew something was wrong."

"Maybe she was sleeping," suggested the detective.

"Her face was white . . . gray." Paul begins to pace. "I knew she wasn't sleeping."

"You didn't check her pulse, check to see if she was breathing?"

"He said no," I say, defending my dad. "Look . . ." I get tears in my eyes. "Why don't you leave us alone? Haven't we been through enough without you poking around?"

The detective nods solemnly. He says, "I'll be brief."

We don't answer him. We stay in the living room while he searches. A half hour later the detective comes back carrying all of Mom's pills in a plastic bag. He says, "Mind if I take these with me?"

Paul says go ahead. As soon as he leaves, I notice Paul is white. I take his hand and ask him what's wrong. He whispers, "Your fingerprints were on the bottle."

I smile and shake my head no. "I wiped everything clean."

Paul smiles and calls me beautiful. God, no one has ever called me beautiful. Want to know something weird? Paul's a much better lover than he is a father. We make it right there on the couch, knowing it's a stupid and dangerous thing to do, but we don't care. An hour later we go to bed.

The fucking asshole pig comes back a week later with all of his piglets. Paul is enraged, but the pig has all the papers in order—the search warrant, the this, the that.

Paul asks, "What is going on?"

"Complete investigation, Mr. James."

"Of *what!*"

"I don't believe your wife's death is an accidental overdose."

"Why not?" I ask.

Paul glares at me. The detective ignores me and I don't repeat the question.

"What do you think it is?" Paul asks.

"Intentional overdose."

"Suicide?" Paul says, "No note was found."

"There isn't always a note," the detective responds. "Besides, I didn't mean suicide, I meant homicide."

My body goes cold when he says the word. The pig asks us if we mind being printed or giving them samples of our hair. Paul nudges me in the ribs and answers, "Of course not," for the both of us.

Then he adds, "We have nothing to hide."

Now I'm thinking that was a real dumb thing to say.

They start to dust the Chippendale, spreading black powder over the fabric. Paul goes loony and screams how expensive the chair is. No one pays attention to him.

He stalks off to his bedroom. I follow.

"What are we gonna do?" I whisper.

"You wiped away all the prints?" he whispers back.

I nod.

"They've got nothing on us, babe." He inhales deeply. "We'll just have to wait it out. Now, get out of here before someone suspects something."

I obey.

All the pigs leave about four hours later. They've turned our home into a sty.

Paul is becoming a real problem. He's losing it, and that's bad news for me. When I confront him with what a shit he's being, he starts acting like a parent. Can you believe that? He fucks me—his daughter—then when he's losing it, he starts acting like a parent.

Yesterday he didn't come home at night. That really pissed me off. I reminded him that we were in it together. That pissed *him* off, and he claimed the entire thing was *my* idea and that I was a witch and a whore. Man, what a battle we had. We're all made up now, but let me tell you something, we watch each other carefully.

Real carefully.

They arrested me this morning for the murder of my mother. They leave Paul alone for now. Apparently whatever they have is just on me and not him.

To tell you the truth, I'm kind of relieved.

The same detective asks me if I want to have a lawyer present. I say yeah, I'd better, knowing that Paul will get me the best mouthpiece in town. He has to, 'cause he knows that it's only a matter of time before his butt is on the line. I'm left waiting in this interview room for about an hour. Just me and the detective. Finally I say what I know I shouldn't say.

I say, "How'd you find out?"

"Find out what?" the detective answers.

"About my mom being murdered and all."

His eyebrows raise a tad.

"You mean, how'd I find out you murdered your mom?"

I know it's a trick, but what the fuck. I don't care anymore. I nod.

"Did you kill your mom, Kristine?"

He asks the question like real cool, but I can see the sweat under his arm pits.

"Yeah," I admit. "I offed her."

"How?" he asks.

"I laced her coffee with her own Seconal," I say. "When that didn't do the trick, I injected her with more. That finished her off."

"Where'd you inject her?" he asks.

"Under her tongue."

He nods. "Smart thinking," he says. "No marks." Then he pauses and adds, "So you're a hype, huh?"

I shake my head. "Recreational," I say.

"Ah."

"So how'd you find out?" I ask again.

"Two other things set an alarm off in me," the detective said. "The autopsy report showed bruises on the inside of your mom's right wrist. Like someone squeezed her."

"Maybe someone did," I say.

The detective says, "Yeah, like someone was feeling for a pulse. Yet your dad denied touching her."

I say, "Maybe she was playing a little game with one of her lovers."

"I thought of that," the detective says. "She went to a pretty wild party. But then the bruises would have been on both of her wrists."

I don't say anything right away. Then I say, "You said two things. What was the second?"

"Your mom had loads of Seconal in her body, along with booze and coke. She also had just a trace amount of heroin. Too little if she actually shot up a wad."

"My needle," I say. "I forgot to clean it."

"It's hard to remember everything, Kristie," the detective says. "I found it when I searched the house the first time, but I couldn't take it with me for physical evidence because I didn't have the proper papers. I waited a week until I had the search warrant in hand, then took it. We analyzed it, found traces of Seconal and heroin. People don't normally shoot Seconal. You should have dumped all your evidence."

"I never was too good at throwing things away. Mom used to yell at me for that. Called me a bag lady, always keeping everything."

I sigh.

The detective says, "Also, we powdered your mom's meds and found they had been wiped free of prints. If your mom had committed suicide, her prints would have been on the bottle."

"I should have thought about that," I admit.

"Well, you did okay for your first time out," the detective says. "The marks on the wrist were a giveaway. Started me thinking in the right direction. You—or your dad—shouldn't have squeezed her so hard. And you should have used a fresh needle. And gloves instead of wiping away the prints."

He leans in so we're almost nose-to-nose.

"Close but no cigar. You're in hot shit, babe. Want to tell me about it?"

"What do you want to know?"

"Why'd you do it, for starters," he asks.

"'Cause I hated my mom."

"And why did your dad help you?"

"What makes you think my dad helped me?"

"The bruises on your mother's wrist were made by fingers bigger than yours, Kristie. It was your father who felt for the pulse, even though he emphatically denied touching her."

"You can't prove who made those bruises," I say.

The detective doesn't say anything. Then he sticks his hands in his pockets and says, "It's your neck. You could probably save it by turning state's evidence against your dad."

I don't say anything.

"Look," he says. "I understand why you offed your mom. She treated you like shit. And your dad offed her so he could marry his girl-friend—"

"What girlfriend?" I say, almost jumping out of my seat.

"The cute little blond chickie that was on his arm last night."

"You're lying," I say.

He looks genuinely puzzled. He says, "No, I'm not. What is it? Don't you get along with her?"

I feel tears in my eyes. I stammer out, "I . . . I don't even know her."

"Don't cotton to the idea of your dad making it with a young chick?" he asks.

"No," I say.

"Why's that?"

I blurt out, "Because *I'm* his girlfriend. We're *lovers*."

I hear the detective cough. I see him cover his mouth. Then he says, "You want to talk about what happens when you turn state's evidence?"

I shrug, but even as I try to be real cool, the tears come down my cheeks. I say, "Sure, why not?"

Old Paul is on death row, convicted of murder along with rape and sod-omy of a minor.

Me? I'm in juvie hall and it ain't any picnic. The food is lousy, I'm with a couple of bull dykes, and everybody steals. So I can't make any headway in the money department. A couple of gals here say they were raped by their fathers, and they wanted to kill their mothers too. They talk like we have a lot in common. I tell them to leave me alone. Some-times they do, sometimes they don't. But it's cool. I'm beyond caring what the hell happens to me. Just so long as I don't die from boredom.

All that attention. It was really exciting.

I've got to get out of here.

They assigned me a real sucker for a shrink. An older man about my dad's age who gives me the eye.

I mean, he really gives me the eye.

The other day he told me he was going to recommend my release to the assessment board. He says I have excellent insight and a fine prognosis.

The other day he also asked me why I became a hooker.

I mean, what's on *his* mind? I wonder.

Yeah. I have insight.

And I know what's on his mind. And I'll do what I have to in order to get out of here.

I need freedom.

At least juvie hall was a new experience for a while.

Just like killing my mom and fucking Paul.

I hate to be bored.

JAMES ELLROY
(b. 1948)

There are no heroes in the novels and stories of James Ellroy, nor are there any true villains. For the term "villain" still has a lingering aura of Victoriana about it, as if the vague possibility still floats in the air of ugliness somehow transformed at the end of the tale, redemption achieved. With Ellroy, ugliness merely gets uglier, no one is redeemed, and villainy simply doffs its hat in mocking salute. Ellroy's is the darkest world possible in late-twentieth-century terms: a Boschean hell of violence and corruption and betrayal and dreadful night, the continuum of what might be termed the new nihilism and the new brutalism.

Yet Ellroy has a comic genius as well, a humor that is black as hag's midnight but highly developed and splendidly anarchic. Only he would have the gall to feature a third-rate, real-life 1950s squeeze-box player as a hero in the novella Dick Contino's Blues (1994). Rather than elicit disgust, his serious bad taste will often provoke helpless hilarity. This jaunty (on occasion, necrophiliac) black humor certainly helps keep the blues at bay.

At one stage, Ellroy's life was as dark and seemingly doomed as the lives of any of the demonic characters about whom he writes. Yet he managed to survive great tragedies; indeed, they appear to have nourished his peculiar vision, causing him no regret. Much of his writing has been profoundly influenced by the murder of his mother in Los Angeles in June 1958. A cause célèbre at the time, the crime was never solved. Ellroy fictionalized the terrible incident in his second novel, Clandestine (1984).

His masterwork thus far is the Los Angeles Quartet, a series that comprises The Black Dahlia (1987), The Big Nowhere (1988), L.A. Confidential (1990), and White Jazz (1992). This massive roman-fleuve is a brilliantly fictionalized account of crime and corruption in the City of the Angels from the end of World War II to the election of John F. Kennedy to the presidency. It is a vast, sprawling, and epic canvas, densely written in an increasingly frenetic, wired-out prose that reaches minimalist proportions toward the end, but is still a compulsive read. The one problem Ellroy seems to have in his larger works is character delin-

eation: it seems that when he writes in shorthand, however electrifyingly, character is inevitably lost.

Ellroy's shorter fiction often has the feel of something sliced from a longer work, a literary outtake that is readable but leads nowhere. On very rare occasions, however, he writes a little jewel of a tale, with a beginning, a middle, a fine twist, and a big finish. "Gravy Train," the small saga of Stan "the Man" Klein and his love affair with Basko the pit bull, is rude, at times crude, nerve-gratingly and gratuitously vicious—and hilarious.

J. A.

1990

GRAVY TRAIN

Out of the Honor Farm and into the work force: managing the maintenance crew at a Toyota dealership in Koreatown. Jap run, a gook clientele, boogies for the shitwork and me, Stan "The Man" Klein, to crack the whip and keep on-duty loafing at a minimum. My probation officer got me the gig: Liz Trent, skinny and stacked, four useless master's degrees, a bum marriage to a guy on methadone maintenance and the hots for yours truly. She knew I got off easy: three convictions resulting from the scams I worked with Phil Turkel—a phone sales racket that involved the deployment of hard core loops synced to rock songs and naugahyde Bibles embossed with glow-in-the-dark pictures of the Rev. Martin Luther King, Jr.—a hot item with the shvartzes. We ran a drug recovery crashpad as a front, suborned teenyboppers into prostitution, coerced male patients into phone sales duty and kept them motivated with Benzedrine-laced espresso—all of which peaked at twenty-four grand jury bills busted down to three indictments apiece. Phil had no prior record, was strung out on cocaine and got diverted to a drug rehab; I had two G.T.A. convictions and no chemical rationalizations—bingo on a year County time, Wayside Honor Rancho, where my reputation as a lackluster heavyweight contender got me a dorm boss job. My attorney, Miller Waxman, assured me a sentence reduction was in the works; he was wrong—counting "good time" and "work time" I did the whole nine and a half months. My consolation prize: Lizzie Trent, Waxman's exwife, for my P.O.—guaranteed to cut me a long leash, get me soft legitimate work and give me head before my probationary term was a month

old. I took two out of three: Lizzie had sharp teeth and an overbite, so I
didn't trust her on the trifecta. I was at my desk, watching my slaves
wash cars, when the phone rang.

I picked up. "Yellow Empire Imports, Klein speaking."

"Miller Waxman here."

"Wax, how's it hangin'?"

"A hard yard—and you still owe me money on my fee. Seriously, I
need it. I lent Liz some heavy coin to get her teeth capped."

The trifecta loomed. "Are you dunning me?"

"No, I'm a Greek bearing gifts at 10 percent interest."

"Such as?"

"Such as this: a grand a week cash and three hots and a cot at a
Beverly Hills mansion, all legit. I take a tensky off the top to cover your
bill. The clock's ticking, so yes or no?"

I said, "Legit?"

"If I'm lyin', I'm flyin'. My office in an hour?"

"I'll be there."

Wax worked out of a storefront on Beverly and Alvarado—close to his
clientele—dope dealers and wetbacks hot to bring the family up from
Calexico. I doubleparked, put a "Clergyman on Call" sign on my windshield and walked in.

Miller was in his office, slipping envelopes to a couple of Immigration Service goons—big guys with that hinky look indigenous to bagmen
worldwide. They walked out thumbing C-notes; Wax said, "Do you like
dogs?"

I took a chair uninvited. "Well enough. Why?"

"Why? Because Phil feels bad about lounging around up at the Betty
Ford Clinic while you went inside. He wants to play catch up, and he
asked me if I had ideas. A plum fell into my lap and I thought of you."

Weird Phil: facial scars and a line of shit that could make the Pope
go Protestant. "How's Phil doing these days?"

"Not bad. Do you like dogs?"

"Like I said before, well enough. Why?"

Wax pointed to his clients' wall of fame—scads of framed mugshots.
Included: Leroy Washington, the "Crack King" of Watts; Chester Hardell,
a TV preacher indicted for unnatural acts against cats; the murderous
Sanchez family—scores of inbred cousins foisted on L.A. as the result of
Waxie's green card machinations. In a prominent spot: Richie "The

Sicko" Sicora and Chick Ottens, the 7–11 Slayers, still at large. Pica-resque: Sicora and Ottens heisted a convenience store in Pacoima and hid the salesgirl behind an upended Slurpee machine to facilitate their escape. The machine disgorged its contents: ice, sugar and carcinogenic food coloring: the girl, a diabetic, passed out, sucked in the goo, went into sugar shock and kicked. Sicora and Ottens jumped bail for parts unknown—and Wax got a commendation letter from the ACLU, citing his tenacity in defending the L.A. underclass.

I said, "You've been pointing for five minutes. Want to narrow it down?"

Wax brushed dandruff off his lapels. "I was illustrating a point, the point being that my largest client is not on that wall because he was never arrested."

I feigned shock. "No shit, Dick Tracy?"

"No shit, Sherlock. I'm referring, of course, to Sol Bendish, entrepre-neur, bail bondsman supreme, heir to the late great Mickey Cohen's vice kingdom. Sol passed on recently, and I'm handling his estate."

I sighed. "And the punch line?"

Wax tossed me a keyring. "He left a twenty-five million dollar estate to his dog. It's legally inviolate and so well safeguarded that I can't con-test it or scam it. You're the dog's new keeper."

My list of duties ran seven pages. I drove to Beverly Hills wishing I'd been born canine.

"Basko" lived in a mansion north of Sunset; Basko wore cashmere sweaters and a custom-designed flea collar that emitted minute amounts of nuclear radiation guaranteed not to harm dogs—a physicist spent three years developing the product. Basko ate prime steak, Beluga caviar, Häagen-Dazs ice cream and Fritos soaked in ketchup. Rats were brought in to sate his blood lust: rodent mayhem every Tuesday morning, a hun-dred of them let loose in the back yard for Basko to hunt down and destroy. Basko suffered from insomnia and required a unique sedative: a slice of Velveeta cheese melted in a cup of hundred-year-old brandy.

I almost shit when I saw the pad; going in the door my knees went weak. Stan Klein enters the white-trash comfort zone to which he had so long aspired.

Deep pile purple rugs everywhere.

A three-story amphitheatre to accommodate a gigantic satellite dish that brought in four hundred TV channels.

Big screen TVs in every room and a comprehensive library of porn flicks.

A huge kitchen featuring two walk-in refrigerators: one for Basko, one for me. Wax must have stocked mine—it was packed with the high-sodium, high-cholesterol stuff I thrive on. Rooms and rooms full of the swag of my dreams—I felt like Fulgencio Batista back from exile.

Then I met the dog.

I found him in the pool, floating on a cushion. He was munching a cat carcass, his rear paws in the water. I did not yet know that it was the pivotal moment of my life.

I observed the beast from a distance.

He was a white bull terrier—muscular, compact, deep in the chest, bow-legged. His short-haired coat gleamed in the sunlight; he was so heavily muscled that flea-nipping required a great effort. His head was perfect good-natured misanthropy: a sloping wedge of a snout, close-set beady eyes, sharp teeth and a furrowed brow that gave him the look of a teenaged kid scheming trouble. His left ear was brindled—I sighed as the realization hit me, an epiphany—like the time I figured out Annie "Wild Thing" Behringer dyed her pubic hair.

Our eyes met.

Basko hit the water, swam and ran to me and rooted at my crotch. Looking back, I recall those moments in slow motion, gooey music on the sound track of my life, like those Frenchy films where the lovers never talk, just smoke cigarettes, gaze at each other and bang away.

Over the next week we established a routine.

Up early, roadwork by the Beverly Hills Hotel, Basko's A.M. dump on an Arab sheik's front lawn. Breakfast, Basko's morning nap; he kept his head on my lap while I watched porno films and read sci-fi novels. Lunch: blood-rare fillets, then a float in the pool on adjoining cushions. Another walk; an eyeball on the foxy redhead who strolled her Lab at the same time each day—I figured I'd bide my time and propose a double date: us, Basko and the bitch. Evenings went to introspection: I screened films of my old fights, Stan "The Man" Klein, feather-fisted, cannon fodder for hungry schmucks looking to pad their records. There I was: six-pointed star on my trunks, my back dusted with Clearasil to hide my zits. A film editor buddy spliced me in with some stock footage of the greats; movie magic had me kicking the shit out of Ali, Marciano and Tyson. Wistful might-have-been stuff accompanied by Basko's beady browns darting from the screen to me. Soon I was telling the dog the secrets I always hid from women.

When I shifted into a confessional mode, Basko would scrunch up his brow and cock his head; my cue to shut up was one of his gigantic mouth-stretching yawns. When he started dozing, I carried him upstairs and tucked him in. A little Velveeta and brandy, a little good-night story—Basko seemed to enjoy accounts of my sexual exploits best. And he always fell asleep just as I began to exaggerate.

I could never sync my sleep to Basko's: his warm presence got me hopped up, thinking of all the good deals I'd blown, thinking that he was only good for another ten years on earth and then I'd be fifty-one with no good buddy to look after and no pot to piss in. Prowling the pad buttressed my sense that this incredible gravy train was tangible and would last—so I prowled with a vengeance.

Sol Bendish dressed antithetical to his Vegas-style crib: tweedy sports jackets, slacks with cuffs, Oxford cloth shirts, wingtips and white bucks. He left three closets stuffed with Ivy League threads just about my size. While my canine charge slept, I transformed myself into his sartorial image. Jewboy Klein became Jewboy Bendish, wealthy contributor to the U.J.A., the man with the class to love a dog of supreme blunt efficacy. I'd stand before the mirror in Bendish's clothes—and my years as a pimp, burglar, car thief and scam artist would melt away—replaced by a thrilling and fatuous notion: finding *the* woman to complement my new persona. . . .

I attacked the next day.

Primping formed my prelude to courtship: I gave Basko a flea dip, brushed his coat and dressed him in his best spiked collar; I put on a spiffy Bendish ensemble: navy blazer, gray flannels, pink shirt and penny loafers. Thus armed, we stood at Sunset and Linden and waited for the Labrador woman to show.

She showed right on time; the canine contingent sniffed each other hello. The woman deadpanned the action; I eyeballed her while Basko tugged at his leash.

She had the freckled look of a rare jungle cat—maybe a leopard–snow tiger hybrid indigenous to some jungleland of love. Her red hair reflected sunlight and glistened gold—a lioness's mane. Her shape was both curvy and svelte; I remembered that some female felines actually stalked for mates. She said, "Are you a professional dog walker?"

I checked my new persona for dents. My slacks were a tad too short; the ends of my necktie hung off kilter. I felt myself blushing and heard Basko's paws scrabbling on the sidewalk. "No, I'm what you might want to call an entrepreneur. Why do you ask?"

"Because I used to see an older man walking this dog. I think he's some sort of organized crime figure."

Basko and the Lab were into a mating dance—sniffing, licking, nipping. I got the feeling Cat Woman was stalking me—and not for love. I said, "He's dead. I'm handling his estate."

One eyebrow twitched and flickered. "Oh? Are you an attorney?"

"No, I'm working for the man's attorney."

"Sol Bendish was the man's name, wasn't it?"

My shit detector clicked into high gear—this bimbo was pumping me. "That's right, Miss?"

"It's Ms. Gail Curtiz, that's with a T, I, Z. And it's Mr.?"

"Klein with an E, I, N. My dog likes your dog, don't you think?"

"Yes, a disposition of the glands."

"I empathize. Want to have dinner some time?"

"I think not."

"I'll try again then."

"The answer won't change. Do you do other work for the Bendish estate? Besides walk the man's dog, I mean."

"I look after the house. Come over some time. Bring your Lab, we'll double."

"Do you thrive on rejections, Mr. Klein?"

Basko was trying to hump the Lab—but no go. "Yeah, I do."

"Well, until the next one, then. Good day."

The brief encounter was Weirdsville, U.S.A.—especially Cat Woman's Strangeville take on Sol Bendish. I dropped Basko off at the pad, drove to the Beverly Hills library and had a clerk run my dead benefactor through their information computer. Half an hour later I was reading a lapful of scoop on the man.

An interesting dude emerged.

Bendish ran loan-sharking and union protection rackets inherited from Mickey Cohen; he was a gold star contributor to Israel bonds and the U.J.A. He threw parties for underprivileged kids and operated his bail bond business at a loss. He lost a bundle on a homicide bond forfeiture: Richie "Sicko" Sicora and Chick Ottens, the 7–11 slayers, Splitsvilled for Far Gonesville, sticking him with a two million dollar tab. Strange: the *L.A. Times* had Bendish waxing philosophical on the bug-out, like two mill down the toilet was everyday stuff to him.

On the personal front, Bendish seemed to love broads, and eschew birth control: no less than six paternity suits were filed against him. If the suit-filing mothers were to be believed, Sol had three grown sons and three grown daughters—and the complainants were bought off with chump change settlements—weird for a man so given to charity for appearance's sake. The last clippings I scanned held another anomaly: Miller Waxman said Bendish's estate came to twenty-five mill, while the papers placed it at a cool forty. My scamster's brain kicked into very low overdrive. . . .

I went back to my routine with Basko and settled into days of domestic bliss undercut with just the slightest touch of wariness. Wax paid my salary on time; Basko and I slept entwined and woke up simultaneously, in some kind of cross-species psychic sync. Gail Curtiz continued to give me the brush; I got her address from Information and walked Basko by every night, curious: a woman short of twenty-five living in a Beverly Hills mansion—a rental by all accounts—a sign on the lawn underlining it: "For Sale. Contact Realtor. Please Do Not Disturb Renting Tenant." One night the bimbo spotted me snooping; the next night I spotted her strolling by the Bendish/Klein residence. On impulse, I checked my horoscope in the paper: a bust, no mention of romance or intrigue coming my way.

Another week passed, business as usual, two late-night sightings of Gail Curtiz sniffing my turf. I reciprocated: late-night prowls by her place, looking for window lights to clarify my take on the woman. Basko accompanied me; the missions brought to mind my youth: heady nights as a burglar/panty raider. I was peeping with abandon, crouched with Basko behind a eucalyptus tree, when the shit hit the fan—a crap-o, non–Beverly Hills car pulled up.

Three shifty-looking shvartzes got out, burglar's tools gleamed in the moonlight. The unholy trio tiptoed up to Gail Curtiz's driveway.

I pulled a non-existent gun and stepped out from hiding; I yelled, "Police Officer! Freeze!" and expected them to run. They froze instead; I got the shakes; Basko yanked at his leash and broke away from me. Then pandemonium.

Basko attacked; the schmucks ran for their car; one of them whipped out a cylindrical object and held it out to the hot pursuing hound. A streetlamp illuminated the offering: a bucket of Kentucky Colonel ribs.

Basko hit the bucket and started snouting; I yelled "No!" and chased. The boogies grabbed my beloved comrade and tossed him in the back seat of their car. The car took off—just as I made a last leap and hit the pavement memorizing plate numbers, a partial read: P-L-blank-0016. BASKO BASKO BASKO NO NO—

The next hour went by in a delirium. I called Liz Trent, had her shake down an ex-cop boyfriend for a DMV runthrough on the plate and got a total of fourteen possible combinations. None of the cars were reported stolen; eleven were registered to Caucasians, three to southside blacks. I got a list of addresses, drove to Hollywood and bought a .45 automatic off a fruit hustler known to deal good iron—then hit darktown with a vengeance.

My first two addresses were losers: staid sedans that couldn't have been the kidnap car. Adrenaline scorched my blood vessels; I kept seeing Basko maimed, Basko's beady browns gazing at me. I pulled up to the last address seeing double: silhouettes in the pistol range of my mind. My trigger finger itched to dispense .45 caliber justice.

I saw the address, then smelled it: a wood-framed shack in the shadow of a freeway embankment, a big rear yard, the whole package reeking of dog. I parked and sneaked back to the driveway gun first.

Snarls, growls, howls, barks, yips—floodlights on the yard and two pit bulls circling each other in a ring enclosed by fence pickets. Spectators yipping, yelling, howling, growling and laying down bets—and off to the side of the action my beloved Basko being primed for battle.

Two burly shvartzes were fitting black leather gloves fitted with razor blades to his paws; Basko was wearing a muzzle embroidered with swastikas. I padded back and got ready to kill; Basko sniffed the air and leaped at his closest defiler. A hot second for the gutting: Basko lashed out with his paws and disemboweled him clean. The other punk screamed; I ran up and bashed his face in with the butt of my roscoe. Basko applied the *coup de grâce:* left–right paw shots that severed his throat down to the windpipe. Punk number two managed a death gurgle; the spectators by the ring heard the hubbub and ran over. I grabbed Basko and hauled ass.

We made it to my sled and peeled rubber; out of nowhere a car broadsided us, fender to fender. I saw a white face behind the wheel, downshifted, brodied, fishtailed and hit the freeway doing eighty. The attack car was gone—back to the nowhere it came from. I whipped off Basko's muzzle and paw weapons and threw them out the window; Basko licked my face all the way to Beverly Hills.

More destruction greeted us: the Bendish/Klein/Basko pad had been ransacked, the downstairs thoroughly trashed: shelves overturned, sections of the satellite dish ripped loose, flocked velvet Elvis paintings torn from the walls. I grabbed Basko again; we hotfooted it to Gail Curtiz's crib.

Lights were burning inside; the Lab was lounging on the lawn chomping on a nylabone. She noticed Basko and started demurely wagging her tail; I sensed romance in the air and unhooked my sidekick's leash. Basko ran to the Lab; the scene dissolved into horizontal nuzzling. I gave the lovebirds some privacy, sneaked around to the rear of the house and started peeping.

Va Va Va Voom through a back window. Gail Curtiz, nude, was writhing with another woman on a tigerskin rug. The gorgeous brunette seemed reluctant: her face spelled shame and you could tell the perversity was getting to her. My beady eyes almost popped out of my skull; in the distance I could hear Basko and the Lab rutting like cougars. The brunette faked an orgasm and made her hips buckle—I could tell she was faking from twenty feet away. The window was cracked at the bottom; I put an ear to the sill and listened.

Gail got up and lit a cigarette; the brunette said, "Could you turn off the lights, please?"—a dead giveaway—you could tell she wanted to blot out the dyke's nudity. Basko and the Lab, looking sated, trotted up and fell asleep at my feet. The room inside went black; I listened extra hard.

Smutty endearments from Gail; two cigarette tips glowing. The brunette, quietly persistent: "But I don't understand why you spend your life savings renting such an extravagant house. You *never* spell things out for me, even though we're. . . . And just who is this rich man who died?"

Gail, laughing. "My daddy, sweetie. Blood test validated. Momma was a car hop who died of a broken heart. Daddy stiffed her on the paternity suit, among many other stiffs, but he promised to take care of me—three million on my twenty-fifth birthday or his death, whichever came first. Now, dear, would you care to hear the absurdist punch line? Daddy left the bulk of his fortune to his dog, to be overseen by a sharpie lawyer and this creep who looks after the dog. *But*—there has to be some money hidden somewhere. Daddy's estate was valued at twenty-five million, while the newspapers placed it as much higher. Oh, shit, isn't it all absurd?''

A pause, then the brunette. "You know what you said when we got back a little while ago? Remember, you had this feeling the house had been searched?''

Gail: "Yes. What are you getting at?''

"Well, maybe it *was* just your imagination, or maybe one of the other paternity suit kids has got the same idea, maybe that explains it.''

"Linda, honey, I can't think of that just now. Right now I've got you on my mind.''

Small talk was over—eclipsed by Gail's ardor, Linda's phony moans. I hitched Basko to his leash, drove us to a motel safe house and slept the sleep of the righteously pissed.

In the morning I did some brainwork. My conclusions: Gail Curtiz wanted to sink my gravy train and relegate Basko to a real dog's life. Paternity suit intrigue was at the root of the Bendish house trashing and the "searching" of Gail's place. The car that tried to broadside me was driven by a white man—a strange anomaly. Linda, in my eyes a non-dyke, seemed to be stringing the lust-blinded Gail along—could she also be a paternity suit kid out for Basko's swag? Sleazy Miller Waxman was Sol Bendish's lawyer and a scam artist bent from the crib—how did he fit in? Were the shvoogies who tried to break into Gail's crib the ones who later searched it—and trashed my place? Were they in the employ of one of the paternity kids? *What was going on?*

I rented a suite at the Bel-Air Hotel and ensconced Basko there, leaving a grand deposit and detailed instructions on his care and feeding. Next I hit the Beverly Hills Library and re-read Sol Bendish's clippings. I glommed the names of his paternity suit complainants, called Liz Trent and had her give me DMV addresses. Two of Sol's playmates were dead; one was address unknown, two—Marguerita Montgomery and Jane Hawkshaw—were alive and living in Los Angeles. The Montgomery woman was out as a lead: a clipping I'd scanned two weeks ago quoted her on the occasion of Sol Bendish's death—she mentioned that the son he fathered had died in Vietnam. I already knew that Gail Curtiz's mother had died—and since none of the complainants bore the name Curtiz, I knew Gail was using it as an alias. That left Jane Hawkshaw: last known address 8902 Saticoy Street in Van Nuys.

I knocked on her door an hour later. An old woman holding a stack of *Watchtowers* opened up. She had the look of religious crackpots everywhere: bad skin, spaced-out eyes. She might have been hot stuff once—around the time man discovered the wheel. I said, "I'm Brother Klein. I've been dispatched by the Church to ease your conscience in the Sol Bendish matter."

The old girl pointed me inside and started babbling repentance. My eyes hit a framed photograph above the fireplace—two familiar faces smiling out. I walked over and squinted.

Ultra-paydirt: Richie "Sicko" Sicora and another familiar-looking dude. I'd seen pics of Sicora before—but in this photo he looked like someone *else* familiar. The resemblance seemed very vague—but niggling. The other man was easy—he'd tried to broadside me in darktown last night.

The old girl said, "My son Richard is a fugitive. He doesn't look like that now. He had his face changed when he went on the run. Sol was going to leave Richie money when he turned twenty-five, but Richie and Chuck got in trouble and Sol gave it out in bail money instead. I've got no complaint against Sol and I repent my unmarried fornication."

I superimposed the other man's bone structure against photos I'd seen of Chick Ottens and got a close match. I tried, tried, tried to place Sicora's pre-surgery resemblance, but failed. Sicora pre-plastic, Ottens already sliced—a wicked brew that validated non-dyke Linda's theory straight down the line. . . .

I gave the old woman a buck, grabbed a *Watchtower* and boogied southside. The radio blared hype on the Watts homicides: the monster dog and his human accomplice. Fortunately for Basko and myself, eyewitnesses' accounts were dismissed and the deaths were attributed to dope intrigue. I cruised the bad boogaloo streets until I spotted the car that tried to ram me—parked behind a cinderblock dump circled by barbed wire.

I pulled up and jacked a shell into my piece. I heard yips emanating from the back yard, tiptoed around and scoped out the scene.

Pit Bull City: scores of them in pens. A picnic table and Chick Ottens noshing bar-b-q'd chicken with his snazzy new face. I came up behind him; the dogs noticed me and sent out a cacophony of barks. Ottens stood up and wheeled around going for his waistband. I shot off his kneecaps—canine howls covered my gun blasts. Ottens flew backwards and hit the dirt screaming; I poured bar-b-q sauce on his kneeholes and dragged him over to the cage of the baddest looking pit hound of the bunch. The dog snapped at the blood and soul sauce; his teeth tore the pen. I spoke slowly, like I had all the time in the world. "I know you and Sicora got plastic jobs, I know Sol Bendish was Sicora's daddy and bailed you and Sicko out on the 7–11 job. You had your goons break into Gail Curtiz's place and the Bendish pad and all this shit relates to you trying to mess with my dog and screw me out of my gravy train. Now I'm beginning to think Wax Waxman set me up. I think you and Sicora have some plan going to get at Bendish's money, and Wax ties in. You got word that Curtiz was snouting around, so you checked out her crib. I'm a dupe, right? Wax's patsy? Wrap this up for me or I feed your kneecaps to Godzilla."

Pit Godzilla snarled an incisor out of the mesh and nipped Ottens where it counts. Ottens screeched; going blue, he got out, "Wax wanted . . . you . . . to . . . look after . . . dog while him and . . . Phil . . . scammed a way to . . . discredit paternity . . . claims . . . I . . . I . . ."

Phil.

My old partner—I didn't know a thing about his life before our partnership.

Phil Turkel was Sicko Sicora, his weird facial scars derived from the plastic surgery that hid his real identity from the world.

"Freeze, suckah."

I looked up. Three big shines were standing a few yards away, holding Uzis. I opened Godzilla's cage; Godzilla burst out and went for Chick's face. Ottens screamed; I tossed the bucket of chicken at the gunmen; shots sprayed the dirt. I ate crabgrass and rolled, rolled, rolled, tripping cage levers, ducking, ducking, ducking. Pit bulls ran helter skelter, then zeroed in: three soul brothers dripping with soul sauce.

The feast wasn't pretty. I grabbed an Uzi and got out quicksville.

Dusk.

I leadfooted it to Wax's office, the radio tuned to a classical station— I was hopped up on blood, but found some soothing Mozart to calm me down, and highballed it to Beverly and Alvarado.

Waxman's office was stone silent; I picked the back door lock, walked in and made straight for the safe behind his playmate calendar—the place where I knew he kept his dope and bribery stash. Left–right–left: an hour of diddling the tumblers and the door creaked open. Four hours of studying memo slips, ledgers and little black book notations and I trusted myself on a reconstruction.

Labyrinthine, but workable:

Private eye reports on Gail Curtiz and Linda Claire Woodruff—the two paternity suit kids Wax considered most likely to contest the Bendish estate. Lists of stooges supplied by Wax contacts in the LAPD: criminal types to be used to file phony claims against the estate, whatever money gleaned to be kicked back to Wax himself. Address book names circled: snuff artists I knew from jail, including the fearsome Angel "Fritz" Trejo. A note from Phil Turkel to Waxman: "Throw Stan a bone—he can babysit the dog until we get the money." A diagram of the Betty Ford Clinic, followed by an ominous epiphany: Wax was going to have Phil and the real paternity kids clipped. Pages and pages of notes in legalese—levers to get at the extra fifteen million Sol Bendish had stuffed in Swiss bank accounts.

I turned off the lights and raged in the dark; I thought of escaping to a nice deserted island with Basko and some nice girl who wouldn't judge me for loving a bull terrier more than her. The phone rang—and I nearly jumped out of my hide.

I picked up and faked Wax's voice. "Waxman here."

"Ees Angel Fritz. You know your man Phil?"

"Yeah."

"Ees history. You pay balance now?"

"My office in two hours, homeboy."

"Ees bonaroo, homes."

I hung up and called Waxman's pad; Miller answered on the second ring. "Yes?"

"Wax, it's Klein."

"Oh."

His voice spelled it out plain: he'd heard about the southside holocaust. "Yeah, 'Oh.' Listen, shitbird, here's the drift. Turkel's dead, and I took out Angel Trejo. I'm at your office and I've been doing some reading. Be here in one hour with a cash settlement."

Waxman's teeth chattered; I hung up and did some typing: Stan Klein's account of the whole Bendish/Waxman/Turkel/Ottens/Trejo scam—a massive criminal conspiracy to bilk the dog I loved. I included everything but mention of myself and left a nice blank space for Wax to sign his name. Then I waited.

Fifty minutes later—a knock. I opened the door and let Wax in. His right hand was twitching and there was a bulge under his jacket. He said, "Hello, Klein," and twitched harder; I heard a truck rumble by and shot him point blank in the face.

Wax keeled over dead, his right eyeball stuck to his law school diploma. I frisked him, relieved him of his piece and twenty large in cash. I found some papers in his desk, studied his signature and forged his name to his confession. I left him on the floor, walked outside and pulled over to the pay phone across the street.

A taco wagon pulled to the curb; I dropped my quarter, dialed 911 and called in a gunshot tip—anonymous citizen, a quick hangup. Angel Fritz Trejo rang Wax's doorbell, waited, then let himself in. Seconds dragged; lights went on; two black & whites pulled up and four cops ran inside brandishing hardware. Multiple shots—and four cops walked out unharmed.

So in the end I made twenty grand and got the dog. The L.A. County Grand Jury bought the deposition, attributed my various dead to Ottens/ Turkel/Trejo/Waxman *et al.*—all dead themselves, thus unindictable. A superior court judge invalidated Basko's twenty-five mill and divided the swag between Gail Curtiz and Linda Claire Woodruff. Gail got the Bendish mansion—rumor has it that she's turning it into a crashpad for radical lesbian feminists down on their luck. Linda Claire is going out with a famous rock star—androgynous, but more male than female. She admitted, elliptically, that she tried to "hustle" Gail Curtiz—validating her dyke submissiveness as good old American fortune hunting. Lizzie Trent got her teeth fixed, kicked me off probation and into her bed. I got a job selling cars in Glendale—and Basko comes to work with me every day. His steak and caviar diet has been replaced by Gravy Train—and he looks even groovier and healthier. Lizzie digs Basko and lets him sleep with us. We're talking about combining my twenty grand with her life savings and buying a house, which bodes marriage: my first, her fourth. Lizzie's a blast: she's smart, tender, funny and gives great skull. I love her almost as much as I love Basko.

LAWRENCE BLOCK
(b. 1938)

New York City is the prototypical American urban jungle. More novels and short stories have been written about its ever-changing mean streets, past and present, than about those of any other major city. No writer has done a better, more insightful job of capturing the dark side of Manhattan from 1975 to the present than Lawrence Block in his razor-sharp series about Matthew Scudder, former cop, recovering alcoholic, and part-time private detective.

Scudder was created for the paperback market in the mid-1970s, and first appeared in a trio of novels: The Sins of the Fathers (1976), In the Midst of Death (1976), and Time to Murder and Create (1977). After a four-year hiatus, he reappeared in A Stab in the Dark; a year later, Eight Million Ways to Die was awarded a Shamus by the Private Eye Writers of America for best novel of 1982. Six more Scudder novels have been published since then, as have several short stories (one of which, "By Dawn's Early Light," was awarded the Mystery Writers of America Edgar for best short story of 1985). "Scudder has changed some over the years," Block has written, "but then, who hasn't?"

Block has been writing high-quality crime fiction for more than thirty-five years, ever since the appearance of his debut short story, "You Can't Lose," in the February 1958 issue of Manhunt. His first two novels, Mona and Death Pulls a Doublecross, were published in 1961. Thirty have followed under his own name, and another five under the pseudonyms Paul Kavanaugh and Chip Harrison. In addition to Scudder, Block is the creator of three other notable series characters: unrepentant burglar Bernie Rhodenbarr, hero of five novels; Evan Tanner, the spy who cannot sleep, in four titles; and the Nero Wolfeian Leo Haig and his sex-hungry Archie, Chip Harrison, in two adventures published as by Chip Harrison. The best of Block's short stories can be found in three collections: Sometimes They Bite (1983), Like a Lamb to the Slaughter (1984), and Some Days You Get the Bear (1993).

"Batman's Helpers," which first appeared in Playboy in 1990, is a perfect portrait in microcosm of New York City in the 1990s. It is less a crime story than a sociological indictment of that place and this time. Block knows Manhattan, and so will the reader (as much as an outsider

can ever know it) after walking its streets with Scudder and the people
who inhabit his world.

B. P.

1 9 9 0

BATMAN'S HELPERS

Reliable's offices are in the Flatiron Building, at Broadway and Twenty-third. The receptionist, an elegant black girl with high cheekbones and processed hair, gave me a nod and a smile, and I went on down the hall to Wally Witt's office.

He was at his desk, a short stocky man with a bulldog jaw and gray hair cropped close to his head. Without rising he said, "Matt, good to see you, you're right on time. You know these guys? Matt Scudder, Jimmy diSalvo, Lee Trombauer." We shook hands all around. "We're waiting on Eddie Rankin. Then we can go out there and protect the integrity of the American merchandising system."

"Can't do that without Eddie," Jimmy diSalvo said.

"No, we need him," Wally said. "He's our pit bull. He's attack trained, Eddie is."

He came through the door a few minutes later and I saw what they meant. Without looking alike, Jimmy and Wally and Lee all looked like ex-cops—as, I suppose, do I. Eddie Rankin looked like the kind of guy we used to have to bring in on a bad Saturday night. He was a big man, broad in the shoulders, narrow in the waist. His hair was blond, almost white, and he wore it short at the sides but long in back. It lay on his neck like a mane. He had a broad forehead and a pug nose. His complexion was very fair and his full lips were intensely red, almost artificially so. He looked like a roughneck, and you sensed that his response to any sort of stress was likely to be physical, and abrupt.

Wally Witt introduced him to me. The others already knew him. Eddie Rankin shook my hand, and his left hand fastened on my shoulder and gave a squeeze. "Hey, Matt," he said. "Pleased to meetcha. Whattaya say, guys, we ready to come to the aid of the Caped Crusader?"

Jimmy diSalvo started whistling the theme from "Batman," the old television show. Wally said, "Okay, who's packing? Is everybody packing?"

Lee Trombauer drew back his suit jacket to show a revolver in a shoulder rig. Eddie Rankin took out a large automatic and laid it on Wally's desk. "Batman's gun," he announced.

"Batman don't carry a gun," Jimmy told him.

"Then he better stay outta New York," Eddie said. "Or he'll get his ass shot off. Those revolvers, I wouldn't carry one of them on a bet."

"This shoots as straight as what you got," Lee said. "And it won't jam."

"This baby don't jam," Eddie said. He picked up the automatic and held it out for display. "You got a revolver," he said, "a .38, whatever you got—"

"A .38."

"—and a guy takes it away from you, all he's gotta do is point it and shoot it. Even if he never saw a gun before, he knows how to do that much. This monster, though"—and he demonstrated, flicking the safety, working the slide—"all this shit you gotta go through, before he can figure it out I got the gun away from him and I'm making him eat it."

"Nobody's taking my gun away from me," Lee said.

"What everybody says, but look at all the times it happens. Cop gets shot with his own gun, nine times out of ten it's a revolver."

"That's because that's all they carry," Lee said.

"Well, there you go."

Jimmy and I weren't carrying guns. Wally offered to equip us but we both declined. "Not that anybody's likely to have to show a piece, let alone use one, God forbid," Wally said. "But it can get nasty out there, and it helps to have the feeling of authority. Well, let's go get 'em, huh? The Batmobile's waiting at the curb."

We rode down in the elevator, five grown men, three of us armed with handguns. Eddie Rankin had on a plaid sport jacket and khaki trousers. The rest of us wore suits and ties. We went out the Fifth Avenue exit and followed Wally to his car, a five-year-old Fleetwood Cadillac parked next to a hydrant. There were no tickets on the windshield; a PBA courtesy card had kept the traffic cops at bay.

Wally drove and Eddie Rankin sat in front with him. The rest of us rode in back. We cruised up to Fifty-fourth Street and turned right, and Wally parked next to a hydrant a few doors from Fifth. We walked together to the corner of Fifth and turned downtown. Near the middle of the block a trio of black men had set up shop as sidewalk vendors. One had a display of women's handbags and silk scarves, all arranged neatly on top of a folding card table. The other two were offering tee-shirts and cassette tapes.

In an undertone Wally said, "Here we go. These three were here yesterday. Matt, why don't you and Lee check down the block, make sure those two down at the corner don't have what we're looking for. Then double back and we'll take these dudes off. Meanwhile I'll let the man sell me a shirt."

Lee and I walked down to the corner. The two vendors in question were selling books. We established this and headed back. "Real police work," I said.

"Be grateful we don't have to fill out a report, list the titles of the books."

"The alleged books."

When we rejoined the others Wally was holding an oversize tee-shirt to his chest, modeling it for us. "What do you say?" he demanded. "Is it me? Do you think it's me?"

"I think it's the Joker," Jimmy diSalvo said.

"That's what I think," Wally said. He looked at the two Africans, who were smiling uncertainly. "I think it's a violation, is what I think. I think we got to confiscate all the Batman stuff. It's unauthorized, it's an illegal violation of copyright protection, it's unlicensed, and we got to take it in."

The two vendors had stopped smiling, but they didn't seem to have a very clear idea of what was going on. Off to the side, the third man, the fellow with the scarves and purses, was looking wary.

"You speak English?" Wally asked them.

"They speak numbers," Jimmy said. " 'Fi' dollah, ten dollah, please, t'ank you.' That's what they speak."

"Where you from?" Wally demanded. "Senegal, right? Dakar. You from Dakar?"

They nodded, brightening at words they recognized. "Dakar," one of them echoed. Both of them were wearing western clothes, but they looked faintly foreign—loose-fitting long-sleeved shirts with long pointed collars and a glossy finish, baggy pleated pants. Loafers with leather mesh tops.

"What do you speak?" Wally asked. "You speak French? Parley-voo français?" The one who'd spoken before replied now in a torrent of French; Wally backed away from him and shook his head. "I don't know why the hell I asked," he said. "Parley-voo's all I know of the fucking language." To the Africans he said, "Police. You parley-voo that? Police. *Pólicia*. You capeesh?" He opened his wallet and showed them some sort of badge. "No sell Batman," he said, waving one of the shirts at them. "Batman no good. It's unauthorized, it's not made under a licensing agreement, and you can't sell it."

"No Batman," one of them said.

"Jesus, don't tell me I'm getting through to them. Right, no Batman. No, put your money away, I can't take a bribe, I'm not with the Department no more. All I want's the Batman stuff. You can keep the rest."

All but a handful of their tee-shirts were unauthorized Batman items. The rest showed Walt Disney characters, almost certainly as unauthorized as the Batman merchandise, but Disney wasn't Reliable's client today so it was none of our concern. While we loaded up with Batman and the Joker, Eddie Rankin looked through the cassettes, then pawed through the silk scarves the third vendor had on display. He let the man keep the scarves, but he took a purse, snakeskin by the look of it. "No good," he told the man, who nodded, expressionless.

We trooped back to the Fleetwood and Wally popped the trunk. We deposited the confiscated tees between the spare tire and some loose fishing tackle. "Don't worry if the shit gets dirty," Wally said. "It's all gonna be destroyed anyway. Eddie, you start carrying a purse, people are gonna say things."

"Woman I know," he said. "She'll like this." He wrapped the purse in a Batman tee-shirt and placed it in the trunk.

"Okay," Wally said. "That went real smooth. What we'll do now, Lee, you and Matt take the east side of Fifth, and the rest of us'll stay on this side and we'll work our way down to Forty-second. I don't know if we'll get much, because even if they can't speak English they can sure get the word around fast, but we'll make sure there's no unlicensed Batcrap on the Avenue before we move on. We'll maintain eye contact back and forth across the street, and if you hit anything give the high sign and we'll converge and take 'em down. Everybody got it?"

Everybody seemed to. We left the car with its trunkful of contraband and returned to Fifth Avenue. The two tee-shirt vendors from Dakar had packed up and disappeared; they'd have to find something else to sell and someplace else to sell it. The man with the scarves and purses was still doing business. He froze when he caught sight of us.

"No Batman," Wally told him.

"No Batman," he echoed.

"I'll be a son-of-a-bitch," Wally said. "The guy's learning English."

Lee and I crossed the street and worked our way downtown. There were vendors all over the place, offering clothing and tapes and small appliances and books and fast food. Most of them didn't have the peddler's license the law required, and periodically the city would sweep the streets, especially the main commercial avenues, rounding them up and fining them and confiscating their stock. Then after a week or so the cops would stop trying to enforce a basically unenforceable law, and the peddlers would be back in business again.

It was an apparently endless cycle, but the booksellers were exempt from it. The courts had decided that the First Amendment embodied in its protection of freedom of the press the right of anyone to sell printed matter on the street, so if you had books for sale you never got hassled. As a result, a lot of scholarly antiquarian booksellers offered their wares on the city streets. So did any number of illiterates hawking remaindered art books and stolen bestsellers, along with homeless street people who rescued old magazines from people's garbage cans and spread them out on the pavement, living in hope that someone would want to buy them.

In front of St. Patrick's Cathedral we found a Pakistani with tee-shirts and sweatshirts. I asked him if he had any Batman merchandise and he went right through the piles himself and pulled out half a dozen items. We didn't bother signaling the Cavalry across the street. Lee just showed the man a badge—Special Officer, it said—and I explained that we had to confiscate Batman items.

"He is the big seller, Batman," the man said. "I get Batman, I sell him fast as I can."

"Well, you better not sell him anymore," I said, "because it's against the law."

"Excuse, please," he said. "What is law? Why is Batman against law? Is my understanding Batman is *for* law. He is good guy, is it not so?"

I explained about copyright and trademarks and licensing agreements. It was a little like explaining the internal combustion engine to a field mouse. He kept nodding his head, but I don't know how much of it he got. He understood the main point—that we were walking off with his stock and he was stuck for whatever it cost him. He didn't like that part, but there wasn't much he could do about it.

Lee tucked the shirts under his arm and we kept going. At Forty-seventh Street we crossed over in response to a signal from Wally. They'd found another pair of Senegalese with a big spread of Batman items—

tees and sweatshirts and gimme caps and sun visors, some a direct knockoff of the copyrighted Bat signal, others a variation on the theme, but none of it authorized and all of it subject to confiscation. The two men—they looked like brothers and were dressed identically in baggy beige trousers and sky-blue nylon shirts—couldn't understand what was wrong with their merchandise and couldn't believe we intended to haul it all away with us. But there were five of us, and we were large intimidating white men with an authoritarian manner, and what could they do about it?

"I'll get the car," Wally said. "No way we're gonna shlep this crap seven blocks in this heat."

With the trunk almost full, we drove to Thirty-fourth and broke for lunch at a place Wally liked. We sat at a large round table. Ornate beer steins hung from the beams overhead. We had a round of drinks, then ordered sandwiches and fries and half-liter steins of dark beer. I had a Coke to start, another Coke with the food, and coffee afterward.

"You're not drinking," Lee Trombauer said.

"Not today."

"Not on duty," Jimmy said, and everybody laughed.

"What I want to know," Eddie Rankin said, "is why everybody wants a fucking Batman shirt in the first place."

"Not just shirts," somebody said.

"Shirts, sweaters, caps, lunch boxes—if you could print it on Tampax they'd be shoving 'em up their twats. Why Batman, for Christ's sake?"

"It's hot," Wally said.

" 'It's hot.' What the fuck does that mean?"

"It means it's hot. That's what it means. It's hot means it's hot. Everybody wants it because everybody else wants it, and that means it's hot."

"I seen the movie," Eddie said. "You see it?"

Two of us had, two of us hadn't.

"It's okay," he said. "Basically, I'd say it's a kid's movie, but it's okay."

"So?"

"So how many tee-shirts in extra large do you sell to kids? Everybody's buying this shit, and all you can tell me is it's hot because it's hot. I don't get it."

"You don't have to," Wally said. "It's the same as the niggers. You want to try explaining to them why they can't sell Batman unless there's a little copyright notice printed under the design? While you're at it, you can explain to me why the assholes counterfeiting the crap don't counterfeit the copyright notice while they're at it. The thing is, nobody has to do any explaining because nobody has to understand. The only message they have to get on the street is 'Batman no good, no sell Batman.' If they learn that much we're doing our job right.''

Wally paid for everybody's lunch. We stopped at the Flatiron Building long enough to empty the trunk and carry everything upstairs, then drove down to the Village and worked the sidewalk market on Sixth Avenue below Eighth Street. We made a few confiscations without incident. Then, near the subway entrance at West Third, we were taking a dozen shirts and about as many visors from a West Indian when another vendor decided to get into the act. He was wearing a dashiki and had his hair in Rastafarian dreadlocks, and he said, "You can't take the brother's wares, man. You can't do that."

"It's unlicensed merchandise produced in contravention of international copyright protection," Wally told him.

"Maybe so," the man said, "but that don't empower you to seize it. Where's your due process? Where's your authority? You aren't police." Poe-lease, he said, bearing down on the first syllable. "You can't come into a man's store, seize his wares."

"Store?" Eddie Rankin moved toward him, his hands hovering at his sides. "You see a store here? All I see's a lot of fucking shit in the middle of a fucking blanket."

"This is the man's store. This is the man's place of business."

"And what's this?" Eddie demanded. He walked over to the right, where the man with the dreadlocks had stick incense displayed for sale on a pair of upended orange crates. "This your store?"

"That's right. It's my store."

"You know what it looks like to me? It looks like you're selling drug paraphernalia. That's what it looks like."

"It's incense," the Rasta said. "For bad smells."

"Bad smells," Eddie said. One of the sticks of incense was smoldering, and Eddie picked it up and sniffed at it. "Whew," he said. "That's a bad smell, I'll give you that. Smells like the catbox caught on fire."

The Rasta snatched the incense from him. "It's a good smell," he said. "Smells like your mama."

Eddie smiled at him, his red lips parting to show stained teeth. He looked happy, and very dangerous. "Say I kick your store into the middle of the street," he said, "and you with it. How's that sound to you?"

Smoothly, easily, Wally Witt moved between them. "Eddie," he said softly, and Eddie backed off and let the smile fade on his lips. To the incense seller Wally said, "Look, you and I got no quarrel with each other. I got a job to do and you got your own business to run."

"The brother here's got a business to run, too."

"Well, he's gonna have to run it without Batman, because that's how the law reads. But if you want to *be* Batman, playing the dozens with my man here and pushing into what doesn't concern you, then I got no choice. You follow me?"

"All I'm saying, I'm saying you want to confiscate the man's merchandise, you need you a policeman and a court order, something to make it official."

"Fine," Wally said. "You're saying it and I hear you saying it, but what I'm saying is all I need to do it is to do it, official or not. Now if you want to get a cop to stop me, fine, go ahead and do it, but as soon as you do I'm going to press charges for selling drug paraphernalia and operating without a peddler's license—"

"This here ain't drug paraphernalia, man. We both know that."

"We both know you're just trying to be a hard-on, and we both know what it'll get you. That what you want?"

The incense seller stood there for a moment, then dropped his eyes. "Don't matter what I want," he said.

"Well, you got that right," Wally told him. "It don't matter what you want."

We tossed the shirts and visors into the trunk and got out of there. On the way over to Astor Place Eddie said, "You didn't have to jump in there. I wasn't about to lose it."

"Never said you were."

"That mama stuff doesn't bother me. It's just nigger talk, they all talk that shit."

"I know."

"They'd talk about their fathers, but they don't know who the fuck they are, so they're stuck with their mothers. Bad smells—I shoulda stuck that shit up his ass, get right where the bad smells are. I hate a guy sticks his nose in like that."

"Your basic sidewalk lawyer."

"Basic asshole's what he is. Maybe I'll go back, talk with him later."

"On your own time."

"On my own time is right."

Astor Place hosts a more freewheeling street market, with a lot of Bowery types offering a mix of salvaged trash and stolen goods. There was something especially curious about our role as we passed over hot radios and typewriters and jewelry and sought only merchandise that had been legitimately purchased, albeit from illegitimate manufacturers. We didn't find much Batman ware on display, although a lot of people, buyers and sellers alike, were wearing the Caped Crusader. We weren't about to strip the shirt off anybody's person, nor did we look too hard for contraband merchandise; the place was teeming with crackheads and crazies, and it was no time to push our luck.

"Let's get out of here," Wally said. "I hate to leave the car in this neighborhood. We already gave the client his money's worth."

By four we were in Wally's office and his desk was heaped high with the fruits of our labors. "Look at all this shit," he said. "Today's trash and tomorrow's treasures. Twenty years and they'll be auctioning this crap at Christie's. Not this particular crap, because I'll messenger it over to the client and he'll chuck it in the incinerator. Gentlemen, you did a good day's work." He took out his wallet and gave each of the four of us a hundred-dollar bill. He said, "Same time tomorrow? Except I think we'll make lunch Chinese tomorrow. Eddie, don't forget your purse."

"Don't worry."

"Thing is, you don't want to carry it if you go back to see your Rastafarian friend. He might get the wrong idea."

"Fuck him," Eddie said. "I got no time for him. He wants that incense up his ass, he's gonna have to stick it there himself."

Lee and Jimmy and Eddie went out, laughing, joking, slapping backs. I started out after them, then doubled back and asked Wally if he had a minute.

"Sure," he said. "Jesus, I don't believe that. Look."

"It's a Batman shirt."

"No shit, Sherlock. And look what's printed right under the Bat signal."

"The copyright notice."

"Right, which makes it a legal shirt. We got any more of these? No, no, no, no. Wait a minute, here's one. Here's another. Jesus, this is amazing. There any more? I don't see any others, do you?"

We went through the pile without finding more of the shirts with the copyright notice.

"Three," he said. "Well, that's not so bad. A mere fraction." He balled up the three shirts, dropped them back on the pile. "You want one of these? It's legit; you can wear it without fear of confiscation."

"I don't think so."

"You got kids? Take something home for your kids."

"One's in college and the other's in the service. I don't think they'd be interested."

"Probably not." He stepped out from behind his desk. "Well, it went all right out there, don't you think? We had a good crew, worked well together."

"I guess."

"What's the matter, Matt?"

"Nothing, really. But I don't think I can make it tomorrow."

"No? Why's that?"

"Well, for openers, I've got a dentist appointment."

"Oh yeah? What time?"

"Nine-fifteen."

"So how long can that take? Half an hour, an hour tops? Meet us here ten-thirty, that's good enough. The client doesn't have to know what time we hit the street."

"It's not just the dentist appointment, Wally."

"Oh?"

"I don't think I want to do this stuff anymore."

"What stuff? Copyright and trademark protection?"

"Yeah."

"What's the matter? It's beneath you? Doesn't make full use of your talents as a detective?"

"It's not that."

"Because it's not a bad deal for the money, seems to me. Hundred bucks for a short day, ten to four, hour and a half off for lunch with the lunch all paid for. You're a cheap lunch date—you don't drink—but even so. Call it a ten-dollar lunch, that's a hundred and ten dollars for what, four and a half hours' work?" He punched numbers on a desktop calculator. "That's twenty-four forty-four an hour. That's not bad wages. You want to take home better than that, you need either burglar's tools or a law degree, seems to me."

"The money's fine, Wally."

"Then what's the problem?"

I shook my head. "I just haven't got the heart for it," I said. "Hassling people who don't even speak the language, taking their goods from them because we're stronger than they are and there's nothing they can do about it."

"They can quit selling contraband, that's what they can do."

"How? They don't even know what's contraband."

"Well, that's where we come in. We're giving them an education. How they gonna learn if nobody teaches 'em?"

I'd loosened my tie earlier. Now I took it off, folded it, put it in my pocket.

He said, "Company owns a copyright, they got a right to control who uses it. Somebody else enters into a licensing agreement, pays money for the right to produce a particular item, they got a right to the exclusivity they paid for."

"I don't have a problem with that."

"So?"

"They don't even speak the language," I said.

He stood up straight. "Then who told 'em to come here?" he wanted to know. "Who fucking invited them? You can't walk a block in midtown without tripping over another super salesman from Senegal. They swarm off that Air Afrique flight from Dakar, and first thing you know they got an open-air store on world-famous Fifth Avenue. They don't pay rent, they don't pay taxes, they just spread a blanket on the concrete and rake in the dollars."

"They didn't look as though they were getting rich."

"They must do all right. Pay two bucks for a scarf and sell it for ten, they must come out okay. They stay at hotels like the Bryant, pack together like sardines, six or eight to the room. Sleep in shifts, cook their food on hotplates. Two, three months of that and it's back to fucking Dakar. They drop off the money, take a few minutes to get another baby started, then they're winging back to JFK to start all over again. You think we need that? Haven't we got enough spades of our own can't make a living, we got to fly in more of them?"

I sifted through the pile on his desk, picked up a sun visor with the Joker depicted on it. I wondered why anybody would want something like that. I said, "What do you figure it adds up to, the stuff we confiscated? A couple of hundred?"

"Jesus, I don't know. Figure ten for a tee-shirt, and we got what, thirty or forty of them? Add in the sweatshirts, the rest of the shit, I bet it comes close to a grand. Why?"

"I was just thinking. You paid us a hundred a man, plus whatever lunch came to."

"Eighty with the tip. What's the point?"

"You must have billed us to the client at what, fifty dollars an hour?"

"I haven't billed anything to anybody yet—I just walked in the door—but yes, that's the rate."

"How will you figure it, four men at eight hours a man?"

"Seven hours. We don't bill for lunch time."

Seven hours seemed ample, considering that we'd worked four and a half. I said, "Seven times fifty times four of us is what? Fourteen hundred dollars? Plus your own time, of course, and you must bill yourself at more than regular operative's rates. A hundred an hour?"

"Seventy-five."

"For seven hours is what, five hundred?"

"Five and a quarter," he said evenly.

"Plus fourteen hundred is nineteen and a quarter. Call it two thousand dollars to the client. Is that about right?"

"What are you saying, Matt? The client pays too much or you're not getting a big enough piece of the pie?"

"Neither. But if he wants to load up on this garbage"—I waved a hand at the heap on the desk—"wouldn't he be better off buying retail? Get a lot more bang for the buck, wouldn't he?"

He just stared at me for a long moment. Then abruptly, his hard face cracked and he started to laugh. I was laughing, too, and it took all the tension out of the air. "Jesus, you're right," he said. "Guy's paying way too much."

"I mean, if you wanted to handle it for him, you wouldn't need to hire me and the other guys."

"I could just go around and pay cash."

"Right."

"I could even pass up the street guys altogether, go straight to the wholesaler."

"Save a dollar that way."

"I love it," he said. "You know what it sounds like? Sounds like something the federal government would do, get cocaine off the streets by buying it straight from the Colombians. Wait a minute, didn't they actually do something like that once?"

"I think so, but I don't think it was cocaine."

"No, it was opium. It was some years ago—they bought the entire Turkish opium crop because it was supposed to be the cheapest way to keep it out of the country. Bought it and burned it, and that, boys and girls, that was the end of heroin addiction in America."

"Worked like a charm, didn't it?"

"Nothing works," he said. "First principle of modern law enforcement. Nothing ever works. Funny thing is, in this case the client's not getting a bad deal. You own a copyright or a trademark, you got to defend it. Otherwise you risk losing it. You got to be able to say on such and such a date you paid so many dollars to defend your interests and investigators acting as your agents confiscated so many items from so many merchants. And it's worth what you budget for it. Believe me, these big companies, they wouldn't spend the money year in and year out if they didn't figure it was worth it."

"I believe it," I said. "Anyway, I wouldn't lose a whole lot of sleep over the client getting screwed a little."

"You just don't like the work."

"I'm afraid not."

He shrugged. "I don't blame you. It's chickenshit. But Jesus, Matt, most P.I. work is chickenshit. Was it that different in the Department? Or on any police force? Most of what we did was chickenshit."

"And paperwork."

"And paperwork—you're absolutely right. Do some chickenshit and then write it up. And make copies."

"I can put up with a certain amount of chickenshit," I said. "But I honestly don't have the heart for what we did today. I felt like a bully."

"Listen, I'd rather be kicking in doors, taking down bad guys. That what you want?"

"Not really."

"Be Batman, tooling around Gotham City, righting wrongs. Do the whole thing not even carrying a gun. You know what they didn't have in the movie?"

"I haven't seen it yet."

"Robin, they didn't have Robin. Robin the Boy Wonder. He's not in the comic book anymore, either. Somebody told me they took a poll, had their readers call a 900 number and vote, should they keep Robin or should they kill him. Like in ancient Rome, those fighters, what do you call them?"

"Gladiators."

"Right. Thumbs up or thumbs down, and Robin got thumbs down, so they killed him. Can you believe that?"

"I can believe anything."

"Yeah, you and me both. I always thought they were fags." I looked at him. "Batman and Robin, I mean. His *ward,* for Christ's sake. Playing dress-up, flying around, costumes, I figured it's gotta be some kind of fag S-and-M thing. Isn't that what you figured?"

"I never thought about it."

"Well, I never stayed up nights over it myself, but what else would it be? Anyway, he's dead now, Robin is. Died of AIDS, I suppose, but the family's denying it, like what's-his-name. You know who I mean."

I didn't, but I nodded.

"You gotta make a living, you know. Gotta turn a buck, whether it's hassling Africans or squatting out there on a blanket your own self, selling tapes and scarves. Fi' dollah, ten dollah." He looked at me. "No good, huh?"

"I don't think so, Wally."

"Don't want to be one of Batman's helpers. Well, you can't do what you can't do. What the fuck do I know about it, anyway? You don't drink. I don't have a problem with it myself. But if I couldn't put my feet up at the end of the day, have a few pops, who knows? Maybe I couldn't do it either. Matt, you're a good man. If you change your mind—"

"I know. Thanks, Wally."

"Hey," he said. "Don't mention it. We gotta look out for each other, you know what I mean? Here in Gotham City."

ED GORMAN
(b. 1941)

Ed Gorman is among the best American crime writers to have entered the field in the 1980s and 1990s. His novels and short stories provide fresh ideas, characters, and approaches. Told with genuine feeling, in an often lean, deliberately rough-edged style, his tales are an amalgam of pure entertainment, social commentary, symbolic statement, and indepth studies of people whom he has described as "outsiders trying to make their peace with the world."

Beginning with his first novel, Rough Cut *(1985)*, Gorman has created a number of series characters—outsiders and misfits all. The first and most prominent, Jack Dwyer, is a former cop, part-time actor, and security guard who has been featured in six novels, perhaps the most satisfying of which is The Autumn Dead *(1987)*. Other noir creations include an older, more complex private detective, Jack Walsh, who appears in The Night Remembers *(1991)*; and Tobin, a five-foot, five-inch film critic with an explosive temper who is the protagonist of Murder on the Aisle *(1987)*.

Gorman is arguably at the apex of his talents in the nonseries shortstory form. His 1992 collection, Prisoners and Other Stories, *contains twenty-two uniformly excellent dark-suspense tales, one of which is* "The Long Silence After." *Its protagonist, Neely, is a quintessential Gorman character, while the story itself is a quintessential modern hardboiled tale—at or very near the limit to which the form has evolved to date. As Gorman himself states in his introduction to* "The Long Silence After" *in* Prisoners: *"We kill so many people in our stories that I worry we have no sense of real death, or the true spiritual cost of dying. In this story, I wanted to give death at least a little dominion." He has.*

B. P.

1992

THE LONG SILENCE AFTER

The flight from Baltimore was bumpy. Not that Neely cared much. Not now.

At Hertz he asked for a city map. The counter woman, sweet in her chignon and early evening exhaustion, smiled sadly. As if she knew why he'd come here. She gave him the map and a brand new Buick that did not yet smell as if somebody had barfed in it and then covered up the stench with Air-Wick.

He had one more stop to make. The Fed-Ex office near O'Hare. A package waited there for him. He did not unwrap it until he got back to the car.

Inside the red white and blue wrapping, inside the well-lined box, he found what he'd sent himself here last night; a snub-nosed .38. From the adjacent small box he took the cartridges. He would never have gotten this stuff through airport security.

Finally now, he was ready.

He spent four hours driving. Street names meant nothing. Sometimes faces were white, sometimes black. He wanted a certain section. Three times he stopped at gas stations and described the area. How there was this drugstore on one corner and a Triple-XXX theater directly across the street and (cheap irony here) a big stone Catholic church a couple blocks down.

Finally, one guy said, Oh, yeah, and told him where he'd find it in relationship to Rogers Park (which was where he was now).

Around nine, just before he saw the drugstore and the XXX-theater, it started raining. Cold March rain. Beading on the windshield, giving all the neon the look of watercolors.

He found a parking garage. A black guy who had a big chaw of chewing tobacco kept spitting all the time he was taking the keys. And kind of glaring. Fucking suburban white dudes. Motherfuckers anyway.

In the front of the XXX-theater was a small shop where you could rent videos and buy various "appliances" (as they are called). He was never comfortable in such places. Probably his strict Lutheran upbringing. These are places of sin.

The man behind the counter had bad teeth and a wandering left eye. Somehow that was fitting in a place like this.

He described the woman he was looking for but the counter man immediately shook his head. "Don't know her, pal."

He described the woman a little more but the man shook his head

again. "Sorry," he said exhaling Pall Mall smoke through the brown
stubs of his teeth.

He didn't expect to get lucky right off, and he sure didn't. He started at
the west end of the street and worked down it: three bars, a massage
parlor, a used clothing store, a tiny soup kitchen run by two old nuns,
and a bar with a runway for strippers.

And nothing.

Sorry, my friend. Sorry, buddy. Sorry, Jack.

Never seen/heard of her. You know, pal?

And so then he started on the women themselves.

Because of the rain, which was steady and cold, they stood in doorways instead of along the curbsides. The thirty-four degree temperature
kept them from any cute stuff. No whistling down drivers. No shaking
their asses. No jumping into the streets.

Just huddling in doorways instead. And kind of shivering.

And it was the same with them: no help.

He'd describe her and they'd shrug or shake their heads or pretend they were thinking a long moment and go "Nope, 'fraid not,
friend."

Only one of them got smart-mouth. She said, "She musta been somethin' really special, huh?" and all the time was rubbing her knuckles
against his crotch.

Inside his nice respectable topcoat, the .38 was burning a fucking
hole.

Around midnight he stopped in this small diner for coffee and a sandwich. He was tired, he already had sniffles from the cold steady rain,
and he had a headache, too. He bought his food and a little aluminum
deal of Bufferin and took them right down.

And then he asked the counter guy—having no hopes really, just
asking the guy kind of automatically—and the guy looked at him and
said, "Yeah. Betty."

"Yes. That's right. Her name was Betty."

Through the fog of four years, through the fog of a liquored-up night:
yes, goddammit that's right, Betty was her name. Betty.

He asked, "Is she still around?"

The counter man, long hairy tattooed arms, leaned forward and gave
him a kind of queer look. "Oh, yeah, she's still around."

The counter man sounded as if he expected the man to know what he was hinting at.

"You know where I can find her?"

The counter man shook his head. "I don't know if that'd be right, mister."

"How come?"

He shrugged. "Well, she's sort of a friend of mine."

"I see."

And from inside his respectable suburban topcoat, he took his long leather wallet and peeled off a twenty and laid it on the counter and felt like fucking Sam Spade. "I'd really like to talk to her tonight."

The counter man stared at the twenty. He licked dry lips with an obscene pink tongue. "I see what you mean."

"How about it?"

"She really is kind of a friend of mine."

So Sam Spade went back into action. He laid another crisp twenty on the original crisp twenty.

The tongue came out again. This time he couldn't watch the counter man. He pretended to be real interested in the coffee inside his cheap chipped cup.

So of course the counter man gave him her address and told him how to get there.

Fog. Rain. The sound of his footsteps. You could smell the rotting lumber of this ancient neighborhood now that it was soaked. Little shabby houses packed so close together you couldn't ride a bicycle between some of them. One-story brick jobs mostly that used to be packed with Slavs. But the Slavs have good factory jobs now so they had moved out and eager scared blacks had taken their place.

Hers was lime green stucco. Behind a heavy drape a faint light shone.

He gripped the gun.

On the sidewalk he stepped in two piles of dogshit. And now the next-door dog—as if to confirm his own existence—started barking.

He went up the narrow walk to her place.

He stood under the overhang. The concrete porch had long ago pulled away from the house and was wobbly. He felt as if he were trying to stand up on a capsizing row boat.

The door opened. A woman stood there. "Yes?"

His memory of her was that she'd been much heavier. Much.

He said, "Betty?"

"Right."

"Betty Malloy?"

"Right again." She sounded tired, even weak. "But not the old Betty Malloy."

"Beg pardon?"

"I ain't what I used to be."

Cryptic as her words were, he thought that they still made sense.

"I'd like to come in."

"Listen, I don't do that no more, all right?"

"I'd like to come in anyway."

"Why?"

He sighed. If he pulled the gun here, she might get the chance to slam the door and save herself.

He had to get inside.

He put his hand on the knob of the screen door.

It was latched.

Sonofabitch.

"I need to use your phone," he said.

"Who are you?"

In some naive way, he'd expected her to remember who he was. But of course she wouldn't.

"Could I use your phone?"

"For what?"

"To call Triple-A."

"Something's wrong with your car?"

"The battery went dead."

"Where's your car?"

"What?"

"I asked where your car was. I don't see no new car. And you definitely look like the kind of guy who'd be driving a new car."

So he decided screw it and pulled the gun.

He put it right up against the screen door.

She didn't cry out or slam the door or anything. She just stood there. The gun had mesmerized her.

"You gotta be crazy, mister."

"Unlatch the door."

"I ain't got no money, man. I ain't got nothing you'd want. Believe me."

"Just unlatch the fucking door or I start shooting."

"My God, mister, I don't know what this could be about. I really don't."

But she unlatched the door and he went inside.

He closed and locked both doors behind him.

He turned around and looked at the small living room she stood in. The first thing he noticed was that she had not one but two velvet paintings of Jesus above the worn and frayed couch. There was a 17-inch color TV set playing a late movie with Sandra Dee. There was a pressed wood coffee table with only three legs, a stack of paperback books substituting for the missing leg.

She sat on the couch.

He pointed the gun at her.

She said, sounding exhausted now, "You look crazy, mister. I can't help but tell you the truth. You really look crazy."

And now he had some idea of how much weight she'd lost. Maybe forty, fifty pounds. And her facial skin was pulled drum-tight over her cheekbones. And her pallor was gray.

There was a bad odor in the place, too, and he didn't have to ask what it was.

"You fucking bitch," he said, waving the gun at her. She'd been right. He heard his words. He was crazy.

She looked up at him from sad and weary eyes. "I'm so tired, mister, just from walking over to the door that I can't— What do you want anyway?"

"You know this is pretty goddamn funny."

"What is?"

He started pacing. For a time he didn't talk. Just paced. She watched him. The floorboards creaked as he walked over them.

"You destroy me and you don't even remember who I am? That's pretty goddamned good."

And then she said, seeming to know everything suddenly, "Oh, shit, mister. Now I know why you come here. And all I can say is I'm sorry."

He turned on her, seized with his fury. "I've got a wife and two children. I've got a good business. I'm not gay or some junkie or—"

She said, and now her breathing was ragged, and she looked suddenly spent: "How long have you known?"

But he didn't want to answer questions.

He wanted to shake the gun in her face, the gun that signified how trapped and outraged he felt.

And so he shook it. He went right up to her and shook it in her face and said, "You fucking bitch, couldn't you have had yourself checked out before you went on the streets?"

Because that was how it had happened. Him visiting Chicago for an insurance convention. Some executive friend of his from Milwaukee who really liked slumming bringing him down here for a little "black poontang" and—

And a week ago his family doctor, just as incredulous as he was, told him. "David, Jesus Christ, these tests can be wrong sometimes but right now it looks as if—"

Only once in eighteen years of marriage had he been unfaithful.

In Chicago.

Insurance convention.

Black woman.

And now he stood above her. "I can't tell you how badly I want to blow your fucking head off, you bitch."

She looked up at him and said, "Maybe you'd be doing me a favor. I got maybe six months to go myself, mister, and this is some hard way to die, let me tell you." Again she sounded completely spent.

"The worst thing is, I may have infected my wife."

"I know," she said. "My old man left me when he found out. But it's probably too late for him, too."

"You fucking bitch!" he said, no longer able to control himself.

He brought the gun down hard across her jaw.

Almost immediately she started sobbing.

And then he couldn't hit her anymore.

He heard in her tears the inevitable tears of his wife and children when they found out.

And he couldn't hit her at all anymore.

She just sat there and sobbed, her whole body trembling, weaker with each moment.

He said, "I'm sorry."

She just kept crying.

He started pacing again.

"I can't believe this. I keep thinking that there's no way I could—"

He shook his head and looked over at her. She was daubing at her nose with an aqua piece of Kleenex.

"Do you get help?"

She nodded. She wouldn't look at him anymore. "The welfare folks. They send out people."

"I'm sorry I was so angry."

"I know."

"And I'm sorry I hit you."

"I know that too."

"I'm just so fucking scared and so fucking angry."

Now she looked at him again. "The anger goes after awhile. You get too tired to be angry anymore."

"I don't know how I'm going to tell my wife."

"You'll do it, mister. That's the only thing I figured out about this thing. You do what you've got to do. You really do."

He dumped the gun in the pocket of his respectable topcoat. And then he took out his wallet and flicked off a hundred dollars in twenties.

"You really must be crazy, mister," she said. "Leavin' me money like that."

"Yes," he said. "I really must be crazy."

She started crying again.

He closed the doors quietly behind him. Even halfway down the walk, even in the fog and even in the rain, he could still hear her crying.

There was a three o'clock flight to Baltimore. He wasn't sure he had nerve enough to tell her yet but he knew he would have to. He owed her so much; he certainly owed her the truth.

He walked faster now, and soon he disappeared completely inside the fog. He was just footsteps now; footsteps.

CREDITS

Alexander, David: "Mama's Boy" by David Alexander was first published in *Manhunt*, May 1955. Copyright © 1955 by Flying Eagle Publications, Inc. Copyright renewed by David Alexander in 1983. Reprinted by permission of Russell & Volkening as agents for the author.

Appel, Benjamin: "Dock Walloper" by Benjamin Appel is from *Dock Walloper* published by Lion Books in 1953. Copyright 1953 by Benjamin Appel. Copyright renewed 1981 by Sophie M. Appel. Reprinted by permission of the Estate of Benjamin Appel.

Block, Lawrence: "Batman's Helpers" by Lawrence Block was first published in *Playboy*. Copyright © 1990 by Lawrence Block. Reprinted by permission of Knox Burger Associates, Ltd.

Brackett, Leigh: "So Pale, So Cold, So Fair" by Leigh Brackett was first published in *Argosy* in 1957. Reprinted by permission of Spectrum Literary Agency on behalf of the Estate of Leigh Brackett Hamilton.

Brewer, Gil: "Home" by Gil Brewer was first published in *Accused*, March 1956. Copyright © 1956 by Atlantis Publishing Co., Inc. Reprinted by permission of the author and the author's agents, Scott Meredith Literary Agency, L.P., 845 Third Avenue, New York, NY 10022.

Burnett, W. R.: "Round Trip" by W. R. Burnett was first published in *Harper's Magazine* in 1929. Copyright 1929 Harper & Brothers. Reprinted by permission of H. N. Swanson, Inc., on behalf of Whitney L. Burnett, executrix of the Estate of W. R. Burnett.

Cain, James M.: "Brush Fire" by James M. Cain was first published in *Liberty*, December 15, 1936, issue. Copyright 1936 by MacFadden Publications, Inc. Copyright renewed 1963 by James M. Cain. Reprinted by permission of Harold Ober Associates, Inc.

Cain, Paul: "Trouble-Chaser" by Paul Cain (Peter Ruric) was first published in *Black Mask*, issue 17, no. 2 (April 1934), 60–71. Copyright © 1934 by Pro-Distributors Publishing Company, Inc. Copyright renewed © 1962 by Popular Publications, Inc. Assigned to Keith Alan Deutsch and reprinted by special arrangement with Keith Alan Deutsch, proprietor and conservator of the respective copyrights and successor-in-interest to Popular Publications, Inc. *Black Mask* and the distinctive logotype © 1994 by Keith Alan Deutsch.

Chandler, Raymond: "I'll Be Waiting" by Raymond Chandler was first published in *The Saturday Evening Post* in 1939. Copyright © 1939 by The Saturday Evening Post. Copyright © Philip Marlowe B.V. Reprinted by permission of Ed Victor Ltd. Literary Agency.

Cole, William: "Waiting for Rusty" by William Cole was first published in *Black Mask*, vol. 22, no. 7, October 1939. Copyright © 1939 by Pro-Distributors Publishing Company, Inc. Copyright renewed © 1966 by Popular Publications, Inc. Assigned to Keith Alan Deutsch and reprinted by special arrangement with Keith Alan Deutsch, proprietor and conservator of the respective copyrights and successor-in-interest to Popular Publications, Inc. *Black Mask* and the distinctive logotype © 1994 by Keith Alan Deutsch.

NAME INDEX

Numbers in boldface refer to pages on which a story appears.